Tears of the Sea

Mike King

Pearl Press

First published in Great Britain by Pearl Press

ISBN 978-0-9563076-9-9

Typeset by TW Typesetting, Plymouth, Devon

Printed and bound by Good News Press, Ongar, England

Dedicated to all those who have connections with the Armed Forced, past or present

I would like to extend my acknowledgements to my wife, Elaine, for typing the original script and the staff

Contents

Foreword

My dad was in the Royal Navy for over twenty years and I know that he'd have loved this book because it captures the sights and the sounds and the scents of life at sea. My dad would have enjoyed the layered plotting, and he could have settled down with the book in those long hours as his ship rode out a storm. The war years still have a fierce hold on our collective imaginations and Mike King uses that fascination to paint a broad and vivid canvas of the times.

This book is carefully and enthusiastically written by someone who knows their subject. It almost makes me want to follow my dad into the RN. Almost, but not quite.

Ian McMillan

Prologue

'Will there be any oaks on tonight's bonfire?'

From first light, the waters of the Solent had been alive with small boats scurrying back and forth towards, between and away from the ranks of grey-hulled warships anchored in their set positions. As the sun came up, its rays shone on the well-scrubbed superstructures and helped to light up the flags of every description and colour that flew in the breeze as it whipped the waters into isolated specks of foam.

A signal gun fired. Steaming into the anchorage came the Royal Yacht *Brittania*. Sirens boomed. On shore people cheered in celebration. Bells in numerous churches began to ring. In the pubs extra special pints of commemorative ale were poured to their frothy brims in thousands of glasses. But this was really the day for grey-haired veterans. Some in wheelchairs. Others leaning on a stout stick. All with well-polished medals glinting on their chests. Women joining the ranks of the ex-servicemen. Groups from the armed forces that had served their country so well fifty years previously. Rank on rank they passed the saluting bases. Royalty, Lord Mayors or just the local vicar or council leader acknowledging the collective array of salutes and tramping feet. Tears on faces of those who remembered comrades who could no longer be with them-or of comrades lost before peace had come. Multitudes of ordinary citizens watched and cheered these old veterans. They were saying 'thank you' for fifty years of relative peace. Fifty years after the last great all-European madness.

A madness called war.

A single powerful black-hulled launch moved purposefully into the grey sea. To those who lived near the shore this stretch of sea was almost permanently grey. Rarely the child-image colour of bright blue. There was a child on that launch. She was seven years and four days old. She wasn't really aware of why she was on board. Only because mum and dad were there. As well as grandma and grandad. Who were there because of Great Grandma Andrea. And she was there at the invitation of the Colonel, who like great grandma had passed his three score years and ten. Like the boatman seated at the wheel, staring impassively ahead. The other person in the boat, seated next to the Colonel in the warm, comfortable lounge insulated from the biting breeze whipping across the restless waves, wore the habit of a Catholic priest. His black cassock flapped from under the duffel coat he wore round his thin shoulders and the sole splash of colour was the purple stole with gold embroidered crosses that extended under the coat as well. He was the fourth person over seventy years old on board. All four of them had known him. Two of them had originally met him as their captor. Yet all four of them had been friends with him for nearly fifty years. Until his death three weeks previously. They were here, on this stretch of water as requested in his will and by courtesy of the Colonel.

Where he had been fifty years ago. Not the colonel but the boatman, the priest and Great Grandma Andrea. On these waters that had once been full of grey warships. Deciding the possible fate of the nation. May 1916. Row upon row of smoke-pouring battleships with their attendant lines of cruisers and destroyers. Returning, but not all of them, with the scars of a fierce conflict.

Twenty five years later the big ships had left again. Not into the North Sea but westwards to the long rollers of the North Atlantic. Their target this time wasn't a massive fleet but one single warship. Reputed to be the most powerful individual afloat. Again they hadn't all returned. The Royal Navy's biggest warship had not been amongst the returnees.

But it was all empty now. Still grey. Still cold. Still uninviting. So it was seemingly strange that on this particular day that just this one boat pushed its way. Past a buoy that tinkled deeply and mournfully as it gave to the pitch of the tossing waves.

'That'll be the old *Oak*', commented the boatman as the launch thrashed past.

Little seven-year old Sophie didn't understand that statement. 'Oaks don't grow in the sea, do they mummy?' and then with the total butterfly logic of a child added 'Will there be any oaks on tonight's bonfire?'

Her mother hushed her and shook her head. 'Quiet dear, we're nearly there!'

The launch was indeed slowing down. Approaching another marker buoy with a lighter zing to its bell as it too tossed up and down.

'We're here now' said the boatman. 'I'm putting the launch on slow speed and auto-pilot, sir.' This latter remark addressed to the Colonel, who stood up and announced 'Come on all of you, time to carry out his last wish.'

Everyone followed the Colonel out into the stern of the launch. A few bubbles frittered into the general maelstrom of choppy waves and the strong breeze whipped at their faces as they gazed at the grey waters.

The old Catholic priest intoned some words and then invited everyone to say the Lord's Prayer. Sophie thought his English accent strange but joined in with her mum and dad. Then the priest nodded to the Colonel who took up in his right hand a small two handled-pot with Great Grandma Andrea holding the other handle. The priest removed the lid and then the pot was slowly lifted upside down over the gently bubbling wake, its grey ash content fluttering slowly to settle briefly on the grey sea and then to gently subside below the heaving surface.

'It was his wish' said the Colonel.

'Now can we go to see the fireworks?' piped up little Sophie barely understanding what had just taken place. On those cold, grey waters.

'Not quite my dear' said her mum.

The Colonel stood up with a wreath, of laurel with red and yellow roses. He then threw it into the water over where the ashes were floating to their final rest. Up came his right arm. The boatman did as well. Army and naval salutes. Silence apart from the gentle chugging of the engines of the slow-moving launch.

Then the boatman lowered his right arm. The Colonel nodded. 'Right, back to base if you please.' The launch's engines growled as the boatman pushed open the throttles and left that tiny splash of green, red and yellow floating by itself on that cold, grey water.

Red, yellow, orange, white and green flares of colour soared above the castellated roofs of the cliff-top hotel. Sophie gasped in admiration. This is really what the old man which her mum and dad called a Colonel had promised her. In the hotel's courtyard a ceilidh band with pipes in support played a whole host of merry tunes, including many a gallant Scottish reel. Kilted lasses and lads danced and swirled. Gay Gordons, The Dashing White Sergeant. Names that Sophie didn't know anything about but in turn the boatman and the Colonel had shown and guided her in what to do. Old and young. Together, on that evening of 8th May 1995.

The bonfire in the courtyard centre subsided into a gentle glow of sparkling embers that faded as the dark night sky enfolded over the landscape. Then as the last rocket whooshed, sparked, glittered and exploded into a puff of smoke the music stopped and a single piper, up on the hotel's upper balcony played the Scottish lament 'Flowers of the Forest'. Its tune had wailed for those lost at Culloden; for those lost on the Somme and at Passchendaele and now it wailed to remember the loved ones who hadn't returned fifty years ago but by their love had given their life so that children like Sophie could dance and enjoy their lives to come. The Colonel put his arms around the little girl as she gazed up at the fading rocket and murmured 'Come on, little one, time for bed' and despite his age, picked her up and carried her into the log-fire warmth of the hotel's sumptuous lounge.

There the boatman waited and taking Sophie by the hand said 'Come on my brave little girl, you are going to bed and I'll tell you one of my stories.' Sophie had heard one of the boatman's stories before and gave a huge smile. She thought that his stories were very funny. So with mum, the three of them made their way upstairs whilst the Colonel ushered the others to a circle of comfortable chairs by the fire. A white-coated waiter entered the lounge and one by one the Colonel made sure that all his guests had a drink and were seated in the warmth being thrown out by the blazing logs.

'You know why I've invited you all here. Because of him. Strange isn't it? Fifty-three years ago I faced death in a bullet-ridden launch when he and his ship came along. At first I was just grateful but he recognised the gallantry of my lads after he'd learnt what we'd been through and as a result he kept us out of the hands of his supposed allies and in due course under the auspices of the Red Cross, we were repatriated back to England. By then, I counted him as a friend. Not an enemy. All of you are relatives of Andrea. She became a friend of his as well. His wife, for those of you who don't know, couldn't bare children but she baby-sat for nearly all of you, excepting little Sophie. He settled in this country with me as a near neighbour when it was all over. His final wish was to entrust this scroll to me but I am not worthy to keep it so I pass it onto you. It's a rather special one and I trust that you, as a family will ensure its safe keeping. You may look at it.'

Grandma received the scroll. She'd never seen it before. Only Great Grandma Andrea. She untied the gold tie-ribbon and unrolled it.

'Goodness gracious me!' she gasped.

She read the calligraphic script but it was the signatures at the foot of the scroll that made her gasp again.

George VI – King
Clement Attlee – Prime Minister.
Winston Churchill – Leader of the Opposition.

She couldn't take it all in. He had been on the other side. The enemy. He'd even held her mother as a prisoner. She'd often been told about him by her mother but not once had this scroll been mentioned.

'But why us? Why have we to keep this?'

'It was his wish. In his will. He held Andrea dear in his thoughts and you, when you were a baby, in his arms' replied the Colonel. 'However, it really is a very long, long story. Someone ought to research it and write it all down. I'm a bit surprised it hasn't really been the subject of a book. I suppose the end bit was too much to believe.'

'Yes, perhaps it should. From what little I've heard, it really is a remarkable tale' replied grandma.

'Well I suppose it's bed-time. Off you all go. I'll just sit here a little. It's been a long day for all of us and for me. I have been most pleased that you all came.' With that the Colonel stood up and bade all of them, personally, a good night's sleep and he'd see them at the breakfast table. All except Great Grandma Andrea.

She stayed sitting in her chair watching the flames of the log-fire die gently into red glowing embers, a tear or two dribbling down either cheek as she recalled the man and her long connection with him. Ending with looking at a gentle fire.

The Colonel sat next to her and leant over to her. 'Now Andrea, compose yourself. I know. We knew him longer than the others apart from the boatman and the priest. Perhaps I'll find a writer to research the story. All those sacrifices and we live in a world that still hasn't stopped its arms races and its killings. Even he, like me, was once part of that stupidity but yet in the midst of it all he wanted was to make friends. With you. With me. Even when we were supposedly enemies. And since it all happened, we've all been friends.'

The fire in the grate was burning low and the two old friends, lulled by its glow and by the slow ticking of the venerable grandfather clock in the corner, lapsed into silence, closing their eyes.

It had been a long day. For the Colonel. For Great Grandma Andrea. For all of them. Of memories.

About him.

Chapter 1

'Our leader has escaped our naval weather'

March 1915. Leutnant Wilhelm Canaris stood very still by the compass binnacle of the beleaguered German light cruiser *Dresden* anchored in the lee of the hills that surrounded Cumberland Bay, part of the once-romantic island Juan Fernandez off the Chilean coast. Robinson Crusoe may well have planted his footsteps on the sandy beach less than half-a-mile off the anchorage site but there were no romantic illusions in the mind of Canaris or his captain, Fritz Ludecke as their isolated ship with less than eighty tons of coal in her bunkers had simply nowhere to go. Not with three larger British cruisers closing in on them from the seaward side of the sheltered bay.

There just wasn't enough fuel for an attempted escape and the willingness to fight had gone. Indeed those members of the crew who could be spared had already made their way ashore unseen by the crews of the approaching British cruisers. One of them was in no mood for niceties. She'd already fired her six-inch guns at the stationery German warship which made no reply from her out-ranged four point one's (10.5cm).

The fight had gone out of her after that ever so long, sunny, clear day off the Falkland Islands when somewhat inauspiciously the commanding admiral of the German East Asiatic Squadron of which *Dresden* had been a member, had decided to attack the British-held islands only to discover, to his horror, that in Stanley Harbour were the fighting tops of two British battlecruisers. Ships that could outgun and out-speed the German squadron's two largest cruisers. Ships that had accompanying light cruisers that could do the same to the three smaller German light cruisers in Maximilian Graf Von Spee's squadron.

Nemesis overtook four of the five German ships before the cloak of darkness was able to hide the escape of *Dresden* who with her boilers almost bursting and her engines at full speed, managed to outrun her pursuers who in turn, concentrated their attention to the light cruiser's slightly slower companions *Leipzig* and *Nurnberg*. The last that Canaris saw of either ship were the flames and smoke issuing from their shell-wrecked decks as the evening wore on giving them no respite from their eventual destruction. Earlier the two bigger armoured cruisers, *Scharnhorst* and *Gneisenau* had gamely turned towards the British battlecruisers in what turned out to be almost total annihilation. *Scharnhorst* went down with all her crew. Less than a quarter of *Gneisenau*'s were rescued after she'd also been sunk.

Now that three-month delay of nemesis had caught up with *Dresden*. The first fingers of it had stretched out a week beforehand when the little cruiser was chased by HMS *Kent*, a larger but slower cruiser. The high speed effort to escape Kent badly depleted *Dresden*'s coal reserves and there was no supply collier anywhere near to replenish her bunker. It was the same *Kent* that now fired her main guns at *Dresden*. Harshly Ludecke ordered Canaris, 'Get a boat and sail it towards our enemy. Wave a white flag. Slow them down. It could give us a few more minutes.'

When the *Kent* and the other British ships saw the small boat rowing towards them with a white cloth attached to an oar, they stopped firing. Then another flag appeared. From *Dresden*'s foremast it fluttered in surrender. Canaris, sitting stiffly at the stern of his rowed boat, did not see his cruiser's white flag. He didn't even alter his position when boats from the British cruisers rowed past his own, their crews intent on boarding their German opponent.

Too late.

Explosions shook the German cruiser. Scuttling charges going off even as Ludecke and the rest of his crew launched the last boat, intent on reaching the shore.

The British boats were recalled. They took no notice of Canaris and his men as they returned to their own ships. As Canaris passed the sinking *Dresden*, her bows dipped under the still waves, the stern reared up and moments later, what had been his home since even before the start of the war, vanished under the surface. Last to disappear was the German naval ensign that had been flying at the stern of the sinking light cruiser, now swallowed up in the cool, dark green waters of the bay.

March 1935. Admiral Wilhelm Canaris stood very still on the launching platform of the naval dockyard in Kiel. The leather-coated, jack-booted leader of the new National Socialist Germany punched a button that hurled a bottle of German champagne on to the bows of Germany's newest warship. Adolf Hitler yelled 'I name this new cruiser, *Dresden*. May she be a proud symbol of the might of the new Germany and serve her country well in the future.' But the thoughts of Canaris were half-a-world and twenty years back in time. Even as the warship to bear this new one's name was sinking and as he'd passed over her watery grave, the initial ideas of creating a new ship to replace her were forming in his mind. Lithe. Fast. Guns. Torpedoes. Oil-fired. Not sulking in a deserted bay. A ship to expunge the shame of Ludecke's abject surrender. Now here were his dreams becoming a reality. She was sliding into the water for the first time. His ship. His ideas. Then his thoughts took him back to the time when he'd met the naval design architects and he'd sketched out for them the ideas of this ship. Soon they produced the ship for him on the drawing boards, ones that also had the plans for the new Panzerschiffes on them. The small battleships *Deutschland, Graf Spee, Admiral Scheer.* His ship was an extension of them. Still six eleven-inch guns but in three twin turrets, two forward, one aft. Bigger, unladen at nineteen thousand tons. Fully laden another seven thousand. Twin rudders. Triple propellers. And she was fast. Thirty three knots. Maybe a bit more if really pushed. Canaris likened her as a fast light battlecruiser. Like the British idea of their Great World War naval supremo, Fisher and the three ships *Courageous, Furious* and *Glorious.* But these heavy-gunned ships were converted to aircraft-carriers soon after the Great War ended. But the new *Dresden* was to be the only one of her type. Already, plans were advanced for two larger battlecruisers to be named after Spee's defeated armoured cruisers at that now distant Falklands engagement. A bigger development of *Dresden.* So Canaris knew for certain that this new warship was the only one that he could say was his. There'd be no more. Already his work in charge of Germany's Secret Service, the Abwehr, was dominating most of his thoughts and work.

The band struck up 'Deutschland uber alles.' Hitler and his sycophantic entourage jerked up their stiff extended right arms in the now all-too familiar Nazi style of saluting but Canaris and the other Kriegsmarine representatives ignored their gesture by saluting the new ship with the traditional German naval salute as the *Dresden* with her full length settling under guidance of the tugs fussing around her, felt water for the first time under the whole length of her keel.

Maybe Hitler thought he'd launched a new heavy cruiser, a sister for the already launched *Admiral Hipper.* At least that's what the World's press representatives had been told in a pre-launch briefing directed by the Propaganda Ministry. At the thought of that group of out-and-out liars, led by the scrawny-necked Joseph Goebbels, Canaris was almost sick. Already his Abwehr department was experiencing differences with the Goebbels gangsters. But then his thoughts began to sway back to the slowly disappearing new addition to Hitler's fledgling Kriegsmarine's surface fleet. Canaris was preparing for a conflict with France and Britain again as possible enemies. The new *Dresden*, unlike the cruiser that he'd once served on, was designed as a raider. Not to fight in fleet actions but as an independent unit, albeit with a chain of supply ships in attendance as and when needed.

She should be able to out-gun any cruisers that would inevitably be summoned to chase after her; outspeed not only them but any of the battlecruisers that could in turn out-gun her. Fast. And highly manoeuvrable. With a better radius of action than the three 'panzerschiffe's or pocket battleships', this latter term being bandied around the Western press. How far was it? Halfway round the world at seventeen knots. Twelve thousand miles. She'd be able to remain at sea for a year or so providing her supply ships were well placed. It was his department that was already probing the ports and harbours of the world for supply bases, depots and shelter for *Dresden* and the other raiders that in a possible new war Germany would again put into action.

A ship capable of lightning strikes against the enemy convoys or single ships. To be used with aggression. The only way to win. Graf Von Spee's raid against the Falkland Islands had been so badly flawed even before it had started. Why hadn't he divided his ships into two or three smaller groups to chase after Allied ships in the Atlantic? Harder to find.

So his thoughts wandered on this special day. As for Hitler and his cronies they'd soon dispersed, strutting off the platform to the specially-prepared luncheon and reception for the new ship. Cronies who could see no further than tanks and bombers to fight a land war but to defeat Britain, Germany would need a strong naval arm. Kriegsmarine chief Grand Admiral Erich Raeder had his plans but too much of them concentrated on the creation of super-battleships.

How could they be ready unless another ten years was to elapse? Canaris had already read secret documents that seemed to point to a war by nineteen-forty. What the German navy needed were ships designed to attack the mercantile strength of Britain and her allies. Fast battlecruisers. Maybe an aircraft carrier or two.

Canaris cared little for the politics of Hitler and his entourage but he did care for a strong Germany. He watched his ship being manoeuvred into the fitting-out basin. His new ship. Free of any Nazi influence. He'd had Raeder's word on this matter. No party members as crew on her. No jack-booted smart-arses on his ship.

Sleet showers began to sweep across the bay. The crowds were moving away. The band had long since dispersed but as Canaris stood gazing across the choppy waters a stern-sounding voice cut into his thoughts 'Good show Wilhelm, I see that our leader has escaped out of our naval weather.'

Canaris turned to look into the etched lines of the face of Grand Admiral Erich Raeder. A grave unsmiling face. Similar in political views to Canaris knowing that he had to keep them well inside to himself. Already at odds with them over his plans for the new Kreigsmarine. Construction of the expected new ships was way behind his fervent hopes. But at least another new one had just been added to his fleet.

'Well, Wilhelm,' continued Raeder 'I hope that your ship proves her worth. She's the only one of her type. An interim step between the panzerschiffe's and the two small battleships.'

Canaris gave a faint smile. 'Thankyou Erich. I know that the new battlecruisers are larger, have more guns but we will need a lot more of them. And aircraft carriers. That is if we're to give the Royal Navy a real headache the next time round.' Raeder grunted. He knew that to get the navy he wanted was going to be a difficult task. Hitler was nothing but a jumped-up lance-corporal with a big mouth whose main war aim was to avoid the horror of protracted trench warfare. One in which fast-moving tanks aided by dive-bombers acting as a flying arm of the artillery would pulverise a shocked defending army. The new Kriegsmarine was a mere offshoot to what to Hitler would be a land campaign. A disgraced offshoot at its best. Nearly all its major First World War counterparts had ended up scuttled in the deep waters of a hostile Scapa Flow. Useless when afloat. Only useful when sunk, to the team of intrepid scrap-dealers who had raised the hulks from the dark depths and sold them to aid of all things British metal foundries. Even the Kriegsmarine's vital weapon of submarines that nearly won the Great War had hardly started in new production. It was if Hitler didn't want to upset Britain as yet. Perhaps he even thought that the island country would stay out of what to him would be essentially a mainland European affair. They'd get jittery, so he would argue with Raeder, if they thought that a new German Fleet, of aggressive ships, was being built in order to challenge their Royal Navy. It was much quicker, cheaper and easier to build up squadrons of tanks and bombers. Easier too to hide them from prying eyes. Ships, especially big warships always attracted attention. Like as if they were status symbols. In Germany's case, symbols of an emerging Kriegsmarine.

Raeder came out of his thoughts little realising that in many ways they were paralleling those that Canaris held. 'If and when war comes, our new *Dresden* must do her best. I hope that she'll not be needed for quite some time until Germany has the balanced fleet she requires. Look after her well, Wilhelm, in between all your other duties. Set the timetable to work her up keeping her in the Baltic away from prying British or French eyes if at all possible. We must try to hide her true characteristics for as long as possible. Only I can over-ride any of your decisions. She's your ship.'

'Yes Herr Admiral, she's my ship. A very special ship.' Canaris replied quietly. Almost whispering.

His superior saluted and left to join in the celebration luncheon. Canaris watched him go and then turned to look across to where his new ship was now securely berthed. He turned not to eat with the officials but back to his car and for his office. Some-time later with a cup of black coffee and lighting up a cigarette, he drew out the plans of his special creation.

The light battlecruiser KM *Dresden.*

The war with Poland was barely two days old. Already two of Germany's oldest warships, pre-dreadnoughts, had fired their guns on Polish forts. Two of the panzerschiffes were in the wastes of the North and South Atlantic. *Deutschland* and *Graf Spee.* Two of the light cruisers were waiting orders, as soon as they came, to dash across the North Sea and lay the first minefield in British waters. *Leipzig* and *Nurnberg.* Names echoing that Falklands conflict in the Great War.

But another name from that South Atlantic affray was silent. *Dresden* was in dry dock. In Kiel. A long exhaustive trial around the Baltic, through the Kiel Canal and into the North Sea had ended in near humiliation when an error by the Chief Engineer caused a major breakdown in the engines. Towed by three tugs back to Wilhelmshaven and then by a smaller one through the Kiel Canal, she'd finished up in the Kiel dock for a major overhaul and refit. Just as the war for which she'd been planned started. Her captain, feeling disgraced tendered his resignation and Raeder, not Canaris, immediately replaced him with a staff officer, Von Munke, who was given the simple instruction 'Get her ready for sea but no more errors, this time, or else we'll lose her.' Von Munke, a cautious man at the best of times, took these words to heart as he settled himself into his main cabin on board *Dresden.*

Canaris himself was in his offices in Berlin and despite his major pre-occupation with Abwehr business, still had on his desk a photograph of the battlecruiser taken whilst she was on her speed trials. What was it? 35.37 knots over the measured distance. Full speed. Faster than her planned speed of 33 knots. Then came the news of her damaged engines followed shortly after by the appointment of Von Munke. Canaris's upper lip curled up in a snort of disgust. A staff officer with limited ambition. Not one that was really required to be in charge of a speeding raider. A ship that had been scheduled to go out in mid-October to the North Atlantic to replace the *Deutschland* and then further south to cover the return of the *Graf Spee*. Ships out there a-raiding as soon as the German High Command gave the go-ahead.

Then Canaris looked at the photograph of his family. No more summer holidays on the beaches of North Germany. No more cruises on the Strength-through-Joy liners now being requisitioned for use as depot ships and other uses that the Kriegsmarine would require from them. Summer was giving way to autumn. War with Poland was fully underway. Peace was becoming a distant memory.

The door to peace finally slammed shut on this fateful Sunday morning soon after the clamour of bells calling the faithful to worship ceased in Berlin, Paris and London. The wireless sets, some placed especially in public places, gave out the news even before the Sunday roasts had finished being cooked that Germany was at war, not just with Poland but the United Kingdom and France as well.

Canaris sighed as he stared at the two photographs and smoked yet another cigarette. He wished that he was with his family but he rarely took a break from his duties. Now with the war against the two principal West European nations, holidays would become a rare luxury. Even for him.

As he stared at the photograph of the speeding battlecruiser he just couldn't get *Dresden* out of his mind. Suddenly he reached for the desk telephone. 'My car, Now. To the station. For Kiel.' His secretary soon rang back with the arrangements.

By late afternoon he was on *Dresden*'s deck planking forward of Anton turret, the foremost of the twin eleven-inch (28cm) guns. He leant over her still bows, stuck fast in the dry-dock imagining her at full speed with waves creaming in a white wash on either side of her flared bows. Bows so designed to make her more seaworthy. His idea. Incorporated into the two new big battleships still building as well as the new heavy cruisers *Blucher* and *Prinz Eugen*.

Dimly down below, as he walked along her deck, he could hear the sound of hammering as the dockyard workmen together with the ship's own engine-room staff toiled on the job of removing the badly-twisted shaft to her port-side propeller. With him was Von Munke still affecting a high wing collar to his uniform shirt. Stiff. A man whose ideas dreamed of a fleet action as had happened at the Skagerrak battle, which the British called Jutland, some twenty-three years earlier. A man who stuck to the rule book. Canaris didn't like Raeder's choice for he felt that this man would lack the flair needed to be in charge of a raider. *Dresden* was a raider. Not a battle-fleet ship. Still he was very courteous and polite. Also dull and unimaginative.

He smiled at the grave-faced captain, 'Soon, Von Munke, you'll be out at sea and you'll be able to show us all what this ship, my ship, can do. After the British merchant ships. Use her well.' With that he saluted *Dresden*'s captain and turned to go back down to his car waiting on the dockside, 'Cunning sod' thought Von Munke, 'Wants to see how I'm running this ship. I'm answerable to Raeder, not him.'

The war had been in progress for eighteen months. The nature of Western Europe was completely changed. With horrifying speed, German tanks and jack-booted soldiers, together with their advance force of dive bombers swept the astonished, and in some cases, panic-stricken defenders into a rush of successive capitulations almost as if they were a pack of collapsing dominoes. Denmark, Norway, Luxembourg, Belgium, Holland and France. Bloated Mussolini with his black-shirted Fascists joined the Axis pack and Allied sea-routes in the Mediterranean were now under threat.

Only the United Kingdom resisted. Stubborn island race. Their navy gave the Kriegsmarine a bloody nose as sea battles raged off the indented Norwegian coastline. Three cruisers and ten destroyers sunk. Then it rescued a major portion of the British and French armies by picking them off the sandy beaches around Dunkirk and carrying the exhausted soldiers off to the safety of Dover and Ramsgate. Then that same country's air-force reduced the Luftwaffe to a mere night-raiding menace and severe as the bombing in the Blitz had been, and still was, the country showed no signs of surrendering. The citizens of London, Coventry, Liverpool, Sheffield, Hull, Swansea and many others were unbowed. Further afield, the war at sea was fiercely contested. Both sides experienced their successes and reverses. The Kriegsmarine's proud panzerschiffe *Graf Spee* was scuttled off the River Plate despite severely damaging two of the three opposing cruisers. She was forced to run for Montevideo and four days later, her captain blew his ship upon a sandbank before committing suicide. Then the Luftwaffe stupidly sank two German destroyers whilst they were on an operation against British coastal shipping. With the losses from the Norwegian campaign the German Fleet was in a precarious position to support the projected invasion of Southern England. To Raeder's immense relief the project was postponed.

Nevertheless, the small number of German submarines, or U-boats as everyone called them, scored some outstanding successes. The aircraft-carrier *Courageous* was sunk in the English Channel, the old battleship *Royal Oak* in Scapa Flow and off north-west Scotland, convoy SC40 was utterly decimated.

Meanwhile battlecruisers *Scharnhorst* and *Gneisenau* accounted for an armed merchant cruiser as well as the carrier *Glorious*, and panzerschiffe *Scheer* scattered another convoy, HX84, as well as sinking its escorting armed merchant cruiser and five other ships.

But, so far as Canaris was concerned, an even greater success was scored early in this new year of nineteen forty-one. A squadron of six German and Italian motor-torpedo boats were cruising off the Libyan coast at a very low speed when three British warships, silhouetted in the lighter western sky one evening were sighted, one of them being a cruiser.

This cruiser, a sister to the *Exeter* that had fought so gallantly in the River-Plate action, was taken totally by surprise when two torpedoes crashed into her bows and then the whirl of roaring engines as the Axis boats burst into life with the accompanying spate of tracer-fire. A wild melée then occurred with the two escorting destroyers trying to get back at their swiftly manoeuvring opponents. Suddenly after less than ten minutes it was all over with five of the Axis boats disappearing at full throttle into the darkening seas chased by the two destroyers. One of the German E-boats though, stayed behind in the lee of the damaged cruiser, HMS *Southwell.* The bigger ship was in serious trouble with all but one of her senior officers dead or wounded following the raking of her bridge by their enemy's machine guns. Painfully the sinking cruiser had turned towards the Libyan coast only some two miles away with her young and inexperienced fourth lieutenant in charge trying to reach shallow water before his ship sank. Unfortunately for him, *Southwell* ran onto an unexpected off-shore sandbank just as her engines failed due to the engine-room being flooded. Lieutnant Schultze, on his nearby E-boat, still not sighted by the dazed cruiser's crew, closed with engines throttled down and then, when within a quarter-mile, switched on a search-light and opened fire with three machines-guns. Utterly helpless, and expecting more torpedoes, most of her crew jumped into the shallow-water and made for the shore. From the bridge a white-sheet of surrender was hastily draped over the side. Schultze ordered 'Cease fire' but did not close the stricken cruiser until daybreak. Italian and German aircraft arrived to circle over the cruiser and in the growing light, Schultze noticed unusual aerials in the mast abaft the cruiser's bridge. Taking his boat alongside, he hurriedly boarded the stranded British cruiser and with six armed sailors, rushed up to the bridge to investigate. As an auxiliary Abwehr agent, he guessed that what he'd seen was the evidence that the cruiser carried one of the new highly efficient radar sets that the Royal Navy was thought to possess. The information that *Southwell* possessed an undamaged new radar set was radioed back to Schultze's headquarters in Sicily and then on to the Abwehr offices in Berlin.

A sleepy Canaris grunted as the telephone shrilled its alarm by his bedside but he was soon wide awake as he read the report of the coded teleprinter message. Very soon, three of his top Abwehr agents were in a Junkers 52 tri-motored transport lifting off from Templehof Airport in Berlin. Six hours later, in the sunnier climes of Sicily, the aircraft was fully refuelled and with an escort of three fighters took off for Libya. The agents quickly transferred to the scene of *Southwell*'s grounding to find that camouflage netting was already spread over the grounded cruiser.

Schultze's boat, alongside a flimsy pier some two miles further down the coast took the agents the short sea journey to the cruiser. Following Schultze they boarded the ship and climbed up to the bridge structure to a door labelled 'RDF'. Inside was the brand-new set. Quickly assessing the situation, the agents called for help from Schultze's mechanics who carefully removed the set within the next two hours, together with all it's wiring and aerials. Amazingly all the manuals as to how the set worked were recovered as the radar's sole operator was unable to destroy the set after *Southwell* grounded. A machine-gun bullet early in the action grazed his skull as he'd emerged from the nearby 'heads'. Consequently, somewhat dazed and disorientated, he'd failed on coming back to consciousness to activate charges in order to destroy the set.

Schultze's boat soon set sail with the radar set covered in canvas sacking and the agents left to return to Sicily leaving instructions for the Italians to tow the cruiser off the sandbank and then sink her offshore as soon as possible. Already two tugs were on their way from Sicily under escort to carry out the required job of ensuring *Southwell*'s disappearance. She'd only been able to give out a call that she was sinking before power to her wireless failed. A mis-calculation of some thirty miles as to her true position had not helped her cause.

When the Royal Air Force set up a limited search they failed to find the cruiser. The tugs soon pulled her off the sandbank into deeper water where she sank aided by extra scuttling charges.

When Schultze's boat arrived in Sicily, German lorries were waiting to load up the radar set and take it to the waiting Junkers 52 where with the three agents, it was flown back to Berlin. Canaris himself almost drooled with delight when he saw the set and instantly knew as to its eventual destination. On his ship *Dresden*.

But his ship was in disgrace. Her captain, Von Munke, had become the battlecruiser's second captain to tender his resignation for after a foray into the Atlantic, the ship returned to Kiel and Von Munke hurriedly left the ship, resigned his commission in the Kriegsmarine and returned a broken man to his family estate in North Prussia.

Just six weeks after *Scheer*'s success against Convoy HX84, *Dresden* was sent out under Von Munke to the same area. Careful work by Abwehr agents in Halifax gave the information that a small convoy of a dozen ships with a weak escort had set sail, practically the only one at that time without a battleship or cruiser escort because *Scheer*'s attack prompted a reluctant Admiralty to give as many of the North Atlantic convoys a principal warship as escort, no matter how stretched the resources were to cover the convoys as well as patrol the passages from the Arctic Ocean and North Sea into the North Atlantic. This small convoy had only an armed merchant cruiser the *Runswick Castle* as well as two corvettes as its escort and to keep up a reasonable speed comprised of ships that would make at least twelve knots. Relatively fast for a North Atlantic convoy, it was still no match for the speedy German battlecruiser.

Shadowed by a U-boat that had already expended all its torpedoes, *Dresden* approached the convoy but was sighted by *Runswick Castle,* which with the two corvettes, swung out at seventeen knots to ward off the approaching enemy ship. Even when still out of range of her six-inch guns, the ex-liner opened fire, in company with the single four-inch guns of each of the two corvettes. Von Munke, thinking that the corvettes were destroyers, turned *Dresden* away and in exposing *Dresden*'s full length the ship was hit by a fluke shell from *Runswick Castle* that skimmed across the waves as if it was playing 'ducks and drakes'. Thoroughly alarmed, Von Munke retired at full speed and fled for the Denmark Strait where even worse, his ship sighted by a patrolling cruiser. Still at full speed, *Dresden* was able to avoid the cruiser and then vanished into the cold, misty Arctic seas and soon via Norway, returned to Kiel.

Canaris knew all this and realised that his ship needed a new, dynamic, forceful captain to replace Von Munke, He had a man in mind and outlined his ideas to Raeder. For once, the Grand Admiral agreed with him, even admitting that his choice of Von Munke had turned out to be an appalling error. Especially when the other heavy German ships were beginning to show signs of their worthiness in the Kriegsmarine. Admiral Lutjens had already sailed to replace the disgraced *Dresden* with the two larger battlecruisers *Scharnhorst* and *Gneisenau.* Heavy cruiser *Hipper* despite engine problems had already seen North Atlantic service and panzerschiffe *Admiral Scheer* was continuing her cruise reaching the Indian Ocean. In the Baltic, new battleship *Bismarck* was preparing for exercises with the equally new heavy cruiser *Prinz Eugen* for a raid into the North Atlantic.

Dresden had to show her mettle with one more chance with a new captain. Otherwise Canaris knew that his ship would be confined to a negative training role in the safe waters of the Baltic. His new captain would have little time to work up the battlecruiser but Raeder was approving of Canaris's plan to get *Dresden* through a hard working set of trials and back into the Atlantic to follow-up any success that Lutjens could produce and also to keep up the pressure on the Royal Navy's already stretched resources.

Chapter 2

'Anyway mate, who are you?'

A grey afternoon with flurries of sleet turning increasingly to snow lashed Berlin as the lights came on in the office where Canaris was in the process of crushing out yet another cigarette when there came a knock on the door and one of his aides, a grey-suited elderly sergeant in civilian clothes, entered to tell the Abwehr Chief that his guest was outside in the corridor.

The man didn't know why he was in Abwehr's headquarters waiting to see '*someone important*' as he'd been originally informed. George Reitz had been born in the decade of growing German dominance prior to the Great War and had last seen his father in early May 1916. Later he learned that his father had captained his destroyer in a desperate dash against the battleships of the British Grand Fleet as they'd challenged the Kaiser's High Seas Fleet off the Skagerrak. As the Grand Fleet turned to avoid the threat of the destroyer charge and torpedoes, the defensive fire of the battleships caught up with his father's little ship and literally blew it apart as it was in the process of launching its sleek, lethal missiles. There'd been no survivors. Somehow his mother struggled in the Germany that was being gradually strangled by the British-inspired blockade to bring her growing son into his teens and towards manhood. The post-war years seemed endless and French troops marched past his home in their occupation of the Ruhr in 1923. Two years later Reitz, who had gained entrance to Munich University to study Geography and English, found himself in his final year seconded to Aberdeen University where he was to perfect his English. This was the time of the Weimar Republic and the happiest days of that post-war era. Reitz made many friends at the Scottish University and was able to go with friends to Edinburgh and on one notable occasion as far south as the walled city of York where, like so many others, he'd marvelled at the superb dominance of the city's medieval Minster of St Peter.

Fluent in English, he'd gained his university degree with flying colours but then became attracted to the idea of following his father's footsteps. So he joined the tiny Kriegsmarine naval force as an officer cadet. Entrance was relatively easy. Not only did he have his top class degree but his father was a Kriegsmarine hero. Eventually in 1929 he found himself as a junior midshipman on board the newish cruiser *Emden* when she sailed on a World cruise flying the flag of a peaceful Germany. His geographical knowledge, combined with newly-acquired navigational skills helped him a great deal during the cruise and in his spare time he studied the available books about the escapades of the cruiser's Great War predecessor as well as that of other notable German raiders such as cruiser *Karlsruhe* as well as the disguised merchantmen *Moewe* and *Wolf*.

Steadily he rose in rank concentrating on improving his seamanship, and not on the changing face of German politics as the ex-corporal leader of the National Socialists took charge in 1933. More and more new ships joined the growing Kriegsmarine and by September 1939 he was appointed captain of a new Z-class destroyer. His ship was soon in action, escorting light cruisers as they dashed across the North Sea in sowing mines, and then he went on night attacks against coastal convoys coming under fire as the tracers of both sides lashed across at each other. In the spring of 1940 his destroyer was attached to the screen escorting heavy cruiser *Admiral Hipper* off the Norwegian coast. He'd been involved in trying to chase the brave, elusive little British destroyer *Gloworm* as she twisted, turned and finally rammed her much larger opponent. Reitz stopped his ship and helped some of the British destroyer's survivors to safety as their shattered smoking vessel sank from underneath them. Then he'd joined the German destroyer force in the actions against more British destroyers off Narvik where his destroyer drove an opposing enemy destroyer ashore.

Again Reitz stopped his own ship to pick up survivors from the British ship that jumped into the icy water as their vessel lurched off the rocks and sank in deeper waters. Days later, and short of fuel, he'd taken his destroyer into a narrow fjord as the Royal Navy sortied to exact a grim revenge on the stranded German destroyers by sending in battleship *Warspite* with a strong escort. One by one the German ships were winkled out of their hiding places, forced into battle and shattered by the big guns of the battleship or the torpedoes of her escorts. Reitz's ship, on trying to close the *Warspite*, was torpedoed in her engine room and drifted out of the battle towards the nearby shore. Most of his crew were ordered to leave his slowly-sinking command but then his chief engineer regained some power in the engines and Reitz with a reduced crew once more turned to try and engage the British force as it left the fjord steaming hard to regain the open sea. With smoke drifting over the surface of the water, Reitz was able to get within a mile of the great battleship and four torpedoes were fired. To their utter dismay, the Germans saw all four torpedoes explode prematurely when perfectly in line to score hits on the *Warspite*. Their presence discovered, his part-crippled destroyer was soon overwhelmed by a score of small and medium calibre shells and it turned over and sank leaving Reitz and the remaining men on board to escape their shell-wracked ship and desperately swim in the icy waters for the shore but quarter-of-a-mile distant. Their destroyer vanished into the dark depths of the fjord and some of the swimmers also gave up the struggle as the icy coldness numbed their weakening bodies but Reitz and half of the men with him were able to make it to the stony shore. Help was soon at hand and after a short spell in hospital and a two-weeks leave, Reitz found himself appointed captain to another destroyer, that although surviving the Norwegian campaign, had lost its captain when Fleet Air Arm fighters machine-gunned its bridge. More action soon followed in fresh skirmishes off England's North Sea and English Channel Coasts following the withdrawal of the British and French armies from Dunkirk and Northern France. Then his destroyer was recalled to the Baltic to assist in war-exercises involving first of all the larger battlecruisers *Scharnhorst* and *Gneisenau*, then with *Dresden* and now soon to be with the new battleship *Bismarck*. On the day before sailing he was told, without warning, to report to the Abwehr headquarters in Berlin.

Where he was. Sitting. Waiting. In a corridor by a door marked 'Abwehr Commander, Wilhelm Canaris.' He didn't know why he was there. Nor did he know much about Canaris. He could remember of the connection between the Great War light cruiser *Dresden* with Canaris but not of the intense interest that Canaris held in the current battlecruiser of that name or in him.

The elderly sergeant opened the door and beckoned Reitz to enter the office. As he entered, Canaris looked up at the newcomer. Having read over his file many times he was still intrigued by the presence of the six-foot tall captain in front of him. A man of a darkish complexion with dark brown eyes and a mop of overlong dark brown hair too long for the military purists. But it wasn't just his appearance that Canaris was interested. It was the man's record. The heels clicked. The naval salute was immaculate.

'Sit down Kapitan Reitz. Smoke?' Canaris offered a cigarette. Reitz shook his head. Canaris winced. He should have realised that in the record he'd read so often was a reference to the death of Reitz's mother. Lung cancer. Also the clear words 'non-smoker'. 'Do you know why you are here Kapitan Reitz?'

'No, sir.'

'Well, I've a job for you. It could be dangerous; most likely with periods of high excitement and possibly a chance to be away from Germany for at least a year, if not longer.'

Reitz stared back at Canaris. Impassively. Why was the Chief of the Abwehr briefing him? Surely if something was important should he not have been before the Grand Admiral himself? Behind him the civilian-clad sergeant was closing the black out curtains. Shutting out the steady snow that was falling silently over the darkened German capital. Despite the vanity of that bumptious oaf Goering and his scrawny-necked side-kick Goebbels, British bombers had already bombed some of the side-streets of the city. Canaris, watching Reitz as well as the sergeant, contemptuously sneered in his mind at these thoughts. Loyal German that he was, he had no intention ever of getting involved with, to him, the insane leaders of the country. Then he whirled his mind back to Reitz. 'Very soon our armies will be fully on the march again with the advent of spring. Our bombs will renew the offensive against the stubborn British and at sea, our big surface ships will be striking against the North Atlantic convoy routes. We have every hope of success in all fields. It is at sea that we need to win this war. We must cripple the Royal Navy sufficiently so that it cannot effectively guard against those convoys. A strike is being planned to bring this to fruition. It will involve new battleship *Bismarck* and other heavy ships, together with the U-boats, striking at those convoys. It will send a shudder through the ranks of the Allies and particularly the British.'

Canaris paused to take a puff at his cigarette. He needed a cigarette even if Reitz was a non-smoker. He also needed a breather for his words had tumbled out. Reitz, outwardly composed, felt that an appointment to *Bismarck* or as captain to one of her escorts was why he'd been brought to this office. Or was it? Was it something else?

Canaris blew out smoke and then said 'Ever heard of Von Munke?'

'Mmm' nodded Reitz. The disgraced captain of the fast light battlecruiser *Dresden*, The big ship that he'd been escorting during a recent gunnery exercise. Bloody awful. Hadn't once hit the slow-moving target. Almost as if the gunners hadn't really been trying.

Then through his thoughts he heard Canaris saying 'Kapitan Reitz, you are to be the new captain of the battlecruiser *Dresden*. She's my ship. That's why you're here.' Another pause and then in a strong whisper, Canaris continued 'My ship. I helped design her. You may be aware that she's the only one of her type in our navy, never mind any other navy. High speed, torpedoes and guns; excellent endurance. Every factor required for the need of a fighting warship raider.' Louder he continued, getting up from his desk as he did so. 'At the moment, thanks to Von Munke, she is languishing as the laughing stock of the Kriegsmarine and for me, it has been a bitter pill to swallow.' Another pause. Another puff. Then standing to face Reitz he added 'You, Kapitan Reitz, are to change all of this. Plans are in hand for you to take my ship out on an offensive cruise when you will engage the enemy – and not run away from piffling armed merchantmen and corvettes!' Reitz nodded. He wasn't a 'run-away' man as had been Von Munke. He'd not flinched in the North Sea, off the English coast or in the Norwegian fjords near Narvik. However he kept an impassive face as Canaris battled into his thoughts. 'I know your record. That is why Grand Admiral Raeder gave me the honour of telling you of your new task. He'd blundered when he appointed Von Munke, against my advice I may add. Now I have the choice and I have chosen you. To restore *Dresden*'s and the Kriegsmarine's honour. We need to hold our heads above the rotten levels of the Schultzstafflen or the slimy Gestapo whose thugs follow up the gains of our Wehrmacht with rape and murder. They are scum. The Kriegsmarine must never lower itself to that level. I know that your record of rescuing enemy survivors whenever it has been possible is one that I am sure you will render correctly when out there.' Here he unrolled a large wall map of the North Atlantic and stuck his right forefinger in the centre of that ocean. 'Here the sea is our enemy. Not the filth of the Nazi regime. I have made as certain as I can that no card carriers of the Party are enrolled as crew members on board *Dresden.*'

Steady on, Reitz thought. Walls have ears. Gestapo ones. He guessed that Canaris, like himself, was no Nazi. Like the little Admiral, he wanted a strong Germany but not at the expense of senseless murder and destruction due to the whims of an ex-corporal who didn't understand the nature of sea warfare.

Canaris looked at him quietly and said 'First, Kapitan Reitz, you will need to restore my ship's morale. I have a new programme of a fortnight's work of intensive trials followed up by what I hope will be quite an unusual final practice. Right now, her first officer, by the name of Hiltzern, is trying his best to raise the efforts of what is a demoralised bunch of men, some of whom have just been drafted to the ship to replace the more promising personnel who have gone to more active ships, such as *Bismarck* or to our escort vessels or even into submarine training. Your job is to weld them together as a disciplined unit and make them all realise that once more *Dresden* has a real purpose. Briefly, exercising in the Baltic and then it'll be out into the Atlantic where you can appear and disappear. Use her speed. Use her new radar. Use her three aircraft. Use her high degree of manoeuvrability. You will attack, withdraw, attack. An elusive sprite of war on the high seas.'

Reitz stared at him. Expressionless. As earlier. Giving nothing away even though twinges of excitement as well as apprehension coursed though him. Canaris was really telling him that he'd better make a success of *Dresden* or else the underlining truth could lead to searching questions about possibly the whole future of the Kriegsmarine. *Dresden* had to be successful as a prelude to *Bismarck* and other potential raiders. Yet he could only see the dismal performance at the recent exercises he'd attended when on his destroyer as he'd escorted the battlecruiser on her recent gunnery trial. Two hours of desultory fire, rarely coming near the target. Then they'd steamed back to Kiel.

'Well?' barked Canaris shaking him out of his thoughts.

'Could take more than a month to get the crew into shape' replied Reitz, somewhat unconvincingly as he struggled to get his thoughts together.

Canaris shook his head. 'No, not possible. *Dresden* has to be sailing for the North Atlantic by the middle of April, if not earlier. You'll get all the chances you'll require out there to finally shape the crew together. The programme for you is all in this folder', he said tapping a large package on his desk '– and we've even sorted out as I earlier said a final, somewhat special rehearsal for you. A bit unusual. Not even the Kriegsmarine thought this one up, I did. If it fails, then *Dresden* fails, you fail, I fail.' Reitz furrowed his brows. Canaris lit another cigarette, despite the grimace from his new battlecruiser captain.

'Right now, *Dresden* is stocking up with fuel, stores, ammunition-practice and live torpedoes and three brand new Arado 196 float planes. You'll be off on your trials on April fifth – that is, a week from today. However, take a few days leave. Read. Think. Digest all I've said. Here. Rail and hotel tickets. Bavarian alpine region. Sit down whilst you go fishing. Work it all out. How to prove that my ship is a worthwhile investment for our country. One in which we can believe in. Not a ship to be lied about by that cretin Goebbles nor any of his twisted propaganda team. God, why do we have such nonentities in charge of our destiny? But you, Kapitan Reitz, will have the destiny of *Dresden,* of the Kriegsmarine and maybe of Germany at your hands to shape. To me, you and my ship are that important. *Dresden* is that important.'

Reitz again inwardly grimaced at the manner in which Canaris lampooned the Nazi hierarchy. The one thing he didn't want to be involved with was a slanging match with the political leaders of Germany. He was employed to do his best as a warship captain in the service of his country just as much as his opposite numbers in the Royal Navy looked on their approach to serving the Allied cause.

The little Admiral seemed to read his thoughts 'Kapitan Reitz. You take this short break and come back refreshed at the prospect of proving my ship to be a worthy unit of the Kriegsmarine. By the way, you'll find fishing gear at the hotel. One of my lads runs it and he'll see to all your needs. Go on. Prove yourself!' At this, Canaris extended his right hand. The interview, such as that it had been, was over. Reitz stood before him, shook the proffered hand, stepped back, saluted and left the diminutive Abwehr chief still smoking a cigarette. Somehow deep down he felt that he'd never see the man again.

Seven days later, wreathed in clouds of dingy brown smoke, a dirty overworked locomotive chugged out of a Berlin railway station into an hysteria of swirling flakes of snow at the start of its journey to Kiel hauling eleven coaches full of service personnel going back to their war duties. Reitz was crammed into a corner of a compartment of the rear carriage surrounded in the main by noisy U-boat men who'd been enjoying their respite from the arduous strain of dangerous patrols in the North Sea, English Channel or further afield in the deep-troughs of the heaving waves typically experienced in the North Atlantic. Huddled in his naval greatcoat, *Dresden*'s new captain seemed to just merge within this seething mass of noisy humanity. Not for him the relative calm of the forward two carriages which were reserved for officers as well as members of the SS or Gestapo. Rarely did a Kriegsmarine officer, unless he was one of the rare few in the service who was a Nazi-Party member, mix, unless it was totally unavoidable, with the murky toads who carried out their Leader's rapacious orders to the extreme if so required.

Reitz himself preferred to mix anonymously with the ordinary sailors and other ranks of his country's armed forces when he was on leave or returning back to duty. His officer's cap and rank badges were hidden from sight-either in his luggage or underneath his scuffed dark-blue naval coat which was devoid of any markings at all. As he sat in the corner of the compartment his mind still twirled with the events of the short leave but also with the appointment to *Dresden.* However he was soon distracted by the extremely loud belching of the heavily bearded sailor opposite him. Too much beer and schnapps thought Reitz. Suddenly the man lurched to his feet, opened the sash window and leaning outside parted company with the contents of his stomach for them to splash onto the side of the track and also partly back on to the carriage window through which Reitz was staring.

'Sorry for that mate!' rumbled the navy man.

'Mate indeed!' thought Reitz.

'Bin celebrating my brother's wedding although why 'e 'ad ter gerrer in t' club, I ain't a bleedin' clue.' Reitz winced at the rough accent. 'Now the silly bugger's gone off to fly 'is soddin' Stuka in Yugoslavia. Prob'ly get shot down straight into a Serb knocking shop. Silly sod. Anyway mate –' that word again '– sorry fer messin' up yer window. Me, I've gorrer sober up. Been assigned to that dumb battleflop that's known for doing 'nowt but run away. Some new captain's been appointed ter knock it into shape. Trouble is, so I've 'eard, the props can only go one way – backwards. Anyway, I'll just 'ave to lean on me spanner cos' I'm 'er new chief Engineer. Albert Herzog's mi' name.' The drunken oaf stretched out an airy salute somewhat mockingly in Reitz's direction and heavily sat down. Then the mouth opened, a dirty grease-stained hand went inside, scraped away some spittle, came out and waved another vague salute 'Anyway, t'owd Adolf's prob'ly got 'is one ball waggling at us not knowing what way we'll shit next. Serve the jumped-up fart right if we fire our guns at 'im. I 'ear that the bloody gunners are that bad. Fer revenge e'll jump up and down in his over polished jackboots and say "Ve vill turn you into a million Stookas".' The accent was deliberately rude and the bearded officer laughed heartily at his joke. No-one else in the crowded compartment joined in. 'Eh, come on! Good joke. Eh? Anyway, mate –' addressing Reitz 'Who are you?'

'Oh just another sailor going back to the war.' Reitz smiled inwardly to himself.

'Well mate, I were previously on t' *Nurnberg*. Anyway her skipper weren't all that pleased at the prospect of me joining *Dresden*. Wasn't quite sure if I could find enough grease to be able to coax 'er engines into a forward motion when she's released from the dockside bollards!'

'Oh I dare say a drop of schnapps in the fuel should do the trick' was the dry comment from Reitz.

Herzog heartily laughed again 'By heck, that were a good joke' and then promptly put his head back as he fell asleep, soon, snoring in vociferous blasts. Much later he woke up to find the compartment empty. Only an old cleaner, a man in his seventies, was shaking him. 'Come on, sailor, time to get up and go off to war!' almost repeating the statement uttered by Herzog's new, but unknown to him, captain.

The locomotive had long since shuddered to a halt in a cloud of smoke and vaporising steam. Reitz left the station relieved to be away from the steamy, smelly, overcrowded compartment. Mingling with the still noisy crowd, he showed his naval pass to the bored-looking sentry at the entry gates to Kiel's naval dockyard. Dimly in the evening light he could see the cranes and gantries, silent, as if guarding their warship charges below their curved motionless hooks.

He approached the dockside staring up at his new command. A myriad of gun-turrets, the imposing bridge structure, the aerials atop the bridge looking strangely alien to the clean lines of the ship from the flared bows, to its capped funnel and down to the rounded stem. So much bigger than his last command and yet, somehow, even from the dockside despite it being a ship of war, it was a ship graceful in design. Every part seemingly blending with each other. He tried to visualise her at speed-what had Canaris written in his notes? Thirty-five knots. Two knots faster than his Z-class destroyer. Visions of the last time he'd taken the destroyer into action. A wild melée attacking a British coastal convoy in the North Sea ploughing southwards to its London destination. Torpedoes exploding. Starshells and orange smoke from the defending escorts. Fast, difficult to hit motor torpedo boats from both sides weaving intricate wash patterns as they criss-crossed each other in the gloom and smoke. A launch coming into their path being hit by one of the five-inch shells. It exploding. Vanished. As if it had never been. Then the hurried withdrawal and high-speed dash back to their base on the Dutch coast. Trying to reach its relative security before dawn and any avenging British aircraft. Woe betide any stragglers!

But this ship? What was it again that Canaris had printed in those notes? 'Treat her like a large destroyer.' Except that she had six big guns. Maybe not as big as the powerful capital ships that she might encounter. Yet, here silhouetted on that late winter's evening she looked like all three types of main surface ship-battleship, cruiser, destroyer. All rolled into one genius of a ship. But she was a ship of shame and it was his job to restore her fortunes. As he neared the ship he looked across the basin. He could make out the outlines of another gracefully-designed new heavy cruiser. *Prinz Eugen.* To become the consort to battleship *Bismarck.* His ship was to act alone, not in company. But like the new cruiser it seemed as if *Dresden* wasn't ready for action. A few dozy sailors were lounging over the rails of the battlecruiser as Reitz began to climb the connecting gangplank that led up to her mid-ships deck from the quayside. If they were the guard duty, thought Reitz, they don't seem to be all that bothered about their new captain. Perhaps its because I'm a day earlier than expected. Tough!

A burly Petty Officer tried to assemble the men into some sort of order as Reitz neared the top of the gangplank. Reitz heard his growl

'Sorry sir or whatever, but what's your business in boarding our ship?' Reitz glared at the man with his cold brown eyes almost shrivelling him to a complete non-plussed standstill. Casually he flipped open his anonymous blue coat, produced his captain's cap, let the Petty Officer see his array of medals and the Oaks Leaves to his Knight's Cross, together with the distinctive Narvik ribbon. Then quietly, but with steely firmness in his voice he said 'My business is that of captain of this ship.' The Petty Officer hastily clicked his heels and threw up as smart a naval salute as he could muster but his efforts were interrupted as the quiet but icy voice continued 'And where is the duty officer? Get him. Now!'

Junior Leutnant Karl Anders was having a quick smoke near one of the secondary gun turrets when Schenke, the Petty Officer blundered up to him 'Sir, new skipper's here. He's come on –'

'– Oh shit and thrice shit' spluttered Anders, desperately attempting to stamp out his cigarette.

Schenke jerked his thumb but was stopped as Reitz pushed his bulk to one side. 'You!' This time his voice was loud. Almost shouting. 'Are you the Duty Officer?'

'– Er – er – yes sir.' Anders still desperately stamping out his dropped cigarette but Reitz was quicker as he savagely ground it flat to the deck. 'You lazy young man. I could have been an Allied spy for all the care and attention that you are giving to your duty. Pull yourself together you apology of a Kriegsmarine officer and tell me who you are?'

Andes stepped back a pace, tried to click his heels and salute his new captain but somehow he knew he'd even messed up this elementary part of his disciplined training. Strewth the crew had been told that the new captain wasn't due for another twenty-four hours. What was he doing here? How the hell could this misfortune have been his lot? Somehow he stammered 'Sorry Sir, I mean, Herr Kapitan. I am Junior Leutnant Karl Anders, officer of the watch. Sir!' This time, the click of heels and the salute were much better.

Reitz glared at him. 'Well, Leutnant Anders. I'm going back down that gangplank. Then I shall turn round. By the time I reach the deck, I shall expect a Bosun's Party piping me aboard and all to be immaculate order. As befits my standing as your new captain.'

'Yes, yes, yes, Sir, Herr Kapitan' stammered Anders who was feeling hopelessly flustered. He knew it was his fault but no-one seemed to care. *Dresden*'s performance at the gunnery practice had been so bad. Even worse than the failure of their Atlantic cruise. So it seemed. And now this. The new skipper a day early! What a bloody shambles!

Hastily he assembled the guard as Reitz slowly walked down the gangplank. Eyes were straight ahead as the guard faced each other. Heels clicked as one as Reitz stepped aboard his new command for the second time.

'Pipe our captain aboard. Now!' shrilled Anders, maybe a trifle too enthusiastically.

The pipes wailed their plaintiff trills. Reitz saluted and then to Anders he said 'All of these men at 0600 hours tomorrow morning on defaulters parade. And you as well. You can leave this lot standing to attention for the next hour. Our new Chief Engineer will be along soon. I'd hate to have him so sloppily welcomed as I was. Now, show me to the officer's wardroom. Not to my cabin but to their place of so-called comfort. Perhaps they're all asleep for no-one but us seems to have heard the trilling of the pipes.'

Anders saluted yet again, turned and led the way across the deck, past unmanned anti-aircraft guns, silent motor launches, round the base area of the ship's single funnel and then through a steel door into the lower half of the bridge structure.

Down a corridor to another door.

'Here sir, this door.'

Reitz pushed Anders to one side and jerked the door open.

A fog of smoke swirled around him as he strode into the room. Knocking some empty glasses from off a nearby table with his gloves he shouted 'Achtung! Schnell! To your feet. Gentlemen. Now!'

A voice through the fog sneered 'Piss off, Gestapo whore!'

'Silence. All of you. I am your new captain.'

'Good grief, we –'

'Stand to attention. All of you! Now!'

As the awesome realisation hit the assembled officers that this was no joke, they shuffled to their feet. One of them knocked over a bottle of beer. It gurgled in the growing silence as the men stood rigidly staring ahead of them. At their new captain. Reitz of Narvik. None of them had seen him in the flesh but they knew of him and his face. A hero of Germany continuing to fight off superior British forces whilst his ship sank beneath him.

'So you are the officers of *Dresden*. What a shower! Can't keep a proper duty watch! Not even a sentry on duty by the entrance door. Don't you know harbour regulations? None of you? What a disgrace to the Kriegsmarine! No wonder you run for harbour just so that you can smoke and drink yourselves into an uncaring oblivion. But –' Reitz paused and looked at the sea of faces, many now with downcast eyes, full of shame at their captain's biting words '– soon all that is going to change. By the time I've finished with you lot, you are going to be proud to have served on this ship even if it means working and hopefully, fighting this ship harder than ever you could have imagined.'

The assembled officers gazed bleakly back at Reitz, each wondering just what their new captain had in mind.

In a lower voice, Reitz continued 'In case any of you numbskulls don't know my name, it is George Reitz although you will always address me as "Herr Kapitan" when on duty. I'll see all the officers, including any not here or not yet arrived in here tomorrow at 0700 hours after defaulters parade which will be held outside my sea-cabin an hour earlier. See to the required arrangements for that and also see to it that this place is tidied up by yourselves. Not the stewards. You lot. And there'll be no smoking before or during the meeting. So get those filthy ashtrays cleaned and put away. I expect my officers, like myself, to be part of the whole team, however menial the task. See to it. Now!' With that, Reitz turned and left the bemused men. Taking Anders, he ordered the young officer to lead him to his main quarters.

Behind him the shaken officers tried to gather themselves together. 'Bloody shit and hell's bells' remarked the corpulent acting commander of the ship, Ulrich Hiltzern 'So that's Reitz. I guess he's going to be a massive improvement on the gutless ratbag we had in Von Munke. Yes, he's going to drive an active ship. He wasn't at Narvik fighting for nothing whilst we were pissing around trying to avoid the enemy.' He looked around him 'Well come on. Don't stand gawping around. Tidy this mess up. Open a port-hole or two. Let the night air gush in. Sod the blackout. And get on cleaning this mess. Come on. The Kriegsmarine needs gash-bucket officers at the double!' With that, he hurried as fast as his heavy bulk could take him after his departed captain.

Hiltzern caught up with the new captain at the entrance to his main cabin.

'Sir, if only we'd known' he said, half out of breath.

'Save your excuses' snarled Reitz. 'Who are you, anyway?'

He actually knew of Hiltzern. The description of *Dresden*'s acting captain was clear and precise in the folder that he'd avidly read during his short leave. Canaris had provided him with not only photographs but also a short portfolio of all his senior officers of the battlecruiser.

'Hiltzern, sir, acting commander.'

'Well, you had better come in. Leutnant Anders. You will see that my baggage is brought here. Now. Get along. Back to your guard duty. And no more smoking!' This time, the heel click and naval salute were immaculate. Just as if on parade. Improving already thought Reitz as he watched the tall, broad-shouldered young officer turn and march off to his post. Inside the partly furnished cabin – Von Munke had taken all his home comforts with him – Reitz waved the ship's former acting captain to one of the four chairs – 'Tell me, Hiltzern, what's the true situation as you see it?'

The officer wedged himself into the sole armchair that was available. He looked up, his small piggy-like eyes beneath heavy eyebrows fixing their vision on a point above where Reitz was still standing, and somewhat hesitantly began 'Er, well sir, we're known as the "runaway" ship. Run from this. From that. After the shambles that was our last cruise, a good quarter of the ship's company applied and most of them secured transfers to other surface vessels or for U-boat training. For the rest of us we seemed to have hit rock bottom so far as morale is concerned. If you've come to sort us out then you've one hell of a job.'

Reitz had by now lowered himself on to the swivel chair at the main desk and table in the cabin. Rocking slightly from side to side, he steepled his fingers under his chin and leant forward guessing that Hiltzern had more to say.

Which he had.

Hiltzern held his arms out and his right hand punched the air. 'Sir, this ship has bags of potential. She's fast. She has powerful guns and torpedoes. We haven't even fired them in anger. Would you believe it? Eighteen months and still we've not opened fire on the enemy!' He lowered his arms and his voice dropped. His gaze went to the carpeted floor. 'You see sir, the fault was the captain. Von Munke. Him. Always him. Took the memos from our Supreme Leader to heart. Something like "Do not stand in to danger nor even engage enemy surface forces if there's any likelihood of damage." What the hell' raising his voice and hand to look at Reitz directly '– do you expect in war? We expect danger. Dammit sir, that's what we've got guns for – to fight the enemy with and if possible sink them before we ourselves are placed in danger.'

He paused. As if some terrible cloud had come over him. A cloud of shame. Of self-despair.

'We were off Narvik in company with the *Scharnhorst* and *Gneisenau* when they were chased by Renown with us less than fifteen miles away. We should have closed with the British battlecruiser and, between the three of us we should have been able to finish her off. But what did Von Munke do? Having sighted Renown we turned away. I don't think that the British actually saw us. But we turned away and even worse Von Munke actually claimed later that we were too far off the British warship when she was firing at *Gneisenau.* Piffle! I actually saw the gun-flashes of Renown. Then we steered south and then saw the *Warspite* and the British destroyers steering hell-bent for Narvik. What did the silly sod do? Kept radio silence and again steered away. Christ, Sir, excuse the religious expletive, we should at least have made a high-speed challenge, fired off a few salvoes and then turned away. You know what happened to our destroyers.'

'I do. I was captain of one of them.'

'Von Munke even altered my observations in the log claiming that he'd been unable to identify the sighted squadron. Then a bit later on we were supposed to have linked up with S and G but somehow we didn't link up with them until after they'd sunk carrier *Glorious* and her two escort destroyers. By that time *Scharnhorst* had been torpedoed. So when we returned after the Norwegian campaign I should think that we were the only major unit involved in that campaign that had not fired guns at the enemy nor even gone to full action stations.'

Reitz's face became really serious with frowns knitting across his upper forehead.

'Aye there's worse to come' Hiltzern was continuing. 'We refitted having suffered some minor heavy weather damage and in December we were on our own again and came up with *Runswick Castle.* Von Munke immediately veered us away reckoning that the armed merchantmen must have heavier back-up and that was why she was firing her guns even when out-of-range. So we upped our speed and ran away. The humiliation! I turned on the slimy toad and we had one hell of a row on the bridge. He tried to threaten me with dismissal but I stood my ground and so did the other officers on the bridge with me. Suddenly he broke and fled for this very cabin where he stayed for the rest of the voyage home. I know that I had no choice but to bring *Dresden* back to Kiel but as soon as we tied up alongside the quay, naval police came on board and escorted Von Munke off the ship. I hear that he pleaded a nervous breakdown and so has been retired. Good riddance. He just weren't up to the demands of war.'

At times Hiltzern lapsed into his Ruhr Basin vernacular.

Reitz still held his fingers steepled together. 'I have heard something of all this but I'm glad that you've told me.'

'Well, now you're here I take it that we are going back to war and not on any more pointless three hour cruises around the bay.'

'Yes, Commander. It'll mean a lot of hard work. As from tomorrow we will be back on a war footing and we'll set sail as soon as possible. We will exercise everything. I want to get the feel of this ship and that radar set which we have. There are plans for a new cruise in April and I intend, despite the short notice, to raise morale and fighting pitch as high as is possible. So go and get some rest and I will do the same. By the way, do I have a steward?'

'Probably ashore. He's good. He'll be back tonight I expect. Von Munke didn't deserve him. He'll soon have you organised' remembered Hiltzern, his anger evaporating and giving way to the realisation that Reitz was the captain that the sleek battlecruiser really needed. 'Well, I reckon that's it so I best be getting off to make sure the night duty staff are in place.'

'Yes commander, thank you very much. You've given me a most valuable insight as to what has been the problem with this ship. Good night and I'll be up soon after five in the morning.'

Hiltzern mumbled his farewells and shambled out of the cabin in order to get those night watches organised.

But not quite quick enough for the captain's steward for at that moment he was in conversation with the helmeted sentry at the very gates that Reitz had so recently negotiated.

'Halt! Who goes there?'

'Stuff it Franz, it's only me.'

'Identify yourself.'

'Piss in your gob, Franz. Here, have a little favour from Rudi of the *Dresden*.'

'Attention you drunken slob of an oaf. Surprise, surprise your new skipper's already arrived and unless you sober up I guess you'll be having a night in the cells.'

'Franz, my sober pal, you're a real mate.'

'So', Rudi thought, 'skip's in a day earlier. Mind, I've had a brilliant leave even if I am a bit shattered. That raven-haired tart was really warm work! It all had left him feeling really pleased for she'd told him that he was way ahead of any of her other clients. At the inn she'd shown him the well-stocked liquor store. 'Here' she'd said 'take what you can as a form of payment for being so good.'

So Rudi staggered out with a well-laden work bag full of excellent bottles of a wide range of spirits. How he'd been able to avoid running into some nasty nosey load of Gestapo shit-makers he hadn't really fathomed out but here he was slipping into the hand of the sentry one of those illegal bottles.

Then he was off scuttling across the slush of the quayside and up the gangplank where the watch party that had been standing to attention for the past hour were in process of rubbing their aching limbs having just been dismissed by Anders. In the confusion Walters slipped behind them and faded into the shadows of a gun turret just as the sonorous tones of a petty officer was yelling the new duty watch into their position.

Walters breathed a sigh of relief. 'Blimey! Things is getting a bit keen. Must be the new skipper.' Still clutching his work bag he made his way to the small cabin that was his headquarters as he put it to every other crew member. He fumbled at the door with his key, pushed it open and in the gloom fell over a pair of outstretched legs.

'What the –'

'Nice of you to drop in steward.'

Walters adjusted his bleary eyes and made out the form of what he suspected to be his new skipper who stood up over his prone figure and switched on the cabin light.

'Sorry sir, you have the advantage.'

'I'm your new captain, George Reitz. Here, get up and introduce yourself.'

'Rudi Walters, sir' was the steward's response as he airily sketched a lazy salute. 'Fresh from a damn good fleshpot ashore complete with a bag of goodies. At your service, sir.'

Reitz observed the little man's features. A shock of hopelessly untidy red hair, numerous freckles and red cheeks. His unbuttoned shirt leading down to many creases in his trousers and badly scuffed shoes.

The little man was saying 'What's your tot? Schnapps, bourbon, rum, gin, brandy or even Scotch? Me? I either have 'em here or can get them if you give me an hour ashore' and saying that he tapped his stub of a nose and dropped a wink with his right eye.

'Whisky. Scotch. Not Irish.' Reitz said somewhat weakly.

'Mmm, yes. Different from Von Munke. French cognac was his taste. Even drank it when 'e were asleep. Pissed most of the time. That's why we 'ad to run away from trouble cos' 'e was allus in t'heads.'

Rudi swayed as Reitz grinned helplessly at the man's sense of crude humour. The little man was continuing 'Ah guess Von Munke didn't want a shell to hit this cabin. What would 'e 'ave done wi'out 'is bit of French stuff? Anyway, do you want a little nip of Scotch. Got some here in this bag. Glen Morangie, I think it's called.'

Reitz proffered a glass as soon as Rudi opened the precious amber bottle. 'Have one yourself.'

'Nah, sir, beer's my brew' smiled Rudi.

'Well, steward, cheers.' Reitz raised his glass. 'Now tell me, what about you? Your name again for starters.'

'Rudi Walters, sir. My mum's from Hamburg. Me dad was an American soldier who married 'er in January nineteen-nineteen when 'e settled in t'city after the Great War. Then 'e gets the flu 'an pops off before I were born. Then I growed up and went to work in an Hamburg bar when I were fifteen. Then decides ter join the Kriegsmarine on account of better pay. They polished up mi' manners. When war started I were drafted to this ship an' 'ave been here ever since.'

'So, Walters, seeing you are my right-hand man, have you any opinions about this ship?'

'Not really fer me ter say but if you wants a candid opinion Von Munke couldn't have ever organised a piss-up in the world's best-stocked brewery except 'e'd get hisself sloshed whilst everyone else were forced ter remain sober. 'E 'asn't done too much fer morale!'

'Quite.' Reitz took another sip at the whisky. 'Ten year old malt. Where did you say you could get a further supply?'

'I didn't sir, but I 'as a nose fer the stuff like as when I did a run on a coaster ter Leith. Had a snifter of it over there, recognised a good spirit and some bottles came back with me across the North Sea.'

'Mmm' was the captain's response suddenly feeling very tired. 'Guess I'd better turn in.' I'll take a light breakfast at eight bells. Goodnight, Walters.' With that Reitz returned back to his more spacious cabin, throwing his jacket on to his bunk and then himself on to it, falling asleep in seconds.

Reitz awoke to find himself tucked in to his bed wearing just his underclothes. When his eyes focussed he saw that he had a clean set of clothes neatly pressed on a nearby chair. He could hear the distant shouts of petty officers sorting out the morning watch. Eight bells. Four in the morning. The changing of the watches. A gentle knock and then in came Walters smartly attired in his white steward's uniform.

'Morning sir. Brought in a spot of breakfast. Thought you might like it before getting up.' Walters placed a tray on a side table, drew it up to the side of the bunk, shook out a napkin, gave a slight bow and left Reitz to savour his first meal on board his new command. A roll of warm brown bread, a bowl of what looked like Scots porridge with a dash of honey, two soft boiled eggs, a dash of marmalade and toast as well as a pot of tea. Just as he'd tasted when in Aberdeen. How could Walters have known? The eggs were perfect, the porridge with just the right thickness in it. No wonder Hiltzern said that Von Munke didn't deserved the ginger-haired man as his steward. When, precisely a quarter-of-an-hour later Walters re-entered the cabin, Reitz asked him how he knew of his liking for Scottish breakfast. 'Simple sir, you likes their liquid gold; so you must 'ave acquired a taste for their breakfast – but don't ask me where I gets the stuff,' He added tapping his stubby nose again. 'Oh, an' by the way, your uniform's in your main locker. I unpacked your case whilst you were asleep.' Reitz shook his head in amazement. 'Thankyou, Walters.' And the little man took up the tray and vanished back into his cubby-hole of an headquarters.

Making his way to the bridge Reitz noticed that the sloppiness of the night before had vanished. The bridge gleamed; smart salutes and cheerful greetings from officers and seamen alike abounded. Word of his sharpness of arrival had obviously spread. The Master-at-arms stood outside his sea-cabin at the rear of the bridge standing smartly to attention with the previous evening's defaulters. The sloppy watch that had been so ill-prepared. Now they stood smart and clean, almost as if outwardly at least, proud to be on default. With the six sailors was Junior Leutnant Anders. Reitz looked them up and down as they filed into his much smaller sea-cabin. 'Yesterday you were a disgrace but today is a new day. I do not tolerate any sloppiness at all whatever the situation. You will be docked one day's pay and the next time we return to Kiel, you will all stand an extra watch. Now, get back to your duties and be proud to be on this ship. Leutnant Anders, you stay here! The rest of you are dismissed.'

Some other defaulters followed. One late from leave, two for coming aboard in a state of unacceptable inebriation, another for being involved in a fight with a Wehrmacht soldier on leave ashore and finally one for spitting on deck – unfortunately in the unexpected presence of Hiltzern.

Quietly he dressed them down and handed out the summary punishment of loss of pay or privileges as well as doing extra duties and when they'd left, he turned to deal with Anders. He told the young officer that he expected the very highest standards from him and that from now on that the punishment for him was that he was to be at Reitz's' beck and call whenever required.

Then he visited the bridge where he found Hiltzern instructing a group of junior officers on how to be in charge of the ship whilst their senior counterparts were waiting for Reitz in the wardroom. 'Good morning sir, I am just explaining to these children as to how to look after this ship whilst she's still attached to the dockside. They mustn't be too overawed by their responsibilities and must not disturb us unless big man Grand Admiral Raeder or his toady corporal boss dear Adolf should decide to come along to work out what a real warship looks like. I've also added that if fat Goering or weedy Goebbels turns up that they should find a few gash buckets and chuck these idiots of our political leaders into them. Waste not, want not, I say.' Then the big man started laughing at his satirical jokes until Reitz, with a wry smile on his face, clapped him on the shoulder 'Come on Commander, time we went below.'

The wardroom was clean and sparkling, all traces of the last evening's smoke and mess completely gone. The portholes had been opened to clear away the smell of the smoke and sweat. Reitz nodded at the assembled officers who all came smartly to attention when he entered the room. Then he waved them to their seats. There were one or two slight chuckles and even a few smiles at this introduction.

'Good morning gentlemen. It's very much more pleasing to come in here and be able to breathe and also that I can see you all.'

After a short pause, Reitz continued to outline his own career and his thoughts of *Dresden*'s current war record. He watched their faces as he went on 'Today we shall fully stock up with fuel and ammunition. Barges will be alongside very soon. By evening we shall have the feel of the Baltic beneath our keel. At first light, just twenty-four hours from now we shall begin a series of meaningful exercises in our role as an independent raider and not as part of some imaginary non-existent battle fleet. Our targets, below, on and above the water will be both real and imaginary. We will practise with everything as well as fire and damage drills, air-raid alerts, bombing avoidance tactics, in short, the lot. This ship will become a proper fighting unit of the Kriegsmarine in less than three weeks. That's all the time we have. There will be no more "*Runswick Castles*" again when eventually we run into the Atlantic' – and then he thumped on the table in front of him, 'for run we will, not away but for the enemy. However, we need to be fully prepared so these exercises will be as real as Admiral Canaris and I have been able to make them. During them I shall get to know all of you as well as I can within your own sphere of operations before we set out for deeper waters, one final exercise and then into a true warlike cruise. This cruise will show *Dresden*'s real potential. It's her, and our, last chance or else we'll end up like cruiser *Emden* on a permanent training schedule for the Kriegsmarine's new recruits.' He looked at the expectant faces. None of them were downcast. Perhaps they sensed that Reitz was so different from Von Munke. They'd heard of his efforts at Narvik and elsewhere, even if he'd only been captain of a destroyer rather than on this major unit of the Kriegsmarine.

He was continuing. 'Yes, I know I am a destroyer man but this ship can really combine three vessels in one – destroyer, cruiser and battleship. She has the speed, the endurance and the weapons to give the Allies a very nasty surprise. It is my job to see that she gives a good account of her capabilities. If you have any complaints please let me know, or Commander Hiltzern, although whether I shall act on them remains to be seen.' There was a further slight ripple of repressed laughter.

Reitz looked over them again. 'Believe me, the next three weeks will involve us all in real hard work. Now to it. All of you. We sail at eight bells of the afternoon watch. Oh and by the way, if you wish to smoke or booze yourselves to death in here, then do so if the portholes are open and the ship is not in any foreseeable action. Otherwise, I want everyone of you on the alert all the time. Once we've been in a scrape then by all means kill yourselves by having a cigarette if your nerves can't stand the change of direction that this ship will be taking.'

Perhaps this was a tough joke but the assembled officers knew that this new captain of their ship meant business. Proper warlike business.

Reitz then left the men to discuss the import of what he'd just said before they went off to their various stations on the ship. Back on the upper bridge he motioned to Anders 'Leutnant in ten minutes time I'm going to tour this ship. You will assist me together with two armed sailors. See to it. I'll meet you here when you have your men ready.' Down in the wardroom just two of the officers were left, Surgeon Commander Wilhelm Lebers, another small man who wore spectacles and whose main form of relaxation was to have the chorales of J.S. Bach echoing around the ship's hospital berth, was in conversation with the ship's chaplain, Padré Erich Jervaulx a former curate of a Roman Catholic parish in Munich. Lebers commented 'I see we have a new broom padre, eh, what?'

'God works in mysterious ways, His wonders to perform.' quoted the cleric who had long since noted that he shared with the fleet's supreme chief a common Christian name. He also realised that it was Raeder's insistence that the big ships of the Fleet all retained a naval chaplain as well as one at the bases for the smaller ships. Jervaulx also wore rounded glasses and his hair, thinning on top, was turning prematurely grey. Born in Saltzburg he'd qualified as a Catholic priest two years before the war had begun.

Once it had, he'd asked his bishop to release him from the parish in Munich as he felt the calling to join the chaplaincy division within the Kriegsmarine. After a quick training course into the ways of the Navy he'd been appointed to the new heavy cruiser *Blucher*. The ship had been mistakenly sailed into the narrow Lombaks fjord approach to the Norwegian capital of Oslo and there torpedoed by the gallant Norwegian resistance to the German attempts to take the area by force. Somehow he'd survived as the heavy cruiser capsized and sank. Despite the cold water he'd swum for the shore and had been rescued by a Norwegian family who'd seen, with surprise, his clerical garb as he lay gasping, alone, on an isolated section of the narrow shingled shore some half-mile downstream from where *Blucher* had sunk. They'd helped him to recover and in gratitude to them he'd never given them away once he'd returned to the newly-established German authorities in Oslo. Soon after, he'd been posted to *Dresden* once she'd returned from her North Sea activities and was on board her during her brief Atlantic sortie and the meeting with *Runswick Castle*. During the return to Kiel and even when tied up to the quay he'd heard many sailors in confession give vent to angry thoughts about the validity of Von Munke as a captain and as to how they'd dispose of the now disgraced former captain who'd brought so much shame to their ship. He looked up at Lebers and continued 'Perhaps we have exchanged a scared wimp for a very determined whip!'

Lebers nodded. 'Maybe. Mind if he does take the ship into battle perhaps we may have more than just pretend headaches and the occasional cut finger to deal with – maybe your funeral book will have to be dusted, eh?' With that ironic comment the surgeon heaved himself out of his chair and wandered off to check his ever-so clean medical instruments, the likes of which he had yet to use in earnest.

Navigating Officer Oberleutnant Alfred Serle accompanied Reitz into the chartroom as soon as he'd reached the bridge. The list of charts that the captain wanted were numerous and he wasn't sure that they were all in stock – the South Atlantic, Indian, Pacific and even the Antarctic Oceans. Serle queried the requests but was told somewhat curtly by his new captain that if any were missing then he was to get hold of them immediately from shore-based supplies.

Then with Anders as his guide and the two armed sailors flanking him or bringing up the rear of the small group, Reitz next went up to the gunnery control room to have words with Morge Halder, the officer in overall command of *Dresden*'s guns, from the big eleven-inch ones down to the smallest calibre machine-gun. He left Halder in no doubt that the big guns would be fired in anger and that on the new exercises they'd better get used to hitting not only slow-moving targets but much faster ones as well, even if the battlecruiser was shaking herself to bits at full speed.

Onto the radar room. Reitz marvelled at the array of dials and the various screens and control buttons. The two radar operators told him that they were still going over their newly-translated manual that the Abwehr had provided for them and that they were looking forward to its full usage once *Dresden* was out at sea. Both men had been transferred from *Scharnhorst* which had the best radar so far in service with the Kriegsmarine but from what they could already work out, this British machine was far superior. 'Best keep the fact that we have it a secret so no talking about it when, and if ever when, you go ashore. It could be the difference between success or defeat when we engage the enemy, and we will engage them have no fear – Your information in detecting the enemy will be of the utmost value.'

There were four operators in the wireless room although two of the men weren't officially on duty. Reitz enquired as to the range of their instruments and was duly impressed by the replies that were given. Did they know how to jam enemy transmissions?

Yes, they felt sure that they could but under Von Munke they'd never had the chance. Reitz assured them that they would get that chance.

Anders then took him outside on a tour of the numerous anti-aircraft guns and via some of the secondary gun turrets eventually reaching the torpedo tube control area where Theodore Seizel was the officer in charge. As with the gunners the message was the same. If they hadn't been fired in anger, Reitz promised them that he would find them work on the next cruise but to Seizel he also added that the torpedoes on *Dresden* were just as important as the big guns.

'You know that this ship can sail as fast as any destroyer so I intend to use a destroyer's main offensive weapon – these' and there on, Reitz patted the practice torpedoes that were currently in position '– except they won't have dummy warheads but the real ones.'

He visited the rear main gun turret, named Cesar with the same remarks as before that once out on the cruise the big guns would soon have the chance to fire in real earnest. Down then into the main interior of the ship. To the damage control section where the men controlled the whole ship in their enclosed room of dials, levers and wiring. 'Vital this area,' Reitz remarked 'and yet so remote from anything.' He knew that the armour around the controls was especially thick to try and prevent the section becoming damaged in the heat of a battle.

On and on, to the kitchens and storerooms. Head chef, Peter Merke also doubled up as an anti-aircraft gunner if so required and jokingly remarked 'I can always provide useful ammo if we run out of the real thing – hardened sausages – "bangers" as the English call them. Ha! Ha!' Reitz smiled realising that a new spirit was obviously spreading throughout the ship as a result of his arrival, encouraging words and tour of the whole ship. Merke was continuing 'Oh we have a line in extra lifebuoys – extra light and large pancakes. Worked out a special recipe especially if we decided to float off Von Munke!'

Reitz grunted. Here was a character who knew how to tell really awful jokes – just the sort needed in a real emergency to help keep up morale.

Then it was down into the engine room where he met up again with his erstwhile railway companion, Chief Engineering Officer Alfred Herzog as well as his deputy Arthur Luth, a long – faced sombre looking man who'd been with *Dresden* since she'd first been in commission. Reitz knew little about engines or the men that served them with their array of oil cans, grease guns, spanners, hammers, wrenches and the various other paraphernalia of their trade at hand except to know that this area was the real hub of the whole reason for the battlecruiser. Already the engines were gently rumbling. 'Are we ready to go?' asked Reitz to Herzog.

'Aye, aye sir, with or without a dram in the fuel!'

Another character with a brand of humour hinting of Reitz's preference for the amber liquid from Scotland.

'Well, make sure you keep these babies in perfect order' replied Reitz patting an engine casing and with that climbed back up the ladders following an apparently untiring Anders. Constantly opening doors, climbing ladders, pushing hatch bars and always in the lead. His physique was still in excellent shape. He hadn't won the Junior Physique title of Germany without a lot of training. This tour only reinforced his high standard of physical fitness.

Reitz said to him 'Not getting tired Anders?'

'Not yet sir seeing I'm fully fit.'

'Well, you're doing very well. Anywhere else?'

'The sick bay and the padré.'

'Padré?'

'Yes sir, we have one. Decent fellow although I'm not particularly religious myself.'

'Well, let's go and see.'

Anders once again led the way to the centrally placed Sick Bay with its rows of neatly made beds. In the office off the main ward, he met Doctor Lebers, his two principal attendants as well as Jervaulx the padré, who also doubled up as an extra male nurse for he'd qualified as one before joining the Catholic ministry.

Reitz was impressed by the sense of peace and quiet in the berth. Its immaculate cleanliness making it veritably shine. 'I trust that you are a good surgeon' Reitz remarked to Lebers 'and are knowledgeable about tropical diseases. Please make sure that you have a good supply of the necessary inoculations, malaria tablets and quinine – we may well need them on our forthcoming cruise. Go as discreetly as you can to the nearest Abwehr office – they will have the required stocks ordered for you by the next time we dock – in plain cartons so that Allied spies don't get the idea that we're actually going to sail away to far-off seas!'

Lebers nodded 'Well sir, it'll be a change for us to do some real work!'

To Jervaulx, Reitz said 'Padré, let me know of all your church services and whatever else you require – and try to become acquainted with the Anglican burial service. You never know when it will be required!'

'Not to worry sir! I do believe in the ecumenical service of the whole church. We have on board as well as Roman Catholics, a mixture of Lutherans, Baptists and even a couple of Orthodox adherents. As for the Anglican church, one of the engineers is from such a church in Wurtemberg – apparently his mother is English – and he has quite a divided view of the war.'

Reitz looked at the eager face of his ship's chaplain. 'I note that from your war record, that you served on *Blucher* making you one of the very few men on this ship to have not only been under fire but to have had to swim for your life, like myself, eh?'

'Yes sir, the water of that fjord was a bit chilly!'

'Well, it's good to know that there are at least two of us who have inadvertently swum in Norwegian waters. Maybe we shall all be under the enemy's fire one day but hopefully we won't need to realise how good our swimming powers are – or that we shall have need too much of ours or the Anglican's funeral orations!'

'As you say sir.'

'Right padré, I think that's all. Can't say that I've had too much in the way of a religious connection recently although I was known to pull a bell-rope or two in my youth at my local church. Knowing Herr Hitler he'll probably want to take all the bells down for scrap metal and turn them into shells.'

'I hope not sir, Bell metal isn't all that useful for anything other than making bells.'

'Really? Well I mustn't get involved in that sort of conversation. Too much to do. Goodbye all – and I trust that hopefully we won't shake your neat berth to bits when the guns open fire!'

The tour of the ship took nearly four hours to complete but Reitz was pleased he'd done it. Behind him the men were all that much the better realising that the stories that they'd heard about him must have held some truth. The dynamism that he possessed was already spreading throughout the ship as it prepared to get out to sea. Back in his main cabin Walters appeared with two substantial beef sandwiches as well as a small apple pie with cream – all washed down with strong tea – and all as if just cut and brewed the moment he'd entered through the door. As he munched his way through the sandwiches he pondered yet again over the turn of events that had befell him over the last fortnight. The departure from the Z-class destroyer, the interview with Canaris, the few days of leave and then his arrival on *Dresden*, a ship now almost straining to be off to sea. But it was his leave that he lingered over the longest.

Far away so it seemed. In the foothills of the Bavarian Alps. The war had seemed millions of miles away with the snow covered mountain tops glistening in the morning sun. The mountain stream dropping down the waterfall by which he had been fishing. Thoughts of his new command were humming through his mind as he'd waited for a bite at the end of the extended rod over the rippled water.

Canaris. 'She's only really a big-gunned destroyer. Use her like one. Not the ponderous out-dated battleship that Von Munke thought that she was. She's got speed.'

Then the whine of the fast Focke-Wulfe 190 interrupted those thoughts. A test pilot jubilantly testing the new fighter to its limits swooping down over the valley.

Scaring the brown chestnut mare.
And its rider.
Elle.

Only moments earlier he'd seen the horse and rider picking its way along the streamside path but then the rod wriggled indicating a probable bite by an unsuspecting trout.

The horse reared.
Throwing Elle into the pool.
The deepest part.

Without hesitation he'd flung off his coat, discarded his long fisherman's waders and dived in gasping at the coldness of the water. The girl was thrashing desperately. He reached her as her head was going under water and then frantically back-pedalled holding her head above the surface. Her panic had made the swim to the edge of the pool doubly difficult but somehow surprisingly it was soon reached. She didn't struggle as he pulled her out of the water. He tried his best to rub her as dry as possible without giving her cause for any embarrassment. Eventually she opened her eyes.

'Hullo – and thanks.'

'A bit of a surprise, that fighter wasn't it?'

'Yes – and a wet one!'

'Look, my name's George. What's yours?'

'Elle, Elle Chemnitz.'

'Well, have a nip of this.' With that Reitz gave her his hip flask. Full of neat schnapps. Elle spluttered and coughed as the rawness of the spirit hit the back of her throat, but she still swallowed it. Then she struggled to her feet, with Reitz's, help even though her jacket, sweater, jodhpurs and riding boots were soaked. Reitz gave her his fishing coat and a spare blanket and held her close as she began to shiver.

'Please get me my horse.'

Fortunately it had recovered from the shock of the noise of the aircraft and it stood contentedly munching lush meadow grass and Reitz, good horseman that he was, approached it and was able to catch hold of its bridle. Docilely it followed him and with a still sodden Elle, the bedraggled couple walked back down the valley to the inn at which Reitz was staying.

The innkeeper's bustling wife took Elle in and after she'd undressed and bathed, she gave her a long woollen night-dress and a huge dressing gown. Meanwhile Reitz mounted the horse and it trotted back up to the fishing pool from where Reitz collected all his fishing gear. Then he rode over to the inn in the next village where he'd learned that Elle was staying. The landlady there rummaged through some of Elle's spare clothes and packed them into a small suitcase. Arrangements were made with the horse's owner to collect it from Reitz at the inn to which he returned, still in his damp clothes. By the time he'd returned, Elle now with her long black hair dried out, was now sitting on a padded stool in front of a blazing log-fire. He quickly changed into drier clothes and by the time he'd come downstairs the innkeeper had a meal ready for them both – hot sausage pie, beetroot, cabbage and boiled potatoes followed by warm sponge with cream. Elle didn't say too much during the meal but every so often she raised her face and her black eyelashes fluttered as she looked across at Reitz.

Then as the last of the hot sponge was swallowed and two coffees laced with brandy were poured by their genial host, Elle began to talk.

'You know, George, that I already am aware of who you are. You see, I work for the Abwehr although I was unaware of your presence in this area. I'm also on a short leave, shortly to be transferred to our operations in Brest as part of the naval liaison team. Your fame has spread being a Narvik hero.'

Reitz grinned, fascinated by the relaxed features of Elle as she looked at him. She continued 'I'm a Cologne girl although my parents have moved to a suburb of *Dresden.* They've a bit of money and dad managed to get a new practice – he's a dentist – in that city.'

Reitz intervened, 'How many more co-incidences are we going to get today? You see, my new ship is the battlecruiser *Dresden* and the man in charge of my appointment is also your ultimate boss, Admiral Wilhelm Canaris.'

It was Elle's turn to smile 'Well you never know, my work could be involved in plotting your ship's position if it is ever ordered out into the Atlantic.'

Reitz gave a faint smile and then gently steered the conversation to non-warlike items as they sat gazing at each other or at the flickering flames of the log-fire.

The innkeeper cleared away the dishes and whispered to Reitz that his car was available in order to take the lady back to her hotel. So, in a very relaxed state, George returned Elle to her rooms, lightly kissed her on the cheek with a promise to return in the morning and take her down to the railway station.

Wistfully they held hands on the platform as the decrepit old tank engine hauling two equally ancient carriages trundled and hissed its way into the branch-line station. As it laboriously chugged its way out with a cloud of belching black smoke and swirls of white vapour, Reitz stood on the platform waving to Elle as long as was possible before the train slowly crawled round a bend three hundreds yards down the track from the station.

Then he'd returned back to the waterfall, the fishing rods came out again and he sat on the accompanying basket staring into the waters thinking of her.

Of Elle.

The last drops of a 'wee dram' were drained from the glass as Reitz rose to leave his cabin in order to make his way to the bridge. Strange, he thought, that the liking of an enemy's liquor was so much to his taste. It was difficult to think that the Scottish or the English were 'enemy' for he'd so thoroughly enjoyed his time in Aberdeen or touring their country. He'd even returned when his friend, Charles Sugden, had invited him over in 1937. They'd gone, with other former university associates to the Naval Review of Spithead. The array of British naval power had been most impressive. Not even the pride he'd felt on seeing the new smart appearance of the *Graf Spee* was able to wipe away the fact of the overwhelming strength of the numerous Royal Naval warships as compared to the limited contribution to the Review by the fledgling Kriegsmarine. Was it a sheer co-incidence that Germany's first major naval loss of the war had been that self-same *Graf Spee*, now little more that a rusting, shattered hulk on a sandbank off the Uruguayan port of Montevideo?

He reached the bridge and knew that thoughts of Elle, or of the 'enemy' had to be pushed to one side as he prepared to take *Dresden* out to sea. Two tugs hovered by the battlecruiser but Reitz sent a signal for them to move away. He did not want their assistance. He meant to con *Dresden* out to sea as if she were nothing more than his previous Z-class destroyer command.

Mind, she was a bit bigger. Say, eight times.

The ropes that connected her to the quay were slackened off and cautiously and carefully Reitz gave out his orders. 'Slow ahead.' 'Port rudder.' 'Starboard engine only.' 'Stop.' 'Slow astern.' 'Stop.' 'Slow ahead starboard.' Until at last her bow swung well clear of the quayside. 'Slow ahead all engines. Ten degrees port rudder.'

Something nagged at him as he concentrated. To Halder who

wasn't in his gun control position but instead, at his side, he asked 'Are the anti-aircraft gunners at their positions?'

'Yes sir, they are' was the reply. The swell of the Baltic was to beginning to make itself felt as the harbour walls were falling astern when the bridge intercom crackled into life 'Wireless room to bridge; air alert for Kiel.'

An escorting minesweeper pulled over to allow *Dresden* to pass, her captain noting, as did the tug men, how much better handled that the warship was now showing. Von Munke's departures had always been under the hawsers of two or sometimes four tugs. She was even putting on more speed than usual. Reitz wanted sea room before the bombing attack was going to begin.

There were fifty-three bombers from the Royal Airforce over Kiel in that snap raid. A mixed force of Whitley, Wellington and Hampden bombers, they bombed from a safe height, at the upper limit of the town's heavy anti-aircraft guns. The bombs fell somewhat haphazardly over a wide area around the port but none hit a major naval target although three whisked down to crash into the water some sixty-feet from cruiser *Prinz Eugen* causing some slight damage from the resultant splinters.

Fifty-one bombers returned. The flak managed to bring two raiders down. The rest rumbled back to their bases in East Anglia and Lincolnshire with their crews unaware as to how close they'd been to seriously damaging or even sinking *Dresden.* One small patrol boat berthed immediately astern of where *Dresden* had been moored, simply vanished under a hail of bombs although all her crew were ashore at the time.

Kiel reported this fact to Reitz and he smiled. Maybe he was bringing new luck to the battlecruiser. He pushed his ship up to twenty-five knots and the crew of the escorting minesweeper watched her go away with a frothy stern wake as the sign of her departure into deeper waters. Her crew, as one man wished her good luck. So far *Dresden* had been a failure but now with her new captain, Reitz of Narvik, then perhaps her fortunes would change. For the better . . .

The battlecruiser pushed into the Baltic. Northwards and then eastwards. On into the night.

Eight bells. The end of the first watch of the next day. Reitz, already up after only a few hours sleep was in the radar room. 'You shall pick up a blip fairly soon' was his directive as he stared at the illuminated screens. Just under an hour later the radar operators sent a message to Reitz who was back on the bridge 'Strong double echo off the port bow. Range about fifteen miles.' Already the two men were realising that the captured British set was far superior to anything they'd ever worked on before. Reitz pushed the Action Stations button on the bridge. The klaxon sounds echoed throughout the ship. Urgent and strident. Booted feet echoed all over. Water tight doors were slammed shut. Divisions throughout the vessel began to send reports to the bridge that they were all already. Guns. Torpedoes. Engine-room. Damage control. Sick berth. Within three minutes the ship was closed up and fully ready.

'Not bad' murmured Reitz.

Then a lookout yelled 'Target and smoke in sight!'

'Bearing man, what's the bearing?' snarled a petty officer.

'Thirty-two degrees off the port bow.'

A smudge of smoke could be seen as binoculars and telescopes focussed on the distant objects. A tug belching smoke and about a mile astern a target vessel under tow.

'Full ahead. Guns open fire with main armament.'

The forward two turrets, Anton and Bruno opened up. Raggedly and inaccurate. Halder, still trying to come to terms with his repeater screen from the radar had underestimated by nearly two thousand yards the target that showed up as a blurred green blip on the screen. He desperately re-adjusted the range requirements and the next time, the salvo from the forward turrets was not only in time together but the practice shells fell only a few hundreds yards in front of the target.

'Up two hundred. Fire.'

This time, at least one of the four shells hit the target. Halder readjusted yet again making allowances for *Dresden*'s speed and Reitz's change of course as he turned the ship so as to bring the third turret, Cesar, at the stern, into position so that it too could open fire.

Eight salvoes from each turret were fired as *Dresden* continued to turn and keep at a range only suitable for the big guns.

Then Reitz ordered 'Cease fire,' brought the battlecruiser in a tight turn back towards the target and closed in, ordering the secondary five point nines and the heavy anti-aircraft four point ones to fire when in range, first the port batteries and then, after another tight turn, the starboard ones as well.

Another turn again and this time it was up to the torpedoes to show their merit.

The four port torpedoes fired, scoring one hit. Another tight turn. The starboard battery scored three hits. Torpedo Officer Seizel felt much better. It was like scoring with that fat Hamburg wench in the sleazy whore-house he'd visited during his last leave.

Time after time Reitz flung *Dresden* around the target until the practice ammunition for the big guns was exhausted and the sea around the target was full of floating cases and practice torpedoes. The astonished tug master couldn't believe that the ship he'd been watching on exercise was the same one that had so desultorily fired on the same target with such limited success only a few days back, never mind earlier on. He'd heard that the battlecruiser had a new captain. Obviously he was making a considerable difference.

He watched the sleek warship over the horizon, her broad wake indicating that she was still travelling at a high speed. At least twenty-five knots.

Reitz knew what he was doing. It was all in the exercise dreamt up by Canaris. No-one else did. An hour passed. Radar reported 'five blips just off starboard bow.'

The men, who'd been stood down, were once more sent to their action stations as the alarm bells rang.

An alarm for the four neutral Swedish merchantmen who to the astonishment of their lookouts and officers on watch alike, they saw the shape of a powerful warship rapidly bearing down on them. Their escort, a veritable relic of a tired-looking torpedo boat of 1911 vintage, belched out heavy smoke as she turned towards the speeding newcomer, flashing a 'stand-off' message as she attempted to ward off *Dresden*.

Reitz maintained his course with Halder giving the guns the ranges as they fell rapidly. Suddenly Reitz yelled 'Hard-a-starboard!' taking the battlecruiser away from the T-boat and her charges. Then, as the ship seemed to be widening the range he snarled 'Hard-a-port' and *Dresden* executed a heeling turn once again towards the ships, aiming to pass between the escort and her charges as Reitz ordered the helm to be straightened up. One of the Swedish ships began to lag behind somewhat erratically as her helmsman was watching the antics of the battlecruiser rather the course he was supposed to be keeping. To his horror he saw that his wanderings had taken his ship on an apparent collision course with *Dresden*.

The T-boat, belching even more smoke as her stokers piled on coal in a bout of frenzied activity also began to swing to try and ward off the battlecruiser.

Dresden slipped between the two ships with only about two hundred yards to spare on either side as she steamed rapidly whilst executing yet another sharp turn so as to not only cross the bows of the erring merchantmen but also manoeuvre behind the sterns of the other three ships.

Reitz had known about the convoy although he hadn't bargained for the wandering merchantman whose witless helmsman was knocked away from the wheel by the ship's first mate who pulled the ship to her original course and straight into the frothy wake that spread out behind *Dresden*'s rapidly disappearing stern.

Pots and pans, hammers and paint tins; anything loose were sent clattering even though Reitz in the earlier gun practice had warned that loose items must be stowed away but he'd not given them any warning of the violent twisting and turnings around and now between the vessels of that small convoy.

'God, I thought that we were going to hit them.' Hiltzern gasped as *Dresden* began to draw away.

'Not really. This ship has three screws, twin rudders and the qualities of a large destroyer, not some ponderous battleship' came the riposte from Reitz who gave out such an aura of relative calm.

'I still think sir that we were taking too great a risk.'

Back came a comment 'Just think of the situation had we been shooting our weapons whilst dashing between the serried or more likely scattering ranks of ships in an Allied Atlantic convoy'.

'But, but, we've never done anything like that before. Certainly not with Von Munke.

'Ah, but you should have done. *Dresden* is a ship with so much potential.'

'Well, er yes, sir, we can see that now.'

Then to Serle he gave the orders for the course to be sent to the north-west again. Back to the tug and her larger ship. More firing tests. At full speed, at low speed, at one gun at a time, even when reversing. Every so often, the big tug fished out the practice ammunition for it to be handed back to *Dresden* when her cranes had the chance to practise whilst on a swaying platform. As Reitz put it 'Wait until we're alongside a supply ship. Then the practice will be seen to be very useful, very useful indeed!' There was even a grim chuckle as well.

As the practice went on the target became more and more battered as Halder's gunners scored more frequently than they'd ever done in any practices under Von Munke. Only darkness brought relief for the gun crews as well as a scarcity of usable practice ammunition.

The battlecruiser cruised quietly until shortly after daybreak. Grey clouds scudded in a fresh wind from the north-west bringing squally sleet and rain showers. Even so the radar boys were in early with a warning of a fleet of aircraft.

They came in low, towing drogues. As each aircraft took it in turn to fly over *Dresden* the light anti-aircraft guns opened up peppering the drogues with tracer and shells. All the time Reitz made frequent changes of course to try and throw the gunners off balance but they stuck determinedly to their task. After all, Reitz pointed out that Allied aircraft wouldn't expect them to sail obligingly in a straight line at a constant speed whilst they dropped their bombs. Reitz knew that the greatest danger to his ship would be from carrier-borne aircraft, not from other battleships. Those he could outspeed but compared to a carrier plane, *Dresden*'s top speed was really quite a laborious crawl.

The following day Reitz practised simulated damage to all areas of the ship. Fires were lit using oil-soaked rags all over the place without warning on instructions passed, not through the senior offices, but via a team led by Anders. Even in the engine-rooms where smoke flares were set off to try and give the staff down the ship's most vital area a reality they'd never even practised before but Reitz knew just how vital it was for the engineers to keep the ship on the move. First-aid parties were sent all over the ship practising rescue techniques and then carrying the injured via tortuous routes back to the Sick Berth or other sites designated temporary wards. One of the first-aid men became a genuine case as he gashed his elbow on a sharp projection when Reitz ordered a violent change of course.

Even the canteen staff weren't excluded. Reitz stopped the ship and had all the power switched off. The canteen men then had to make four sandwiches each for the twelve hundred men in just one hour in a darkness only dimly lit by a few oil-lamps and candles. And distribute them as if the crew were at actions stations.

'Well done' was the only thanks they received. It was enough. The ship's engines were also in the picture with the machinery they controlled being disabled. One rudder damaged. Both stuck at right angles. Steering using the propellers only. Then with two of the propellers damaged. Every possible combination.

'Just in case' said Reitz when queried. 'Supposing a submarine or aircraft-launched torpedo hits us there. It's *Dresden*'s Achilles-heel you know.'

On a calmer day they practised evacuating the ship using the boats and rubber floats leaving only a skeleton crew on board.

Again as Reitz said 'I did this at Narvik only we hadn't practised it beforehand!'

The humour was there. So was the lesson.

Seven exhaustive days and nights. At last Reitz swung *Dresden* back to Kiel. To refuel and also to restock ammunition supplies with live ammunition. As well as a full load of torpedoes.

By the time they'd made fast to the quayside, Reitz again declining any help from tugs the crew noticed that *Prinz Eugen* had left her berth. She'd too gone into the Baltic to begin a series of exercises with new battleship *Bismarck*.

By mid-morning of the next day *Dresden* was on the move again fully stocked up with fresh, frozen and tinned food as well as all the other items needed for a long cruise which Canaris provided upon Reitz's requests. She turned for the north. The Skagerrak and Kattegat. Keeping as far away from the Swedish coast as was possible. When at their closest, Reitz slipped *Dresden* through at night. No-one realised that the battlecruiser had passed by. Upon reaching an offing from the southern Norwegian coast, Reitz once again called a conference of his senior officers.

The junior officers were in charge yet again for in one of the exercises Reitz had practised a simulation of all the heads of department either killed or injured by ordering them into the Sick Berth. Doctor Lebers was somewhat sarcastic when they all turned up pretending to be ill or worse. Only Reitz had stayed on the bridge or nearby in his sea cabin observing as to how the younger men coped in a situation in which the speed was reduced to twelve knots, both forward turrets were out of action and that the ship had been torpedoed with a list of five degrees to port. Anders had even taken upon his own initiative to order a transfer of the heavy ammunition to the stern turret so that it could keep firing as well as to put out a thick smoke screen to cover their withdrawal from the 'pretend enemy,' in reality the small destroyer that was really their sole escort. Now Anders was in sole charge for Reitz was with his senior men in the still very clean wardroom.

'Gentlemen,' Reitz began 'so far, very good. We have such little time left. We are on the way out into the Atlantic providing we get through our final exercise. An unusual one to say the least but one in which I hope our torpedo men will come up trumps again, with I say, practice warheads. As our role in the Atlantic will be to attack real convoys we will in this exercise be attacking one of our own convoys. The principal escort will be of the opinion that we are an attacking Royal Navy cruiser. She will open fire with real ammunition –' there were some astonished looks at this statement '– but it's unlikely that she will be able to register any hits – Abwehr agents have tampered with her range-finder as well as her gun-sights so as to make them hopelessly inaccurate.' He paused to look around but only met the steadfast gaze of all those present. 'I concede that this practice does have an element of danger but it will give the crew, for the first time, an idea what it could be like to be under heavy gunfire, even though, I trust, it to be hopelessly inaccurate!' A slight ripple of laughter went through the gathering. 'My head and that of Admiral Canaris are on the block if this exercise fails but it is my intention to torpedo that major escort as if she were a genuine Allied warship – our practice torpedoes will dent its venerable hulk but not seriously damage it. The ship is the old pre-dreadnought *Rugen* which is currently employed escorting iron ore ships across the open sea before reaching our own waters. Her captain does not know of our role although the three torpedo-boats that are also in the escort force are in the picture. Speed, subterfuge and surprise. Weapons that we will require out in the Atlantic. Any questions?'

Second Officer Oberleutnant Helmut Brautsch stood up, nervously twiddling his officer's cap. 'Sir, what if we do sustain a hit by the *Rugen*'s shells?'

Reitz knew that this question was bound to come up. He'd often thought about this when he'd read about it in the file that Canaris had given him. 'Good question. The answer is that we shall carry on our mission for you see *Rugen*'s shells are not all armed ones. The Abwehr men have been very busy making sure that the first twenty shells she could well fire will all be relatively harmless apart from a bump or two should they hit. All personnel on deck will be under armoured shelter by the time she will be firing in our general direction. Remember we need our crew to be acclimatised to the fact that this ship fights sailing towards the enemy. Not away!'

'Captain, will we be using our radar?' Hiltzern this time.

'Yes. They will be plotting the convoy's course.'

'And the Arados?'

'Sorry, but I will be using them later in the Atlantic and elsewhere.'

Reitz paused. There were no more questions.

'Right gentlemen, it's time to go to our positions. Instruct all your departments to get some rest. We will, if Serle's navigational team will need to correct me on my own calculations, go to Actions Stations at 0530 in the morning.'

In his main cabin Reitz gazed at Elle's photograph that stood on his large desk to which he'd seated himself to pore over the large chart of the south-west coastline of Norway indented with its numerous river valleys and fjords but the warmth of the meal provided by Walters as well as the 'wee dram' dulled his senses and diverted him to looking at Elle. His mind wandered back to their last short meeting. After *Dresden* had tied up for her last recent visit to Kiel, he'd received a message that she'd be arriving at Kiel Railway Station. Over a mug of coffee and a plate of cakes at a nearby café he learned that Elle was about to go to Brest in North-West France in her new position as a clerk in the Naval Intelligence Department of the Abwehr. There she would be collecting information that would be of assistance to the surface raiders in the North Atlantic as well as further afield. She'd humorously remarked that Reitz and his battlecruiser could be one of those mercurial will-of-the-wisps. Reitz gave her a hint of a smile at this more than accurate thinking by the raven-haired girl who was nearly ten years his junior. A hurried last drain of their coffee, a smart walk back to the station platform, a lingering kiss and then the carriage door was shutting, the guard was blowing his whistle and the labouring locomotive with whooshes of steamy white vapour clouds and an ever-increasing curtain of dark brown smoke pouring up to the station roof pulled the heavy train on to its next major destination, that other great German naval port of Wilhelmshaven. Elle leaned out of her carriage window for as long as she could see the new naval man who'd come into her life beginning in the clear mountain air and deep cold waters of that Bavarian Alpine stream. A man whose destiny she already knew for a top official of Canaris already told her that within a few weeks, *Dresden*'s plan of action would see the ship in the heaving swells, troughs and wave patterns of the ever restless North Atlantic Ocean. What she nor Reitz would ever know, or could even say with any certainty would be when they'd ever meet again.

'Actions Stations' sounded their strident cacophony at seventeen minutes past five that next morning. Radar had picked up the convoy that Reitz knew would be there. It was time for their last practice. An idea that Canaris knew had an element of risk but so far as he could see, the majority of *Dresden*'s crew needed to realise the real meaning of being under fire.

The twelve and a half thousand ton bulk of *Rugen*, a pre-dreadnought battleship for the developing navy of the Kaiser's Reich, first entered water in the late January of 1903. Equipped with four eleven-inch guns in twin turrets fore and aft, numerous secondary guns of a smaller calibre poking out on either beam and with a top speed of eighteen knots she was soon engaged in warlike manoeuvres when she carried out exercises in the Baltic with the Russian Navy of Tsar Nicholas as her most likely target, but the Tsar's battle-fleet unexpectedly sailed through the Baltic and then halfway round world only to be annihilated off Tsushima by their waiting, more capably organised opponent, the Imperial Japanese Fleet under Admiral Togo. *Rugen* then joined up with her sisters in a mundane existence totally over shadowed by the new dreadnought battleships being built in the race for supremacy against the Royal Navy of the British people across the grey waters of the North Sea. The older, weaker, slower battleships were soon relegated into the Kaiser's Reserve Fleet and merely helped to train the new crewmen who were soon drafted to the bigger, faster units. Even so, when Admirals Scheer and Hipper decided on a trial of strength in May 1916 with the Royal Navy, they were forced to call upon the older battleships to add their gun-power to try and level terms with the British Grand Fleet. *Rugen* and her sisters went out to battle with Rear-Admiral Mauve in command and when Scheer ordered a one hundred and eighty degree reversal of course, the old ships instead of being at the rear of the line of battleships found themselves the nearest large units of the Kaiser's Fleet to their opposite numbers in the Grand Fleet. Despite the near-darkness, searchlights and star-shells illuminated them during their gun-battle. One of Mauve's ships failed to see a destroyer closing in with a salvo of torpedoes and the *Pommern* simply blew up in a blinding flash. There were no survivors from her devastated crew as *Rugen* and her sisters, in the wild melée, raced for the safety of home waters. Before it was over *Rugen*'s guns helped to drive off the British destroyers and one nearest to the battleship limped away with smoke streaming from at least three savage shell-hits.

After the briefest of refits, *Rugen* waddled back into the Baltic to form part of the patrol line against possible incursions into the German-Swedish merchant trade route by the ships of the Tsarist Navy, her original would-be opponents for which she had been built.

In October 1917 she encountered an equally slow Russian battleship still flying the Tsarist flag even though the country was under the new revolutionary government of Kerensky. The battle in which *Rugen* was the principal escort of a group of German military supply ships turned out to be a scrappy affair but one in which the Russian battleship was forced to retreat coastwards before running aground on a small sandbank. One of the Russian's last shells scored a damaging blow that hit *Rugen*'s after turret completely knocking it out causing a serious fire. Her captain turned his badly-damaged ship back to her base in East Prussia but like his Russian enemy, *Rugen* ran aground on to a mud-bank outside the port when her engines failed.

She was abandoned by her crew and her captain faced a charge of incompetence but for him Germany's pre-occupation with staving off defeat meant that he was simply retired out of the service, as was his ship. Abandoned. To sit on that mud bank rusting away. Forgotten in the turmoil of defeat. By her own people as well as the Allies. Most of the main ships of the Kaiser's Navy were sailed off to Scapa Flow to swing at their anchors for nearly half-a-year before one ignominious June day their remaining crews scuttled them. The few ships left in German waters were little more than a dispirited coastal force headed by two of *Rugen*'s sister ships, *Schlesien* and *Schleswig-Holstein* that were destined twenty years later to serve in the new Third Reich's Navy.

One July week-end, whilst on holiday in the area, a former gunnery officer of the *Rugen*, but now a captain in the revitalising Kriegsmarine of the Weimar government, Otto Franke was amazed to find his old ship still on the same mud-bank that she'd been stranded on when he'd last been a member of her crew. He hired a boat from the nearby harbour which took him out to the battered old battleship. Boarding her, he probed around the decks and despite eight years of neglect he worked out that basically the ship was repairable and perhaps could become a valuable training ship for the emerging new navy that had just launched a new cruiser, the *Emden*. Lovingly, almost, he rubbed his hands over the scarred stern rail with its rusting damage from that last Russian shell. Then the idea had come stronger to him. Could the discarded veteran really be saved? A vein of excitement and hope ran through his mind as he made his way back to the harbour in the launch.

It took some persuasion but the naval authorities within a few weeks were giving permission for first an inspection and after that, with the aid of tugs in early September, the *Rugen* was pulled off the mud-bank and with pumps working to prevent her from sinking, the old ship was taken to the nearest dry dock for the second stage – to make sure that she could float without the need of these pumps and then slowly she was towed across the Baltic to Kiel amidst as much secrecy as could be managed. The world was at peace and no-one, apart from those naval authorities, could really be bothered if the Germans were dragging a pre-Great War relic off a sand bank and into a harbour to be refitted for training purposes.

Franke supervised the whole repair job. As soon as it was possible, he lived on board the battleship watching and urging on the restoration work. Her aft turret was replaced by a twin-turret of old 5.9 (15cm) inch guns and her secondary battery of similar guns were reduced to only three single guns on either beam. The coal-fired boilers were cleaned out and augmented by oil-fired ones. Eventually a crew, captained by Franke with a few old-hands and the rest new trainees, took the old ship into the Baltic to test fire her guns and try out the restored and renewed engines.

With the trials behind her she was re-commissioned back into the Kriegsmarine and was soon in full employment training the steady trickle of new recruits as the Kriegsmarine began to develop under Grand Admiral Raeder. Back and forth she waddled as more and more trainees came and went. Occasionally she had the briefest of overhauls and maintenance checks but she held up well. Franke remained her captain for he had nowhere else to go. His wife and young daughter had died in the vicious influenza epidemic that swept across Europe shortly after the hostilities of the Great War ended. *Rugen* was now his main concern and somehow he felt that he could and would not desert his old girl.

When ex-corporal, now Fuhrer of Germany, Adolf Hitler upped the stakes of war with his Austrian 'anschluss', *Rugen*'s work increased. New gun crews were ever in demand for the trio of Germany's panzerschiffe's, the new light battlecruiser *Dresden* and even for the two larger battlecruisers *Scharnhorst* and *Gneisenau* – and the old ship, with Franke, helped to train the growing influx of naval recruits. Early in 1939 she went in for a full overhaul and came out on 30th August bound for the Polish coast at her working top speed of thirteen knots. Two mornings later on Friday 1st September she opened fire on real targets that even fired back at her.

Not that armed trawlers and two ancient coast-defence ships could offer much resistance and to the relief of Otto Franke, his bigger guns forced the surprised Polish sailors to hoist surrender flags. Perhaps it also helped that *Rugen* had as an escort two of Germany's newest destroyers.

The war turned an extra twist just two days later when Britain and France joined in, without effect, to assist Poland. Soon any naval action in the Baltic died down and *Rugen* continued in her task of training new recruits either on training exercises or escorting some small convoys across the Baltic to and from Swedish territorial waters.

Into nineteen-forty and Germany, once the ice had melted across the Baltic, began a new phase of the conflict with her sea-borne invasion of Denmark and Norway, in which the Kriegsmarine lost, of her modern ships, three cruisers and ten destroyers. Consequently the navy had to resort to their older ships to fill the gaps in much of the more mundane work of escorting the iron-ore carrying merchantmen bringing the vital raw material through the Norwegian leads and across the Kattegat to German ports. One of the ships called up to provide big gun support against possible, although, considered unlikely, incursions by British cruisers was Franke's venerable warship.

It was escorting some of the ships sailing on their first part of the voyage back to Narvik that *Rugen* found herself as a bright green spot on *Dresden*'s radar screen as the battlecruiser surged towards the unsuspecting group of ships at a speed of just over thirty knots. Somewhere on the waters off south-west Norway, near Stavanger.

A young lookout on *Rugen* yelled 'Ship on port beam, bearing seventy-five degrees.' Franke, even at the age of fifty-four years, was quick to react. The stranger was approaching from the west. Seemingly, as he took its shape in his binoculars at a very high speed. 'British cruiser!' he yelled. 'Main turret to engage as soon as you can bear. Open fire!'

As the stranger rapidly approached, Franke's memory quick-flashed him back to the destroyers attacking Von Mauve's squadron of pre-dreadnoughts. *Pommern* exploding. Yet Franke did not flinch. He wasn't afraid. He'd been there before. He knew he had to delay the stranger.

The forward turret seemed to take an age to turn to face the oncoming warship. Then the twin eleven-inch (28cm) guns opened fire. Hopelessly wide. Odd though, the stranger hadn't as yet replied.

Still it came on swinging broadside on before showing her stern.

The forward turret boomed again.

Then Franke saw four white streaks of water coming towards the port flank of his battleship. 'Hard-a-port!' he yelled.

Ponderously *Rugen* swung her bows towards the tracks. An aeon of time too late.

Thud! Thud! Thud! Thud! Franke couldn't believe it. The strangers missile's were all failures. They hadn't exploded. *Rugen* was still turning. Then Franke, was attracted by an astonished lookout yelling 'They're lowering their flag.' 'The White Ensign'. Even more astonishing, up the flag mast rose the Kriegsmarine's own naval flag.

But the shocks weren't over.

A light began to flash from the stranger. 'KM *Dresden* to KM *Rugen*. Thanks for the practice. Best wishes. Hope we haven't dented you too much. Cheerio.'

Then with a flurry of foam at her stern the battlecruiser turned away, back to the Western horizon.

Franke felt hopelessly weak at the knees. 'Good heavens above' he thought 'we fired live ammunition at her. What if we'd hit her? Who the hell dreamed up this exercise? Why wasn't I told?'

One of the smaller escorts began to follow the old battleship and was already slowing down to pick up the practice torpedoes now just floating on the surface.

Reitz murmured to Hiltzern 'Did you see that? The captain of that old veteran wasn't afraid. He turned his ship towards us trying to protect his convoy.'

Hiltzern replied 'A good thing then that his guns had been tampered with or else we might have been hit.' He didn't sound all that pleased at the apparent success of the exercise. *Dresden* had been under fire by one of her own Navy's warships.

Reitz merely grunted 'I know but we've proved one thing – if we can take the enemy by surprise, using our speed, even their older battleships will be vulnerable. Unlike Lutjens and his two battle-cruisers who I gather turned away from old British battleships, defending their convoys we shall, if the opportunity arises when we're out in the Atlantic, go in, attack, and not run away.'

Then to Serle, his principal Navigating Officer, he said 'Lay out a course for twenty miles off Trondheim at a cruising speed of fifteen knots. We will be rendezvousing with a supply ship.' Then he paused over a paper with scribbled co-ordinates. 'There, at that position.' Serle clicked his heels and went to work in the chart-room.

Dresden steadied on to her new course taking her into waters where a year previously Reitz had witnessed the courageous act of the British destroyer *Gloworm* when, despite severe damage, her captain had rammed his ship into the side of the heavy cruiser *Admiral Hipper*. Now here he was again but this time in charge of Germany's fastest main warship with a mission to prove that she was still a valuable asset for the Kriegsmarine.

Back in his main cabin he removed his sea boots and jacket, flung himself on his bunk realising that soon such a rest would be a luxury. Six hours at least to the rendezvous. For now the other officers could see the ship to the rendezvous. Hopefully the threat of British submarines was no longer prevalent as they had been when panzerschiffe *Lutzow* was torpedoed by one during the Norwegian campaign.

Five hours later Walters entered the cabin to find his captain awake. He'd laid out a cold weather uniform on the chair and asked if Reitz would like a bath. Only the captain had this privilege on board *Dresden.* A rare luxury. Fresh water wasn't, for the ship had her own desalination machinery for washing purposes.

As Reitz rubbed himself dry he watched Walters set out a simple meal on the table – beef stew with cabbage followed by fruit pie and cream. As he ate it, in his solitude, Reitz thought that for some time to come this could well be his last decent meal. He pondered whether his officers and crew knew of *Dresden*'s future course of action. Walters came in with a coffee and a small tot of Scotch so Reitz asked him again, 'Where do you get this stuff –' indicating the whisky '– from?'

'Oh, here and there sir. I have my contacts. By the way you're drinking from a bottle brought in by one of our raiders so it really is courtesy of Winston Churchill himself, like.'

'Mmm' murmured Reitz and then he removed his bath-robe and dressed in what would be his regular rig for the days to come. Long under-drawers and long-sleeved vest, thick shirt, roll-neck sweater, leather trousers and jacket which men in the U-boats also wore, waterproof coat with hood. Thick socks and his long sea boots completed the ensemble, together with his captain's cap. A last sip of the whisky-flavoured coffee sent his thoughts back to England and a last touring holiday with his friends on a hired motor-cycle. There'd been four of them, three motorcyclists and he'd also had a pillion passenger. What was her name? Ah yes, Elizabeth MacBryde. Ginger coloured hair curling down to her shoulders. An infectious laugh. The four of them had stayed at various boarding-houses on a tour that took them in a run to Edinburgh, Newcastle and then York. Then across country via Chatsworth House and Coventry to Stratford-upon-Avon. Back up north via Chester and Blackpool with its famous tower. The last stop-over had been in Glasgow.

Yes, he mused, he knew Britain so well and it saddened him to be in charge of a ship that was now at war with that country. So full of tradition and history. He'd written to Elizabeth when he'd returned to Germany but she hadn't bothered to reply. Now, after so many years of his own company, Elle had arrived. Carefully he picked up the photograph of her and stashed it into an inside pocket, meaning to transfer it to his sea cabin aft of the bridge. There she was, now, probably in Brest. Perhaps even plotting the progress of *Dresden* as well as the courses of Germany's other sea raiders, some of which were in the guise of an innocent merchantman. Ships captained by Bernhard Rogge of the *Atlantis* or Felix Kruder of *Pinguin*, the latter ship having captured almost all of the Norwegian Whaling Fleet in the Antarctic. Reitz wondered if ever he could match their record or even of Theodore Krancke who'd commanded pocket-battleship *Scheer* in a five month cruise that had taken the regular warship into the Indian Ocean. Only recently returned.

The speaker above him clicked on 'Captain to bridge.' He acknowledged and left his cabin.

On the bridge closed staring through the rain-lashed windows stood Hiltzern. 'Radar, sir, three blips almost stationery about fifteen miles ahead.'

Reitz nodded 'Nothing to worry about. They are expected. A sort of final exercise for the crew.' Hiltzern raised his right eyebrow but said nothing. Soon a lookout reported a large merchantman with two small warships on either beam.

The ship, a tanker, came up close and began signalling '*Berengia* at your service.'

Reitz nodded again. To Hiltzern 'She's our supply ship. Instruct Luth to have the oil hoses slung out on derricks. She's going to top up our tanks.'

The big tanker, 13,439 tons unladen was down to her load line as she manoeuvred within two hundred yards of the now near motionless battlecruiser. She was a former British tanker captured at Rotterdam when German troops had taken control of the docks. She'd survived the bombing of the city being unable to make her escape to safety due to a serious fault in her engine room. Despite desperate efforts by her engineers they were unable to complete their work before the city's capture by the invading forces. She was towed to Wilhelmshaven, taken over by the Kriegsmarine and fully refitted, became a new supply ship for the German sea-raiders. *Dresden* was her allocated vessel.

So there she was, a black-hulled ship rolling in the grey waters with her two small minesweeper escorts bobbing up and down like demented corks in a mill-race, tiny and diminutive in contrast to their solid-looking charge.

Three hose-lines were made fast and the vital fuel oil flowed into *Dresden*'s tanks to fill them to capacity. The two ships made a forward progress of around three knots during the fuelling but Hiltzern, keeping a careful watch, never allowed the ships to come closer than forty feet despite the swell that surged back and forth between the two ships.

With the fuelling complete, the two ships slowly swung apart with *Berengia* signalling 'See you in broad acres.' She set course for the south to cross the eastern North Sea but *Dresden* shaped her way north-westwards and as night fell, Reitz ordered an increase in speed to twenty knots.

Aiming for the North Atlantic background. North of the Shetlands to meet the cold waters of the Arctic. Well to the north of the British Isles and then a run westwards before turning south. But this time, as *Dresden* pushed into the steepening seas there was a difference. She was going to attack whatever the consequences. She wasn't going to run away as she'd been so directed under Von Munke. With George Reitz in charge, the crew could sense a change had come over them. In just over three weeks. It was as if they were on a different ship even though it was the same one. Even the movement of the vessel itself felt different. Almost as if she was straining at the leash rather than dragging her feet.

'Yes gentlemen, this time it is going to be different.' Reitz was once again addressing the senior offices in the still sparkling wardroom. 'We are going through into the Atlantic, not via the Denmark Strait but through the passage between the Faroes and Greenland where, so I am led to understand, the Royal Naval patrol line consists of weaker ships and I trust, whatever we meet, we shall brush them aside and be into the Atlantic rollers before the Royal Navy's big ships in Scapa will have been able to haul their anchors out of the mud of their so-called snug anchorage.' Only Herzog and Serle had been very far into the Atlantic being on other ships before their appointment to *Dresden*. Even Reitz hadn't penetrated these waters in war-time. 'We are in charge of Germany's finest sea-raider. Six heavy guns, reliable and fast engines when so needed, otherwise very economical, a high degree of manoeuvrability and what has this ship achieved so far? Nothing!' Hiltzern's eyes were down-cast gazing at the simple blue carpet on the floor. He could still see Von Munke yelling 'Goods heavens Commander, those escorts of that cruiser are destroyers! One torpedo hit and we are finished!' He'd been screaming, his face pinched white. Hiltzern hadn't hit him despite an anger surging inside him. Only a very iron naval discipline had kept him in control but then he yelled 'Why the hell don't we open fire on them?' before turning his back on the screaming Von Munke, just as

Dresden had finished her own turn away and with increasing speed had fled from the Runswick Castle and her two slow corvette escorts. Then he'd heard the man say 'Right, now that we're getting away from danger I am going below. You con the ship back through the Denmark Strait' and Von Munke had then left the bridge, never to return to it. With a heavy heart Hiltzern had taken the battlecruiser north about, avoided any searching British cruisers, safely reaching Norwegian and soon after, German waters.

Reitz's voice cut into his thoughts 'It is in the reaches of the North Atlantic where this ship will create an impact by attacking Allied convoys sailing to or from the British Isles and sinking them. But more importantly it is the hope of Admiral Canaris, whose ship this really is as well as of Grand Admiral Raeder, that we create such a hornets nest so as to divert the attention of the Royal Navy on to us and away from battleship *Bismarck* which, with the new heavy cruiser *Prinz Eugen*, will be breaking into these waters some three weeks or so after us. We are the elusive bait. They will be the hammer blow.' Here Reitz clenched one fist into the palm of the other hand. 'To possibly back them up, battlecruisers *Scharnhorst* and *Gneisenau* will come out from their Northern French bases.' He paused, taking a sip of water, looking at the now earnest faces in front of him.

'We shall strike. Appear to retreat. Be chased. Elude them. And strike again. Simple isn't it? Our advantage will be our speed and the eyes of our radar.'

'Sir, if we're running at high speed –' bespectacled Leutnant Hans Goethe from the supplies department butted in 'We shall require fuel oil and other necessities. Do we have a supply ship rendezvous in the plans?'

An awkwardly stated question. Reitz smiled. 'Don't worry. Admiral Canaris has detailed our recent friend to be our supply ship. At present she is on course for a passage through the English Channel, steaming through the Dover Straits at night and then laying up by day in convenient French ports until she leaves Brest for a rendezvous with us in due course off the Azores. If she doesn't make it, we shall have to find our own supplies from any captured British merchantmen and relieve them of their materials.'

'How do we slip into the North Atlantic sir?'

'By using our speedy engines, Oberleutnant Brautsch.'

'Sorry sir, I mean, are we going to adopt a disguise?'

'Yes, I guessed at what you were driving at. Sorry for the sarcasm.' Reitz smiled at his second most senior officer. The man whose job he'd decided would be to board stopped enemy ships.

'With our gun arrangement we are from a distance, providing the carpenters can rig me up a dummy funnel, a passable imitation of *Repulse* or *Renown*. We will also fly the Royal Navy's "White Ensign" up to the moment we open fire. I also have a flag very much like the Imperial Flag of the last war that from a distance also looks like a White Ensign. It does incorporate our National Socialist leader's crooked cross in the centre but not too prominently!' There were a few grim laughs at this for most of the company were only too aware that the 'Swastika' was becoming a hated emblem to the Allies. Reitz concluded the meeting with a final stirring message 'Gentlemen. We shall fight with honour. With fairness. We shall aim to be victorious but once the enemy has surrendered we shall treat our prisoners with respect. The Royal Navy are highly experienced and very worthy opponents but it is our job to sink their ships before they can do us damage. It will be up to all of us. This time there will be no more *Runswick Castle* episodes. Soon we shall be altering course for our breakthrough. The trials are over. The real conflict so far as we are concerned has now begun. I cannot tell you when we shall write the final chapter. Our first chapter is over and the main event is now before all of us.

Chapter 3

'What do we know of her?'

The brisk cold north-westerly wind whipped the long North Atlantic rollers in the grey waters at the southern entrance of the Iceland-Faroes passage into white-spumed vicious crests. Into them plunged the straight prow of the reduced Hawkins-class cruiser HMS *Byrne* as she smashed her way into them with a sickening unpredictable motion during what to her morose crew seemed to be a never-ending monotonous, damp, boring and wasted experience of the life that was their lot of an Allied warship on patrol in seas as remote as could be from the regular shipping lanes but in waters that needed to be watched on the off-chance that a German surface raider may choose to pass through them on its way to, or from, more nefarious activities, such as sinking Allied merchantmen.

Those angry grey and white seas washed regularly round, over and across the pointed bow surging and swirling upwards and towards the next obstacle, the forward single-mounted turret of 'A' gun, a seven-point-five inch weapon that was virtually useless in these crashing seas. Then, dissipating, the cold very wet water sloshed even higher to do its best to totally submerse even the higher-placed 'B' turret before dispersing into smaller globs and sprays that beat into the miserably damp faces of the unfortunate crew members on watch on the exposed upper bridge. Having done its worst, the freezing cold water slurped on to pervade into the rest of the labouring old cruiser. Over the midships section and then into the gangways and messes of the upper structure, around and aft of the two funnels, the latter seemingly a thinner afterthought of the forward squat one. Permeating even deep into the lower decks. A ship that was wet. Cold. Damp. Sodden. Everything and everywhere.

She was old by the standards of her day. New in 1917 when first designed as a convoy escort to Germany's a-raiding light cruisers. Then it was thought that her four heaviest guns would see off the raiders but the war ended before she was even commissioned. By 1920 she was drafted off to serve on anti-pirate patrols on the China Station based in Hong Kong and then later off the Malayan Coast and Singapore. She'd then flown the flag on peace-time visits with other warships around the Mediterranean and for part of the time, as an escort to the big battlecruiser *Hood*'s world cruise in the early 1930s.

Then Europe's war-clouds darkened and plans to put *Byrne* into reserve were shelved as the Royal Navy, desperately short of modern cruisers, needed all its older ships that hadn't as yet been consigned to the scrap-heap, to help train the new recruits and reservists for the war that was surely coming. A hasty refit in July 1939 and two months later *Byrne* became part of the Northern Patrol group of the Royal Navy ships trying to prevent any German raiders reaching the North Atlantic undetected. Many of her companion ships were hastily converted former passenger liners equipped with up to half-a-dozen six-inch guns and given a grand title 'Armed Merchant Cruiser.' Totally inadequate, at least on paper, if regular Kriegsmarine cruisers came out on to the high seas. Captain Kennedy and his crew on the 16,000 ton *Rawalpindi* put up a brave, heroic and in the end, for them, a totally inadequate fight against their bigger opposing enemy battlecruisers but at least they'd been able to send out a warning causing the Germans to return to their home waters. *Byrne*'s crew had heaved a collective sigh of relief. They'd been but a hundred miles to the west when the one-sided action started.

It was those two German battlecruisers that had briefly appeared in a snow squall near *Byrne* on the starboard flank of the Royal Navy's bigger but older battlecruiser, HMS *Renown* off the North Norwegian coast in April 1940. The *Renown* had given chase leaving *Byrne* hopelessly behind but the two German ships eluded their pursuers.

Somehow *Byrne*'s crew seemed, by some fortune of war, to be attracted to the timings of *Scharnhorst* and *Gneisenau*, those two big potential raiders. Whilst patrolling the western sector of the seas into which she'd now come, plunging and rolling, the two German battlecruisers had again sailed within a hundred miles of *Byrne* as they steamed undetected through the Denmark Strait.

She returned from that patrol only for her moribund crew to have their leave curtailed. The German raiders were thought to be attempting to return to home waters via the northern passages and the cruiser was needed to get back out on patrol. Out she went but nothing was seen. Only those empty, very wet, long grey Atlantic rollers breaking over the forecastle. Time after time.

Three weeks she'd spent there. Three very long weeks at a slow economical (so said the Admiralty) speed of just ten knots. North. East. South. West. Up. Across. Down. Across. Always wet. Always cold. Always tired. Always aware that if the enemy was sighted that they were to retire out of range and sight. Then report. And then, again in the words of the Admiralty 'to shadow' the enemy until re-inforcements arrived. As their Lordships pointed out, the *Byrne* was equipped with a radar set. Except that it didn't work very well because its two operators were inexperienced in its electrical circuitry and these often failed because of that almost permanent wetness into it which caused them to frequently malfunction.

So it was nine times out of ten, up to the keenness of *Byrne*'s lookouts whose super sharp eyes, so their Lordships added in the operational orders, would be able to see the enemy first as Royal Naval personnel was far superior to anyone serving in the Kriegsmarine.

Except that after three monotonous long weeks those super sharp eyes were dulled with salt spray, cold, aches, drips, spots, dizziness, blurring and over-tiredness. Coupled with being linked to brains bored out of their common senses.

So the *Byrne* pitched and rolled and plunged.

Albert Snodland was port lookout one grey morning as the ship plunged slowly like a very wet chronic surfaced whale to the northern point of her patrol. Albert sported a long heavy moustache that permanently drooped and dripped making his mournful appearance even more lugubrious. Albert hated the pitiful and ceaseless lot of the plunging cruiser. He hated the war. Still, he'd survived eighteen months on this 'old tub of a war bucket' as he called the cruiser but rarely had he been troubled by the thought of anything even remotely exciting. Only once when *Byrne* was on the extreme starboard wing of *Renown*'s escort screen off Norway had there been anything to excite any of her crew but Albert, even though ostensibly on watch had sneaked off into the heads as he put it 'for a quick fag in the fug' and 'in a position of contemplative thinking' when the cry went up 'Enemy in sight' from his mate, Pete Farrell who'd been covering for the wretched Albert. Stumbling out still trying to adjust his trousers into the correct waist-holding position, he'd shouted 'Where? Where?' trying to follow his pal's pointing finger but the enemy, presumed to be *Scharnhorst* had already disappeared into a snow squall. Some time later, based on Farrell's quick sighting, they'd seen the flashes of Renown's guns as she'd opened fire on that German ship and her companion *Gneisenau* scoring hits on the latter vessel. But the excitement soon died down as the German ships simply vanished into more snow squalls with their ability to steam at a higher speed than *Renown* or any of her escorts could manage.

Then the *Byrne* was re-assigned back to the drudgery of the Northern Patrol, reinforcing the armed merchant cruisers trying to plug the gap in place of the regular warships. One of them was some twenty miles east of *Byrne* but all Albert could see were towering grey seas smashing their fury at the labouring cruiser. His thoughts wandered to his thin-faced wife in their back-street terraced home in Liverpool's dockland. The last time he'd been on leave, arriving at the front door on Christmas Eve, he was sure as he'd kicked it open that he'd heard the back door closing but his wife held him in her arms but only briefly before she broke off having seen his scruffy boots and yelled at him 'Get them mucky things off and get thi'sen inter tin bath cos' you stink.' Some welcome but he was sure it had been nothing but a cover for her previous guest. Maybe a German bomb would come down and hit her on the head. Mind, Albert thought, she was that thick it'd probably bounce off her nut, roll outa' back door and into the alley where the snotty kids would use it as a new kind of football. Serve 'em right if it bent their big toes out of joint. His mind continued to wander to his present predicament where the wind and sea-water spray combined weren't doing his 'tache any good at all. Now then, where's my cocoa?

'Wakey, wakey, Albert! Tha's bin dozing ageean.' Farrell's broad Yorkshire tones with its Barnsley accent burst into Snodland's semi-numb dumb cells of what may have passed as a brain. Farrell was as thin as Snodland was broad and as ever was two minutes early before the watch-change. As Albert's thick-fingered hands clasped the mug of cocoa, both of them could hear the distant chime of eight rings on the bridge bell. 'Nah then, Albert, gerrit dahn thi' afore it freezes over.'

Why Farrell, an alert nineteen year old despite his accent, should be best of pals with Albert Snodland who was, as the rest of the crew reckoned, really only put on to the ship to give it extra ballast weighting and not for much else, no-one could ever really fathom. Albert bent his head down to slurp at the cooling liquid that vaguely resembled cocoa when Farrell burst out:

'Crikey, Albert, ar tha' bin dozin as usual, eh?'

'What about it?' came the morose reply from Albert still with his head over the mug of cocoa.

'Well, Albert, there's summat outa theear that'll be a reight sore sight for thi' eyeballs, that's what.'

'So?'

'Look!' Farrell swung his right arm over the side of the look-out position. 'See, there's this ruddy great big ship outa theear.'

Even dozy Albert could see it. Emerging out of a rain squall. Probably not more than two miles away. Flying a flag which to him looked like a Royal Naval 'White Ensign'.

'Anything from t' wireless room?' he asked Farrell. ' Or from t'radar? Prob'ly not. It's allus jiggered.' Albert's tone of voice didn't suggest any high degree of concern. To him, wireless and radar, when either or both were working and sending him messages via snarling petty officers, suggested too much like extra work. Like straining his eyes or exercising the few cells that still had life in what most other crew-members thought was dead wood in his skull.

The two friends continued to stare at the strange warship as it rapidly closed the distance between it and the cumbersome *Byrne*. They watched the sleek warship's flared bows flinging back in a contemptuous fashion the same waves that washed so regularly over their ship. They saw its two forward twin turrets aiming in their direction. Was it, wasn't it *Repulse* or *Renown*?

God in heaven above, what if it was an enemy ship?

Suddenly a brain cell in Snodland's upper head sparked into life. Shouting, via his loud hailer, he yelled 'Strange warship on the port beam.'

'Range and bearing you stupid man' snarled the savage riposte from a very young Second Lieutenant (reserve) who was just beginning the new watch. Feeling very raw and cold. This was the first time on the patrol that he was standing watch alone as the most senior officer on the bridge.

Farrell seized the hailer from the dithering hands of his friend.

'Three hundred degrees, about two and a half thousand yards, sir.'

The young officer soon had the stranger in his binoculars. 'Christ, she's a bleeding Jerry' but before he could even press the Action Stations buzzer he saw to his horror the enemy warship's forward guns flash yellow and orange. Directly at *Byrne*. Seconds later shells crashed into the cruiser. One on to the defective radar room, another blew apart the wireless room, a third hit the bridge structures and the fourth shell smashed into the base of the forward funnel.

The very young lieutenant, Pete Farrell and virtually everyone else on that upper exposed bridge simply vanished. Blown into immediate nothingness. Apart from Albert Snodland. Something told him to dive flat on to the planks on which he'd been standing. Perhaps this was the first sensible action he'd ever performed in his whole life.

Behind his prone figure the bridge caught fire. So too did 'B' turret below him. And its ready store of ammunition which in its force-field of an explosion blew the hapless Albert Snodland up and clear of the now keeling ship. Briefly Albert registered many more explosions including at least four one after the other in rapid succession along the whole length of the dying *Byrne*. More by luck than by chance Albert had remembered to have been wearing his orange-coloured life-jacket. A souvenir, his dad had said, from a lifeboat man. No-one had ever bothered to reprimand Albert for wearing a non-regulation life-jacket. Now it was saving him. As he bobbed up and down, he gasped at the sudden change of his miserable fortune from a slurp of luke-warm cocoa to a very cold mouthful of salty sea-water. Together with the fact that he was being tossed up and down in the heaving waters instead of being on the likewise former heaving upper bridge of the *Byrne* but where was the bucket? Snodland couldn't see her, not even when he was at the crest of a wave. All 7,503 tons of an old, wet and tired cruiser had gone. As if she'd never been. The only trace a bit of scattered wreckage and Albert Snodland. The cruiser's sole survivor.

Vaguely he heard the sound of the enemy ship's engines slowing down, then he saw the wash of that same ship roll over across the waves to him and as the engines deepened and the ship put on speed he was aware of a yellow life-raft floating close to him. Another brain-cell sparked into life and Albert began to thrash desperately for it and after a dozen strokes of his arms he bumped into it, grabbed it and scrambled into it with all the grace of a floundering hippopotamus. Albert flopped into the bottom of the rubber raft still trying to work out what had happened. Vaguely a phrase from a training officer came to him – 'cruisers are tough ships, they take a lot of sinking.' Not that old bucket. Thirty seconds without as much as even opening fire back at the Jerry. Funny though. This raft must be from that Jerry. But then realisation set into another brain cell of Albert Snodland which told him that he was alone, cold and shivering and that unless he was soon rescued he'd just float on and on until oblivion came.

Just aft of the main control centre on the bridge of the armed merchant cruiser, HMS *Forfar Castle* was the sea cabin of her captain, in which just munching on some toast was that self same man, Charles Cockburn. The ex-liner's 11,317 tons plunged and rolled in the Atlantic's troughs although not quite as sickeningly as the motion experienced so recently by her now sunken companion, HMS *Byrne* but even so, Cockburn still had to maintain a firm grip on his mug of sweetened tea as he washed down the last crumbs of the toast. Just how often he'd contemplated the vulnerability of his supposed warship which was his position to command he'd probably lost count. Supposedly on patrol to possibly deter the disguised armed merchantmen that the Germans were known to be employing as dangerous raiders with her six six-inch guns and her nineteen knot top speed, Cockburn knew that his ship could only put up a brave hopeless fight if faced with one of the Kriegsmarine regular major warships. Even the crumb of comfort that *Forfar Castle*'s sister ship just a few months earlier had deterred one of the Kriegsmarine's would-be raiders, largely supposed to be their fast light battlecruiser. Cockburn pondered. What was its name? Ah yes. *Dresden*. Ah well, I musn't think too much. It won't happen. Not here. Their big stuff used the Denmark Strait. Well away from his ship's patrol area.

He wiped the last crumb off his upper lip, fitted his cap to his head, tightened a scarf around his neck, shrugged himself into an oilskin coat and ventured out on to the bridge to see what the morning would give. If anything. He didn't know that at the moment he closed his cabin door that his wireless operator, nor his assistant who'd just come on for his four-hour stint, were both deeply worried. On the hour, at the watch change-over the required regular coded signal to *Byrne* had been tapped out. There'd been no response. The assistant duly noted this fact in their log and said that he'd try in five minutes time. As a reservist he didn't feel all that alarmed at *Byrne*'s non-reply. 'Probably had to go and have a long session in the heads' was this his initial laconic comment. But not five minutes later. Still no response from the old cruiser. Not after three repeats. His chief stayed listening all the time. 'Best call the bridge.' The response was 'Keep on trying.'

Cockburn reached the bridge. 'Anything?' he asked.

'Well sir,' the junior fourth officer who'd been standing the watch and inwardly feeling a bit peeved at the captain's lateness, 'we've had a call from the wireless office – apparently *Byrne*'s not responding to our usual contact calls.'

Cockburn raised his eyebrows 'Not responding?'

'No, sir.'

'Do we know *Byrne*'s latest position?'

'About here, an hour ago' the young officer said pointing to the cross he'd made on the chart. 'Steering due north.'

'Right'.

Cockburn issued orders to alter course to an estimate of *Byrne*'s probable position, ordered 'Actions Stations' and the engines to full ahead.

Ten minutes later with the liner corkscrewing across the send of the rollers at her fullest speed of nineteen knots, a lookout sang out 'Unidentified warship. Off port beam. Range about fifteen thousand. Steering south by west, high speed.'

Cockburn turned to the man on the bridge wing – 'Is it *Byrne*? One of ours?'

The man shrugged. 'Can't say for definite. Possibly flying a "White Ensign" but whatever she was, she's now disappeared behind a storm squall. Don't think she's seen us.'

'If she wasn't *Byrne* or one of ours, what ship was she?'

'Looked like a cruiser, sir.'

'Mmm. Maintain present course. Pass the word round to everyone for extra vigilance. We'll keep radio silence for the time being. If she's enemy and picks up our transmissions, she'll turn round and come looking for us.'

Sleet showers lashed down at the plunging liner in vicious squally bursts before lifting and clearing the ship.

Almost an hour passed and Cockburn was fretting. Nothing had been sighted but at least the strange ship, whoever or whatever she was, hadn't reappeared. Then a lookout on the foremast rang a warning bell and via his 'phone, rang across to the bridge.

An officer took the message 'Yellow life raft ahead. Fine on starboard bow.'

Eyes strained as Cockburn ordered 'Slow Ahead.' Then the life-raft bobbed into sight topping the rollers in a corkscrewing motion. A bright splash of colour amidst the seething greyness. It was a miracle that the life-raft had even been seen but soon it was in the lee of the heaving liner. A motor-boat was launched and Albert Snodland without resistance was hauled out of it wearing just his underclothes and a life-jacket. He didn't hear the rescue boat being lifted out of the water. He didn't feel the willing hands hoisting him onto a stretcher. Nor did Albert in the armed cruiser's sick-bay realise that Surgeon Lieutenant Haslett give a wry smile that indicated that he was still alive, even if only just.

Soon after *Forfar Castle* had begun to move ahead again, another lookout yelled 'Wreckage off starboard bow!' There wasn't much for the motor-boat crew to pick up. Some timber, a lifejacket, a float and a briefcase with the initials C.N.A.

Cockburn looked at the wreckage after he'd been summoned down to the deck. 'C.N.A.' he murmured. 'Charles Northcliffe Arbuthnot. Captain of the *Byrne*. Late captain more like it.'

'You know what that means?' muttered his first officer as the two men made their way back to the bridge.

'Yes. *Byrne*'s been sunk and unless their Lordships tell us something different, the vessel that's sunk her is that warship that was briefly seen by our look-outs meaning that she wasn't Royal Navy but a German raider of at least cruiser size and is probably heading towards the convoy lanes at this very moment. If not, then *Byrne*'s been sunk by a U-boat which at this moment could be eyeing us up via their periscope. So full ahead it is and zig-zagging on an easterly heading for the next two hours whilst I go and work out an appropriate coded message for their Lordships!'

Having coded the signal he gave it to the wireless operators, both of whom were on duty together sensing the gravity of the situation. Then Cockburn went down to the Sick-Bay to consult Haslett about the sole survivor of the *Byrne.* Haslett could only shake his head when asked if the man had said something but he then added that he reckoned that the man, according to his identity disc, was named Albert Snodland, seaman, Royal Navy but no other clue to his identity. It was odd though for the orange life-jacket was RNLI issue and the yellow life-raft had no markings at all except some that had been scrubbed out. It certainly wasn't of Royal Naval design.

Scapa Flow was its usual grey grim self. Grey waters topped with white crests as the north-easterly bitched at the anchorage's waters with numerous gusts that lashed at the moored warships, each straining on their anchor chains as if eager to get away. All of them were waiting for the news of the breakout of any of the big capital ships that the Germans could use as sea-raiders. So far their role had been only in the realms of scaring off the German warships or at least keeping them well clear of Scapa.

Tugging at one of her bow anchors was a sixteen inched gunned thirty-four thousand ton battleship which also doubled up as the flagship of Admiral Sir Kenneth Ronald Charles Collins. And the Admiral was clearly a worried man as he stared at the charts of the North Atlantic, North Sea and the Baltic spread out in front of him. The news wasn't very promising. The new battleship *Bismarck* had been reported to be loading an extensive amount of stores in the Polish port of Gdynia. Apparently the new heavy cruiser *Prinz Eugen* was also in the same port, again loading. It seemed probable that the two ships were being prepared to come out on a foray against the Atlantic convoys.

Then he moved his gaze to the French port of Brest. Docked there, no doubt undergoing a refit after their recent Atlantic cruise, were the two battlecruisers *Scharnhorst* and *Gneisenau.* What was it? Twenty-two ships in less than two months at sea and it was no comfort that Admiral Lutjens had veered both ships twice away from convoys covered by one slow old battleship. Now if they were to join forces with *Bismarck* and her accompanying cruiser there would be one devil of a job to stop them from creating absolute havoc.

What else? Pocket battleship *Scheer* and heavy cruiser *Hipper* were both in Germany, supposedly also refitting after their attacks in the Atlantic and in the case of the former warship, even the Indian Ocean. What if they came back out as well?

There was a knock on the door and in stepped his aide. Flag-Lieutenant Matthew John Rimington-Smythe. A thin bespectacled and balding individual who had been seconded to flag duties having been declared medically unfit for active service. Behind the somewhat bland face there actually existed a very keen alert administrative brain which assimilated detail to an amazingly high degree of perfection.

Collins looked up and barked 'Yes, what is it?' sensing bad news.

'Sir, grim news has come in from *Forfar Castle.*

'What ship, and where? Show me!'

'She's one of the a.m.c.'s of the Northern Patrol covering the Faroes Gap. She has sent in a signal that an enemy raider of at least cruiser size has sunk her companion patrol cruiser the *Byrne* somewhere round about here' . . . whereupon the lieutenant's thin forefinger landed on the chart in the area of the southern opening of that Faroes passage.

'Which one?'

'We're not absolutely certain but my guess is that the raider is the *Dresden.* All the other German ships of cruiser size and above are in harbour or were when last reported in the Eastern Baltic. Apparently *Dresden* left Kiel some ten days or more ago and hasn't been seen since.'

'What do we know of her? Wasn't she the German warship that veered away from a.m.c. *Runswick Castle*'s convoy some three or so months ago?'

'Yes sir, but she now has a new captain.'

'Who is?'

'Goes by the name of George Reitz. Apparently a destroyer skipper who has served the Kriegsmarine with distinction – in raids off our East coast, off Norway against *Gloworm* and at Narvik. Seems from what we can evaluate, that his destroyer, despite severe damage managed to fire torpedoes that would have hit, and possibly sunk, *Warspite* had they not all prematurely exploded.'

'A man of some guts, and bad luck, eh?'

'If you say so, sir, but if it is him and he's in charge of *Dresden,* then he's out there. Now. In the North Atlantic.'

'Have we anything that could catch him, even now? Say *Hood*?'

'Unlikely. *Dresden* is even faster than *Hood* or any of our eight-inch gunned cruisers. Anyway we need these ships to guard against the threat of *Bismarck* and the battlecruisers they've got in Brest.'

'What else?'

'Only our six-inch cruisers. None of the aircraft carriers – there's *Victorious* here and *Ark Royal* with Force H in Gibraltar. Both carriers need to be within a hundred miles of an enemy ship before we can send their aircraft off on an offensive mission – and as I've said before, the orders are to keep them in their bases until *Bismarck*'s intentions are known.'

'Damn, this couldn't have broken out at a more opportune moment. I bet he's guessed that we're tied up looking and waiting for the "Big One" and hey-ho, off he'll go and play merry havoc with whatever he can find, inviting us to go and get after him.'

'And sir, leave the gap wide open for *Bismarck*.'

'By God, Rimington-Smythe, that's just it. If we send ships to chase after him, then *Bismarck* will have a much freer hand.'

Collins stopped to re-light his pipe. Once he'd got it going to his satisfaction he said to his aide 'Get this message to all ships. "Suspect enemy raider, probably *Dresden* in North Atlantic. Convoy escorts to keep a special lookout. Home Fleet ships and Force H to stay at base, repeat, at base for further instructions."'

Rimington-Smythe saluted and left the Admiral to ponder over his charts. Collins was tired. Every day there were pleas from his superiors to allocate more escorts to the North Atlantic convoys but he was trying to read the German mind. If *Bismarck* was going to break out it would have to be by mid-May at the latest. Much later and the lighter nights and calmer weather could well deter the Germans from risking their biggest warship into the convoy battles for fear of her being found by a Royal Naval Task Group that would remorselessly hunt her down regardless of losses. The only thing that he could do was to send out another old cruiser to plug the gap so tragically left open by *Byrne*. Just in case *Dresden* turned back but somehow he felt that this time, under her new captain, things would be different. If Reitz was to repeat his destroyer efforts, then this could mean that he'd handle his light battlecruiser just like one.

Rapid attacks. Perhaps even with torpedoes and then if a defending cruiser threatened his ship he'd simply retire out of range only to reappear at another target.

He ran his hands through his shock of grey-hair that was thinning, took off his horn-rimmed glasses and proceeded to wipe them as if to make his vision clearer. But nothing could clear his mind.

Rimington-Smythe reappeared. 'Sir, *Forfar Castle*'s just signalled. The *Byrne*'s sole survivor has regained consciousness with these words – ahem – "Shit and hell, she's a bleedin' Jerry" and then relapsed into unconsciousness again. No sign at all of the raider. They've asked if any cruiser is leaving to come out and plug the gap?'

'Yes, yes' Collins snapped 'Look send this signal – "Most Immediate to captain of Dorian. Complete refuelling. No leave. Sail at 10.00 hours for rendezvous with *Forfar Castle*."'

'They won't like that sir, having only just come in from patrolling the Faroes-Shetland Gap.'

'We're not playing at seaside trips' Collins snapped again. 'This is a bloody war and if *Dresden* chooses to return via the Iceland-Faroes passage, then we need an extra ship to look for her but not to engage her. Add this –' Collins lowered his voice –

'Manchester will relieve you as soon as possible.'

'Damn you, Reitz. You've picked your moments. But I'm not chasing after you. What warships out there protecting the convoys will have to suffice – until you show your hand.' Collins thought as his aide saluted and left the cabin, yet again, at his superior's bidding.

Kapitan George Reitz was also thinking as he ate a light supper. Three days and two nights after sinking the *Byrne* and as yet, apart from the patrolling a.m.c. that they'd briefly seen, and her wireless messages, no doubt for help, the Royal Navy was keeping reasonably quiet. So, for once, *Dresden* had been a success. Perhaps the enemy didn't even realise for certain that it was his ship that had sunk the old British cruiser. How apparently easy it had been. The radar sighting. Then closing in, via those sleety shower squalls, to overwhelm her with accurate gunfire and the salvo of torpedoes. She'd succumbed so quickly to the unexpected onslaught. Then they'd seen just the one orange-jacketed survivor, waving his arms. Good work to get that life-raft so close to him. He'd regretted leaving the lone man but it had been with some relief that they'd seen him climb into it – at least, one good thing out of the viciousness of that one-sided engagement. He knew that he needed to get away into the North Atlantic wastes as quickly as possible before the Royal Navy's cruisers in Scapa could start to search for him.

Soon after the sinking, Reitz, with Anders and his men toured the ship, remembering the pleased look of the crew members, although one or two did remark that it was a pity that there weren't more survivors. Reitz generally replied that the *Dresden* had fought well and hard to earn her victory and that the enemy should have kept a better lookout. He stressed that when on duty, every man should do their work with much diligence.

When the tour was complete, the one fact in the captain's mind that stood out was the feeling that the crew were behind him one hundred percent. They'd taken on a unit of the Royal Navy and it had been overwhelmed. They hadn't avoided it. They hadn't run away.

And now they were here. Powering southwards to intercept the North Atlantic convoy routes.

'Captain. Wireless room here' sparked his ever-open intercom speaker.

He acknowledged.

'Sir, a patrolling U-boat has found a convoy.' The position was given. Reitz looked at it on the chart. One hundred and twenty miles to the south-east. Hurriedly he grabbed a jacket and went up to the bridge where Serle's mournful-looking deputy, Ernst Gruber, was keeping the navigational watch. 'Work out, Gruber, speed and course for a dawn position some twenty miles ahead of the convoy. I shall want to have an aerial reconnaissance at first light. I need to know more of her escorts. The U-boat's report isn't definite enough.'

Gruber soon had the figures ready. Reitz nodded his thanks, spoke to Luth, Herzog's second in command via the engine room telephone connection and then left the bridge to try and snatch some sleep. Gradually *Dresden* steamed into the darkness to approach the expected rendezvous early next morning with the convoy. One she was going to attack. Not run away.

Rimington-Smythe handed another message to Admiral Collins. From *Forfar Castle* re-inforcing the definite news that the raider had been the *Dresden.* The sole survivor had recovered his senses and had given quite a graphic description.

From it Collins began to develop a respect for the German commander. It seemed so different from all the previous clashes by German surface units when so far away from their bases ever since Langsdorff's *Graf Spee* had accepted battle off the River Plate when his clash with the three Allied cruisers eventually led to his own ship being scuttled. It was the manner of the utter destruction of *Byrne.* Less than two minutes. No chance to radio that she was under attack. *Dresden* must have closed in fast and fired at point-blank range. Probably finished the hapless cruiser off with torpedoes. If so, Collins knew that the success Reitz had enjoyed with his destroyers was now becoming seriously evident with his handling of the *Dresden.*

Dangerous. Yes, he thought, but not as serious a threat to Allied shipping as was *Bismarck.* She was the bigger menace. Not *Dresden.* He didn't have the resources to adequately deal with both raiders. *Hood* had steam-up, so did the new untried battleship *Prince of Wales* but they'd have to stay at Scapa. Waiting for the bigger German ship. Together with their attendant and patrolling support cruisers and destroyers. The convoys at sea would have to manage. Nearly all of them had at least a cruiser as their main warship escort. Should be able to keep *Dresden* at bay, now that they knew she was on the high seas.

But where would she reappear?

Rimington-Smythe was still hovering. The details of all the convoys at sea. One, HX97, had been tailed by a U-boat that had been radioing in a code not yet broken by the Allies. It was presumed to be calling in other U-boats. Forbes looked at the Admiralty message.

'Charts, here, now!'

His aide produced them. Already marked. HX97.

'What escort for this one?'

Once again his efficient aide had the answer 'Light cruiser, *Macclesfield*, an R-class and a much older destroyer and five smaller corvettes and sloops; one rescue tug. Guarding eighteen merchant-men and two naval tankers.'

'Hmmm' grunted Collins. Then his finger wandered up the chart to the *Byrne* sinking. Rimington-Smythe it seemed had worked it out. 'Yes, sir, *Dresden* could be intercepting that convoy. Say at 0600 tomorrow.'

'Hmmm' Collins wondered if he ought to send out *Hood*. No. He couldn't. She'd not get there in time. There was an eight-inch gun cruiser in a convoy going in the other direction but it was three hundred miles away. Again too far. Even at thirty knots it couldn't reach HX97 until at least 10.00 hours. Damn! If *Dresden* was responding to that U-boat, then a dawn attack could be probable. She was probably in that area. Yes. She wouldn't risk a night attack. If it was going to be any time, it would be at dawn.

'Send this message to *Macclesfield* – "Expect dawn attack by German battlecruiser. Scatter convoy if required. Hold off Jerry until re-inforced."' Then, acting on a hunch, a further message to be sent to the *Wellington*, that heavy cruiser, ordering her to steam at full speed from her convoy for HX97. At once!

'Damn, damn, damn! Jerry's got us by the short and curlies!'

Born in Hamilton, New Zealand, Richard Hoggard, captain of HMNZS *Wellington* received the signal from Collins with a sense of perplexity. It was his job as a senior escort commander to guard the thirty ships under his charge and particularly the six escort vessels. He was a New Zealander in charge of his country's only heavy cruiser. It was with considerable pride that he'd accepted the position as captain of his country's main warship – a considerable coup as the Australians already had *Canberra*, a similar County Class cruiser, of the same lineage as the Royal Navy's *Berwick* which only a few months ago had driven off Germany's *Hipper* in a clash on Christmas Day when the German cruiser attempted to attack a convoy. At that time Hoggard had been rounding Cape Horn with a troopship convoy from the two Anzac countries. Now he was escorting the current convoy to Canada before returning with Canadian troops and then a troopship convoy to round Cape Horn for the Middle East.

'So the Royal Navy wants to chase after a possible – note the word "possible" – German raider that is suspected to be near HX97 which we passed, relatively speaking only yesterday.' Hoggard was consulting his navigating officer who was soon busy with slide-rule and note pad working out the most direct course and time, assuming twenty-eight knots, to the aid of the possibly threatened convoy. Hoggard murmured 'We must be the nearest heavy unit. It appears that HX97 has only a light cruiser as its principal escort.' Already *Wellington*'s bows were swinging and the froth under her counter was bubbling ever more furiously as she began to pick up speed from the wallowing nine knots of her convoy.

Eight bells of the dawn watch struck on the *Dresden* that early May morning in the mid-North Atlantic as the German warship cruised steadily at seventeen knots some twenty miles ahead of the presumed course of HX97. The bell's strident ringing aroused Reitz as well as the new watch closing up in readiness. Radar within ten minutes picked up the convoy at eighteen miles. 'Strong echoes. Suspect convoy' went the message to Reitz via his cabin speaker as the *Dresden*'s captain fastened up his jacket and swallowed a mouthful of coffee that Walters had made ready for him.

'Aha, a fine day for it, Herr Brautsch' addressed Reitz to his second-in-command. 'Here, these are the co-ordinates. Get off down to the Arado lads and ask them to go aloft. We'll launch one of them into the morning air within the next five minutes. Go on, get on with it, please!' Brautsch saluted and hurriedly made his way to the hanger, sited to the rear of *Dresden*'s sole funnel. Already one of the three Arado 196s was warming up on the catapult with the fliers and mechanics anticipating possible orders.

The orders were passed over to Senior Pilot Leutnant Arthur Stein. He beckoned to his junior navigator and observer Heinrich Stolle. 'Come on, Heini, let's get up and go. These are the co-ordinates.' Both men clad in their fleece-lined grey leather jacket and trousers tucked into thick flying boots clambered up onto the gently throbbing float-plane. Adjusting their flying helmets and goggles, the two men settled into their seats. Stein went through the pre-flight check as quickly as possible. This was it. Action for them at last!

The propeller began to turn as a mechanic pushed it into life and then with a roar, the little plane rushed off the catapult ramp, dipped a little and with the revs increasing pulled up and away from its parent ship climbing for the thin cloud cover above it.

Stolle looked around him in sheer amazement. Soon *Dresden* was a tiny speck on a wide empty ocean. This was his first-ever time on an action flight away from exercises in the Baltic. Stein, who'd served in a similar position on *Graf Spee* and who, via a blockade-runner had made it back to Germany, spoke to the nineteen-year old observer 'Come on, Heini, stop daydreaming. Let me know when you see the convoy. Look for their escorts.'

Stolle began to panic a bit. What if the convoy's escorts fired up at them? Hit them. Unable to get back to *Dresden*. He peered over the starboard side.

'There! Down there!' he yelled. 'Convoy. Enemy destroyer.'

Stein climbed desperately for a thin area of cloud. As they entered it the air below them flickered with red sparks and dirty-brown puffs of smoke.

The destroyer's lookouts saw what they first thought was an aircraft and without a second's hesitation the order was given to the gunners of 'A' and 'B' turrets to open fire. Without the captain's permission. Not that it would be the first time that Navy guns had opened fire on anything that resembled an aeroplane. Crews on Royal Navy warships were notoriously poor on recognition techniques – be it a seabird or an enemy aircraft. The gunners simply reasoned that it was better to open fire, scare the sod away or shoot it down rather than let whatever it was continue to fly at its own leisure.

Captain Robert Marson stormed on to the bridge 'Who the hell gave the order to open fire? And at what?' He was still wearing his pyjama trousers, having hurriedly pulled his uniform jacket on over the tops.

'Lookouts reported what they thought was an aircraft. Could be from the enemy raider. So, I ordered the guns to scare it away,' the destroyer's gunnery officer replied.

'Really. Are we expecting the enemy so soon? Are you sure it was an enemy aircraft or just one of those birds that our gunners seem so eager to take pot shots at, eh?' Marson was really being sarcastic. On a previous convoy, when just out of Liverpool, the gunners had fired at a flock of seagulls, claiming that they were German bombers. Four seagulls, at least, had been shot down, much to the amusement of everyone else on the crew of *Reward*. 'Well, er, sir, I think it was an enemy plane.'

'Well, look at that. Whatever are those floating down? Bits of Jerries, eh?'

Marson pointed to a couple of feathered wings and other bits fluttering ahead of them in spirals down to the sea ahead of the speeding destroyer.

'Feathers. Not a bleedin' Jerry!' was the continued heavy sarcasm from Marson.

Unseen and now well away hidden in the thin clouds, the little Arado flew hastily back to *Dresden*. Stolle muttered somewhat.

'Gosh, that was a bit nasty of them.'

'Don't shit yourself. With a bit of luck, they'll think they've shot down a seagull,' retorted Stein 'I chucked over the side one of cook's bag of chicken feathers. If they drop near that destroyer they'll think that we were a bird. If not, well, let's see!'

'You're a clever one boss.' Stein then heard Stolle give a short laugh into the intercom.

Ten minutes later they were back on board the battlecruiser and reporting to Reitz and Brautsch who were waiting for them as they clambered out even as the floats were still dripping from their landing in the lee of the battlecruiser as she'd stopped to enable the aircraft crane to hoist the little plane back on to the hanger decking.

Stein and Stolle both saluted their captain, 'Sir, the convoy has a destroyer leading with the ships in three columns. Smaller escorts on either wing and to the rear. One warship, possibly a cruiser, also on the port side. Oh, and we were shot at but I used a bag of feathers as a ruse in our escape.' Stein reported to Reitz showing his position of the convoy on Stolle's chart.

'No damage?'

'No sir. Possibly brown stains in Stolle's trousers. He was a bit frightened!'

'Not to worry. We shall attack at once, meeting the convoy at full speed ahead.'

To Brautsch he said 'Sound "Actions Stations" and order full speed ahead.' *Dresden* surged forward, a white water wake creaming arrow straight from her flared bows and her frothing stern.

Light cruiser HMS *Macclesfield*, with ten five point two five inch (13.5cm) dual purpose guns, was on her first war cruise. Her captain, Neville Rickards, had positioned her on the port wing of the convoy. The northern edge. Specifically on the advice sent from Admiral Collins. A German raider, of at least cruiser size, was thought to be in their vicinity. The R-class destroyer, HMS *Reward,* was patrolling the starboard flank just in case the Jerry was circumventing the convoy and wanted to make an approach from the side she was least expected. The third principal escort, an old V and W destroyer, the *Variant,* was now ahead of the convoy. Three of the sloops covered the rear section and the two corvettes were patrolling the central part of the phalanx of merchantmen. It was the best Rickards could think of in a counter to the possible attack. In six hours a heavy cruiser would be reaching them so hopefully Jerry wouldn't attack. But would it? Was it just a bird that *Reward*'s enthusiastic gunners had shot down or had they really been firing on say a float plane from the raider? They were known to have them.

The convoy's image flickered on *Dresden*'s radar screen. Reitz had worked ahead of the convoy and was aiming to attack on the convoy's south-eastern flank. As he'd pointed out to Hiltzern, the Allies, if they suspected his presence, could well reason that he'd approach the convoy from the north and as the convoy's cruiser escort was aware of them, it could well be watching the northern flank.

Which the lookouts on *Macclesfield* and radar operators were. Then one of the operators caught on his set a momentary glimpse of a faint echo to the south-east. When the impulse went round again he gasped. The echo was considerably nearer. But was it Jerry? Or the reinforcing cruiser? Then the convoy's ships confused the picture. Their echoes were distorting the southern flank. The operator wasn't sure. He hesitated. Fatally. Eventually he rang through to the bridge. 'Echo, sir, about ten miles off starboard flank. Unable to relocate it.'

Rickards swung round. 'What? How long ago?'

'Three minutes, at least,' reported the now embarrassed operator. 'On the southern flank. Possible echo. Ten miles. Fast speed. Could have been a U-boat on the surface that has now dived.'

'Or' Rickards snarled 'it could be that bleedin' Jerry raider and that your fancy bag of tricks could have a blind spot.'

Rickards felt uneasy. He couldn't dare leave the northern flank just in case the radar operator had been right. But what if it was the raider? He called *Reward* up on the short-wave ship-to-ship voice radio.

Captain Robert Marson was equally nervous and had been so since the shooting at the so-called bird. Now here was Rickards suggesting that Jerry was possibly on the convoy's southern flank. Closing fast. Would his lookouts keep their eyes peeled?

The rising sun glinted over the long Atlantic swell which raised and lowered most of the convoy's ships as easily as matchsticks on a rippling pond. Rolling, plunging, rearing ever eastwards with a number of their varying crews watching either *Reward* or *Macclesfield* putting on extra speed in a flurry of thrashing foam at their sterns without any of them really sure as to the reason for the hasty manoeuvring. Always showing off were the big Navy boys. The other escorts were maintaining Convoy HX97's mean speed of just under nine knots. Every so often the small corvettes would simply bury their bows into the dips of the swell, creaming white water up and around their small control bridges. But some of the merchantmen simply just ploughed their way through the swell, each heavily-laden with a variety of cargoes – the two Navy tankers full of crude Venezuelan oil; other ships with West Indian rum, sugar and fruit; two with spare machine parts for the tanks and artillery destined for the British Army bases in the Mediterranean. Every ship playing its important role, no matter how seemingly small in the overall situation.

Marson's attention wasn't on the merchantmen. It wasn't really on anything other than the possibility of the raider but no-one of his crew could see the *Dresden*'s line of approach coming directly out of the glare of the rising sun.

Not until it was too late.

'Sir! Warship four miles off starboard bow! Ten degrees!' yelled a lookout.

Marson swung up his binoculars. 'Full ahead. Starboard twenty. Guns, open fire!'

Too late!

Whoosh! Whoosh! whoosh!

Three columns of yellow-stained water climbed alongside the sleek destroyer but a fourth shell in that opening salvo had landed aft. Near X-gun. Catching the destroyer before she could complete her turn towards the onrushing *Dresden*.

Reward's turn began to wobble alarmingly. The helmsman reported that steerage was becoming difficult to control. Marson dashed to the rear of the bridge. The shell hit had set off ready-store ammunition and the stern area was already horribly on fire.

Three more shells again fell alongside. Again the fourth in the salvo hit. This time on the starboard wing on the bridge. Splinters whizzed around the men standing on the upper bridge. Marson ducked flat on to the bridge boards but his first officer was too slow. So also was the helmsman at the wheel. Both collapsed with shards of metal thudding into their hapless bodies. *Reward* lurched out-of-control and presented herself broadside on to the oncoming German battlecruiser. Marson saw *Dresden* clearly as he struggled to peer over the side of his battered command. Through the swirls of smoke he saw the enemy ship sparkle with gun flashes all down her length. Feebly 'A' turret fired in the vague direction of the destroyer's assailant. To no avail. The next salvo of shells completely wrecked it, as well as 'B' turret and the single funnel abaft the now burning bridge. Then two violent explosions shook the ailing destroyer.

Marson knew what they were. Torpedo hits. He realised that *Reward* had virtually come to a complete halt and was keeling over on to her starboard side.

'Abandon ship' he croaked in a disembodied voice. Virtually no-one heard him. *Reward* was mortally wounded and those crew members still alive and able to do so were already jumping into the sea and striking madly in their endeavours to escape the now rapidly sinking destroyer. In just three minutes. Turning over and going down by her stern.

Dresden's shells began to drop amongst the startled and slowly-scattering merchantmen. Within a minute two of them received shattering blows as the plunging shells tore their unprotected sides and decks apart. One of them, a tanker, suddenly burst into a terrifying glare of orange, yellow and red flames as the fuel in her tanks ignited. Pyres of black smoke tipped the flames as the twelve-thousand ton ship disintegrated. Burning oil spread over the sea catching the few men who'd been able to jump overboard.

'Come on, open fire!' yelled Rickards as his light cruiser tore across the fleeing merchantmen with the gunnery officer desperately trying to lay his guns on the swift-moving German raider that had assaulted the convoy's southern flank. Ahead of *Macclesfield*, old *Variant* exuded heavy black smoke from her funnels as she tried to lay a smoke screen to cover the leading merchantmen. Rickards, to his chagrin, even saw a gun flash from *Variant*'s stern as her captain flung his little destroyer in a tight turn away from the oncoming *Dresden*.

The German battlecruiser seemed to be ignoring the little destroyer and soon it was apparent as to which ship was her next target. *Macclesfield*. Shells splashed ahead and on either side of the light cruiser as she made her challenge.

Her forward turrets blossomed as her guns at last opened fire. For their one and only salvo for *Dresden*'s next salvo caught 'B' turret and totally wrecked 'C' turret above and severely damaged the lower 'A' turret. On the bridge the blast from that salvo had knocked down all the personnel. When Rickards cautiously regained his feet into a working order and forced himself to peer over the rail he saw to his astonishment that the German warship was showing her stern and was actually veering away from the convoy's disorganised array of ships.

Her boiling stern wake seemed like a mocking salute at the inefficiency of the convoy's defence. Rickards couldn't work it out.

Just when the German ship had the convoy at its mercy, it was turning away.

A boy messenger from the wireless room helped to support Rickards as he slumped heavily aware for the first time of blood oozing from his right shoulder. 'Sir! *Wellington* will be here in two hours time. She heard our calls for help. The German captain must know that she's close-by so he's scarpered, like, sir.' Rickards gaped at the seventeen-year old who had more naval logic in his head than seemingly he and any of his dazed surviving men around him.

Indeed Reitz did know of the approach of the heavy cruiser. Which was why he was turning away. To entice not just it but any other nearby British heavy warships to chase after him. Except that his ship was faster. *Dresden* was undamaged. None of the enemy's shells had fallen anywhere near his ship. With two of the main escorts sunk or put out of action, U-boats could well close in and find the targets easier to get at without serious fear of retaliation.

With the convoy's smoke columns fading away Reitz addressed the crew 'Well done, all of you' the firm voice came over the loudspeakers 'We are making a tactical withdrawal having inflicted quite severe damage on the enemy – one cruiser badly damaged, one modern destroyer sunk, and at least two merchantmen, one of them a tanker also sunk; possibly three others damaged – our wireless boys have picked up a nearby transmission that indicate that a heavy cruiser, HMNZS *Wellington,* is about thirty miles away. Whether she'll chase after us remains to be seen as we're making less than her top speed. Just to see if she will attempt to close in on us. So for the next two hours, we'll remain at Action Stations and if *Wellington* doesn't chase after us, we'll go to normal cruising routine. Well done, again. All of you. Thankyou.'

The speakers clicked off. Without any prompting one man began to cheer. Soon other members of the crew joined in and when Reitz looked over the port wing of the bridge to see what the hubbub was about, arms began to wave up at him from all the upper exposed positions of the ship.

'They're cheering you, sir.' Brautsch saluted.

Reitz nodded and in reply simply said 'We are now a real fighting warship. Perhaps for the first time!'

The messages relayed by Rimington-Smythe to his admiral weren't at all encouraging. The only gratifying aspect about the *Dresden*'s attack was that she'd turned away probably after picking up the wireless *en-clair* messages from *Wellington* to the crippled *Macclesfield.* Hoggard hadn't been at all pleased when the message from Collins reached him 'Round up the convoy. Stay with them. Do not, repeat, do not attempt to chase *Dresden.* Take convoy to Gibraltar and there await further instructions.'

Collins looked at his chart. There was something very ominous about *Dresden*'s efforts. Her gunnery was extraordinarily accurate. Two Royal Navy warships both sunk before they could make a worthwhile reply and with cruiser *Macclesfield* also facing major repairs after her battering, the score was – *Dresden* 3 Royal Navy 0.

What was worse was the fact that *Bismarck* and her consort had not returned to Gdnyia nor Kiel. An unconfirmed report had them in the Skagerrak but as yet nothing definite. If the Big One was on the move, and she linked up with the battlecruisers in Northern French ports as well as with *Dresden,* the effect on the North Atlantic convoys could well be catastrophic.

He couldn't afford to relax Home Fleet ships or the Gibraltar-based Force-H squadron to leave their bases – yet. Not until he knew where the *Bismarck* was and where she could be headed.

So what else could he release to chase after *Dresden*? His mind wandered across the Atlantic to cruisers based in the West Indies that were earmarked to escort convoys following the track of HX97 which was diverting to Gibraltar trying to reach safety before *Dresden* re-appeared. Even with *Wellington* the convoy was only just adequately protected.

Collins looked at the list of ships on the Caribbean station. All lined up to escort valuable convoys. Merchantmen whose food cargoes as well as Venezuelan oil were desperately needed to succour the ration-booked population of his own beleaguered island nation. It looked a thin list. Not one modern heavy unit amongst them. The biggest in guns was a full-sized Hawkins cruiser, of the same vintage as the recently lost *Byrne*, and the fastest was a Town-class light cruiser with six-inch guns, only marginally more powerful than those so recently blasted by *Dresden* on the *Macclesfield*.

'Hmmm!' thought Collins. 'Not much there although if they were all concentrated in one group they could between them maybe. and only maybe, score a damaging hit on the German. But where will she strike next?' Collins looked at all the Atlantic convoys then at sea. All protected by at least one heavy cruiser and in some cases, by one of the older battleships. It had been a valuable tactic when Lutjens and his two bigger battlecruisers twice sheered away when about to attack a convoy protected by such powerful guns. But was Reitz so different? Where would he go next? Perhaps he was short of fuel and ammunition. Or he'd make one more strike. Then his fingers, and his mind wandered to the south-east sector of the Atlantic Chart. To the convoys running from Freetown up to Gibraltar. There was a slow convoy currently at sea with two armed merchant cruisers as its principal escort. Yes, that was it. He had to give it more protection. Oh dear, that's not going to please those New Zealand chaps. HMNZS *Wellington* was the nearest available heavy cruiser. Captain whatever his name would just have to lump it. There was a war on. Comfort came second place to duty. The convoy needed protection. Just in case.

He had to try and stop *Dresden*. Reitz was doing just what he'd probably planned. Come on Royal Navy, here I am. The trouble was where. Then no doubt he'd pop up somewhere unexpected. Smack the Navy on the nose and then vanish. *Dresden* was playing a war game.

'Hit, run and chase me. Well, I'm not going into whatever he wants me to do. Gosh! I'm tired.'

Outside the wind blew in an even chillier blast across the grey waters of Scapa. Weather to match the mood that Collins was in and neither it, nor his mood would change, so it seemed until . . . *Dresden* and *Bismarck* were eliminated.

For good.

Throughout the next three days *Dresden* pushed south-eastwards. No radar blip indicated a chasing cruiser. SKL (Seekriegslatung – the Kriegsmarine's war at sea command group for the surface raiders and also their supply vessels) had already, from Brest, signalled not only their congratulations but also that there was a convoy sailing from Sierra Leone relatively weakly escorted. A U-boat in the area, having rid itself of all its torpedoes was now assigned to intercept and shadow it.

The main problem that worried Reitz was whether to go for the convoy or to re-supply from *Berengia* but it didn't take the captain long to make up his mind.

'Gentlemen' he addressed Hiltzern, Brautsch, Herzog, Halder and Serle in his sea cabin. 'We have a convoy here.' He indicated an area off West Africa. 'We shall close with it and attack tomorrow. The procedure will be the same as before. An aerial search to determine the opposition and then an attack before their crews have woken up to the new dawn.'

'Sir!' It was Brautsch. 'What about our re-supplying? We'll be needing fuel and ammunition fairly soon.'

'Don't worry, Helmut. So far as we are reliably being informed, the escort is not very considerable. Perhaps an a.m.c. and a few small warships. It will be another quick strike and then retreat to here – off the Azores – to re-supply.'

Herzog muttered 'Two more days of hard steaming – that's all we've got left so captain, if we do as you say we'll just about get to *Berengia*. Now I must be off and see to my babies down below' and with that he lumbered out and down the various steps and ladders to the labyrinth of machinery, pipes and dials that comprised his beloved engine-room.

Hiltzern proffered 'Sir, what if the escort is a strong one?'

'Then we'll engage and withdraw when expedient, as I said earlier' came the riposte from Reitz. 'This ship fights, weighs up the opposition, smacks them on the nose and then disappears before they can gather their strength into a united force. Hit and run! Keep them guessing!'

Soon after the officers dispersed to their stations, each with his own thoughts on the tactics that their captain seemed to be developing.

In the evening, radar reported the presence of various echoes. Just where they should have been. An hour to darkness. Reitz adjusted the battlecruiser's course to circle the convoy so as to intercept at dawn, head-on. As before.

The Gibraltar-bound convoy had been re-routed on its course from Durban and its last port-of-call, Freetown, in Sierra Leone, only very slightly from its original track as the Admiralty reckoned that it was out of projected sphere of operations of *Dresden*. It was a desperately slow one. Seven knots. Three U-boats off Freetown had already sunk four of the merchantmen and damaged another before retiring, leaving one of their number to shadow it and send off the coded reports which SKL assimilated. By midnight Reitz possessed enough information to work out that the escort comprised of definitely one armed merchant cruiser and possibly another six smaller ships. Nothing big or really of a major threat to his raider.

On board the main escort, the 18,373 ton armed merchant cruiser HMS *Rillington Belle*, her captain, Eric Wishart, felt a certain degree of apprehension as the long dark hours of the night ticked inexorably onwards. The Admiralty told him that a U-boat had been sending off coded messages which had then been decoded to reveal that the enemy submarine was sending details of the convoy and course to presumably its Northern French headquarters base. To reassure Wishart, the Admiralty sent a brief message to the effect that a heavy cruiser *Wellington* and two destroyers would be sent to bolster up the escort until the convoy was in range of air patrols from Gibraltar. Perhaps in another twelve hours. Mid-day. An aeon of time away. Wishart knew how vulnerable his slab of a liner was, especially if the reported German battlecruiser was to heave itself over the darkened horizon. Without warning.

Restlessly he'd slept. Fitfully. Seeing the gun flashes on the horizon. Waking only to hear the seemingly normal ship sounds of his command carrying on. As usual. But the tension was there. He left his cabin and made his way to the bridge as the first faint streaks of dawn began to lighten up the eastern sky.

'Anything?' he said to no-one in particular, although all on the bridge heard him. His second officer merely shook his head, yawned and stumbled off the bridge. It had been a long night. Wishart gazed round the convoy as the light of the new dawn began to assert itself. His ship was on the port side of the convoy. Nearest to a possible threat from a raider coming in from the Atlantic. A smaller armed merchant cruiser, the 12,157 ton *Portland* was on the starboard flank. Leading the phalanx of some thirty ships was the old 1916-launched V and W destroyer, HMS *Ventress* with two corvettes on either beam carrying out U-boat sweeps. Bringing up the rear was the minute Hunt-class destroyer HMS *Candid* with an armed trawler as her additional back-up. Seven inadequate escorts for the twenty-three merchantmen. Inadequate to deal with a big surface raider. So far the U-boats had only taken ships on the edge of the convoy. It was still in its formation.

With the exception of one ship.

A Greek tramp with the all but improbable name, in Wishart's mind, of Olympia D. Stallamaroucous with an ever-increasing out pouring of dirty black smoke coming from her thin spindly funnel as she began to lose station astern of *Portland*. Destroyer *Candid* fussed up to her signalling her to close the gap up to the main formation but ascertained only an exasperated wave of arms from a grubby-looking officer on her decrepit bridge.

It didn't matter.

Shells from *Dresden* using the thick funnel smoke as an aiming point crashed into the sea around the Greek without warning. One shell hit the base of the reeking funnel. It simply toppled over. The next salvo accounted for the grubby officer, the decrepit bridge and most of the fore section of the already staggering merchantman. *Candid* reeled away like a riddled sieve caught in the hail of splinters from the awesome shells crashing around her. Miraculously she was still afloat. Just.

The third salvo from the raider bracketed *Portland* as, with some of her ancient six-inch (15cm) guns opening fire, she desperately turned towards the German battlecruiser. Trying to draw the fire and allowing the convoy time to painfully scatter. Just as had *Jervis Bay* when challenged by the *Scheer*. Brave. Futile. The gunnery of *Dresden* was much more accurate and devastating than that wrought by the *Scheer*. Two salvoes were enough to bring *Portland* to a shuddering halt as shells smashed their way into her engine-room and set her central super-structure a-blaze along its whole length.

Wishart, stunned by the incredibly deadly attack, quickly ordered *Rillington Belle* up to full speed and weaving across the slowly-scattering convoy he knew he had to help the already sinking *Portland.* Even though his ship would probably be pounded to bits with her equally old six-inch guns unable to even reach the attacking enemy raider.

'Damn' he thought 'the bleedin' Jerry's gone right round the convoy attacking us from the east and out of the rising sun. Can hardly see the blighter. Shit, she's bloody accurate with her damned gun-fire.' Wishart looked over the port wing of his two-funnelled liner, making smoke, and saw a flash from one of the liner's ancient guns as it opened fire. Hopelessly out of range. But at least a gesture of defiance. He also knew that by the action of that gun and the simple fact that his prominent two-funnelled slab of a ship was steaming towards, and not away from the enemy, would cause that gun-crackling grey menace to fire at his ship. A liner once loved by the pre-war Mediterranean socialites who'd cruised so sedately on her cruises from Gibraltar to Genoa, to Naples and then to Palma before returning to base port. Laughing passengers drinking wines, playing deck quoits and eating lavishly in the beautiful centrally-placed saloon-restaurant. Even now her old cruising area was in a war zone. Just like here off the West Africa coast. Warm and hot. A Sahara wind blowing out to sea. And a grey, fire-spitting warship firing guns which even as *Rillington Belle* juddered across the sea had brought two more hapless merchantmen to a flamed-wreathed sinking halt.

Then the ancient gun below the bridge fired. Again. Desperately trying to draw *Dresden*'s shells away from the merchant ships. Even so, one of them fired from its stern-mounted four-inch gun, Wishart looked around for possible assistance from the little *Candid* but she was nowhere to be seen. *Rillington Belle* was alone. Way behind his cumbersome liner a plume of smoke pouring out from the funnels of *Ventress* began to drift across some of the fleeing merchantmen. A semblance of cover. But not where the exposed liner was making her blundering course trying to distract the raider from the convoy. Not when three eleven-inch shells crashed alongside *Rillington Belle*'s starboard side, the water spouts mingled with splinters causing the brave gunners to duck trying to escape their lethal hail. The protective shields around their guns weren't at all adequate if there was a direct hit or an explosion of a shell behind them as when the fourth shell of the salvo did so behind battery number two blasting its crew into oblivion and the gun off its mounting.

Then two more shells smashed into the liner's superstructure between the two tall funnels penetrating into the saloon below which caught fire, rapidly attacking the carved ceiling and its supporting oak pillars. Peering through the smoke billowing up from the wrecked gunnery battery, Wishart was astonished at the apparent closeness of the German ship. More ripples of flame flashed out from the attacker all along her length but amazingly before Wishart could comprehend, the raider abruptly altered course away from his already battered ship. Feebly a single gun fired from the starboard aft battery. Suddenly *Rillington Belle* shook along her whole length. Two brown and yellow columns of water soared up from her amidships section. Wishart felt his former liner shudder as she lost her way as water poured rapidly into her ruptured, torpedoed flank. She was doomed. Listing.

On fire. Sinking. Slowing down.

A dishevelled wireless operator, with blood seeping from a gash across forehead staggered on to the bridge 'Sir, help's on its way. HMS *Wellington*'s left Gibraltar coming at full speed fer us.'

Wearily Wishart gazed at him 'Too late. Too bloody late.'

'No sir, she left yesterday. Be here within a couple of hours so. T'old girl might last out 'til then,' the operator added hopefully.

'Still too bloody late. See, we're already at a fifteen degree list. Nothing can stop us from sinking.' Looking up, he added 'Odd though, the German's high tailing it.'

'Must've been *Wellington*'s signal. She nearly blasted mi' eardrums off!'

'Thanks. Go back. Get your life belt. We're going to abandon ship in five minutes if the pumps can't keep us afloat but it does help if Jerry is steaming away.'

Dresden's wireless room had indeed picked up *Wellington*'s '*en-clair*' signals and realising that they were close they rang through to the bridge.

'What distance do you think?' asked Reitz.

'About twenty to thirty miles away, sir' came back the guarded response.

'Anything on the radar, Leutnant Brautsch?'

'Nothing reported as yet sir' answered Brautsch.

'Better if we break off now rather than risk a heavy unit catching us and landing us a damaging blow so early in the cruise.'

'Shame sir, the convoy's at our mercy.'

Not only Wishart and his surviving crew on the sinking *Rillington Belle* but the collective minds of all the crews of the as yet not sunk or even damaged ships of the scattering convoy all sensed a surge of relief as they saw their attacker abruptly alter course and steam off to the south-west. Just when it seemed that the German raider had them all at its mercy. Now it was sailing away.

Rillington Belle was struggling to stay afloat although Wishart knew that she was doomed. Carefully and as orderly as possible, the port-side lifeboats were lowered, despite the ship's increasing list and the surviving crew swarmed down ropes and hastily positioned scrambling nets in order to get down to them.

'Come on, sir!' yelled one of the crew as he saw Wishart gazing out from the wing of the bridge as it teetered over the water but a few feet below it, but if the captain heard he gave no sign. The engineers from down below were the last crew members to hurriedly jump into the sun-dappled waters and desperately start to swim away from the ever-more rapidly sinking armed merchant cruiser as her twin funnels hovered perilously above them.

Suddenly, she lurched completely on to her port side, her funnels smashing into the water with a massive splash catching some of the struggling crew members as they tried to escape from the tumbling mass of funnels, masts, wires and ropes. *Rillington Belle* seemed to wallow horizontally like an ungainly hippopotamus and with internal explosions renting her still showing superstructure, she turned completely upside down with gouts of air escaping in huge dissipating bubbles. Then bow-end first, she made her fatal plunge to the sea bed, her twin screws and rudder being the last to vanish below the seething water.

Just as heavy cruiser *Wellington* reached the area. Hurriedly she stopped, launched boats and picking up speed, sailed off in the direction of the now vanished battlecruiser but to no avail and soon Captain Hoggard gave up the chase and returned to pick up his cruiser's boats as well as those from the sunken *Rillington Belle.*

Captain Wishart was not amongst the survivors, even though the boats from *Wellington* searched as carefully as they could amongst the wreckage. Grimly the boats were recalled.

Hoggard shuddered as his second officer, in charge of the rescue operation gave him the number of survivors from the sunken former liner. 'About half the ship's total company.'

Yet again it was his cruiser that was picking up the debris left behind by the damned German raider. Wearily he ordered the news to be sent to Gibraltar and then to HQ in London, Scapa Flow or anywhere else.

On board his flagship, Collins studied the latest messages sent from Wishart's doomed command as Rimington-Smythe hovered nearby.

'Same as before, sir. Smash and grab and as soon as the real heavy weight of the law threatens to make things a bit hot, burglar Reitz buzzes off, pardoning the expression.' Collins sighed, 'Yes, you're right. *Wellington* will be there, late again. Just like last time. Virtually a repeat. What's the losses this time?

'Mmm. Assuming the loss of *Rillington Belle*; she's been torpedoed and is sinking, the convoy's lost two armed merchant cruisers, a destroyer and five merchantmen. In about twenty minutes of action. *Dresden*'s gunnery must be good and in less than twenty days she's already sunk almost as many ships as any other surface raider of the main ships in the Kriegsmarine.

'Remind me?'

'*Byrne*, *Reward*, *Candid*, the two a.m.c.'s and seven merchantmen, together with severe damage to *Macclesfield*.'

'Quite a tally, eh?'

'Yes sir. A dangerous customer.'

'Ah, but not as much as the *Bismarck*. Where is she, now?'

'Possibly in the Skagerrak unless she's doubled back after being sighted outside Swedish territorial waters.'

'If she's sailing north about, she's going to call into a Norwegian fjord. Warn our agents.'

'Already done, sir.'

'She's a bigger menace than Reitz and his battlecruiser. We can't afford to send too many ships after *Dresden*. Got to keep them in case the Big One comes out.'

Rimington Smythe said nothing. After all he was only a glorified messenger boy. It was up to Collins to make the decisions, however painful. Inwardly he agreed.

'Hmmm. Not an easy choice, eh? Look here, *Wellington*'s scared Reitz away for the second time so tell me, where will he head?' Collins jabbed a finger over the Azores. 'That's where. And further to the west. Towards here –' his finger landed in the area of the approaches to the Caribbean Sea. 'Our weakest sector. No capital ships. Just those few cruisers, none of them individually capable of standing up to him but as a group? Now then, what can we afford to spare? Go on, remind me yet again.'

'Well, er, sir, we have two convoys forming up with three cruisers to each of them. Could divert the convoys to Halifax with destroyer escort and detach the cruisers into hunting groups. If either group has at least one Walrus between them and with *Wellington*'s Walrus astern we could sandwich *Dresden* between the groups with her being air-searched before the combined groups could engage.'

'Sounds good but can we make it work?'

'Only if Reitz sails where we think he will!'

A messenger arrived. Rimington-Smythe read it, grimacing.

'Well?'

'Sir. The message is from *Wellington*. It reads "Have reached convoy. Few survivors from naval ships sunk. Own aircraft has engine trouble. Can you fly out spares or do we return to Gibraltar?"'

'Oh damn bloody Reitz' exploded Collins 'He's going to get away from us. *Wellington*'s aircraft is a key point to our hunting group idea. Signal back "Will have spares flown out to you if you sail within range of Gibraltar. Will arrange for transfer of survivors in due course." Yes, that should do.'

Then to the map of the Caribbean which the alert Rimington Smythe had just unrolled on to the chart desk.

'Well, let's have it. Just what really is our strength out there?' he gruffly asked. Something had crawled under his skin, as it were. The growing realisation that Reitz was handling *Dresden* in a manner so differently than had so far been shown by German commanders during their raiding cruises in charge of the major surface units of the Kriegsmarine. It seemed that Reitz used dash and daring, attributes usually assumed to be the sole preserve of the Royal Navy, particularly with their own cruisers and destroyers.

If Reitz handled his ship in the manner he'd so far chosen, then nothing short of an overwhelming concentration of heavy cruisers, capital ships or numerous aircraft from at least two aircraft carriers would be able to stop him. Collins knew that he had to have such a force to stop the *Bismarck*, not the elusive ship that Reitz commanded.

Grimly he nodded as Rimington-Smythe bleakly said 'We've already discussed the available forces. And their disposition.' Lamely he added 'It's all we've available to confront *Dresden* if you are keeping to your practice of holding the bigger ships to watch for *Bismarck.*'

Steaming steadily westwards across a calm sunlit ocean *Dresden* sailed towards her expected rendezvous with *Berengia* with Reitz unaware of the ideas Collins was planning.

An Arado was flown off when the radar picked up a near stationary blip in the area where the supply ship was expected. To make sure, Reitz ordered the little float plane to double-check and then to sweep the area to make sure it was clear of any Allied warships.

Rubens, the *Dresden*'s second pilot snapped in his throat microphone to Stolle 'Come on, wake up. What's that I see down below?'

A single funnelled tanker-like ship flying a Spanish flag came larger and larger in view as the seaplane flew lower down towards it.

'Fire the recognition signal!'

From the ship below, to the airmen's delight came answering flares. Green, white and orange. They flew lower and Rubens waggled the plane's wings as he circled the supply ship from which some of the crew were waving from the decks having only moments earlier being largely hidden behind the ship's protective guns.

Rubens contacted the out-of-sight *Dresden* on his short-range wireless and then circled the tanker before flying off to patrol the seas in a thirty-mile radius sweep.

Soon Kapitan Wilhelm Theider could see the approaching battlecruiser as she loomed into sight over the horizon. Lamp signals were exchanged and within half an hour *Dresden* was alongside the big tanker with thick fenders draped on the adjacent sides as she prepared to take in the vital oil-fuel needed to replenish her now almost empty bunkers. As Herzog had said somewhat petulantly to Reitz only hours earlier 'We've only about two days cruising or about three hours mad-dashing left in the tanks. Pray we don't meet up with a nasty Allied warship wanting to bash ten bells all over us cos' we'd 'ave to signal it to "hang on", can't give you a fair scrap 'cos we've run out of piss!'

All that day *Berengia*'s cranes also hoisted the varied supplies from her cavernous holds to be deposited on *Dresden*'s decks. Supply officer, the ever-so neat Hans Goethe meticulously ticked them all off on his prepared list before crew members carried the boxes and tins to their appointed store place below decks. After six hours the sun began to set and both captains called it a day. Like the old days of coaling ship, virtually everyone not on watch was involved. Reitz himself joined the chain of men in passing the boxes along to their store-house and when *Berengia*'s captain crossed over even he joined the chain for fifteen minutes before both men retired to Reitz's main cabin where with navigator Serle and his chart, they worked out the course for *Berengia* towards the next rendezvous.

To the south-west. Clear of the Azores to meet off the north-eastern coast of Brazil.

In a month or so's time. Not into the North Atlantic where *Bismarck*'s chain of supply ships was already in position. Waiting anonymously for the Big One's breakout. Reitz told Theider that he was aiming for a strike in the Caribbean Sea area to try and stir the Royal Navy to come chasing after him, leaving the convoy routes to the north more exposed to the menace of *Bismarck*.

Darkness fell and for the first night since last meeting up with the battlecruiser off Norway the crew of the supply ship could to some extent properly relax. After that earlier parting a few weeks previously with *Dresden*, they had dashed each night from harbour to harbour. Amsterdam, Boulogne, Cherbourg, St. Malo and eventually to Brest. Occasionally her escort brushed with the Royal Naval light forces but *Berengia*'s top speed of seventeen knots helped her to escape into the darkness and the relative security of the next port on her route whilst her escorts kept the attackers at bay.

As soon as Theider had taken his ship out of Brest, the RAF came over the area bombing from quite a height, somewhat inaccurately, in their attempts to neutralise the two bigger German battlecruisers *Scharnhorst* and *Gneisenau*. The bombs missed their two principal targets but one particularly large stick of bombs plastered in and around the berth so recently vacated by *Berengia*. It wasn't until Theider reached Bordeaux did he and his crew begin to relax, safe in the knowledge that they were out of range of the possibility of serious air attacks or even sea directed attacks. Mind, Theider thought, had it come to it, the ship's four five-point nines (15cm) would have given a good account of themselves but throughout the voyage they had remained hidden behind their quick-dropping disguised flaps.

Now here they were. In company with their charge again. A ship whose exploits were being much discussed and admired by all in the Fatherland. Slowly through the stillness of the night,the two ships cruised at a leisurely ten knots and as dawn lit up the ocean once again activity broke out on both ships and from the battlecruiser, an Arado was again catapulted to resume a widespread patrol.

Two hours later into their patrol and about forty miles west of their parent ship, observer Stolle yelled into his throat microphone

'See those three ships down on our starboard side?'

'Yes' came the reply from Stein his pilot. 'Enemy cruisers, I think' and saying this he turned the little plane around and clawed for height on the flight back to *Dresden.*

Not one lookout on any of the three warships below saw the little aeroplane. Little did they suspect that its parent ship was the ship that they were seeking. The German raiding battlecruiser KM *Dresden.*

The leading warship was a 1920 vintage Hawkins-class cruiser HMS *Hereward* with eight seven point five-inch guns. Commodore Alfred Lachmann on board snatched a quick bacon sandwich and a mug of hot sweet tea before climbing to the main bridge. To a signalman he ordered 'Send out – "Spread out to daytime stations. Our Walrus taking off on search patrol at 0530."' Twenty minutes. The two other ships, the small D-class cruiser *Dunchurch* and what was really an irrelevance in such a patrol group, the thirteen thousand ton armed merchant cruiser *Ranjit Star* began to churn to a position ten miles abeam of *Hereward.*

Lachmann, a student of maritime history at his university shivered despite the warming rays of the sun. He looked across to Les Brightmore, the captain of *Hereward* and nodded grimly 'Could be the day that the Jerry raider we're searching for turns up and what do we have? Three ancient out-gunned has-beens to stop him. Just like Admiral Kit Craddock on board his out-dated cruiser the *Good-Hope* searching for Admiral Von Spee's squadron off the

Chilean coast in November 1914. Again he also had an out-gunned light cruiser *Monmouth* and an armed merchant cruiser for his searching group. Not dis-similar to the current situation. All I have are three ships to this lone Jerry raider but not one of them capable of outgunning or out speeding the *Dresden.*'

History could be repeating itself. He knew that the rendezvous with the more southerly-placed hunting group expected within the next twelve hours would even up the odds but even so, despite the presence of the modern Town-class cruiser *Chelmsford,* he felt extremely apprehensive about their capabilities of stopping the *Dresden* on what had been so far a somewhat successful raiding cruise for the German warship.

The rising sun spread its golden rays over the upper works of the *Hereward* as she plunged steadily through the gentle swell of that morning at sixteen knots.

'Message sir,' A midshipman saluted him. Lachmann read it with a rising sense of despair. The Walrus had a fault in her engines. Couldn't take off for about an hour. The mechanics were doing their best to effect repairs.

'Is the radar working?'

'Bit dodgy, as always' came a grinned response from the cruiser's first officer.

'Meaning?'

'Well, sir, it works now and then. Depends whether the operators have found a piece of sticking plaster to keep it in one piece.'

'Really! Don't be such a fool!'

'Only joking sir, but it hasn't really worked in a reliable manner for some time.'

'Hmm.' Lachmann snorted 'Well, tell the lookouts to keep their eyes peeled.' He paced angrily to the port open wing of her bridge and glared out to sea to where the *Ranjit Star* was pushing her way into her allotted position.

'Useless bit of flotsam' Lachmann thought to himself.

So what next? Always decisions. Even his promotion to Commodore was only temporary. Just for this cruise. He thought back to the flight in the rattly old Sunderland across from Gibraltar via the Ascension Islands to refuel. To join *Hereward* just before the cruiser set sail on this, to him, desperate venture. To seek out and to shadow the German raider. Some bright braided desk bound gold braided fart in the Admiralty had no doubt thought it up!

'Sir. Cuppa' up.' A seaman jerked Lachmann out of his wandering thoughts whilst doing his rounds of the bridge personnel.

'Thanks.' Then to Brightmore he petulantly snapped 'Is the Walrus ready yet?'

'Aye, aye, sir. Just had a message to confirm its readiness.'

'Stand by to launch in a minute's time. Course and position will be –'

Lachmann never finished giving his orders. Suddenly and without warning there came the sound of a host of express trains. Swift and with a nasty bite to them. Hitting his ship. Pulverising the forward turrets and smothering the bridge in a sheet of searching flames.

The horrified upperworks crew on the still trailing *Dunchurch* watched the *Hereward* just simply disintegrate. Splitting in half as fresh explosions simply blew her midships section asunder, seemingly from the insides outwards. Her masts collapsed, her twin funnels crashed overboard and her aft turrets were blown into the air spiralling as they crashed into the sea boiling behind the disintegrating warship. Sinking rapidly. The stern section, what was left of it, hanging precariously afloat for a few extra seconds after the rest of the old veteran had vanished.

Somewhere forward, a six-inch gun fired from *Dunchurch* over the sinking wreckage. But at what? No-one on the cruiser had ordered the gun crew to open fire for they hadn't as yet seen the target. Then from beyond the cloud of smoke disappearing from their shattered squadron flagship the above deck officers and men on the little cruiser saw the long lean dark menacing silhouette of *Hereward*'s assailant. Spitting flame. At them. From bow to stern of the German warship's starboard side, orange flames jutted in rapid succession. Before an order to try and swing the *Dunchurch* away could be given came a horrifying series of crashes into the sea abeam of the bows and with two explosions bursting inboard adjacent to the forward funnel, the German shells seemed to obliterate all such evasive manoeuvres out of the minds of the shocked crew. Further shells that smashed into the superstructure caused gouts of black smoke to curl up into the blue sky above, edging the quickly bursting expanse of the midships flames. *Dunchurch* lost speed, slewed heavily into the long Atlantic swell and from her stern began to sink with a horrible certainty.

Sixty years old and captain of HM's armed merchant cruiser *Ranjit Star*, Harold Ronson was in the process of issuing orders to turn away from the tragic events unfolding off his starboard beam. Desperately full speed orders of only nineteen knots were given and black smoke was belching furiously as the ship's engineers attempted to create a smokescreen to cover the ex-liner's possible escape. Too late! Shells from *Dresden* slammed into the sea on either side of the fleeing ship. A perfect bracketting.

'Stop engines! Prepare to abandon ship' yelled Ronson trying his best to avert a third tragedy. If the two regular Navy cruisers could be so rapidly overwhelmed what chance did his hopelessly outgunned, out-ranged command realistically have? *Ranjit Star* slowed down. Even the White ensign was lowered as a sign that the ship was not only stopping but surrendering as well.

'Sir, t'enemy's signalling.' One of the signalmen on the bridge yelled out to Ronson. 'It's in our lingo like. Says – "Don't abandon. Pick up survivors. We will not sink you. Please confirm. Reitz. Commander of KM *Dresden*"'

Ronson could scarcely believe his ears. Not sinking us? Rescue survivors? Hoarsely he asked the signalman to flash back a message of compliance. 'Oh, and add "thanks" at the end with my name and that of this ship.'

Ronson, his fellow officers and available crew watched the German battlecruiser cross behind their stern, saw her increase speed with a bubbling froth from her wake as she withdrew towards the north-western horizon. Seeing her disappear, Ronson ordered the starting up of the engines and manoeuvred towards the sinking *Dunchurch* which by now had dipped her starboard deck into the water as she slowly sagged towards her final watery grave.

Boat crews swarmed into *Ranjit Star*'s lifeboats and rafts as they were hurriedly lowered in an attempt to get over to rescue *Dunchurch*'s survivors now leaping overboard. Six of the armed merchant cruiser's boats managed to reach alongside the sinking cruiser to pick up men, still disciplined, directly from the decks as they gradually slithered underwater. Hurriedly backing off and all full with grateful men, the boats turned away as the light cruiser sank behind them leaving the usual surface litter of the flotsam of a sunken ship. Abandoned lifejackets, timber spars. Mementoes of family photographs. Drifting into the debris of the war at sea.

Picking up speed, Ronson took his ship to where the *Hereward* had sunk but as he slowed his command down yet again there was no sign of any survivors at all. A bit of scattered wreckage but of the sunken cruiser's crew, nothing. All gone. He launched two of his boats for the men to search but it seemed a hopeless task. And so it was to prove. Sick at heart, Ronson turned *Ranjit Star* back to the area of the now also sunken *Dunchurch* but the news of her survivors was much better. When they were all safely back on board his first officer reported that of the cruiser's four hundred and fifty-seven crew, all but forty-three had been saved, although amongst the lost were her captain and his first officer.

Ronson worked out a message in code and then, *en-clair*, he added, so that their German assailant could pick it up 'Thanks to Jerry sparing us we have rescued most of *Dunchurch*'s crew.' Let their Lordships puzzle that one out!

Reitz nodded when his wireless operators informed him of the a.m.c.'s signal. It was something, he thought, to give the British Admiralty to work out. Naughty Nazi raider actually not killing Allied sailors when they could have all been massacred.

The contents of *Ranjit Star*'s message did cause Collins to raise his eyebrows. Suddenly he felt really old. One of the hunting groups eliminated with, so far as he could ascertain, hardly causing the *Dresden* any trouble at all. Even worse, the RAF had reported that Grimstak Fjord was empty. *Bismarck* and her Hipper-class cruiser consort were at sea. Presumably Atlantic bound. To try and prevent these two German warships from reaching the convoy routes he'd already ordered to leave Scapa the darling ship of the Royal Navy, the service's current largest serving warship, battlecruiser *Hood* with Vice-Admiral Holland in charge, accompanied by the new battleship *Prince of Wales* together with destroyers as escort. To meet up with heavy cruisers *Norfolk* and *Suffolk* at the southern entrance of the Denmark Strait. In two days time.

He was giving Admiral Tovey the battleship *King George V* and the slower battleship *Rodney*. A third group would be his battleship with the relatively new aircraft carrier *Victorious*. Other capital ships and heavy cruisers from various convoys were now on 'stand-by'. But nothing substantial was spare to hunt for *Dresden*. Not even Force H based at Gibraltar with aircraft carrier *Ark Royal*, battlecruiser *Renown* and light cruiser *Sheffield*. Already this group had been placed at a moment's readiness to leave for the Northern Atlantic should *Bismarck* break past Vice-Admiral Holland's ships. Ideally placed to intercept *Dresden* should Reitz's ship sail northwards yet Force H needed to be in readiness for the greater threat.

Rimington-Smythe had charts at the ready. 'Yes' he said, '*Wellington* could again be diverted to chase after the German battlecruiser. Hopefully the New Zealand cruiser could reach *Chelmsford* and the two C-class cruisers in time to make an effective force. Say in three days time.

'Three days' groaned Collins.

In came another staff lieutenant. 'Sir, problems with the troopship convoy at Freetown. Main escort, battleship *Resolve*, has engine trouble. They've requested additional support if at all possible.'

Collins shook his head. 'Damn!' The expletive came out almost like a snake's hiss of anger. 'There's only *Wellington* and she's haring off to support Froggatt in *Chelmsford*. Just signal the convoy to wait a day or two until *Resolve* sorts out her engines. No – wait – tell them to set sail immediately and at full speed. Could well outdistance *Dresden* – that is if she turns east. Yes – it's the risk we'll have to take. What've they got as escort, hmmm?'

'A light cruiser, an a.m.c. and four destroyers plus six smaller escorts. Collective top speed of fourteen knots.'

'Bit weak. But it'll have to do, for the time being!'

The lieutenant looking perplexed, hurriedly left. His boss just didn't have a bee in his bonnet, it was a perceptible wasp's nest. Collins did have a hornet's nest of responsibilities. The North Atlantic convoys vital to Britain's survival. Troops hurrying from South Africa and Australasia to help reinforce British forces in the Mediterranean. Due to tranship at Gibraltar for Malta and thence to Greece. Some to stay on for training in Britain.

Where, oh where, were the spare Royal Navy ships? Gloomily he stared at the Atlantic Chart spread out in front of him seeing the endless rolling waves, then the groups of merchantmen and finally the gun flashes of a German warship on the horizon.

His head spun. Decisions. None of them right but they had to be taken. Call it instinct. Intuition. He had to stop *Bismarck*. The greatest danger. Yet *Dresden* so far had already given the Royal Navy a number of bloody noses. Not a knockout punch but her exploits were hurting. Hard. Seemingly always where the Navy had its weaker ships. As if Reitz was probing for the weak spot. Time after time. Dashing, from one quick attack to the next. What if Reitz did turn back? And not for the Caribbean? Or north to link up with *Bismarck*? It came to him. Blazing troopships. Soldiers screaming for their lives as the heavy shells crashed into the sea. Around them.

'Tell that lieutenant to signal *Wellington* to reinforce their Freetown convoy. Then to signal Froggatt that if he sights *Dresden* that he's to shadow and not to engage until re-inforced. Repeat not to engage. Yet.'

It had been a long tiring day. 23rd May 1941.

Just four hours after the sinking of *Hereward* and *Dunchurch*, Leutnant Brautsch reported to Reitz that radar had sighted a large stationary object, thought to be a ship at about seventeen miles distance.

'Best send up an Arado.'

The pilots reported back saying that the object was a tramp ship with a long thin funnel out of which curled a spiral of smoke although the ship was stationary, there being no trace of a wake.

'Let's investigate. Sound Actions Stations.'

Reitz listened to the hurried sound of booted feet running to their positions. Still eager after the recent action against the cruiser force. Everything seemed to be going so well. Such a contrast from the dispirited feeling that had pervaded the ship when he first climbed aboard. Then she'd been a ship of shame. And now. A ship to be proud of her efforts. Acton had been joined when other Kriegsmarine units would have avoided even the weaker odds that had so far been the opposition for *Dresden*. As the ship altered course towards the now visible plume of smoke his mind wandered yet again to the mail that he'd received when the *Berengia* had so recently met them. Elle had written three letters with cuttings of the battlecruiser's exploits being so subtly exaggerated by the Nazi-manipulated papers. Odd, thought Reitz, that a ship crewed by non-party members should be receiving such prominent press reports under the direction of that most deviously cunning of all the Nazi leaders, Joseph Goebbels. Out here his thoughts continued, the ship was free from the tainted evil that surrounded his country's political leaders. It was almost a shame that so far, apart from the failure to subdue the island nation, that the military campaigns waged under the swastika banner had been basically extremely successful. Perhaps they would soon be able to present peace terms to the British and then the war would end.

Thoughts that Elle hinted at so thinly so as to avoid the censor's black ink but Reitz knew what she was thinking about. The good news for him was that she was now working in Brest in a liaison capacity with the Kriegsmarine's surface forces in the SKL. She was following every detail as much as she could about the cruise of his battlecruiser.

'Sir!' a shout from a lookout shook him out of his thoughts. 'Ship is clearly in sight. Giving off lots of smoke. Must be coal-fired.'

Reitz looked at the stationary steamer that was hoving ever clearer into view. She was indeed coal-fired and entered the water for the first-time in 1896 under the name of *Rampleton*. New and clean then, but now a very dirty tired trampship. Shuttled around in her career to all parts of the world despite one Great War and now another. Humping filthy cargoes such as her present load of corrugating iron sheeting bound for a new roofing scheme in the Falkland Islands, a remote British dependency that in the Great War, proved to be such a fateful attraction for *Graf Spee*'s Asiatic squadron of cruisers. She'd been in a convoy from Liverpool to Gibraltar but for the rest of the voyage had been independently routed. Plodding southwards at a mundane eight knots she'd reached this area only for one of her boilers to break down under a stream of foul-mouthed oaths from her hammer and spanner wielding filthy engineer. As *Dresden* approached, he was doing his best to switch to the remaining boiler in the hopes that the rust bucket could stagger up to five knots. It seemed, though, that his equally dirty captain couldn't care less. For the three hours that *Rampleton* had wallowed in the gentle swell Cedric O'Flanagan had taken to his Irish whiskey bottle. 'Open target for any crackpot U-boat skipper who wants to waste a kipper on us! Might as well go down pissed.' That was his philosophy and three hours later, he was quite simply very drunk. Incapable of any clear thought at all. When his engineer reported that he'd been able to connect up the other boiler into some semblance of order and that the steamer could get under way again to a speed of five knots, O'Flanagan had gazed blearily back at him and had then told his engineer to sod off and sort his filthy boilers out for himself and just leave him to get on with his boozing.

Rampleton was just getting under way with the First Mate in charge – O'Flanagan just lolling in a corner of the unkempt open bridge, bottle in hand – and with gouts of dirty black smoke rolling out of her spindly funnel when gunner Denzil Davis, RNVR, the only sober, and some would say, sensible member of the tramp steamer's morose and extraordinarily lazy crew, sighted a large warship coming up rapidly on the stern starboard quarter. Signalling 'Stop your ship.'

And flying what looked like a 'White Ensign'.

Davis wasn't taking anything for granted so using his size twelve boots he kicked the shins of his two dozy gun assistants and shouted 'Warship bearing down. Could be the enemy. Man the gun!'

The gun. A four-incher made new in 1914. The only clean object on the *Rampleton.* Davis spent hours polishing it. Oiling it. Making sure that his gun would be ready when required. Now this ship had appeared. Not a very friendly ship, thought Davis. Just my chance to fire this gun. At it.

'Get ready with the ammo you lazy sods.' Size twelves threatened.

'Balls' was the reply from one of the still comatose filthy gunlayers. 'Yon ship's one of ours an' if it in't then it's ter big fer us to fire at.' Truculent as always was Jack Smith, ex con-man at London docks before the war had thrown him on to this very dirty ship.

The big warship slowed and was preparing to launch a motorboat.

'Gerrup, yer lazy sod.' The literary standard of Gunner Davis wasn't exactly varied. Not being stretched very far on *Rampleton.*

The reply wasn't really of a literary standard seeing it was mixed in with a howl of pain as a size twelve thudded into the ribs of Jack 'the lad'.

The boat came alongside.

No-one from *Rampleton*'s dirty crew helped the smart white-uniformed pistol-wielding officer as he clambered over the midships guard rail. Nor did they help the armed sailors who were also coming aboard. Gunner Davis and his size twelves vanished. Perhaps he was the only person of the tramp's crew who realised that the visitors weren't Royal Navy. No way was he going to be taken prisoner by a load of square-headed Krauts. O'Flanagan, with his near empty bottle of Jameson's in his right hand belched at the top of the bridge rail and airily hurled the bottle at Brautsch yelling 'Oy, you there, have the rest yourself. Bloody Navy man.' Then he stumbled and fell down the flight of steps to land in a sprawled untidy heap at the feet of the advancing Germans, knocking himself virtually unconscious.

Jumping over the inert body of the tramp steamer's captain, Brautsch swiftly climbed up to the wheelhouse where an extremely dishevelled helmsman, leaning on the useless, lifeless wheel, greeted him with the words 'Watcha, matey. How's yer doin'?'

Brautsch snorted with disgust and motioned the helmsman to get out of the wheelhouse and on to the open bridge from where he shouted 'This ship is now in German hands. All crew to assemble on the forward well-deck.'

Scruffy characters emerged from the various sections of the ship like rats scuttling out of their holes, some clutching a bag of equally dirty possessions. Two of them picked up their inert skipper and without much ado threw him unmindfully into the boat below. It seemed that all of them, especially Jack Smith with his sore ribs, were quite happy to be leaving their dirty former home. No-one lamented the potential loss of the SS *Rampleton.*

Except the still hidden gunner Denzil Davis RNVR.

The tramp's cargo was of little value to the quickly searching boarding party and soon, with their prisoners, they and two other boats that had come alongside were on their way back to the battlecruiser. Two of *Dresden*'s tertiary four point ones (10.5cm) opened fire. Four shells were enough. *Rampleton* began to topple over on to her starboard side.

Then gunner Davis, shaken by the firing emerged and was seen to be swinging the stern gun round to point it at the German warship. Seemingly too late, one of *Dresden*'s 4.1 guns swivelled round to fire but Davis was first to the race.

'Gotcha you Jerry b –' he yelled as he pulled the firing lever but he never completed the sentence as the gun blew up in his face shredding Davis to bloodied fragments and hurling itself off its deck mounting.

Gunner Davis had always been a careful man. The gun's tampon closure was rarely removed in case rainwater got into the barrel of his ever-so clean gun and caused it to rust. A pity that it had still been there when Gunner Davis at the crowning moment of his very limited career had chosen to pull the firing-lever. So the fuse-cap of the shell hit the cover, exploded, causing the barrel to burst and shred both itself and Gunner Davis, into many pieces.

The old ship sank very quickly after two of *Dresden*'s four point one inch (10.5cm) guns fired a further shell each at its waterline. It wasn't mourned by its crew. Nor by *Dresden*'s men. Just a dirty stain on the water. Some bits of wreckage. Soon to be dispersed by the restless waves of that section of the Atlantic Ocean.

The scruffy crew survivors were glad to be on board a ship that was much, much cleaner than their late home. Even if it did belong to the enemy. Apart from them, Brautsch and his men hadn't brought anything from the former 4,313-ton dirty ship, that had been full of coal, dust, rats, rust and iron sheeting. Hardly worth the bother of sinking except for the practice of stopping and searching a would-be prize. Maybe she had an extra cargo underneath the outer veneer of all their filth and dirt. Maybe her drunken captain knew. Maybe not. Reitz thought on these lines as *Dresden* gathered speed away from the site of the sinking.

On impulse, Reitz left the bridge and went down to deck level where Brautsch had just poured a bucket of cold sea water over the inert ex-skipper of *Rampleton.*

'Wake up, my friend,' he urged O'Flanagan who began to shake his shaggy semi-shaven head. Spluttering some base oaths, he stirred himself into a sitting position.

'Where the hell am I?' he croaked.

His eyes focused on Reitz's immaculate white naval trousers and polished shoes.

'Aah, Aah! So the captain wakes up.' O'Flanagan looked at the German captain, his eyes gradually focussing.

'You're not one of my crew, are you?'

'Forgive me. I am Captain Reitz, commander of the Kriegsmarine's battlecruiser *Dresden.*'

'Not Royal Navy are you?' came O'Flanagan's response.

'No my friend. We are Germans and we have just sank your very dirty ship.'

Brautsch interposed 'Sunk with all the filth that was on board. But we wonder, was there anything else on board? Steel props? Concrete or cement powder? She sank very quickly.'

'Silly bleedin' square heads,' snorted O'Flanagan. 'Don't yer know why I was having a bevvy?' The latter word was lost to the Germans standing by, except Reitz.

'A bevvy means a glut of drinking!' he commented dryly.

'Well, you bleedin' Nazees. My ship were a bullion carrier. Gold bars to safe-keepin' in t' Falklands. 'Neath all that muck and stuff. So read in a manifest produced by –

'Me yer bloody nutcase – 'fer a joke.' A little man with a thin face spoke. 'Yes, me, the bosun. Cos' we don't like yer an' decided to get yer sloshed whilst t'engines was bein' repaired.'

'Enough of this nonsense. Put this man –' Reitz indicated to O'Flanagan '– into a solitary cell and the rest can all give their version of this silly, sorry episode at a more convenient time.'

Brautsch mused 'Even if they'd had gold on board, there's no way that we're going to get it, nor anybody else!' but his thoughts were interrupted when the ship's loudspeakers crackled into life 'Captain to the bridge. Urgent!'

It was a radar report indicating that three ships were about fifteen miles to the north-west and closing at an increase of their speed from twenty to an estimate of twenty-five knots.

'Could be a fresh hunting group of cruisers and we're the target' was the response from Reitz. 'Right, increase our speed to twenty-five knots, alter course to one-hundred and eighty-five degrees and let's play with them. See if they alter course and if they do then we'll let them chase us.'

Which radar reported that the three following ships had done but at the speed of twenty-five knots they were not closing with *Dresden*.

Maybe because darkness was falling. Maybe they were just following orders to shadow the German ship until dawn, close in, verify their suspicions and then either force an action or hope that possible reinforcements would arrive to help them trap their opponent.

To help lull the possible cruisers into a false sense of realism Reitz during the night reduced the battlecruiser's speed back to twenty knots but kept on the same course as previously, before turning in to get a few hours rest before dawn. He stood down as much of the crew as he could feeling that at first light the chasing cruisers would try to close in to force an action. Radar reported that they too had correspondingly slowed their speed although they had closed to within about twelve miles.

Dawn.

Reitz was alert and refreshed on the bridge relieving Anders who had stood the night watch until eight bells of the first watch. Radar reported that the three potential cruisers were closing in with an increase in their speed. The wireless room also reported that one of them was sending out a long coded message. Reitz commented that the message could well be that they were closing in on a suspected target. Them. Probably to the Royal Naval Headquarters in London.

The crew of *Dresden* were fully closed up and the stern turret, Cesar, had its twin eleven-inch (28cm) guns already at maximum elevation seemingly sniffing at the as yet unseen target. Anton and Bruno had also been swivelled round in preparation for the contest.

Then at 5.17 a lookout shouted 'Enemy in sight! At one hundred and forty-seven degrees on the starboard rear quarter.'

Halder already had the range worked out. If they were cruisers, they were still out of Cesar's reach, never mind being in the range of the guns of those cruisers.

Reitz held his course but ordered a very gradual increase of speed to almost match that of the British cruisers. To make it hard for them to chase their target. To entice their commander to attempt to close the range.

In Scapa on board his battleship Collins knew that the group of cruisers under Commander Robert Froggatt on board the Town-class cruiser *Chelmsford* had the German battlecruiser in sight and were closing the range. He also knew that Vice-Admiral Holland on board the Royal Navy's largest warship, the battlecruiser *Hood* was also in sight of Germany's largest warship, battleship *Bismarck* together with a heavy cruiser, off the southern exit to the Denmark Straits. Three German surface raiders. In sight. There was the chance to nail all three of them.

Vice-Admiral Gunther Lutjens was a stern taciturn sailor of the strict Prussian mentality. Firmly believing in *Bismarck*'s superiority as she pushed her way through those cold North Atlantic waters he received her consort's message of 'Two battleships in sight' with a feeling of grim satisfaction. Then came a message from the radio room picked up from *Dresden* that an enemy cruiser force was attempting to close with her off the Azores. He turned to the battleship's captain Ernst Lindemann.

'You see, here we have the enemy in sight. *Dresden* is doing her job further south. Now is the time to prove our worthiness and deal a double blow to the British. Tell our guns to open fire as soon as possible.'

Chelmsford's accompanying warships, the older and slower C-class cruisers *Castleton* and *Caerphilly* were beginning to fall astern of their more modern companion as they strained to speed up beyond twenty-seven knots, three knots slower than Froggatt's ship. Already Froggatt had urged his Chief Engineer to screw down the safety valves as he strove to close the gap between his ship and the now clearly defined *Dresden*.

The evening before Froggatt's airmen had caught *Dresden* napping when the cruiser's Walrus float-plane sighted the German with *Rampleton* after they'd been spotted on radar at extreme range. After recovering the Walrus which the Germans had failed to sight, he'd closed the gap to about fifteen miles when radar reported that one of the blips had vanished and that the other had moved off, increasing speed all the time before steadying as darkness fell at twenty-knots. Froggatt was unwilling to fight a night action and settled instead for a pursuit with the intention of surprising the German with a dawn attack. His previous ship, of the same class, the Sheffield had already fired her guns at an Italian battleship so when he'd transferred from her to *Chelmsford* to take over from her previous captain who'd gone down with a severe tropical fever, he'd relished the chance to chase after the German battlecruiser whose appearance in the Atlantic had been so dramatic.

Not for him to be taken by surprise. The thrill of the chase took him back to his youth flying along the country fields in red coat, white jodhpurs and black riding boots astride his big black stallion as he raced after hounds pursuing yet another twisting, cunning red fox. He gripped the rail of the open upper bridge with a white silk scarf draped round his neck urging the cruiser to close with his fleeing fox. Only this time it had nowhere to hide. No hedges. No ditches or culverts. No midden piles in farmyards in which to roll. No. Not this fox. She was there. In sight on the open sea. What he missed was the cry of 'Tally-ho' and the blast of the hunting horn. The wake of the fleeing fox could be clearly seen. Arrow straight.

Unlike the fox, the target he was chasing had extra large vicious teeth. Not white. They glared red and orange. Two of them. Together with a dragon's breath of grey and brown smoke. Aimed at *Chelmsford.* Whistling their missiles through the air. Nastily. Landing just a hundred yards ahead of the cruiser so that she was lashed with their falling spray as she rushed forwards.

Then those teeth glowed again with the shells landing adjacent to the cruiser's bows. Splinters flew in and across the fore section of the cruiser clanging and gouging at her thin metal skin of protection.

'Damn good shooting by them' yelled Froggatt's first lieutenant.

'Maximum speed. Hold our course. We must close them' snarled his captain, seemingly oblivious to the threat posed by the German ship which was altering course. Then he yelled 'Guns. Open fire. Now!'

'A' and 'B' turrets crashed out a full six-gun salvo. Even though they were virtually out-of range. But the gap was closing for Reitz was turning *Dresden* so as to bring his forward turrets to bear. Anton and Bruno. Six eleven-inch guns against the six forward six-inch guns of *Chelmsford.*

Dresden's next salvo was of all her big guns firing at the light cruiser.

Far away to the north eight-inch (20.5cm) shells from *Prinz Eugen,* the German battleship's consort, had already hit the *Hood* starting an amidships fire on the British battlecruiser but then *Bismarck* with a fresh fifteen-inch (38cm) gun salvo was to shatter the Royal Navy's darling warship for they hit the *Hood* with such an appallingly destructive power that they created a mighty explosion which ripped the big warship into two halves amidst a massive eruption of destroying power. It was just ten minutes after the guns had opened fire. *Hood* sank rapidly and her consort, the new battleship *Prince of Wales* was forced to take desperate avoiding action in order to escape a fate similar to that which had so devastatingly shattered the *Hood.* Seven heavy shells were to crash aboard her as she turned away.

Off the Azores at the same time as *Hood* was blowing up, parts of *Chelmsford*'s superstructure were also being reduced to scrap metal as *Dresden*'s full salvo crashed aboard, smashing B-turret off its runners and flames began to probe into the lower section of her bridge. Froggatt staggered back from the devastating blow but steerage was lost as the helmsman collapsed with a splinter smashing into his right arm. Although a reserve helmsman sprang forward in the smoke to take the wheel he couldn't immediately gain control. Then another salvo crashed alongside and two of the shells landed amidships.

'Make smoke. Steer from the emergency system' croaked Froggatt. Just four salvos and his cruiser was out of the chase. The other two cruisers, about a mile astern couldn't hope to catch the now disappearing German battlecruiser which at full speed was outstripping them.

Reitz smiled 'That'll do. They can't catch us now. Hold our course until we lose them off our radar and then alter course to the south-east.' To Serle he indicated the new course. Then the wireless room buzzer sounded. The news was electrifying. *Bismarck* had sunk the *Hood* and forced another battleship to turn away severely damaged. Yet even as Reitz announced their bigger companion's success over the intercom as well as praising his crew's efforts at beating off the recent challenge of the British cruiser, he had a nagging doubt despite the cheering of crew members, that something wasn't quite right. The news of *Bismarck*'s success had been picked up '*en clair*' from a Royal Navy ship. The German battleship it seemed was holding her course. Surely the Royal Navy would try to seek to avenge the loss of *Hood.* Perhaps he ought to turn north to try and link-up with *Bismarck* but then he'd run the risk of running into the Royal Navy units seeking out the big German battleship so the nagging doubts gnawed at him. Then later that day SKL sent out instructions for *Dresden.* To keep clear of the northern area so as to leave it free for the other two German ships and anyway, they were scoring successes where they were and soon the Atlantic would be clear of enemy shipping. Lutjens had scored a huge success and was seemingly bent on expanding it. But Reitz had his doubts. Even as darkness closed his wireless operators picked up numerous Royal Navy warship signals indicating a build-up of forces to the north of them. All seemed to indicate that their target was *Bismarck.*

Admiral Collins woke up to find himself in an Inverness hospital. Bleakly he stared up at a crisp white-starched uniform. Matron Audrey McCutcheon. Spinster. Very stern-faced. Collins was in her care and she would see to his rapid recovery that was hoped for by the Navy who'd sent him to her, yes, her hospital. The Navy had been somewhat alarmed on hearing the news that he'd collapsed after suffering a mild heart attack, brought on by the double blow within minutes to the Navy's pride. Firstly the demise of the *Hood* and then the crippling of *Chelmsford.* The result – three dangerous German raiders at large at the northern and southern entrances of the North Atlantic.

A civilian, with a briefcase, entered the room. Matron McCutcheon blanched when she saw the name on the card.

'Is he well enough to talk?'

For the first time in her life, Audrey McCutcheon stammered, somewhat weakly 'Well sir, er yes, well, yes.'

The civilian spoke 'Now, Bernard, I hope that you will soon recover. We'll need you to help us catch *Dresden*, not *Bismarck.* Enough of our resources are being assembled to catch the big one including carriers *Victorious* and *Ark Royal* as well as five battleships and numerous cruisers and destroyers that are sailing from Gibraltar, the Home Fleet and the various convoys in the area.'

Collins unable to recognise the civilian or even register the fact that the man had somewhat familiarly used his Christian name, dimly nodded as the civilian looked directly at him having now seated himself by the bed and thereupon he'd opened his briefcase pulling out a file labelled *Dresden* and her captain, George Reitz.

'Well, Bernard, what of *Dresden*?'

Still bleakly looking around him, Collins blurted out 'Yes, get her. She could be far more dangerous than *Bismarck*. Faster, better captained – no admiral interfering like on her big sister – and very dangerous. Longer range too. Could go anywhere, that is if you've lost her.'

The civilian nodded. Collins continued.

'Reitz will not turn north to help *Bismarck*. He'll have already guessed that we'll pull out all our stops to halt the battleship. No. He'll sail south, lie low and then return after the fuss has died down – if it ever does. But you're right. Lutjens must be nailed although if he's still in the North Atlantic I'm surprised. If I'd been him I'd have turned round and gone back to Norway. He no longer has the element of surprise. We are expecting him. My guess is that he'll go for France. Our best chance of getting him.'

Collins sounded breathless when he'd finished, but after a moment or so he continued 'Get Reitz as well or we'll suffer more losses. So far he's outguessed us and will continue to do so unless he too is brought to account.'

All the time the civilian had been making notes but then he straightened and patted Collins on the shoulder 'Alright Bernard, get some rest. We'll get Lutjens first and then hunt for *Dresden*.' Then he left the room passing Matron McCutcheon on his way out. A matron perturbed that her patient had been talking far too much with this civilian, however important that he was. The Ministry of Defence. Sir whatever on his card. Collins is my patient. She merely snorted at the civilian as he tipped his bowler hat at her as she left the room. Looking down on her patient she saw that he'd closed his eyes. Seemingly asleep. Summoning a junior nurse to watch over him, she flounced off in the direction of the main ward.

On board *Chelmsford* the damage control teams worked hard all that long day extinguishing the flames around 'B' turret, the lower superstructure of the bridge and the amidships section, and then they set to cut away the mangled wreckage and clear away the remains of the crew members who'd perished in the shambles. In a somewhat distracted manner Froggatt went to see the damage but he knew that he had failed. He should have held back and shadowed the German ship but instead he'd charged in. Wireless messages informed him that heavy cruiser *Wellington* had been diverted away from her convoy duties and that she was on her way with a possible back-up of a battleship, an old R-class one, *Resolve* with two destroyers. But what was the use? The *Dresden* had now vanished to the south. He was sick in the pit of his stomach as the cruiser's padré went through the motions of a burial service for the bits and pieces in their weighted canvas bags. He lost count until the padré finished by saying.

'We commit all these sixty-seven members of our crew to the deep.' Then they heaved them overboard. Worst of all he had to keep *Chelmsford* on station with her two 'C'-class consorts on an East-West patrol line until the *Wellington* made her appearance. *Dresden* was not to be allowed to link up with the *Bismarck* which it transpired had manage to shake off her shadowers as well. If *Dresden* or God forbid, *Bismarck* came across them they were to engage. Engage! What did those chair-bound arseholes think they were? Half his main armament out of action and severe damage that needed urgent dockyard work and Their Bleedin' Lordships were telling him to engage the enemy! Must be severely blinkered. Froggatt was to stay on station. Until the enemy re-appeared but hopefully not before *Wellington* arrived and then possibly much later, the old *Resolve* and her escorts.

Unknown to Froggatt. *Dresden* sailed much further to the south than anticipated. Reitz had taken the battlecruiser well away, guessing that due to his actions with the cruiser groups, the British would be sending re-inforcements to guard against him linking up with Lutjens and his battleship. A battleship trailing a streak of oil and pushing for a French port rather than turning back for Norway. Attracting avenging Royal Navy warships.

An attraction that Reitz decided to avoid. He'd done his utmost to get the Royal Navy to chase him but it was the bigger catch that they were after first, not his ship.

Early next morning radar reported a slow-flying aircraft circling some fifteen miles astern.

'Think you can shoot it down?' Reitz asked Stein, one of the airmen who flew the Arados.

'If it's a Walrus and we can get higher above it before it sees us.'

'Well try. Don't want it to see us if at all possible.'

A desperate move which soon resulted in the Arado being catapulted off for the chase. No tricks with bags of feathers. Just a single nose-mounted machine-gun.

The aircraft, which was as rightly guessed, a Walrus, had been catapulted from heavy cruiser *Wellington* some one hundred miles to the north. Then the Walrus's crew sighted a ship below them in the distance to the south.

'Ship sighted. Am flying to investigate' came in the message to the wireless operators on the heavy cruiser. No position. No positive identification. Moments later came another 'Hell, we've be –' and then nothing else.

Only silence.

Stein's machine gun, at short-range ripped into the unsuspecting Walrus as its crew concentrated on closing with the *Dresden*. Then, to their horror, they heard the firing and saw their aircraft burst into flames. With a slam of water and surge of spray, the Walrus hit the sea still burning furiously. Desperately her crew excepting their dead wireless operator, scrambled into an inflatable dinghy and as hurriedly as possible, paddled away watched by Stein and Stolle as they flew above them.

Reitz took his battlecruiser to the scene of the crashed Walrus but it had sunk to a watery grave by the time Brautsch and his launch raced over the waves in order to rescue the three naval airmen still somewhat dazed by their unfortunate turn of events. In order for them to be questioned. One of the airmen said rather cockily 'It'll be your turn for the chop when old Wellie gets you.'

Brautsch interposed 'He means the County-class cruiser HMNZS *Wellington.*' And then to the airmen 'Well we know she's more than twenty miles away so we'll soon outspeed and outdistance her. We aren't the slower pocket-battleships, you do realise that don't you?'

So *Dresden* fled for ten hours at full speed. Due south. A long way from the drama unfolding further north. Re-discovered, *Bismarck* was attacked by aircraft from the carrier HMS *Victorious.* Lutjens and his battleship were being hunted remorselessly. Not to escape. Not like Reitz and his luck with *Dresden.*

Chapter 4

'Been with you lot before'

Yet another hot day was developing as Padré Jervaulx came to the end of his sermon on that morning in the Petty Officers Mess. His joke that Hell was perhaps even hotter than the current weather that the battlecruiser was being welcomed into that Sunday morning had gone down better than he'd thought – some of the nearly two hundred men crammed into the room tittered as their sweating padre did his best to describe that the tortures of that foreboding realm took place in an area hotter than their mess. More chilling were the prayers uttered for their comrades on board battleship *Bismarck* much further north than they were.

They all knew that the Royal Navy was closing in on the big ship. That she had been in action against carrier planes, cruisers and destroyers although she still floated despite her damage. Somehow they sensed that the big ship was facing her final *denouément*. Jervaulx had done his best. He'd thanked His Presence that they had, with their captain's guidance, so far, not been severely worsted by their enemy and that they were putting the earlier disappointments of previous cruises behind them with the successes so far gained in this current foray.

Reitz thought of Elie as he accepted the communion wafer. The other crew members no doubt thought of their loved ones as well but felt that the Royal Navy was, in its action against *Bismarck*, barring their way back to German held waters. At least for the time being.

Only Reitz knew different.

There was a contingency plan in case of a disaster to *Bismarck* and that was for *Dresden* to run into the South Atlantic, take what prizes came their way and then to await further orders. Since the shooting down of *Wellington*'s Walrus and the immediate high-speed dash to the south, Reitz had cruised his ship steadily ever south-eastwards towards the centre of the Atlantic 'Narrows' between north-east Brazil and the western coastline of North Africa. Clear of the crowded mess room he paused to gaze over starboard rail near one of the torpedo tubes. He looked at the deceptively peaceful blue waters. Wistfully he hoped that perhaps, if he and his ship survived this protracted struggle he'd sail these waters again, tension free and perhaps with Elle at his side. How was she coping with his absence? But his thoughts were interrupted when Junior Leutnant Anders came running up to him 'Sir' he blurted out, hurriedly saluting, 'urgent message, in code, for you from the wireless room.'

Reitz took the signal flimsy. From SKL. 'URGENT. CAPTAIN OF *DRESDEN*.' Then a jumbled series of letters. He'd need his code-book.

The message was stark in its content. Bleak. – '*Bismarck* sunk. Go to South Atlantic – Rhine's supplies drying up'. Reitz knew that this last sentence to be the code jargon for *Bismarck*'s supply ships. Probably being caught by the searching Royal Navy's cruisers. He continued to decode. 'Keep up the good work and radio silence unless in an emergency. Contact later within next thirty days. Canaris and E.'

Elle must have sent out the message. Her initial at the end. His heart fluttered at the impact that she'd sent out this communication. Whilst trying to digest the reality of the words the speaker above his desk crackled into life. 'Captain to bridge. Have a merchantman in sight.'

Reitz picked up his cap and arrived on the bridge with part of him wanting to tell all and sundry of the news of the demise of their big brother.

Hiltzern saluted him. 'She's going in fits and starts. Like sending Red Indian smoke signals. Shall we close her?'

Reitz nodded. 'Yes. We'll pretend to be Royal Navy. We'll try to capture her, send a boarding party over and see if she's worth keeping. Looks to be quite a modern one, even at this distance.'

Dresden closed in on the slow-moving merchantman. The ship grew increasingly clearer in the sight of the Germans. She was modern. British. All 7,213 tons of her. Tyneside built and completed in 1936. A refrigeration ship out from Buenos Aires and bound for Gibraltar to join a convoy to take her to England and eventually her home port of Bristol.

But the ship had a problem.

Three hours earlier she'd developed defects in her engine-room which restricted her speed to five knots. Bearings had run hot and the ship's engineer had no white metal to make a permanent repair. At the time when *Dresden* was making her approach, her captain, Richard Smithson, was in the engine-room discussing with his Chief as to whether their ship, the *Arabian Nights* could make it to Gibraltar or whether she should run for Freetown on the West African coast. He'd left a very young junior second officer on the bridge. It was his first ever solo time on the bridge, a factor that made twenty-year old James Nalton feel very important yet at the same time, somewhat nervous. What if something further went wrong? What would 'the old man' say as a result? His nerves twanged up and down his spine as he watched the fast-approaching warship bear down on the lumbering freighter. A freighter full of valuable foodstuffs – refrigerated and frozen. Vital in the fight to keep fed members of the island race for which she was bound.

He knew it wasn't the *Bismarck*. She'd been sunk. He didn't realise that the approaching ship was *Dresden*. Captain Smithson would have possibly guessed that it could be the German battlecruiser but the last report he'd had of her was that she was possibly going north to assist *Bismarck*. But he was down in the engine-room. Not on the bridge helping Nalton. Anyway the approaching warship was clearly flying a White Ensign. The warship flashed a signal 'HMS *Repulse* here. Stop your engines. Am coming to check your papers.'

Perfectly normal behaviour. You had to obey the Royal Navy in wartime. It's what he'd been told at training school. What he'd forgotten to do was to have sent off a signal from the wireless room that an unidentified warship was closing them. He really also should have told Captain Smithson.

Not that it would have made any difference. *Dresden* was far too close for anything but compliance with her demands which were continuing. 'No wirelessing. Boarding party on its way.'

Smithson's first intuition that something was wrong was when the engine telegraph jangled into a stop position. He indicated to his Chief that he was going topsides but even as he reached the deck level, Brautsch and several armed sailors were already on board.

'Bloody Germans aren't you?' snarled Smithson not particularly relishing the machine-pistol being waved in his direction. 'I hate bleedin' Nazis!'

'Yes we are German but not Nazis. There is a difference' smiled Oberleutnant Helmut Brautsch of the Kriegsmarine battlecruiser *Dresden*. 'Now you must be?'

'Captain Smithson. The ship's *Arabian Nights*. No good to you lot. Something wrong with our engines. You'd best come up to the bridge.'

Two of the boarding party had already reached the bridge and Nalton and the crew members there were now under guard. Other armed men had stormed into the wireless office and also down below to the engine room. Quickly the crew were assembled on deck whilst signals were being exchanged. 'No casualties. Valuable cargo of foodstuffs. Crippled engines. Send Luth to see if he can repair them. White metal needed.'

Reitz acknowledge the news with a grunt of dismay. Could he dare to linger whilst Luth and his team attempted to repair the engines? True, a very valuable prize if only she could be repaired but was it worth the risk? Was the heavy cruiser they'd avoided still chasing them?

It didn't take long for him to come to a decision and soon Second Engineer Luth, his men and their tools and spare white metal were clambering down into the merchantman's engine-room whilst from the battlecruiser an Arado took off to fly a circular patrol to the north beyond radar range with instructions to return as soon as they sighted an enemy warship.

The crew of the *Arabian Nights* were taken to the battlecruiser with a certain degree of trepidation amongst them for they had all been made fully aware of Smithson's hate for the Nazis and to them, the ship that loomed ever closer was probably crammed full of them.

One sailor muttered within earshot of Brautsch 'Don't let these bleedin' Jerries get to us lads, look what happened to their almighty *Bismarck*. Same'll 'appen to their rust bucket.'

'Quiet!' snapped Brautsch whose command of English was perfectly good enough to fully understand the underlining of the truth in the sailor's mutterings. He'd learnt the language whilst touring England with friends from Wittenberg University in those pleasant days in the early 1930s when the world was still at peace and graduate students could taste freedom before starting out on their various careers. He took his duties as boarding officer very seriously but it had been with a sense of relief when, having burst into the wireless office that the man at the set had put his own gun down on the table rather than trying to brazen it out in what would have been a futile show of resistance.

Once on board *Dresden*'s decks, Brautsch organised the freighter's crew into four columns where each man came forward to give his name and rank as well as to be relieved of their bulkier possessions not essential to their every-day existence. To their surprise they were each given a receipt for these possessions. Brautsch explained that when the crew members were transferred to a supply ship *en route* to Europe their possessions would be returned.

Those that wanted a job on *Dresden* doing menial tasks were offered one. Better than doing nothing at all, one man said. All the seven Lascar seamen accepted without batting an eyelid. One ship was the same as any other. Humping cargo. Cleaning decks and storerooms. Five others, all Chinese, said that they'd work in the ship's laundry and two of the Greeks of the mixed crew offered to work as waiters/stewards to the officers, just as they'd been doing to Captain Smithson and the officers of *Arabian Nights*.

For Smithson, Brautsch received instructions to take him up to see Reitz so somewhat reluctantly the British merchant captain trailed after the German officer. Memories of his last time as a German prisoner passed through Smithson's mind. Twenty-four years earlier he'd been a junior officer and just like Nalton he'd been on the bridge when a merchantman hove into sight flying a Red Ensign. Approaching them at a closing range and then suddenly the German flag fluttered up the mast and a gun sent a warning shot. It was another success for the raider *Wolf* and he and the rest of the crew were taken prisoner. A long, dreary existence followed as the *Wolf* stayed on the seas for a further seven months before she eventually returned to Germany.

After his release and that Great War's ending, Smithson returned to the merchant ship service and via a succession of ships rose to captain's rank and in August 1939 he took charge of *Arabian Nights* for her regular runs between Buenos Aires, Montevideo, Gibraltar and Bristol.

All ships sighted were regarded as a potential enemy when he was sailing independently so he steered away from them using the refrigeration ship's top speed of seventeen knots as the means to avoid these other ships. Only recently he'd even outrun a surfaced U-boat using the ship's stern gun to fire at the submarine until *Arabian Nights* was out-of-range of the threatened danger. Even then, Smithson still pushed his command for a further twelve hours of hard-steaming. Ruefully he mused that perhaps that push to escape had added extra strain on the coupling that had crippled his ship and so had brought it within the range of the German battlecruiser on whose decks he now trod. As he climbed up to the bridge he looked across the three hundred yards to where *Arabian Nights* heaved gently in the Atlantic swell. In between the two ships were a number of small boats shuttling across laden with easily accessible goods taken from his ship or returning for another load. He could but guess at the activities going on in the engine-room as the German engineering officer and his team strove to effect the repairs to make their valuable prize a going concern again.

'Three hours I've given them, Captain Smithson' called out Reitz as the merchant-ship skipper reached the bridge. 'Please come and watch. Please also to be reassured that we have hopefully no intention of harming your ship and definitely none of your crew. Come, please!'

Reitz could see the wariness of Smithson but he still held out his hand in a gesture of friendship. Smithson, surprised at the warmth of attitude that generated from the German captain, stuck out his right hand. In a shake of reluctant friendship.

Then Reitz took him to his sea-cabin at the rear of the bridge where Walters was ready with a good quality filter coffee. 'From your ship captain. Milk? Sugar? A little dram?' Smithson, still somewhat bemused, nodded glumly and muttered 'Two sugars. I like brandy, rather than whisky.' Walters, who understood enough English to know at least all the more common liqueurs quickly produced a cognac and poured a generous measure into Smithson's cup before retreating to his little store-room. Smithson took a sip of his coffee and then studied the German. Dark lines around his eyes; curly black hair that couldn't be hidden by the rakish-angled naval cap. Medium height and a slim, almost athletic, build.

'Now, captain.' Reitz was speaking. In excellent English thought Smithson. 'My steward is quite a marvel. Here I am with a Glen Moray malt in my glass. You have an excellent French cognac in your coffee. What could be better, even though you've lost your ship?'

'Been with you lot before.'

'How do you mean?' Reitz quickly guessing the answer and the reason for the English captain's reticence.

'On radar *Wolf* in the last war. Now you lot.'

Reitz nodded. 'Yes, your crippled engines certainly brought you into our sphere of operations.'

'Aye, you could say that.'

Changing tack, Reitz said 'Well, captain, your experience of sea life is much deeper than mine. This is only the second time I've ever been in these waters.

'Aye, enjoy it while you can because now that *Bismarck*'s gone, it'll be your turn next' growled Smithson 'Your advantage is that you're down here and not up there.'

'We are aware of the situation and once my three hour limit on repairing your ship is up, we shall be off-going further south and if your ship isn't repaired, then we shall, reluctantly I may add, have to sink her. I dare not, as you say, stay in these waters too long or else it will be our turn.'

'You don't want to sink my ship, do you? She's too valuable a cargo on board, eh?'

'Quite so. Now I must be back to my duties. You may stay here for a bit longer. I have even a few books for you to browse through. In a short-time a guard will collect you but in the meantime, my steward will top up your cup or glass should you so require. I must now return back to my duties. You may stay here for a bit longer. Your quarters are sharing ones – with two officers from a ramshackle tramp we sank a few days ago but not with her captain. He's in our punishment cells for his own protection. Apparently his crew didn't like him all that much! Please feel at ease as much as you can.'

'Not to worry, captain. My war days are over so it seems. Cheers.' Smithson raised his glass as Reitz clicked his heels, gave a slight bow and left his own cabin to catch up with the news of his newly-acquired prize. It was re-assuring. Luth's team had signalled that they expected to be finished within an hour.

Eventually Luth signalled again 'Repairs completed. Starting up engines. Time to be off. Twelve knots. Just in time for one of the Arados was back in sight. Signalling 'Heavy cruiser sighted.' The pilots reported. 'Forty miles to the north-east. Three funnels. County-class heavy cruiser. Probably doing about twenty knots. Coming in their direction.'

Reitz decided to draw the cruiser's direction to him but away from his new prize. So accordingly he steamed steadily to the north-east and when *Wellington*, for it was this cruiser, appeared at the edge of the radar screen he altered course, first due east and then by various points to east-south-east.

Tension began to mount as the blip marking the cruiser came slightly more towards the centre of the screen. Lookouts posted on high points were straining through their telescopes and binoculars at the horizon.

'Masthead in sight! 045 degrees' yelled one of them.

Reitz focussed his binoculars on the thin line. 'Alter course to one hundred degrees. Further round to the south-east.'

The masthead came a little clearer, especially when puffs of smoke appeared.

'She's increasing speed' muttered Hiltzern.

Then a lookout yelled 'She's turning away.'

'Check the radar plot' snapped Reitz.

On board *Wellington* Captain Hoggard, despite the loss of his one workable Walrus, was carrying out a sweep following a hunch developed from a precautionary message about the presence of a fast food freighter scheduled in their area. He'd been given an approximate position for the freighter which carried the romanticised name of *Arabian Nights*. Hoggard had the thought that *Dresden*, if in the area, could also find that freighter. He hoped that she could. Three times now the German had eluded him. If busy with the freighter Jerry could be caught napping.

'Radar sir! Have picked up a vessel on a course of roughly north-eastwards' reported the seaman watching the radar repeater, a facility as yet denied to Reitz on his ship.

Hoggard stared at it, not trusting it fully. 'Order the lookout to keep a watch. We'll see if it's that freighter or the bloody German. What's the contact's speed?'

'About fifteen knots. Probably a bit more' the seaman replied. Fifteen minutes later a lookout shouted 'Smoke sir, faint wisps. Bearing 125 degrees.'

South-east of the cruiser. About twelve miles away. Hoggard lifted his binoculars. There was a cough, directly made behind him.

'Yes, what is it?'

It was a midshipman. 'Sir, message from the radio room. Marked URGENT but the rest is in code.'

Hoggard groaned and rushed for his code-books.

'Damn' he muttered.

Hurriedly he returned to the bridge. To the navigator he snapped 'What's the plot?'

'Target's turned a bit away from us sir. Speed has also slightly increased.'

'What can our lads see?'

'One of them has a thin mast, he thinks, in sight.'

'Well, we have now to turn round and head at full speed for Freetown. Pronto. Yes! Now! At once!' snarled the increasingly irritable Hoggard. 'That message has ordered us to escort a convoy of troopships going to Cape Town. Apparently their Lordships think that the needle in the haystack, that may not be that smudge of faint diesel smoke and a thin mast could well slip into the South Atlantic and decide to have a go at those troopers and hey ho, we shall be there to meet it. In other words, turn this bloody ship round chop, chop and forget that merchantman or whatever it is, and get me an accurate course, mister navigator for Freetown, and at twenty-five knots tell me when we'll get there. We must keep their bleedin' Lordships happy and not go looking for a needle in a haystack.' Hoggard sounded grumpy. He was grumpy. He'd lost time in the last few days, or was it weeks, that his overstrained cruiser had received contrary orders. And always the same ship. His *bête-noir*. The German flippin' battlecruiser, KM *Dresden*.

Heavy cruiser HMNZS *Wellington* turned abruptly to the north-east. Away from the prize she'd be sent after. She'd never be as close again. Or would she?

It was true. The heavy cruiser's smoke and masthead turned away. Out of sight.

Reitz couldn't work it out. Why had she turned away? She must have seen *Dresden*'s faint smudge of diesel smoke even though Herzog had only gently opened the throttles, as it were, on the big steam-turbine engines that were now his pride and joy. The gap between the two ships increased until radar reported that the blip representing the cruiser had vanished altogether. Reitz stood the crew down excepting those on watch. It was time to sail further south for a further rendezvous with *Berengia* as well as the new prize, *Arabian Nights*.

Collins was sitting up in bed feeling much better, talking with that civilian again. The news of *Bismarck*'s demise had certainly cheered him up. Also, from the French Resistance had come news that heavy cruiser *Prinz Eugen* had docked in Brest so at least her whereabouts was also known. But then he asked the civilian the awkward question. Where was *Dresden*? The civilian could but shake his head.

Nothing had been heard of her since her brush with *Chelmsford* and the possible shooting down of *Wellington*'s Walrus although there was no definite proof. It could have been downed by a surfaced U-boat. The civilian assured him that most single ship sailings had been suspended for the next two weeks, irritating that it was to schedules! Once *Dresden*'s potential source of victims had dried up, the civilian felt sure that the battlecruiser would be ordered to return to Germany. All the Atlantic convoys would have at least a heavy cruiser as principal escort. Even the fast troopships convoys were receiving such an escort on their route to rounding the Cape with reinforcements for the Army in the North African Desert where fighting was intensifying now that the German general Erwin Rommel was organising an offensive with his Afrika Korps. Three such convoys were being planned over the next six months. The first had already sailed with *Wellington* soon to be its escort, the cruiser having now joined it at Freetown. The cruiser was better employed in this duty having failed to find *Dresden*.

Then the man in the grey suit was talking again. 'Sister McCutcheon says that you can leave this hospital later today so take time off over the weekend. Then we'll give you something else to do. Be a bit quieter for you. You can even forget *Dresden* for the time being. Take charge at the Simonstown naval base. We'll fly you down there. You'll get there by the time *Wellington*'s convoy comes in for refuelling. Then see the other two convoys through, at least. Be quite a restful change from the cut and thrust of the North Atlantic. Max Horton's going to get better escort groups organised for the Western Approaches because now that *Bismarck*'s gone, the Jerries will probably concentrate on their U-boats.'

Collins grunted in reply. Somehow the civilian had got it wrong. *Dresden* was still at large. But how could he argue the case for a fresh hunting group situation like the one that eighteen months ago had caught *Graf Spee* off the Plate Estuary? There just weren't enough spare ships to chase after a shadow. But she wasn't a shadow.

Dresden was real. Bound to be out there as a potential threat. Reitz wasn't a quitter.

'Well, old chap. Matron McCutcheon will be along soon to give you a final check-over. 'Bye for now.' The civilian nodded, placed his bowler hat on his head, picked up his briefcase and marched out without as much as a backward glance.

Matron McCutcheon marched in and held Collins' right wrist.

'Mmm. Just about normal. Have your lunch, Sir Bernard and then it's off to your home, I should think. Don't forget the air-sickness tablets I've brought in for your flight to South Africa.' And with that she flounced out of the room, as she always did. Bustling back to the main ward. Getting on with her job. Leaving Collins to ponder over his move to Simonstown. Over his thoughts about *Dresden.*

The battlecruiser had her two accompanying merchantman on either side and two of her Arados were on patrol looking for any Royal Navy units but the seas were clear. Six hours passed as the fuel flowed into *Dresden*'s tanks and some of the food from *Arabian Nights* was transferred to both ships. Carpenters hammered away on *Berengia* converting her now emptying holds into quarters for the prisoners and before the ships drew apart, Reitz ordered all his prisoners except Captain Smithson to be transferred, together with their armed guard, across to the big supply ship. Fresh coded orders had reached Reitz. In due course he was to take his ship into the Indian Ocean. To replace sunken raider *Pinguin* that had conducted a very successful career until caught by the heavy cruiser *Cornwall* and after a short exchange of fire, she'd blown up with a heavy loss of life to her crew and prisoners on board at the time.

The three ships parted company, the re-supplying over. The two merchantmen to make their way, independently, to a rendezvous east of Madagascar in July, joining trade routes, to act out under disguise a role of being a normal Allied merchantmen. The two patrolling Arados also returned but one of them came back with quite a startling message.

'Large freighter twenty-five miles to the south-west. On fire. Crew wanting to be rescued.'

Reitz asked Stein and Stolle to show him the position of the ship. He didn't take long to come to a decision. *Dresden*'s bows swung round on a course for the ship. How could he ignore a ship in obvious distress-even in wartime?

Radar reported the echo of the ship when the battlecruiser was just over fifteen miles away. Reitz sent up Stein and Stolle up again in their little seaplane but with Royal Naval roundels on it this time – so as to allay any fears that her survivors may show if they realised that it was a German ship coming to their rescue.

As the airman closed the burning merchantman they came to the imminent conclusion that the flames had become worse as they engulfed the aft section from the stern to the central bridge structure. Stolle signalled 'Rescue is nearby' but whether any of the few people on the fore peak understood was doubtful although at least one of them waved a white rag at the seaplane. Stein leaned out of his seat pointing to the direction from which *Dresden* was coming but couldn't really work out whether the people on deck could understand. Another puzzling feature to both the airmen was that the survivors on the ship appeared to be entirely women. Stolle took the Arado in as close as he could noting the name *Arades* on the bows of the freighter. With a waggle of the aircraft's wings, they flew towards their out-of-sight battlecruiser.

One of the women on the forepeak said to the others 'It'll be alright soon – that plane has come from one of our warships.'

Another woman, in reply, said, somewhat tersely 'Ah, but are you certain?'

They could but wait and see for there was no viable escape from their burning ship. All the boats had gone as well as the liferafts – shot, shelled, destroyed or burnt beyond any further useful purpose.

Arades was a medium sized tramp freighter of 8,317 tons and her usual pre-war wanderings from port to port her had been restricted to ones in the South Atlantic before connecting with a port in the United Kingdom. Her cargo of South African, Argentinian and Brazilian meat, fruits and other wares, packed in numerous crates, filled her holds to capacity. Since the start of the war her master preferred independent sailing but by perforce of the current situation in the Atlantic had reluctantly been persuaded to join convoys in the final phase of her steaming into British waters.

Two days after leaving Rio de Janeiro on her current voyage, *Arades* was challenged by a long-range surfaced U-boat with its main deck gun pointing directly at the freighter but her master, expecting such an occurrence, attempted to escape. The U-boat's guns opened fire and the opening round was a direct hit on the freighter's bridge killing all the upper deck officers as well as wrecking the wireless office. Slowly, despite the shelling from the U-boat, *Arades* swung her stern round and her gun crew, at last, despite the furious flames, could see through them and over across to their opponent, and sighting their gun, opened fire and to their surprise, saw their first shell hit the base of the submarine's conning-tower as well as blasting the deck gun into instant scrap-metal. Only able to fire three more shells, the raging flames forced the heroic gun crew to jump overboard from the still slowly moving freighter. Flat on their stomachs in the freighter's saloon were eight British nurses all answering the call for help from their Motherland, who had joined *Arades* when she'd docked at Buenos Aires. Now they were part of an ever-expanding horrific nightmare, Paralysed by fear and shock. The surviving crew members of the burning merchantman rushed to launch their sole remaining lifeboat with nary a thought for the terrified women. One of them heard the squeak of the lifeboat falls lowering away and coming out of her stupor she shoved open the saloon door only to see the damaged boat bob away and then slowly sink leaving the struggling crewmen shouting and screaming for *Arades* still had a considerable, to the swimmers, forward movement. The nurse, Andrea Cantrell, could hear those desperate cries for help as they gradually grew fainter and fainter until the roar and crackling of the aft deck fire blotted them out of her hearing.

It was only then that she realised her predicament. The U-boat had sunk, there were no lifeboats left and the fire was gaining strength as it crept inexorably closer to the saloon. In sheer desperation she rushed back into the saloon shouting at her seven friends – 'Come on, come on, get out on to the forward deck.' Only one other nurse seemed able to help. Together they took hold of the other six, one by one and dragged, pulled, pushed, cajoled them on to the forward well-deck, still free of the furious flames.

No other crew member appeared to help them. They were alone. But not quite. None of them saw the tiny seaplane circling high above them nor did they see it disappear to the north.

They did see the plane when it returned and flew much nearer sporting Royal Naval roundels. Andrea and her fit friend, Elfrida Ramsdale, waved vigorously to it and in response they saw it waggle its wings before it flew over them.

'That's a British plane' whispered Andrea. 'Help must be on its way. Its mother ship must be quite close.'

Elfrida wasn't convinced. She'd seen a Walrus flying-boat before carried by cruisers. The plane that had over flown them was much smaller. However, she felt, it would bring help.

Helplessly the women waited as the fire gradually began to attack the central section of the freighter. The heat from the flames grew more intense as the women tried to back further away towards the forepeak. Four of the nurses had nasty wounds in their legs caused by flying glass shards from the shattered windows of the now blazing saloon and it was with great difficulty that Andrea and Elfrida dragged them as far as they could but climbing up the access ladders to the forepeak was too difficult for them. They couldn't leave them on the foredeck whilst they scrambled for a few extra minutes of life.

'Look!' cried Andrea, as she stared desperately over the starboard rails 'there's a ship coming towards us.'

'Yes I can see it too,' muttered Elfrida. 'And it's one of ours. It's flying the "White Ensign".'

They watched the strange warship slow to a near halt about three hundred yards away. It then stopped broadside on to them. A boat was launched and they could see white uniformed sailors in the boat as it approached. A voice shouted 'Keep clear ladies. We're going to throw a grappling hook.'

Andrea, puzzled at the accent, motioned to Elfrida to back away as the voice had suggested but as she did so, she again whispered 'I think that they're Germans. Didn't you notice that accent?'

'Oh God, no! They'll probably shoot us like those damned U-boat men.'

'We've no choice. Look! One of them's clambering over the rail.'

To Helmut Brautsch it had seemed very strange to see just women at the rail of the foredeck of the freighter, whose aft and midships section were truly well ablaze. Where were the crew? Had they just abandoned the ship and if so, where were their lifeboats? What had caused the freighter to catch fire? The crew of the Arado had not reported any other vessel nearby. No distress calls had been picked up by *Dresden*'s wireless operators. If she had been attacked by a U-boat, where was it now?

Desperately he clambered up to the deck trying to shield his face from the heat as he climbed over the rail quickly followed by two more of his men. He muttered, in German. 'Quick hoist up the stretchers. There's at least four wounded women. And send Ernst and Frankel as well up to the deck to help carry the women to the rail.'

Then he went over to the women and in the best English that he could muster, he spoke to them 'Ladies, you need help. We are here to give it to you. Quick, let my men help you to the rail. This ship hasn't got too much longer to survive, I think!'

Standing there in his smart white uniform and cap, with holster and pistol, he made quite a handsome sight causing Andrea to momentarily feel a little flutter as she looked up at him. 'Come, quick ladies, you mustn't hesitate,' he urged again.

'Four of our companions are badly injured. All the crew have abandoned us. I think that their lifeboat sank whilst this ship was still moving forward. I heard them shouting for help.' Andrea said somewhat tersely.

'Please, madam, come. We shall look for those crew members after you've made the journey to our ship. Look, here are my men with stretchers.' He put out his right hand to guide Andrea to the rail. Without realising her actions, she automatically took it and went with the German to the rail.

'Please, madam, climb down the rope-ladder.'

Andrea carefully descended down to the waiting launch followed by Elfrida and two of the other less wounded nurses. They gasped as the first stretcher with one of their companions was lowered rather quickly and Andrea turned to one of the sailors.

'Hey, you, take more care!' The sailor muttered something that Andrea couldn't at first understand but then something whizzed in her brain. She was sure the man had spoken in German. She whispered to Elfrida 'I think that these men are Jerries.'

'So what? At least they're saving us'

One by one the other three stretcher loads were lowered down to the launch, followed quickly by Brautsch shinning down the last rope as quickly as he could. One of the sailors cut the rope as soon as his feet touched the launch's planking, the motor throttled into life and the boat turned to retrace her course back to *Dresden.*

'Are you German?' Andrea asked Brautsch somewhat accusingly 'because if you are, then it's a bit odd. One minute one of your U-boat is shelling us to bits, then the next minute you lot in some bloody big warship play heroics to rescue us! It seems at odds with our ideas of Nazis. You know, all shooting first and asking questions afterwards.' Andrea's voice sounded bitter.

'Yes, madam,' came back the answer 'we are German. I am the

senior boarding officer Oberleutnant Helmut Brautsch but madam, we are not Nazis. We sail the seas to sink Allied ships, that is true for we are at war, but if at all possible, providing that our own ship's security is not threatened, then we will endeavour our best to rescue the survivors, take them prisoner and eventually send them back to Europe. Civilian personnel, like yourselves, will be released to the authorities of any neutral country.'

'Fine words, Herr Brautsch, but will you abide with them?'

'Madam, I do not know your name.'

'It's Miss Andrea Cantrell and my friend is Miss Elfrida Ramsdale. We, and the other six ladies are all qualified nurses trying to reach England. They're needing us but first your U-boat and then you have meant that we're in your hands, not still sailing towards Gibraltar.'

'I'm sorry Fraulein Cantrell that your journey has been interrupted but look at your freighter now for if we hadn't come, you'd all have perished.'

Andrea followed Brautsch's arm. The foredeck of the *Arades* was now well alight.

'Herr Brautsch. We are grateful and I'm sorry that I've been a little petulant.'

'Well, we're nearly at our ship.' Andrea looked up as the bulk of *Dresden* loomed up above their relatively tiny launch. Even as it was being hauled out of the water, four medium guns opened fire, one after another causing Andrea and Elfrida to cry out sharply.

'Ladies' they heard Brautsch say, 'we're finishing off the burning freighter, making sure that she sinks. Look, she's going.'

Amid the tortured sounds of rending metal and hissing steam as the sea poured into the stricken *Arades*, they watched the freighter rear up her bows, half turn and then quite quickly and with relatively little fuss, slide under the surface. Soon the grey and white cloud of smoke and steam dispersed and all that could be seen were a few bits of wreckage bobbing about as flotsam on those restless Atlantic rollers.

Carefully the wounded nurses were lifted out of the launch and carried down to the Sick Berth where Doctor Lebers was waiting.

In German he said 'Aha, what have we here? Wounded female survivors. How unusual.'

'Not so unusual, Herr Doktor' responded Andrea in excellent German 'We're all nurses and this is Fraulein Elfrida Ramsdale and I am Fraulein Andrea Cantrell. We will assist you. Now where are your clean dressings and medications?'

Lebers took a step back and peered over his horn-rimmed glasses. 'My, my, ladies with spirit. Of course you may help!'

'Thankyou, Herr Doktor!'

So, rolling up their sleeves and finding aprons, they both set to with Doctor Lebers and his two regular Sick Berth Attendants at cleaning and washing the six wounded nurses, four of whom were badly injured with two of them barely conscious.

They felt the ship tremble as she began to pick up speed away from the scene of their traumatic experience. Suddenly Reitz appeared with Brautsch and Anders into the Sick Berth.

'Greetings ladies' he said in his excellent English. 'My name is Kapitan George Reitz and I am in charge of this ship. I am sorry that you've had such a harrowing ordeal. I believe the one called Andrea could fill me in with the details. Which one of you is Andrea?'

Andrea nodded.

When she'd finished her account of the ordeal of *Arades* at the hands of the U-boat, as well as of the bravery of the gunners which compared so much to the actions of the rest of that ship's crew, Reitz nodded gravely. He hadn't interrupted once although Anders made notes having had the main outlines translated to him by Brautsch. Then Reitz repeated that once they were all fit he would release them.

Andrea stepped forward 'Captain Reitz, thank you for rescuing us. The two of us, Elfrida and myself, who weren't injured at all in the shelling, would like to continue to assist in the work of this Sick Berth, if we may.'

'Well, Fraulein, I am sure Doctor Lebers would welcome any assistance. So far he hasn't had too much to do except smack the malingerers, pop pills into reluctant mouths for head and toothaches and occasionally deal with a few minor injuries. You ladies are his first real patients.' Then with a click of his heels, he bade them farewell. As Brautsch turned to go, he smiled at Andrea and to her astonishment Andrea found herself smiling back at him. She also felt the hot flush of a blush begin to spread over her face.

Two days later *Dresden* was in the same latitude of the river Plate. An area of ocean which had seen the battle between the German panzerschiffe (pocket battleship) *Graf Spee* and three smaller Allied cruisers leading to the eventual demise of the German warship. The day was hot and sunny without a cloud in sight.

It being a Sunday, Padré Jervaulx had set up his altar on the deck aft of turret Cesar and was holding a memorial service as *Dresden* cruised through the waters at twelve knots. All men who could be spared assembled to attend the service to remember the men on both sides who'd died in that first major sea conflict of the war. Captain Smithson who'd been retained on board the *Dresden* as well as Andrea and Elfrida had agreed to attend representing the Allies. After two hymns and a Bible reading, Jervaulx uttered prayers for the dead and then one of reconciliation that when the war was over, both sides could come together as friends in the sight of their Lord. Smithson then read the twenty-third Psalm, in English, with Reitz providing an immediate translation into German.

After the reading, tough man Otto Schenke threw a wreath of artificial roses over the stern and then Captain Smithson was invited to do the same but he declined by passing the wreath to Andrea, murmuring 'For the brave gun crew of *Arades* as well.' She nodded and then walked to the stern and with Helmut Brautsch at her side, she hurled the wreath into the bubbling waters. Brautsch murmured 'Thankyou, Miss Cantrell' before she turned back to join Smithson and Elfrida. Reitz then came down and shook the hands of all the three English representatives, nodding his thanks for their attendance.

The converted *Wellington* bomber rolled to a stop on the tarmac of Gibraltar's air-strip. Blasts of hot June air hit Admiral Collins as he stepped out during a couple of hour's stop-over whilst the aircraft re-fuelled for the next stage of its flight to Cape Town via Freetown, Nairobi and Johannesburg with its twelve passengers, all of upper-ranked military personnel *en-route* for South Africa to help co-ordinate the movement of the convoys that were now being re-routed around the whole of Africa rather than risk them across the Mediterranean which was becoming a dangerous battleground of the Axis airforces versus the Royal Navy which had recently taken a heavy battering in the waters around Crete.

Collins was shown the way to the naval offices adjacent to the airstrip and after the minimal of introductions he brusquely demanded as to the whereabouts of the *Dresden*.

No-one could give him a reply. Heavy cruiser *Wellington* was now with the departed Freetown convoy. The battered *Chelmsford* had been withdrawn for a full-scale repair and refit and was sailing back to England with a small convoy. Even Force H's ships, having scoured the North Atlantic, with those based in the Home Fleet, had failed to find the elusive battlecruiser although they'd had considerable success at finding *Bismarck*'s fleet of supply ships.

Nothing had come in from the various Allied agents scattered in France or Norway. The big three German ships at Brest were already receiving extra attention from the RAF in order to scare *Dresden* away, as someone laconically noted. All the other main German surface ships were known to be in their own home waters. But nothing was known about the one ship that mattered to Collins.

Battlecruiser *Dresden*.

An aide came up to him 'Time to go, sir, your aircraft's ready for the next stage of the journey.' Damn, thought Collins, nothing definite about Reitz and his ship. Where was she? Why didn't I concentrate heavier cruisers earlier on to catch her? What if she's returned to Norway? Or gone south? Where is she? He tried to put the matter to the back of his mind when the roar of the *Wellington*'s engines burst into full power hurtling it down the runway on its take off for Freetown.

SKL contacted Reitz in a series of brief coded messages and the result was that they ordered *Dresden* to avoid contact with any Allied ships as she pushed her way southwards. For the best part of a fortnight at a speed of fifteen knots, or thereabouts, she continued what to the crew was a most mundane progress after all the excitement of the previous few weeks since their ship's breakout into the North Atlantic. On one of the days *Berengia* appeared to top up the battlecruiser's tanks whilst the ships remained moving alongside each other. No more of *Dresden*'s prisoners were transferred across to the supply ship. In fact, two of the nurses from *Arades* were giving Doctor Lebers cause for concern for their injuries were proving to be problematical and just not healing up at all. Then *Berengia* parted company and moved off to round the Cape of Good Hope posing as an Allied merchantman as well as to spy on shipping movements in the area.

So the battlecruiser pushed into the cooler waters well to the south of the Cape of Good Hope. Seas which grew ever more steeper and greener in colour with white spumed tops. Frequent rain squalls lashed the ship as she plunged into the heaving waters. Everything was battened down. So far as the world was concerned, the German warship had vanished. Disappeared.

Even Collins thought this as he went to the Naval HQ office that was to be his scene of operational planning in Simonstown. When he asked about *Dresden* there had been no fresh news at all. U-boats were known to be active in the South Atlantic shipping lanes and were moving into the area off Cape Town and even into the Indian Ocean itself. Perhaps they had supply ships to support them but so far none had made its presence known to the Allies. The trouble was identifying them. The Germans seemed very apt at the art of disguise. The same with their merchant-ship raiders. Cunningly armed and camouflaged. The authorities told him that probably at least three of them were roaming the World's trade routes in the Southern Hemisphere.

But *Dresden* was more dangerous than all of them, U-boats included. She had speed, a long range, probably radar and aircraft as well as her guns and torpedoes. A very elusive and cunning opponent. She had to be found. But no-one at the Cape had heard of her since her brush with *Chelmsford.* A few ships had gone missing in the South Atlantic but their disappearance was put down to U-boats or a disguised merchant-raider. Not *Dresden.* No wireless messages for 'help' had been received from at least three of them, including a valuable modern refrigeration ship. Gone as elusive as the dream conjured up by her name of *Arabian Nights.*

His thoughts wandered to as many possibilities as he could. Already the next troopship was preparing to leave Gibraltar bound for the Cape. Would the battlecruiser have a go at it? Even if it had an old battleship as principal escort? What else was there spare? An 'Exeter' class cruiser? Armed merchant cruiser? Destroyers? So Collins pondered. What if these ships could be kept in Indian Ocean or Far Eastern waters? There were political murmurings that the Japanese were becoming increasingly restive. The Allies would need to have some forces in the area to counter any threat that the Japanese Imperial Fleet might pose. What of more modern ships? Or *Repulse* or Renown, the Royal Navy's two remaining battlecruisers? Fast enough and powerful enough to challenge most of Japan's older capital ships, their heavy cruisers and definitely *Dresden.* Damn that German ship. Always there in his thoughts. Even when thinking about the Japanese Navy. She just wouldn't go away, where ever she was. He hoped that her presence would soon be announced that she was definitely in European waters. It would be one less thing to worry about. He should have dealt with the damned ship when she'd first broken into the Atlantic. Careful now, old Matron McCutcheon will be having me back in her starched hospital sheets if I get too het-up about *Dresden.* Collins sighed. Above his desk he had a framed photograph of the German battlecruiser. A pre-war shot of her on her trials. For a warship, quite graceful. But menacing. Powerful. A picture that belied her real strength. Now that she'd been given Reitz as captain, Collins knew that this beautiful battlecruiser had to be brought to heel. Soon. She'd done more than enough damage already.

What Collins didn't realise was how relatively close the subject of his thoughts was at that precise time. She was there, in the wild seas to the south of Cape Horn where the swells of the South Atlantic, the Indian and Antarctic Oceans meet in a constant maelstrom and welter of spume and spray. It was here that the *Dresden* was plunging her steady passage. Grey clouds scudded across a laden sky. Cold winds from the Antarctic ice-caps whipped up the wave-tops into foaming white horses that tried their best to break over the flared forecastle of the battlecruiser. With her radar shut down for its own protection and the Arados confined to their hangers, only the salt-streamed eyes of the look-outs trying to peer into the confused seas could warn the German warship of any possible rare incursion into the area of an Allied warship. On the other hand it would indeed be a rare sight if there was one in the area for this was the perfect weather for the battlecruiser to disappear from sight. No Allied ship or aircraft in their senses would have been ordered to search for the battlecruiser unless they knew for certain that she was there. Which they didn't.

So Reitz guessed as he huddled on the bridge in this 'U-boat' uniform as he called it – long waterproof cape and sou'wester over two thick sweaters and grey leather trousers tucked into long sea boots watching the spray lash over the flared bows that rode most of the heaving water so extremely well. He was mulling over the momentous coded messages that SKL had sent him over the last fortnight. Short bits of information so that the Allies wouldn't be aware of his position or to even which ship it was being sent to – that is if they'd picked up the brief messages at all. Reitz had the knowledge that Lutjens had sent a long message from *Bismarck* before that ship's eventual horrendous end. A mistake that had helped the Allies pinpoint that ship and thus send it to its final *denouément* So far he hadn't disclosed the content of SKL's messages to his officers but it was momentous. But the men would have to wait until he deemed it appropriate to disclose the contents of those coded messages. Right now it was coming to the end of June and there'd been the other news to occupy not only Reitz's mind but also those of the rest of the crew's especially for all who had relatives in the Wehrmacht for on the twenty-second Hitler ordered his armies to attack Russia and in the first few heady days of the onslaught the German Army scored some spectacular successes.

Reitz could not help harking back to his scholarly days at school when the class with their venerable schoolmaster had studied the Napoleonic Wars. The old teacher had given a graphic description of the horrendous retreat of the once victorious French Army in the winter of 1811/12 when it had trudged its way out of Moscow, harried all the time by Russian armed forces which had been thought to have been beaten but using 'General Winter,' they had hammered time after time in the driving snow at the unprepared and often starving French troops. Would the same happen to the German Army if it failed to breach its objectives before the winter approached? The thought wouldn't go away, even as he watched yet another wave crash against *Dresden*'s flared bows and disperse back into the ocean as it was flung aside. He thought of the train journey he'd once made to Leningrad. It had seemed interminable. Endless miles of open countryside. Plenty of space even for a beaten army into which to withdraw and then re-group. But back to the problems in hand. Here, right at the edge of the Antarctic. Lookouts twice reported icebergs but the warship was swung steadily away to the north-east and the white blocks of menace receded into the distance. Gradually the course of *Dresden* altered to directly northwards, towards the warmer weather, and the calmer waters of the vastness that is in the Indian Ocean. It was now July the first.

Then, as the air cleared and the seas abated a lookout called out 'Smoke in sight!'

'What's the bearing?' shouted an irate petty officer.

'020 degrees. Off the starboard bow.'

'Can't see it.'

'It was there.' Young seventeen years and two days old Karl Prebke, junior lookout and a gunner's mate, persisted.

Five minutes passed.

Then, Prebke the youngest member of the crew again shouted out, 'Smoke. 023 degrees. And a mast.'

No-one else had picked up the supposed ship. The radar hadn't yet been refitted so it was still upon the accuracy of the lookouts that the safety of *Dresden* depended so much.

No-one was expecting a ship in these waters. The capture of the Norwegian whaling fleet just over seven months beforehand by Felix Kruder's raider, HK33, otherwise called *Pinguin* was presumed to have deterred the Allies from having a fleet of that nature in those waters unless it had a warship escort.

Prebke had indeed sighted a ship for when Reitz reached the bridge he decided to at least get close enough to verify Prebke's claim. Sure enough a ship began to emerge taking on the outlines of a tanker. Behaving rather oddly. Every so often a plume of diesel smoke belched out of her stern-placed funnel with a short movement in the water, and then she'd come to a halt. Reitz took *Dresden* on a circuitous route around the tanker, keeping the merchantman's stern nearest to his ship. But nothing changed. No frantic burst of speed to try and escape. No wireless messages. Just the same odd activity.

'Close in' ordered Reitz.

'The crew's already at action stations' murmured Hiltzern.

'Up White Ensign on mainmast.'

Still no reaction. Not one sailor on the tanker reacted at all, not even when *Dresden* closed to within a mile of the ship. To all intent and purposes, it seemed to the Germans that the tanker was totally unaware of their presence.

When the battlecruiser edged to within three hundred yards of the labouring tanker, Reitz ordered a blank to be fired from one of the smaller guns.

No immediate response.

'Fire another shell, this time across her bows and flash a signal asking what her name is and that we're sending a boat across to her.'

The spout of water from the fired shell was collapsing into the waves when at last a response came from near the tanker's bridge. Laboriously it spelt out.

'Who the hell wants to know?'

Reitz laughed. 'Reply HMS *Renown*.'

'Which Renown?' came back the reply.

'The Royal Navy one.'

'OK. Suit yourself. Come aboard.'

'Thanks. We will.'

No-one leaned over the tanker's stern port quarter when Brautsch and his boat-load of armed sailors arrived. A grappling iron and line was quickly made fast to the railings, Brautsch hauled himself up followed quickly by two of the ratings onto the stern boards before dropping down a rope-ladder and making it fast to the rails. More armed men scrambled up and under Brautsch directions scattered across the decks.

No-one wanted to shoot at them. Indeed, it almost seemed as if the arrival of *Dresden* hadn't caused the slightest bit of interest amongst the tanker's crew.

Brautsch and three men climbed up to the bridge and pushed the door open.

'What is thees? You're bluddy rude for Breetish Navee' came a somewhat truculent voice in rather poorly accented English.

'And you, are, sir?' replied Brautsch carefully modulating his English.

'Captain Carl Larsen Royal Norwegian Naval Reserve' came the answer.

'At your service' mocked Brautsch 'But not for long I fear. Allow me to introduce myself. Oberleutnant Helmet Brautsch of the Kriegsmarine warship *Dresden.* You and your crew are now our prisoners and this ship is our prize. Please captain –' here Brautsch waved his Luger pistol '– no heroics. I have plenty of well-armed men.'

'Not bloody Nazees. You can not be ' Larsen said somewhat incredulously 'No, no, not Nazees. There is no Nazee ships round here. London told me so.'

'London was wrong, Herr Kapitan. We are from the *Dresden* but you will receive fair treatment from all of us. My captain, myself and all the crew. We may be German but none of us are Nazis.'

'Sheet! You really are Jerries.' Realisation was at last grasping into the mind of Larsen.

'Yes! Now. Captain Larsen, why your odd progress? Are you expecting Royal Naval ships? You didn't seemed too surprised or agitated when we tried to attract your attention.'

Larsen snorted, his English improving all the time. 'Well we're early. Supposed to be on hand to refuel escort vessels which will be on hand to protect Allied whaling ships in thees area. Can't have you lot nabbing off with the fleet like one of your bleedin' raiders did last time round.'

'Ah, yes, that was the raider *Pinguin.*'

'So when we sees your White Ensign, we deed not panic. Thought at first that you were a beeg destroyer.'

'Come here, Captain. You see the flag we are now flying. Even looks like a White Ensign.'

Larsen looked across and saw the flag that Reitz had designed. 'It ees like the Imperial German Flag your lot flew in the last war with the Breeteesh.'

'Nearly. Not quite.' murmured Brautsch. 'Now I'd like to see your cargo manifest.'

Reitz was highly pleased when he learned that the captured tanker, by name of *Olaf* was laden with about twenty thousand tons of top-grade fuel oil. Just the prize that he'd need if *Dresden*'s cruise was to go on for a long time. Quickly he organised a prize crew to take over the functions of running the tanker although a further signal from Brautsch gave the indications that some of the Norwegians on board were quite prepared to carry on working rather than waste their time on *Dresden* as prisoners. Apparently there was ample food on board for at least a further three months.

When Brautsch returned to *Dresden* he had even more information from the now talkative Captain Larsen. Apparently *Dresden* was supposed to be returning via the North Atlantic to Norway for repairs. Both Berlin and London radio stations had given out this information.

Collins had even heard of *Dresden*'s return to Norway. A copy of a German newspaper had been flown put to him from Sweden. True the photograph of a warship anchored in a Norwegian fjord could well have been faked but resistance agents as well as a long-ranged RAF reconnaissance aircraft had seen a large warship anchored under the lee of an overhanging ledge in an isolated fjord. It had to be *Dresden.* All the other big Kriegsmarine units were already accounted for so far as Allied Intelligence was aware. In German or Northern French ports.

The Admiralty in its London Headquarters though requested a double-check on this vessel that the Germans were so keen to tell the World of its whereabouts. Normally their big ship movements were kept as secretive as possible. They'd already lost *Bismarck* partly because of her prolonged stay in Grimstak Fjord which had first definitely alerted the Allies to her exact whereabouts. Now here they were actually praising the fact that their heroic *Dresden* had eluded all the Royal Navy's efforts at catching her at sea and with such an impressive list of successes to her name, had reached German-controlled waters with, as they put it, relatively minor damage following action with 'numerous units of the Royal Navy'. Not superior, but numerous.

But was it the elusive battlecruiser? Was it just another ploy by the Goebbels propaganda machine to pull the wool over their enemy's eyes?

The Admiralty sent out a message to its agent nearest the Trondheim Fjord where the supposed *Dresden* was said to be anchored. The agent was to get as close as possible, make an accurate sketch and then pass it to the regular Swedish contact. Elsa Sergen hated the Nazis. They'd brutally shot her father when he'd failed to report during a security check. 'How could he?' he'd protested when he was up in the hills trying to round up errant sheep. The Gestapo chief of police thought otherwise. Eric Sergen was avoiding arrest due to subversive practices. He had failed to report within the twenty-four hours notice given to his village. Thus he, and two others, one a seventy-year old widow were lined up against the wall of the village hall and shot by a firing squad.

Elsa hated them. Anything German. Anything stinking of the Nazi stench of injustice. The swine had even taken her father's camera.

What they didn't know was that Elsa was a superb artist. And that she could ride her father's motorcycle, hidden up in the hillside in a sheep barn. Together with a stock of twelve petrol cans, all full bar three of them. A motorcycle used only at night. For patriotic journeys. Such as the one she was going to make that night. The message had reached her via the village's schoolmaster. The wireless set was hidden amongst the timbers of the church's bell tower. The schoolmaster also helped to wind up the clock. Seemingly perfect cover. So far the Nazis hadn't tracked down the wireless. Perhaps it was the metal of the two bells in the tower that distorted the search-waves of their detector van. Whatever it was, the instructions were quite plain. Find the Nazi warship. Draw it. Get it to 'our friend across the border.'

Elsa shrugged into her dark overalls and climbed up the hillside as the evening light faded with the sun setting over the western range of mountains. Donning goggles she kick started the motorcycle into life and set off via green country lanes as much as possible rather than main roads. Even so, twice she had to hurriedly jump off and run into a nearby field entrance as she saw the dim lights signifying a German patrol. When within a mile of her destination she pushed the bike under a bush and then carefully descended down the fjord side until she came to an over hanging rock that made for a cave-like aperture. She'd known that it existed for she and her father had often sat there before the war looking out over the still waters of the deep fjord below them watching the cruise-liners and ferry-boats ply the waters that now harboured various units of the Kriegsmarine. Anything from patrol launches to destroyers, E-boats to cruisers.

And now this. Germany's raiding battlecruiser. Even in the darkness Elsa could see the hooded lights over the decks of a largish warship with another vessel moored alongside. Then they went out. It was nearly midnight. It was going to be a long wait until morning. She unrolled her sleeping bag and fell asleep. A guard dog barking woke her up. Five-thirty and the first hint of a new dawn. She stretched and cautiously looked over the ridge. There it was. Shrouded in both an early mist and what looked like to be camouflage netting. As the light grew stronger she worked out various floats and buoys surrounding the mystery vessel. Her father had told her that these probably supported anti-torpedo nets. Only rigged around important warships.

Taking an apple from her coat pocket she munched on it watching the scene below. A number of patrol boats pushed their way across the fjord looking like water beetles, with their red and black naval flag flapping at their sterns. As the sun rose Elsa watched the mystery ship very carefully. Two big twin gun turrets forward. A largish bridge. Tall mast. A single funnel emitting smoke but beyond that she couldn't really say for the camouflage netting hid the details. Taking out her sketch pad she worked on the drawing of the warship as well as noting down the positions of the anti-aircraft batteries in the hills overlooking the fjord, as well as the timings of the patrol vessels. Towards mid-day she saw a destroyer steam down the fjord. Overhead slow patrol aircraft scanned the area. Elsa kept very still whenever she heard them. Foot and motorcycle patrols were also noted to be frequent in occurrence on the main road that ran round the edge of the fjord far below her vantage point.

With only a bottle of cold water and a cheese sandwich for further sustenance, Elsa watched during the whole of that long day keeping her movements to a minimum so as not to attract attention. In that she succeeded. Not one of the German military forces under her scrutiny suspected even the remotest inkling of her presence so that when again the light faded, she eased herself upright and flexing cramped muscles, she made her way slowly and carefully back to her hidden motorcycle. Relieved to find it still intact, she again kick-started it into life and made her way to the Swedish frontier some forty-five miles to the east.

Two hours later and she was handing her drawings and notes over to Pers Lindstrorm, her Swedish contact. Five minutes later she was on her way back over the mountain track and by keeping her speed at reasonable levels and looking again carefully for any sign of German night patrols she was able to slip back to her shepherd's hut as dawn's first faint touch of light began to wipe away the cloak of the night's darkness.

Lindstrorm, at about the same time, by catching the night milk train to Stockholm, was leaning on the entrance door bell to the British Embassy. The guards knew him well and so did the Ambassador's clerk.

'Well, Lindstrorm, what have you this time?' he asked. Lindstrorm handed over Elsa's sketches and notes.

Three days later, via the diplomatic bag, they landed on Admiral's Pound's desk. As Commander-in-Chief of the Royal Navy they interested him a lot. He didn't understand the Norwegian notations but a translator did.

'Hmm, very thorough work' he commented. 'And this, is this the *Dresden*?

'Looks like her. The agent is reputed to be an excellent artist. We've had sketches from her in the past.'

'Can we get an air-strike at her?'

'No sir, she's out of our land-based attack range for heavy bombers.'

'Damn. Jerry will repair her and she'll get back to home port.'

'Well at least we know where she is.'

Three days on and Collins was looking at a copy of Elsa's drawings of the ships in that far-off Norwegian fjord. A world away from his office in Simonstown but yet, sharing a common enemy. He stared and stared at it, feeling a sense of admiration for the way she'd captured the scene, wondering how she'd been able to do it without being detected. As good as any camera. What dangers the resistance agents must be going through in Occupied Europe. He didn't know that the artist's father had been executed by the Gestapo.

But something wasn't quite right. There was nothing obviously wrong with the artistry. The warship in the centre, bows on, looked like *Dresden*. Collins nagged his brain. Then it hit him. He'd remembered in his Great War days sailing in and out of Scapa Flow just how many extra battleships there'd been seemingly attached to the Grand Fleet. Always there. Mock-ups of timber and canvas screenings moored in the centre of the Flow. Not too close to shore for an accurate scrutiny. All on unwanted merchant-ship hulls. To fool, it was hoped, any active German spies. Moored there when units of the Grand Fleet were out at sea. That was it. Supposing that ship so superbly illustrated was just that. A bit of careful trickery. Probably thought up by the Abwehr. Of course, the Abwehr, headed by Admiral Canaris. The designer of *Dresden* so it was widely believed. The cunning sod, thought Collins. He's created a '*Dresden*' to fool us. That's not *Dresden.* And if not, where is she? Out there, somewhere. South Atlantic? Indian Ocean? Where was she if that ship wasn't her? His mind was racing. Thoughts jumbling over and over. Should he tell London? They'd think he was paranoid over the German battlecruiser. He'd failed to set in motion efforts in the North Atlantic to catch her whilst concentrating on the bigger, more dangerous threat of *Bismarck.* Deep down he knew that he'd been right but yet the thought just wouldn't go away. If that ship in the Norwegian fjord wasn't *Dresden,* then she was still on the high seas looking for fresh victims. He knew that the big troopship convoys were well escorted with at least a heavy cruiser or a battleship as the main escort. Enough to drive off the likes of Reitz. But was it? Surely *Dresden* wouldn't dare to attack a heavily escorted convoy. *Wellington*'s convoy had by now reached Aden, unharmed. The New Zealand cruiser which had come closest to catching the German battlecruiser on more even terms than all her other opponents would soon be sailing for Colombo and then to her home waters for a long overdue refit and leave for her war weary crew. The next convoy, due in soon, had the old *Resolve* as its big-gun escort, a B-class cruiser (sister ship to the gallant *Exeter* of the River Plate action) and a modern Mauritius-class cruiser. Plenty there to scare off *Dresden.* Should be. If she was out there. Thinking of attacking the troopships. Carrying men and material vital for the defence of Allied interests in North Africa and the Middle East.

He took a long, long look at the maps pinned to the wall, seeing in his mind the endless stretch of restless waves stretching from one horizon to the other but always, never going away was the speck that grew in size. Dark, long, menacing, spitting red and orange flames at its target. A hapless troopship crammed with Allied soldiers.

Then he stopped. No. It was his imagination going riot. *Dresden* wasn't out there. It was her in that Norwegian fjord. Under the care and attention of the repair ship moved alongside her. It was too much to expect of Canaris and his staff to think up of such an elaborate ruse.

Or was it?

The subject of his thoughts was out there. Three hundred miles off the East African coast. Steaming where the raider *Pinguin* had met her demise at the hands of heavy cruiser *Cornwall*. Not without a fight. She'd gone down, guns firing, when an eight-inch salvo had smashed into her hold full of mines. Few of her crew and the prisoners on board had been able to escape. Those that did were picked up by *Cornwall* in the spirit of the chivalry of sailors for fellow strugglers. That, where possible, in a war situation, survivors would be picked up. A code that Reitz knew that he would follow wherever possible. SKL was moving its raiders around – *Dresden* off East Africa to be joined by *Skua*, another disguised armed merchant ship raider, currently operating off Western Australia. Replacing *Skua* would be *Kormoran*, currently in the Atlantic and due for a rendezvous with Bernhard Rogge's *Atlantis* which had, so far gained, the most success of all the disguised raiders.

With *Dresden* and *Skua* were *Berengia*, *Arabian Nights* and *Olaf*, making the concentration off the Horn the greatest that the Kriegsmarine was able to muster outside home-controlled waters. Only Reitz knew why they were soon to concentrate their efforts. Secret coded messages in short sections at a time had built up for him the requirements demanded by SKL and Canaris. All of them signed with the letter 'E'. Elle. How Reitz, in his few quiet moments, pined for her. So near in his thoughts.

So far away in her physical presence.

The bulk of the 32,000 ton R-class battleship *Resolve* looked impressive as she and her fellow escorts sailed into Simonstown's naval base for refuelling and re-victualling. The convoy was intact.

No losses at all since leaving home waters. Collins watched the scene and felt sure that if *Dresden* was waiting for the convoy, she wouldn't dare to attack her heavier gunned opponent nor her two cruiser escorts, never mind the ten smaller warships. Would she? If she was there at all.

Then his mind flitted to that brave Norwegian agent's drawing. Even Admiral Pound had declared himself satisfied that the ship that Elsa had so carefully drawn was most likely to be the *Dresden.*

No need to worry, Collins told himself. No need!

Chapter 5

'You did your best old girl'

Late one evening Andrea and Elfrida had just come to the end of their duties for the day in the Sick Berth during which one stoker's two gashed fingers were cleaned and bandaged and another crew member, a young kitchen hand was treated for a burnt wrist when it had come in contact with a hot dish being drawn out of the oven. *Dresden* had unexpectedly lurched in a large Indian Ocean swell more than usual and hot dish and wrist had come into contact with each other. Earlier in the day, soon after midday, two men had come down, red-faced after a reprimand from Commander Hiltzern. They'd been rather careless with their lookout duties and thought that acquiring a suntan was better than searching for the rarely seen smoke of a carelessly engineered merchantman. It was just their bad luck that the Commander had seen them from the lofty bridge without their shirts on during their duties.

It had thus not been too strenuous a day for the two English women and they were just about to retire for bed when a call came through for Doctor Lebers to attend a senior officers' conference. Lebers raised his eyebrows on hearing the summons. It was now so late on in the evening when the previous conferences had been held in the morning to noon watch. Andrea and Elfrida were getting on well with the Austrian-born medical officer. Earlier he'd told them that he'd moved, with his parents, to ironically the beautiful city whose name had been given to this battlecruiser on which he now served. In July 1939 he was drafted for service in the Kriegsmarine, although only qualified as a doctor for just two years. Quickly appraised of the requirements of naval discipline, he was appointed to the *Dresden* shortly before her abortive Atlantic foray under the weak leadership of Von Munke. Fortunately the unhappy crew had seen the removal of Von Munke and now under Reitz everyone it seemed was doing their utmost to help each other and crew the ship to a high degree of efficiency. Certainly the largish number of malingerers that had usually been in the Sick Bay whilst Von Munke was captain had vanished soon after Reitz had taken charge.

He bade the ladies farewell and was soon in the still neat, tidy and smoke free wardroom. Not a cigarette in sight a-glowing or with wisps of blue smoke curling up from ones that could have been in the ashtrays. Not a cigar. Nor a pipe. The rules that Reitz had laid down for officer conferences ever since that famous initial outburst that now seemed light years ago, were still in force even though the ship was sailing the high seas on a war footing.

The air was clear and despite the lateness of the hour the assembled officers had an air of expectation about them. Eager. On tenterhooks. Guessing that something very important was about to be revealed to them. Perhaps a breakthrough back to Germany? Or an extension to their successful raiding cruise further into the Indian Ocean and maybe even across to Australian waters?

Reitz entered and all the officers stood smartly to attention. The captain eased them down on to their chairs with a wave of his right hand.

'Gentlemen' he began, 'it is time to tell you of the plans that SKL have sorted out for us in conjunction with *Berengia*, *Arabian Nights* and the Hilfskreuzer *Skua* which is sailing to rendezvous with us having been in action in Australian waters where she has recently been laying mines off some of their busiest harbours, besides sinking a number of Allied merchantmen.' Reitz paused. The officers knew a bit about the role of the disguised merchantmen which were now in service with the Kriegsmarine armed with hidden guns and torpedo tubes. With a pointer Reitz showed the assembled officers the expected rendezvous. Two hundred miles south-east off the Horn of Africa.

'Here gentlemen. So far as we can ascertain, unless a convoy is in the area, the waters are only infrequently patrolled by Royal Naval warships and even more less by long-range Royal Air Force or even civilian aircraft. In other words an ideal area for us to concentrate our strength.'

Herzog raised a hand.

'Yes, Chief?'

'For what purpose are we concentrating this strength of the Kriegsmarine's ships?' He, as well as most of the others present were aware that the wireless office had been receiving messages, in code, destined for Reitz and no-one else. Something was in the air but what? Even the desperate loss of *Bismarck* and their lonely progress towards these waters had still not shaken their belief in their captain's leadership qualities. He'd not only completely turned round the fortunes of their ship since the start of the current cruise but he'd raised the ship's morale and had kept it up for the past four long months. So many ships sunk or captured. Yet no-one had even tried to bring up the subject when they would be turning for the home run. Here they were, sailing northwards adjacent to the East African coast. But for what purpose? 'Gentlemen, our ship is designed as a fast, hard hitting surface raider. Yes, I know that we've had set-backs. *Graf Spee* and *Bismarck* have been sunk. Our other fellow regular navy big ships are now sheltering in German or French harbours. We're the only major Kriegsmarine surface unit still at large on the high seas, a fact that we are all fully acquainted.'

He paused. Looked around. Not a man moved. All eyes and minds were locked on to him. He had their full, undivided attention.

He continued, waving his pointer to the lowest edge of the wall map.

'Down here – probably on the floor if we follow the scale on the map –' there was a hint of a titter of laughter from one or two of the men '– is the British naval base of Simonstown. Assembling there, for a refuel and revictualling stop-over, is an Allied troop convoy consisting of, so we are reliably informed, ten liners carrying three thousand soldiers each sailing to re-inforce the British army in Egypt. Thirty thousand re-inforcements together with their weapons, including tanks and field guns being carried in, so far as I have also been informed, about ten other supporting merchantmen. A convoy taking men who would help to slow down the progress of our own troops of the Afrika Korps led by Erwin Rommel who even now are making steady progress towards Egypt and the Suez Canal. If we deny the Allies of these re-inforcements, then Rommel's progress towards his goal will be made all that much easier, with or without the help of our somewhat erstwhile Italian allies.' Again a slight titter or two. Even so isolated from the mainstream of the war nearly all the men present were aware that the Italians had only made progress in their advance when supported by German air and land forces.

Even the numerically stronger Italian navy had made little impact in halting Mediterranean convoys that were only now under threat due mainly to German air and U-boat attacks. Not from the Italian battle fleet which with more effort could have brought about the possible cessation of the Malta convoys.

But still no-one dared express the even remotest idea in their mind that Reitz was thinking of attacking this assembling troopship convoy. Surely it must have a strong escort. So they waited, iimpassively, to hear out their captain.

'No-one wondering what I'm getting at? Too unsure to ask? Mmmm?' Reitz looked round and then waved his pointer at the map.

'Well, this is where we are. One tiny speck in a vast ocean. A potential dagger at the supply lines of the one enemy that has so far not surrendered, The United Kingdom together with her Empire friends. They halted our Air Force whilst this ship was resting in a German harbour. Their stubborn soldiers almost stopped our paratroops assault on Crete. They delayed us in Greece having withdrawn their men almost a year earlier at Dunkirk. But it's their Navy that has done us most damage so far. Three smaller cruisers stopped the cruise of our panzerschiffe *Graf Spee* off the River Plate. A destroyer force wiped out ten of our destroyers at Narvik. I know. I was there. Their ships, despite all odds, carried out successful evacuations off Dunkirk, off Greece, off Crete. Despite many losses their spirit has not been broken. Often outgunned they fight on. Look at their brave armed merchant cruisers Rawalpindi and Jervis Bay. Outgunned by superior Kriegsmarine units they turned to fight. Not run away like this ship did when confronted by the Runswick Castle. What shame that incident brought upon those of you who were aboard at that time. But since then, we have improved. We've honed our fighting skills to match those displayed by the Royal Navy. I consider this ship now to be the best fighting vessel of the Kriegsmarine.'

The men looked up again. Some had downcast their eyes when Reitz mentioned Runswick Castle. Somehow they felt he was dangling an idea in front of them like a fisherman teases a hungry trout.

But was the bait that convoy?

Reitz continued 'The Allies think that we are in Northern Norway. Damaged but still a going concern. That is why I had to allow that Town-class cruiser to get almost in range so that she could fire her guns at us. The hope is that the Allies, mainly the British, will think we sustained some damage and we are now sheltering in a Norwegian harbour with a repair ship. Don't ask me how, but our old friend *Rugen* is up there disguised as us!' This time there were quite a lot of laughs. How the old pre-dreadnought could be made to look like their sleek warship seemed almost beyond sensible comprehension.

'Gentlemen, order please! The ruse may not last very long but it will be long enough for us to carry out our orders, for surprise will be our biggest weapon – at least in the initial stages.

'You see, gentlemen, we are going to attack that troopship convoy when it reaches this area here –' the pointer smacked onto the map in the sea region off the Horn of Africa. 'In about a week's time the ships of that convoy will come within range of our guns and torpedoes. This time we shall not hit and run. This time I intend to sink or damage as many of their ships as is possible, if necessary until we run out of ammunition or are sunk ourselves.' There it was.

Bang on target. No ifs or buts. Quite simply. The biggest target to come *Dresden*'s way.

Hiltzern raised a hand and asked 'What's the convoy's escort?'

Reitz responded 'One R-class battleship the *Resolve* with eight 38 centimetre guns. You know, bigger than ours! But then,' with a wry smile 'we are about ten knots faster than its top speed of around twenty knots and can fire our main guns at least three times faster than she can. SKL have also told me that there's a Cathedral-class B-cruiser the *Llandaff*, a sister ship of the *Exeter* that so rattled our *Graf Spee* and another new light cruiser of the Mauritius class with a speed of thirty two knots together with twelve thirteen centimetre dual purpose guns as her main armament. Nearly as powerful as was our last Royal Naval opponent but a shade quicker, so I'm informed. Then there's about ten smaller escorts, some only going as far as Mombasa and the local escorts there will probably take over for the final run to the convoy's destination of Aden or even on to Alexandria with the troopships.'

Hiltzern grunted 'Seems a heavy escort sir.'

The response came firmly. 'Yes. But we'll have a number of advantages. First, we're hoping the enemy don't know where we are.

Secondly, our speed coupled with our record so far on this voyage. One bang from *Resolve*'s guns and they'll expect us to run but they'll be wrong. We shall close with the enemy – a surprising enough move as it will appear to our Royal Naval opponents. But not to any of us. Thirdly, U-boats are in position in the Mozambique Channel, through which the convoy will sail and hopefully our submariner friends will fire torpedoes and sink or seriously damage some of the escort ships. Those ships are their prime target, not the troopships. Hopefully the Allies won't connect the attacks on the escorts with our intended move against the convoy. The U-boats will maintain wireless silence until after their attacks and only if they can confirm the convoy's course, speed, position and torpedoed ships will they signal, in a prearranged code to us on a set frequency. If the Allies pick up the transmissions we hope that again they will attach no special significance other than the message being a standard U-boat report.'

Again Hiltzern interposed 'Aren't we running a risk engaging the *Resolve* even if we can achieve surprise? One of their big shell hits on us could force us out of the battle.'

'Commander. That is a risk that we shall have to face but I intend to attack so quickly so as to outmanoeuvre the battleship and get in close enough to sink her by torpedoes. Remember our practice with old *Rugen*? Well, that is how we shall go for *Resolve.* No running away like Lutjens did with *Scharnhorst* and *Gneisenau* when they spotted an old battleship escorting North Atlantic convoys. We will go in and engage. To attack. To win.'

There it was. No question about it. Straight in. Smack! On the nose.

Reitz continued ' Soon we shall be meeting up with *Skua.* Her job will be to go for the slower merchantmen. Our other ships *Berengia* and *Arabian Nights* will close in when it is safe to do so in order to pick up survivors. When we've finished depleting *Berengia* of her stores, she will be fully converted to a prison ship and after the engagement with the convoy, she'll be returning to France to offload the prisoners. Hers will be no easy task but then neither will ours.'

'Survivors, sir?' Padré Jervaulx this time.

'Yes, Padré. When, and only when, it is safe, we will rescue what survivors we can. Once the fighting is over the rule of survival at sea and common humanity must, and will, be exercised. This ship will not be known for its brutality – an epithet too readily applied to the SS and Gestapo as I am sure we are all well aware of in our own thoughts.'

Jervaulx smiled. Nervously.

'You've have all been given sealed envelopes. In it are the details of our rendezvous with our fellow ships as well as to the priorities of your departments. Please open them after I leave this room.'

'Does the rest of the crew know?' came another question.

'No doubt. They seem to know everything before you and I do!' came the humoured reply. At this the assembled officers could see that their captain was smiling. Then raising his glass of water, Reitz asked the men to rise. 'Gentlemen! To the success of this ship. My ship. Your ship. Our ship.'

They all stood and cheered heartily as their captain turned and left their wardroom. Soon echoing cheers could be heard throughout the ship. It was obvious that the ship's 'telegraph of news' amongst the crew knew that something really big was in the offing. Men came up to Reitz to salute him and some to clap him on the shoulder as he made his way to his main cabin aft via the midships decks of the battlecruiser.

Nurse Andrea Cantrell was up soon after dawn next morning and decided to take a stroll on the deck adjacent to 'Bertha's' turret on the starboard side where the sun's rays were already warming the metal side railings.

'Good morning to you, Miss Cantrell.' Reitz, speaking in English, surprised her as she gazed at the yellow-dappled streaks amidst the blue waters.

'The same to you, Captain Reitz,' replied Andrea, nodding her head as she turned to see the German smiling at her.

'You are well, Fraulein?'

'As well as can be. Like your crew. We haven't had many of them down in the Sick-Bay as yet.'

'Yes, that must be so. You get on well with Doctor Lebers?'

Another veiled question thought Andrea. 'Yes, captain, I do. He is so kind. So professional. None of your crew have given me any cause for concern, which after my experience of the U-boat attack on *Arades* has come as a most welcome turn of events. Even Herr Brautsch comes down to the Sick Berth to make sure that the crew are behaving correctly. And here I am. Not as a celled prisoner for I am allowed to stroll your decks in my leisure time.'

'Yes, I know that you do but you will find armed sentries posted at the sensitive parts of this ship – not only will they stop you but also any member of the crew who has no right to be in that region of the ship. My men aren't all angels although those that do step out of line are quickly on defaulters parade and the most serious ones are sent to the punishment cells. Two such men in there now will be transhipped back to Europe as soon as is possible. They are not worthy members of this crew. In their bouts of enforced idleness during our slacker periods of activity they stole from fellow members. I do hope that this doesn't alter your views of my crew. I do my best, and so do my officers to keep the men occupied, at duty times and in their off-duty periods but we can't be on top of them all the time. However, I am pleased to tell you that they are behaving honourably to you!'

'My, my captain. What a speech!'

'Ah well, I must be off then. I except you will know that soon we will have plenty of activity in the very near future.' Andrea nodded and gave a thin smile. 'Well, you'll see soon enough. We'll meet up with our support ships in a day or so and then you and your companions can be transferred if you so wish. You can, of course, remain here and I'm sure Doctor Lebers will be grateful. For added charm I'm quite sure Leutnant Brautsch will continue to see to your welfare.'

Andrea blushed, feeling a redness come to her cheeks. How could this German captain know that she was beginning to develop a real liking for *Dresden*'s boarding officer? After all, Helmut Brautsch was enemy. Wasn't he? Reitz smiled again at her.

'You see Miss Cantrell, even I know!' and with that he clicked his heels, gave a slight bow and turned to continued his own pacing of the decks.

For some inner reason Andrea looked up towards the upper bridge. There she saw Brautsch looking down at her. He inclined his head and even raised his left hand in a wave. She blushed again and straightening her skirt she turned and hurried back to the Sick-Bay. 'Damn, damn, damn. I'm falling for him and he knows it too as well!'

Preparations for the forthcoming attack on the troopship convoy kept everyone busy for the rest of the day. Brautsch was unable to find time to visit the Sick Bay until late in the evening but when he did get down, Lebers motioned him to silence whispering

'The two fit nurses Andrea and Elfrida have been cleaning all the instruments and checking out all the bandages for me. They are real angels, but now they are asleep.' Brautsch nodded and asked the doctor to pass on his thanks.

Soon after sunrise the next morning radar reported a stationary blip which soon appeared over the horizon as *Berengia.* Once she was alongside hoses were soon pumping her tanks empty of her remaining precious fuel oil and passing it to fill the tanks of the battlecruiser. From *Dresden* carpenters swarmed on board to start turning empty holds into prison rooms, once they had been flushed as clean as possible with copious amounts of sea-water. The hammering and sawing of compartments and bunks filled the air for the next three days on board the big supply ship.

The next arrival came on the third of those days. A blacked-hulled freighter flying a Dutch flag at her bows, and also at the stern, the name of Van Helmdijk. She was in reality Hilfskreuzer *Skua* with her taciturn, somewhat narrow-minded Prussian captain Artur Bock who since leaving German waters in December of the previous year hadn't exactly endeared himself to his fellow officers or crew. He tended to shoot off his guns in ferocious night attacks whether or not the enemy ship had ceased using its wireless. If any of the victims managed to launch a boat, Bock rarely took prisoners, whom he despised preferring to give the men in the boats little more than a map, a compass, a bit of food and water and telling them to head for the nearest land. Not until SKL had told him that when these surviving crew members landed and given a description of his raider to the Allies did Bock desist from such harsh tactics. This was re-inforced when two slightly faster ships than his veered away even when *Skua* signalled them to stop engines. Despite the raider opening fire, both ships escaped from his clutches and so to safeguard his vessel Bock had been ordered to lie quiet in Antarctic waters for three weeks before moving into the West Australian sea-lanes to release three hundred mines that her holds carried off the approaches to West Australia's main port of Fremantle.

Bock, at least on paper, had a record of successes for under his command *Skua* had sunk eleven ships, captured one to be used as a prison ship and three vessels, including an Australian destroyer were sunk on his mines before the local naval authorities discovered the extent of his black-horned field and had swept them clear before they could claim any more victims.

In practice, his tactics were harsh and morally questionable.

When Bock lowered the Dutch flags and started to raise the 'Swastika' emblem on *Skua*'s mainmast a curt signal from Reitz ordered it to be lowered and replaced with the self-same Dutch flags. 'After all' as he pointed out to his men who were on *Dresden*'s bridge, 'we must pretend to be Allied ships in case either a British submarine is in the area or that by some quirk of fate, an offshore Allied aircraft sees us even though we are three hundred miles off the coast.'

So when Bock climbed aboard *Dresden* later that day, followed by Wilhelm Theider from *Berengia* and together with Karl Neumans of *Arabian Nights* which had arrived soon after mid-day, the raider's captain wasn't in the best of moods even though his crew were far more at ease. For the first time in their long cruise they could relax under the protection of the big guns of the battlecruiser.

Reitz met the three captains in his main cabin together with Hiltzern, Herzog, Brautsch, Halder and Serle. Bock was the only one who proffered the Nazi salute but it was Herzog who rumbled 'No Nazis on this ship, mister, so give the captain the proper naval salute, see!'

Bock glared furiously around him but realising that he was in a minority of one, hastily sketched a salute more to the taste of the other men present.

Walters was soon amongst them with a tray of drinks. Schnapps, cognac or whisky. 'All pressies you see from Neumans' ship' he announced with glee, as well as thrusting for first offers, the tray under Bock's nose. *Skua*'s captain was the only one who chose a schnapps.

'Gentlemen, please be seated' announced Reitz as soon as Walters had disappeared into his pantry. 'Now to the details as to why you are all here and to the adventure before us. This is how I propose to mount my attack.'

Very much further to the South, Admiral Sir Bernard Collins watched the huge bulk of battleship *Resolve* slowly churn out of the Simonstown naval base to rejoin the other escorts for the troopships re-assembling in the approach waters. Four hours earlier he'd said farewell to the battleship's captain, a rotund heavily-bearded sixty year old whose rounded stomach could not be contained by the crumpled white shorts that he'd been wearing. The Honourable Robert Wills-Wilson may have looked comical but he was a true

Royal Navy man when as a lieutenant commander, he'd come under fire on board the same *Resolve* as she faced a succession of German battleships firing at her during the battle of Jutland twenty-five years earlier. Then he'd been the ship's gunnery officer. Now he was the oldest naval officer of the escorting ships but was not in overall command. Far too often Wills-Wilson's mind had taken him back to that murky May evening. Gun after gun aboard *Resolve* had been knocked out and as Wills-Wilson had toured the guns after the battleship had extricated itself out of danger he'd been appalled at the carnage wrought by the German shells. Somehow Wills-Wilson, as senior surviving officer, had taken the battered ship back to Rosyth dockyard where she limped in after Beatty's flag ship, battlecruiser *Lion*.

As temporary captain of *Resolve* Wills-Wilson had fretted whilst the battleship remained in dockyard hands. Eventually with repairs still not completed he was drafted to command a light cruiser for nearly fifteen months and once again had been in action guarding a convoy from Bergen in Norway to Newcastle when it had been attacked by three German light cruisers. Somehow he'd fought them off although his own ship had been severely damaged. To his relief, he was re-appointed back to the repaired *Resolve* as her new first officer (next to the captain) and was with her when she'd bombarded German sea defence guns in Belgium. Finally at the end of hostilities he watched the German High Seas Fleet sail to Scapa to surrender. In early 1919, *Resolve* waddled off to act as distant support for Royal Naval units involved in the extremely unsatisfactory post-Great War conflict against the Russian Communists in the Baltic. He left the ship when she docked for a long overhaul and refit. Peace-time saw him again in command of various light cruisers until after a flag-waving cruise in company with battlecruiser *Hood* he retired from the active list.

It wasn't until August 1939 with the war clouds over Europe becoming increasingly more threatening that Wills-Wilson volunteered his services with the Navy again. The authorities were surprised that he asked to be considered for command of the now veteran battleship *Resolve* as the old ship's commanding officer had just been promoted to one of the new King George V battleships as her captain upon completion They'd readily accepted his request and Wills-Wilson found himself striding the old ship's decks once again as she lay at anchor in the bleak fleet base of Scapa Flow. Was it by chance that he'd taken the battleship out on exercises for her gun-crews the day before Gunther Prien in U-47 had torpedoed her sister ship *Royal Oak* on that dreadful October night just two months into the war? And then, by chance he was escorting a convoy across the Atlantic when *Scharnhorst* and *Gneisenau* had appeared and veered off when seeing the outline of his command.

It was perhaps as well that the two German ships had turned away for *Resolve* had been in the Reserve Fleet until December 1938 when a hurried refit saw just a few extra anti-aircraft guns and some strengthening around her upper bridge-works as the only attempt to modernise her in time for the rapidly approaching conflict. She looked more robust than she really was for altogether with her relative lack of modern armoured protection, *Resolve*'s engines were in need of serious attention when the war had broken out and it was only by the valiant efforts of her Engineer Commander and the recent hurried refit at Freetown that the veteran warship was able to even start out as the main escort for this vital convoy. It was the threat of her eight fifteen-inch guns that the Admiralty was relying on to scare away any possible attack that could be posed by a major unit of the Kriegsmarine, however unlikely, should it dare to even approach the convoy. At best Wills-Wilson reckoned that a top speed of twenty knots, if that, could be relied upon if required. Even the convoy's overall speed of fifteen-knots was proving a strain on the veteran's overworked machinery.

Collins took to the battleship's captain right from the time they first met at the conference called for the escort commanders. Wills-Wilson was only three years junior to Collins but ten years older than any of the other men at the conference. Despite this seniority in age and being captain of the biggest guns of the convoy, their Lordships had deemed to not to make Wills-Wilson the man to lead the convoy nor for the battleship to be the flag-ship. Instead, leading the convoy, was in Collins' opinion, a bumptious oaf. Rear Admiral Henry Robert Hallett who chose to fly his flag on the most modern of all the convoy's escorts, the new light cruiser *Cocos* of the Mauritius class which was named after an island in the Indian Ocean. In November 1914 the highly successful German light-cruiser *Emden* was battered into a wreck after she ran aground on *Cocos* Island when facing the bigger HMAS *Sydney.*

As Hallet remarked to the press at Gibraltar – 'That ship has a name that rankles with old Jerry and should any of them wish to tangle with me whilst I'm on board then they'll have to be rankled again, eh what!' When questioned why his flag wasn't flying from the battleship's mainmast, his rebuff was 'Must have dash to get at the enemy, you can't expect me to stride aboard a clapped-out slow tortoise, can you, eh, what!' It was a remark that hadn't endeared him to Wills-Wilson who'd sat tight-lipped at the meeting. He knew his beloved *Resolve* didn't have speed, but she did have those eight big guns. Hallett had gone on to say that if there was any Nazi raider hell bent on attacking the convoy it was in his opinion that the Nazis were pressing on their self-destruct button should they wish to tangle with the sleek *Cocos.* Collins had found Hallett just as obnoxious at the conference he'd held with him, Wills-Wilson and the other main-escort captains. Leonard Codrington of the *Cocos* and Angus MacLeod in charge of the *Llandaff*, a Cathedral Class B-type heavy cruiser, sister ship to the famous *Exeter* and the less fortunate *York* which had been torpedoed in Suda Bay off Crete. Like *Resolve*, the *Llandaff* had been much used on escort duties and was desperately in need of a total refit of her engines.

MacLeod was promised that, after escorting the convoy to Aden, the ship would receive an overhaul there at the naval dockyard before a full refit upon the cruiser's return to England. On the other hand Codrington had no quarrel about his new cruiser which was on her first wartime mission but neither did he care too much about having to host Hallett and his staff.

Collins duly welcomed the captains and formally detailed the course the convoy was to take. It was when he began to outline possible German attacks that the attitude in the conference room took a distinct air of unreality as Hallet scoffed at almost all of the warnings that Collins was giving. The very idea that the Germans had a pack of long-range U-boats waiting for them caused him to scoff 'Pah! If yon Jerries had wanted to attack the convoy they'd have done so off the Skeleton Coast, not off the more distant eastern coast'. Armed merchant cruising raiders were easier to dismiss. All their victims so far in the war had been unescorted lone merchant ships but as Collins tried to point out 'You never know, chaps, one of them just might decide to sidle up to the convoy in disguise, fire off her torpedoes and then try to get away – especially at night-time.' Hallet snorted at such, to him, preposterous thinking.

It was when Collins suggested that *Dresden* could be in the area that Hallet really saw red.

'Stuff and nonsense man, she's in Norway. Even poor old Dudley has stated that it's the German battlecruiser.' Collins had winced. 'Old Dudley' was no less a personage than the Admiral of the Fleet, Sir Dudley Pound. The casual use of his name by Hallet shook Collins. Pound was the Navy's top man. In overall charge of every Royal Navy warship afloat. Every naval operation. Including the composition of this troop convoy.

Collins just wasn't convinced that the ship said to be *Dresden* was in fact that ship. To him it seemed, even for the Nazis, to be overt propaganda. Just that bit too brash. The Kriegsmarine had made no boast when *Scharnhorst* and *Gneisenau* docked in Northern France. So why now with *Dresden*? Collins knew that the battlecruiser was the idea of Wilhelm Canaris. Loyal German maybe but Canaris was not a member of the Nazi Party. Why should his ship suddenly become a story for the vile propaganda machine run by the sinister figure of Joseph Goebbels?

He wasn't convinced at all.

Neither were the bemused crew of the *Rugen*. To them it seemed as if the Kriegsmarine 'big wigs' had completely lost their senses. Never mind that seemingly crazy exercise that they'd had earlier with the *Dresden*. Now they were supposed to be pretending to be that self-same warship.

Assigned to the Skagerrak escort run across the western entrance to the Baltic, they'd suddenly been ordered into Norwegian waters. At Tromso they'd fully refuelled with both coal and oil, said their leave of the trainees who'd been posted to her before they left to more active units of the Kriegsmarine (about a third of her whole crew) and then had trundled northwards towards the Arctic Circle keeping about thirty-miles off shore. Ahead of her was a distant escort group that kept away any local fishing boats or coastal steamers although most of these vessels kept much closer inshore.

Late one evening the *Rugen* put on full speed, about thirteen knots, and Franke and his ship were escorted into a deserted fjord by four E-boats. The few Norwegians in the area were quickly removed and at the fjord entrance, the Waffen SS were in charge of newly positioned anti-aircraft guns. Soon after she'd dropped anchor, a decrepit-looking cargo vessel came alongside laden with piles of plywood. In no time at all sawing, hammering and drilling from a swarm of workmen filled the area adding a dummy turret forward and one aft together with dummy twin eleven-inch guns. Two of *Rugen*'s three funnels were painted so as to merge with the fjord's dark rocky sides and the forward one repainted a lightish grey and a funnel casing added to it to make it look more like the ones carried by the major surface units of the Kriegsmarine. One of her two masts was cut down, dummy anti-aircraft guns appeared; her secondary guns were blanked off and the whole creation was then painted battleship grey with streaks of artificial rust.

A Kriegsmarine captain, senior to Franke in rank but about half his age bluntly told the *Rugen*'s captain what he'd already guessed. Only for about two weeks would *Rugen* be in that fjord, the captain said. Franke snorted but accepted the position. With the Waffen SS around he knew that protests about the way his beloved ship was being altered would get him a transfer – probably never to return. So he bit his lip when an SS Colonel arrived on board with some men who proceeded to even dismantle *Rugen*'s radio, watched by the Kriegsmarine captain whose face looked increasingly glum. Franke asked him why all these measures were being taken and all he could get as an answer was 'security'. More vessels arrived – a boom-net layer, three trawlers bristling with anti-aircraft guns and a repair ship that was warped alongside. Small launches came and went, light aircraft flew overhead and when the plywood and paint-work was to the Kriegsmarine captain's satisfaction he withdrew, with his staff. The launches disappeared and no more aircraft flew over. The last one had taken numerous photographs as well as a cine-film before it, with its crew, disappeared to land at a base out of sight of the disguised old warship now masquerading as Germany's most successful main warship raider of the high seas, KM *Dresden*. This was the ship that Elsa Sergen had so carefully illustrated in her sketches, copies of which Collins now studied. Scoffed by Hallet for being so pessimistic. 'Damn it, man, even the RAF's taken photographs of that bloody ship. It's that damn Nazi raider that's there. The Navy or the RAF will get those glory boys when she tries to sneak round Southern Norway and then Reitz with his merry Krauts will be saying "Hello" to all those Norwegian cod that swim around.' Then wagging his right forefinger at Collins he'd brusquely added 'Now I've got a convoy to get to Aden. I don't run my affairs on a swivel chair in some bloody office!'

Collins reply was merely a raising of his eyebrows and a resigned glance at Wills-Wilson. Ever since Pound's quick acceptance that the so-called *Dresden* was the actual *Dresden* some sixth sense in the mind of Bernard Collins couldn't accept the fact that this Canaris supported warship was the one being so hyped-up by the Nazi propaganda machine.

But he had no proof.

Nothing concrete.

Only a recurring vision of blazing troopships and screaming soldiers.

Then Hallett just upped and left the conference. So Collins took the senior captains – Wills-Wilson, MacLeod and Codrington to one side – 'Look, chaps' he said, 'I know you may think I've a bee in my bonnet but I must stress to you that I have this hunch that the *Dresden* will try to get at the convoy, somewhere North of Madagascar and South of Mombasa. I think that the Jerry raider's out there and not in Norway but I've no proof so keep a good look out, eh!'

It was with some ill feeling inside him as he watched *Resolve*'s huge ponderous bulk gradually reduce in size as the old battleship churned her way towards the waiting troopships in the distance. *Dresden*. A ship on his mind. A ship that wouldn't go away. Somehow he had the feeling that he'd never see *Resolve* ever again. A feeling about a ship that he'd never had before. What he needed was proof. The proof he needed that *Dresden* was out there waiting for her moment. Proof that he simply did not have.

But was she out there? Waiting? For the convoy?

Reitz finished outlining his plan of attack and then went on to detail *Skua*'s role. 'Kapitan Bock, you will keep well clear of the convoy until you receive my signal to move in. Your job will be to try and catch any of the merchantmen fleeing to the south. Following you will be Theider and Neuman whose ships will have the main task of picking up survivors.'

'Survivors?' queried Bock.

'Yes. To be taken prisoner, if at all possible, but only if our vessels are not under any threat of attack by any of the surviving convoy escorts. We don't want them to be later rescued by Allied ships after we've gone, now do we? If we don't pick them up they may well turn up, having been later rescued, in fighting form against Rommel's forces. Of course the other reason, Herr Bock, is that I also believe in the common humanity that binds all sea-forces in that if it is at all possible to effect a rescue of our fellow human beings in distress in the water or in lifeboats, then we shall do so to the best of our capabilities because one day it may be our turn to be rescued.'

Bock kept a tight lip. Did Reitz really know of some of his tactics against Allied merchantmen?

His mind was refocused when he heard Reitz mention his ship. 'With *Berengia, Skua* after this last fling will be returning to Occupied France where any prisoners we've picked up will be handed over for transit to camps for the duration of this war.'

Reitz paused. An oft-repeated tactic at his conferences. It seemed to give him his audience time to focus their minds, just as Bock's mind had been so targeted. He also paused to eye ball Bock but *Skua*'s captain's eyes gazed unwaveringly straight ahead. In that moment Reitz felt he hadn't Bock's full attention so he decided to give him, as well as the others, a recent history lesson.

'Gentlemen, the idea behind this attack was sown in the desolation of Chilean waters when Admiral Canaris, then a lieutenant, watched his ship, the light cruiser that bore this ship's name sink beneath the waves under the gaze of an overwhelming British cruiser force. Outgunned, outrun, out-manoeuvred. Quite something for him to work on when nearly twenty years later he found himself being responsible for the initial design of this ship. You've all, with the exception of Kapitan Bock, seen how I've run this ship. What is different with my approach is that this ship does not avoid conflict with our opposite numbers in the Royal Navy. So far, panzerschiffe *Graf Spee* and battleship *Bismarck* have opened fire on major units of the enemy and have been worsted in such actions. When earlier Admiral Lutjens faced battleship-escorted convoys in the North

Atlantic he chose to turn away rather than split up our two bigger battlecruisers and thus divide the enemy's fire. We shall not turn away. A high-speed dash towards the enemy, a tactic that I hope will confuse him so much that by the time he's worked out that our boldness really does mean business, we will have delivered a knock-out blow to the main surface escorts. Speed. Guns. Torpedoes. And tactics.' He paused again.

After a sip of his malt whisky he continued – 'When we've completed our surprise initial attack – the final details of the plan are in your folders as I've earlier said-and it really depends on you all following these directions to the letter-then you'll be able to exercise your discretionary powers as to how to use your ships, in the hope that we shall achieve a victory over the enemy so that his forces in the future will be unable to resist sufficiently well enough to halt Rommel's Afrika Korps. That is all gentlemen. We are facing the Kriegsmarine's greatest triumph or if we fail, then I'm afraid, yet another bold, brave but in the end, useless gesture –' he thumped the table '– but we shall not fail. Success will be ours!'

All the officers, except Bock started to applaud infected with the daring and the enthusiasm of the plan. Reitz smiled, bowed and tucking his folder under his arm, turned and left his cabin to take a stroll on the decks of his ship. He gazed over the ship's port rail looking out to the gentle swell of the seemingly endless Indian Ocean. Steadily *Dresden* pushed a north-north-westerly course towards her destiny.

At the southern entrance of the Mozambique Channel the crew of U-177-A, one of the newest submarines with the longest range in the Kriegsmarine were relaxing whilst their boat cruised gently on the surface. The boat's captain, Kapitan Leutnant Ernst Aarlberg was smoking a thin cigar having just come up the conning tower. He was, by nature, a nervous, cautious man. Seemingly unsuitable to be a U-boat commander but he'd disposed of eighty-thousand tons of Allied shipping so far before this command which had sent him clear of the Atlantic convoys, round South Africa and now on patrol to wait for a special target. The instructions were all in a sealed folder on his desk. Locked up. Only he knew what SKL told him. A messenger came up the conning-tower 'Herr Kapitan, message for you from the wireless room.'

Aarlberg dropped down the ladder and went to his cabin to decode the message. In a new code. Decipherable only from the code-book given to him just before he'd left the boat's Lorient base. After decoding it he knew what it said. 'Special target had left nearest base. O.S.E.2.' Open Sealed Envelope number 2. Aarlberg duly did so and knew what he was supposed to do next.

A fast motor-launch came alongside *Resolve* just as she was about to rejoin the convoy. A metal canister was thrown on to the deck to be caught by a petty officer waiting by the gangway at the top of the boarding steps which had hurriedly been lowered. It wasn't every launch that flew a vice-admiral's flag. 'For Captain. Urgent' read the label on the outside of the container. Wills-Wilson was on the bridge when the petty officer reached it, saluted him, and said 'For you sir. Came from that launch.' Wills-Wilson retreated to the rear of the bridge and broke open the container. 'To Captain of *Resolve*. Treat each dawn after leaving Mozambique Channel with utmost care until you reach latitude of Mombasa, at least. Suspect German battle-cruiser *Dresden* may attack convoy. Have your gun crews at the ready. Try to warn MacLeod. Collins'

As Reitz leaned over the rail watching the phosphorescence of the bow-wave, mesmerised almost by its consistency of bubbles, a seaman came to him. 'Guests are leaving, sir. Also message from wireless room.' Reitz tore the envelope open. He knew the code by heart. 'SKL to R. Target in open sea.' Hurriedly he made his way to where the three captains were waiting to board their ships. 'Gentlemen' he said 'the convoy has just left Simonstown.'

Thirty hours later as darkness crept over the sea, Aarlberg's U-boat was again on the surface with her captain out on the conning tower. A telephone rang. 'For you, Herr Kapitan' announced the officer-of-the-watch.

'Yes?'

'Sonar reports strong propeller noises to the south. About eight kilometres (6 miles) distant.'

'Dive the boat' ordered Aarlberg. 'To periscope depth!'

Cautiously Aarlberg manoeuvred the submarine to a position where the convoy would be silhouetted against the lighter western horizon. Dark shades loomed up in his view.

'Standby torpedo tubes. Open bow doors.' Then he both heard and saw it. What looked like a charging destroyer suddenly loomed up.

'Fire one and two! Then crash dive!'

The submarine shook slightly as the two torpedoes sped towards the onrushing warship. As U-177-A slid rapidly downwards, light cruiser *Cocos* with Rear-Admiral Hallett, Captain Codrington and the rest of her crew blissfully unaware of the submarine's presence brushed over her diving shape a hundred feet below their ship's churning propellers.

Until an explosion briefly flared up nearly a mile behind the cruiser's stern.

Where a torpedo almost at the end of its run crashed into the bows of a South African manned corvette out on the starboard wing of the convoy.

And another more muffled explosion below water that indicated that the second torpedo's self-destruct mechanism had caused it to explode. Harmlessly.

Hallett turned to Codrington 'Must be stray mines. We haven't had any reports of U-boats, have we?'

'Not that I know of, sir' came back the response from Codrington who knew exactly what had caused the explosions but so careful was he not to contradict the Rear Admiral that he simply made a mental note that when he could leave the bridge, he'd make his way to the wireless room to ask Simonstown as to whether they'd received news of any U-boat activity in the area.

Whilst, in the meantime, a badly damaged corvette, minus three feet of her bows, turned away with another of the small escorts in attendance, barely able to move at more than two knots. A slow and possibly perilous journey with Simonstown at least four days away.

The convoy continued to plough northwards at fifteen knots. As if nothing had happened.

U-177-A surfaced once the propellers had passed overhead. Her lookouts failed to see the slow moving crippled corvette and its escort some four miles to port. Aarlberg ordered full ahead to try and close the convoy but gradually the bulky shapes of tall slab-sided liners and their accompanying merchantmen and escorts drew out of range. In the set coded message, he radioed on the pre-arranged wavelength to SKL, who in turn, relayed on a different wavelength the message to *Dresden.*

Reitz received the news and having decoded it, with Serle, pinpointed the convoy's course, speed and position adding the fact that one vessel, not known, had been possibly damaged.

Collins snorted when Codrington's message came through giving Hallett's view that the corvette's damage was thought to be from a drifting mine. Then he smiled as he perused the last sentence. 'Suspect mine to be a U-boat. C.'

U-boat? Were there others waiting ahead?

One of the base's wireless operators said that they'd picked up probably the tail-end of a message in an unknown code. The approximate bearing, and at best, an intelligent guess for the message had been too short for accuracy, was somewhere in the area of the convoy. Collins put two and two together. A U-boat had attacked the convoy, possibly at long-range and then had re-surfaced behind the ships and sent off a coded signal. Course. Speed. For other U-boats ahead? Or maybe even *Dresden*? But what proof did he have? None of the usual U-boat chit-chat had been detected. And no-one had heard of *Dresden* since her engagement with *Chelmsford.* It could be possible that the Germans had withdrawn her to Norway. But then she could have gone south. The troopship convoys going round the Cape were certainly a tempting target. His mind whirred with the possibilities of the naval situation.

After much thought, he sent a coded message to Wills-Wilson. 'Take care. Suspect U-boats ahead. Collins.'

It was with some dismay when at noon, Wills-Wilson saw from *Resolve*'s high bridge, the light cruiser *Cocos* suddenly surge from just ahead of his ponderous battleship to overtake the leading ship of the convoy and take up a new position a quarter of a mile further ahead.

'What's the fool up to now?' he wondered. 'If there are U-boats ahead he's going to be the first obvious target.'

Codrington was wondering too but steeled his mind to put it mildly he thought that Hallett was, well, to put it crudely 'a jumped up fart' but such thoughts, as a captain and thus Hallett's junior in rank, could not be said out loud. So he complied with the Rear Admiral's order to place *Cocos* at the head of the convoy.

'We're going to sweep ahead of the convoy, not sulking behind fat merchantmen or ungainly liners. We need to be ahead. If there's an enemy raider out there it's us who need to get at him first. Not that there is. Collins was pissing in the wind simply to put the fright on us. If old Dudley says *Dresden*'s in a Norwegian fjord then that's good enough for me,' Hallett snapped at the cruiser's captain as if reading the latter's thoughts.

Codrington bit his lip. The words at the conference had been 'perhaps she's that ship in a Norwegian fjord.'

Hallett was continuing. 'We're far too clever for any Jerry raider. Records show that *Dresden*'s no better than any other of them. She'll run as soon as she's been threatened. *Chelmsford* must've scored a damaging hit to send him limping to base. Look what Harwood's ships did to *Graf Spee* and see where Lutjens and his super battleship are now. In Davy Jones's locker and that's where we'll put her if she's daft enough to show up!'

Codrington bit his lip. Again. What was *Dresden*'s tally so far? Three cruisers, a modern destroyer, two a.m.c.'s and over a dozen merchantmen? At least!

Instead he asked 'Then why haven't we a destroyer with us. What if there are any more U-boats in the Channel?'

'Pah, there aren't any U-boats and if there are, we're too fast for them. We shall be conducting vigorous sweeps in a zig-zag pattern and any old Jerry periscope watcher is going to be cross-eyed and sea sick simply just trying to keep track of us. One or two of our destroyer escort will from time to time leave the screen and join us. Don't worry, Captain, no-one will ever touch us. After all, this is the flagship of the convoy!'

Codrington loathed the bumptious upstart. Ever since he'd first boarded the cruiser at Gibraltar. At the head of the bosun's party had been the cruiser's first officer. Half-an-hour earlier he, with one of the anti-aircraft gunners had just completed a messy overhaul of one of the cruiser's pom-pom guns when the announcement had come that Hallett was due to board when everyone had assumed, incorrectly, that the flagship for the naval escorts would have been *Resolve*. The first officer had hastily exchanged grease-grimed overalls for his tropical whites, but an errant spot of grease had found its way on to the front crease of the left leg of his shorts. There hadn't been time to even borrow another pair. Hallett had come aboard to the usual trill of bosun's pipes but even as the notes had just ended he'd seen that grease-mark. Hallett had gone almost beserk when reprimanding the cruiser's first officer in front of the assembled party. Everyone there knew that the officer had hardly been off duty during the potentially hazardous run from Southampton. None of the cruiser's crew had taken a liking to the Rear-Admiral since that incident and the men on duty on the cruiser's bridge when Hallett was expounding his unsound naval theories took an even further and deeper dislike.

They utterly detested him and when one of the watch-keepers stuck two fingers up in the air in the traditional Anglo-Saxon manner as Hallett left the bridge to go to his cabin, as he put it, 'to plan my strategic manoeuvres', others smiled. Even Codrington. 'So the others think as I do!'

On his previous cruise in the North Atlantic, Korvettan Kapitan Braun Minsche torpedoed three ships in a ten-minute flurry of activity during a sixty-day patrol. He then took U-673 back to Lorient, and then after only a week's leave whilst his boat was hurriedly refitted, reprovisioned and refuelled, he set off once again but this time with strict instructions to avoid contact with any ships whatsoever until SKL designated him to meet a supply ship when he reached the latitude of Southern African waters. One such meeting took place deep in the South Atlantic and then it was on again – surfacing at night but diving at dawn when his boat was within range of possible air-patrols at the edge of South African waters. This was all so different from those previous five consecutive patrols in the North Atlantic when the constant battling with mountainous seas had been the main problem. Now all he had to do was to reach the Mozambique Channel and then open the last of the sealed envelopes.

U-673 reached her position three days ago. SKL had relayed Aarlberg's initial report and Minsche had manoeuvred his boat to the area through which he reasoned the convoy would pass. 'Sometime that evening' he reckoned given the estimated speed.

Minsche was down below having just finished his mid-day meal when the alarm button in his tiny cabin sounded. Three times. Hurriedly he raced up to the conning tower and immediately reeled from the heat of the blazing sun. The clear blue sky was reflected by the flat calm surface of the Mozambique Channel's waters.

'What's the matter?' he asked.

'Herr Kapitan, one of the lookouts has seen smoke. Lots of it. Over there to port' came the reply from the officer on watch.

Minsche snapped binoculars to his eyes. 'Mmm. Lots of ships. Looks like our target. A troopship convoy. Somewhat earlier than what I expected. Right.' He lowered his binoculars. 'Careful dive to periscope depth.'

U-673 slid gently below the surface with hardly a ripple to denote her former surface presence.

Minsche swivelled the attack periscope in the convoy's direction. A fast-moving warship came into view at the head of the advancing phalanx of ships. A light cruiser. Astern of her was a small destroyer.

He remembered his orders. 'Attack the escort vessels.' It was the first time ever that he'd been ordered to attack such warships in a convoy as the priority target. The cruiser was such an ideal target.

'Right rudder ten degrees. Open bow tubes one to four. Range three thousand metres and decreasing. Stand by. Steady. Fire.'

He pressed the attack button.

At three second intervals the four deadly torpedoes slid out of their tubes and at forty knots veered off towards the as yet unsuspecting *Cocos*.

U-673 dropped lower into the depths, her crew waiting. Counting. Counting the seconds to hear if the torpedoes had found their target.

Rear-Admiral Hallett was at ease with the world. As he'd put it earlier to Codrington the noisy U-boat, if that is what it was, had been left far behind. The convoy was nearly half-way through the Mozambique Channel. No more alarms so everyone could relax. No raider would dare to attack with such limited sea room. He'd taken his lunch and the Cockburn's port was going down very well as a superb after-meal tonic. Maybe not as fast going down his throat nor as lethal as the rapidly approaching quartet of amatol warheads coming towards *Cocos* at a combined speed of nearly sixty knots. Coming closer every second as the flavour of the port seeped into the taste buds of the Rear-Admiral.

That the wirelessing U-boat was on its own was not an opinion shared by Leonard Codrington. It had been odd that Hallett even agreed that the wirelessing that *Cocos* had picked up had come from a U-boat when his first opinion was that the South African corvette had hit a drifting mine. Although the wirelessing had been in code, it was obvious that its contents must have been referring to the convoy. But to who or what? Codrington guessed that it was to other U-boats. With Hallett having his lunch – Codrington's had been a hasty sandwich and a mug of sweet tea on the bridge-he'd signalled the old V and W destroyer astern of them to take up the lead and carry out an Asdic sweep. HMS *Whimple* surged ahead as Codrington reduced his light cruiser's speed to match that of the convoy.

It was this reduction in speed that almost saved his cruiser. As she slowed, the calculations that Minsche had made were somewhat thrown off balance.

A flashing light from *Whimple*'s bridge was the first warning. Then a look-out yelled in alarm. 'Torpedoes off starboard bow!'

'What the hell?' snarled Codrington. 'Hard a starboard! Full astern!'

Too late. Four faint streaks of bubbles were streaking arrow-like towards the cruiser. The combination of the drop in speed by the cruiser and Codrington's desperate orders caused the two streaks of bubbles furthest away from the *Cocos* to pass ahead of the turning bows. The next one in line clipped the cruiser's bows and diverted, plunging its deadly load to the seabed. The fourth slammed its lethal, explosive cargo some twelve feet in from the bows. There was a vicious spout of flame, smoke, water and splinters and the cruiser's course was forced away from the original into confusion, causing her to slew heavily into the swell.

'Close all watertight doors. Stop engines!' snapped Codrington

'Already done sir' came a reply.

'Report damage.'

Not that it was needed for with an ominous grating from the bows of metal bending and cracking under severe strain the whole of the torpedo damaged forward section with an appalling screech of tortured metal simply just sheared off and vanished leaving the bows truncated to just forward of 'A' gun turret. Down below, the first officer's damage control party were already shoring up where needed and the remaining bulkheads seemed to be holding up as well as the horrendous circumstances allowed. Even so, the men worked desperately hard to ensure that their ship could at least stay afloat.

'Try slow ahead' muttered Codrington after hearing the reports from the damage control parties. Slowly at little more than a knot the cruiser began to move forward.

But much too slowly for Rear-Admiral Hallett who somewhat belatedly had clambered to the bridge smelling of far too much port and swaying on his feet.

'What the bloody hell has happened Cap – tain Cod – ring – ton?' his voice shrilling higher with each pronounced syllable.

'Torpedo hit. We've lost about ten feet off the bows.'

'So this ship's a bloody cripple, eh, what?'

'Yes sir. Emergency repairs are in progress. Destroyer *Whimple* is dropping depth charges to keep the enemy quiet although my guess is that the U-boat has already gone deep under the convoy.'

'Yes and look what's happening to it. Passing us at full speed whilst we sit here like some clapped-out wreck!'

'Well, once repairs have been completed we may be able to make five to ten knots. Could be an hour or so before we're ready'.

'Far too late. You'll have to return to Simonstown. Detail *Marigold* to act as escort –' indicating a small Flower-class corvette assisting *Whimple* in dropping depth charges. – 'Well I need to be with the convoy. Signal *Llandaff* now to come alongside and I will transfer to her.'

'Not *Resolve* sir?'

'No! No! No!' shrieked Hallett his face effusing red and purple blotches.

'But sir –'

'Don't but me. Do as I order! Now!' Hallett slapped his hand on the adjacent chart table, his face even further suffused as his rage welled within him. He turned to Codrington whose mind was on saving his ship. 'You bloody fool Codrington! I cannot control this convoy from either this cripple nor that ancient wallowing tub. I need speed. I need dash. Only *Llandaff* can fulfil either of these qualities even though she isn't as quick as this cruiser was before this recent misfortune that seems to have befallen her.'

'Misfortune! You stupid fool!'

Codrington somehow kept his control to within his own troubled thoughts.

'Well, Cap-tain! Has *Llandaff* responded?'

'She'll be alongside within ten minutes.'

'Well I must go and get my things. Have your men ready for my transfer,' and with that Hallett turned and clattered away down the exit steps.

Codrington's coxswain stuck up two fingers behind the Admiral's retreating back. His captain nodded and simply said 'Ditto. We'll be well rid of him.' His mind was focussed on his damaged command. Not with a slanging match against Hallett. Dully he said to the second lieutenant standing next to him 'Go on. Get the boat's crew organised, and try not to push the Admiral into the brink when he turns up to board it!'

'Aye, aye sir.'

A short time later *Llandaff*'s rust-streaked sides came into range and without getting wet at all, Rear Admiral Hallett, declining to offer even a word of thanks to Codrington, let alone a backward glance to the damaged *Cocos*, boarded the Cathedral-class cruiser which as quickly as possible set off back to the disappearing convoy leaving *Cocos* and the little *Marigold* to struggle painfully back on course for Simonstown.

Minsche and his crew heard one explosion signifying a torpedo hit as their boat dived deep, headed as correctly guessed by Codrington, for the disturbed wakes of the churning propellers of the convoy's ships. Distantly they registered the desperately dropped depth charges but as these faded away together with the propeller sounds of the convoy, Minsche cautiously ordered his boat to the surface to see if he could ascertain what damage his torpedoes had caused.

As the periscope probed above the surface, Minsche was surprised to see the near stationery and badly damaged *Cocos* little more than two miles away. Then he saw the corvette circling the cruiser in an anti-submarine sweep but as the corvette moved to a position on the other side of the crippled cruiser, Minsche ordered another full spread of four torpedoes to be fired.

This time none of them missed. One after another they struck in succession along the length of the portside of their target.

It didn't take long for *Cocos* to sink as she broke into two halves.

When *Llandaff* caught up with the convoy observers on her saw the flashes of the explosions on the helpless light cruiser. A desperate message from the little *Marigold* reported the loss of the *Cocos* and a bit later, another message gave the grim news that the corvette had picked up only about sixty survivors, but Captain Leonard Codrington wasn't amongst them, nor was the first officer. Hallett read the messages when a copy was sent to him but having perused them he simply crumpled them up and tossed them into a nearby waste paper bin in the main cabin of the cruiser's captain who had hastily vacated the room, preferring to spend what little spare time he had in his sea cabin abaft the main bridge controls. Like Codrington, Captain Angus MacLeod cared little about Hallett and the more he could make the Admiral stay in the comparative comfort quarters of his main cabin, so much the better.

U-673 again dived deep but only after Minsche had seen all the four torpedoes hit. He watched as the cruiser broke up in flames and began to subside below the waves. Then he saw *Marigold* approach and dove his boat. After about half-a-dozen discernible crumps of exploding depth charges he stayed down for a further two hours before bringing the U-boat to the surface by which time *Cocos* had long since sunk and *Marigold* was but a tiny blob on the southern horizon trying to reach Simonstown as quickly as she could as a number of the cruiser's survivors were seriously injured and in desperate need of urgent hospital treatment. Minsche sent off his brief coded report and within the hour, Reitz on *Dresden* knew that the convoy was minus its most modern major escort, as well as its position, estimated speed and course.

The third U-boat, of which Leutnant Karl Renke was its first officer was late into its intercepting position and badly handled. The now thoroughly alert lookouts on the starboard wing destroyer escort of the convoy saw the submarine crash-dive little more than a mile further out in a welter of foam as the evening shades began to envelop the calming waters. Hurriedly the destroyer's captain, without waiting for orders from Hallett who but an hour previously had signalled all the escorts on the short-range transmitter/receiver systems that they had to follow his orders explicitly, swung his lithe warship in a direct line to the diving submarine and with a well-grouped pattern of depth-charges brought it out of control back to the surface. A hail of shells from the destroyer hitting in and around the shaken submarine suddenly caused it to sink rapidly stern first. Karl Renke, who'd been first up on to the machine-gun lashed conning tower, and a seaman were washed overboard as the sinking U-boat slid under water. Both men were picked up by a following escort which diverted again without Hallett's instructions, to assist in the hoped-for destruction of the U-boat. When questioned, Renke gave his rank and name but on further questioning as to why the U-boat had been in the area all he said was that his captain did not divulge his instructions as to the operations of the boat to anyone. His job, as first officer, was to ensure that the crew did their jobs according to the captain's orders. Renke didn't even know that in the few moments that the U-boat had wallowed on the surface after the depth-charging that her wireless operator had been able to give a short signal of its approximate position before the boat had filled with water.

Hallett rushed on to *Llandaff*'s bridge as soon as he'd heard the crump of the distant depth-charges.

'What's going on MacLeod, eh? No one's bothered to come to my cabin to tell me. Perhaps you can!'

'Look over there sir. It appears that we're sinking a U-boat.'

'What? Why? How?'

'Destroyer *Whimple* surprised it as it was seen crash-diving. Dropped a few depth charges. Corvette Drayton is assisting.'

'So we've got one, eh?'

'Yes sir.'

MacLeod was a captain of few words, especially when it came to talking to Admirals. A dour Northerner, he'd been skipper of the cruiser since the start of hostilities and he, like his ship, was in desperate need of a long rest. To him, Hallett was an unnecessary idiot who should have been removed from the Navy before he'd even applied to join the service.

The unnecessary idiot was speaking again. Giving orders for *Llandaff*, with two destroyers abeam of her to sweep ahead of the convoy. Like Codrington, MacLeod kept tight-lipped as his over-worked cruiser sped up to twenty knots until she reached a position some quarter-of-a-mile ahead of the main convoy.

Back in Simonstown, Collins received the news of the convoy's latest brush with the U-boats. To him it seemed strange that the U-boats hadn't made a combined attack. The fact that the three interceptions they'd made appeared to be at more or less regular intervals led him to make the accurate assumption that their interventions were according to a plan set up by the Kriegsmarine's High Command. But for what purpose? Apart from the attack on *Cocos* none of the interventions had been aimed very accurately for as yet none of the troopships had been targeted. The loss of *Cocos* was serious for with her high speed she was the only major warship in the escort which could match *Dresden* for speed. *Dresden.* Why that ship again? London had already signalled that they didn't have the aircraft or the resources to mount yet another immediate reconnaissance of that Kriegsmarine unit in that remote Norwegian fjord. The ship was the battlecruiser and that was that! Royal Naval units at Scapa were waiting to hear if that ship was going to attempt her break back to Germany but until she did, all they could do was to wait.

Collins looked at the chart. Another twelve hours and the convoy would be clear of the Mozambique Channel. Perhaps then they'd be able to steam clear of any waiting U-boats, if there were any more of the underwater menaces still in the area. Hallett had made no major deviations in course and the speed was constant. Almost as if he was doing precisely how the Kriegsmarine expected. But for what? Were those U-boats plotting the convoy for a waiting *Dresden*? Were any more U-boats waiting to attack that convoy?

At the northern exit of the Channel idling on the surface in the early hours of the next morning, as surmised by Collins, cruised a fourth U-boat under the command of Kapitan Hans Schmidt. His boat, U-877-B, had been on patrol for nearly a fortnight in that area and directed there, via a long detour into the Indian Ocean, after laying mines in the approaches to Cape Town harbour for the U-boat was principally a minelayer and only carried half-a-dozen torpedoes. Expecting a quick return to France, Schmidt was ordered to rendezvous with a tanker flying a Norwegian Flag and calling itself *Olaf* in a remote part of the Indian Ocean. He'd not been asked aboard but had stayed on his own boat whilst the refuelling of U-877-B's tanks was completed. As soon as the hose pipes were hauled back to the tanker, the bigger ship increased speed on a course to the north-east whilst Schmidt's new orders brought him after a six days slow cruise to this part of the Mozambique Channel. Then the wireless reports had started to come in. Schmidt knew that the convoy was due. He broadcast to the crew giving them time to prepare. Unlike Renke's captain, he told the crew everything about the tasks ahead. Mines to be laid. Ships in sight. Weather conditions. Course taken.

'Sir, propeller noises to the south – just where we were expecting them' the principal sonar operator reported when he'd picked up the faint sounds of the approaching ships.

'Dive the boat. Periscope depth.'

U-877-B was a cumbersome boat and it took almost three minutes for her to slip carefully and slowly below the waves. Schmidt's adrenaline began to course through his veins. Memories of an attack in October 1940 came flooding back when in one memorable hour he'd torpedoed five ships, one after the other, in one of the much smaller VII-B boats.

He'd never attacked a convoy with such a big cumbersome boat under his command. Perhaps SKL had no more suitable attack submarines available. Gradually the ships became clearer. A heavy cruiser flanked by two escorts followed by a large three-funnelled liner, itself with two merchantmen on either side. Beyond that, in the funnel haze, he thought he could see the bridge structure and control tower of a battleship. Carefully, remembering his orders, he worked out his attack. Go for the cruiser in the lead and then, if undetected, the battleship. Not the big liner.

As Schmidt gazed at the approaching ships still undetected, Hallett was crowing to MacLeod over the recent success against the U-boat. 'You see. I was right. Be forceful with our escorts and we will have success. You see, Captain, deep down Jerry is yellow. Alright his subs have had some success but his surface raiders have no guts whatsoever. Just before they promoted me to this position I was captain of a light cruiser as escort to a battleship. As soon as puny Lutjens poked his head in our direction and saw us, he turned off and ran with Salmon and Gluckstein. Buggered off, eh what! So, you see, Captain MacLeod, that is why I need to have a cruiser in the lead. Scares the shits out of Jerry's pants as soon as he sees me, eh!'

MacLeod didn't answer. He didn't have to for how could he ignore the double thumps and water erupting on the starboard side of escort destroyer *Catchpole*. Even as *Llandaff* surged ahead on his command of 'Full ahead, hard-a-starboard', the little Hunt-class destroyer broke in two and vanished under the swell of that beautiful sunny dawn. Nor could Hallett even ignore the distant thump of the morning's third explosion abaft the forward holds of merchantman *Sela* which was on the starboard side of the big three-funnelled liner. It had been a torpedo aimed for *Llandaff* which, on missing the cruiser, struck the unfortunate *Sela* right at the end of its run. The ten thousand ton merchantman seemed to stagger as she received the blow but by great fortune the torpedo hit was into a large hold crammed with the spare, as well as additional, uniforms for the troops dispersed amongst the liners in the convoy. Although the hold began to fill with water, the uniforms acted like a huge sponge, expanded and then effectively blocked the inrush of water to such a degree that the pumps were able to nullify the effect of the damage. Even so, *Sela* staggered slowly out of line and began to steer for the nearby Portuguese-held Mozambique coast, her captain hoping to either reach a suitable harbour or a part of the coastline where he could safely beach his stricken ship.

To prevent the U-boat making a fresh attack, Hallett, with at last something approaching common-sense, ordered *Whimple* to drop more depth charges, at random if nothing else, so that as with the recent attack which had seen *Cocos* stricken so badly, the U-boat would stay down until the convoy had out-run it. Schmidt stayed deep slowly crawling at four knots away from the mainly ineffective barrage put out by *Whimple*. After an hour the little destroyer having dropped thirty-six charges and emptied her racks, turned for the convoy to catch them up soon after mid-day.

Hallett was quite pleased with *Whimple*'s safe return and report that debris, possibly from a damaged submarine had floated to the surface towards the end of the barrage. The destroyer's crew had been temporarily fooled by one of the oldest tricks in the book of survival for U-boat crews. A discharge via one of her torpedo tubes of a collection of dirty washing, empty food cartons and long out-of-date magazines had made Schmidt chuckle and to no doubt he and his crew would have been even happier knowing that for once the old trick of rubbish and a bit of fuel had served to bring the depth-charging to an end. They weren't to know that *Whimple*'s depth-charge racks were empty and also that her captain had received a stark wireless message ordering her back into position escorting *Llandaff*. When Schmidt deemed it safe to return to the surface, the convoy had long since gone and even the slow-moving *Sela* had been able to limp safely towards the darker background of the distant African Coast. On *Llandaff*'s bridge, MacLeod endured the bombastic attitude of Hallett who proclaimed that the convoy's brushes with the four U-boats could be counted as a success. One, if not two of the menaces had been sunk. 'Fifty percent of what Jerry could throw at us is down on the bottom of the sea. Not bad, eh what!'

MacLeod could only grimace. What was it? One modern cruiser and a destroyer sunk. Seven hundred sailors lost. Two other escorts sent off back to Simonstown. The crew of *Sela* still struggling to make it to the nearest harbour. He shuddered when Hallott went on to loudly assert that now that the U-boats had been thrown off the hunt, the convoy was as good as safe at its destination. None of Jerry's merchant-ship raiders would dare to attack and as for the mythical *Dresden*, no-one had any confirmed sightings of her except of the warship that the Nazis had crowed over about being anchored in a Norwegian fjord. 'So you see, MacLeod,' Hallett concluded 'we're just about home and dry. Mission almost accomplished. No need to call Actions Stations any longer. The lads deserve to relax, eh, what!' and with that he left the bridge and retired to MacLeod's main cabin.

The response to his departure was more or less the same as had been witnessed on the bridge by the crew of *Cocos* when Hallett had been aboard that so recently lost warship only this time it was slightly different. The two finger sign was initiated by MacLeod who also added 'And may it hit you right in the balls!'

Schmidt sent off his coded report and then turned his big submarine to the east where he set course to circumnavigate Madagascar before entering cooler waters to round the Cape of Good Hope and then alter course nothwards and then take the long haul to the boat's base at Lorient, France.

Reitz received the coded report with some satisfaction. Another escort sunk. Calculating the convoy's speed he, with Serle, worked out that in two days time it would be in their area. He even, without knowing, guessed that in order to conserve fuel for the smaller escorts, the convoy's commander would more than likely to keep to fourteen or so knots.

Soon it would be time to officially inform the crew as to the real purpose of all the waiting. Of the cruise itself. 'Blue Danube' was being relayed at a gentle volume over the ship's loudspeaker system. Quite often Commander Hiltzern resorted to playing popular songs and what were euphemistically termed the light classics during times of relative relaxation. What were banned, on his, as well as his captain's orders, were the rabble-rousing Nazi speeches and marching songs. Oddly, enough, when it came to requests, Souza's 'Washington Post' and Elgar's 'Pomp and Circumstance No1' featured just as often as Strauss Waltzes, Beethoven marches or songs such as 'Lili Marlene'. Reitz nodded as the music swept over the ship and mused that sometime during the next day he would tell his crew of the momentous tasks ahead of them.

The next dawn saw the convoy roll over the horizon in sight of Neumans and his prize crew on board *Arabian Nights* as she in turn ploughed steadily northwards at a speed of about thirteen knots. Neumans became tense when one of his lookouts reported that one of the wing escorts divert to close with them. It was with some relief that when it came within a mile and saw their Red Duster flag flapping gently at the stern and their adopted name Sandisland displayed clearly at their stern as well as on the port bow, it sheered off, without even signalling them, and scuttled back to its position on the starboard wing of the convoy. Through binoculars, Neumans and the watch lookouts noted the position of a heavy cruiser in the lead, the imposing outline of the R-class battleship in the centre and the largest liner, a three-funnelled one, leading all the others. They also counted the whole phalanx of ships as slowly they began to overtake the disguised freighter.

As he re-focussed his glasses on the bigger liner, Neumans recognised her due to the fact he'd once served on her as a steward when she'd done a run from Hamburg via Southampton to Cape Town. He knew that she was a real beauty. A twenty-eight thousand tonner. *Aspen Castle.* Union Castle liner. Soon to be attacked. Probably carrying up to five thousand troops. A prime target. He hoped that he wouldn't witness her destruction. Gradually the convoy hauled off to the north at a collective speed which Neumans guessed to be at about fifteen knots. As it became hull down on the horizon, Neumans raised his own command's speed to almost match that of the disappearing ships. A one-letter signal to *Skua* in position to the north soon had her Heinkel float-plane coming into sight. As it circled the freighter Neumans sent off a lamp signal to it giving the course, speed and disposition of the convoy. Cautiously the float plane's airmen took their aircraft to a distant view of the rear of the convoy but due to the clear skies they kept well away and then carefully turned away after confirming that the convoy was still on course. The plane, by a circuitous route flew over *Skua* and then on to *Dresden.* Without landing, they signalled the fresh information from *Arabian Nights* where it was assimilated by Reitz and his senior officers.

No-one on the convoy's ships caught a glimpse of the little float-plane although one lookout on a freighter thought he'd seen a flash of light but on reporting it to a deck officer, he was told that it was probably a trick of the equatorial sun. Only Captain MacLeod of the labouring *Llandaff* was feeling uneasy. With one of the engines of his cruiser coughing and spluttering at irregular intervals he felt that it could well seize up entirely if called upon to achieve full power. A situation that could arise if the *Dresden* was in the area. Suppose that she was. Without realising it, he had, like Collins traced an estimated course since the last known position of the German battlecruiser's action with *Chelmsford.* He came to the same supposed theory that the warship raider could have quite easily reached the area that the convoy was now approaching. But what proof? Even the superb code-breakers at Bletchley had as yet been unable to work out the new cipher messages from the recently encountered U-boats. Nothing affirmative from London or Simonstown at all. Nothing definite. Yet he felt uneasy. Call it sixth sense but somehow he felt that the German battlecruiser was out there. Just waiting for the ships to roll into range. All that long day they'd overtaken three merchantmen. All bound northwards. Not once had Hallett bothered to order one of the convoy's escorts to really close in and investigate. Two were flying the 'Red Ensign'. The last one a Dutch flag. All about three hours apart. All three travelling at just below the speed of the convoy. He felt sure that the flashes of light from the last merchantman's bridge had been sunlight reflecting from high-powered binoculars. Watching them. Or perhaps it was just curious mercantile officers gazing at the splendid sight of so many large ships.

MacLeod was so uneasy that without informing Hallett he personally went down to the cruiser's wireless office and ordered a coded message to be sent off to Collins at Simonstown. Back came the reply within half-an-hour. Had Hallett flown off either *Llandaff*'s Walrus aircraft or *Resolve*'s? To investigate. Well, no he bloody well hadn't and besides it was now getting too dark. Night time was encroaching. MacLeod's reply shocked Collins. It seemed that Hallett was ignoring even the simplest of precautions. If the merchantmen had been German ships in disguise, they would have been easily overwhelmed by the fire-power of the convoy's escort. But Hallett had made no move against them and the fears that were lingering had not been allayed. So it was no wonder that Angus MacLeod as well as Wills-Wilson on the battleship were beginning to feel really uneasy. Call it intuition but they somehow sensed that something ill was in the wind.

Reitz knew that the positioning of his three support ships had been a risky part to his plan but as he'd agreed to his officers, boldness always carried a degree of risk, as well as rewards. What he now had was an accurate plan of the disposition of the convoy's ships. Neither had it altered its course or speed all day. Apart from the cursory inspection of *Arabian Nights* not once had the convoy's escorts deviated from their general patrolling positions. The heavy cruiser was still in the lead, followed by the big three-funnelled liner. Towards the centre of the convoy came the old R-class battleship. It hadn't been pushed forward at all. Even its big guns had remained solidly pointing in the rest position – forward or aft. Everything was as he had hoped. As the sun dipped below the western horizon he decided that this was now the time to speak to the crew.

'My loyal crew' he began, after Hiltzern informed the ship over the loudspeakers that the captain was about to speak, 'may you all find time to sleep tonight. Tomorrow at dawn, all our practising, all our efforts, all our working together as a team comes to a climax. Our guns and torpedoes will be aimed and fired at a large enemy troopship convoy. Our friends of the U-boat service have depleted the escort of one light cruiser and up to three of the smaller warships. There is still a cruiser of the Exeter class as well as an old R-class battleship and we shall engage these ships first. No doubt this will cause the ships of the convoy to scatter. Due to their relative high speed some of the troopships will more than likely escape. Hopefully the slower merchantmen in the convoy will come within range of the guns of *Skua* and maybe even *Berengia* as well.' Here the voice fell silent. To give the crew time to digest the news that most of them suspected something bigger was coming. Then Reitz continued, firmly but a shade quieter. 'It may well be the case that we shall sustain casualties ourselves should our initial assault fail but before we do I will ask all of us to attend to our duties to the highest degree possible. Our aim, knowing that we will all be ready, is to destroy as much of this convoy as we can. Should we succeed, our brothers in the Afrika Korps fighting in North Africa will find their tasks so much more the easier. It is what this ship was planned, designed and built for in the event of war. To attack, engage and destroy enemy shipping. That is our aim. That is what we shall be doing come the dawn. I trust that success will be ours. Thank-you. All of you.'

With that the speakers clicked off. Then, from the bridge and spreading over the whole ship came the repeated sounds of men cheering. As he looked out to the midships section from the port wing of the bridge he could see men waving their arms and animatedly talking to each other.

Next, Reitz decided to tour the ship. Gathering Brautsch and Anders whom he'd just summoned to the bridge together with three of the battlecruiser's naval policemen, he went first to the radar room where one of the operator's was watching the glowing green screen. Round and round went the repeater dial. Nothing at all. The captain put a hand on the man's right shoulder 'Paul, you and Heine are my eyes. As soon as you pick up the convoy probably at around eight bells of the first watch in the morning, you will let me know. Directly. I am relying on your super machine.'

Paul nodded 'Jawohl, Herr Kapitan.'

On to the wireless room where he knew the men listening would soon have their work cut out recording all the distress messages from ships under attack – as well as trying to catch any incoming calls.

Down some ladders with Anders opening all the doors to the Damage Control Section. Amidst all the fuse boxes, dials, switches and lights in the enclosed area. Reitz knew that if the British battleship was able to range her guns, then it was this room that really controlled the ship, not the bridge. Vital to their continuing operation in the heat of the battle. Hopelessly cut off if the ship was left out of control and sinking. Trapped by their sealed watertight doors. Along more corridors he and his group went eventually reaching the magazine compartment below the forward turrets. The men down there knew that if one of the British battleship's shells exploded amongst the racks of the numerous shells that they'd be the first of *Dresden*'s crew to be blown to smithereens. Not much chance of survival for them. Yet they were patiently greasing the hoists and testing their equipment. All to give *Dresden* as high a rate of fire as was possible.

Reitz and his group climbed up the ladders to visit the gun crews of 'Anton' and 'Bruno'. They knew that they'd be the first of *Dresden*'s weapons to fire at the convoy. Reitz told them that their target could well be the Exeter class cruiser but this time, unlike with the *Graf Spee*, they would be responsible for knocking out their British opponent in less than ten minutes, if at all possible. The men there knew of their responsibility and they said that Reitz could trust them.

Then it was down the ladders along corridors and down even more ladders that led into the engine-room where he found Herzog with Luth and their engineers, greasing and oiling where needed at the engines that, although only at slow ahead looked, imposing as the steam turbines whirred round as well as the gleaming shafts that led to the propellers which ceaselessly revolved. Reitz patted an engine casing and smiled broadly at Herzog and the men who'd gathered around. 'These are our key. Keep them all in good order lads, for tomorrow we shall make them work extra hard. In return I'll do my best to keep you informed as to the situation topsides.' Herzog grinned.

On and on the group went eventually to reach the Chief Quartermaster, Chief Petty Officer Hans Goethe and his team of clerks. Goethe was a very neat man. A very straight centre parting to his short cut brown hair. Tie immaculately fastened. Uniform always looking as if it had just been cleaned or pressed. Shoes ever gleaming. Even after so long at sea but Reitz never queried his efficiency nor his supply lists so neatly tabulated and filed. In Goethe's own beautifully neat handwriting. It was due to his efficiency that Reitz always had accurate figures about the state of the ship's level of supplies – in food, fuel, ammunition and a host of other requirements that a major warship on a war cruise required. Goethe's team knew exactly when an item was running short in supply. So vital to ensure *Dresden*'s success.

More corridors. More storerooms and then it was to the upper decks. To Serle's men at the torpedoes tubes. Reitz patted one of the so-potentially lethal missiles in its rest position. 'Tomorrow, baby, you and your pals will sink a battleship. Not in practise but for real,' and then to the men 'Aim true lads or we ourselves will be on the receiving end.' Upwards next, to the gunners of the secondary and lighter guns. To each of them a word of encouragement even if the gunners felt that they wouldn't be in action. 'Don't worry, lads,' was his reply. 'I'll do my best to get close enough. If not, just keep an eye open for any planes that the enemy may try to launch.' So it was on to the hanger where *Dresden*'s Arados were housed. All three aircraft were being checked over for the next day's hectic round of flying. They knew that at first light a plane was to be flown off to search for the convoy and once found, the other two planes were to take it in turns spotting the fall of shot, tracking fleeing ships and trying to persuade some of them to surrender to *Skua* or even *Berengia*, with weighted messages to be dropped on their decks if required. The mechanics assured their captain that all three aircraft and their pilots, would be ready.

The group's last top-deck visit was to the aft gun turret, 'Cesar'. Even at that late hour, turret gunnery officer Robert Koch was still training the turrets to imaginary targets and was in the process of practising localised control with half of his gun crew pretending to be out of action when Reitz entered the dark shell of the turret's interior. Reitz nodded in agreement when Koch told him what he was doing but then added that he hoped that the forthcoming engagement wouldn't lead to such a state of affairs. He then advised Koch to stand the crew down. 'There'll be plenty of real work for you all come the morning. Get some rest, all of you!' Koch, a serious minded twenty-seven year old, nodded in agreement but kept his own council. Of all the officers on the battlecruiser he was the only one who had anything approaching affinity with the Nazi party although he'd very quickly realised that voicing such support just did not curry flavour at all with other men in the ship. So, he kept these thoughts to himself but when in his own cabin he played, albeit very softly, on his own gramophone some of the records of Wagnerian opera, a taste of music that he knew was very much in favour with those who shared his secretly held political views.

Back down to the kitchens the group went to the ship's main gallery where Reitz spoke to Ernst Lau, the assistant cook, a thin rancid-looking man who'd been a chef at a top Hamburg hotel before being called up to serve on *Dresden* via an almost perfunctory course in the ways of the Kriegsmarine. Since the capture of *Arabian Nights* he'd been able to once again put on food that made him think more of those meals prepared for the top society in the clientele of Hamburg's upper echelons. He assured his captain that it would be a breakfast of scrambled egg and sausage as the pre-battle meal and ham sandwiches as and when required in the hours that followed with ample amounts of coffee or tea when needed, even cold fruit squashes. Reitz remarked that it looked as if Mr. Churchill looked after their needs as well as that of the enemy. Lau grinned so much that to his men it seemed as if his thin face had split in two.

Finally, at nearly midnight the group entered the Sick Bay where Andrea hushed them to be quiet. Doctor Lebers and his three SBAs were all asleep, as was Elfrida and their three patients. She'd just been asleep and was standing the night watch. Reitz murmured his thanks 'Fraulein, You are a very brave woman to stay here with us. Tomorrow, this place may be filled with many of my men. Even myself. Perhaps we may not even be here. My grateful thanks to you in advance. Goodnight!' As the group left, Helmut Brautsch was the last to go, and as he closed the door, he smiled at Andrea and closed his left eye in a slow, quite deliberate wink. Then he was gone and all she could do was to feel confused. About herself. About her being still on his warship. But above all about Helmut. 'Damn, damn, damn. He's enemy but I can't help it. I'm in love with him. But I can't even dare to tell him. Why, oh why? Why am I feeling like this? Damn, damn, damn!' She nearly spoke out loud even though she was only whispering the words to herself. One of the men in a cot groaned in his sleep but try as she might, Helmut Brautsch would not go away from the swirling of her mind in her head.

The group dispersed, tired after the exhausting tour of their ship. Even so, as Reitz left each area, the men felt that much better for his visit. They knew that he cared for them in a way that Von Munke could never have done. Now here they were only hours away from what could be their finest hour or from an undeniably horrible death. Reitz had pulled no punches in what lay ahead. The men were prepared and gladly all who could have gone to rest and sleep with their collective morale as high as it ever could be. Soon after Anders had heaved his weary body into his bunk with his arms aching from operating so many watertight doors, the ship fell relatively silent as only a skeleton watch remained on duty through the night hours.

At Simonstown, Collins received a signal from London that left him even more puzzled – 'The big warship has moved from her Norwegian base.' Reported by Norwegian Resistance to be moving south. Destination believed to be Kiel. Collins had been doing his homework delving much deeper into the movement of Germany's warship of cruiser size or above. Apart from the three big ships in Northern France, all the others were known for certain to be in

German waters except two. *Dresden* and an old pre-dreadnought battleship, normally used for training purposes, called *Rugen* which had, until two weeks previously, been seen in Tromso and then reported to be on the move, destination unknown. She hadn't been seen since. Collins had pursued this apparent piece of useless information and came to a startling, supposed piece of logical thinking but again he had no proof. He'd remembered again that in the Great War, even old merchant ships were disguised as Grand Fleet battleships to try and fool German spies keeping watch on Scapa Flow. Now, he thought just suppose the Germans had done the same with *Rugen*. Put her out of sight, altered her appearance and then anchored her in an almost inaccessible fjord pretending to be *Dresden* whilst the real battlecruiser was in fact off the north-east African coast waiting to attack the troopship convoy. But what proof? Only those recent words of a brave but also possibly frightened Norwegian agent desperately tapping at a furtively hidden wireless set scared of the door being blasted in by the Gestapo.

Collins did not hesitate. As darkness fell he contacted the naval base at Colombo. Yes, they said, heavy cruiser *Wellington* could sail for the convoy rather than go on escort duty to Singapore and thence to her home base in New Zealand. Yes, they said within the next few hours. She was the only major naval unit within reach of the convoy even though at full speed she could only be up with the convoy within about thirty hours. Collins sent off a signal for the heavy cruiser to set sail as soon as possible having informed London of his suspicions. Then he sent a message direct to MacLeod in *Llandaff* and Wills-Wilson in *Resolve*.

'Am sending heavy cruiser *Wellington* to give you a helping hand. Suspect *Dresden* is in your area. Collins.'

When MacLeod received the message from the wireless operators all he could do was to say 'Well, be better than nothing but'll probably be too late anyway if this mythical *Dresden*'s in our area. We'll just have ter see for the old girl's engines are being a bit asthmatic at present. Still, with an Admiral on board, how can we come to any harm?' Then, seeing it was near on midnight and that he'd been on the bridge for the past sixteen hours he muttered 'I'll be off to me mansion. Wake me up at eight bells at the end of the first watch. Can't miss out on a beautiful sunrise, can I?' and saying that he shuffled to the rear of the bridge to his sea cabin, shut the door and pausing only to remove his shoes, threw himself on to his bank still dressed in the rest of his tropical uniform of white shirt and shorts.

It was after midnight that Collins also went to bed. His aides had checked with the ships that had left Mombasa in the last twenty-four hours. It seemed probable that the three merchantmen that MacLeod not Hallett, had reported that the convoy had overtaken, could all have been ones that had been independently sailed from the port bound for either Aden of Colombo. He couldn't get it out of his mind that the worst scenario could be that the ships were Germans disguised as Allied vessels. Maybe he should contact Mombasa again but he was tired. Perhaps there was nothing wrong at all. Maybe Hallett was correct. 'Everything going well. All troops intact. U-boat shaken off. Expect to be in Aden within forty-eight hours. Hallett.' That had been twelve hours previously.

The sun rose in a steady but nevertheless as usual, fascinating spectacle over the Eastern horizon, etching the starboard sides of the convoy's ships in a yellow glow. Just twenty miles from the phalanx of ships came the sleek battlecruiser raising her speed to thirty knots, slicing the waves with an arrow-straight precision. The convoy had just come on to the edge of her radar screen. 'Actions Stations' had sounded and all her crew were at their positions. An Arado catapulted into the air was soon circling to gain height above her speeding parent-ship. Forward gun turrets 'Anton' and 'Bruno' seemed almost to be sniffing the air as they angled over the warship's port bows at their near maximum elevation. Reitz, alert and clean-shaven came onto the bridge as soon as the radar had reported the convoy's presence.

'Soon,' he remarked to Brautsch 'soon we shall see the real fighting capabilities of this ship. We'll only get this one chance and then the British will build a ship like us just so that we can't do it all over again!' A grim joke but it did help to ease the tension.

Then, quite suddenly, a cry went up, 'Smoke sir! Thirty degrees off the port bow.' It was the convoy.

MacLeod had also risen with the dawn but not in quite the same mood as the German captain on the as yet unrealised approaching battlecruiser. Soon after he'd stumbled on to the bridge with a bacon sandwich in one hand and a mug of tea in the other when the bridge telegraph rattled.

'Is yon captain there?' asked a disembodied voice, sounding far away. The third officer, unable to guess who the voice belonged to, snapped back 'And who wants to know?'

'Don't bugger me about laddie, I wants the skip. It's Fergus down here.'

Fergus Ronaldson was the cruiser's Chief Engineering Officer, part Scottish, part English and part just plain awkward, He was Captain MacLeod's best friend although to hear them talk gave listeners a totally wrong impression.

'Now then, Fergus, what is it?' snapped MacLeod down the voice pipe.

'This bucket's 'ad it. I must close down the starboard engines because we've gotta red-hot bearing and coupling that's just about knackered' came the response.

'Fergus, we have to maintain convoy speed.'

'Nay, Angus, we'll just 'ave ter do without such extravagances. I've got to shut the bloody thing down or else we'll 'ave to ask fer a tow.'

'Can't do that, Fergus, wouldn't be form.'

'Sir,' came an anguished cry on MacLeod's right,

'Not now,' came the irritable reply 'we've got engine problems.'

'But sir!' The voice again. From a very anxious junior midshipman, aged barely eighteen years but gifted with a very good pair of eyes.

'Now Fergus.' MacLeod was speaking quite firmly 'How long?'

'To shut down and repair, well, let one say about four hours.'

'Four hours!'

'Aye but with the port engine running gently an' some fine work of steering by the Cox'n, we mebbe can give you about six or seven knots.'

'Sir,' the voice of that very anxious junior midshipman cut sharply into MacLeod's thoughts but this time it went on 'I have a fast approaching warship some twenty degrees off the starboard bow.'

'Warship? Already? We only had word last night that we were getting a County class cruiser replacement for *Cocos*. From Colombo. Not expected – not – not –' MacLeod's voice faded and faltered '– Oh no, if you're right.'

'Angus!' bleated the engine room voice-pipe.

'Not now, Fergus, we've a suspicious warship in sight!'

MacLeod peered through his binoculars to where the midshipman was pointing. There, he'd found it. Barely a thin speck but even as he stared, it began to assume the white moustache at the bows indicating high speed and above those bows the bridge-works of a large warship.

With big guns forward angled at his cruiser. He stared at it. Mesmerised. The bridge structure was not that of a County Class heavy cruiser. Where the hell was Hallett? Probably scoffing his breakfast.

Llandaff shuddered. The engines were failing. MacLeod groaned and swore under his breath. Aloud, he ordered 'Send *Whimple* off to investigate the stranger and also sound Action Stations.'

The old V and W destroyer on their starboard flank turned, put on speed and with smoke pouring from her two thin stacks, she began to close with the fast oncoming warship.

Which soon announced its non-friendly intentions when, still in sight in MacLeod's binoculars, orange flames blossomed forward of its ever-growing bridge structure. The sort of flames associated with large naval guns opening fire.

For that is what they were.

When turrets Anton and Bruno of KM *Dresden* opened fire at 06.07 on 4th August 1941 directly aimed at HM heavy cruiser *Llandaff*.

Where some twenty or so seconds later, with the sound of tearing silk, or manic express locomotives or whatever other wrenching sound the shocked crew members of that cruiser could think of recalling, three of the four shells smashed into the sea just fifty yards ahead of the bows of the labouring and already slowing-down warship. Like it or not, the starboard propeller shaft's coupling glowed white-hot and then burnt out before the engine-room staff could stop the shaft. An aeon too late for them and far too late for any avoiding action for the fourth shell slammed on to the fore-peak, severed the starboard anchor chain and sent it rattling with its anchor down to the sea bed.

Llandaff's forward turrets, trained directly forward slowly began to revolve on their mountings to face the now clearly identified enemy warship. As they steadied on their mountings with their shells in the breeches, MacLeod watched angrily as *Dresden* fired again, this time her aft turrets also blossoming flame. Along the length of the German battlecruiser other small stabs of orange flame sparked out. Her smaller guns aiming for *Whimple* whose two forward single-mounted four-inch guns briefly sparked flame in a puny attempt to match their enemy.

The 'open fire' gong rattled tinnily in *Llandaff*'s forward turrets but it was the last sound that the gunners in their metal boxes ever heard as their world literally blew apart as three of *Dresden*'s incoming salvo of six shells crashed on and through the roof of 'A' turret and also down on to 'B' turret. Another shell smashed into the base of the bridge and a further one landed somewhere near the aircraft hanger setting it immediately alight. Flames, smoke, explosions and debris hurtled up and around the suddenly seriously crippled cruiser. The sixth shell failed to explode but it did land in a remarkable place. Penetrating close to 'C' turret it spiralled to land outside the cabin where Rear Admiral Hallett was amazingly still having his breakfast. No-one had bothered informing him of the sighting of *Dresden*, nor of her opening fire nor of the crippling damage to *Llandaff*'s over-worked, non-maintained engines. So engrossed was he with his breakfast that he'd even failed to register the shell hit that had smashed the anchor up forward but the shell that smashed into his door with the resulting pressure and shock-waves caused Hallett to crash backwards in his chair striking his head onto a locker door and knocking him out for a few seconds. When he came to, smoke from the fiercely burning aircraft hanger above his cabin was pouring through the open door and together with explosions above and below him, he lay cowering on the floor mortified beyond his gutless wits. *Dresden*'s third and what proved to be final salvo of shells crashed into the mid and aft sections of the ship as MacLeod desperately tried to turn his shattered vessel stern-first to their German assailant in order to try and get the aft turret to bear. Down below Hallett continued to cower with real fear whimpering like a badly-hurt puppy. A fear that he had never known before.

Dresden shifted her fire to the three-funnelled *Aspen Castle* for even with the crippling of *Llandaff* in those vicious four minutes no order had yet been given for the convoy to scatter. The cruiser, belching flames and heavy gouts of grey and black smoke was out of the battle slowly lurching forward at hardly any speed at all. Her sole contribution was a single salvo from her aft turret fired by local control before a final shell from *Dresden* had hit the ammunition hoist depriving the turret of any further shells as well as jamming the turret with the twin barrels pointing at right angles to the starboard side. The big liner, captained by a doughty sixty-year old from Hull, Albert Morris, put on speed and her funnels were spewing smoke as she attempted to put distance away from the shells hurtling towards her from her German assailant. *Dresden*'s smaller guns were in action aimed at the little *Whimple* which bravely continued to try and close the gap but numerous hits raked all along her length and the destroyer came to a stricken halt still about four thousand yards short of the German warship, having being unable to get in an attempt to torpedo the attacking battlecruiser. With flames, smoke and steam spouting out of numerous holes, she suddenly capsized on to her starboard side and quite quickly gave up the struggle and vanished below the waves. What astonished her few survivors in the water was that the *Dresden* altered course towards them whilst still firing her big guns at the fleeing *Aspen Castle* and when within a quarter mile of the swimming men dropped two large orange floats. Reitz even saluted at the swimmers as *Dresden* swept past them. 'Such bravery' he murmured, 'so hopelessly outgunned yet they kept coming.' To the men in the water they didn't know quite what to do – give the traditional Anglo-Saxon two-fingered salute or just wave their thanks as they swam towards the floats.

Wills-Wilson was in his sea-cabin having a cup of tea and the ubiquitous bacon sandwich when the alarm bells began to sound over his lumbering battleship. He hurried as fast as his corpulent frame could take him to the control bridge where the ship's commander tersely told him that an unknown vessel was firing on *Llandaff* and that the cruiser had been hit. As she was almost four miles ahead it wasn't all that easy to see but guessing at the smoke and flashes of shell hits on the cruiser the commander surmised that the enemy could well be of heavy cruiser size, at least. Wills-Wilson snarled 'Hell, it isn't! It's the bloody *Dresden.* I take it that our guns are being prepared to open fire wherever the blighter is? Are they? What's the range? Have we the enemy on our radar.'

The commander replied '"Guns" is having to guess where *Dresden* is, as smoke is obscuring visual sighting and the radar is currently working only intermittently and they've not been able to accurately pin-point the German ship.'

'Tell "Guns" to open fire. Hopefully our big bangs might scare the sod away' growled Wills-Wilson.

Resolve shook from stem to stern when her two twin forward turrets opened fire. Over to starboard. Hopefully in the direction of the German ship.

Then to the horror of Wills-Wilson, they saw orange flames shoot up amidships on the *Aspen Castle.*

'Good heavens, Jerry's after the civilian ship thinking she's our main trooper. Why the hell isn't Hallett ordering the convoy to scatter? Well, we'll order them to scatter. Go on, now!'

Three more shells hit the big liner as she tried to turn away, the last one wrecking part of the engine-room and bringing her to a crippling standstill. On seeing her slow down, Reitz switched his attention to the *Resolve* as the battleship was trying to make her presence felt. Her first salvo had been a long way off target but the second one sent up huge columns of water only half a mile away. Reitz gritted his teeth. He knew that his attack could well fail unless *Resolve* was eliminated. Just one crashing salvo of the battleship's one ton shells could disable his ship. He had to close the range. All his big three gun turrets ranged on the battleship but *Dresden*'s eleven-inch shells wouldn't be able to stop the advance or the menace of their older, slower and heavier opponent.

To his chagrin Wills-Wilson's hope that the *Resolve*'s big guns would scare away Reitz's ship collapsed like a snowball thrown into a blazing bonfire for he saw for the first time that the German ship was rapidly closing the range. 'Probably to score some hits on my ship,' he thought, 'before turning away.' Smaller sparks of flame flashed along the German's length. Using her secondary guns as well 'Mmm! We'll use ours.' Aloud he ordered 'Secondary starboard guns open fire. Now!' he yelled.

The casement guns, having last fired in anger at the Battle of Jutland crashed out with one of their opening salvo of shells landing but fifty yards off the bows of the speeding German battlecruiser now barely three thousand yards from the *Resolve.* Some of *Dresden*'s shells bracketed *Resolve* and then at least two hits were observed by the Germans on their British opponent. Some ready-use ammunition by an anti-aircraft gun amidships was hit and flames began to flare viciously into life.

'Aim for the flames.' yelled Reitz.

'Get those flames out!' snarled *Resolve*'s second lieutenant in charge of a damage control group of seamen. Hastily they dragged their hoses and aimed the nozzles at the flames. Wills-Wilson ordered a turn slightly to port so that his aft main turrets could get a better view of their opponent but in so doing exposed *Resolve*'s fuller length to his German opponent. The battleship's big guns crashed out again and their huge shell splashes seemed to jump out of the sea close to the speeding German warship, but she emerged from the collapsing geysers of water apparently unscathed.

'She's turning away' cried a young midshipman on the starboard wing of *Resolve*'s bridge.

'By crikey, she's had enough. That last salvo must have scared the balls off her' commented Wills-Wilson.

'Sir! Torpedoes coming in on starboard side' shouted another startled lookout.

'Shit!' exploded Wills-Wilson suddenly understanding the tactics of the German ship. 'Hard a starboard, full rudder.' But it was too late. The bows of *Resolve* had barely begun to turn in a desperate effort to comb the path of the onrushing missiles when one after another three horrendous explosions crashed along the battleship's starboard side. The old ship shook like a demented whale in a fatal harpooning. Wills-Wilson felt his ship first shudder and then begin to take on an alarming list to starboard as tons of water poured into her badly ruptured plates. Moments, maybe even a millisecond later as he stared transfixed at the falling debris of the torpedoing, horrendous red and yellow flames began to jet out above the stern turrets. The rearmost magazine was exploding and in turn set off concurrent explosions which ran along the whole length of the ship.

Desperately Wills-Wilson yelled 'Flood the bilges and the magazines!' but although men were trying even before that command to do exactly what he'd ordered, their moves were doomed to failure. Power from the flooding engine-room was rapidly being lost and *Resolve* was literally disintegrating. Blowing up progressively from stern to the midships section before Wills-Wilson's horrified gaze. His beloved old warrior. In her death throes. Then 'X' turret blew up and flew with a massive thrust into the air twisting and turning before dropping with a heavy splash into the sea. The single squat funnel split into two halves to topple with the mainmast as *Resolve* burst apart.

Wills-Wilson, along with some other members of his crew who were topsides suddenly found themselves being blown overboard by the convulsions of the rapidly sinking veteran battleship, blowing up beneath them.

Reitz stared aghast at the sight of *Resolve* ripping apart and coming to her violent end. Suddenly he barked, 'Hard a starboard! Head for that doomed battleship and throw some more life rafts for there may be some survivors.'

Wills-Wilson, semi-conscious, surfaced some fifty yards from the now capsized hull of *Resolve*. Amazingly, some ten or so members of her crew were stepping from the upturned bows into the sea and swimming as fast as they could before they too followed the rest of the ship under the waves for the section forward of the funnel stayed afloat some twenty seconds longer than the now vanished stern and midships sections. With an obscene burst of trapped air and oil bubbling to the surface, the remnants of *Resolve* gurgled their way under the surface down to the ocean bed.

'Blimey, they're coming for us' gasped an anti-aircraft gunner struggling in the water as he could see their German opponent bearing down on them. Dazedly Wills-Wilson looked up but to his amazement he saw the *Dresden* sharply turn away and although at full speed, and despite her wash, he also saw three orange rubber rafts being overboard.

'They've dropped rafts' shouted a petty officer. 'Come on lads, swim for them.'

As *Dresden* thrashed her course away from the swimming survivors, Reitz looking aft at the pitifully few of them, was able to see at least one sailor reach the rafts. Then his attention swung back to the task in hand. Sinking troopships.

Wills-Wilson sagged heavily on the life-line of one of the rafts, shivering with cold. Even on a warm tropical morning the Indian Ocean was still a cool place in which to be taking an involuntary dip. Two burly petty officers and the gunner lifted him into the raft. Maybe it was the shock of it all. Losing his beloved ship. So violently. So quickly. Eventually sixty-seven other men from the *Resolve* reached those rafts.

Nearly eight hundred did not. Drowned. Blown apart. In just a few seconds of sheer unadulterated horror. Flotsam of war. It was now just 6.21.

Dresden's next target was another small destroyer of just over a thousand tons. Similar to a diminutive 'Hunt' class, the little *Tintagel* was laying a smokescreen to try and cover the almost stopped *Aspen Castle*. Every so often her captain, Lieutenant Commander David Swift brought his ship out of the screen to fire her guns at the German battlecruiser hoping to draw Reitz's ship into the smoke. Unfortunately his desperate foray soon after *Resolve*'s shattering end found his ship bracketed by a salvo of shells. But one eleven-inch shell crashed into the engine-room reducing *Tintagel* to an instant cripple. With the smoke of his own ship's fires now mingling with the slowly dispersing screen, Swift turned *Tintagel* painfully back into what smoke was still hanging over the water and slowly sailed after *Aspen Castle* determined to protect the liner if *Dresden* returned but the battlecruiser was after other targets having reduced his destroyer to an apparent incapable wreck of a warship. As the smoke dispersed, Swift could see the German warship firing on other targets. Before *Dresden* disappeared he grimly noted three separate columns of smoke which no doubt indicated three more crippled ships. *Tintagel* painfully crawled closer to the *Aspen Castle*, Swift could see the amidships fire on the liner still burning although white clouds of vapour seemed to indicate that hoses were playing on to the flames. A signal lamp began to flash from the liner's port bridge wing. 'Hello little brother. Join the bashed-in club. Our fires are now coming under control. Engines damaged. Not many casualties. How are you?'

Swift sent back 'Thanks big pal. Once we're repaired we'll help to protect you. Can we shelter on your quiet side?'

'Come on. We'll keep you away from nasty pals.'

Swift manoeuvred his little destroyer close to the side of the big liner and as the sun's heat rose on that shimmering death-ridden part of the Indian Ocean the crews of both damaged ships drew a sort of strength from each other as they set to in attempting to repair some of the destruction wrought on them both from *Dresden*'s shattering shell-fire.

Three hours passed. In that time four troopships and two freighters all succumbed to *Dresden*'s gunfire. One of the troopships sank very quickly as four eleven-inch shells struck on her waterline creating a big hole and causing the sixteen-thousand ton liner to capsize rapidly trapping most of her crew and military personnel. The other three caught fire and sank much slower enabling a good portion of their crews and soldiering passengers to escape in lifeboats or rafts, even though some of *Dresden*'s secondary and smaller shells were landing in and around them whilst the bigger guns sought fresh targets. Another ship, an ammunition ship burst asunder in a vast explosion, much to Reitz's dismay, for now that the main Royal Naval opposition had been dealt with, he had hoped that once shelled, the merchantmen would stop and surrender. Only one did, flying a white flag and an Arado flew over signalling it to stop and help pick up survivors and then to wait. Soon *Berengia* hove into sight, with *Arabian Nights* and the crews of all three ships were soon busy shepherding boats and rafts so that the survivors could be brought to safety.

Five of the troopships were able to escape due to their twenty plus knot speed attained as their engine-room staffs extracted the last ounce of power out of their machinery as the various captains set them on a scattering course once they'd received the desperate order from the now long-since vanished *Resolve*. One of the slower liners, an eighteen-knotter settled for a south-easterly course but at noon was sighted by a searching Arado. Within ninety minutes the liner's crew sighted the now familiar shape of *Dresden* steaming towards them but the trooper had company. An armed merchant cruiser of fourteen-thousand tons, the *Peveril Dyke* once of the same line as the fleeing trooper *Saffron Stream* but now in Royal Naval hands.

Reitz assumed that he now had two troopships in view although he was perturbed somewhat when one of the vessels began to put out a smokescreen and two flashes of flame from stern-mounted guns could be seen even though his own ship was well out-of-range. Then the rearmost ship began to turn completely round trying to obscure the other ship. As he stared at it through his binoculars Reitz soon realised the purpose for the manoeuvring. A huge 'White Ensign' was fluttering from the mainmast of the liner and then from her port side came four flashes. 'She's an armed merchant cruiser which is going to try and stop us getting the other one. Oh the bravery of these Royal Navy sailors. When will they ever give up?' Then he ordered his big guns to open fire. Soon the eleven-inch shells were crashing into *Peveril Dyke* rending aside her relatively thin sides and exploding deep inside the ship. Once again flames began to devour a brave ship but her captain refused to surrender even though within five minutes of the German battlecruiser opening fire his ship was heavily on fire, taking in water, losing speed and three of her port guns had been knocked out. Sluggishly *Peveril Dyke* attempted to turn to starboard so as to bring her unaffected guns into the battle but Reitz brought *Dresden* up quickly and again Serle's torpedoes were launched. Two of them struck the armed merchant cruiser before she could complete her turn and the end came quickly as she capsized on to her port side.

Again, her struggling survivors were amazed to see orange life-rafts bobbing in the battlecruiser's wake as she chased after the trooper which was making her forlorn effort to escape. All to no avail as *Dresden*'s shells began to crash on board. A single gun at the stern made a valiant reply before being blasted away by an exploding eleven-inch shell. The *Saffron Stream* slowed down and raised a white flag, visibly sinking at the bow. Reitz sent a message across – 'Get into your boats and await rescue. It will come.' Even as *Dresden* circled the burning doomed liner, they saw her suddenly dip her bows into the sea and quite rapidly lift her stern out of the water. Men could be seen jumping overboard in their desperate haste to escape the sinking ship. Some were to be grateful for once again, two large orange-coloured rafts were left in the battlecruiser's wake as Reitz ordered full speed ahead in his search to the north for the crippled liner which had been his first mercantile victim, as well as for the heavy cruiser. Both ships had been reported to be still afloat some forty miles to the north by an Arado but it failed to spot the little *Tintagel.* Reitz, from the positions reported by the airmen, guessed it would take him about two hours to reach the liner and possibly a further half-hour to the cruiser.

He'd celebrated his sixtieth birthday the previous day had Captain Albert Morris of the convoy's biggest merchant vessel, the now badly crippled *Aspen Castle.* Eight hours earlier his liner's engine-room was almost wrecked by the German raider but his Chief Engineer had just reported that despite the appalling wreckage he could get limited power using the port engine only to a speed of about three knots. The fires were out and the wreckage from their flames that had burnt away at the amidships cabins and former first-class dining saloon were now mostly cleared away by his surviving crew and many of the civilians on board the ship. Morris had hated the decision by Hallett to put his vessel to the forefront of the convoy because nearly all of his passengers were non-combatant and civilian personnel *en route* to Colombo or to Singapore and not to North Africa. He knew Hallett had reasoned that if there was to be a surface attack his big liner could well be Jerry's first target. As the callous Rear-Admiral had remarked 'Better your lot get killed or shot at rather than the real fighting lads in the other ships, eh, what!' Now by some miracle, not only was *Aspen Castle* still afloat but she was beginning to move again, albeit jerkily and slowly, through the water. And she had Royal Naval company. The crew of the diminutive *Tintagel* had also repaired the main damage to her engines and she was now little more than three hundred yards away on her starboard side. Morris was eager to get away for he could still see in his mind the catastrophic destructive end of the old battleship even though her sacrifice had diverted Jerry from sinking his ship. The ship's doctor had reported only six crew and thirty-four civilians killed plus about twice as many wounded. Morris didn't want the rest of the three thousand souls under his care to be blasted to pieces by the enemy warship, if she returned. There were no other signs of the scattered convoy apart from one thin column of smoke to the east of them. It had been there all during that day. Probably from the Royal Navy's other heavy escort ship. What was her name? Ah yes, *Llandaff*. Must be still afloat although heavily damaged. Trying like us to limp to safety.

Morris was tired. Still badly shocked at the day's events. His crew were also tired. From the engineers to the fire-crews and even to the chief cook in his partly burnt out canteen. Somehow on the one stove still operable with but two of her plates, the canteen staff were able to boil up water for tea, coffee or even cocoa. Sandwiches of tinned meat or cheese they'd prepared and cut for the liner's complement, still shattered themselves at their predicament with some having not just lost their friends but also their cabins and possessions when the amidships fires had been at their worst. Many of the passengers gathered, huddled in various groups with most of them worn out after their exertions with the crew in getting the fires to abate and finally go out.

Morris was just about to take a second gulp of a sweet weak cup of tea when one of the bridge lookouts burst out to say

'Smoke, sir, on the horizon. Not much. Just a bit.'

'Keep yer eye on it, lad' growled Morris. 'Could be one of the troopers that's escaped Jerry – she must be miles and miles away by now.'

'No she in't, sir' gulped the lookout, a mere youth of seventeen. 'It's a warship sir. Prob'ly 'er sir, the Jerry.'

Morris snatched up some binoculars, 'Could also be a Royal Navy cruiser coming to help us instead.' But as he stared at the enlarging shape those looking at him saw his shoulders slump and then he snarled 'Damn, it's 'er alright. Gorra a white flag or summat? We are surrendering but what our little pal does is 'er business. Go on, one of you, flash a signal to *Tintagel* an' tell 'er we've got nasty company approaching.' Then he went to the engine telegraph, rang it and yelled down the voice-pipe 'Stop engines! Now!'

Aspen Castle hadn't been making much speed. Now she gently drifted to a halt in the lazy afternoon swell. A shimmering sea but not a friendly one for on it, slowing down with her guns trained on the hapless liner, was the menacing shape that Morris and his crew knew only too well.

'Come ter finish us off?' growled the captain. 'Check ready what few life-boats and rafts we have left!'

'Sir, she's signalling.'

'Well, what's the sod saying?'

'Stop your ship. Prepare to abandon. *Dresden*.'

'Reply that we are a civilian ship, that we have wounded, cannot make more than three knots and have insufficient boats to take off all our passengers and crew. Oh, and that we have surrendered but not our little pal.' Morris added 'That'll fool Jerry a bit.

Perhaps *Tintagel* can get away on our blind side. Oh shit! What the bloody hell is that destroyer doing?'

Dresden's radar had failed to pick up the little destroyer. So had the earlier reports from the searching Arado. As Reitz digested the liner's signal wondering what 'our little pal meant,' suddenly *Tintagel* appeared streaming smoke as her engines still damaged as they were, strove to reach a speed of about ten knots. To Reitz and the men on watch they stared transfixed at the emerging destroyer little more than three thousand yards away.

Dresden's engines were slowing down. Unexpectedly down below in the engine-room Herzog saw the bridge repeater dials spin round the order 'Full ahead.' On the bridge the helmsman, dozing for a little for the first time during that long tiring day took a shade too long to react to the order 'Hard-a-port!'

Seconds in which *Tintagel* drew clear of the big liner and turned towards her much bigger adversary which was exposing her full length as she tried to turn away. Along that length bronze flames began to stab out as *Dresden*'s smaller guns opened fire but it took the weary gunners time to get the range. As *Tintagel* tried to complete her turn, Reitz knew what her commander was trying to do. Launch torpedoes before being overwhelmed.

Swift was yelling down the now repaired phone-line to the petty officer in charge of the two torpedo tubes still in working order that could range on to the German from the destroyer's starboard flank. 'Fire when you bear – and hurry!'

Dresden's shells began to lash the destroyer which shuddered under the onslaught. At least two 5.9inch (15cm) shells whistled over to crash into the sea between *Tintagel* and the liner.

Reitz grimaced when he saw those shell splashes but he knew that the little destroyer had to be eliminated. Rapidly. His mind flashed sparks in his brain cells 'Oh, the bravery of the Royal Navy sailors.'

He'd seen it all before when the *Gloworm* had closed in, under heavy fire, to ram heavy cruiser *Hipper* before his own destroyer could close in to help finish off *Hipper*'s tormentor.

Shells swept over, around and crashed on board the advancing *Tintagel* raking into her midships and bow sections but by her torpedo tubes, one of the deadly tubes was fired by its brave crew a split second before two heavy shells slammed on to the tubes, wiping the torpedo crew out and setting off the second tube in a vicious explosion that shattered the little warship into two halves. When the smoke and immediate flames of the blast dissipated only the forepart forward of the funnels was still afloat. The stern section had completely vanished. For twelve seconds the forward part moved with its own momentum through the rolling waves and then quite suddenly it toppled over and vanished beneath the surface. A few survivors, to the incredulous gaze of the watchers from *Dresden*'s upper decks were seen to be desperately trying to swim clear and some were supporting wounded colleagues.

Then, 'Torpedo approaching!' An ear-piercing shout from a keen watcher. This sharp yell of an agonised lookout concentrated the minds of the crew members. The menacing line of bubbles of the torpedo's wake was seen to be closing towards the after part of the German warship. Lighter guns were quickly depressed and began firing at it. Sailors appeared on the deck abaft the aircraft hanger firing machine guns and about six were armed with short-fused stick grenades. In clusters they were hurled at the torpedo's track. On the bridge, Reitz gripped the rail in front of him, his knuckles white with tension. Suddenly there was a vast explosion. The torpedo and grenades going up in one massive upheaval. Just twenty yards from the side of *Dresden* but with sufficient force for the blast to split some thirty feet of hull plating between the hanger and Cesar's turret. Even deck boards were badly splintered and scarred. Two of the grenade hurling seamen were blasted overboard, three more were thrown back to the unyielding sides of the hangar. Damage control teams were quickly in position with their pumps and within five minutes, Hiltzern's deputy, Johannes Luderitz was reporting, via a phone link, to his captain that only one small storeroom was full of water but that it had been sealed. The pumps were clearing other parts where water had pushed its way through the fractured plates but Luderitz knew that in those areas, the situation was well under control.

Although the initial sight of the explosion had been severe, Reitz's nerves were put at ease with the reassuring report from Luderitz. It seemed as if the battlecruiser had, by sheer good fortune, avoided the serious damage that had always been at the back of his mind throughout the day. The telephone link rang again. This time it was Doctor Lebers. Fifteen men were receiving treatment to head and leg injuries, broken arms and ankles; burns and scarring. None life-threatening but serious all the same. The two English ladies, as he called them, were of a tremendous help. So far as he knew the crewmen blown overboard could have survived but one man hurled against the hanger's housing had died. Ritter Feldt. Assistant cook and gun-loader for one of the smaller guns.

'Launch boats' snapped Reitz 'Anders – you look for our two lads; another to search for the destroyer's survivors. Brautsch – get ready to get over to the liner.'

To *Tintagel*'s pitiful few survivors it seemed perplexing. One second they'd witnessed the apparent massive blast close to the German ship. Now a few minutes later, sailors from that self-same enemy vessel were dragging them to the temporary safety of a rescuing lifeboat.

Taking *Dresden* nearer to the stationary *Aspen Castle*, Reitz flashed a message across – 'Do not try to abandon ship. We are sending boats. Any military personnel to surrender their weapons or we open fire. Please comply.'

'Have we got to trust the bleedin' Jerries, sir?' growled the liner's first officer, Fred Quince, his left arm in a sling having had a piece of shrapnel slice across the lower half earlier in the day.

'We'll 'ave to' muttered Morris. 'At least they're not shooting at us. Look, here they come.'

'Pity about the little destroyer. Do you think Jerry will turn nasty on us?'

'Somehow I think not for how were we to know that the destroyer would turn for *Dresden*? My thoughts were that she'd tried to hide behind our bulk to try 'an get away.'

'Sir, Jerry's lowering more boats' remarked a young lookout.

'Aye, but their guns are still pointing at us' remarked Quince.

Dresden came to a halt about a quarter-mile off and four of her motor-boats were soon approaching *Aspen Castle*. One contained twenty armed crewmen, a second a set of engineers under the leadership of Second Engineer Garth Luth and in a third boat were two of the Sick Berth attendants as well as Andrea and Elfrida. With them was Helmut Brautsch. The fourth boat had been hurriedly provisioned with some food and drink supplies. Brautsch's boat drew alongside the liner on her undamaged port side coming to a halt at the side ladder and entrance port. When Brautsch reached the port a young merchant navy officer saluted him. 'Come with me. I'll take you to the captain.'

'No need, I'm here' announced Morris who had hastily descended from the bridge.

Brautsch saluted him 'Herr Kapitan, my name is Oberleutnant Helmut Brautsch, boarding officer of the KM *Dresden*. We are not here to sink your ship but rather, now that the fighting has stopped, to assess your damage, give medical aid where required and to pass on to you some of our own food supplies.' Morris was astonished. Not only that the Jerry officer was speaking in reasonably good English but also by the content of his message.

'How do you know?'

'My captain has made a quick assessment of your needs. The fires we regrettably caused may be out but you have serious damage to your engine room and maybe even your kitchens as anywhere else!'

'You're right there.'

'Furthermore captain, it is eight hours since we shelled you. Your ship has made very little progress. Maybe ten or so miles. Your engines must be damaged. My engineers will try to carry out some repairs.'

'Bloody hell. One minute you shoot the hell out of us. Now you try to repair us!'

'Ah well captain. The fortunes or misfortunes of war. We did not know that you were a civilian ship in the forefront of a troopship convoy. Perhaps there are wounded. Mmm?'

'Yes, but mercifully you stopped shelling us before too many were killed but we do have some wounded'

'Well perhaps an English voice will help. These two ladies here –' Brautsch waved his hand at Andrea and Elfrida '– should be able to help. We rescued them from their burning drifting ship, some time back and they've been assisting our ship's doctor ever since. We hope to send them back to Europe in due time.'

'More surprises, eh!' responded Morris.

'One more question, captain, which person was responsible for placing what seems to be a mainly civilian liner, the largest in the convoy, as the leading merchant vessel? One that would make it the most prominent target for either a surface or indeed, a submarine attack?'

'Oh a simple question! That burp of an admiral, bleedin' ruddy 'allett. Rear Admiral Hallett in proper language!'

'Was he on the battleship?'

'Nah.' Morris grunted in his East Riding accent. 'E's on the first ship you lot clobbered. The *Llandaff*. Probably that column of smoke that we been seein' nearly all day. To the north-east. Gone now. Either she's sunk or she's put 'er fires out. Nowt we could do about it seein' your lot went an' crippled us an' all!'

Brautsch had some difficulty in understanding the English of the liner's captain but Andrea, who'd been standing near to him quickly translated into German the gist of Morris's blunt wording. Morris in turn raised his eyebrows.

'Tha' speaks in German an' all, lass?'

'Yes I do captain. Spanish and even Japanese, if you so wish.'

'Ah well, lass, tell thi' German lad I meant no harm in talkin' in mi' accent. Been a long day.'

To his astonishment, Andrea went over to him and kissed him on his left cheek 'Yes captain, it has and now show me where your wounded patients are.' Gently she took his right hand and he responded by squeezing the hand that now held him. 'Right, lass, follow me.'

'Two hours' yelled Brautsch as Andrea glanced over her shoulder at him before she disappeared into the passageway where Morris was taking her. It led to the first-class dining saloon where many of the wounded sat on chairs or were resting on hurriedly retrieved mattresses from the liner's undamaged cabins.

Llandaff was still afloat. Her earlier fierce fires had been extinguished by the survivors of that plucky cruiser after *Dresden*'s shattering attack. The hours seemed endless as the men, who emerging from the horror and who were capable of trying to save their ship, had toiled long and hard to not only put out the fires but also to restore life to pumps, as well as restoring a limited electrical supply and now a near miracle. *Llandaff*'s engines were turning over again after hours and hours of more than exemplary labour by her engineers often working waist deep in dirty oily water. With an awkward series of gut-renching thumps, the pistons began moving. Two knots and an erratic course as the port propeller was virtually useless and the rudder in a similar precarious state. But the cruiser was moving. Erratically. Slowly. Dragging her badly shattered hulk perhaps to eventual safety. Captain MacLeod, his left arm in a sling and a bandage around his head, gave a grim smile when he heard the engines thumping gaspingly into action. He knew his ship wasn't a major fighting unit any longer. A few light guns worked but not one of her big three turrets, except the aft turret which the gunners couldn't repair, but if a target came at right angles to them on the starboard side maybe they'd be able to fire just one salvo to take the enemy by surprise! The cruiser had barely covered a mile when an agonised shout came from a lookout standing as high as he could on the truncated main mast.

'Ship ahoy! Off the port stern quarter. Merchantman steaming hard.'

MacLeod acknowledged the message with a nod and stared at the approaching overtaking vessel. In his binoculars he could see no flag. It didn't look like any of the convoy's ships. Tersely he said to the nearest signalman 'Signal the blighter. Ask who she is and what she's doing.' Just as the lamp began to chatter it suddenly came to MacLeod where he'd seen the presumed Holt Steamship Company's vessel. Just before darkness of the evening prior to *Dresden*'s attack.

'Man any gun that can bear if we have any! She's a bleedin' Jerry' he growled.

To confirm his suspicions the stranger, now directly on the port side and little more than a mile distant, raised two flags – one on her main mast and the other at her stern. The hooked black cross on a white background with red surrounds. The 'Nazi Swastika'.

'She must be one of their disguised raiders. Six-inch guns and torpedo tubes. *Cornwall* sank one of them in this region last May' perked up a keen sub-lieutenant.

'Aye, I know about 'em son' came MacLeod's blunt response. 'We'll try and get our stern round to them. Maybe "X" turret can fire one salvo at them.'

But to no avail. The German raider, for it was *Skua*, kept pace with the crippled cruiser. As if teasing the British captain. With her guns, not hidden but in full view and men waiting by her clearly visible torpedo tubes. Waiting to fire an overwhelming salvo.

Knowing that the battered slow-moving cruiser had seemingly no effective means of reply.

Under Bock, *Skua* had achieved relatively little so far in dealing with the fleeing ships of the convoy. A crippled tanker was ruthlessly torpedoed and another damaged merchantman was sunk in a fury of rapid shell-fire even after it had stopped, showed a White flag and had tried to lower its boats. Two fleeing troopships near the hapless merchantman quickly veered away and Bock had been far too slow to give the orders to switch the fire of his gunners who were firing excessively into the already sinking freighter. Both the troopships escaped before Bock could get *Skua*'s guns firing at them but by then it was too late. They were well out-of-range and vanishing hull-down over the smoke-shrouded horizon. Then one of his two floatplanes was hit by shrapnel by one of the escorts and had only just been able to ditch near *Arabian Nights* that stopped to rescue the crew. The airmen were able to guide Neuman's ship to the site of the few survivors of Bock's now sunken victims. Meanwhile the other Arado, circling further to the north, discovered the then motionless *Llandaff* and immediately the airmen flew back to report their find to Bock who, instantly seeing that the sea around him was now empty, gave orders to sail the raider to what could well be a major coup to complete his cruise. Sink the enemy cruiser and then sail, triumphantly, back for Europe and home. Putting on full speed, Bock hurried towards what he assumed to be an easy target. The enemy cruiser had been badly knocked about, still exuded smoke from the last of her internal fires and had a slight list to port as well as being low down at her stern. If the airmen were right, *Skua* would be able to close in to deliver an overwhelming coup-de-grace. As the raider drew closer, Bock could see that the cruiser looked to be in a very battered state-of-affairs. Arrogantly he closed his ship to within a mile. There was no visible response from the badly shattered *Llandaff*.

Gunner Robert Mills was feeling very very tired. Despite the heat of the day and the flames of the burning *Llandaff*, he was still in position by a dual-purpose four-inch gun adjacent to the port side of the badly-holed aft funnel that bore all the signs of a direct hit from one of *Dresden*'s shells. Splinters had clanged around him and one very small one had lashed across his forehead just missing his left eye. As he'd dived for cover other splinters rattled on to his tin helmet. All that had seemed a long long time ago but yet he didn't abandon his gun. He couldn't. It was his post. Just like he'd read in one of his history books about a young lad aboard a cruiser in the battle of Jutland in 1916. He'd never left his post. Oddly enough he could never quite remember what that lad's name had been. Jack Cromwell? John Cornwell? That lad's gun had still been in working order. So was his. What Gunner Mills didn't know was that it was the only big gun on the cruiser still in working order. But then no-one else on the shattered cruiser knew that it still was in working order. Either. The heat of the flames and of the noonday sun, together with his general exhaustion had all combined to make Robert Mills very tired. So he dozed off.

But then Robert heard shouting. Sluggishly he opened his eyes. The outlines of a ship swam in front of him. Slowly he focussed his eyes on it. A freighter. With red and black flags. Nazi swastikas. Mills peered through the gun's range-finding telescope. Yes, an enemy ship with what looked like guns and torpedoes. Pointing at *Llandaff*. Then Robert remembered his mate Harry. The gun-loader who curiously had grown a third eye earlier that day between his two normal ones. Where was he? Harry had placed a shell in the breech. The gun was ready to fire. There was no-one around him to give the order to fire. He tried the telephone. There was no response. The line was broken. Robert decided what to do. Very carefully he trained his gun a couple of degrees to the right and down a few inches until the Nazi-beflagged ship swam, as it were, into full sight in the centre of his view. Men by the ship's torpedoes could be seen and a white-capped officer appeared to be giving orders. He then watched tubes being adjusted as if they were pointing directly at him.

'Not bloody likely you bleedin' Huns' he growled and jerked at the firing lever. The gun roared and flashed out its defiance. Even

Captain MacLeod was taken by surprise and he turned to say 'What the hell?' to the petty officer at his side. But before he could even complete his sentence, a massive explosion shook the armed merchant raider that had been their close companion for the past ten minutes. *Skua* was erupting as if she were a thousand Roman Candles all rolled into one concussive blast. Robert's four-inch shell had landed right on top of the torpedo tubes all primed and ready to fire their lethal missiles at *Llandaff*. The warheads had simply blown up in a simultaneous explosion which instantly spread in a vicious blast to other parts of the ship . . . to ready stacked ammunition as well as down the hoists that loaded the raider's main five point nine inch guns (15cm) to blast the stored explosives there blowing *Skua* into numerous pieces that hurled themselves into all directions. The guns sheared off their mountings, the bridge flew apart, the tall central funnel toppled over the disintegrating port side and the two masts with their shredded flags collapsed in towards each other as *Skua*'s keel plate broke in two parts causing the bow and stern sections of the ship to sink inwards. Within thirty seconds the raider sank and apart from a cloud of smoke drifting slowly skywards and the flotsam of scattered wreckage littering the disturbed water of the sea's surface, it was as if she had never existed. Mills stared incredulously at the result of his firing of *Llandaff*'s sole portside gun capable of making a serious response to the presence of the German raider. Shortly after the explosions that had caused *Skua* to disintegrate, the waves of their disturbance began to rock *Llandaff* but despite her dreadful damage she rode the turbulence although she heaved from side to side quite violently until the waves subsided and the cruiser lay relatively stable in the gentle swell of the ocean. Cautiously MacLeod ordered the engines to stop so that the engineers could check whether the rocking had caused any further harm. Damage control parties were again checking the ship to see if any more of the cruiser's plating had cracked under the strain of not only the heaving but also the blast of that violent explosion.

MacLeod could also see medics checking for any further wounded for scattered bits of *Skua*'s wreckage had crashed on to the cruiser's superstructure. MacLeod also asked for someone to find the gunner who had fired the gun. 'Such initiative needs rewarding' he added.

Even over the horizon whilst his ship was assisting *Aspen Castle*, Reitz heard the explosion that signified *Skua*'s demise and then saw the smoke cloud lift itself over the horizon. Perhaps it was the heavy cruiser that they had so seriously damaged earlier in the day. An Arado crew's report of three hours previously had the warship in roughly that area. Rubens and Stolle had only just returned from an extensive search for further crippled victims but had missed Bock's *Skua* on her way to intercept *Llandaff* but fresh orders from Reitz found them scrambling into their flying gear and soon after they were shooting off the battlecruiser's catapult in their hastily-checked and refuelled Arado on course for the source of the explosion.

Stolle tapped Rubens on his right shoulder. 'Look, down there. The English cruiser.' They flew nearer and even at their height of two hundred feet they could see the damage that *Dresden*'s shells had wracked on the warship's superstructure. Then Stolle yelled again 'Over there! Wreckage.'

MacLeod and his men watched helplessly as the little float-plane circled the wreckage. Quite accurately MacLeod said 'Well, *Dresden* has sent her little bird to see what was the big bang. Seein' it's not us, Jerry will be having a fit. She'll be here in next to no time, mark my words. Before sunset at least.'

Then the Arado flew off in a westerly direction towards the sun which even then was beginning to drop down towards a clearly etched horizon.

When Rubens gave his report, Reitz reasoned that probably Bock had tried to intercept the cruiser. The last they'd known was that the cruiser had been on her own. Crippled. Grimly he worked out that the only possible solution was that *Skua* had approached the shattered cruiser too near and that had given either a gunner or one of the torpedo men on the cruiser crew their one chance to sink Bock's ship. Using the short-range transmitter he asked his operators to call up *Berengia* and when she replied that she was only twelve miles to the south of *Llandaff*, Reitz ordered her to steam for the cruiser so as to observe but not to get too close. Then he flashed a message across to Brautsch and his men still on board the *Aspen Castle*. 'Finish off as soon as you can. We sail in half-an-hour.'

The reply was encouraging 'Luth has engines able to work. Nurses have wounded ready for transfer. Jervaulx is conducting burial service.'

Captain Morris was most surprised when the German officer asked him for an English prayer-book. 'Was this a macabre twist to their efforts?' he thought. Aloud, he said 'Now what on earth do you want that for?'

'To carry out a burial service for your dead. Our ship's chaplain understands a little English and will help you. He's also one of the medical team,' came the response from Brautsch.

'First you shoot at us. Then leave us. Then you come back. Tend our wounded. Help us with our engines. And now, a service of burial. You do surprise me!'

'We do our duty, Herr Kapitan. After the fighting we follow the rules of rescue as much as we can. If our own ship is not in danger, then we assist survivors of the ships we've stopped. You have far too many on board for us to care for and besides, they are mainly civilians. My captain does not wage war on helpless civilians. Ask nurses Andrea and Elfrida. We rescued them from a burning ship that had been shot up by one of our U-boats. Now they help us to help you. Now please, Captain, your prayer book!'

A young apprentice boy, during Brautsch's little speech, had silently run to the captain's cabin and even as the German officer finished his little dissertation, re-appeared, a little breathless on the bridge and handed Captain Morris a battered copy of the Book of Common Prayer. Brautsch motioned for the British captain to follow him which he did. Passing the burnt remnants of part of the midships section of the battered liner, the two officers, the apprentice boy and three armed German sailors met up with Jervaulx and other German sailors together with some of the civilian passengers as well as members of the liner's crew already assembled at the stern. On the aft deck under a number of sheets surmounted by a Union Jack flag lay the bodies of thirty-nine members of the liner's crew and passengers.

In German, Brautsch called his men to attention and then in English asked Morris to begin. Shakily at first, but gaining strength as he went along, Morris recited the twenty-third psalm 'The Lord is my shepherd' which Andrea translated for the benefit of the German sailors. Just before they continued with the final burial, Jervaulx gave a benediction in Latin and blessed the canvas sheeting with drops from a phial of holy water. He even intoned, in English, with Captain Morris, the Grace. Then, one by one, the weighted bundles were dropped overboard and the German sailors fired a volley into the air over the stern. Brautsch saluted Captain Morris and said 'Thank-you Captain. May the next time we meet be in peacetime when we can be friends. For now, your ship is free to go to Mombasa. We have taken prisoner thirty military personnel as well as the most severely wounded. All will be transferred in due course to a supply vessel bound for France. The wounded will be exchanged under a Red Cross agreement. Your ship, so my engineer tells me, is capable of about five knots. I'm afraid we've destroyed all your wireless sets except a small emergency one in the number three lifeboat. However when we are clear of the area, my captain will transmit a signal to the Allies giving your position as you steer towards Mombasa. You must go there Captain Morris. It is your nearest port.' Then Brautsch put out his right hand and to his surprise Morris found himself shaking it. Morris then replied 'You did your worst at the start of this day but now you've done your best. I thank you for not destroying my ship and all on board her. So long, mister' and with that he turned round and stumped off to his position on the bridge whilst behind him Brautsch and the rest of his men together with Andrea and Elfrida clambered down to their waiting launches.

Even as Morris reached his bridge position he could see the last of the battlecruiser's boats being hoisted aboard and the warship begin to move. 'Good luck for Mombasa' came the signal as she drew away. On *Aspen Castle*'s decks some of the passengers were even waving at her grateful that they were not only afloat but still free to journey to the safety of Mombasa. It had been an extraordinary day for all of them and all who could, stayed at the rails of *Aspen Castle* watching *Dresden* become smaller and smaller until at last, with the sun hovering over the horizon they watched her vanish. Almost as quickly as she'd arrived in those dawn hours of that self-same day.

On board *Llandaff*, the beleaguered Royal Navy men warily watched a big tanker as she sailed slowly round them at a distance never nearer than ten miles. After an hour they caught sight of her signalling to as yet an unseen ship.

'Bet that'll be the blasted *Dresden*' snarled MacLeod. 'Coming to finish us off. Well, no heroics this time.' Like Gunner Mills, whom MacLeod had warmly congratulated for his brilliant shooting of the one shell that had devastated *Skua*, the captain had been treated by the ship's doctor for his left arm wound, it now being held by a sling so as to reduce the pain. Coxswain Chief Petty Officer Alfred Erskine stood next to him with a bloodied bandage around his forehead.

'It's 'er alright' Erskine muttered as the shape of *Dresden* became bigger, clearer and closer to the hapless *Llandaff*.

'Have we any means of signalling Jerry?' asked MacLeod.

'Aye sir, ah've got mi' big 'and lamp.'

'Well use it. Tell them we're surrendering and ask them to assist with our survivors. Tell them we're sinking as well. I fear our pumps aren't keeping pace with the water sloshing around and in us. The explosion from their raider did us more underwater damage than expected.'

A lookout on *Dresden* shouted that the British cruiser was signalling but couldn't make out the message.

'Fire a shell from our forward port secondary gun.' ordered Reitz.

'Let's see if that produces a "White Ensign" or a white flag' as he watched the almost stationary British cruiser.

The shell crashed into the sea some fifty yards from *Llandaff*'s starboard side.

'Seems that's tellin' us something, sir,' growled Erskine. MacLeod didn't want to but knew that he had to give the order. What remained of the White Ensign still fluttering from the stump of the cruiser's mainmast had to be hauled down or else *Dresden*'s next shells would literally blow his ship away.

'Have we a white flag?'

'Aye sir, ah knows where ther's one doin' nothing useful' grunted Erskine who turned and hurried off the bridge. With his heavy boots ringing out loud, he raced along the deck, clambered down a short set of steps and unceremoniously kicked open the door of the cabin where Rear-Admiral Hallett still cowered like a frightened dog, whimpering to himself. Ignoring the wretched man, Erskine whipped off the white tablecloth scattering the broken crockery on it to the floor and charged out again. Hallett hadn't even noticed him. He just stared up vacantly. A broken man. Utterly useless. Out of his mind.

''Ere we are sir' blurted Erskine, as panting for breath he arrived back on *Llandaff*'s broken bridge. ''Ave they fired any more bricks at us?'

'No.'

'Well, t'Admiral didn't object. Mind it's first decent thing he's ever done since comin' aboard. Where shall we fly 'is Lordship's offerin' sir?'

'Drape it over the edge of the bridge' said MacLeod. 'Perhaps they'll see it.'

From *Dresden* they could see a new tiny patch of white fluttering from the bridge. The remnants of the 'White Ensign' were also observed to have been lowered.

Reitz snapped 'Send this signal – "Stop your ship. Assemble crew on deck".'

Erskine reported this to MacLeod who told his coxswain to reply in the affirmative, to say that *Llandaff* was slowly sinking and that could the *Dresden* send boats to take off the men.

Then they saw the German battlecruiser edge much closer but her big gun turrets were trained directly on them.

'Can't trust us. Think that Gunner Mills is going to have another go. Signal them again to hurry up.' MacLeod spoke in a harsh whisper as *Llandaff*'s stern lurched heavily as a swell in the otherwise calm ocean swashed against the weakening metal plates.

From the German ship they could clearly see the plight of the British cruiser. *Dresden* closed within two hundred yards and began to lower her boats. *Berengia*, already filled with many rescued survivors, also came closer and then began to lower her boats as well.

The first boat to reach *Llandaff* contained not just Brautsch and his usual boarding crew but nurses Andrea and Elfrida, with Jervaulx acting as an extra assistant to the expected medical needs of *Llandaff*'s survivors.

Erskine saluted Brautsch as he clambered on to the cruiser's decks. 'My skipper's on the bridge, mister. Follow me.'

Brautsch hurried after the bandaged burly coxswain. MacLeod saluted the German as he clambered on to the bridge 'I am Captain MacLeod of HMS *Llandaff*. I surrender this ship to you but we're sinking albeit slowly. Can your men be as quick as possible to help evacuate my wounded?'

'We've already started. I have professional medical aid personnel doing the job already.'

To their surprise, dazed crewmen of *Llandaff* heard not only a voice in English but a woman ask them 'Where are your wounded?'

A midshipman stepped forward 'This way, Madam Fraulein, this way' and motioned for Andrea to follow him. In the cruiser's wardroom lay nearly sixty men on makeshift beds and stretchers.

Hurriedly the German sailors with fit members of *Llandaff*'s crew began to lift them and take them up on to the deck. Many willing hands soon lowered them into the boats that shuttled them across to *Dresden* where Lebers and his assistants then took them down to the battlecruiser's sick-berth. Here the facilities for caring for them were far better than the hell that had been their experience on board the now sinking *Llandaff* during her day-long ordeal.

Brautsch, standing near the side of the cruiser from where the wounded were being trans-shipped, turned to MacLeod and asked 'By the way, is your Admiral still on board or has he been killed?'

'Aye, mister, the sod's still on board. It were his tablecloth what we waved at you lot' came the terse reply from MacLeod in his broad vernacular that Brautsch again just about understood.

'Where is he? Show me!'

'Can't see the point. Might as well let the bastard drown when this old girl goes to Davy Jones.'

Brautsch didn't understand what Davy Jones had to do with the Admiral or *Llandaff* but he persisted 'Where is the Admiral?'

'Erskine, you show our German pal where his bleedin' Lordship is.'

Erskine led the way to the cabin where Brautsch could see the huddled shape of the cowering Admiral.

'There, that's what you've come for. 'Im. Brainless clot!'

Erskine fair spat out the words. Brautsch flicked a finger and two burly German sailors yanked the whimpering Hallett to his feet.

There was no resistance. No bluster. No arrogance. Just meek compliance. It was as if he couldn't work out who the two men grabbing at his arms and hoisting him to his feet were, nor the fact that one of them spoke to the other in German, a language he didn't understand. Even as they marched him along the corridor to the upper deck he simply complied with the direction in which he was being propelled but suddenly when at the top of the rope leading down to a boat ladder he tried to break free. Realisation swept over him. These men weren't British sailors. They were vile Nazis. He began to scream 'Bloody Huns!' but before he could utter anything else, one of his guards hit him across the face and the force of this blow sent Hallett over the side, the other guard releasing his grip. The Admiral crashed into the water alongside the waiting boat. The German sailors in that boat leaned over and hauled the spluttering soaked man into the boat when he again tried to break free. Only when the crushing blow of a rifle butt hit him across the back of his head did he fall silent, collapsing on to the stern-sheets in an untidy sprawl.

Just ten minutes later as the sinking cruiser's stern dipped under the surface, the boat with Brautsch, Andrea, Elfrida, Jervaulx and the last of the wounded as well as Captain MacLeod and CPO Erskine on board, motored away from the side of *Llandaff*.

In the gathering darkness, illumined by the afterglow of the last few signs of the setting sun, *Llandaff*'s bows came clear of the water. Then, tilting slightly to port, the cruiser sank stern first, increasing speed as her after section filled rapidly with the encroaching waters. Loose machinery and other assorted debris began to break free within the dying warship and MacLeod on hearing the death rattles of his beloved command, suddenly stood up and gave as smart as a salute that he could muster, tears welling into his eyes and then streaming down his cheeks. 'You did your best old girl' he said quite clearly and then he could restrain his sobbing no longer. Andrea stood up and put a blanket around him and gently encouraged the grief stricken man to sit down. 'Aye, lass, she was a tough old bird and many a good man has gone down with her as well, includin' mi best pal, the Chief Engineer.'

Dresden's searchlights were lighting up the scene as *Llandaff*'s bows dipped under gurgling and bubbling as they did so in the water around them. Darkness was falling quickly and Reitz was in a hurry to get away after his mercy missions.

Brautsch led MacLeod and Erskine up to the bridge where, despite his tiredness, Reitz saluted them and then shook both men by the hand. 'You are both brave men. I salute you.'

'Thankyou, captain' responded MacLeod 'thankyou for coming just in time to rescue my surviving crew even though earlier in t'day you did thi' best ter sink us!'

Reitz winced at the vernacular twang and smiled. 'Yes captain and maybe one day, if the roles are reversed, the same courtesy will be given to us if an Allied warship sinks my ship.' He looked directly at MacLeod.

'Tha' wants ter know summat else. Like who sank your upstart cocky armed raider, eh?' perceived *Llandaff*'s captain.

'Maybe, Captain MacLeod, although by the inference in your voice it is not hard to guess. But first, you said just in time! I'm sorry for the delay. We were detained by the *Aspen Castle*.' MacLeod frowned. 'No, no captain! We haven't sunk her. She is at this moment sailing for Mombasa. Her badly wounded, like yours are in our Sick Berth. My second engineer and his men helped to give running repairs to her engines. She can make about five knots. My padré helped at the burial of her dead. And –' here Reitz paused as if the words were difficult to say and then continued '– and all this despite minor damage to this ship when a torpedo fired by a brave destroyer called *Tintagel* blew up alongside us. Not enough to seriously damage us but enough to cause us to revise our future strategy. No, what I was really angry about was that here was a large civilian ship, the biggest merchantmen in the convoy, mixed in with troopships and other supply vessels all carrying war materials. Please, I must know, why? Was Rear-Admiral Hallett really responsible for the disposition of the ships?'

'Bloody Hallett. Pity he didn't go down with poor old *Cocos* yer know, the Mauritius-class cruiser that one of your U-boats copped off Madagascar. Course it were his idea to stick *Aspen Castle* in t'front. You still got 'im on board? Well, I tells thee, chuck the bugger overboard.'

Reitz again winced inwardly at the vehemence of *Llandaff*'s captain who had just seen his own ship go down.

'I seem to have struck a sore point. It is my intention to question Rear-Admiral Hallett when he recovers. You see we thought that *Aspen Castle* was the major troopship in the convoy. That is why we tried to stop her even before dealing with the battleship. By the way we have the battleship's captain on board but not the *Tintagel*'s. That brave man and all but a handful, which we rescued, went down with his ship. I know what it's like to be sunk. *Warspite* and her destroyers sank my ship when she went down off Narvik.' Reitz stopped as if remembering the sight of his destroyer sinking and his own desperate swim for the nearby shore in the cold icy waters of that fjord.

'You see, Captain MacLeod, I do know what it is like to lose a ship due to the apparent incompetence of others higher up the chain of command.' Again the German paused, a momentary tired glaze coming over his face. 'Now, one more question to which I think I know the answer. How did your ship sink the *Skua*?'

'You mean the arrogant disguised merchant raider flying dirty great big swastikas?'

'Yes, that ship. Largish, tall, black funnel.'

'Aye, that were 'er. Well, she came up to us to within about a mile. No signalling. Just had her guns and torpedo tubes trained on us, like. Why she didna' finish us off at a more extreme range I canna' say. P'raps wanted ter mek sure, like.'

'Go on. I can understand quite well your Scottish-cum Yorkshire dialect. I have spent quite some time in both areas in the United Kingdom.'

'Well, she came up close to us. About a mile or so. Slowed right down. We feared the worst. She seemed to be toying with us. What she didn't know, nor I for that matter, was that one of our four-inch guns was still capable of firing a shot and more ter point, Gunner Mills were itching ter fire a shell at 'er like.'

'Yes.'

'Well, without orders from anyone, he carefully sighted 'is gun and pulled the firing lever. Yon shell hit your bleedin' raider an' up she went like a big Roman Candle. Must 'ave 'it her torpedo tubes or ammo stored on deck. Anyway she sank right quick and if there were any survivors we could do 'nowt about 'em seein' predicament we was in. Not that I thinks there were any like.'

'No, if she blew up, there probably weren't. Thanks for that information. What does intrigue me Captain MacLeod is that you speak with a predominant Yorkshire accent with a slight Scottish lilt yet your name if I'm not mistaken, is of a strong Scottish clan. You see, I spent some time at Aberdeen University. Do you mind telling me why?' Despite his tiredness and the loss of his ship and many of his crew, MacLeod was beginning to warm to the sincerity of the German captain. Strangely enough, before he could reply, Erskine butted in. 'Well Captain Reitz, Mi' skipper's grandad were a Scottish fisherman what visited Scarborough and took a fancy to a local lass. Stayed and bought his own boat and Cap'n MacLeod's dad were born theear. Then when his dad grew up he married and Cap'n MacLeod was a result of their union. I were t'dad of Mrs MacLeod's sister. You see, me and Cap'n MacLeod is cousins, like. Well 'e went off ter Hull and met a lass whose parents lived in Barnsley. She were a typist at the Merchant Navy Training School. When first war came, 'e were skipper of an Hull trawler that were given a gun, a Royal Navy Skipper an' off she sailed to protect our East Coast convoys. I were chief bosun. So we is both back-door Navy men. Anyway t'skipper were killed when we tangled in t'channel wi' some of your destroyers and Captain MacLeod took over. When t'war ended, Navy kept 'im on like and bit by bit 'e went up t'ladder. Me. I stays right wi' 'im, as a CPO Then when this 'ere war started 'e were appointed ter *Llandaff* an' of course, I follows 'im. So we is 'ere, like.'

'Thankyou, Chief Petty Officer,' gasped Reitz, amazed at the speech. 'It seems strange, I know. I started the day trying to knock hell's bells out of your ship and yet here we are, as tired as can be, you telling me your family background. When I've the time, I'll return the compliment. Now I must bid you both as comfortable a night as is possible. You, Chief, will be with the other officers who we have rescued and taken prisoner. The other ranks are with many others on my big supply ship. But have no fear, Rear Admiral Hallett is in solitary confinement. In one of the ship's punishment cells. He has behaved somewhat irrationally since capture and for his own sake we felt it would be better if he was by himself. Goodnight!' Reitz saluted them both, clicked his heels and motioned for the armed escort to lead both men down to their quarters.

Quietly Reitz gave his orders. Twenty-two knots speed for a meeting with *Olaf* in a remote part of the Indian Ocean. *Arabian Nights* was to off load her prisoners on to the captured freighter and then to catch up with *Dresden* at the rendezvous. The freighter, with a large crew and with much of her military cargo dumped overboard was to sail with *Berengia* for Occupied France. It would be a difficult haul for both ships but as luck would have it, the freighter did have enough fuel for a twelve-knot run to the South Atlantic where a supply tanker would top up both her and *Berengia*'s tanks. Should an Allied warship intercept them, both ships had instructions not to offer any resistance. With around twelve hundred prisoners, Reitz didn't want any more addition to the enormous casualties, in ships and men, that had occurred during that most eventful and for many, horrendous day.

Outwardly and if observed from a distance, the Royal Navy's base at Simonstown carried on as normal all that same day even to the extent of a naval band playing 'Sunset' as the colours were lowered at sundown. The sentries as always at the entrance gates checking vehicles in and out. Sailors in uniform saluting as they passed each other going around the base. Chief Petty Officers, as they seemed to do the world over were bawling out orders at the top of their voices no matter what navy they represented and at Simonstown that day, at least that naval order of protocol carried on being observed to its fullest on the parade grounds of the training base as new recruits were being marched up and down.

However if the visitor had been able to eavesdrop into the main operations room he or she would have been aware that the conversation and general order was dominated by one topic and only one topic.

That topic was the German battlecruiser KM *Dresden*. Ever since being made first aware of her initial stunning attack on *Llandaff*, the personnel at the base's operations centre had collected more and more data from the desperate wireless signals coming from the stricken fleeing vessels of the troopship convoy.

First *Llandaff*'s signals had ceased to transmit and soon after *Resolve*'s, half way through a long signal. Other smaller warships and then the troopships. One by one. 'Am being shelled.' 'Am abandoning ship.' 'Am being fired on.' 'Sinking.' With their position if they'd had time. Then other details. References to more than one ship firing at them.

After midday one of the Hunt-class destroyers acting as escort in company with two fleeing troopships escaping northwards for Aden sent in a long signal which filled in some of the missing gaps of the traumatic events.

And all the time Admiral Sir Bernard Collins had been thinking of one theme all the time. The sheer audacity of the German naval attack led by, without doubt, their leading protagonist – George Reitz. And his ship. KM *Dresden*. How well it had gone for the German ship. And how he was left to try and neutralise his brilliance. But with what? HMNS *Wellington* cleared Colombo just as the news of *Dresden*'s attack reached Simonstown but even at full speed. which wasn't likely, as the heavy cruiser was long over due for a refit, she would take at least another thirty hours to reach the area by which time any German ships would have long since disappeared into the vastness of the Indian Ocean.

So what else?

RAF mechanics were patching up a Sunderland flying boat at Mombasa hoping for a dawn fly-off the next day. What aircraft they had at Aden were inadequate in range and certainly couldn't mount a search for the German ships. How many had been involved? *Dresden* and possibly one, or two others. What had they disposed of? It made very grim reading. One R-class battleship, one B-class heavy cruiser, one armed merchant cruiser, at least four of the eight smaller escorts, four or five of the troopships, five of the slower merchant ships and worst of all, the large personnel ship *Aspen Castle*. None of the missing ships were transmitting despite frequent requests from Aden, Mombasa or Simonstown.

The loss of life just simply could not be contemplated. Ten thousand perhaps? Maybe more? It depended on efforts at getting into life boats, the speed at which the ships sank and even as to whether the Germans had made any attempt at rescuing survivors. All that day Collins asked so many questions to himself, to his aides or to other staff members but as the days events unfolded and were pieced together with the accuracy of a sixty percent completed jigsaw. Collins wearily resigned himself to the basic base-line fact that Reitz and his battlecruiser for the first time ever by a Kreigsmarine unit in what was already a harsh, protracted war, had scored a major triumph over theoretically stronger Royal Navy opponents. In theory, *Resolve* and *Llandaff* together with at least three of the escort vessels should have been able to turn the German raider away or if it had come to a gun conflict, should have been able to overwhelm *Dresden* by the sheer weight of shell. Instead, thanks partly to Hallett's poor disposition of his warship escorts but mainly to the sheer brilliance, or so it seemed, of the tactics employed by Reitz, the Royal Navy was having to come to terms with perhaps its darkest day so far of the war. Off Norway in June of the previous year it had lost carrier *Glorious* and two destroyers in a surface action with the two large German battle-cruisers; three months earlier in this year as Collins so well knew, battlecruiser *Hood* had blown up in the action by the *Bismarck* but this, well, it was beyond belief. Not only the warship losses but the troops and the troopships. And then, the *Aspen Castle*.

Collins felt the apparent loss of the big liner and its mainly civilian passengers just as keenly as the loss of *Resolve* and the other naval vessels.

He stared up at the clock ticking away above the main chart showing the Indian and Atlantic Oceans. Nearly midnight. Just about eighteen hours since the opening of the day's momentous events. A messenger came up to him as he stared again for the umpteenth time at the map.

'Sir.'

'Yes, what is it?' Collins was tired. Irritable. And now this. Another message. Was *Dresden* still sinking ships? There'd been no distress calls for almost ten hours.

'A message for you, sir.' The rating handed a note. It was from the wireless centre. Sealed envelope. 'For the Admiral' hastily scribbled on the front. He tore the flap open. The typed script seemed to leap out at him.

FROM KM *DRESDEN* TO NAVAL BASE, SIMONSTOWN. HAVE VICE ADMIRAL HALLETT PLUS CAPTAINS *RESOLVE* AND *LLANDAFF* PLUS TWO DESTROYERS ON BOARD. ALSO SEVERELY INJURED SURVIVORS OF THESE SHIPS AND *ASPEN CASTLE*. SAFE PASSAGE GIVEN TO *ASPEN CASTLE*. TO MOMBASA. REITZ. COMMANDING OFFICER.'

Collins read it twice. Then he turned to the rating and snapped, 'How long ago was this sent? Did they get a bearing?'

'Don't know sir. Shall I send for the wireless operator?'

'Yes. At once!'

'Aye, aye, sir.'

When the operator appeared, Collins asked the same question. The reply was that the message had occurred only ten minutes previously from a ship guessed at approximately one hundred miles east of the convoy battle.

Collins went over to the big operations chart on the central table. Three men were leaning over it. They stood to attention as Collins bent over the chart and moved the marker-ship, letter 'D' with the swastika over it. He pushed it across to the right.

'There gentlemen is where *Dresden* could be. If she continues heading east or even south-east at say twenty knots by dawn she'll be approximately here' – he pushed the marker into the appropriate place – 'Now then, let's assume *Wellington* is here at dawn. Gentlemen, if *Wellington* launches her Walrus will it be able to find our elusive little Jerry war-monger, eh?'

'Shall we signal her with the approximate co-ordinates?'

'Yes. At once. To launch aircraft at dawn.'

Twenty minutes later, Collins received the script of *Wellington*'s coded reply. 'Sorry chaps. Your German shot my bird down ages ago and no-one has given us a replacement.'

Collins grimaced at the message. Of course *Wellington*'s Walrus had been shot down. Two months ago. He should have remembered. Damn the Admiralty for their inefficiency. He was very tired and feeling utterly despondent. It was time for bed.

Perhaps he'd be able to snatch a few hours sleep.

Next dawn *Dresden* was more or less where Collins had thought she would be although he didn't know it, heading steadily south-south-east at twenty knots on a gradually curving course to a rendezvous with *Olaf*. During the hours of darkness all of her exhausted crew were able to get some sleep after the exertions of the previous day although in the Sick Berth, Lebers, the two nurses, Jervaulx and three attendants were the last to retreat to sleep. Operating, injecting, bandaging, calming and watching over their patients, German and Allied alike, as each one of them came to terms with their wounds and predicament, in some cases knowing, that for instance that a limb would never work properly again or had even been removed. After twenty hours since the first salvo from *Dresden*'s main guns had shattered the atmosphere of that now so long ago dawn, Elfrida succumbed to the need for sleep. Two hours later Andrea, the last to give in, lay down on a cot adjacent to the main ward and closed her eyes. As she did so Helmut Brautsch came into the dim-lit ward area, went to her cot side and murmured gently in her ear, 'You are an angel. Your efforts are really appreciated by all of us.'

Dimly Andrea heard the words and then came more aroused when she felt the pressure of lips on her face. She made no attempt to withdraw her head for she raised her right arm around his neck and whispered into his ear as she pressed gently up to his neck 'Thank-you my love. You know Helmut that I'm falling in love with you. I don't know why, you're supposed to be my enemy. You all are. But I don't see it that way despite all this pain and hurt around me. Somehow when this dreadful war ends I know that we shall be together, if not before. I do not want to lose you. Not now. Not ever.'

'Thankyou my liebling. You must now sleep. We shall be together. I will not lose you for I love you as well.'

'Yes. All of us will be brought together. Friends again. Even the British prisoners here are grateful for being rescued. They can't believe that we are trying to get them as well again as is possible even on this, to them, an enemy warship. They thought that they were going to be abandoned.'

'Rest love, please. You really must. I'll be back as and when my duties allow me time to come and see you!' Gently he eased himself upright, released his hand from hers, kissed her on the forehead and turned, leaving a room of comfort, fresh hope and yes, even love. The first two feelings as a result of the efforts of all the medical staff inspired as they were by the two English nurses. The latter feeling because of the growing bond between himself and one of those nurses. A mousey blonde-haired gentle lass called Andrea.

By the next morning despite all the attentions of the medical staff, three of the wounded in that Sick Berth succumbed to their injuries. One of them was one of the German sailors caught by the torpedo blast from *Tintagel*, the other two being civilians, one a woman, from the *Aspen Castle*. Padré Jervaulx conducted a burial service aided by Angus MacLeod. Reitz asked Wills-Wilson and the two destroyer captains to stand with him on the aft deck of the battlecruiser for the short service. In tribute to the liner's former passengers, the ship's band played the sole English sea tune they knew 'Hearts of Oak' as the two weighted bundles were dropped over the side. A sad German sailors' tune was played for the lone *Dresden* crewman as he also descended to the deep. Reitz held his right arm in the German Naval salute and the four British captains likewise saluted as the bodies were committed. So also did CPO Erskine.

Reitz then saluted the British officers and had just started to return to the bridge when one of the ship's guards, with a petty officer, came rushing up, skidded to a halt, threw up a hasty salute and said 'Sir, the British Admiral!'

'Yes, what about him?'

'Sir, he's hung himself!'

'Show me, now!'

'Sir, this way!'

They found Hallett hanging from the cell-door with his braces looped through the bars and tied tightly round his neck. Doctor Lebers had already been summoned and felt the man's pulse.

'No life in it, sir.'

Reitz asked the guard, as to the circumstances.

'It must have been after we had served him his breakfast, sir. He sort of looked up at us and seemed alright. Like us orders, sir, we checked on 'im every half-hour. Well, we did but on us check at just about the time the burial service was ending, it were to see 'im like this. We rang for Dr. Lebers and I came running to tell you, sir.'

'Better cut him down and ask Padré Jervaulx to prepare for another burial. However, –' this remark to Hiltzern who'd also been summoned '– this time we'll not reduce speed. I don't want to lose any more time getting clear of the possible Allied warships and aircraft searching for us. We also need to make our rendezvous with *Olaf* on time.'

Admiral Wilhelm Canaris was feeling very pleased. At last his creation, his ship, had made a massive impact in the war at sea. Although the Allies had been reluctant to release full details of the disasters that had befallen the troopships convoy it was obvious, that despite the apparent loss of *Skua* and only the briefest message from *Dresden*, that at least half the convoy had been sunk and that the loss of troops to the Allies, as well as war material, would take quite some time to recoup.

His ship. His battlecruiser. KM *Dresden*. Not that Goebbels and his side-kicks in the Propaganda Department had made much of the coup. They simply didn't understand naval warfare. They were too busy hailing the Wehrmacht's triumphal progress into the depths of the might of Soviet Russia. Perhaps he was the only senior member of the National Socialist Government of Germany who realised, despite the enormous successes of the Wehrmacht, that to attack Soviet Russia would be such a severe strain on the resources of the country. If the expected victory hadn't come by early autumn, then the successes would be reversed into a deteriorating failure of men and materials.

As yet he hadn't made public his private concerns of the direction of the war campaign but after the failure to force the United Kingdom into surrender, the attack on Russia seemed to him to be one move too far for Corporal Hitler. Canaris knew, that at any time, his own Abwehr could well be investigated by that duo of vile creeps, Himmler and Goebbels, never mind the other big oafs in the Nazi hierarchy – Goering, Bormann and their minions. Perhaps as well the failures of the Abwehr were being put to one side, partly due to the successes of the Wehrmacht in Russia and to a lesser extent the success of *Dresden*. It had been surprising that some members of the government had left messages of congratulations about the efforts of the battlecruiser.

He thought about the meeting only a few hours earlier he'd had with Grand Admiral Erich Raeder. The Kriegsmarine supremo had, for once, been ecstatic. At long last, a major unit of the surface fleet had been able to justify the massive financial outlay spent on building and crewing it. *Bismarck* and *Graf Spee* had briefly shone before they'd been sunk via Royal Navy actions. The two bigger battle-cruisers had veered away when faced with Royal Navy ships of similar or just below par strengths and were now sulking in north-western French harbours. So far heavy cruiser *Hipper*'s career was at best enigmatic with her engines being so problematical.

The same could be said about *Prinz Eugen* even though she'd avoided the net thrown by the British after the *Bismarck* debacle. Only panzerschiffe *Admiral Scheer* had been able to attack Allied commerce successfully during a five month cruise but the efforts of all of them combined were not even matching that of the career of the rejuvenated *Dresden*. She was, at sea, the Royal Navy's Public Enemy Number One. Raeder had listed the ships that *Dresden* had now sunk. A battleship, three heavy cruisers, two light cruisers, three armed merchant cruisers and at least ten escort vessels. Never mind the troopships and merchantmen. Over two hundred thousand tons of Allied shipping. No wonder Raeder had been beaming when up to this point in time, the Kriegsmarine's surface fleet had been little more than a serious threat on paper but not really in full practice. Now *Dresden* had shaken her opponents. More than likely they'd pull out all the stops to catch her so as Raeder agreed, it was time for the raider to disappear, give her crew a rest and then to possibly return to home waters in the winter months early in the next year.

The echoes of the dawn bugle at Simonstown had faded away long since the second morning after the convoy battle. Admiral Collins, having breakfasted lightly on toast and tea, took up his position in the main chart-room. Fifty-two hours since *Llandaff*'s first desperate warnings of *Dresden*'s attack. Only now was any encouraging news coming through to the base. The five surviving troop-ships had all safely berthed at either Mombasa or Aden. So also had three of the merchantmen. Two others, damaged, were in range of the Aden escorts having detoured first eastwards and then in the cover of darkness northwards and by good fortune had escaped in their flight for safety.

But what of the German warship or her accompanying protagonists? Nothing substantial had emerged from the belated Royal Air Force searches from Mombasa or Aden. One of the Sunderlands, hastily repaired, had even found survivors clinging to wreckage. Landing nearby, the aircraft's crew launched their dinghy to eventually rescue twenty-three survivors. Further searches discovered a number of lifeboats making for the Kenyan coast and rescue vessels left Mombasa and the other small ports to pick up these survivors.

At the edge of its search area one of the aircraft sighted *Berengia* but on seeing a British flag flew off without getting close enough for fear of running out of fuel. The air-crew assumed that there would be merchantmen in the area running for port. The ship they had seen had been steaming quite fast as if trying to distance itself from the battle area.

None of the aircraft had yet sighted the *Aspen Castle*.

London naturally sent Collins a stream of messages, not just relating to the disaster that had overtaken Hallett's convoy but that the next convoy would be guarded by the battlecruiser *Repulse*. This policy it was hoped would deter *Dresden* from attacking it – if she was still in the Indian Ocean by the time the ships would arrive. One of Admiral Pound's better ideas thought Collins. Poor old duffer. Shouldn't really be the First Sea Lord. Still at least the gist of messages laid the blame fairly and squarely on Hallett's shoulders. It was obvious that he'd ignored all the advice given to him by Collins and his actions had led to the debacle of the convoy's defensive tactics.

Then a near miracle.

As Collins sipped a mid-morning coffee still pondering over the inadequacies of the convoy's defence and the air search for both survivors as well as the German ships, a messenger came up to him, saluted and handed him yet another flimsy from the wireless room.

Collins read it briefly, smiled and handed it to his flag-lieutenant, Arthur Carlson.

'It's *Aspen Castle*. Apparently a civilian aircraft, commandeered by the RAF has just sighted the liner slowly limping for Mombasa. Speed about three knots. Says she's information about *Dresden*.'

Carlson raised his eyebrows as he fully read the message.

'It says she's damaged.'

'But it doesn't say how badly.'

'No sir. The liner's due in Mombasa in about seventy hours. She's currently about two hundred or so miles north-east of the port. Here.' Carlson jabbed a finger at the map.

'Warn the local escorts. Ask them, no, send them an order from me that two of them must sail at once to bring her in safely. Now!' Collins paused – 'can we signal the liner?'

'I'll check via Mombasa.'

Five minutes later Carlson was back.

'Well?' queried Collins.

'She has no wireless. All messages were relayed to the aircraft by hand-lamp.'

Collins frowned. '*Dresden* could be either far away or possibly limping south to try and sail round us here. Step up all air and sea patrols. We must catch her. Meanwhile we will both go to Mombasa. When's the next flight?'

Carlson, having anticipated such a request, was soon ready with the answer.

'I've already booked. Two seats, sir, on the next RAF flight to Kenya. Goes tomorrow morning. We should reach Mombasa about twenty-four hours ahead of the liner.'

'Good man. I don't suppose you know the name of the liner's captain? We shall need a first-hand account from him.'

'Yes sir. He's a rather craggy individual. A mercantile equivalent of *Llandaff*'s captain. His name is Morris, he's sixty years old, he came from a ship-builders in Selby and then trained as a deckhand on a Hull trawler. One of Union Castle's top captains now. He rose through the ranks by hard graft and stern discipline. Can be a bit blunt, so I've heard.'

'Mmm.' Collins dug out his pipe and filled the bowl. As he tamped the tobacco into place he grunted 'Well, we'd better not upset him too much but if he can fill us in how badly *Dresden* is damaged it could help us in knowing where she's heading. My guess is for a quiet spot in the Indian Ocean before attempting the breakthrough for Germany.' He stopped to light his pipe and satisfied that it was going well enough, he continued. 'But then of course Reitz might take his ship to Japan and try to provoke a *Goeben* incident.'

Carlson pursed his lips '*Goeben* sir?'

'Ah yes, bit before your time young man.' Collins smiled but then continued 'She was a German battlecruiser under the command of an Admiral Souchon in the Mediterranean at the start of the Great War. Souchon evaded a plethora of British battlecruisers, armoured cruisers, light cruisers, destroyers – the lot – and reached Constantinople. Within days *Goeben* was incorporated into the Turkish Navy and Souchon handled his ship so well that it was partly due to him that the Turks threw their lot in with Germany. Now if Reitz goes to Japan who knows what the result will be. We know from intelligence that German merchantmen and some captured Allied merchantmen with German crews have been using Japanese ports to refuel or stock up with goods. A notable one was the ex-Norwegian tanker Ole Jacob that exchanged her cargo of aviation oil for one of fuel oil and then set sail – no doubt to refuel raiders, blockade runners, U-boats and the like before running for Western France.'

'So do we inform Singapore?' asked Carlson.

'Of course, and the Dutch in Java. They've a few cruisers which with our ships could block off the entrance to the South China Sea.'

'What ships do we have?'

'Not much. A few old 'C' and 'D' cruisers, some clapped-out destroyers and about half-a-dozen gunboats but then, Carlson, you should have known.'

'Well, sir, I did but we really need something to stop *Dresden*'

'Keep this under your hat, Carlson, but London is moving, albeit slowly. A new Far Eastern Task Force may be formed in the near future to discourage not only Reitz or anymore of his pals but also the Japanese from any hopes of jumping on to the Axis bandwagon.'

'Too late to stop *Dresden* if she does go eastward, sir.'

'Any reports of her possible support ships?' Collins asked, switching tracks.

'Nothing we can verify. Ships in South African air range have all been checked out sir. We have three South African frigates patrolling up to a two-hundred mile limit off-shore but they're widely spread out and can't approach every ship in those waters but with aircraft we hope that they'll intercept most of the ships rounding the Cape.'

'Mmm. Well, I suppose we'd better get ready to fly up to Nairobi' and with that, Collins took another look at the large chart, jabbing his right forefinger on to the centre of the Indian Ocean. 'Now then, Herr Kapitan Reitz, just where the bloody hell have you gone? Eh!'

A South African *Wellington* bomber on her air-search actually flew over *Berengia* but fortunately for the big supply ship she had only a few of her prisoners on deck. Theider knew that to give a lot of prisoners exercise on deck in broad daylight before he could escape into the wastes of the South Atlantic would be tantamount to exposing his ship to the Allies as to what his mission was really about. With over a thousand prisoners on board he knew that to keep them underneath the main deck all the time could probably lead to a potential riot so Theider decided to allow ten of them at a time, for ten minutes in rotation with two armed guards in attendance. If and when aircraft flew over the ship the few men seen strolling on the deck would be seen as little more than spare crew.

The *Wellington*'s own air-crew did see the big merchantmen and also the 'Red Ensign' flying at her stern. They didn't fly too closely to investigate but continued with their patrol waggling the wings of the bomber as they flew northwards, the pilot noting the merchantman in the aircraft's log but did not report the matter immediately to base. After all, his instructions were to find a German battle-cruiser, not a merchantman sailing on what appeared to be her normal legitimate business of trade.

Another aircraft the next day took off from Cape Town. On board were Admiral Collins and Flag-Lieutenant Carlson. A long tedious flight to Johannesburg and thence to Nairobi. The final stage, at the end of the day, was in an RAF Hampden, converted to carry passengers that flew the two naval men to Mombasa. Early next morning the two officers were driven to the dockside to await the arrival of the *Aspen Castle* which had anchored off the harbour in the early hours to await the dawn, a tug and the pilot.

As she slowly entered the harbour, curious onlookers who'd heard of her imminent arrival were gathered on or near the harbour walls to watch the obviously damaged liner limp to her berth. Collins registered some sense of shock when he saw the badly twisted central upperworks blackened and distorted by what must have been a fierce fire. To his amazement lining the rails on either side of the damaged superstructure he could see the passengers waving and shouting to the onlookers, no doubt highly relieved that the ship had finally made it safely to port.

As the lines were thrown to the waiting longshoremen for them to haul round the securing bollards, a gaggle of eager pressmen surged forward waving their passes and all seemingly demanding an exclusive right to an interview but their efforts to board the liner, once a gangplank had been positioned, were thwarted by a solid line of armed Kenyan police who quickly formed a double cordon, acting on the request of the harbour master as well as the naval authorities.

From their clearly marked Royal Navy car, Collins and Carlson emerged near the gangplank accompanied by the self-same harbour master who quickly ushered the two naval officers, resplendent in their smart white tropical uniforms and peaked caps, through the cordon and up the boarding plank to the scarred deck of the liner.

Morris hurried down from the bridge having received a tersely worded message from the increasingly harassed harbour-master. 'Expect top Royal Naval visitors as soon as you berth.' The liner's captain didn't particularly like the top brass types especially from the Royal Navy. The last time he'd met them, at Simonstown, the Admirals there had assured all the merchant ship captains that the convoy was about to start its last and safest leg of the long haul – and as Morris thought 'See what a shambles has happened since. What was it that the convoy had lost? – the battleship, escorts, troopships, merchantmen and countless personnel.'

He wasn't in a good mood as he stood near the gangplank glaring down at the two Royal Naval officers approaching him. 'Morning. I've nowt against t'*Dresden.* Only your lot fer not protectin' us like,' he gruffed out making no effort to salute his visitors.

Collins however did salute *Aspen Castle*'s master and introduced himself and his flag lieutenant. 'Can we talk? We need to know as much as you can tell us about the German battlecruiser. It's a matter of urgency!'

'You'd best come to mi' cabin' grunted Morris and gestured to the two naval officers to follow him. They noted the scarred decks, cabins and central superstructure; the flaked and charred paint on the three big funnels; the gaping holes where *Dresden*'s shells had struck which had only been hastily patched up in parts with bits of plywood. Even the stench of the long-extinguished fire still pervaded the area that they walked past and didn't fully disappear even after they'd been ushered into the captain's cabin within the main bridge superstructure.

Morris's steward had a pot of tea with digestive biscuits waiting for the visitors. Morris never offered his visitors anything stronger or more substantial. He was strictly teetotal and short on what to him were unnecessary provisions.

After stirring his cup wishing that a tot of gin was also on offer, Collins started quite bluntly with the question 'Well, Captain Morris, what was the condition of *Dresden* when she left you?'

'It were bleedin' 'allett's fault' came the non-committal response.

'Captain Morris, I repeat, what damage had been caused, if any, to the German ship?'

Morris looked at Collins with a blank stare. 'Damage? We 'ad lots of it and they then caught us up an' 'elped us ter repair some 'onnit. Like as they were sorry!' He'd lapsed quite deliberately into his broad Yorkshire vernacular. 'You see, mister, 'allett 'ad all 'is warships in't wrong place so Jerry could pick 'em off one by one. We was 'it reight early on and seein' we was ablaze like an' crippled, Jerry then left us alone cos' *Resolve* were tryin' to 'urry an' 'elp us like but she were ter slow, like, an' got torpedoed an' blew up wi' a reight big explosion an' then Jerry went off an' left us 'cos 'e were busy shootin' up all t' other ships an' then all t'action disappeared over t'orizon an we was left by 'ussens for 'ours until like some returnin' avengin' reaper 'e turns up ageean but this time we 'ung out a white flag 'cos I knew I 'ad all mi' civvies ter tek care on like so 'e stops quite close.' Morris stopped for a big breath. The words had quite simply tumbled out. Like a school-boy telling his teacher an account of a tense football game only that it wasn't a game. Ships had been sunk. Many men were killed. Drowned. Injured. But somehow Morris skated over the horror of that appalling day. He continued to stare straight at Collins. 'Nah then, weear was I? Ah yes! T'owd Jerry stopped. We'd stopped. But not our little pal. She'd been 'it reight bad by prob'ly three big shells. Been wi' us nearly all day tryin' ter repair 'is damage like we was ours. *Tintagel* – ever bin theear? Ah did once, in mi' teens. Went wi' a Cornish mate o' mine. T'owd Arthur's supposed ter 'ave 'ad 'is castle theear! An' t'owd post office. Way, it's all twisted like.' Morris was wandering. His eyes seemed to glaze as he suddenly stopped his apparently extended explanation. When he restarted the glazed look had gone. So also had most of his broad Yorkshire accent. He was back to reality.

'Well, when Jerry had stopped, our little destroyer pal came out from behind us and went as fast as it could go. About ten knots. Straight for *Dresden* who began to fire her guns as fast as fury. Little *Tintagel* was hit over and over again but just before she was overwhelmed, somehow she must have fired at least one torpedo. It blew up against the side of *Dresden* and as I later learned, this was due to grenades thrown at the torpedo. Some Germans were killed in the blast but despite that, *Dresden* still stopped, lowered boats to search for *Tintagel*'s survivors and sent other boats to come over to us.'

Collins looked at Morris who was now staring out of one of the cabin's portholes. Carlson piped in with the next sentence. 'This incident with *Tintagel* must have been very similar to when *Gloworm* attacked the *Hipper* off Norway and was sunk after damaging the German cruiser which stopped and picked up survivors of the sunken destroyer. Pity that the *Scharnhorst* didn't do the same for *Acasta*'s survivors later in that campaign.'

'Aye maybe you're right mister. You see the captain of *Tintagel* was my best mate's eldest son. The mate who before the war took me to see that Cornish village. Little did I realise then just what that name would mean to me.' A tear rolled down from the left eye of the suddenly aged, worn face of the liner's captain. He didn't even attempt to wipe it away.

'Aye, the Germans were good to us. After all that killing and shooting, they showed real humanity and let us go. Quite surprising. They even had a chaplain who helped me conduct a funeral service for all those lost, not just on our ship but also during the whole of the convoy battle. He wasn't too clever on his English but at the end he managed to say our English Grace. I know they're on the other side, as it were, but I hope that one day I can meet their captain. He'd stayed on his own ship. When they'd done their best in two hours for us, he took his ship off at quite a fair rate of knots so he couldn't have been too much damaged, now, could he?'

'I suppose not' snapped Collins, suddenly irritated by the blunt Yorkshire man. He'd heard what he wanted but also a good deal more. It was amazing that, despite the severe damage to the *Aspen Castle*, as well as the loss of all the other ships and their crews in the convoy due to the *Dresden*'s attack, the man hadn't really a bad word going at all against the German battlecruiser, her captain or her crew.

Suddenly he stood up. 'Well, thank-you Captain Morris. Come on Carlson, we must be off' and with a quick salute, left the cabin and clattered down the paint-blistered ladder to the equally blistered decks, followed hastily by a surprised Carlson who was somehow taken aback by his superior's sudden departure. So also was Morris. 'Huh, bloody naval men. No manners at all.'

His steward came in. 'Aye sir, they hasn't them 'an also they hasn't hardly touched their tea. Waste of a good cuppa'. 'Ah doubt they 'eard that they is a war on sir? You know – waste not, want not.'

Morris merely shrugged his shoulders and even as he reached his cabin door and looked down he could see that the two naval officers had already reached the quayside.

Collins was indeed in a hurry. Straight to the harbour-master's office he strode and entered with little more than a peremptory knock

'Now then man, your chart if you please, of the Indian Ocean. Come on, quickly' he ordered, snapping his fingers at the bewildered official.

Nervously Carlson piped up 'Sir, no need to ask. I've one here in my folder.'

'Well, hurry up! I must try to work out where the bloody German's taken his ship. It appears that he's hardly been damaged. You, man, any dividers? Right, now then. What's the scale? Right, mark off four days estimated sailing at say eighteen knots. Good grief! She could be trying to get round the Cape right now.'

Carlson intervened 'Or be approaching the Dutch East Indies. Or even Australia.'

'Do you have to make it even worse? You, man, what radio facilities do you have? What! Under repair! Oh! they've one at the Army's base. Right, we must get to it. How far? Two miles. Car still there. Right, come on Carlson, let's go!'

On their way, Collins snapped at Carlson. 'Come on, man, tell me again. Just what are our resources again for catching *Dresden*?'

Carlson replied at once, without even referring to notes. 'An old aircraft carrier at Trincomalee but her aircraft, only two dozen, are all needing a major overhaul, three heavy cruisers including *Wellington* which is even now in the convoy area but hasn't sighted the German warship and another of the two is undergoing engine repairs. The third arrived yesterday having escorted a troop convoy from Australia. She'll be going with these ships on their next stage to the Red Sea. Two other light cruisers are currently returning to Australian waters having been on escort duty. Both are due for a quick refit. In Australia, heavy cruiser *Canberra* is in dry-dock for a general overhaul. The Dutch have three light cruisers in their part of the East Indies based in Surabaya. We have three old light cruisers at Singapore together with a scattering of old destroyers and lighter craft between Penang and right round up to Hong Kong.'

Pausing for breath he looked up at Collins having had his eyes fixed on the jeep's floor. Then he resumed. 'The South Africans have but a handful of destroyers and frigates with lighter craft all on anti-U-boat patrol together with two of our a.m.c.'s. From the UK, sir, the next big troopship convoy has *Repulse* as its escort but she won't reach Cape Town until the end of the month. And that's about it. Our outer sea defences, away from the North Atlantic and the

Mediterranean are currently, to put it mildly, somewhat thinly-stretched. *Dresden* could slip past with ease wherever she chooses!'

'Well, as soon as we have radio contact with Simonstown, I want a full air search with RDF fitted aircraft to be mounted for the next fortnight on at least a five-hundred mile radius of the ocean from Cape Town. If we don't get her then, I fear that the *Dresden* will have slipped through and be sailing towards the North Atlantic convoys. Who knows what will happen then! We were fortunate enough to nail the *Bismarck*. I'm not so sure about success against Reitz and his ship. He seems to have a far more grasp of naval affairs than the rest of the bloody German Fleet put together!'

Collins lapsed into silence. His mind brooding firmly on the problem of the *Dresden*. It was beginning to become part of his own reason for existence. It ate into everything he did. He knew that he wasn't responsible for the appalling debacle of the convoy. He couldn't be. He hadn't been on the spot. Yet, deep down, he felt responsible for all the ships that had been sunk, for all the lives that had been lost and for all the families so anxiously hoping, against hope, that their loved one was not amongst the casualties. How banal had been the BBC's World Service News – 'One of our convoys with re-inforcements for our armies in North Africa has been attacked by units of the enemy's Kriegsmarine. It has yet to be established about the extent of Allied losses but at least one, if not more, of the enemy ships has been sunk and the others have all retreated from the scene of the battle with varying degrees of damage.'

No mention of the complete debâcle, nor of the principal attacking Kriegsmarine unit. No admittance of the disaster that had befallen the Royal Naval ships was the worst that they had suffered in one incident so far in this dreadful war.

The shades of the third evening after the departure from the convoy area were flickering in ever darkening shadows across the superstructure of that Kriegsmarine unit as the *Dresden* cruised steadily south-eastwards. Earlier in the day she'd met *Olaf* and had refuelled filling her near empty tanks but now the warship was again surging steadily on her course. At peace again and yet at war. The radar teams constantly kept a watch on their glowing screens. The Arados, in turn, were sent aloft but apart from a glimpse of a speeding cruiser that in reality was the *Wellington* when the plane itself was at the extreme edge of its radial flight from *Dresden*, there was no sign of the aircraft having been seen by the crew of *Wellington*. The cruiser was sighted sailing a course at right angles to that of *Dresden* and when Reitz received the airmen's report he made no alteration to his steady course to the south-east. No speck on the radar screen showed up and at first light the next day the airmen flew their plane to check the area as far as they could go but there was, to their relief, no sign at all of the cruiser. So Reitz refuelled as scheduled and then continued his steady south-easterly course.

In the Sick Berth all the wounded, Allied and German, were responding well to treatment and towards the end of that day, Andrea decided to go up out on to deck for a welcome breath of the cool evening air. As she gazed out at the sunset near a guard-rail by Cesar's silent guns, she watched the beautiful orange, purple and red glow begin to fade away. So immersed with the spectacle of what was one of the best sunsets that she'd ever seen, she failed to hear the approach of Helmut Brautsch until he discreetly coughed when almost within touching range.

She turned; startled a little until she saw whom it was standing there, smiling at her. 'Oh, it's you' she whispered, trying to be as calm as possible even though she felt her cheeks reddening a little and inside her, the thumping of her heart suddenly seemed to become louder and more insistent. Something about this German excited her. Not just his blue eyes or finely chiselled features. No, it was something about his physical presence. Ever since he'd helped her into the boat away from the burning *Arades* she'd begun to have feelings for him. After all, the Germans didn't have to risk their lives just to rescue her and her companions. They could have just let the flames devour the ship. Now here she was on the battlecruiser's decks and this German stirred up emotions that she'd never had about a man before. Here he was, smiling at her.

'Good evening, Miss Andrea. A beautiful sunset is it not?' he said with a slight bow. 'Are you well?'

'Er, yes. Thank you.' She stammered. 'It is a lovely sight.'

'And all your patients?'

'They're progressing well. None are on the death-risk list. I think that they'll all recover.'

'Yes. War can be undeniably horrible at times. Doctor Lebers thinks highly of your professional capabilities. He says that you are very good at surgery. Seems to think that you are a doctor in disguise!'

'Maybe so. I qualified in England four years ago but wanted to work overseas. After a short time in Japan I took up a post in an English-run hospital in Buenos Aries, that dealt mainly with ex-patriots working in Argentina. Unfortunately some of them had a very snobbish attitude and it was with a sense of wanting to return home to work in a hospital in my own war-torn country that with Elfrida and the other nurses we decided to take our chances and board the *Arades*. The rest you know. First the U-boat.

Then you lot turning up to our gallant rescue and now I'm here. On your ship. Helping the wounded and sick. German and Allied. Feeling not afraid. Maybe a bit confused.'

'It is awkward for you to be helping us Germans on a German ship of war?'

'Yes and no. You see, Leutenant Brautsch, I've treated all nationalities – British, Americans, Brazilians, Japanese, Chinese, French. It's only the places that have changed. Admittedly I didn't expect to be carrying out my professional duties on a warship be it either Allied or German!'

Brautsch smiled, nodded as if in agreement with her and then, perhaps impulsively he took her by the hands and lifted them both to his face, gently kissing them before releasing them. To his utter astonishment, she once more brought her right arm round his neck and drew his face to her's before kissing him quite passionately, lips to lips for what seemed, to him, to be an eternity. Quite suddenly she pulled away, her urge of desire spent and whispered somewhat hoarsely 'There, Leutnant, something for you to think about as you do your rounds.' Then she sagged limply into his now enfolding arms and he was able to hold her in a gentle embrace as the sun still glowing red, orange, purple and yellow, sank below the horizon and darkness, as it had every night of the *Dresden*'s long cruise, began to creep over the restless ocean through which the warship pushed her way. Ever onwards. South-eastwards.

When Brautsch eventually released her, he reached out and held her at arm's length. 'Look, Andrea, here is something for you from me to let you know that I love you,' and saying this he removed a ring from the smallest finger on his right hand and pressed it into her hands. Stepping back, he gave a little bow, blew a kiss and walked out of sight round the big gun turret. Andrea, feeling somewhat heady and shaking with an unexpected shiver of excitement looked at the band of gold and on impulse tried it on the forefinger of her right hand. It fitted just about perfectly. He was supposed to be enemy but he'd done two things that had utterly confounded her. The ring and saying 'I love you'. In return she'd kissed him. He wasn't enemy. He was her new love. In her life. Shivering slightly with the drop in temperature and the closing darkness she traced her steps back towards the Sick Bay unaware that Reitz, high on the rear of the bridge, had seen most of the episode. It pleased him to realise that his second officer had made such a personal development in his growing friendship with Nurse Andrea but it hurt him that the love of his life was halfway across the world. Elle. Constantly in his thoughts yet the hopes of seeing her again were as remote as they could get for his ship was *en route* for a remote set of islands where the *Dresden* could recuperate, repair her damage and wait for further instructions. SKL had bleakly put in their coded messages that the North Atlantic was humming with too much Royal Naval activity based at Gibraltar or its home ports. To bring *Dresden* back until the winter's storms could hide her would be to possibly invite her own destruction. Better to keep her in an isolated setting that had previously been used with success by merchant ship raiders *Pinguin* and the most successful of them all so far, *Atlantis*. So Reitz smiled wistfully to himself thinking of Elle in far off Brest whilst the ship forged ever nearer to her destination of refuge.

An isolated wind-swept group of uninhabited islands

The Kerguelens.

Chapter 6

'Come I'll take you up to the waterfall'

In as lonely and isolated area of the World as anyone could find are the remote Kerguelen islands. A French man hopelessly off course happened, by chance, to discover them in the late eighteenth century. Inhabited in the air by screaming seagulls and on the shores by wallowing sea-lions and seals, they had resisted, even after one hundred and eighty years of being known to humans, any attempt to establish a permanent human presence and one had never been seriously attempted. Somehow rabbits had been introduced by visiting whale-men as a source of alternative meat supply as well as sport in rare moments of leisure. The whale-men had long since given up trying establish a living on the islands and had left behind them a collection of rusting corrugated sheeted huts. Perhaps the name of the main shelter for the occasional visiting ships, Desolation Bay, had only helped to emphasise the futility of the islands of trying to become a leading well-known part of the World to visit. Yet for elusive German raiding warships or their individual supply ships to call in and temporarily make a stop over, the islands were, despite their lack of facilities, ideal as a place in which to anchor, take a rest and re-stock or repair worn machinery. Felix Kruder had called at these islands before penetrating further south into the wastes of the Antarctic with his raider *Pinguin* to capture, virtually intact, the whole of the 1940 Norwegian whaling fleet. Raider *Atlantis*, under Bernhard Rogge, also visited the area but his ship ran onto an unchartered rock and their stay was extended as a result whilst the damaged raider's hull was repaired. Rogge, via a supply ship that returned to France, had given details of the anchorage and it was these that Reitz now studied. For it was to this isolated place that the *Dresden* was approaching to repair her battle damage to restock and refuel. Yet Admiral Collins did not include the Kerguelen Islands as a possible refuge for *Dresden*. As yet the Allies hadn't realised that the islands had been used as a base for German raiders, however temporary. Collins was still of the opinion that the battlecruiser, not significantly damaged, was making for the South Atlantic and then the run northwards to Occupied France. If seriously damaged he was guessing that *Dresden* would be bound for Japan.

Seven days. A week ago since *Dresden* had swung away from the site of the sinking *Llandaff*. A week of a long curve of a cruise and now the battlecruiser was only a few hours from the Kerguelens. Reitz retreated to his main cabin to collect his thoughts and to write a letter to Elle. He'd sent her a quick note in the mail that was now on board *Berengia* but he'd been unable to find the time to really write about the cruise so far nor of the tensions of the convoy battle. He'd also written a report, typed up by the ship's writers, for Admiral Raeder. A factual one. Ships sunk. Course taken. Ammunition and stores used. Prisoners taken and policy plans to hide in the Kerguelens for a short time whilst waiting for orders. This was to go on the next available supply ship returning to France.

Elle, he knew, was now in the Abwehr's department at Brest, working as a liaison officer with the main naval headquarters. She'd even heard Frenchmen cheer the efforts of *Dresden*. It seemed that French naval men still in Brest had been very bitter when British warships fired on their ships based in North Africa in July 1940. She learned quite a lot from their attitude. Almost daily she was in receipt of news of *Dresden* and she compared it with the camouflaged hulks of the two bigger battlecruisers as well as heavy cruiser *Prinz Eugen.* Hiding from the RAF's constant raids. Incredibly with comparatively little damage.

Sulking, Staying in harbour rather than face the enemy in the North Atlantic. Yet they still remained a potent threat. So far, the French underground movement had done little to disrupt naval affairs in Brest or at St Nazaire where *Scharnhorst* had been berthed for some time. Part of Elle's job was to keep track of the underground resistance fighters in their efforts to occasionally disrupt the work of repairs, not only to the big ships but also to the U-boats that were now carrying the main effort of the naval war in the convoy battleground amidst the surging Atlantic rollers.

As Reitz wrote his reply he thought of her letter that he'd often glanced at in his few spare moments. He thought of that first meeting. Unexpected. The clean air flowing off the steep mountain sides. Matched by the clear water of the stream. That stream in which he'd dived in to rescue her. The roaring log fire in the inn where they'd shared their first meal together. It all seemed so long ago. He found it difficult to compare it with the life he'd led on *Dresden* during her now prolonged cruise. He wrote of the comradeship on the ship. How the crew was working so well, that 'Captain's Defaulters' was almost an unknown occurrence. Of the prisoners but not of the growing relationship between Brautsch and nurse Andrea. Vaguely he'd written of the convoy battle but hadn't gone into detail. He knew, that even before Elle would read it, maybe three, four months from now, that the Nazi-censors would claw over every word. So he let little out and anyway, if the letter fell into Allied hands, he didn't want them to know how well *Dresden* was facing up to her cruise. Finally he signed it wishing Elle all the best and to keep up her spirits. With love. George. He wrote Elle's name in kisses.

Then as he laid his pen down after writing the envelope, the speaker above his head clicked and intoned 'Captain to bridge. Kerguelen islands in sight.'

Hurriedly he pulled on oilskins and sea-boots and wrapping his white muffler around his neck, so much favoured by U-boat and small warship skippers, he stomped his way up to the bridge sensing the coldness coming at *Dresden* from the Antarctic wastes further to the South.

As he reached the open upper bridge, rain began to lash across the surging waves. He was glad he'd put on his oilskins and muffler. It was so much colder than even the previous day.

'A passing shower, Herr Kapitan' growled Hiltzern and so it proved. The low mound of an outlying island began to take shape. Part of this desolate group over six hundred miles from the Cape of Good Hope. Reitz nodded to the navigator, Alfred Serle.

'Are we on course?'

'Yes sir. Same as Rogge's *Atlantis*. We'll be lowering motorboats soon to make sure of our soundings. Can't afford to run aground.'

'Indeed not. We'll anchor a bit further out than *Atlantis* but by all accounts, the main bay is quite deep.'

Two miles from the main bay *Dresden* lowered three boats which spread out taking regular soundings. About five hundred yards from the shore, the anchors were dropped. For the first time since her departure from German-held waters nearly seven months previously, part of the battlecruiser was in contact with land, even if it was ten fathoms beneath her keel. Only a gentle swell rocked the warship as her main engines came to a halt. Soon Herzog came up on to the main deck abaft the funnel to meet Reitz. With him was a team of divers. They were scheduled to survey the underwater damage caused by the exploding torpedo from that brave destroyer *Tintagel.* Another task was to check the propellers for any damage. Herzog suspected that a blade, at least, on one of the triple propellers had been slightly bent.

Suddenly Reitz said 'Fetch me a suit. I'll go over first. Then the men can follow me – if they want!' Herzog raised his shaggy close-knit eyebrows but the other men laughed and cheered their captain.

'Don't worry, Chief, I used to dive quite a bit – albeit for fun, in my younger days.'

Someone handed him the thick diving suit and soon after, Herzog himself screwed the helmet in place. Reitz, the first man over the side, dropped down into the cold but clear waters that lapped against the damaged plates of the anchored battlecruiser. Petty Officer Schenke splashed into the water next to him and with a powerful underwater torch he showed Reitz the full extent of the blow that *Dresden* had received. Two other men followed with a tape measure and between the four of them they traced the extent of what was needed to be repaired. Across and down. Diagonally as well. Schenke, with a specially equipped throat micro-phone spoke carefully into it and with Herzog at the receiver on the deck, the extent of the damage was converted into a rough sketch.

Three minutes, then four. Almost five before Schenke was satisfied. With a tug of their connecting ropes, he, with Reitz and their two assistants were hauled up to the surface where they were dragged spluttering with cold, despite their diving suits, into a waiting motorboat. Then the boat was steered to the falls, hooked on and hauled up to deck level. Schenke helped his captain out of his diving suit and the two men went forward to where Herzog was waiting. Walters was also there and thrust a hip flask full of Scotch whisky at his captain. Reitz took it neat and then passed it round to the three men who'd accompanied him. 'Here men, have a taste of what my favourite enemy can provide!' Then to Herzog he asked 'Well, Chief, can we repair the damage?'

'It'll take time but it is possible if we careen the ship to an angle of about fifteen degrees or probably better still, we could demolish one of those shore huts and using the sheeting and bars, build a coffer dam around that part of the hull, drain it and then work without having to disturb the trim of the ship. Mind, we'll have to hold her hard-to on all our anchors and trust that we'll have a constant state of calm weather. Can we get any nearer to the shore? Say with only two metres under our keel and still hold really tight?'

Reitz liked his Chief Engineer. He'd kept his beloved engines going all the time on this prolonged cruise and he knew that now that they were still, he'd want the chance to really overhaul them but he also knew that the damage to the plating had to be repaired if they were to stand a fair chance of either renewed action or an attempt to reach German-controlled waters again. Thinking of the hoped-for return, something inside him ached for Elle. But he had to think of his ship.

'Alright Chief, we'll make accurate soundings and then edge in as close as possible. Whatever way we choose, we'll be a sitting duck for any Allied ship that may decide to investigate. At least if we're still on level trim we can fire back. I know that a coffer dam isn't going to be easy to build but we'll risk it. I'm in no hurry but the Allies might be, so, get to it, Chief. Organise the boat crews on to the soundings and you take enough men and start stripping one, or more, of those decrepit whaling huts.'

With that, Reitz shook his Chief's hands and turned once again for the bridge. To Hiltzern he said 'I want to see our airmen as well as Halder. We need to set up a gun post or two on the beach as well as to organise our further defences.'

'A gun post?'

'Yes. I intend to have a last line of defence if nothing else. Give any snooping Allied force something to think about before we surrender. Sorry! Not really! I really intend letting our prisoners some landing space as and when we can. Two machine-gun posts covering the beach area should keep them knowing who is still in charge – not that any of them could escape anywhere but I don't want to waste time searching for anyone who decides to be stupid or foolhardy! They will also act as an extension of our anti-aircraft cover.'

'Any other plans, sir?'

'Yes. If Herzog can spare anyone I shall want a water-supply line rigged to tap that stream that I can see over there. See, it comes over a waterfall. We could rig some pipes and by its own momentum, channel the water into our tanks. We're nearly out of proper fresh water. Our own desalination works can't work without full power from our engines and anyway the water we still have isn't really fit for drinking.' Reitz paused and then added 'We've a lot to do – a good overhaul of everything; painting our rusty bits you know. A damn good overhaul. Oh, and the cook could do with some fresh rabbit and seagull meat as well as fish. Anyone of the crew with some spare time can go ashore on an officer-led raiding party. Yes, Hiltzern, we've a lot to do!'

'Ship in sight' came a shout. It was *Olaf* and the crews of the two patrolling guard motor-launches greeted her at the entrance to the bay. Signals from *Dresden* instructed her to keep in the centre of the bay. Reitz couldn't refuel until the repairs to the plating were complete. Even the weight of the extra fuel would upset the battlecruiser's trim.

The Arado pilots reported to their captain. Instructions were given for them to fly patrols to a thirty-mile radius on the hour for every daylight hour of their stay whilst the repairs were being carried out. Reitz couldn't afford to have his ship caught by surprise. Once the repairs were over he'd reduced the circuits so as to preserve the aviation fuel. *Olaf* carried diesel oil and he hoped that perhaps when some of her tanks were emptied to send her to Japan for some aviation fuel. They were to look for any Allied ships and keep an eye for any surfaced submarines as well. If any were seen close to the islands, then the launches equipped with scuttling charges would have to be directed to its position and at least keep the submarine down.

After he'd finished with the pilots, he spoke to Halder. Could Halder take a battery of light anti-aircraft guns to mount on the highest mound of the island? Yes, he could was his reply. From there the crews of the guns could also keep an extra watch. Extend the usual range of the ship. The airmen may not be able to see everything. At dusk the men would be withdrawn, to recommence their duties on the following dawn.

Thus the crew of *Dresden* found themselves fully occupied. Herzog's gang soon got to grips with one of the huts, finding metal spars and corrugated sheeting to make up the coffer dam. A group under Brautsch and Anders went ashore trying to plan the logistics of dealing with the water pipe. The waterfall was nearly half-a-mile from the ship but if the water could be harnessed, *Dresden*'s tanks would soon be full of the clear and clean supply.

The weather kept relatively calm although squally showers would quite suddenly rush across the bay but the anchors held the battlecruiser steady. If they dragged then *Dresden* would soon be aground. *Olaf* edged to within a quarter mile astern of the warship and two strong harnesses were extended from her to assist in keeping the battlecruiser steadier.

The work on building the coffer dam went apace with much hammering and banging despite the difficulty of setting it all up in the water. Herzog was a genius at the ingenuity required and after only two days he had the dam constructed and pumps set out to drain the water away. The twisted plates came into view and the work to straighten them began. With extra plating from an above the waterline bulkhead Herzog then began the work of riveting it all into place. Bang! bang! Bang! The work went on.

Even some spare plating was brought over from *Olaf* to help.

Using all of *Dresden*'s piping plus extra lengths from *Olaf*, a pipeline was constructed to the waterfall. Brautsch, who had engineering as well as navigational qualifications, with help from one of Luth's men, constructed a funnel to direct the water from the waterfall into the pipes.

A week passed. Then Herzog came up to Reitz to report that, although his work wasn't a dockyard job, the damage had been successfully plated and that the battlecruiser could edge out into deeper water. Just as well for the wind was beginning to freshen and even in the bay, the anchor and hawsers holding *Dresden* into position were beginning to strain. Reitz heaved a sigh of relief and instructed Herzog to fire up an extra boiler so as to give the ship enough power to back the ship into deeper water as well as to continue to give power for the refrigeration plant and the electricity points which had been relying on an independently rigged generator whose incessant throbbing could now cease.

Fortunately the bay was well sheltered and the weather had held back from upsetting *Dresden*'s trim or position. Even the prisoners were allowed on deck to see the land but as yet Reitz hadn't allocated them 'shore leave' but now that the heavy engineering work was complete, groups of the crew were allowed to spend two hours ashore if they so wanted the chance to use their land legs again. Not that there was much to do unless the men were avid nature study fans. Rabbits, seals, various seagulls and most sought after, but never killed, the seven foot wing-spanned albatross. Some men hunted rabbits or collected any eggs they could reach but none of them dreamt of ruining their luck by shooting at an albatross. For most of them just the chance of a stroll along the rocky beach was enough. Soon they were back on board immersed in the many tasks that took up their time from painting out the rusted sections to oiling all the gun mechanisms.

Perhaps the crew members at the gun positions on the island had the laziest tasks. Little, if anything, disturbed their minds although one young lad did get excited when he saw whales spouting off the shore and swung his machine-gun somewhat excitedly, yelling nervously 'Commandos. Mini-subs!' before being reprimanded as to his sheepishly-felt error. Others, including those in the two patrol launches as well as any with spare time, tried their luck at line fishing but the haul was relatively limited but one day the cooks did brew up a Kerguelen stew of rabbit, fish and gull eggs together with edible seaweed (or cabbage as the cooks called the substance).

Padré's Jervaulx's services were required to bury the two crewmen drowned in the flooded compartment which was opened up again. Reitz delayed the funeral until the main repairs were completed and then the whole ship's company, apart from a few men on watch and the pilots on patrol attended. A sombre moment remembering the cost of the war, albeit only small in numbers so far to *Dresden*'s crew. Even the padré's's words of comfort couldn't hide the fact that no matter how far from the fighting that *Dresden* was, none of her crew could feel completely safe until the war ended whichever course its swathing path took. All of the Allied prisoners also attended the service and no doubt were remembering their own fallen comrades from the convoy battle as the two canvas shrouded and weighted body sacks were dropped into the grey waters of the bay.

Waters that soon began to whip up into a white-clapped frenzy as a major storm began to blow across the bay. Sheltered as *Dresden, Olaf* and now *Arabian Nights* were, even their anchors began to strain with the onslaught of the wind and short, sharp punches of the disturbed waters. The water-pipe-line had to be disconnected and all exposed work came to a halt as the storm lashed vicious sleet showers across the bay and on to the ships. The picket boats came hurriedly back crashing over the rising waves and the patrolling Arado just succeeded in making a safe landing in the lee of the battlecruiser.

Down in the sick bay the movement of the waves could be just discerned as Andrea began yet another round of the few wounded, including prisoners, that occupied seventeen berths in the room. Suddenly the door burst open and Leutnant Brautsch stumbled in, clutching his left arm. Andrea rushed up to him, full of nervous alarm 'My goodness, Helmut, what is it?'

'Fell down some steps coming off watch. A sudden lurch caught me off balance. Thought I'd better check to see if I've sprained it or worse still, broken my wrist. Please have a look.'

Gently Andrea led him over to a spare cot and having sat him down, she applied careful pressure to the left wrist. Brautsch winced as a stab of pain shot up the arm.

'Try twisting it now, Helmut.' He tried. It moved a little.

'Helmut, you've not broken it but I'll have to put a firm bandage on it to keep it rigid until the swelling has gone down. Then I'll put it in a sling. You'll have to play the wounded warrior for a few days, I fear!'

'Oh Andrea, you're super! If the weather abates I'll be taking you ashore. Our gallant captain has issued instructions to allow all the walking prisoners to have a stretch of their legs on land if they so wish. I was so happy about this when he said all prisoners could go, including you, that I guess I forgot myself when I fell!'

'Helmut, my, that's quite a speech! But, yes, I'd love to get my feet on the land again, particularly if you're there to prop me up with your good arm!'

'But I shall be there! The captain has placed me in charge of all the shore parties seeing I'm also the principal boarding officer. I'm the first German officer to whom the prisoners have contact. I also continue to see to their welfare for as long as they're on board *Dresden.* You're my main concern, Andrea.'

'And you're mine' she quickly replied, not fully realising the implication.'But you'd better go. Tongues will be wagging.'

'They are already. I've overheard my fellow officers who know that I have a soft spot for you!'

'Don't delay Helmut. Please go. I'll be looking forward to our trip ashore with my arm in yours!' Andrea looked into his face and smiled. Brautsch grinned in return. Aloud, so that the others nearby could hear 'Thankyou, nurse. My arm feels much better.'

Then, much quieter, he murmured 'Until our beach trip, goodbye, my cherry blossom.'

Andrea blew a kiss at him and muttered 'Bye for now darling' and with that, Brautsch turned and left the sick bay. Andrea watched the door close and could feel herself shaking with an inner excitement.

How could she? He was the enemy. But yet she'd fallen for him. She couldn't understand but yet she knew.

A wounded English prisoner said as she passed his bed 'Well, well, nurse. You've quite a handsome catch there!'

Andrea hushed him but with a smile and twinkle in her eyes.

Dawn next day and the wind had abated. The skies were much brighter. It was cold but clear. After breakfast Reitz summoned Brautsch and told him to get the prisoners organised.

'You go ashore, Helmut, whilst we restock from *Arabian Nights.* We will then take all the fit prisoners and transfer them to her. Don't worry, the nurses will stay with us for some time. I don't intend to send *Arabian Nights* back to Europe until we've made full use of her ample food supplies and then *Berengia* will probably replace her. Anyway, more of that but for now, be off with you, mind your arm and enjoy your time. We've been here long enough and after restocking, we shall leave. This will be your last chance. So take it.' Then with a wink 'Mind, don't forget to take nurse Andrea with you!'

Brautsch clicked his heels and turned to get his group organised.

The boats grounded on the shingle of the beach. Andrea, dressed in a thick sweater and slacks, with thigh length seamen's boots jumped into the wavelets as they subsided on to the shore's small stones. There'd been quite a competition amongst some of the younger crew members to volunteer their kit for both Andrea and Elfrida. A young deckhand who was one of the smallest crew members had gallantly offered his boots and with thick socks, they fitted reasonably well. Someone else had slightly larger boots on offer for the larger feet and legs of Elfrida. Both nurses thanked their young benefactors with flashing smiles that coloured their faces. As she jumped into the gentle surf, Helmut thought Andrea looked most stunning in her borrowed out-fit.

'Land, land, land' she yelled as she waded out of the surf flinging a handful of pebbles into the air.

The other able prisoners were also laughing like children as they dashed on to the pebble beach. Brautsch shouted to them

'Enjoy your walk, ladies and gentlemen, but don't stray too far. Not beyond the machine-gun posts. Otherwise, have fun and fresh air. We have two hours at the most!'

To Andrea he said 'Come, I'll take you up to the waterfall and our fresh water pipe. Tomorrow we have to dismantle it for soon we'll be leaving for fresh adventures.'

She tugged at his good arm 'Helmut, it is good to be here. On land. Just look at those birds. What type are they?'

'Albatross. Some say that they never go to sleep. Always flying. The winged master of these southern seas. Two metres wingspan or in your measurement, seven feet. Close up I think that they are rather ugly but to see them flying, they are a bird of beauty, romance and luck.'

'Luck, Helmut?' questioned Andrea.

'Yes. It is considered unlucky for a sailor to kill one. Come, this way to the waterfall.'

With some of the other prisoners, as well as Elfrida close behind, they scrambled along the rough path of rock and shingle, past the former whaling huts and on to the expanse of turf and tough grasses. Andrea gasped at the pace and rate of climb that Helmut was setting. She'd been too long at sea but she strode on holding on to his good arm. At last they reached the pool at the foot of the waterfall. Here Helmut brought the group to a halt, showing the members the channel that had been cut to divert water into the laid pipes from whence, by force of gravity, it was fed into the water-tanks on *Dresden* and also to *Olaf* and *Arabian Nights*. Even though they were only were only about three-quarters of a mile away, looking back at the three anchored ships gave to Andrea a sense of detachment. Somehow, the peace and remoteness of the area gave her the notion that perhaps the battlecruiser and her consorts were mere tourists, not instruments of war. She murmured to Helmut 'It's so beautiful here. Remote. We're away from the war. Can't it last?' But he merely smiled and shook his head.

'No, Andrea. Away only for a short time but let us not think too hard. Temporarily we can all re-gather our energies by resting, although some of the men seem to have been working very hard and they might lynch me if I hinted to them that we'd been resting here in these islands! Maybe one day you and I will stand alone on another island when the world has made its peace, without any thought of who is or isn't an enemy. Would you like that?'

She smiled.

Brautsch winced at her non-reply. Had he gone too far? 'Yes perhaps I do wax lyrically at times. Go on too much.' Stumbling.

Suddenly feeling awkward.

Instead, she gripped his good arm. 'I'm only teasing by not replying,' and then dropping her voice, added 'my love.'

Brautsch looked at her and smiled. Winked at her. It was enough. The bond was there. He didn't want it to break. She'd called him 'love'. The best word possible.

As they stared out over the ships they heard *Dresden*'s funnel siren blasting out. Four harsh blasts. A warning. A light began to stab out from the bridge. Brautsch quickly read the message although the siren had been enough. The emergency signal.

'Hurry, all of you! Back to the boats. That's the recall signal. We need to find out what's the matter.'

The group scrabbled down the turf back to the huts and the others in their group who were being shepherded back to the boats. Andrea almost fell in the surf but willing hands hauled her into the boat. The dream had gone. Something was up. The Germans were in a hurry. But why? Another boat crunched on to the gravel. Men piled out of it. Helmut went with them. Then he and the new arrivals were soon going back the way Andrea had just come.

On *Dresden* all was hustle and bustle. Fortunately the loading from *Arabian Nights* was just about completed although there seemed to be a mountain of crates and boxes on the battlecruiser's decks that needed to be stowed away. It transpired that one of the Arados at the extreme range of her patrol had sighted a warship coming their way at about sixty miles distance cruising at about fifteen knots. Already *Olaf* was gathering way, heading out of the bay soon to be followed by *Arabian Nights*. Reitz wanted the pipe to be retrieved as well as the guns and sandbag shelters to minimise the fact that the Germans had been on the island. A group of men were also scouring the beach area for any discarded litter. The area where the hut had been demolished was soon covered in turf and rock.

An hour passed. The hose-pipe had all been collected. Reeled in and loaded on to two of the boats which then pushed off the shingle and headed back to the battlecruiser whose main guns were raised, almost as if sniffing at the threatening air. A third boat collected the gun crews, their weapons and equipment.

Nothing had happened to get the gunners excited. Except for now. To get their guns back on board and remounted as light anti-aircraft defence. For their ship. A ship now hurrying to get away from the islands and no doubt, if successful, back into proving herself again in this protracted war.

As soon as the last boat was hoisted and secured, the anchors were raised and slowly the battlecruiser, guided by two of the four picket boats made her way out of the buoyed bay. Behind her, the other two picket boats collected the temporary buoys that had marked the safe channel for the ships.

As soon as she cleared the last buoy and the feel of deeper water was under her keel, Reitz ordered the warship to stop in order to collect the four motor-boats and also the circling Arado. Stein's report was that the enemy ship was now only about twenty miles away. He thought that it was a large destroyer or maybe even a light cruiser. He'd been very careful not to approach it and so far as he could tell his little plane had not been seen by the enemy warship.

War activity was afoot on *Dresden*. Ammunition hoists were rattling. Anti-aircraft gunners checked their weapons in case the as yet unseen warship had a seaplane itself. Every loose item was being stored away. A chain gang busily stowed the crates from *Arabian Nights* and only just finished their task as *Dresden* once again gathered way. Down in the Sick Bay Andrea and Elfrida divested themselves of their loaned shore rigs and with Doctor Lebers were preparing for a possible influx of wounded if battle should be joined.

The war was back.

Perhaps with a vengeance.

Reitz paced the bridge. He'd dreaded this occurrence ever since he'd taken *Dresden* into the bay. Well it had come and the battlecruiser had nearly been caught with her two supply ships which now churned away to the south-east whilst *Dresden*'s course took her at right-angles, to the north-east on a bearing of 050 degrees from the approaching enemy ship.

He'd overstayed in the Kerguelens. For about eight weeks. Now here at the latter end of October it could be the big crunch time if he didn't get *Dresden* away.

He'd relaxed too much. Dropped his guard. He hoped that Brautsch's party had cleared away as much of the evidence of their visit, just as Rogge's men in *Atlantis* had done a year earlier.

Speed was steadily increased. At least the divers had been able to scrape away most of the barnacles and seaweed from below the waterline. It could give them an extra knot or so of speed if so required. Tension mounted. Radar to bridge. 'Warship is twelve miles off the port beam. It's estimated speed is about twenty two knots.'

Dresden's wake stretched out in a broad frothy band behind her. Twenty knots – 23 – 26 – 27 –

'Masthead in sight. Two eighty degrees!' yelled a lookout. Binoculars and telescopes swing to abeam of the port side. 'She's there alright' murmured Hiltzern.

'I have her. We must get away. Surely she's seen us. Tell Herzog to be careful not to emit any smoke. So far he's doing well to increase our speed with only minimum exhaust gases. She must not see us. Perhaps her radar hasn't picked us up or isn't working properly.' Halder up in his gunnery control position, ascertained that the range of the enemy warship was little more than twenty-thousand yards. Cesar's twin barrels were creaked up to maximum elevation in the direction of their potential target.

Then the thin mast-top vanished.

As if the potential aura of menace had never been there. Radar reported the reason. The stranger's course was taking her directly towards the bay. Which *Dresden* had only recently vacated.

Even so, Reitz continued to push the battlecruiser up to nearly thirty knots. He had to get her away. In secrecy. To keep the Allies guessing of his apparently mercurially positioned where-abouts. Five tension filled hours until nightfall's protective clock of darkness covered the *Dresden*. Then it was time to relax. The chase was over. Back to a mere fifteen knots.

The Australian heavy cruiser, HMAS *Australia*, turned towards that bay, but seeing no visible sign of ships, her captain shrugged his shoulders. 'Nothing there. We'll look around the whole area and lay off a course for Melbourne.' Later, in another bay, boat crews did land. Nothing significant was found. A few rusting tins. Even so, the cruiser dropped a few mines. 'Just in case Jerry comes sniffing around' grunted the captain. Perhaps relieved that his ship hadn't met *Dresden*. From the German ship's record, she was quite a feared opponent for his smaller, slightly slower and lesser-gunned cruiser to face up to on equal terms.

Four days later *Olaf* steamed into sight at a pre-arranged rendezvous and her oil flowed into the battlecruiser's tanks. Next to arrive was *Arabian Nights*. For a week Reitz cruised gently in the area. SKL had given him a new rendezvous. Scheduled for 20th November when they were to meet up with *Skua*'s replacement in

Australia waters. This was the disguised raider *Kormoran* under the command of Theodor Detmers whose ship had taken ten ships in as many months. Together the two ships would make a double-pronged attack on Australian waters where surface opposition would be relatively weak. SKL had warned Reitz to keep out of African and Indian waters for the time being as the British were reinforcing the area.

With a battleship that had fought against *Bismarck*. And had taken its country's Prime-Minister across the Atlantic. And was now leaving Simonstown harbour *en route* for Colombo in Ceylon there to join up with veteran battlecruiser *Repulse* for the final leg together for Singapore. Not because, as SKL surmised, of *Dresden* but as a result of increasing tension with Japanese. The battleship's name? HMS *Prince of Wales*.

Not that the little Admiral in command was bothered about *Dresden*. His main concern was that he might not reach Singapore in time. He and the battleship's captain were agreed that the Japanese were a major threat. Prime Minister Churchill had told Admiral Tom Phillips that he wasn't to waste any time chasing after the mercurial German battlecruiser if she happened to be in the southern oceans until he'd dealt with the Japanese. Indeed it was his opinion that *Dresden* had eluded all Allied ships and was probably back in Norwegian waters or even in German waters but this time without overt Nazi propaganda announcements. Vice Admiral Collins was not so convinced. He felt that *Dresden* had disappeared to a remote area to lick her wounds and refit. But Phillips had said 'Look, Bernard, I'm not here to embark on a wild goose-chase. Now if I had our carrier with us, it would perhaps be different but *Indomitable*'s silly bugger of a captain has run her onto a reef in the West Indies and has damaged her propellers. We needed her for our own protection but as a side-line her planes could have helped in a search for the German ship. But, she isn't here and that's that. Bloody nuisance but we have to put up with the consequences.'

That had been three days ago in a tense conference ashore. Now the relatively new battleship and her destroyer escorts were churning away from Simonstown and Collins could only stand and stare after them until they'd disappeared over the horizon. Collins still had a feeling that *Dresden* was somewhere in the Indian Ocean and not in the Atlantic or back in Germany but where? Nothing had turned up. Not even with the report of the empty bay in the Kerguelens from the Australia with only vague signs of a previous German presence.

So where was she?

What was she doing?

Dresden was approaching her rendezvous with *Kormoran.* Well away from where Collins thought she might have been. Or Tom Phillips if he was sparing any time thinking about the German warship. By a simple code, at a pre-arranged time, *Dresden* was informing SKL as to approximately where she was. Code D-1 told SKL that Reitz was about a day's sailing away from *Kormoran*'s area off Western Australia's distant coast-line.

19th November. Rendezvous for early 20th November. Off Start Point, Western Australia. It was late afternoon. Darkness wasn't a long way off.

'Captain to the wireless room.' The speakers interrupted a late evening meal that Reitz was having in his sea cabin with Hiltzern. It wasn't often that Reitz entertained his Chief Officer solely in his cabin. They'd been discussing the potential rendezvous with *Kormoran* and what little Reitz knew of Detmers he reckoned that he was a careful captain without the haughtiness of *Skua*'s non-lamented commander. So they were looking forward to a bond of close co-operation. But a summons to the wireless room? What now?

Reaching the room of dials and wires housed in their boxes they met up with Rikard Crantz, the principle operator.

'Sir, just picked up an unusual message – "Straat Malakka" under attack by enemy warship.'

'Straat Malakka is a Dutch name,' responded Hiltzern.

'So which warship, sir?' butted in Crantz. 'If it's a warship it is quite near us. Is it *Kormoran* attacking the Dutchman?'

'Odd to say the least. She's supposed to keep clear of any ships until after our rendezvous' came Hiltzern's observation.

'Can you get a bearing? Any position?' Reitz fired these at Crantz.

'Well, yes sir, the message came from a bearing that is to the north-east of us but Straat Malakka didn't give an accurate one. No doubt her wireless roam was damaged in the attack' replied Crantz but he still looked puzzled.

'What is it, Crantz?' offered Reitz.

'Well sir, she repeated her name three times. As if she wanted anyone near by, like us, to know. To hear the emphasis on her name.'

Reitz looked at him and suddenly the dreadful truth hit him. 'It's not an innocent merchant man under attack by *Kormoran*. It's the other way round. Detmers must be sailing under the pseudonym of *Straat Malakka*. It's *Kormoran* under attack and she's trying to warn us without alerting the enemy warship, most likely to be a cruiser.'

'We must go to help her, Hiltzern. Come on. To the bridge.'

The two men thanked Crantz and went up to the bridge. Serle was on watch with Anders. 'How far to our rendezvous at say twenty five knots?'

Serle got busy with his dividers. "'Bout midnight, sir.'

'Warn radar to keep a lookout. Action stations at twenty-two hundred hours. Tell Herzog's gang to be ready for some hard steaming. We'll increase gradually to twenty-five knots by twenty-two hundred hours.'

Orders were issued and *Dresden*, as if the adrenalin was coursing through her veins, picked up her speed and once again began to thrust her way through the swell with a sense of urgency.

'Radar to the captain. Please come to the radar room.'

Walther Badl, the senior radar operator, made the call shortly after eleven that evening. Darkness was full and there was a cloud cover over the area through which the battlecruiser was pushing ahead at twenty-five knots. Badl, knowing nothing of the outside conditions had, on the screens he was watching, picked up a small speck at almost extreme range. He was good at his job and had been extremely pleased with this British radar. Far better than the one on *Admiral Scheer*, his previous appointment. It was a great piece of work for the Abwehr to have captured it from that damaged British cruiser. Even better for Canaris to have had it installed on *Dresden* rather than on any of the other major Kriegsmarine warships. Badl had learnt a lot during this protracted cruise and time after time the apparatus had proved its worth. Now it was showing him a shaky, erratic course for the dot that kept on recurring as the radar picked up its echo. Erratic. Slow. But generally at 350 degrees or so. To the North-West. Slightly away from *Dresden*'s course. It was fortunate that he'd spotted it. So he called in his captain. Reitz surmised that if the object on the screen was a ship, then it was damaged. He gave instructions for *Dresden* to slow down and alter course towards the twenty-mile or so distant echo. Gradually *Dresden* approached Badl's object. 'Range fifteen thousand yards (metres)' intoned the speakers from the radar room. All eyes strained to locate the object. Suddenly a lookout sang out.

'Fine on port bow. Red glow.' Reitz swung his night-sight binoculars and picked up the glow. 'That's a ship on fire. Close in. All guns to be ready. Get the boat-crews to stand by. We may, no, probably we will need them.'

The range closed to five thousand yards.

'That's not *Kormoran*' growled Hiltzern. 'It's the enemy cruiser. She's on fire, all over. It's a miracle she's still afloat.'

'Barely under way' murmured Serle pleased that his work as a navigator once again was so accurate.

'Close her. Signal her. Fire a warning shot.'

The lamp flashed. There was no response on the doomed cruiser. Even when from a thousand yards, the flames clearly seen, jetted gouts of orange, yellow and red all the time. The crew members on exposed upper parts of the *Dresden* could even feel the heat they gave off, even at that distance.

'No sign of life' observed Serle as yet another explosion shook the dying warship. Her funnels lay at grotesque angles, her turret guns pointed haphazardly. Most of the upper works were a complete shambles. Suddenly she lurched over on to her starboard side, the inrush of water causing some of the flames to die out near the stern.

'Sir, look. Is that a signal?' yelled Anders. 'Near the stern. There, there it goes again.'

Reitz, focussing his binoculars picked up flashes of light. Regular. Unlike the flames. 'There is someone on board. Launch a motor-boat. Tell Brautsch to be careful.'

A motor-boat was hurriedly launched but even as it hit the water, the stricken cruiser lurched even more on to her starboard side and with huge columns of smoke and with white vaporised clouds of steam pouring from her in the dying light of the flames, she began to rapidly subside into the waves. Then a final explosion split the ship into two halves and even quicker still they sank to disappear behind the clouds of dispersing smoke and vapour. The area of sinking went very dark as the cruiser sank.

'Searchlights on' ordered Reitz.

The motorboat, illuminated by the battlecruiser's lights swept into the area of the sinking, her own crew also using hand-held torches to sweep the area as well as the power lamp mounted in the bows. Five minutes of desperate searching but nothing.

'Turn back' ordered Brautsch.

'Wait sir, I think I heard something. Yes, over there!' yelled one of the men, pointing over the bows of the boat.

'Cut the engine.'

Then other men, as well as Brautsch heard it. Faint. Definitely a voice.

'He's there sir. Fifty yards off the bows' yelled the rating operating the power lamp.

The motorboat idled down towards the man struggling in the water.

'Get him on board. A survivor, at least, we've rescued one of them.'

The semi-conscious, badly burned man with only shreds of uniform still covering parts of his shoulders was hauled as quickly as the men could into the relative safety of their boat. The man seemingly recovered blurted out 'Thanks lads. Bleedin' Germans caught us by surprise. One of their damned raiders. Mind we gave 'em 'ell as well. Last saw the buggers ablaze and goin' off like a burnt turkey.' Then, this effort being too much for him, the survivor sighed and collapsed into unconsciousness.

They searched for three more minutes but there was no-one else. No-one at all.

Brautsch took the boat back to the battlecruiser and already Doctor Lebers, Andrea and Elfrida were there to meet them. Hurriedly they placed the survivor on a stretcher and took him down to the Sick Bay but despite the careful ministrations of them all, the man never regained consciousness and died some fifteen minutes later.

Brautsch reported to Reitz. The cruiser had obviously approached *Kormoran*. There had been a desperate fight. The cruiser had been mortally damaged but had also inflicted a destructive blow on the German raider.

Nothing more came from the radar or wireless rooms. No calls for help. No blips on the radar.

Reitz decided not to be caught and so with extreme reluctance he turned *Dresden* away from the area. Away from the horror of that dying cruiser.

Sickened by what had happened Reitz realised that he had reached a low point but somehow he had to shake it off. First and foremost he had to get *Dresden* away from the area although something in him screamed at him to search for *Kormoran*. Despite cautious wireless calls on SKL's wavelength for Detmers to contact him, nothing came back in reply. *Kormoran* was sunk although she had been able to inflict fatal damage in return on to her cruiser challenger. Perhaps all her crew had perished as well. There was no way that anyone on *Dresden* knowing at that time that Detmers and three hundred or so of his crew were in boats and rafts slowly making their way for the West Australian coast. There was no way that Reitz would know that they would all eventually be picked up and taken prisoner. There was no way that the men on *Dresden* would immediately know that the Allies were not mounting a search for the protagonists of that epic sea fight because, unlike *Dresden*, they'd not picked up the distress call from the bogus *Straat Malakka*. The raider's survivors were either picked up mainly by passing coasters or after a desperate few days were to land on the coastal area to surrender to bemused police and military officials.

Dawn on the next day and *Dresden* was a hundred and fifty miles south-east of the drama. Reitz slowed the battlecruiser down so that the lone survivor from the cruiser could be buried. Jervaulx once again led a service with the canvas bag covered in a Royal Navy White Ensign. MacLeod read from the Bible and saluted, with Reitz, as the weighted bag of the unknown sailor was dropped over the stern. Reitz had ensured that his prisoners were told of the action. MacLeod, in return, had requested attendance at the cruiser survivor's funeral.

All in all, a melancholy time.

Reitz, in conference with Hiltzern and other senior officers decided to swing *Dresden* away from the West Australian coast-line for at least three days. In guarded coded messages to SKL they told them what had happened. Three days later SKL informed them that the cruiser had been the Australian light cruiser *Sydney* and that the Allies were admitting her loss with all hands. Even worse was to come. Raider *Atlantis*, the most successful of all the disguised merchant raiders so far employed by the Kriegsmarine had been sunk in the South Atlantic by a heavy cruiser. SKL warned Reitz not to attempt a return home, as yet. They told him that for the time being, *Dresden* was the sole regular Kriegsmarine surface warship on the high seas away from European coastal waters. A raid on Australian, British and Dutch shipping off Australian waters and then perhaps a strike at the oil-tanker trade coming out of the Dutch East Indies. What SKL did not inform Reitz was that the political situation in the latter area was looking increasingly towards war between Japan and the Allied nations, and that Germany could well link up with Japanese in an extension of the Axis forces. *Dresden*, so thought SKL, would be a welcome assistance to the Imperial Nipponese Navy and they, in return, could well offer a suitable venue for the possible refit for the battlecruiser. They told Reitz that for the time being that they expected the U-boats to continue, with increasing success, their efforts to wrest control of the Atlantic in favour of the Kriegsmarine. At the end of their series of coded messages they wished Reitz well.

Somehow, the Allies code-breaking teams were unable to pick up the total content of the signals nor able to break the code which wasn't in the form of the signals to the U-boats.

Calling Serle to his sea-cabin along with Hiltzern and Halder, Reitz revealed to disclose to them the contents of the SKL messages.

'Well, gentlemen, we're off to the sea lane approaches to where? Adelaide? Melbourne? Sydney? or even Brisbane? In my cap I have those four cities names on a card. Then I have four numbers on the reverse side of these cards on my table. Whichever one of us picks number three, then that's where we'll go. Please, Commander, shuffle these cards and then even I won't know which is which!' The other three officers all laughed, maybe to ease the tension.

As it was, Serle turned up number three and as his other card had Melbourne printed on it, then it was to the sea-lanes off that city that Reitz planned a quick strike.

Over the next five days *Dresden* pushed her course towards the area, eager almost to get away from the encounter with the blazing *Sydney*.

It was late afternoon on that fifth day when still two hundred miles from Melbourne that one of the Arados on patrol sighted a single ship some ten miles off the coast in parallel to the battlecruiser's position some eighty miles to the south-south-west.

Reitz grunted when he heard the report. 'We could intercept sir, before dusk, given raising our speed to twenty-five knots. Say, in three hours time,' commented Serle.

'Be good to get back into action' remarked Hiltzern watching the bows already swinging towards the Australian coast.

'Hmmm! It seems to me that the Quartermaster is in charge of this ship as we seem to be turning in the direction towards this mystery vessel' observed Reitz. 'Perhaps he knows me too well!' Then he slapped his right thigh 'By heck! It'll be good to get back into business. Come on! Let's go and catch our self an Aussie fish!' The men around him chuckled and then burst out cheering. *Dresden*, her crew and captain were going back into action.

She was but a tiddler of a catch. By name and by size. A small coastal tanker of 837 tons called *Shrimp II*. She stopped when challenged by a large bows-on warship announcing itself as HMAS *Canberra*.

There was no resistance at all when Brautsch and his men clambered aboard and raced up to the bridge. Brautsch discovered that the tanker was carrying fuel oil destined for the naval dockyard at Perth. So swift was the work of Brautsch and his men that *Shrimp II*'s captain had been unable to destroy his code-book or the notes from Melbourne's naval authorities with one sheaf of papers outlining shipping movements.

A light flashed from *Dresden*'s bridge ordering Brautsch to get the little tanker underway. Reitz wanted to sail her clear of the coast and then take what fuel she had in order to top up *Dresden*'s tanks. Brautsch's men soon persuaded the tanker's crew in getting their little ship up to her full speed of ten knots following *Dresden* well away from coast as darkness crept over the relatively still waters. Reitz grunted when a message flashed across from his men aboard *Shrimp II* about the content of the papers discovered aboard the tanker's bridge. 'So, our little prize was worth it. A top-up of fuel and now this, a small convoy of coastal ships to cross these waters in about twenty-four hours from now.'

Hiltzern nodded in anticipation 'We're back in business, captain. No longer hiding but on the go again. The Aussies will be very surprised – and so will our English friends who haven't a clue where we are!'

Five hours later the oil from *Shrimp II* flowed into *Dresden*'s tanks and then scuttling charges were set and the little tanker, with no fuss, slid below the waves.

Later that next morning one of the Arados took off in the direction of the expected convoy.

'See down there. Four ships.' Stolle spoke over the intercom to Stein, his pilot for the flight.

'Only a small warship escort' remarked Stein.

'Well, we'd best get away. I don't think that they've seen us and even if they have, they probably haven't worked out what sort of little bird we are.' chuckled Stolle. So much more confident than the nervous observer of the Atlantic 'bag of feathers' convoy.

Far away. Another world. Almost another period of time. Yet it was only eight months ago.

Back on board, after they'd given their report, they saw Reitz beckon Serle as the two senior office's walked towards the chartroom to plan the battlecruiser's approach to surprise and overwhelm the coastal convoy. For a late evening attack.

It was a target.

Even if it was a relatively small one.

HMAS *Kookaburra* first hit the waters of the Clyde in 1908 and was then a coal-fired eight hundred and forty three ton fishery patrol sloop for coastal waters in the Royal Navy with an original name of Starbrite. She shuffled around the coasts of Britain and Northern France escorting coastal shipping without ever once having to fire her single four-inch gun during the Great War. In 1921 she was sold to the Australian Navy and having made the slow arduous passage to those waters she was employed as a training vessel for the next twelve years. She was laid up just before Hitler's accession to power in 1933. 'Surplus to modern requirements' ran the official jargon, so she was tied up in a quiet backwater near Sydney and idly swung on a rusting anchor and chain for the next six years. No-one came to scrap her and she wasn't even officially de-commissioned. She seemed to have been almost forgotten.

War on 3rd September 1939 changed her life. A tired naval clerk, looking through a dusty file of ships still in commission but not in active service, discovered her, together with a faded photograph. Eventually a work party came aboard and took her to a naval dockyard where they found that her engines and even her gun still worked. Two Oerlikon machine-guns were fitted to make her look more warlike; a depth charge rack was constructed at her stern and HMAS *Kookaburra*, with a scrape down of the rust and then a coat of grey paint went off to her second war to again protect small coastal convoys. A duty she and her crew performed in a slow, nonchalant manner for the next eighteen months. Hardly anything to do. No raiders. No U-boats. Nothing to disturb the apparent tranquillity of those runs from Melbourne to Perth and back again. Good for training but not much else.

Bit by bit, the real action-yearning sailors aboard her applied for transfers and they were all readily granted. *Kookaburra*'s crew became synonymous for the dead-beats or maybe war-shy Australian sailors who wanted a 'cushy' job.

Her captain was nearly always drunk. Fed up with the unexciting routine he took to bottles of lager beer that were in plentiful supply. His only real excitement in his naval career was in the November of twenty-seven years previous when he'd served as a cadet officer aboard the First World War cruiser HMAS *Sydney* which battered the up-to-then elusive, almost mercurial German light cruiser SMS *Emden* on to a coral reef near the *Cocos* Islands in the Indian Ocean. Even so, he was reprimanded with the rest of his gun crew for failing to get their six-inch gun into action quickly enough and so far as the evidence went, for failing to register a hit on the German cruiser until after she became stuck fast as a consequence of running on to that reef. Ever since, he'd borne a grudge against the naval authorities that only saw fit to raise him to lieutenant status by the time the hostilities ceased. Twenty years later he felt drawn, by some strange quirk of fate to return to the Navy and offered his services. As Australia's oldest lieutenant-in-reserve, they placed him in charge of the one active warship that would be unlikely even to test the limited range of his naval capabilities.

As the lack of action began to dull his brain, Henry Wilmot tried to cheer himself up with swigs at bottles of hard liquor or beer. Less and less of his brain cells devoted less and less time to caring about his small warship command. Increasingly he left the running of it to the junior sub-lieutenants who came, saw, never conquered and then rapidly applied for a fresh posting. The naval authorities seemed quite happy with the situation. The junior officers were getting their sea experience and Henry Wilmot didn't care about a transfer.

So they left him on board his slow little warship to trundle up and down the coast.

Junior radar operator Chris Heine reported the four blips when they were about fifteen thousand yards away. *Dresden*'s crew were already at action stations. The forward gun turrets probing the evening air over the port bow sensing for the target.

'Target in sight!' sang out a lookout.

The little sloop leading the three medium-sized coasters came into view. Lieutenant (reserve) Henry Wilmot was half-asleep on the bridge. Midshipman Farrell arrived onto the bridge for the late evening watch. Wilmot grunted 'Good-evenin' pal' and lurched off to the 'heads' at the rear of the little bridge.

Farrell didn't even know what course the sloop was supposed to be on so he simply said 'Steady as she goes.'

It didn't really matter for suddenly violent flashes lit up the southern horizon. Farrell looked up, thinking a tropical storm was closing them but to his terrified feeling of shock and disbelief, he saw the merchantmen immediately astern of *Kookaburra* suddenly stagger and burst into flames. Recovering quickly, he yelled 'Hard-a-port. Gunners. Open Fire!' The little ship began to turn towards the fierce-some object on the horizon that was violently flashing flame. Two more shells crashed into the merchantman and she came to a shuddering halt sinking by the bows. The other merchantmen began to turn to starboard to try and begin a run for the coastline but they too were soon caught by the next series of salvoes from *Dresden*. Each shuddered to a halt, their survivors rapidly evacuating their stricken vessels. Wilmot, his trousers round his ankles, ducked into his sea-cabin, shaking with fear and drunken terror. Farrell, outwardly efficient but inwardly terrified, was responding to the naval discipline of his training days as he gripped the rusty bridge rail. The four-inch gun at last fired a shell in the general direction of their assailant but then, it and its crew vanished as *Kookaburra* sailed straight into *Dresden*'s fourth salvo of eleven and five point nine inch shells. With a horrifying screech of tearing metal, the thin spindly funnel of the sloop toppled over and took away one of the machine guns with it as it crashed down to the rear of the bridge.

'Cease fire' ordered Reitz as he saw the little warship come to a sinking, listing halt. 'Lower boats. Rescue as many as you can.'

Brautsch took his boat towards the sinking sloop whose surviving sailors dazed by the suddenness of events were already jumping into the water trying to swim away from their shattered warship. The other boats made their way to the stopped and sinking merchantmen, the first ship to be hit going under just as the Germans reached the area where her few survivors were clinging to floating wreckage. As darkness fell, the boats switched on their searchlights in an attempt to locate the struggling survivors.

Wilmot, seeing a searchlight and semi-recovering from his far too hasty tumble for shelter, roared 'Put that light out!' and hurled his near empty beer bottle in the vague direction of the offending beam.

It missed the boat's light by a long way. Seeing the failure of his attempt to put out the light, Wilmot staggered towards the rails, but as they'd been blown away, he promptly fell overboard and almost into the boat carrying Brautsch. Thrashing wildly, Wilmot was seized by one of the German sailors and somewhat unceremoniously was hauled spluttering furiously into the boat.

'Blimey!' guffawed one of the Germans.'This bloke, er, um officer, ain't half pissed. You can smell him despite his soaking!'

Then Brautsch was leaping aboard the sinking sloop that probably due to trapped air below wasn't going down as fast as originally thought.

From the bridge a befuddled and dazed Farrell witnessed the antics of his captain and then armed men begin to board his ship which he didn't realise was in danger of sinking. He pulled at his pistol, thumbed off the safety catch and blindly fired it at the incoming Germans, thinking that his ship was being boarded by pirates and that he, Midshipman Ernest Farrell, nineteen years old, had to defend it, even to the last bullet.

The answer came very quickly. One of the German sailors fired a savage burst from his semi-automatic machine pistol. Bullets clanged around and over Farrell's head. He dropped down to the boarding of the bridge and shouted 'OK. I surrender!'

Two German sailors, with Brautsch, rushed up the bridge ladders, seized the bewildered young midshipman and spoke roughly at him 'Alles raus, alles raus!' Farrell, even more confused, allowed himself to be dragged off the bridge. Flashing a torch around, Brautsch could find nothing of immediate real value and then sensing the sloop suddenly beginning what seemed to be her final struggle to stay afloat, he hurried after his men and their young prisoner. Even as his boat backed away, *Kookaburra* lurched suddenly to her port side and then, ever more rapidly by the stern, sank in a flurry of steam and bubbles.

All the launches were busy for the next half-hour picking up survivors of the sunken merchantmen as well as some of *Kookaburra*'s crew who'd jumped overboard after that shattering salvo of shells that had wiped out their one big gun.

It was completely dark when a recall light flashed out from high up on *Dresden*'s bridge. Reitz was beginning to fret over the time taken to try and rescue the convoy's survivors. He felt sure that the convoy's destruction would soon arouse the revenge of the Australian naval authorities but the ship's wireless room reported nothing. Only one of the convoy's ships had begun a desperate message for help but this had stopped after the words – 'Am being sh –' when one of the battlecruiser's shells wiped out the wireless office. None of the other ships had called for help fearing vicious retribution.

The last of the launches with its men and prisoners was safely back in its blocks as the battlecruiser steamed away at over twenty knots directly away from the coast. Reitz was pleased when he learned that only about two-dozen of the convoy's combined crew total of two hundred and seventeen men had perished in the attack. It meant that his sailors led by Brautsch had been able to effect a rescue that came up high on his list of priorities. Save life once the fighting had ended. It had distressed him, and still did, to have witnessed the *Resolve*'s violent end as well as of other ships that by perforce his battlecruiser had sunk in a ruthless manner. So many times this had happened so that to rescue such a large proportion of the convoy's sailors had, in a little way, redressed that balance.

Down in the Sick Berth, Doctor Lebers together with Andrea and Elfrida helped bandage the half-dozen survivors who'd been sent for medical attention. Only two were kept in for observation, the rest joined their bewildered colleagues all bemused by the fact that they were prisoners on a Kriegsmarine warship on which served two English nurses.

Into the night surged the sleek battlecruiser. Away from the shipping lanes. Vanishing into the dark as if she'd never been there at all.

By the next morning *Dresden* was over three hundred miles away from the scene of her attack on the convoy. None of the three merchantmen or even the *Kookaburra* had been able to get out a coherent message, so overwhelmingly rapid had been the battle-cruiser's attack. The coastguards nearest to the attack did report seeing some vague orange flashes and what may have been some faint rumblings but when these were reported it was put down as a rogue thunderstorm. No-one, not even amongst the naval authorities in Melbourne, even remotely suspected an attack by a major surface unit by the Kriegsmarine. As no-one knew for certain where the *Dresden* was, no search was mounted for the little convoy. All the survivors of the convoy had been picked up by the battlecruiser's launches.

Circumspectly Reitz took his command well away from the east coast of Australia but not once did the wireless room report the loss of the convoy being announced either from shore stations or in ship-to-ship or to shore messages. Cruising steadily, *Dresden* entered the south-eastern approaches of the Coral Sea to the north of the Australian mainland at dawn on Sunday, 7th December. Still undetected. Still not even suspected to be in the area. But then events well to the north of her were soon to dominate the lives of all those on board as well as the World at large.

Chapter 7

'Might as well chuck rotten apples'

The calm waters of Pearl Harbor, the main Pacific naval base of the United States of America were rudely shattered when waves of attacking Japanese carrier planes dropped bombs and torpedoes at the moored rows of stately battleships in an act of unprecedented furore on that Sunday morning, 7th June 1941.

The news of the attack surprised Reitz as to its intensity when the wireless room, via the loudspeaker in his main cabin where he'd spent the night trying to relax, relayed the startling news from a near hysterical Australian news-reader broadcasting from Darwin.

Reitz grimaced over his coffee and then, taking the microphone speaker which was plugged into the ship's relay system, he made an announcement to the crew.

'Listen all of you, this is the Captain speaking. I have to tell you, if you don't know already, that aircraft from Japanese carriers have attacked the American Fleet based in Pearl Harbor. As we are in an Axis with Japan, quite soon I expect we shall have an ally with them but in turn we shall have a bigger enemy with the Americans. How successful the Japanese have been in neutralising the American

Pacific Fleet, I don't know but one reason why we are in these waters is to harass Allied shipping as much as we can and probably soon to assist the Japanese Navy. That is all. Be always vigilant. Thankyou.'

There was no cheering at this news. Padré Jervaulx, preparing for his usual Sunday Mass, said a silent prayer for the Americans who'd obviously been killed in the attack and then, as always in his preparations, one for all those on board the battlecruiser.

Suddenly, Reitz put his coffee down. He summoned Brautsch and Anders, telling them to go with him to the prisoners' quarters. He needed to address them. Urgently,

'Gentlemen, officers and crews of ships that we've sunk or captured, I bid you a good morning' Reitz announced to the assembled motley-dressed sailor-prisoners in front of him.

'Yes, I know that it's hot in here but the news that I have is even hotter. This morning Japanese aircraft launched from carriers have attacked units of the American Navy at Pearl Harbor in Hawaii. Have no fear; none of you will be going to Japan to one of their camps. You, and I, know of their efforts in China. Not pleasant. When we link up with our supply ships again we shall make arrangements to have you trans-shipped to Europe where, although our prison camps aren't luxurious, they are better run than those in Japan. When you'll be transferred I'm not sure. Please be patient. Thankyou for listening' and with that, Reitz saluted the prisoners, turned on his heel and left them. MacLeod and Wills-Wilson in return saluted though they felt that Reitz hadn't seen them. What they had seen was sadness lined across his face as he'd spoken. America may have been hurt but in due time she'd fight back with the massive superiority that she'd shown in the last six months of the Great War. That was it. The reason for the sadness. Reitz, even now, sensed that eventually the Axis Powers would be defeated and it showed on his face in his speech to the prisoners.

In the British naval base close to Singapore Admiral Tom Phillips also heard of the Pearl Harbor attack whilst in his cabin aboard the newly arrived battleship, and his flag ship, HMS *Prince of Wales* which lay at anchor, with her destroyer escorts. Summoning the battleship's captain as well as her consort's skipper he made the point, so similar to the one that beset George Reitz, that eventually the full weight of the American war machine would gather its strength to crush the impudent Japanese. Meanwhile the Royal Navy would, with the combined might of the battleship and her consort, the elderly but still powerful battlecruiser, HMS *Repulse*, would soon sally forth to attack the Japanese convoys bearing soldiers intending to further reinforce their invading forces believed to be landing in northern Malaya. If Phillips ever considered the vague warnings that he'd received from Collins when he'd left Simonstown that the *Dresden* could also be in the area, he never mentioned it. When sided up with the array of Japanese aircraft carriers, capital ships, cruisers and other smaller warships that were soon, if not already, poised to attack Allied positions in the area, the German battlecruiser was, relatively speaking, small fry. Perhaps he'd dismissed *Dresden*'s efforts off East Africa just as had the late Rear Admiral Hallett. Perhaps, again like Hallett, he never really understood the enormity of the naval warfare that was staring at him. Directly. Yet he couldn't grasp it so sure was he of the superiority of Royal Naval ships. Properly led, the best in the world. Better than any tin-pot sailed by a little Nip. Or Kraut for that matter.

He, Tom Phillips, was here to defend Singapore.

Singapore.

A city of British Imperial pride.

Fortress Singapore. With huge guns facing seawards as its principal defence. No-one in the city could work out why Japanese forces had, at the same time as the Pearl Harbor attack, launched an invasion of Northern Malaya. Nothing there but dense, impenetrable jungle. A barrier to any land-borne assault on the British possessions to the south and ultimately across the Johore Strait to Singapore.

The conference, such that it was, continued with the two captains of the capital ships sharing none of Admiral Phillips' apparent enthusiasm for a surface attack, even if supported by the four fleet destroyers that had come with them as escort. Leach butted in 'Sir, we haven't any air cover now that *Indomitable*'s suffered damage after her grounding in the West Indies.'

In reply Phillips pointed out that the local RAF Stations would give them support, when needed. Captain Tennant was somewhat sceptical. 'What can a few Hurricanes and out-dated Bristol Brewster planes do? None of them can match the Japanese Zero in air performance!'

Phillips steepled his fingers. 'Listen, both of you. The Yanks weren't prepared. We are. We shall attack the Japanese because they won't expect us.'

Tennant inwardly grimaced. He knew, within hours of his bulk of a battlecruiser tying up to her buoy in the naval anchorage that the probable numerous Japanese spies in the city would have been vying with each other to be the first to inform their Tokyo masters of *Repulse*'s arrival. Never mind the *Prince of Wales*. Two desperately needed capital ships for Home waters yet here they were, half-a-world away, arriving, so their own press put it, to scare off the Japanese from attacking any Allied territory in the area.

Even the civil authorities in Singapore were so confident of the overwhelming presence of the two big ships that they left the city's lights on that first night of this new extension of the war so that when a small force of Japanese bombers arrived they could hardly miss the still brightly lit city below them.

Too late the order for a blackout came but the fires from the first load of bombs acted as a marker for the second group of Japanese aircraft. Only the ships in the naval anchorage remained blacked out. Neither did they open up with their anti-aircraft guns. Phillips didn't want to reveal his newly arrived ships to the Japanese and thus create another Pearl Harbor.

But the attacks had done their damage. Not physically. Morally they'd sent a shiver down even the most hardened military mind. Singapore was in range of air-attack. Not a comforting thought for the native and civilian population.

Two days later, Adolf Hitler led his Nazi Germany into a further extension of the war by declaring war on the United States of America.

When Reitz heard of this latest news he commented to Hiltzern who was standing with him on the upper bridge enjoying a short break with a cup of coffee. 'Remember what I said when we listened to the news about Pearl Harbor. You've heard the news since. Only battleships were sunk there. No mention of the American aircraft carriers. They'll bide their time but I fear the Japanese, and maybe us if they can find us, will be in for a very nasty shock. Our days of major surface raiding will be over if the enemy has air superiority. It will be up to us all to be extra vigilant when those days come. Maybe not today, nor tomorrow or for another year, but the sleeping giant of American capitalism has been aroused. It will stretch, yawn and then produce men and weapons faster, and possibly better than anything that the Axis forces can produce. Do you agree?'

Hiltzern nodded.

Nothing could shake Reitz from his gloomy mood. Not even when a day or two later he learned, via SKL and Allied radio stations, of the grim loss to the British of their two big capital ships off the East Malayan coast. *Prince of Wales. Repulse.* Sunk in a couple hours. By aircraft from nearby Japanese mainland bases. Drowning Admiral Phillips and many of his men because the little man had so fatally underestimated the striking effectiveness of a well-directed air assault on even the best protected of capital ships. Shattering the Royal Navy for unlike the situation when they'd lost the *Hood* to the *Bismarck* and her consort, there was simply no compact force to assemble in the area to combat the Japanese. Just a few cruisers scattered around the East Indies. The intended area of attack for the Japanese forces.

In a series of coded messages, SKL ordered Reitz to take *Dresden* into those East Indian waters to exploit the Allied weakness. Go for merchant ships and attack any of their isolated warships should the situation be favourable. Exploit the debacle of the loss of those two big capital ships. When ordered to do so, Reitz was to take his ship for an overhaul at a Japanese naval base. Then should come a possible return in the winter months to home waters.

Serle laid out a course for Reitz to follow when given orders from his captain who seemed to be recovering out of his gloomy attitude of the previous four days. *Dresden* was on the search. On the attack. At unsuspecting victims because like that brief foray off Melbourne, the warship just wasn't expected.

As she threaded her passage towards the South China Sea via the waters to the west of New Guinea and east of the Philippines, three times *Dresden* approached independently routed merchantmen whilst pretending to be an Allied cruiser. SKL's information that the veteran cruiser of the River Plate action, HMS *Exeter* was based at Singapore and so, it was her name that Reitz used as a pseudonym as the German warship approached the merchantmen. Three times they stopped without using their wireless. Three times Brautsch and his men were able to board the ships with total surprise. Three times the crews were all captured without the loss of a single member. Everything considered useful was taken off them. Twice Luth and his men were able to transfer fuel oil from them into *Dresden*'s emptying tanks for Reitz made no effort to risk his two valuable supply ships into the area preferring as he put it, to exist off what they could capture. One of the ships was carrying a large amount of fresh fruit and all of this was transferred, whilst *Dresden* flew a huge 'White Ensign'. No Allied aircraft flew over them. No Allied warship appeared to disturb the scene of transferring supplies. Even the sea remained calm and blue as each of the three merchantmen were scuttled and sunk with little trace of their presence. Each day the radio broadcast the news of the Japanese advances. Nothing it seemed could stop them. The American carriers were withdrawn to the other side of the Pacific and the Allied cruisers in the area hadn't yet been organised into a force strong enough to be risked chasing after mythical Japanese troop convoys.

Dresden closed in towards the South China Sea entering it, off North Borneo, on Christmas Eve. Reitz announced to the crew that the next day, presents could be exchanged and carols sung – except by those on watch. Even the prisoners were allowed to decorate their somewhat cramped quarters.

Christmas Day. The South China Sea off North Borneo was fairly tranquil as dawn broke. Far from the traditional Father Christmas, snow-covered fir trees and candle-lit churches resounding with the familiar carols. The sun's heat was already making the damp decks steam dry after the night's brief tropical storm. Reitz, as ever served with breakfast by the faithful Walters, laughed as the little steward came in with a red hat and white beard. 'Mornin' sir, Father Christmas with a pressie even for the captain' and saying this whipped off a napkin to reveal a small iced cake in the shape of a ship. 'Compliments of me, via the chef!'

Reitz smiled up at Walters. 'Thankyou Rudi.' Then reaching under his pillow he extracted a card.

'This is for you, Rudi,' It read – 'To the Best Steward in the world. George and Elle.'

Some time later, after standing the day's second watch as the battlecruiser cruised slowly westwards at ten knots some three hundred miles north of the nearest land, Reitz attended a Mass celebrated by Padré Jervaulx on the aft deck, with the music led by the ship's band. Even some of the prisoners attended and Reitz, standing next to Captains Wills-Wilson and MacLeod translated where necessary. After the sweating Jervaulx had given his Christmas blessing, he shook hands with the two captains, wishing them and their men 'Christmas Greetings'. Then, on an impulse when back on the bridge, he decided to address the crew and also the prisoners.

Firstly in German he announced 'My faithful crew. A happy Christmas to you all. I am only sorry that we cannot be with our loved ones at home. We are in this area to intercept any Allied shipping fleeing from Hong Kong and trying to reach Singapore or any of their other bases in the East Indies. But, unless our pals in the radar room detect otherwise, or one of our aircraft does so in two hours time, we shall all have our Christmas dinner in our various messes and think of those we love as we briefly forget this war. I hope, for once, that the Allies will oblige us by not disturbing this hour or so of peace and of jollity. Those on watch will be vigilant, as always for we haven't won this war – yet! My best wishes to you all. I am so proud of you. Happy Christmas.'

Then the voice in the prisoners' quarters changed from German to English. 'Greetings to our Allied prisoners. In an hour or so a Christmas dinner will be served up to you. I am only sorry that you are here and not at home at this special time. Eventually we shall meet up with our supply ships for your transfer but until then, please bear with us and try to enjoy yourselves within the limited facilities that we have. My best wishes to you all.' The speakers then clicked off. Reitz felt that he'd done his best in a far from ideal situation. What came next was totally unexpected for five minutes later; Captain MacLeod was ushered on to the bridge by Schenke and Anders. He saluted Reitz and extended his right hand. Reitz took it and shook hands with *Llandaff*'s former captain.

'Captain Reitz. On behalf of the prisoners I extend our best wishes. Although we are your prisoners we respect your fair treatment.' Then with his left hand he produced a present. A beautifully carved figure-head of an angel. Then a card covered in signatures with the motto 'Christmas Greetings to You from Us.'

Reitz was genuinely touched.

'Thankyou, Captain MacLeod. I hope that one day you and I will meet again when the war is over. I am grateful and rest assured I hope to be able to care for your welfare as well as is possible.'

Then he saluted MacLeod and bade him farewell.

Two hours later, from amidships one of the Arados took off with a roar from its catapult on a search mission.

Dresden was back at war again.

Christmas had been acknowledged albeit briefly.

A precious moment or two. Vital for morale. But this was war. War with a vengeance. With a purpose. For all involved, whatever side. It wouldn't stop just because it was Christmas Day.

Just over an hour later the Arado returned, the crew flashing a signal. Urgently. Soon after the aircraft was hoisted on board, the pilots reported to Reitz.

'Two small fast Allied warships about sixty miles to the north heading south-west. Probably *en route* to Singapore.'

Radar picked them up at eighteen thousand yards as *Dresden* closed in to investigate.

A lookout soon reported 'Mastheads in sight. Ships are destroyers.' Gun ranges were quickly calculated. Speed was increased to thirty knots. *Dresden* was hurtling back into war.

'Guns. Open fire.'

The two destroyers were indeed racing from Hong Kong. One was an American four-stacker, the USS *Robert B. Kitson* the other HMS *Anemone* a small British 1916 built destroyer with three funnels. Two old destroyers built for a previous war but currently seeking refuge from the horrors of the present conflict. That is until they crossed courses with *Dresden*.

Anemone's crew were first to sight *Dresden* but although they went to actions stations, due to the German ship's non-Japanese outline, they first assumed her to be one of the Allied cruisers based in Java coming north to escort them, hoping that it was HMS *Exeter*, or USS *Houston* or even one of the Dutch cruisers. They'd left Hong Kong on 23rd December, rendezvoused with the *Kitson* and now only a day or so's sailing from Singapore had begun to slightly relax after the vicious fighting in the coastal waters off Hong Kong.

Somehow, after crippling three invasions barges and being machine-gunned by avenging Japanese aircraft, the little British destroyer had escaped into the night. Loaded with some scared 'greenhorn' Canadian soldiers who nervously manned their Bren-guns as an extra anti-aircraft defence, she'd found the seas clear of any Japanese warships. Until sighting *Dresden*.

Now here was a fast approaching large warship flying what the *Anemone*'s crew at first took to be a 'White Ensign'. None of them as yet could see that it was Reitz's own adaptation of the flag flown by the High Seas Fleet at Jutland. A small swastika had replaced the Imperial Eagle. At long ranges it could be mistaken and it was for this reason that Reitz flew it. An accepted ruse.

Lieutenant Irwin Briggs, the captain of *Anemone*, was tired. All of a sudden, really tired. Being based at Hong Kong had become increasingly irritating for this rebel in the ranks of officers currently serving in the Royal Navy. His straight light brown hair was far too long, he never wore his tie up to his collar when on shore duty and worst of all, drank brandy, rather than the usual Navy 'tipples' of either gin or rum. He had upset the authorities in Hong Kong with his brashness about trying to get them to recognise the Japanese threat. But he was an excellent captain and a first-rate seaman. Those three shattered Japanese launches that had tried to land their troops had been left utterly wrecked and most of the troops as blasted corpses when *Anemone* had closed in at full speed and her gunners had fired at that close range in the destroyer's brave counter-attack. His crew respected him but like him, now that the surrendered colony was well behind them, they'd begun to relax. Tiredness began to re-assert its presence.

Briggs, alerted by the lookout, stared at the approaching warship with slightly blurred eyes desperately trying to focus through his binoculars. Two twin turrets forward. Could be *Exeter* or the Dutch *Van Tromp*. Certainly not the Jap battlecruisers *Haruna* and *Kongo* thought to be near the Malayan coast. Didn't have their pagoda-like bridge structure. But it couldn't be *Exeter* he thought. This ship approaching had only one funnel, as Briggs swung *Anemone* in a curve towards *Dresden.*

'*Kitson*'s signalling, sir. They're asking if it is one of our's.'

'Reply negative. Suspect enemy. Split up until we're sure.'

Briggs couldn't work it out. Already *Anemone*'s wireless was radioing Singapore asking if the base had sent out a cruiser to escort them in. Singapore was slow to reply.

Had anyone known it on board *Anemone*, Singapore was in the process of having an enormous Christmas binge. As if the city's occupants knew that it would be their last such celebration for a long time to come. Even the naval base's operator wasn't fully sober and utterly resentful about the bleating from *Anemone.* It would take time for him to check.

He needn't have bothered.

Anemone's next message flashed the warning 'Unidentified warship has opened fire. On us.'

Which it had.

Dresden turned her whole length in order to bring rear turret 'Cesar' into play. The forward turrets fired at *Kitson,* and 'Cesar' aimed at *Anemone.* A ripple of fire from the secondary and tertiary guns as well also flashed out and at first nearly all of these seemed to be aimed in a deluge of overwhelming fire at the old four-stacker. The American was smothered in the rain of shells.

'She must be a new bloody Jap!' yelled Briggs as he ordered *Anemone* in a vicious twist to port whilst *Kitson* attempted to veer towards starboard. Too late. *Dresden*'s shells swamped the American and she was mortally hit with the flurry of the relentless salvoes. Then to Brigg's shocked dismay *Kitson* suddenly split into two halves, the section forward of her foremost funnel simply vanishing so quickly that had anyone blinked they'd have missed its going. The aft section only floated for a while longer before, with the screw still turning, it also dove under the surface. Only a few crew men were seen to leap away from the thrashing propeller.

'Make smoke. We'll work round the bastard!' yelled Briggs, his tiredness now gone. Back into action was his keen brain. He wasn't the Royal Navy's youngest destroyer captain for nothing. 'Christ, she's turning with us. How the hell can they try to out manoeuvre us?' Nevertheless *Anemone* led a charmed life for the next three minutes as she twisted and turned to the desperate orders from Briggs. She was in a fight against a superior opponent but by heck, Briggs wasn't going to give in – yet.

'Open fire when you can bear.' *Anemone*'s gun armament of three single four-inch guns came into action firing at *Dresden* as and when they could which wasn't easy due to the wild manoeuvring of their ship.

The officer in command at Singapore's base could do nothing. Heavy cruiser *Exeter* had already left for Java due to the worsening situation and all he had was an old 'C' class cruiser and some smaller warships, ranging from coastal gunboats to armed motor launches. Even had the base officials been fully sober there was nothing that they could do. Nothing to help *Anemone*. She was even out-of-range of the few RAF planes that were still based in the area. There was nothing they could do to suppress what was assumed to be an attack by a Japanese heavy cruiser. No-one knew that it was *Dresden*. Or guessed.

'Still can't make her out' commented Sub-Lieutenant Neeman, Briggs's second officer as he peered through the smoke and shell splashes whilst Briggs turned *Anemone* back on her previous track, hidden in the dense smoke now pouring out from her funnels. For once, *Dresden*'s normal accurate gunfire had as yet not scored a telling hit on the little destroyer although she was beginning to look like a pepper pot thanks to numerous splinters from the near misses frequently landing close by in water-heaving shell splashes.

Her forward four-inch gun fired its third shell when Briggs swung *Anemone* in a tight turn towards the German battlecruiser.

'Christ, we've hit the bugger!' yelled Neeman.

'Might as well chuck rotten apples. We must get in closer to try and torpedo it before she gets us' was the snarl of a reply from Briggs.

The gap closed. Three thousand yards. *Dresden*'s big guns were at full depression and their shells screamed over the speeding destroyer as Briggs closed the gap. Two thousand yards. 'Fire torpedoes!' yelled Briggs as he swung *Anemone* in a tight turn momentarily exposing her full length to the German warship for about fifteen seconds but it was enough. *Dresden*'s lighter guns raked the destroyer over her full length driving the torpedo men away from their lethal missiles. One shell severed the destroyer's steering and she continued to turn in a tighter circle under the bows of the charging battlecruiser.

'Good grief, she'll ram us. We've had it!' yelled Briggs.

There was no reply from Neeman. He'd been hit by a machine-gun bullet and laid spread-eagled and face downwards on the shattered planks of the bridge. The helmsman reported that he'd lost steerage way but even so the now sinking destroyer continued to close the gap with her much bigger opponent.

Dresden towered over her as Reitz clawed his command away from the danger of either ramming the destroyer or it ramming them. It was like *Tintagel* again. Or little *Gloworm* against *Hipper*. Even so, *Anemone*'s tilting mainmast brushed against the battlecruiser's port flank as she turned away to avoid the ramming situation. The little destroyer was now clearly sinking and Reitz ordered *Dresden* around in a tight turn to close the doomed warship.

'Stop ship. Lower boats. Get Brautsch to take the English nurses. We must rescue as many of those brave men as we can' Reitz ordered as *Dresden* began to close the gap with the doomed *Anemone*. Her stern was already under the water and with a gush of escaping boiler steam from her funnels, *Anemone* toppled on to her port side and sank in a flurry of foam and wreckage.

As she disappeared below the surface Brautsch was already in his motor-launch. Hurriedly he'd rung down to the Sick Berth and already Andrea with her medical bag, accompanied by Elfrida and two more sick-berth attendants, all wearing life-jackets were sliding down the ladders into the waiting boat. Then, released from the falls and her engine cutting into life, the launch sped across the quarter-mile to where *Anemone* had sunk. Two other boats were also launched to chase after Brautsch and another boat set off from the other side of *Dresden* aiming for the area where *Kitson* had sunk.

There were quite a number of survivors in the area of water in which *Anemone* had sunk and soon the launches were close enough to begin their rescue mission. One of the first men to be picked up was a long-haired small man who snarled as hands came over the launch's side to haul him up.

'Piss off you yellow bastards! I'd rather drown.'

To his astonishment Briggs heard a woman's voice calling out to him in English 'We're not Japanese. I'm an English nurse and I'm a prisoner of the Germans who've just sunk your ship. Come on, let me help you on board.' Briggs looked up and saw not only Elfrida who'd shouted at him but other European faces. 'Come, come' yelled Brautsch 'Come, we're here to rescue you.'

Briggs looked at Elfrida and gasped 'Christ, bleedin' Germans' and then raised his arms which were seized and somewhat hurriedly he was heaved into the boat where Elfrida began to check him over. Apart from a small gash caused by a splinter in the lower part of his left leg, Briggs hadn't been harmed.

'Are you really English?'

'Ssh! It's a long story. There are two of us.'

The three launches searched for the next half-hour picking up as many of *Anemone*'s crew as they could who lay clinging to bits of wreckage or struggling to float in their sodden life jackets. It was desperate work for many of the survivors were wounded and their blood could attract sharks. A seaman with an automatic rifle fired at what looked like the menace of a dorsal fin but it was only an upturned box. Eventually the three boats set back to return to *Dresden* with a total of sixty-one survivors but some were desperately wounded. Andrea and Elfrida, fighting their own bile that threatened to make them sick, did what they could in their boat hurriedly applying bandages and in three cases, tourniquets.

The search boat for *Kitson*'s survivors found just four survivors, one of whom died before the launch could make it over the increasing swell back to *Dresden*.

Brautsch, with his lips tight, looked down into his boat admiring the way Andrea was working. Only once did his eyes meet hers but apart from a slight wink, she didn't respond. Too much killing. Too much death. On this horrifying Christmas Day.

Andrea had again come face to face with the savage reality of war. It didn't stop just because it was on the day of peace and goodwill. She hated herself, Helmut and everyone around her as she tied the last of the tourniquets into position. Then she looked up at Brautsch and saw his grim face, taut and etched against the late evening light. She then realised that he must be feeling the horror of the recent action as well. Even the German sailors had fallen quiet around her. So long from their own loved ones they obviously felt some twinge of sadness for the position in which the British survivors found themselves. The savagery of the action. Perhaps it had been too much. Then they heard one of the survivors mumbling 'Thank God you're not Japs. Not Japs. Not Japs.'

Soon the launch was hauled up to deck level. Reitz was waiting with Anders.

'Well done, all of you.' Then in English, he turned to Andrea and Elfrida 'Thank you ladies. I'm sure you've been a big help. After all this violence I still think of the real Christmas. Maybe we've all just shown some of its spirit after all.' Then he turned, motioning to Brautsch to make out his report. *Dresden* began to pick up speed, almost as if she too was eager to get away from the region. Aiming to go south of Singapore and thread her way through the various islands to turn north-west for the Malacca Straits in an attempt to intercept any Allied ships reinforcing, or fleeing, Singapore. To the best of SKL's knowledge' the Japanese surface forces were striking further south and east – to Sumatra, the Philippines and eventually to Java and other islands in the Dutch East Indies. Also, Reitz was endeavouring to reach *Olaf* which had steamed round Sumatra's western coast to link up with *Arabian Nights* and so to a rendezvous off the north-west point of Sumatra's elongated coast.

In his cabin Reitz sank to his bed and just allowed sleep to overtake him without undressing. Gently Walters came in and removed his outer clothes and then pulled a blanket over his sleeping captain.

Down in the sick-bay, as the battlecruiser surged on into the night, Doctor Lebers, his attendants as well as Andrea and Elfrida worked on cleaning and bandaging the wounds of the survivors. All were divested of their wet clothes that were duly tagged and sent off to be laundered. No matter how hard they worked, three of the survivors from *Anemone* died before dawn bathed the warship in a grey light.

Reitz woke up and with Padré Jervaulx at his side, together with as many of his own crew and even some of the prisoners including MacLeod and Briggs, the latter in borrowed kit, assembled near the stern of *Dresden* in the shadow of turret Cesar. The ship now slowed down for the funeral of not just the three British sailors but also two of *Dresden*'s crew who'd been killed when the one lone aggressive reply from *Anemone* had struck their anti-aircraft gun as they were firing at the elusive destroyer. The ship's band, now having learnt them, played both national anthems and then 'Stille Nacht' again as the canvas-weighted bundles were dropped over the side. More than one man went away with tears in his eyes. So too did Andrea and Elfrida. Sheer exhaustion hadn't helped. They were so tired. As they turned away, Lebers came to them and said 'No more ladies. Sleep for you both. And, well, thank you.' Briggs was also allowed to talk briefly to them 'Thanks girls. Please come and talk to us when you've rested.' Elfrida looked into his eyes, smiled and then quite surprisingly, kissed him with a sudden impulse, on his left cheek.

Dresden steamed steadily south-westwards weaving her way through the islands to the south of Singapore flying the White Ensign whenever any small boat or coaster was seen. Reitz made no attempt to communicate with them nor to stop them. He was after bigger prey. Late one afternoon he turned north-west and keeping Sumatra to port and an unseen Singapore to the starboard quarter, he pushed *Dresden* at twenty-five knots and entered the southern stretch of the Malacca Straits as darkness fell. The sea in the Straits was empty, just as Reitz had hoped. Once again *Dresden*'s luck was holding.

In Singapore the hangover from Christmas was long felt. The wildness of the celebrations took longer than usual to sober into the stark reality that the Japanese advance though the Malayan jungle was inexorably getting ever closer to the fortress, despite individual brave pockets of resistance.

28th December. At last someone in the naval base reacted to the loss of the two destroyers. A belated air search in the area resulted in nothing. Not even in finding their assailant which at that time was half-way through the Malaccan Straits.

Then, perhaps, a stroke (faint that it was) of fortune, smiled momentarily on the beleaguered Allies. A single lone Hurricane, one of a pitifully few in total at the RAF's base was chasing two Zero fighters that had strafed one of the Coast Defence Force's gunboats on patrol some ten miles off Malaya's west coast. As had been often the ironic fate of the RAF, the Hurricane was too late to prevent the gunboat being severely mauled but as the fighter forlornly chased after the faster Zeros, the pilot, Flight Lieutenant George Hancock saw a smudge of smoke and decided, despite being low on fuel, to investigate. It soon took the form of a large warship steaming northwards through the Straits. Hancock thought that no major Allied warships were supposed to be in the area so he flew even closer to investigate.

Suddenly the warship opened fire. Hancock couldn't distinguish the flag to verify whether it was Japanese. All he could work out amidst the flak bursts was that it had two big gun turrets forward and one aft. He banked his plane into a low dive hearing shrapnel rattling on to the aircraft's fuselage. Racing out of range he tried to radio base but a shell splinter had smashed into the Hurricane's set rendering it useless and it was to be nearly another forty minutes before his wheels hit the tarmac with the port-wheel's tyre bursting on impact. The plane slewed violently and Hancock had to use all of his skill to prevent the fighter from being totally wrecked. It was only when he stopped that he noticed blood seeping through his trousers just above the top of his left flying boot.

Hoisted into an ambulance he was carried to safety. His commander hurried to the makeshift bed in the base's hospital and asked him, somewhat sharply, why he'd made such mess of his landing.

Hancock's reply shook him 'Big Jap cruiser of unusual design for them, two hundred or so miles away steaming north through the Malaccan Straits.'

Despite this incorrect identification there was little the authorities in Singapore could do except send out a general broadcast that an enemy warship was in the Straits.

Admiral Collins assimilated Singapore's message of the unusual 'Jap cruiser' amongst all the other material that came into the Simonstown base. Something nagged him about the warship that had been reported. Sixth sense? He didn't know why but he asked one of his clerks to make out a report to him of all missing ships in November and December, which had been sunk by surface attack in the southern seas. It took some time but he had the list within six hours together with all the dates. He commented on the ones around Australia and casually traced a line to connect them. Although he wasn't aware of it, the trace was yet again an approximate course of *Dresden*. 'Damn!' he swore as the trace became apparent. 'It could be her. Signal Singapore and tell them that it is imperative that they find the warship and properly identify it. Tell them that in our opinion that it's not a Japanese cruiser but the German battlecruiser *Dresden* that is in their area. She'll probably move out into the Indian Ocean and circumvent Sumatra.'

Singapore's response was very gloomy. They simply had no aircraft left for 'search missions'. Most of the serviceable planes were leaving for bases in Java and North Australia.

The naval base at Colombo wasn't very helpful either but as and when the light carrier *Hermes* together with two heavy cruisers arrived they would consider a possible search for *Dresden.*

Suspected, but not realised by Collins, the *Dresden* was more or less where Sir Bernard thought she should be. Not in the Malacca Straits or even in the shipping lanes leading for Singapore. She was at the time that Collins was trying, with no firm evidence to back up his thoughts to determine her real presence, trailing *Olaf*, which was filling her near depleted fuel tanks. It had been a close thing for Reitz for apart from top-ups from *Shrimp II* and the two bigger freighters off the East Indies; the battlecruiser had received no extra fuel. It was a relief for Reitz and everyone on *Dresden* when *Olaf* had come into sight. Soon after came *Arabian Nights* and the rations that had been enforced on everyone, crew and prisoners alike for the past ten days could be relaxed. Some of the merchant seamen prisoners were transferred to the freighter to take new lodgings in one of her now empty cargo holds. Hurried carpentry work had preceded their transfer but even so, the resultant accommodation wasn't entirely satisfactory but the prisoners had no choice but to accept their lot. As Brautsch pointed out to them, they could be transferred to the Japanese if any of them felt like it. No-one wanted such a transfer.

Re-supplying over, Reitz took *Dresden* back to the shipping lanes converging into the Malacca Straits. Wireless traffic by Singapore was becoming increasingly desperate for help and for re-inforcing troops. No troopships were encountered but in four weeks, six merchantmen were all stopped. None of them wirelessed. Again, the pattern from the East Indies was repeated. Anything of value, particularly food, was removed before the ship was scuttled. One of the ships was kept as a suitable prison ship as its cargo of army lorries and machine parts was dumped overboard and the resultant empty holds were converted thanks to the ample supply of timber that the ship, *Aveline Star*, also carried.

The frantic calls from Singapore increased in volume until the wireless office picked up the final message from the beleaguered Allied city.

'Farewell friends. We are surrendering.'

The date: 14th February.

Ninety thousand British soldiers were swept up as prisoners to their astonished Japanese captors.

No more Allied ships would be going to the city. The last few desperate sailings had been fleeing. Away. Nearly all of them sailed southwards. To Java, still in Allied hands.

But one of the last Allied ships approaching Singapore was a big oil tanker. Thirteen and a half thousand tons. Named *Marona* and under the captaincy of a dour Devonshire sailor, Harvey Blissett. He'd been steaming down the Malacca Straits for Singapore but on hearing the bleak news, Blissett turned his ship round in the darkness of that night before the morning surrender of the doomed city and as fast as his over-straining ship's engines could take her, pushed *Marona* back up those Straits. More than once his ship's wireless picked up desperate pleas from bombed and strafed Allied ships trying to dodge the Japanese aircraft and warships amongst the islands to the south of Singapore but failing when caught out in the open sea. Blissett hardened his mind to ignore their calls knowing that his big vulnerable tanker would be easy prey if she herself was caught.

All through the next day *Marona*, at seventeen knots, steamed hard for the north-western exit of the Malacca Straits. Not once was a Japanese aircraft sighted. Night came. Still nothing.

Dawn. Only a few more miles. Then, the wide-open seas of the

Indian Ocean. Harvey Blissett ordered the engines to reduce speed. To a normal cruising of fourteen knots. Already his Engineering Officer had made three requests during the night to slow the whirring machinery as his staff couldn't cool the machinery sufficiently for such a high speed dash.

It wasn't a Japanese aircraft or destroyer that caused the alarm bells on *Marona* to ring. Something a lot bigger was approaching them from the north-west.

Blissett focussed his binoculars on the approaching vessel. Not once did he suspect that the warship coming even closer was anything other than an Allied cruiser. Perhaps it was coming to escort his valuable tanker clear of any Japanese attack. Neither he nor any of his crew had seen *Dresden*'s Arado 'plane above them over an hour earlier. Nor did Blissett ever realise that his ship had been a bright green glow on *Dresden*'s radar screen for the last half-hour.

Then the clearly large warship began to slow down, flashing a signal in the growing light of that 16th February dawn. 'Stop ship. HMS *Exeter*. New instructions.'

Blissett didn't want to stop his ship but, well, the ship was after all Royal Navy and was on the list of Allied warships that he'd been given known to be in the area. Some sixth sense troubled him. Surely *Exeter* had two funnels. Was she as big as this one? Even so, *Marona* gradually came to a halt with a haze of brown smoke pluming from her stern-placed funnel, a haze that floated across the water to the as yet unrealised *Dresden*.

All but one of *Marona*'s lookouts was gazing at the strange warship. But one lookout high on the tanker's bridge heard a noise and yelled 'Aircraft on starboard quarter!' Alarmed at the shout, Blissett dashed to the starboard wing of the bridge. There they were. Four aircraft. Coming in low. Dropping a torpedo each. Swooping towards the stopped tanker.

Desperately, one of the ancient Vickers machine-guns near the keen-eyed look-out opened fire from its sandbagged emplacement. A feeble spurt of flame as the aircraft, with the Rising Sun on their wings, swept over the hapless *Marona.*

Even on *Dresden* the crew topsides were unaware of the approaching low-flying Japanese attackers. Below radar height and masked by the tanker and her funnel smoke, Reitz's men were unable to see the torpedo-carrying aircraft. Until it was far, far too late.

In sheer desperation Reitz shouted 'Raise a Jap flag! Signal them as to what ship we are!'

Desperately Reitz forced his eyes onto the tanker. Knowing that she had no chance for even he could see as the Japanese aircraft climbed up above his ship that their bomb or torpedo racks were empty. Then he and those of his crew able to witness it, saw four columns of spray shoot up above the far side of the stopped tanker. Followed by a massive enormous burst of flames that shot up white-hot, then yellow and orange and finally with dirty brown thick smoke as the fuel tanks of the *Marona* split and caught fire.

'Sir, do something!' pleaded Anders almost screaming at his captain, his young face lined with anguish. As were all the horrified watchers on *Dresden.*

'What bloody fools we have as an ally! Yes, yes, launch the boats – and be bloody quick, for I fear that we will be too late' snapped Reitz and then, turning to the visibly shaken young officer Anders, said 'Remember that you're a serving officer on this ship. I know that the tanker was surrendering to us and that her crew are right now facing a horrible task of trying to escape and that – that –.' Here Reitz just couldn't find the words that fumed in his mind about the crass stupidity of those Japanese fliers.

Anders tried to pull himself together as from the starboard side of the battlecruiser, two launches hit the water with a splash and with engines gunned to their fullest revolutions, and with a white wash creaming from their sides, they surged as rapidly as they could towards the stricken tanker.

In the leading launch Brautsch suddenly waved his hands. 'Don't go any further! She's blowing up! We're too late. Hard-a-port!'

Marona vanished in a white cloud of heat, flames, smoke and finally a vast mushroom of vaporising steam as she broke in half and slid rapidly below the surface.

There were no survivors. Nothing except oil still burning in a widening spread on the surface.

Both boats were rapidly hauled out of the water. Brautsch and his men were visibly shaken.

So too was Reitz as he spoke rapidly on the 'phone to the wireless office. 'Get this message to SKL and also our naval attaché in Tokyo. No time for coding. Let the Allies pick it up for all I care. Message reads "JAP AIRCRAFT SANK BRITISH TANKER SURRENDERING TO US. TRUST THAT THERE WILL BE A SUITABLE EXPLANATION, REITZ. *DRESDEN*." Oh and add the time and our position as "North-West entrance of Malacca Straits".'

SKL picked up the message. So did the German naval attaché in Tokyo. Oddly enough, no Allied station was able to eavesdrop into the message until it was too late. All they picked up was – 'Reitz. *Dresden*'. Nothing else.

Ninety minutes later the four Japanese aircraft all touched down on their newly-acquired Sumatran base.

'Any success?' yelled one of the ground crew to the first pilot to emerge, Flight Commander Hanai Tanaska.

'Yes! We scotched a huge British tanker and had we any more bombs or torpedoes we'd have done a big Allied cruiser that was having the cheek to be pretending to be one of our ships!'

Suddenly the airfield's tannoy crackled into life. 'All four aircrew to report to the Group Commander.'

All twelve men hurried across eager to share their success.

'Fools! Idiots! Stand to attention, you imbeciles!'

Air-Colonel Shimatra screamed, waving a signal sheet. 'Just in from Tokyo. You blundering fools have been responsible for sinking a British tanker that was surrendering to our allies, namely the Kriegsmarine's battlecruiser *Dresden*. You were strictly told by me not to go into the north-western entrance of the Malacca Straits. Well?' The colonel was screaming his head off. Going through various shades of red and purple over his suffused facial expressions. Veins stood out in his neck as his anger seemed like an erupting volcano 'Well? Nothing to say? Any of you?'

All the aircrew stared straight ahead, expressionless. Shimatra continued. 'Well, this is what I have for you all!' Down the line of men he went, ripping off their air insignia badges from the uniform tunic of each man. He was particularly rough with his treatment of Tanaska. Then, having so vented his rage, he shouted 'None of you will fly again! All of you will be sent away from here to act as prison guards. You have shamed your squadron, your air force, your Emperor and me. In ten minutes a truck will take you out of this airfield. Dismiss!'

As one man, they all bowed, their iron discipline still holding them from answering back. Outside, and quite unexpectedly, Tanaska broke from the group now marching under guard, and before the guards could stop him, pulled out his pistol, put it to his mouth and squeezed the trigger, blowing his brains out and collapsing in a heap to the ground.

The other eleven men stolidly continued walking towards their huts. Still expressionless. Fearful of any further retribution. But that was of no consequence to any of *Marona*'s crew who had all perished.

It was perhaps yet the most disturbing episode in the career of the battlecruiser, her captain and her crew.

Thoroughly displeased, Reitz pulled his ship out of the Straits and sailed away from that horror to the planned-for rendezvous. Quite a collection. *Dresden. Olaf. Arabian Nights. Aveline Star*. And the best surprise of all for Reitz and his men. *Berengia*. She'd slipped out of Bordeaux and via the Azores and then the Cape of Good Hope she'd made it to the rendezvous. Her captain, Theider, was in good heart. His soldier prisoners had been well-behaved on the run to Bordeaux and quite a lot had wished him and his crew well before being taken off on their land journey to their various prison camps. But he was also in good heart for not only had he brought a ship well stocked with French wines, beer and fresh food, but also with ample supplies of ammunition, particularly in the shells needed for the big guns. Reitz had known that he couldn't have fought a further protracted action so the appearance of the supply ship was a welcome addition to the prolonging of already the longest cruise for a major German warship.

Most welcome of all were sackfuls of mail for the battlecruiser's crew. Reitz gave everyone, apart from the lookouts and a minimum of watch-members, the next four hours to collect their letters, read them and prepare their replies. With the supply of *Arabian Nights*'s refrigerated stocks at last running low, both she and *Aveline Star* would be attempting the run for Occupied France, the latter ship taking most of the prisoners that had been within the limited spare space available to them on board the battlecruiser.

The three letters that Elle had written to Reitz all wished him well. The crews of the big ships in Brest were known to be chafing at their forced stay in dock but their damage had been repaired. Who knows, one of them or even all three may make the breakout to come and join him or at least relieve his ship so that *Dresden* could return to Germany. Reitz smiled at this supposition from Elle for he doubted whether the British would allow the warships to escape. Neither he, nor Elle, knew that a decision, taken at the Fuhrer's behest, had already been taken to have all the three big ships break through to Germany via the English Channel. Through the Straits of Dover. A daring, secret plan that neither Canaris, nor his Abwehr staff were fully aware of for Adolf Hitler and his Nazi top brass were beginning, mainly under the connivance of Reichs-fuhrer Heinrich Himmler, to distrust Wilhelm Canaris.

She wrote of the time she and Reitz had spent together. Cuttings of *Dresden*'s deeds adorned her office and as she proudly wrote, of many other offices in the Headquarters at Brest. Somehow the cruise of the battlecruiser was still prominent news despite the Army's efforts in Russia and North Africa. She felt, writing her last letter in November, that soon the Allies would be asking for peace and then *Dresden*, her crew and her captain could all come safely home.

She missed him. She loved him. Please come home, soon. She mentioned nothing of the Army's setbacks in the mud and then the snows of Russia. Nor of the Allies holding Rommel away from Egypt. Nor of the entry of the United States for these checks in the tide of Nazi successes hadn't materialised when she'd last written. Germany hadn't won the war. 1942 could be the deciding year. Reitz shivered after he'd read her letters. He knew the real facts. He knew that his ship, after her refit in a Japanese naval yard would probably have to make another major attack to help the progress towards final victory. If not, *Dresden* would become the hunted, not the hunter. Elsewhere in the ship the letters brought varying degrees of news.

Brautsch's older brother had been lost at sea on an E-boat as it had skirmished with British coastal forces. Serle's wife' much to his disgust' had been assigned a job in Gestapo HQ in Copenhagen. Otto Schenke, the toughie of the lower deck, received an unexpected letter. As well as one from his wife he received one from his mother. Father had been killed by the bombs dropped from British aircraft in an air-raid. Good riddance, she'd said, for he was nothing but a lazy, drunken brute. She was sure that Otto would be pleased. Schenke tore the letter up in disgust knowing full well that his mother was delighted because she could now pursue more actively her free life with some of the country's top officials in exchange for the frivolities of war-life – new dresses, fur coats and bottles of French perfume.

Nurses Andrea and Elfrida didn't get a letter for as yet the Red Cross, who'd only been informed by the naval authorities that they'd been rescued by one of their ships, had not yet been able to contact the British authorities to allow any idea of sending a letter. Instead they'd contacted Reitz by letter, urging him to release them as and when he could.

So, it was something of a surprise when Doctor Lebers, having answered the telephone in the Sick Bay, approached them and said they were to report to the captain as soon as possible.

'Sit down please, ladies' Reitz began as they entered his main cabin. 'What can I offer you? Sherry or fruit juice? Maybe gin or brandy?' Elfrida took a dry sherry. Andrea said thanks for a brandy and orange juice. An unusual mixture thought Walters as he made it up.

Then he retired to his adjoining cabin. Both nurses then relaxed on a sofa while Reitz sat on his swivel chair that normally served as his desk chair on the few occasions that he used this main cabin. 'Ladies' he addressed them, turning slightly one way and then the other but with a smile on his face and a twinkle in his eyes, 'Ladies, you have been with us for over six months. My men speak highly of you. Doctor Lebers thinks you're wonderful. But, as you can see, here we are. A covey of German ships, two of which will soon be making their way to Occupied France. For slow merchant ships, strangely enough, they will have a better chance at reaching France than us for they don't attract the attention that my ship would.'

He paused. Both women wondered what was coming next but still took time to take a sip at their drink.

'Ladies, it has been a long, tiring cruise. My ship is in need of an overhaul in a dockyard. I am taking her to Japan. Before that I must make sure that my prisoners go in the opposite direction. You are my responsibility and although German camps won't be all that brilliant, from what I hear, they will be infinitely preferable to those run by the Japanese. Lieutenant Briggs –' here Elfrida began to colour a bit – 'has been able to tell Leutnant Brautsch some details of the indifference shown by Japanese to European prisoners. They are not pleasant.'

Elfrida looked carefully at the German but he seemed not to notice as having taken a sip of his whisky he continued 'The fact is, I'm giving you two and only you two, a choice. You can go on to *Aveline Star* and risk the breakthrough to France or – or you can stay with us on *Dresden*. But not as prisoners.'

'Not as prisoners?' queried Elfrida who, for once, was taking the lead.

'Yes. No longer as prisoners but as serving members of the Kriegsmarine. Ah, you may say, what are women doing on one of Germany's major warships? Well, we do also have a number of female shore-based auxiliaries – very similar to those attached to the Royal Navy. I have had papers prepared and signed by Admiral Canaris – we have some blanks with his signature on – purporting that you've been with us ever since the start of the cruise. You see, Japanese authorities may get suspicious and think that you are our prisoners. You will be paid – as and when we can get back to Germany and upon the ship's return, I shall personally vouch for the Red Cross to afford you safe conduct to a neutral country or in one of the exchanges that I understand are being made via Spain of badly wounded or civilian prisoners. I can't promise anything before then for I don't know as and when we shall try to return to my own country.So, ladies, what's your choice? A prisoner on *Aveline Star* or a prolonged cruise here on board my ship?'

Elfrida gave him a long look through her dark brown eyes 'If we go on *Aveline Star* will Lieutenant Briggs be with us?'

Reitz pursed his lips and lifting just his right eyebrow, murmured 'Ah, Miss Elfrida, you and Lieutenant Briggs get on very well. A very courageous man. Do you know that his ship was the first Royal Naval warship to land a shell on us? Yes, of course. I wouldn't want to break up a budding romance!'

Elfrida said 'You know?'

'My dear, there's not much I don't. Take your friend here, Nurse Andrea. If I'm not mistaken, she and Lieutenant Commander – note,

I have promoted him – Kapitan Leutnant in our terms – Helmut Brautsch are quite close friends. Is that not so, Andrea?'

She, in return, blushed.

'Ah, not an easy thing to admit. Love is a strange thing. Unlike us humans, it knows no boundaries and if needs be, unites those of us who by the circumstances of war, are nominally enemies.

Elfrida spoke, somewhat tersely 'In effect, Captain Reitz, you are giving us three choices.'

'Three?'

'Yes, Captain. We become members of your crew and thus 'traitors' to our own country or we continue as prisoners and take our chances on the *Aveline Star* on reaching Occupied France or we are handed over by you to the Japanese upon reaching Japan. Not much of a choice, is it?'

Andrea interjected 'Elfrida, don't be so harsh on the Captain. We have worked on our own free will on this ship. You know the nursing code. We don't have any boundaries either. Anyone needing treatment whoever they are is given help by us if we can, circumstances allowing. As for Helmut, yes, I do like him and I don't care if he's supposed to be my 'enemy'. I'm not all that keen on being interned by the Japs nor of going to a prison camp in Occupied Europe. I'm quite willing to sign as a nursing auxiliary as long as *Dresden* and Captain Reitz require my services.'

'You can't Andrea. No, I'm going to go with Briggsie and see that he gets my care and attention on the journey to France. He's still not fully recovered from the wounds and sense of shock he received when the captain here and his glory boys smashed his ship to bits on Christmas Day!'

At that moment Walters entered with more drinks. Elfrida turned on him and said 'Stuff your booze, Captain. I'm sorry. I don't want to be on this ship anymore. I'm going on *Aveline Star*.' Then quite suddenly she burst into tears spilling her drink on to the carpet. She realised what an outburst she'd made but through her tear-brimmed line of sight she saw Reitz smiling and heard him say very gently 'Elfrida Ramsdale. You are a very brave woman. I shall transfer you to *Aveline Star* and with you, I shall write a note for the German Red Cross to transfer you and Lieutenant Briggs to a neutral country as soon as they can arrange for such a move. Should an Allied warship stop you of course such a note will not be required. Please, please, both of you, continue drinking. My steward Walters has also a few delicious canapés and ship-made biscuits for your palates. I have to go now to see that our ships are in place for the transfer of supplies and provisions. Farewell.' With a slight bow and a click of his heels, he turned and left the cabin.

Andrea and Elfrida followed him with their eyes and then turned to look at each other. Both knew that this was a key point in their lives. Separation from each other with the man of their own preference. Decisions for each coupled with risk. Andrea knew that deep down she loved Helmut Brautsch but signing for the Kriegsmarine, although this would keep her safe from the clutches of the Japanese, it would mean that technically she was supporting 'the enemy'. She consoled herself with the fact that nurses were neutral in war. The victim whoever he or she was on the operating table or the patient in the hospital or sick-berth bed was someone which her profession had taught her to give her loving care and attention whatever the creed, race or religion to which they were attached. Elfrida felt that she couldn't leave Lieutenant Briggs on his own. He was still severely traumatised by the action of *Dresden* against his little ship. In sight of safety but yet caught on Christmas Day. His physical wounds had almost healed; his mental torment would carry on for a long time to come. Elfrida was determined to be with him to help him get over the tragedy and to face the future whether it was on a German supply ship, in a prison camp or better still, hopefully, in a Red Cross exchange scheme. She wasn't going to leave her 'Briggsie' by himself. Not now. Not never.

Andrea went over to the desk and seeing one of the prepared papers with her name on it she signed it at where Walters, ever helpful, showed her. As she could read German, she perused the sheet carefully. Reitz had added the sentence 'for the duration of the cruise of *Dresden* or until the cessation of hostilities.' Cessation of hostilities. When would that be? Probably next year. Maybe even in 1944. So she appended her signature and with it, in her heart, confirmed her love for Kapitan Leutnant Helmut Brautsch.

Brautsch was, at the moment, unaware of the conversation that his captain had recently held with the two women. Right now his concern, together with Hiltzern was the overseeing of the battle-cruiser's manoeuvrings with *Olaf* on her port side and *Arabian Nights* on the starboard side. Both ships, in the gentle swell were alongside *Dresden* and stores were being transferred. *Aveline Star* was alongside *Berengia* taking on fuel and some stores. Then she would come alongside *Arabian Nights* and help to deplete her once ample provisions even further. What a find that originally crippled ship had been! Similar to one that *Scheer* had found when she'd captured the coal-burning *Duquesa* which went on supplying other raiders in 1940 until her fuel ran out and also when she was towed around for some time after that. Finally depleted of most of her stocks of meat, eggs and other goods, she was reluctantly sunk. Reitz was determined to get *Arabian Nights* to France. On her way home she would supply some of the long-range submarines operating the African and Indian trading routes. Long distance plans could see her back, re-stocked, on further supply work providing that the Allies didn't intervene in the process. Five gentle days passed in that quiet area well to the west of the Sumatran coast. Even the able-bodied prisoners helped when told to transfer to *Aveline Star*. It was with reluctance that some of them went but some also stayed on *Dresden*. Andrea. Some others were recruits of Chinese origin who were working as laundry assistants; two of the Indian lads stayed in the kitchen. Reitz had them all sign on as members of the Kriegsmarine. As he told them, they were members of his crew, not Japanese prisoners, as and when *Dresden* reached Japan.

At last came the day of parting. *Berengia* and *Olaf* with huge Japanese flags on their masts and suspended on their sides sailed for the Straits of Malacca and Singapore. SKL were requested to pass on to the Japanese about the presence of both ships. Reitz didn't want his precious supply ships to suffer the appalling fate of tanker *Marona*. *Arabian Nights* was next to go, bound for her U-boat supply mission. More than one member of *Dresden*'s crew gazed wistfully after her as she churned towards the western horizon. Finally it was Leutnant Anders and his prize crew's turn on *Aveline Star* to wave farewell. Elfrida embraced Andrea with tears on her cheeks before taking the short motor-boat trip with Lieutenant Briggs across to the merchantman. With her, was Captain MacLeod, who before he'd boarded the boat, was allowed to see Reitz.

In his gruff plain-speaking voice he said to the German captain 'Tha' might be mi' enemy but I'm saying this on behalf of all of us – tha's looked after us as well as circumstances allow. Maybe we'll catch your ship and if we do, and you're sunk, I'll mek it mi' business to say that tha' were a gentleman. If tha' not sunk, well, good luck to you and yer crew. May we meet in better circumstances' and with that he held out his right hand and shook the German's. With his left hand he held out a painting of a view from the midships deck up to *Dresden*'s bridge. One he'd done himself during the frequent 'free' time he and fellow prisoners had been allowed. On the back it was signed by every one of the prisoners, including Andrea and Elfrida.

Reitz, somewhat taken aback by the gesture, could only murmur 'Thankyou, Captain MacLeod. As you say, may we meet again when this war is over. As friends.'

With that, MacLeod stepped back, saluted and then with his relaxed lone escort, made his way to the waiting boat.

Aveline Star began to gather speed with her crew and many of the prisoners all waving to *Dresden* until the battlecruiser, gathering speed herself, showed her stern to the converted prison ship.

Dresden steamed steadily south-westwards until she entered the Sunda Straits at dawn on 17th April. She was scheduled for a rendezvous with a Japanese light cruiser and two destroyers. A meeting set up by SKL, in their words 'to further our Axis co-operation and to provide an escort to Japan, if Reitz so required.' Reitz didn't always like the long-range interference by SKL. For all he knew, the Allies could be intercepting the coded messages. Reluctantly he'd agreed for he was aware that his ship needed a good dockyard refit. His crew had done their best at the Kerguelen 'stop over' but further work needed to be done. SKL informed Reitz that two of Germany's merchant-ship raiders were soon to enter the Indian Ocean area to resume the Kriegsmarine's surface presence whilst *Dresden* was refitting.

The battlecruiser turned into the Straits and settled on to her new course as the sun began to lift over the eastern horizon.

The Japanese had already removed the danger of Allied surface warships for in a series of bloody battles off the Javanese coast. Allied war ships had been overwhelmed despite heroic resistance from ships like the cruisers HMS *Exeter*, HMAS *Perth* and the USS *Houston.* Over the next month smaller warships of the Japanese Imperial Navy scoured the bays and narrow channels between the off-shore islets and the main islands searching for escapee Allied military who were still thought to be hiding after the debacle of their main forces – airmen, sailors and soldiers who'd been let down by the inadequacies of their main commanders. Nearly all were gathered up into the Japanese search net. But not quite all of them. Reitz had just begun an early but leisurely breakfast in his sea cabin when the speakers clicked on 'Radar to captain. We have a very small speck almost stationary about ten miles ahead. Should have a visual soon'

Reitz spoke back into the intercom 'Let the bridge know. Advise them to warn all lookouts.' Ten minutes later, Reitz reached the bridge. Brautsch was officer-of-the-watch. 'Seen anything?'

'Not yet, sir.'

Five minutes passed. *Dresden* was only about four miles off the supposed object when a lookout sang out 'Small boat twenty degrees off port bow.'

It was a small boat. A motor-launch. Heaving and rocking gently in the swell.

Colonel Arthur Tibbetts moaned as an urgent hand shook his shoulder. He'd been asleep, like most of the other men in the launch. Asleep. Waiting for death unless a miracle occurred. For what had seemed a lifetime, death's dreaded fingers had been clawing at the men of his battalion. There weren't many more victims to grab at before those clasping fingers took hold of their final few members.

Members of a once proud battalion that had been stationed, somewhat hurriedly on the northern Malayan border in early December 1941. Rushed to the region after being hauled out of the desperate fighting in Crete earlier in the year. A general told Tibbetts 'You're off to the Far East, old boy. It'll be like a rest after your experiences on Crete. We think that there might be a bit of bother with the Japs. Still, it'll be a doddle. Can't expect those yellow-men to be on a par with the battle-hardened German paras and look what we gave them before we were pulled out of Crete, eh, what!'

Tibbetts hadn't bothered to inform the pompous ass that the German 'paras' had given his men a rough ride, that more than half of his own force had been killed, injured, gone missing or taken prisoner. Nor had he bothered to remind the brass hat that the Japanese had been fighting in China for nearly ten years, with considerable success. Some rest cure!

So his battalion was filled up with raw recruits to bring it back to its own numerical strength, shoved on board a troopship and under the main protection of the battlecruiser *Repulse* had set sail in the follow-up convoy to the one devastated by *Dresden*'s attack.

Eventually, they arrived in Singapore in late November and then, without even acclimatising themselves, were transported to Northern Malaya. Within a week a third of his force were suffering from dysentery and malaria. Then the Japanese struck late on 6th December. For nearly two months, Tibbetts and his men proceeded to fight a series of engagements all the way down the Malayan Peninsula. Three thousand men gradually being whittled down. At one point they ambushed over ten thousand Japanese attempting a river crossing. The river ran red with blood as their enemy suffered appalling losses. The next day they were ordered to pull out as the Japanese found an undefended position further downstream and were threatening to cut his battalion off from escape. So back through the dark steamy jungle they struggled. Rarely on the roads. Their motorised transport was soon abandoned, together with their three armoured cars. In the first week. Now it was foot slog with mules and a couple of horses. Grabbing what stores and provisions that they could from hastily abandoned Allied positions and once from an ambushed Japanese supply convoy which had been using one of the few roads that penetrated the tree-covered landscape. By early February they reached the Johore Strait. Two hundred survivors out of the original three thousand. Virtually out of food and ammunition, rifles and grenades. Never mind medicines. They'd lost nine out of ten of their medical staff. These brave men had stayed behind with desperately wounded men after one particularly bloody skirmish with the Japanese. Probably all now butchered presumed Tibbetts but he and his main group had by perforce to leave them behind.

A mere three hours after they stumbled along the road of the Causeway across the Johore Straits it was blown up. Aiming towards Singapore, Tibbetts billeted his men on a golf course to the north of the city and hastily began to form a defensive position. Officials rushed up to him to protest that he hadn't permission to dig trenches. Tibbetts turned round, shocked, and said that the Japanese would soon be crossing the Straits and right now, he nor his men couldn't care-less a penny about spoiling a golf course but they could care about creating a trenched defence post from which to oppose the invaders. The thin strip of water outlining the Johore Straits could easily be seen from their hill-top position. It was perfectly placed for spotting the movements of the Japanese. A few minutes longer than an hour one of those self-same officials returned with a piece of paper headed 'Singapore Military Command.' It tersely informed Tibbetts that any property belonging to the civilian population was not to be tampered with, or altered, unless with the express command of the Military Commander.

'Strange' remarked Tibbetts, 'have the Japanese bothered to ask the Military Command permission for bombing civilian homes? Eh? Oh, I didn't catch your answer! You haven't got one? Well, I have, to quote an Americanism, you ass-hole!!' Taking the headed paper he tore it up into shreds, crumpled these up into a ball and said, 'Well, I think a number nine iron should be able to whack that twenty yards' and then slammed it hard into the breast pocket of the official's golf-club jacket. 'Now, buzz-off! I've a war to be getting on with!'

Just three minutes later the first Japanese shell ploughed into the seventeenth hole. Fifty yards from where Tibbetts and a now thoroughly chastened official were standing. Tibbetts jumped into a trench. The official was nowhere to be seen. He'd vanished. Back to his golf club-house. Possibly now much enlightened as to the seriousness of the war.

For two days the intermittent shelling continued. Bravely small ships of the Coastal Defence Force appeared to fire off their four-inchers and smaller guns at the Japanese on the Malayan side of the Straits but Japanese land artillery as well as their aircraft sank some of the ships and forced the rest to retreat.

Soon after, early in the third morning, the Japanese crossed the Straits in small boats, rafts and rubber dinghies. Tibbetts and his men fired continuously at them but despite their casualties, the Japanese succeeded in landing at various points and were soon finding the weak parts of the Allied defences.

Tibbetts and his men were eventually forced to retreat when supplies of food, water and ammunition no longer reached them in sufficient amounts for them to carry out a defence. Doggedly they retreated, firing at the advancing invaders from whatever strong point that they could find. Retreating towards the city. Taking casualties all the time. Totally ignoring the frequent inane orders sent out to them by the Military Command. Including the last one. 'All units are to put down their weapons as of 0400 hours, 15th February and to surrender to thc Japanese.'

'Balls' was the response from Tibbetts and the sixty-one others of his battalion still left as fighting soldiers. It was the evening of the fourteenth. The battalion was by now on the waterfront. Searching. And succeeding. Four small harbour launches were found still guarded by their bewildered sailors and mechanics. 'Got any fuel for these?' enquired Tibbetts to the Petty Officer in charge.

'Well – er – yes – but '

'Never mind but, my men will help you get it. Now! Quick! We leave in thirty minutes. Come if you want to or surrender to the Nips.'

All four boats, their harbour crews as well as Tibbetts and his men left Singapore just before midnight. Probably the last sizeable contingent of escaping Allied soldiers before the surrender from that burning doomed Allied citadel.

For the next morning, General Percival and ninety thousand Allied soldiers meekly capitulated to a triumphant Japanese General Yamashita. The biggest disgrace to befall a British general in the war so far, and possibly in history.

Whilst Tibbetts and the four launches were trying to find a suitable bay in Sumatra in which to land and hide during the daytime.

'There's a likely place' yelled one of the sailors.

'Aye, and be quick. Jap. planes behind us' shouted another.

The two leading boats made it to the surf, their occupants spilling out and dashing for nearby trees as three Japanese fighters swooped down, machine-gunning the two slower boats. Time after time the snarling Zeros strafed the men from these boats. Tibbetts and his two boatloads crouched at the edge of the dense forest that was only a few yards from the beach helpless to assist. As a last spurt of anger, one of the Zeros swooped over the two-beached boats shooting them up so that they could never be a sailing concern again. Then for good measure on its final run the pilot strafed the edge of the trees bordering the beach into which Tibbetts and his men had sought shelter.

Then the three planes, wings dipping in a mock salute, re-formed and disappeared.

'They'll be back' snarled the Petty Officer. 'Come on, let's see if the boats are not too badly damaged.'

Both of them were in a parlous state. In their engines. Even if they'd been able to repair the smashed planking, neither of the boats would be manoeuvrable. No rudder. No working engines. Beyond anything but a skilled boatyard that with proper facilities could carry out. As the sailors assessed the irreparable damage, seven survivors from the other two boats, three of them with nasty bullet gashes to their arms, struggled ashore.

Tibbetts dashed out of the trees to help them to the beach. 'Any more of you?' he asked.

'Nah, we is the only ones 'ere' replied one of the two sailors to have survived.

When Tibbetts assembled the group, he had but thirty-seven of his own men and six naval personnel. Thirty had perished under the guns of the Japanese aircraft.

'Well chaps, we're not giving in yet. We've twenty rifles between us. We know how to survive in the jungle. My aim is to still reach Java. Somehow. Those who want to stay behind and surrender, can do so. As for me, I'm off.'

Not a man failed to follow him. Finding a track they quickly left the beach and struck inland. For Malayan jungle, it was now Sumatran jungle. The navy men kept up. It was their only chance of survival.

The first village they reconnoitred seemed deserted. It was. The natives had apparently fled. Until Tibbetts and his men found the kampong in the centre. There, lined in a row were eighteen young men. All shot in the head and bayoneted. Twelve of them European. Six were natives.

'That is what we've to expect. Japanese kindness is only one thing. Instant execution for escapee Allied personnel and any native villagers wishing to help them. Right, find what food you can and then we go. No more villages or towns for the time being.' Tibbetts sounded harsh. Inwardly he felt appalled.

It was a long and difficult three weeks. The further south they penetrated Sumatra, the more the presence of the Japanese became evident. Occasionally they ran into Japanese patrols. A quick exchange of fire. No surviving enemy allowed to escape. Once, they heard a truck grinding its way up a steep incline. A convenient recently blown down tree was thrown across the narrow road. The truck-load of Japanese soldiers came to a halt. Then Tibbetts and his men opened fire. In the fierce exchange of fire, four of his men were killed. Twenty-eight Japanese bodies were unceremoniously thrown into a nearby ditch. There were no enemy survivors.

The prize was not only a truck but inside bags of rice and cases of tinned and fresh fruit. Ample to keep them all fed for a further fortnight. Quickly Tibbetts worked out a plan. To travel at night, and then hide up in the day. In the driver's cab was a road map obviously issued for the benefit of the now dead driver. Amazingly its Japanese characters were hand written next to the original Dutch names. Tibbetts was not just a leader of men. He was one of the few officers in the British Army who could speak Dutch. Oh, and French, German and Italian. One of his many diverse talents.

The lorry also carried three drums of petrol and by driving it carefully at a reasonable economical speed, Tibbetts reckoned that they could reach the southern tip of the island. Providing that the Japanese didn't catch them first. In the front cabin the two smallest men as well as Tibbetts himself and the driver all wore uniforms pulled off their recently killed victims, whilst the rest of the men were hidden behind the canvas sides of the truck. Carefully the fugitives set off using a dimmed headlight only. By dawn they'd covered forty miles and with branches draped over and around the truck, the group remained hidden. Japanese aircraft occasionally droned overhead and twice Japanese vehicles rumbled past on the road but Tibbetts and his group were not detected.

As they threaded their way down the island, from time to time, they came across brutish reminders of what would befall them if they fell into their enemy's hands. Even by the roadside, the decapitated corpses of a group of twelve soldiers, bloated by flies, had to be left behind although three of his men pleaded for 'their mates' to be decently buried. 'No, leave them. I don't like it but if we moved them, or buried them, Japs would soon be on our trail. It's almost as if they've left them knowing what our humanitarian feelings would be.' Once again, Tibbetts hated what he had to say but he knew that his decision was the correct one.

So the bodies were left.

So were those of six nurses, all still with red crosses on their uniforms found tied to trees, all bearing numerous bayonet scars. All dead. Causing even the toughest of the group to feel gruesomely nauseated. Again, Tibbetts, equally aghast at such a horror, forced himself to leave them as they were.

When within about sixty miles of their objective the fuel finally ran out. Tibbetts sensed that in just three more days they'd find a harbour. 'All out. Take what food you can. From now on it's more footslog. And for heaven's sake, keep on doing as I say. We're here to avoid capture!'

Twice they skirmished with Japanese patrols killing up to five times as many as they lost but bit by bit, the little group were slowly whittled down to just eighteen men, two of them being the last of the harbour launch sailors. Men who could prove their use if only the group could find a suitable boat equipped with enough fuel and possibly a wireless. Twice they circumspectly investigated two small harbours but there was nothing substantial. Only native prahus and none of them possessed the skill to sail these out-rigger canoes. Then, early one evening almost at the southern tip of Sumatra, they came across a small town.

'This looks better' murmured Tibbetts as he surveyed it from a clump of trees. 'We'll move in when it's dark – in six groups of three. Reach the harbour. Then hopefully there'll be what we want. A smaller coaster, yacht, launch – anything with an engine. There'd better be something here. The Japs know that we're somewhere in the area. Sooner or later our food and ammunition is going to run out unless we risk another ambush. Somehow I feel that our luck, such that it is, could soon run out but as this is the biggest place we've come across, then it should have something. So, go to it, lads.'

The men filtered away. Each threading a separate way through the streets of the small town. A few locals saw them but took no notice. It was drizzling slightly as the eighteen men arrived at various points of the harbour and sea fronts of the town. Plenty of native fishing craft. But then, one major stroke of fortune. About fifty yards away from the harbour wall was anchored a large motor launch. On the quayside, under guard, were at least four drums of fuel. Two other but smaller launches and an ancient coaster were all tied up at the quayside. It was obvious that it was a Japanese launch, for in the slight wind a Rising Sun flag could just be made out in the evening gloom fluttering at the stern. As Tibbetts scrutinised the launch from behind a pile of fishing nets he could see that it was guarded by at least two armed sentries. Quietly his men, using the available cover as well as the gloom of the evening gathered around their colonel who then outlined his plans. Four of the men who could swim well would get over to the launch and deal with the sentries. Four others would creep up to the sentries on the quayside and dispose of them. The rest, on completion of those tasks were to steal one of the native fishing boats and take out their weapons and supplies over to the launch. Tibbetts stressed the need for silent killings. He reckoned that at any time other Japanese patrols might just turn up. So speed was also essential. Silently the four swimmers slipped into the water from behind the cover of one of the native boats. One of the men began to splash when near the launch. Both sentries fell for the trick as they turned their heads towards the distraction that had unexpectedly averted their attention. Moments later, both felt for a microsecond, the sharp feel of a bayonet blade across their throats before they went off to join their ancestors. Silently.

Almost wraith-like, the four men on the quayside rose in the gloom and did exactly the same. A bayonet round the throat and a second one into the stomach. Both sentries, like those on the launch were lowered carefully to the floor and then dropped gently into the water. Then Tibbetts and the rest of his men, with their stolen native boat, picked up their four comrades from the quayside and as quickly as they could without splashing too much, paddled their way out to the launch.

One of the sailors who was also a mechanician, almost drooled when he saw the gleaming diesels of the launch. Her fuel tanks were full. Tibbetts with his men had also brought over more full drums of fuel. 'Should be enough to get us over to a Javanese harbour, perhaps even to one of our own naval bases' the mechanic pointed out to Tibbetts. 'I'll try and start them up as quietly as possible.'

The engines rumbled into life but despite all the efforts to keep the noise down, a patrol of Japanese soldiers marching to the harbour to relieve their now dead comrades on sentry duty, heard the noise and rushing to the water's edge began to furiously fire their rifles in the direction of the dark black shape out at sea.

'Full ahead!' roared Tibbetts and with her throttles wide open, the launch surged forward and with frothing foam broadening from her stern, she soon vanished out of sight round the headland that bordered the edge of the bay.

Totally unbeknown to the escapers, the colonel in charge of the Japanese garrison, when told of the episode whilst enjoying his evening meal, rose from his dining table, summoned the lieutenant in charge of the sentries and the town patrol, lined him up in front of a wall and shouting 'You have brought shame upon our Emperor as well as those of us in this garrison!' shot him through the head at virtual point-blank range.

During the next six hours of darkness the launch powered her way at a top speed of twelve knots towards the objective of the Sunda Straits. Dawn came, but within an hour a single slow patrolling Kawansai seaplane searching for the launch on the explicit orders to sight and report, flew directly from the direction of the sun glaring itself in all its tropical brilliance as it closed with the launch. The pilot, against those explicit orders, guessed that the tiny speck with a definite strong wake streaming behind it was the expected escaping launch. More or less where it was calculated to be. The pilot screamed to his observer, 'Come on, let's shoot the Allied escapees up – for fun of course!'

His observer shouted back 'Sir, our orders?' The pilot didn't reply but gunned the engines of his lumbering aircraft directly at the now clearly visible launch.

It was the sound of those engines that alerted the men on the launch. Despite trying to keep a keen look up towards the skies as well as around them on the blue glistening water, the men on the launch were very tired after three months of hardships and privations as well as seeing the almost total loss of all the original members of their comrades and the sight of many sickening horrors during their retreat through the jungles of Malaya and Sumatra.

'Duck down! Cut the engines! Try to hide, lads!' yelled Tibbetts.

He was just too late with his orders for two men, one at the wheel and the other being one of the lookouts who'd desperately yelled out the aircraft warning. The Kawansai's pilot opened fire with his nose-mounted machine gun and the bullets caught both men, their bodies jerking before toppling over. However, the Kawansai suddenly stopped firing but curiously to everyone, except Tibbetts, continued a steady plunge towards the sea. The colonel, ever alert, had been able to loose off three shots from his Thompson carbine as the seaplane passed over the launch. One bullet hit the aircraft in its fuel tank, the second smashed into the plane's radio and the third, fired vertically, passed through the pilot's seat and then into his stomach. Mortally wounded, the pilot, now screaming his death pain, collapsed, pushing the plane's control column forward causing it to dive into the sea about six hundred yards astern of the wallowing launch. The ruptured fuel tank, leaking fuel and fumes, burst into flames, rapidly enveloping the stricken aircraft. On board the launch those who'd seen the seaplane's descent and crash onto the surface shouted out a few ragged cheers. The Kawansai's horrified and extremely frightened observer released himself from his harness and struggled to get out of his cockpit and succeeding, he jumped into the sea. Upon surfacing he started yelling for help but Tibbetts had him in his sights and fired the Thompson just once. Even at that range the shot was perfect for it drilled a hole into the man's forehead, killing him instantly.

Not for nothing had Tibbetts been a Bisley rifle-champion.

The shooting down of the plane was but a pyrrhic victory for some of the last machine-gun bullets that it had fired had smashed into the launch's steering gear and engine rendering them useless. Without the means of steerage or power the launch was helpless to the winds and currents. For the next few hours they tried everything – paddles from boards and even a makeshift sail from some of the men's tattered shirts but the two bodies of their dead comrades which they'd thrown overboard never seemed to be far off until at last they'd sunk or slowly drifted out of sight as darkness fell. The launch wallowed helplessly for nearly twenty-six hours and the men were resigned to their fate of a slow painful death from the sea or salt-water exposure unless the Japanese found them first and handed to each of them a quick execution. But nothing else came to search for them for the seaplane hadn't been able to send out a radio message. It wasn't missed for about four hours after it had been supposed to return to base and even then the search wasn't made in their immediate area.

Night passed and one by one they all drifted off to sleep. The first hint of dawn saw only private Alwin Esholt awake, the youngest man in the boat for he knew it was his nineteenth birthday this very morning. 17th April. It said so in the tattered diary fastened in his shirt pocket. Still smarting from the Colonel's rebukes for not sighting the Kawansai earlier, he had been awake an hour or so before that dawn. His eyes had often been the key factor in the survival of the other men in that long retreat often seeing and in combination with his alert brain, sensing the presence of the Japanese long before any of the others in the battalion. Perhaps it was the fact that he was the son of a gamekeeper on the Sledmere Estate in Yorkshire's East Riding that had something to do with it for as a younger teenager before the war he'd often been out at night with his father doing the rounds on the estate, helping to catch the poachers who were attempting to ply their trade against the estate's pheasants and other game. Alwin was tired like the rest of them. But not asleep. Through his hazed eyes, heavy with the need of sleep, he first sensed and then saw through the light dawn mist, the emerging bulk of a large, no, a very large warship rapidly approaching the launch. 'Sir,' he began to urgently shake Tibbetts on his shoulders, 'Sir, wake up! There's a bloody great big Jap cruiser coming straight for us.'

Tibbetts stirred. He'd been sleeping the sleep of a dead man. Tired. Ever, ever so tired. Through the mists of reality he heard Esholt's urgent voice. 'Sir, it's slowing down. Came out of the mist or summat. Wake up sir. It's the bleedin' Japs. They're launching a boat.'

Tibbetts woke and saw the approaching launch. Instinctively he reached for the Thompson.

'Stow it, sir, they're armed – and there's more of them than us. They'd shoot us like ducks in a shootin' gallery.' The boy's voice was not only urgent and sharp but full of reality as well. Tibbetts relaxed. What could he do except await his fate? Esholt yelled again 'Sir. They're flyin' the "White Ensign". She's one of ours!' and then the lad stood up waving. Other men in the boat began to wave.

'Don't trust 'em' snarled Tibbetts. 'It's a ruse.'

Which it was, but not with the result he expected.

A metallic voice, via the loudhailer into which Brautsch was speaking came over to them from the approaching launch 'Ahoy. Please to put down any weapons. We are coming to rescue you. We are not Japanese.'

The voice was ever so slightly accented English. It puzzled Tibbetts but not Private Alwin Esholt who found a dirty rag that had once been a clean crisp white handkerchief with the letters AE sown in one corner by his loving mother and given to him on the railway station at Driffield as he'd set off to join the battalion in February 1940. Just over a year ago. So much since then. Crete. Malaya. Singapore. Sumatra. And now here he was on an open, defenceless, helpless launch bobbing up and down in the Sunda Strait under the menace of the guns of an, as yet, unidentified warship.

The motor-boat approached the helpless launch on which sixteen desperate survivors of a four months ordeal were waiting, resigned to what lay ahead.

The voice came over again, this time without the loud-hailer 'I have a nurse with us. Please do not resist. She is here to give emergency medical care. We are coming aboard.'

'A nurse?' queried Tibbetts. 'On a warship?'

As if to answer him he saw her. A light brown-haired nurse in a medical red-cross uniform standing up in the bows of the approaching launch. Behind her, he could see other men with rifles and sub-machine guns pointing at the survivors. Then the nurse spoke as the launch's engines were throttled back and it came alongside 'I am Nurse Andrea Cantrell and I am coming aboard to give you all a quick medical check. I am a British nurse on board the German battlecruiser *Dresden.*'

'Bloody hell, Jerries' gasped Esholt.

'Yes, from *Dresden.* We know of her. She shattered the previous convoy to ours off the East African coast' growled Tibbetts. Before he had time to react further, Kapitan Leutnant Brautsch and two armed men clambered aboard closely followed by Andrea.

'Who is in charge here?' demanded Brautsch.

'I am. Colonel Arthur Tibbetts together with the fifteen survivors of my battalion. Out of an original three thousand. And who are you?'

'Kapitan Leutnant Helmut Brautsch of the Kriegsmarine battlecruiser *Dresden* at your service' came the reply as Helmut fully revealed when he opened his coat to display the Kriegsmarine eagle badge on his uniform jacket. 'Yes, you are now our prisoners. We will not hand you over to the Japanese although we shall be meeting with them fairly soon. Now please, we must hurry to get you on board my ship. Nurse Cantrell will check you all out.'

She had already started and in less than five minutes reported to Brautsch 'Three serious cases of utter exhaustion, two of malnutrition, five of excess sunburn and three others with very nasty wounds threatening to turn gangrenous. Far too dangerous even to transfer them to our launch if we are to get them back to *Dresden.* Even the three fit ones are really very tired. Climbing a ladder will be no fun. Can't we take them in tow and then hook this launch on to our falls and hoist them on board? The wounded can then be stretchered down to the Sick Berth. Please, Helmut.' The look in her eyes was desperate. Pleading.

Brautsch nodded. 'Right. We'll take this boat in tow.' Rapidly, in German, he barked out the orders and soon the helpless launch was taken in tow for the three hundred yard journey back to the towering side of the waiting battlecruiser.

The launch, still with Andrea on board, was quickly fastened to the falls and raised to deck level where Doctor Lebers and his two sick-berth attendants were waiting with other crew men lined up in pairs with stretchers and blankets. As soon as the soldiers had been lifted out of the launch and the wounded carried off on the stretchers, the launch was lowered back into the sea and with two heavy blocks weighting it down, quickly sank when the men from Brautsch's launch peppered it with a quick burst of machine-gun fire. With their own boat back in place on deck, *Dresden* began to get under way as soon as she could. Away from that chance meeting with Tibbetts and his men.

Brautsch, with Otto Schenke as guard, guided Colonel Tibbetts to the bridge where Reitz waited for them.

'Sir, this is Colonel Tibbetts' announced Brautsch. Reitz saluted the bedraggled soldier who nevertheless was trying to keep upright in a proud military bearing. Reitz could see the look of utter exhaustion on the man.

'I'll be quick, Colonel. You look as if you need a good sleep. My name is Kapitan George Reitz. I command this battlecruiser.

You are now my prisoner. We do our best to honour the Geneva Convention. Soon we shall be meeting up with Japanese warships. They know we are here. When I meet them, I will not tell them that we have any Allied prisoners on board providing you and your men keep your mouths shut. You will all be provided with clean shirts, trousers and Kriegsmarine overalls once you're out of bed. I trust that none of you, even when recovered, will give me any trouble. If you do, I shall have to hand you over to the Japanese and what I know of them, your treatment will deteriorate rapidly.'

Tibbetts nodded 'We've already seen their work with prisoners. Not very pleasant, I must say.'

The German captain continued 'For the time being I have reasonable food supplies but we shall be docking in Japan for a refit. With us will be our supply ships. When the time comes, I shall send you back to Europe on one of them and who knows, a Royal Navy cruiser may come and capture the supply ship! Sorry about the ruse. We had to get near to you in case any of you thought about a last desperate act of resistance. When you are recovered perhaps we can have a talk with a whisky or gin in my cabin. Until then, I hope my medical staff will take care of you.'

Reitz saluted Tibbetts and motioned to Schenke to escort the English colonel off the bridge. Tibbetts muttered 'Thankyou Captain', threw up as smart a salute as he could manage and staggered away, with Schenke holding him steady as he climbed down the bridge access ladders.

Dresden, picking up speed, ploughed her course well into the Sunda Straits with a large Japanese flag draped over turret 'Anton' as well as one flying below Reitz's own naval flag.

As she emerged into the wider sea beyond the Straits a fast moving torpedo boat flying a Japanese flag closed within two miles but made no attempt to contact. *Dresden*'s anti-aircraft guns and her four point ones (10.5cm) tracked the torpedo carrying boat which paralleled them for a couple miles before it quickly moved away. Perhaps searching for Tibbetts and his men mused Reitz as he watched it disappear. That had been soon after one o'clock in the afternoon. Later that day two aircraft flew near them with Japanese insignia but it wasn't until the next morning that radar reported two blips ahead of them. Reitz grunted. 'The Japanese reception committee, no doubt. Those aircraft will have reported us and at dawn we shall meet. How dramatic! Too late for them. We've Tibbetts and his men on board if that's what they want!'

As the dawn light filtered across the calm seas and the sun was beginning to make its presence felt over a sea air that was already warm, a lookout yelled 'Warship off port bow!'

A three-funnelled light cruiser and a destroyer with two raked funnels of a more modern design were looming into view. The cruiser, *Tanyo*, was trailing a long dense plume of oily black smoke that began to thin as she approached *Dresden*. Her light began to flash, somewhat ironically, in English 'What ship? I am IJN *Tanyo*'.

Reitz sent back the reply 'KM *Dresden*'.

Back came *Tanyo*'s response 'Please to stop. Am sending officer on board to offer welcome.'

The German warship, towering over *Tanyo* and her fussy escort *Yaguchi*, slowly came to a halt but forcing the Japanese to execute a wide turn and come up astern of her. Reitz did this deliberately. He wanted the Japanese to see the full size of his warship. He also needed time for Brautsch to hurry down to the Sick Berth to see if Lebers and his staff had sedated the sick British soldiers. Not until Brautsch reported that the soldiers were all quietened did Reitz bring *Dresden* to a complete halt. The soldiers who weren't under sedation were briefed to say 'Ach mein herr' or 'Jawohl' or any other brief German sounding utterance in case the Japanese welcoming party chose to visit the Berth.

Lieutenant Imoru Hatsu was twenty-three years old and full of pride having been chosen by Captain Ryoku to represent *Tanyo*. His captain had told him to be courteous and polite but yet to gather as much knowledge as he could about the German warship. Had she, for instance, any British prisoners on board? Hatsu had nodded and was waiting by the rails of *Tanyo* ready to board a rowing boat manned by the cruiser's best oarsmen who only six months ago had won a race in the Imperial Navy's final regatta before the attack on Pearl Harbor. *Tanyo* halted about half-a-mile from the German.

Suddenly Reitz said to Hiltzern 'Commander, have we anyone who can speak Japanese on board?'

'Not sure but I doubt it. Perhaps Brautsch can tell us – he seems to know such a lot!'

'Ah, here he is. Helmut, do you speak Japanese?'

'No sir. I may be fluent in English, Spanish, French and Russian but not Japanese.'

'Hmph. It's just that I don't trust the little yellow blighters.'

'Ah sir, there is someone I know who does understand their language. She reminded me just a few minutes ago. Nurse Cantrell.'

'Well, get her. We don't have much time. They're launching a boat.' Indeed, *Tanyo*'s boat had just hit the water and its oarsmen were soon into their rhythm. Reitz continued 'We've about ten minutes.'

Three minutes later Andrea Cantrell, a little out of breath having hurried after the telephone summons from her work in the Sick Bay, stood on the bridge facing the German captain.

'Ah, Fraulein Cantrell. Do I understand that you speak Japanese? I need an interpreter in case they don't speak German or English.'

'Why?' questioned Andrea, suddenly determined to make a point of seeing the Germans get on edge. Maybe just for a bit of time.

'Well, you see that boat? Those warships? They are the Japanese who are meeting with us. You see, Fraulein Cantrell, I don't trust them. They might want to know if we've picked up any British prisoners. I believe that they've been searching for Colonel Tibbetts and his group.'

'So?'

'Well, they might want to search the ship or converse in their language thinking that we don't understand them.'

'Captain Reitz' responded Andrea. 'You and your men have been very kind to me since rescuing me from *Arades*. You have repatriated all the other women on ships bound for Europe. You have given your word that the Red Cross will look after them if they make it safely to France. On the other hand I have elected to stay on board ostensibly now working as a full member of your crew.'

The rowing boat reached *Dresden*'s starboard side.

'Well, Fraulein?' urged Reitz.

Andrea smiled 'Captain, hold your horses. For two years before the war began I worked in a Roman Catholic hospital in Nagasaki.

I made it my business to learn the lingo. In 1940 I moved to Buenos Aires on a Japanese cargo-liner. Even amongst their crewmen, providing they didn't speak too fast, I could understand the gist of what they were saying. Yes, of course, Captain, I'll listen in and let you know, via Helmut in Spanish, which I also speak but which I suspect they don't, what they may mutter amongst themselves which could be detrimental.'

'Thankyou, Fraulein. I think our visitors are here now.'

Commander Hiltzern together with a bosun's party were lined up as the Japanese officer stepped on to *Dresden*'s decks. Reitz and the others on the bridge could hear the shrill wail of bosun whistles plaintively. Not only a welcome for the visitors but also a warning for Reitz to be ready.

Which he was with Brautsch, Halder, Serle and Andrea. Hiltzern, in German, announced 'Herr Kapitan, the delegation from the Japanese cruiser *Tanyo* led by Leutnant Hatsu.'

Reitz saluted the Japanese and extended his right arm. Hatsu bowed, then saluted and finally shook the proffered hand.

'Pleased to have you on board. Do you understand me?'

Hatsu said, in very poor German 'Sprachen nicht. Nein. Nein. Herr Kapitan.'

Then in English 'But I do speak English. I learnt it whilst at the University in Tokyo and also at San Francisco.' Hatsu's voice had a light tenor tone and came over with an American accent.

Reitz nodded. 'Good. I speak English quite well. Ironic isn't it that we have to converse in the paternal tongue of our enemies.'

'So be it' observed the unusually tall Japanese.

The German captain continued 'You have already met Commander Hiltzern, my deputy and Chief Officer. This is my second-in-command, Kapitan-Leutnant Helmut Brautsch. This is Alfred Serle who navigates us and this is Erich Halder my chief gunnery officer.' Then he introduced Andrea 'This is Fraulein Nursing Officer Andrea Cantrell who has been with us on this long cruise looking after our medical needs with whom I was having a discussion when your ship appeared. I invited her to stay here in case she hasn't met any of your people before.'

It sounded lame. It was a lame effort but it was the best that Reitz could think of at that moment. Hatsu also looked suspicious but replied 'Unusual captain, is it not? A female on board this warship?'

'Perhaps but Admiral Canaris – perhaps you've heard of him – told me to expect women and children as prisoners and that some would need medical help which has indeed been the case. She is also a morale booster for my own sick and injured men. Helps to calm their fears as well as heal their wounds.'

'So, so, Kapitan. My captain wonders if you have seen any escaped Allied militia lately. A boatload of very dangerous men stole an area commandant's launch in Southern Sumatra only three days ago, and was perhaps sighted by a seaplane that has since disappeared. From what we can work out your ship was in their area. We can't find the launch even though we believe it didn't have enough fuel to reach Allied-held areas in Java. Have you seen them?'

'Lieutenant. My business is to disrupt Allied shipping. Not –' Reitz waved his finger at Hatsu '– Not, I repeat, to spend valuable time chasing after desperadoes. What happened to your seaplane I care not one bit. Perhaps the pilot was as stupid as the four pilots who attacked and sank a large British tanker in the Malacca Straits, which we had stopped and were preparing to take as a prize. You may have heard of that incident, Lieutenant?'

Hatsu looked darkly at Reitz. He hadn't expected this harsh riposte from the German. He said, in Japanese to his junior officer

'Be careful. These Nazi scum aren't exactly friendly.' Then, in English, 'Sorry captain, I was translating briefly to my fellow officer. No, I haven't heard of the incident.'

Andrea hissed in Spanish 'The bastard's lying.' Brautsch, out of Hatsu's vision simply raised his eyebrows. Reitz nodded, seeing

Brautsch's signal. Hatsu continued 'My captain has orders to escort you to the Lingga Road-stead south of Singapore.

My information is that two of your supply ships are there under our protection.'

Reitz snapped 'I should hope they are. Can't have any more of your bomb-happy pilots sinking our ships, can we?'

Hatsu flinched. This meeting wasn't going at all well. Of course he'd heard of the *Marona* incident but he'd had to deny it in the hopes that the Germans would forgive their new ally of the incident. Apparently they hadn't.

He spoke again. 'Kapitan Reitz. I must be off. You will please to follow us. I am also informed that your eventual destination is our Kure Naval Base. Destroyer *Yaguchi* will be detached with your group as anti-submarine escort although so far, the Yankee subs are relatively inactive but you never know!' Then in Japanese, he hissed at his junior, unable to control his feelings 'I hope that one of the Yankee subs has this Nazi swine in his cross-wires and shoots accurately with torpedoes.' Then he smiled, bowed to Reitz and turned to leave the bridge.

Led by Brautsch, the Japanese made their way to return to their boat which was still waiting by the battlecruiser's side-steps and boarding platform.

Andrea murmured to Reitz 'He doesn't like us at all. Thinks that you are all Nazi swine.'

Hatsu gave a sketchy salute to Brautsch as he stood on the boarding platform. Quite suddenly, an unexpected swell hit the battlecruiser, just as the Japanese officer was about to get into his boat. All the way back down to the launch he'd been inwardly fuming at being outsmarted. How could these representatives of those Nazi jack-booters who'd trampled over a weak, decadent Europe humiliate him, a warrior of Samurai stock? Samurai sons were now taking on and beating the might of the Yankees. As well as decadent British, French or Dutch incompetents. He'd seen films of the Nuremberg Rallies. Nazi boots and stiff-arm salutes all over the place. But no real steel. All pomp, lights and show. Not one real warrior amongst them. One day, when he'd risen to command one of the giant battleships, which Japan was completing, he'd train its big guns and blow this tin-pot Nazi heap of cow-dung into another heap. Of scrap iron.

So full of inward fury was Hatsu that he didn't realise that the sailors in their boat had lost temporary control with the unexpected surge and where he'd expected the launch to be, Hatsu found nothing but thin air but his momentum swayed him too far forward and with a shriek of anguish he fell into the sea. Surging to the surface he splashed about helplessly, shouting, in Japanese

'Help! Help! I can't swim!'

Helmut Brautsch knew a drowning man when there was one, so he raced down the steps without hesitation and dove into the water to affect a rescue. Grabbing the frantic Japanese officer, he turned him on his back and keeping the man's head above water, back-pedalled as quickly as he could towards the boarding platform where the strong hands of Otto Schenke and his pal Franz Lutz, the tallest man on board whose long arms somewhat unceremoniously yanked at the collar of the Japanese officer and hoisted him, dripping wet, out of the water. Hatsu didn't even say thank-you for he was so angry as well as feeling humiliated and when his sailors brought their rowboat back to the platform he boarded it, somewhat huffily, without a backward glance. Brautsch watched the boat depart in a flurry of dripping oars and then hoisted himself back on to the platform. Lutz snapped 'Some bloody Jap officer. Can't get on a boat. Can't swim. Can't even say thanks.' Brautsch grinned at him before making his way up the steps back on to the deck. Schenke and Lutz supervised and helped with the hauling up of the steps as Brautsch made his way to his cabin to get changed but as he crossed the deck, Andrea having come down from the bridge, rushed up to him and smiling 'My wet hero!' kissed him lightly, before turning to trace her steps back to the Sick Berth. Schenke, seeing the light touch, sniffed at Lutz 'Bloody officers. Some fall in the water. Others play at silly games but him, well, he gets the only bird on this tub!'

Captain Ryoku was not pleased when Hatsu, still very wet, stood in front of him giving his report. The unfortunate boat crew were stood behind rigidly at attention, their faces remained expressionless as Ryoku's severity of words tore into them. 'Call yourselves sailors. What a shower! You have disgraced the honour of this ship and that of the Imperial Navy. A week's pay will be docked for each and every one of you. Call yourselves champion oarsmen. Tch! As for you Lieutenant Hatsu, extra watches from now on until this ship is sunk or the war ends. Go on, get changed and then back on the bridge in five minutes. The rest of you. To your duties!' *Tanyo* began to gather speed and *Dresden* followed the light cruiser with destroyer *Yaguchi* on her starboard flank.

Colonel Tibbetts, cleaned up and refreshed, was resting in Reitz's main cabin as per the orders of Reitz when Walters came in.

'Sir, mister Colonel. The captain would like to see you on the bridge. I'm to take you there.' Tibbetts nodded, replying in German

'Thank-you, steward. Lead the way.'

On the bridge Reitz welcomed Tibbetts. 'There you see an oldish Japanese cruiser and one of their modern destroyers. Part of the Imperial Fleet. You are still here. They asked of your whereabouts and whether we'd seen you. I turned the tables on to them. A British tanker had stopped under my request and we were about to launch a boat when a group of their aircraft came over and torpedoed it. We sent off an immediate protest saying that they had deprived us of a valuable source of fuel as well as wiping out the crew of the surrendered tanker. I gather from Fraulein Cantrell, who was here on the bridge and who understands enough Japanese, that they think that we're Nazi scum. Their officer wasn't too pleased at all when I mentioned the tanker incident. You see, Colonel, we also have seen the Japanese in action.' Colonel Tibbetts grunted and grimaced. Reitz continued.

'I know that some Germans are not very pleasant and I have now learnt about how bad some detention camps for political dissidents are run but somehow I feel that the situation for prisoners in Japanese hands will be very much worse. Have you heard of the Samurai?' Tibbetts nodded and Reitz went on 'Well, some Japanese think that they are true Samurai descendants. The enemy they defeat are worthless. Instead of surrendering they should at least have gone to their deaths in a more heroic mode. That partly and only simply explains their code of practice. Perhaps that British tanker with its little pop-gun should not have surrendered to us, but instead, tried to fight it out. Well, we're not like that. I try to treat my prisoners as fairly as possible. Very soon we shall be in a Japanese naval port. You and your men will not be handed over. You are my prisoners and I will endeavour to return you to Occupied Europe and maybe, under the auspices of a Red Cross scheme, some of your wounded companions will be exchanged for wounded German soldiers. Just keep your heads down and try to look like members of my crew when we reach Japan. Please, Colonel. Please, no trouble!'

Tibbetts looked at the German captain. Somehow his face looked so tired. Perhaps he and his crew were wishing that they were going home. Not to a naval port half-a-world away. All Tibbetts could murmur, though, was his thanks. He saluted the German and this time, unaided, made his way down the bridge access steps. Walters again led him back to Reitz's main cabin.

In the Lingga road-stead *Dresden* met up with her two supply ships, *Berengia* and *Olaf*. Light cruiser *Tanyo* flashed a brief farewell and only destroyer *Yaguchi* stayed with the German ships. After refuelling from *Olaf* and taking on more provisions from *Berengia*, the three German ships as well as *Yaguchi* set sail for Japan and its principal naval port of Kure. Eight days later, with no alarms at all, the German ships dropped anchor in the waters of Kure Bay. Little less than two hours later, a harbour launch, flying a small swastika flag, approached the battlecruiser. Sitting in the stern was the German naval attaché to Japan, Admiral Horst Wenneker, who felt it to be a proud moment in his career in that he was soon to board Germany's most famous raider. The wail of bosun's pipes trilled as the Admiral stepped on to the deck.

Chapter 8

'Get the hell outa' here!'

Drinks and snacks prepared by Walters looked as immaculately presented as always when Admiral Wenneker and his aides entered the main cabin which Reitz rarely used but on this occasion, he was there to offer his welcome together with his principal officers – Hiltzern, Brautsch, Halder, Serle and for a change, a clean Chief Engineer, Herzog. The quick-witted steward disappeared once his duties were accomplished with the guests suitably impressed by the range and quality of the drinks. Reitz's dry comment was that most of them were involuntary presents from the British Prime Minister, Mr. Winston Churchill and that his steward was always a member of the boarding parties when they'd raided captured ships. One of the aides hissed on hearing Churchill's name saying that real German schnapps was the only true spirit that was drinkable. Laconically, Reitz shrugged his shoulders and made the point of pouring himself a further tot of 'Glen Moranje'.

Wenneker raised his glass to toast the success of the exploits of the battlecruiser and her crew. *Dresden*, he pointed out, was the first major German warship to berth in Japan and what a superb example she was of German naval might. He seemed very pleased with himself but was cut short when Reitz commented that the Royal Navy was still in charge in the North Atlantic and that having rid that Ocean of the menace posed by battleship *Bismarck*, it seemed more like a retreat to have to come to Japan for an overhaul and the necessary repairs rather than risk his ship on an albeit dangerous dash to even a Northern French port. Not that these were really safe although *Scharnhorst*, *Gneisenau* and *Prinz Eugen* had escaped back to Germany via the English Channel as their position in those ports was constantly under the threat of the RAF's bombing raids. A new merchant raider, *Michel*, so he'd been informed, experienced a tough fight on her voyage through the Channel before reaching the Bay of Biscay and thence into the Atlantic.

Wenneker's face froze whilst Reitz was speaking. Then he broke into a smile. 'Kapitan Reitz, my dear fellow, you have triumphed over many warships and sunk or captured a lot of Allied merchant ships. I am sure that Germany with her U-boats will soon take full control of the Atlantic and within a year, you and your ship will be able to return in triumph.' He smiled again and before anyone could interrupt him, he added 'So, in the meantime, before your return in the winter months, and in a way of saying thank-you to our host's dockyard facilities, after the repairs, this ship will be attached to the Japanese Imperial Fleet.'

A bombshell! Wenneker, sensing that he had the advantage, smiled again to continue 'However, Kapitan Reitz, you are no longer Herr Kapitan Reitz.'

'What!' exploded Hiltzern 'You mean that our captain's been dismissed? Leaving us? For someone else?'

'Calm yourself! All of you! My orders come from Grand Admiral Erich Raeder. What on earth makes you all think that your captain will be no longer in charge? Why, the very opposite! As from this very moment he will be no longer Kapitan Reitz but –'

He paused. Reitz wondered what the slimy Nazi toad was really getting round to say.

Wenneker reached to an inside pocket and drew out an envelope. From it he produced a typed signal memo and read it out – 'From Grand Admiral Raeder to Wenneker, Naval Attaché, Kure. Inform Kapitan George Reitz that with immediate effect that he is promoted to Konter-Admiral and to command the German Fleet in Japanese waters in liaison with the Imperial Japanese Navy.'

Reitz wasn't impressed. So this was it. He'd been promoted to flag-rank so that at least he'd have a similar rank to some of his opposite numbers in the Japanese Fleet. A fleet that he'd have to co-operate with for the next six months, if not longer. All he wanted was for himself and his crew to sail *Dresden* back to Germany. Via the Atlantic. Where the main sea struggle was taking place. But no. This would mean fleet action, with admittedly a large, victorious fleet against possibly badly demoralised Allied forces. Deep down he guessed that soon the Americans would recover and that the security of his ship would be just as much at risk in the Pacific as it would be in the Atlantic. Dimly he heard Wenneker continuing 'You see, my dear Konter-Admiral, your ship is an heroic symbol of Germany's endeavours. Ever since your victorious convoy battle your deeds have inspired our armed forces to their utmost. We drive on towards Cairo in the North African desert and our armies are deep inside Soviet Russia. Our Japanese allies strike towards India from Burma and are getting close to Northern Australia as well. We should soon be able to take a look forward to –' here he spread his arms outwards '– to final victory.'

Reitz did not smile. Or even acknowledge the simplistic gestures and statement from Wenneker. Instead he thrust both hands behind his back and bluntly said 'Unless the American carrier fleets can be eliminated. I fear that Japan will soon find herself with a very tough fight on her hands. As for the British, they've been able to resume their East African convoys and will be rushing re-inforcements to check our Afrika Korps and soon the Soviets will also recover their strength and fight back.'

Wenneker's smile froze. 'This is defeatist talk! My sources tell me that the Japanese Fleet will soon be challenging the Americans. Four fleet carriers against two of theirs at the most. Backed up by the new battleships *Yamato* and *Musashi* with their enormous guns, the American opposition will soon be sunk without trace.'

Halder interrupted Wenneker from a further expansion of his simple views on Naval strategy.

'Big guns are no longer a deciding weapon. Look at what happened to *Bismarck*. One torpedo, so we understand, delivered by an antiquated biplane from an aircraft carrier, scored the decisive hit. A blow that has caused us to be here in this anchorage rather than back in Germany. We've been very lucky with our own efforts but even we've been told not to attempt a return voyage during the summer months.'

With that Halder came to an end of what for him was a long speech. *Dresden*'s officers were nodding their approval.

Wenneker steepled his fingers trying to control his thoughts. The chat with these heroes of Germany wasn't going quite as he'd expected. Reitz didn't seem at all that pleased with his promotion. His officers couldn't see further than their own private hopes. Alright, of course, they wished to get back to Germany. So did he but at this moment, he knew he had to serve the World-wide interests of his country first. Out here. Helping their new allies. Japan. This was a time of co-operation to aid them to even greater triumphs. Yet Reitz and his men were actually looking at the reality of the war as they saw it. The trouble was that Wenneker knew that they could be right. Could be!

He coughed. 'Admiral Reitz.' The affectation of 'dear' had been dropped much to the relief of Reitz. 'In two days time your ship will be in dry-dock courtesy of our Japanese hosts. Repairs and no doubt your own scheme of maintenance may well take up two months.'

He coughed again, almost unsure of how to proceed. 'Your crew will have plenty of time on their hands, I suppose. Well, be on your guard! I have already had contacts with the Tempai, which is the Japanese Security Police, and anyone without a pass beyond the naval premises will be detained. Hmmmm! No need to be offended. I am sure that we can find some entertainment for all, officers and men alike, can we not?'

No-one spoke in reply. Wenneker was dithering. His thoughts were those of a rambling, incoherent order.

He was interrupted by Herzog who rumbled in his gravelly, deep tones 'No Jap mechanic touches my engines. In fact, I'm not sure whether I can trust them to polish up the propellers!'

Wenneker grimaced.

Then Serle spoke. 'Aye, aren't the Tempai like our bloody Gestapo? Shoot and torture first, then they ask the questions later. Not that the detainee'll be in any fit condition. Some right friends we have here!'

'Well, er, well, it's not really like that' came the feeble response from one of Wenneker's aides trying to rescue the situation – 'you see European faces aren't exactly popular unless they're the Irish monks in the monastic confines in Nagasaki.'

Wenneker intervened. 'Gentlemen, let us not get carried away. Your ship is a national heroic symbol. We must be grateful to our Japanese hosts for all the facilities they've given and will be giving. Surely we must respect them. Their main task is to clean your ship's hull as well as to effectively repair the plating that you patched up in the Kerguelens. What you do with the ship's interior I am sure that your crew will be able to carry out the required renovations.'

'We will have plenty of work for us all' interspersed Hiltzern 'But the crew will need time to relax. Are there any shore barracks where they can take "leave" off the ship and where we can set up some sort of entertainment?'

Wenneker stuttered, 'Er – well – er, yes. I can arrange some shore accommodation with perhaps a pleasure area for the men although it is of Japanese style – not quite up to our Germanic standard, eh?'

He winked at Hiltzern but the battlecruiser's chief officer did not give him the satisfaction of even a hint of acknowledgement at the effort of Wenneker's attempt of crude humour. Hastily the naval attaché continued 'As for the officers, I am sure I can arrange some trips to Mount Fuji and other historical Japanese sites.'

Reitz countered with 'That will have to wait for the time being. My officers and I will be very busy and as to how much spare time they will have for gadding around the Japanese countryside remains to be seen. My main priority is to get my ship back to sea and if possible in the winter months to make the run back to Germany.' The firmness in the captain's words again rocked Wenneker. All his plans to promote *Dresden* seemed to be foundering. He'd hoped to have a propaganda film made of the ship's officers and men enjoying their time in Japan and then sent back to the homeland as soon as possible for the people at home to see their naval heroes on in the cinemas.

He changed tactics. Severely he spoke 'Admiral Reitz, have you any prisoners on board? Haven't I already seen a woman nurse on board? Who is she?'

Serle bluntly replied, for Reitz. He was boiling with internal anger at this Nazi piece of sludge. 'She's one of us. Has signed Kriegsmarine forms. So have all our other prisoners. We ain't 'anding any of 'em over to the Japs, so there.' His broad North German accent was deliberate. Quickly Reitz intervened guessing that Serle was on the verge of losing his self-control. 'Herr Wenneker, my navigating officer is quite correct. Fraulein Cantrell is part of my crew and she has not been coerced. She signed quite willingly in the cause, not of Germany, but of her desire to assist our wounded and of any Allied prisoners that we will be taking in future operations. As for our other British prisoners they have also signed temporary forms to serve on this ship in areas where the security of the ship is not at risk. Two of them are highly skilled decorators and they will be employed in freshening up my cabins as well as that of my fellow officers and crew. I have already, via the prize officer commanders of the two prizes *en route* to France at this moment, stated of my intention of keeping all my prisoners either on this ship or on any other prize in the future. Once these messages reach France they will go to the addressees – Grand Admiral Raeder and Admiral Canaris. So don't try to bluster at me Herr Wenneker. My crew, officers and ship have already done more to serve Germany's cause than any other Kriegsmarine surface warship and please don't treat us like the dog-dirt that can be picked up on our shoes on the quayside or elsewhere on land.'

Wenneker did indeed look down at his shoes feeling very uncomfortable. He had gone too far with this hero of Germany. With the weight of Raider and Canaris behind him how could he, a mere naval attaché, even try to influence this long dark-haired, well-tanned representative of the Kriegsmarine? The cruise of the battlecruiser so far had surpassed the whole of the Kriegsmarine's other main surface warships put together even though some of them such as Panzerschiffe *Admiral Scheer* and the two larger battle-cruisers had already made impressive strikes against Allied shipping but *Dresden* had, under Reitz, easily out scored them. Fifty ships, so he'd been informed, from battleship to small sloop; large liners to small coasters. Over three hundred thousand tons of Allied shipping. Reitz was even understating his own efforts.

He heard somewhat vaguely the new Rear Admiral speaking in a calmer, but still a very firm tone. 'Herr Wenneker. When my ship sails again to join the Imperial Fleet as per the orders of Grand Admiral Raeder, then we shall do our best to carry out the job entrusted to us but at no time shall I place this ship at any unnecessary risk so far as the war situation allows. It will be our intention to slip back to Germany in the winter months and until we do, our actions will be as honourable as can be humanely possible in this awesome struggle. If we take any prisoners we shall be responsible for them. No action we take shall besmirch our name.

One day we may find ourselves being sunk and being rescued by the enemy. May they treat us as well as we would them. Not for us the foul murders of helpless prisoners such as being carried out by some soldiers and the police forces of both our country and that of our hosts. Should the Allies win this war, their retribution for war crimes could well be of fatalistic consequences for the perpetrators. My ship's crew will never ever fall into the category that I have just outlined. So don't ever again mention to myself or my fellow officers as to the treatment of our prisoners.' With this, he wagged his right forefinger in a schoolmasterish manner at Wenneker.

Wenneker at first couldn't reply. All his bluster had gone. Feebly he coughed, stood up and said 'Well, er, Admiral Reitz, I must be gone. Two of my aides will stay with you until you are dry-docked so that they can liaise with our host's dockyard and staff. I wish you all well' and then he clicked his heels and began to bring his right hand up in the Nazi salute with his mouth open to snap out 'Heil Hitler' but thought better of it, quickly altering his salute to the traditional naval one. After all, no moustached portrait of an unsmiling Fuhrer was in evidence. No big swastikas. No Nazi salutes had greeted him. Even Reitz's special flag flew at the top of *Dresden*'s mainmast. The normal naval swastika hung limply at her stern.

Three months later *Dresden* together with *Olaf* and *Berengia* were at anchor in the strong Japanese naval base of Rabaul in New Guinea. This was the Imperial Empire's main southerly base to which the Japanese were sending heavy cruisers and destroyers to help support and hold on to their conquests in the area.

Dresden was in as good a condition as possible. The Japanese dockyard workers, under strict supervision, had worked very well on the new plating, on scraping the hull and repainting it. Even Herzog admitted that they'd done an excellent job at cleaning the propellers and rudder. Internally Hiltzern organised work parties all over the ship getting her back into a full fighting order. The British prisoners had also helped, knowing that their lives were better fed by the

Kriegsmarine rather than facing the bayonets of some of the more brutal guards in the prisoner-of-war camps run by some of the Japanese. When not working on the ship, the crew allocated shore leave found the style of entertainment on offer by their hosts wasn't really up to their liking. All of them were missing their families and friends at home and reliable war news was sketchy. One day a blockade-runner arrived with sacks full of mail. But a lot of the news was censored. It was difficult to piece together the stories that Allied air-raids were beginning to make life difficult. A huge force of bombers had attacked Cologne although the cathedral that stood so proudly near the Rhine escaped relatively serious damage. Those with relatives on the Russian Front were relieved that the fighting had stabilised in the summer months. It seemed that the big South Russian city of Stalingrad was the summer's new objective rather than the previous attack on Moscow. Rommel and his Afrika Korps were battering their way towards the Nile Delta but were facing increasingly stiffer Allied opposition. If only *Dresden*'s success against that East African convoy could have been repeated! Of their fellow surface warships, the three big ships that had been berthed in France were now either in Germany or Norway whilst the North Atlantic was the battleground for the U-boat submarine crews against the Allied convoys.

Heartening news was the arrival of raider *Thor* with her supply ship and one of her prizes. Even so, *Dresden*'s crew had seen little of them for the battlecruiser set off for Rabaul soon after the raider's arrival.

Not so heartening had been the so-called propaganda visit by Reitz and most of his officers to Mount Fuji. The strain of conversing in the language of their enemies, of English, between their hosts and themselves didn't go down too favourably for often the Japanese amongst themselves conversed in their own tongue. Ruefully Reitz wished that Andrea had been in the group but she had, instead, with Helmut Brautsch, gone off with special permission to Nagasaki to try and re-contact the Irish monks in the Catholic Convent in that city where she'd previously worked for two years before taking passage on that Japanese cargo liner *en route* to Buenos Aires. Arriving at the convent, the monks and nuns were somewhat surprised at seeing Andrea again, especially as her companion was a German naval officer. Father Lovatt, who had been Andrea's confessor, effused genuine warmth and welcomed the couple with open arms. Being Irish, and thus a neutral, he'd been allowed with three other Irish monks to stay within the confines of their religious community rather than being interned into a civilian camp. Their American compatriots had wisely left a month before the attack on Pearl Harbor.

Lovatt and his fellow staff entertained the couple to a simple meal of eggs, rice and tea whilst listening to Andrea telling them of her experiences, first on *Arades* and then of the rescue by *Dresden* and also the growth of her friendship for Helmut. Loyatt in return said that he'd heard of the arrival of the German battleship, as the Japanese reports had said, but that he hadn't been expecting a visit from any of her crew, let alone a former member of the civilian medical staff who had only left the religious centre a mere two years previously.

After the meal the three of them went into the centre's chapel and there, Father Lovatt heard their confessions, Andrea first and then Helmut. Independently of each other, both of them told of their love for each other and that marriage was the institution that each hoped would happen to them both. Lovatt pondered the idea. A German officer and an English woman marrying during this dreadful war. Perhaps even here. At this centre. He was grateful for the Catholic Church's rule of keeping confessions utterly secret for if the Japanese Secret Police ever realised that Andrea was English rather than the Spanish identity that she'd assumed, then she'd be transferred to one of the civilian detention camps without any hesitation, even if she was purporting to being of assistance to the crew of the German warship. He knew well enough of the difficulty of anyone with a European face walking the streets of Japan. Only his Japanese monks, nuns and civilian staff dared go out of the confines of the monastic centre and even then Lovatt felt sure that the Tempai were keeping an eye on them because not only were they Christians but were also working at an establishment where Americans had worked up until a month before the Pearl Harbor attack. It was a lot for Lovatt to think about as he said his farewells to the couple as they left to start their journey to return to *Dresden.*

The waiting was over. *Dresden* was anchored slightly apart from the rest of the beflagged ships of the Rising Sun. She was the biggest and most powerful ship in that Rabaul anchorage. The Japanese cruisers, destroyers and support ships were under the overall command of Vice-Admiral Gunichi Mikawa. Some bore the scars of battle for only recently they'd been in a vicious confrontation with Allied cruisers patrolling near a bitterly contested island on Japan's southern border of conquests. Guadalcanal. A long elongated island in the Solomon chain of islands.

The Japanese had started to construct an airfield clearing an area amidst the generally dense jungle vegetation close to the northern shore. They had hoped to use the airstrip for their aircraft to attack Allied shipping off Australia's northern and eastern coasts. The Americans, aware of all this, then invaded the island with little opposition and the Japanese construction engineers had fled into the dense jungle on the western half of the island. Their army units on the island made little or no attempt to stop the Americans completing the airfield which they then named Henderson Field.

At last the Japanese woke up to the danger of this American threat to their southern conquests for during the daytime, American aircraft from Henderson as well as from supporting carriers, roamed over the sea-lanes to the north and west of Guadalcanal bombing and strafing any Japanese ship in the area, to the effect that the Japanese army units on the island could only be re-inforced by destroyers and fast merchantmen during the hours of darkness. To try and stop these re-inforcements building up, the Americans during the night-time, as well as in the daytime, patrolled the seas to the north of Guadalcanal with their own cruisers and destroyers.

It was to oppose these patrol ships that Mikawa had requested the use of not only *Dresden* with her excellent radar, but also the four Japanese battlecruisers in the Imperial Fleet. Big ships with fourteen-inch guns, although none of them had yet arrived at Rabaul.

As soon as *Dresden* dropped her anchors, both *Berengia* and *Olaf* came alongside, the former restocking her with shells for her big guns (that had been delivered by a blockade-runner) and the latter topping up the fuel tanks. Amidst the hustle and bustle, Reitz and Hiltzern were called for a conference onboard Mikawa's flagship, the eight-inch gunned cruiser *Aoba.* When the two Germans arrived, they found the cruiser's wardroom already full with intense looking Japanese naval officers. An English-speaking interpreter took them to meet Mikawa. After the salutes and introductions, Mikawa beamed at them. 'Ah, our famous friends. The inspiration for the news that I have just received. Here, look at the map.' With a pointer he gestured at various places, which below the Japanese characters had their English names below them. Savo Island. Tulagi. Guadalcanal. Lunga Point. Henderson Field. The names reeled off. Familiar names to those involved in the area but new to Reitz, his officers and crew. Mikawa continued to smile at the Germans when he next introduced them to a Japanese Rear-Admiral. Taguchai Tanaka. A smallish, ebullient, bright-eyed, alert naval officer. In command of a destroyer force that almost daily sailed off towards the western edge of Guadalcanal with cargoes of soldiers, ammunition and supplies. A run through the 'Slot' at night to unload and get away before dawn. A tough group of destroyers that had already clashed with their opposite numbers on the American side who in turn called Tanaka's ships 'The Tokyo Express'.

The little Japanese bowed to Reitz and Hiltzern. In American-accented English he said 'Pleased to have you with us. I have heard of your superb exploits. It will be an honour for you to help us strike at the Americans.'

The plan unfolded. Mikawa's heavy cruisers were going to attack and distract the American patrol lines off Savo Island whilst Tanaka's destroyers, after launching their 'Long Lance' torpedoes, would switch to unload their reinforcements and their supplies. In the confusion, and at her highest possible speed, *Dresden* with her escort would slip in between the two groups of ships and power her way to Lunga Point behind which, in the bay, were a dozen American supply and transport ships, which according to reconnaissance aircraft, were suffering delays and likely to be still there during the following night. The Americans seemed to be somewhat lackadaisical in their unloading secure in the hope that their own patrol cruisers, now almost back to full strength, would hold off any Japanese attacks.

In an hour's time the Japanese ships would be sailing. Tanaka grimly told Reitz that without *Dresden*'s speed, firepower and radar, that the chance to sink the American transports could well be abortive. However timing was critical. One run round the bay. Shoot and sink. Then out at full speed in order to be out of range of any American retaliatory air-strikes soon after dawn. Such an attack, if successful, would be of an immense help to the Japanese army which so far had failed to dislodge the impertinent Yankees. Hopefully, with *Dresden*'s help, the army would redouble its efforts. Tanaka wasn't smiling when he finished. He knew that the struggle was a vital one for if the Japanese failed, then the Americans would be in a position to mount further attacks on the islands held by the Japanese to the north of Guadalcanal. Maybe even on Rabaul itself.

In bidding farewell to Reitz, Mikawa said 'We're depending a great deal on your ship.'

Reitz simply nodded, his mind whirling with the fraughtness of the operation ahead of them. Hiltzern ploughed after him as they left the wardroom, his huge bulk seemingly like an elephant amongst gazelles when compared with the smaller Japanese naval men.

Once back on board *Dresden*, Reitz quickly began to issue orders for the action. Serle produced the required charts and began to pencil in the course that the ship would be taking. Herzog checked over his engines with the fuel tanks now fully topped up. Colonel Tibbetts and his lads were transferred to *Berengia* that lay on the other side of the battlecruiser, merging with the members of the German crew who were busy transferring last-minute stores. Earlier Reitz talked to the Kriegsmarine-overalled Englishman of his hope, that once his obligations to the Japanese were over he would then send the Colonel and his men back to Occupied Europe on a blockade-bursting run by *Berengia*. Also transferred, to the escorting light cruiser *Myosho* of the new Noshiro-class, were five of the six Japanese liaison team. He retained the only one who could speak German believing that to translate everything into English could be vitally too slow in the heat of violent action. No-one seemed sorry to see the Japanese leave their ship.

Within the hour, anchors were weighed and the German battle-cruiser churned out of Rabaul's anchorage accompanied by *Myosho* and two destroyers. Already on their way were four of Mikawa's heavy cruisers and Tanaka in turn followed them in his flagship, light cruiser *Jintsu* and eight destroyers. Speed was set at twenty-five knots and the wakes of the seventeen warships bubbled and frothed behind them as they settled on their course bound for the forthcoming contest near the 'Slot', the area of sea that spanned across from the diamond-shaped Savo Island to the northern shoreline of Guadalcanal.

The sun sank behind them in a multi-hued flare of purple, orange, yellow and red as the speeding warships approached the danger area. Soon the light would fade as the darkness of a tropical night encroached the sunset-dappled wavelets of the calm waters, broken only by the wakes of the squadron as it upped its speed to twenty-eight knots.

The ships were seen before the oncoming darkness enveloped them. Their silhouettes were familiar enough to coast-watcher Reuben Benson who was watching for Japanese ships which normally, if on an attack, passed within sighting range of his camouflaged-hide on the fringe of the coastal forest of an island some sixty miles north-west of Savo. For three months he'd been sending out advance warning reports to the Americans on Guadalcanal or on their patrolling ships whenever Japanese surface or air attacks were on their approach run. Somehow he'd always avoided Japanese foot patrols that quite often searched for him and his three native aides. As Benson carefully noted the shapes of the ships with references to his Jane's Fighting Ships guide, he then became astonished. The large warship near the rear of the column was unlike one that he'd ever seen before. Desperately he rippled through the silhouettes of known Japanese cruisers. Nothing tallied with the lean ship he could see through his telescope. Benson though knew he had enough information to realise that this was a Japanese force with perhaps a new fast battleship to help boost their gun-power strength and that he needed to climb down as quickly as possible from the camouflaged hide to his radio set in the thatched shelter at the foot of the tree.

'Not so fast, leetle Engleeshman' came the accented nasal voice, aided by a sharp-pointed bayonet as Benson began to tap his coded message. Suddenly the rifle was reversed and the butt clubbed Benson in the right side of his face. He staggered but before he could even think about reaching for his revolver strapped in its holster, another vicious clubbing knocked him to the floor. Dimly he heard the sound of firing as bullets raked his radio set. Then he felt himself being hoisted up and being dragged out to the base of the very tree he'd just descended.

'Hang him there' snarled the Japanese officer, 'along with those three native brats. They'll make good food for the crows.' Benson could offer no resistance as he felt his hands being lashed and a great pain as the rope around his neck tightened and his feet left the ground. Mercifully, blackness soon followed.

With no advance warning, the arrival of Mikawa's cruisers at the American patrol-lines came as a severe shock to the commanding officers of the ships that were so suddenly attacked with first, blinding star-shells and piercing searchlights soon followed by the crump of the Long Lance torpedoes as they exploded into the leading ships of their patrol line. Two cruisers and a destroyer received their death blasts before the Americans were able to react. And react they did. Vicious gunfire broke out as each side literally exploded into a grim crescendo of violent battle. Shells and torpedoes streaked in opposite directions seeking a victim on their destructive errands. One American cruiser lost fifteen feet of her bows as yet another 'Long Lance' smashed into her. Japanese cruiser *Aoba*, Mikawa's own flagship shuddered under a hail of gunfire and was forced to turn away with her crew desperately trying to get blazing fires under control.

Another of Mikawa's cruisers turning after her flagship, was seriously hit aft of her bridge which engulfed her stern section almost totally in flames. So furious was the exchange that the Americans didn't notice eight of the nine Japanese destroyers as well as light cruiser *Jintsu* slide away to the south-west rather than to the north-east as were the cruisers and their escorts under Mikawa. Tanaka's ships were off to unload their human cargoes on to the shores of north-western Guadalcanal. Neither did the Americans see the fast shape of Benson's 'battleship' as the *Dresden* at thirty-three knots powered her way in the darkness to slip between the American ships still slugging it out with Mikawa's force and the not-too distant headland of Lunga Point. Using only his radar to guide him, Reitz kept *Dresden* fifteen miles away from the conflict aiming for the Point as fast he could take the speeding battlecruiser. A momentary blip on the radar indicated the last destroyer in the

American line hastening to catch up with the conflict with Mikawa's cruisers. It made no sign of having even suspected the presence of the German ship travelling so fast that even *Myosho* and the two escorting Japanese destroyers were beginning to fall behind. *Dresden* powered on with her gun and torpedo crews fully tensed for the targets which all hoped that the radar would reveal once they'd rounded Lunga Point. As she rounded the Point, a rain squall lashed out at her, hiding her from the ships at anchor suddenly showing up so clearly on the radar.

Eight transport ships were still unloading or loading. Four of the smaller ships had already left, their task completed.

Rear Admiral Robert F. Whallen chafed at the delay as he chomped on a stubby cigar whilst pacing the starboard wing of transport *Eastern Wood*, his command ship. Reports of the action with Mikawa's cruisers were reaching him. Reports that indicated that, despite severe losses and damage, the patrol line had seemingly driven the Japanese attackers away. Yet he still felt uneasy at the delays that were occurring in getting the last of the supplies unloaded and in reverse, having the wounded coming aboard and being bedded down. Whallen even risked ordering the deck lights to stay fully lit so as to assist in hurrying up the work. He knew he should have pulled out at sunset and returned in daylight hours but his ships had been delayed in arriving and he just didn't want any further setbacks. Apparently the Japanese recce aircraft had either not been noticed or it had been mistaken for an American plane or else Whallen wouldn't have so blatantly ignored specific orders. He shuffled back to the middle of the bridge to discuss matters with Colonel S. Richard Hallowes, commander of the army personnel being disembarked. ''Bout another ten minutes, Admiral, and then I'll be the last man off your ship. You'll be able to high-trail it out of here then. Just getting the last of the evacuated wounded on board.' Whallen just grunted. All this reinforcement work had taken too long. He paced nervously back to the starboard wing puffing into his cigar as his eyes wandered over to the shoreline. Then another messenger came up to him. The attacking Japanese cruisers were definitely running back to their base. Whallen nodded.

No-one on *Eastern Wood* or any of the other transports saw *Dresden* emerge out at sea from a rain-squall that hadn't even touched the stationary ships. None of the personnel on board these ships suspected the presence of the battlecruiser.

'Good heavens, the Yanks are careless. They've even left their deck lights on for us' murmured Brautsch to Reitz on seeing their targets illuminated against the darker line of the shore.

'Slow to twenty knots. Torpedoes to fire on my orders. No gunfire yet.' Reitz stood calmly issuing his orders utterly amazed at the apparent unwarlike situation now just two miles off the starboard bow.

A lookout on *Eastern Wood* yelled out 'Ship off port side closing fast' as he caught sight of the battlecruiser's dark shape approaching the transports, the white moustache of her bow wave visible but diminishing as the approaching warship slowed down.

Whallen dashed over to the transport's port-wing. 'Must be one of our own cruisers coming back to see if we're still OK.'

Colonel Hallowes wasn't so sure 'Yeah, but why ain't she signalling us?'

'You lands people' sneered Whallen. 'She ain't Japanese. She ain't got their bridge structure like one of their bloomin' temples.

'Anyway, you heard the report, the Jap cruisers have turned back – Good God, what the hell?!'

A loud explosion rocked the outboard merchantman. Then another explosion hammered into the freighter anchored astern of them.

'Shit! Cut the anchors! Get the hell outa' here!' yelled Whallen at the awe-stricken captain of *Eastern Wood* as other vessels began to rock with further explosions. Then the strange dark ship began to spit flame. Shells whistled all around them but *Eastern Wood* bore a charmed existence. Being an inshore ship, she was able to keep the ships already stricken between her and the as yet unknown assailant.

With her deck-lights instantly dowsed, the big transport ship began to lumber her way from the scene of burning destruction behind her, made worse as three more of the transports were hit by shells resulting in flames which seared brightly across their wrecked decks. Flames also burst from the shore as some of the incoming shells began landing amongst the stores still piled up at their dispersal points. Stocks of fuel and ammunition started to blow up in a series of concussive detonations. Men, terrified with the totally unexpected fury of the attack, ran in all directions trying to escape the hell that was suddenly exploding all around them. Even from the burning sinking ships, men were leaping overboard and swimming desperately for the shore before their ships blew up or sank.

The enemy warship, still unidentified, turned but even on her way out of the bay fired further broadsides before to the relief of those still on the wrecked ships or cowering on the shore she passed out of sight round Lunga Point. Following her were three smaller ships that also spat flame and a torpedo from one of them caught another transport that was attempting to escape. Badly crippled, her captain turned his sinking ship shore-wards in an attempt to beach it. Only *Eastern Wood*, having now reached an area of relative darkness at the edge of the flare-up of battered ships and destroyed supplies escaped intact although shell splinter holes peppered her decks and port-sides.

Whallen was a badly shaken man. He just couldn't comprehend the enormity of the disaster. The mystery enemy warship in just two runs across the bay, in about a quarter-of-an-hour, had all but annihilated his command group as well as countless numbers of supplies, never mind the personnel on the ships as well as ashore. He knew that he was facing complete ruin. It had been his decision to carry on unloading. It was his stupidity that had left the deck lights blazing – a perfect aiming point for the initial enemy assault. Even the news that the main Japanese force had retired wasn't even an excuse. Somehow a squadron of their ships led by at least a heavy cruiser had penetrated the patrol line and delivered this appalling catastrophe.

He clattered down from the bridge and rushed to his command cabin, slamming the door shut behind him even as one of the ship's officers and Colonel Hallowes raced after him guessing what was about to happen to the Rear-Admiral. Too late. Even as they put their shoulders to the door they heard the sound of a pistol shot. As Hallowes burst in, Whallen lay down with a pool of blood pouring from a head wound as his body slumped on the cabin's floor. Stricken from this sight, Hallowes turned and raced back to the bridge leaving the junior officer behind him ashen-faced and retching over nearby rails. Ordering *Eastern Wood*'s captain to stop ship, a boat was hurriedly launched so that he could return to the shattered beach and burning ships to try and salvage something out of the horrific onslaught that had so savagely overtaken the supply operation.

Dresden surged away from Lunga Point closely followed by *Myosho* and the two destroyers at a speed of thirty knots. Soon the scene of her attack quickly receded to little more than a flickering glow on the horizon before yet another rainsquall blotted even that out from sight.

'Not bad for such a short action' commented Hiltzern as he returned to the bridge from his damage control position. 'We certainly scored well with Wolle Seizel's torpedoes. It'll give the Americans something to think about!'

Reitz nodded 'Yes. We did well. Took them completely by surprise. Not a shot fired back at us. Like shooting at sitting ducks but we mustn't be complacent. You can guess that their patrol line will have been alerted to look out for our return and no doubt at dawn their aircraft will be taking off in a revenge attack. Until we reach the safety of the approaches to Rabaul we are now the hunted, no longer the hunter. Congratulate the crew by all means but we must remain on full alert. We must avoid any of their destroyer patrols – the radar boys will no doubt keep us informed – and steam as hard as we can for Rabaul.'

Just under an hour after disappearing back round Lunga Point, radar sent in a report to Reitz 'Three ships moving towards us at high speed fifteen miles off our starboard quarter.'

Reitz surmised that the blips represented destroyers and altered course five degrees to port.

Radar's response was that the blips also altered course and were still closing.

The blips were indeed three American destroyers detached from their patrol line in response to a desperate plea for assistance from the shattered supply depot at Lunga. The lead ship picked up *Dresden* and her consorts and altered course to try and intercept, using what her captain assumed to be superior radar in order to close in on what he assumed to be radar-less Japanese ships.

It came as a shock when at a range of six miles star-shells burst overhead the three American destroyers fired from the guns of a fully-prepared *Dresden.*

'Cripes!' yelled a lookout.

'Bloody hell!' shouted another.

Then six huge waterspouts soared just yards ahead of the leading destroyer. Before the little warship could take avoiding action she was caught by two shells from the next salvo. The other two destroyers desperately turned away as shells from not only *Dresden* but also her three Japanese consorts crashed into the sea around them. Riddled with shrapnel they put out smokescreens and vanished into a provident rain-squall.

Fortunately for the first-hit destroyer which was coming to a sinking halt, their enemy's warships didn't follow up with a further attack and so her captain who'd survived the salvo from *Dresden* was able to organise his crew into life-rafts and boats as his ship slowly sank by the bows. One of the other destroyers realising that the enemy force was speeding away from the skirmish turned back and within half-an-hour was on the scene rescuing the first destroyer's survivors as the shattered vessel was swallowed up by the dark waters. She was yet another victim for the area known to the Americans as 'Iron-bottom Sound' on account of the number of ships that had already been sunk in the vicious battles for Guadalcanal.

Dawn. The squally storm clouds of the night had dispersed and the sun peaked its aura over an ever-increasing clear blue sky. The rays shimmered down to the still slightly choppy waters through which *Dresden* steamed through at thirty knots with her consorts also showing arrow-straight frothy white wakes as all four ships streaked for the relative safety of Rabaul still two hundred miles away. Another two hours would see them beyond the range of American aircraft.

Back on Henderson Field and also on two American carriers some fifty miles south of Guadalcanal, American aircraft were indeed warming up to try and catch the raiders of that devastating attack. Mikawa's cruisers and Tanaka's destroyers were already at their extreme range but *Dresden*'s group were sighted by a coast-watcher as they passed his position on one of the smaller islands, a risk that Reitz took aiming to reach safety by the quickest direct route. Hurried flight plans for the aircraft were quickly worked out based on the report that had come in and it was decided that the planes could reach the enemy raiders at just the limit of their range. Despite the risks, the pilots were eager to go in order to have even just one run-in at the enemy that had so surprisingly overwhelmed the carelessly anchored supply ships. Six sunk and one beached out of the eight. The desire for revenge was deep inside the hearts of the fliers.

Eighty minutes later at the extremity of their cruising range the lead aircraft sighted *Dresden*'s squadron steaming hard for Rabaul.

'There they are boys' he yelled over his inter-aircraft intercom 'We've just enough fuel for one run in. Let's go smack 'em!'

The six Dauntless bombers from Henderson arrowed down to the ships below them seemingly immune to the brown puffs of anti-aircraft shell bursts exploding below and in front of them. As they bore in ever nearer to their target, vicious lines of high-velocity tracer fire swished ever closer to them with one of the wing aircraft being a specially selected target as three tracers in an accurate cone punctured it across one of its wings and then into its underbelly. The aircraft suddenly just disintegrated. The bombs began to whistle down. Reitz manoeuvred the battlecruiser like as if she was a lithe destroyer. Down below loose clothing, pots and pans, bottles and crockery were flung from cupboards as the ship switched track in a violent zig-zagging path to avoid the bombs. Andrea clung to a support pillar feeling more terrified than she had when that U-boat was shelling *Arades*.

Suddenly it was all over. Another of the attacking aircraft was shot down. The four survivors streaked low over the waves in making their escape knowing that they'd only just have enough fuel to make it back to Henderson Field. Aircraft from the carriers were forced some thirty miles astern to turn back as they were at the limit of their fuel range.

It hadn't been all one-way traffic. One of *Dresden*'s escorts, a destroyer, took a bomb hit and was slowing down but although damaged she was not in any danger of sinking providing she lost enough speed to enable her mid-ship bulkheads to stand the strain of flooding caused by the hit abaft her forward funnel.

Two of *Dresden*'s anti-aircraft gunners suffered wounds by splinters from a bomb burst off the port-side of the speeding warship. They were taken down to the Sick Berth where Doctor Lebers and Andrea tended to rather nasty gashes across their cheeks and upper-arms. Both men would live to serve their ship again. *Dresden*'s luck had held again and but for the superb handling from Reitz's orders, the ship could have been badly damaged had that bomb landed on board.

Safely back at Rabaul and on battle-damaged heavy cruiser *Aoba*, Reitz told Mikawa of his success which only added to what the Japanese admiral already knew for reports from his recce aircraft told of the seven wrecked ships as well as spectacular evidence of the quick-fire bombardment of the stores on the shore-line depot area. The success of Reitz only served to emphasise what was already going through his mind. What if fast battlecruisers or some of his heavy cruisers could repeat the operation by bombarding Henderson Airfield? Three or four raids of say an hour-long bash at the airfield could render it inoperable and weaken its defences sufficiently for the Japanese troops to follow-up and retake the vital area. Japan had four available fast battlecruisers capable of a sustained effort of thirty knots and with their fourteen-inch guns could fling out such a weight of shells that could well turn the airfield into a pitted morass of mud and wrecked aircraft. Recce reports also gave the news that the Americans had at least temporarily withdrawn their night patrolling of the seas around Savo Island due to the severe losses that they'd been suffering. No doubt they'd be back so Mikawa knew he couldn't delay with his plans.

Within six days of *Dresden*'s attack, the first two of Japan's battlecruisers arrived. The thirty thousand ton *Kongo* and *Haruna* both of 1913 vintage with 1930's modernisations. Mikawa asked Reitz to return to the area to act as the radar guide and to help pinpoint the gunfire assault on the airfield. The three big ships accordingly ploughed their way rapidly south of Rabaul as darkness approached but this time, keeping out of visual range of the islands so as to prevent possible observance by the coast-watchers whose presence was known to the Japanese although in the week since Benson's execution along with his islander friends, no more of the watchers had been caught.

It was nearly midnight when the horizon opposite Henderson

Airfield erupted into flame as the three battlecruisers opened fire. The airfield staff crouched deep in their dugouts whilst the heavy shells smashed into the ground above them flinging nearly half the available aircraft into scraps of shattered steel matchsticks during the hour that the bombardment blasted out. Then the shelling abruptly stopped but it was only at dawn some five hours later that the survivors crept out of their shelters to assess their damaged surrounds. It was like surveying the surface of the moon. They knew that another such night could well see the end of the airfield.

It very nearly did. Two of Mikawa's heavy cruisers shelled the airfield the very next night. Only fourteen of the ninety aircraft based at the airfield were repairable and engineers knew that it would take at least another ten days before they could smooth out all the holes and fill them in safely enough for aircraft to take off. Surprisingly the Japanese army failed to mount an offensive and the work to repair the field was able to continue and soon small fighter-planes from offshore carriers were able to land as re-inforcements.

Also on the Japanese side there were delays. The original two battlecruisers retired back to rejoin the Imperial Fleet further north and their replacements, *Hiei* and *Kirishima*, were delayed. Reitz was ordered by both SKL and Wenneker to replenish *Dresden*'s stores and fuel and to go with the next bombardment group as before, but in the confusion, to slip south past the Americans and into the waters adjacent to Australia's east coast and then across the Pacific on an expected homeward return, coinciding her run through the North Atlantic with the winter storms to help hide her in the breakthrough attempt. As yet, Allied intelligence had failed to pick up the definite whereabouts of the German battlecruiser. Even her non-Japanese outline had only been noted in American reports as a 'new type of Jap battle-wagon'. None of the Americans suspected that the German was with the Japanese warships based off Rabaul.

Although they hadn't recognised the *Dresden*, the Americans were re-cooping their losses on their Savo Island patrol line to the extent in bringing up two of their own new battleships to act as support to the cruisers and destroyers which began to resume their nightly patrol lines to the seas north of Henderson Field in order to try and prevent it being bombarded to its final destruction.

At the same time the two replacement Japanese battlecruisers eventually arrived at Rabaul.

On a November evening, the raiding force set sail. Even *Dresden* seemed to be dwarfed by the bulk of the *Hiei* as the Japanese battlecruiser pushed up the seas from her bows as she followed the German ship at the squadron attack approach speed of twenty-eight knots. *Dresden*'s radar picked up a long line of American cruisers and destroyers when but fifteen miles away from the bombardment area. Reitz ordered full ahead to try and get round the American ships but his ship and the Japanese were sighted by alert American radar operators and soon the distance separating the opposing ships began to dwindle.

The night sky erupted as both sides opened fire on each other at just over a five-mile range. *Dresden* now on the starboard wing of the Japanese ships, took on three targets, one of which was seen to burst into flames. To port, the big bulk of *Hiei* became the main target of the American attacks. Like enraged wasps, she was set upon by eight destroyers. Four of them failed to overcome the return of fire by the Japanese battlecruiser but the rest scored torpedo hits and also hit their enemy's huge superstructure with many of their small five-inch shells that caused numerous fires to breakout. In less than half-an-hour she took in eighty such hits, which forced her commander to turn her away from her bombardment objective. *Dresden* was at the edge of the conflict as Reitz tried to work her round the rear of the American column when radar reported a small blip rapidly closing them from only four miles. US destroyer *Hurst* had been trailing the German warship for most of the sharp battle but had been unable to close with the ship until Reitz ordered a course alteration to take him round the patrol lines. Rapidly *Hurst*, at thirty-four knots to the German's thirty, began to close the gap to what the Americans thought was a Japanese heavy cruiser.

Dresden's guns, of all calibres that could bear on the little American destroyer, opened up a desperate rate of fire to create a veritable forest of shell splashes into which raced *Hurst* on her mission to attack with torpedoes.

Spectres of the brave *Anemone*'s attack on Christmas Day just ten months earlier loomed in the mind of Reitz as he clung to the bridge rail issuing his orders to try and avoid any torpedoes that the approaching American might launch. Shells began to bracket the destroyer and as she turned to try and get away after launching two of the deadly underwater missiles, the German gunners, at last, accurately found the range and the destroyer was literally overwhelmed by the violent hail of shells that raked over her whole length. She shuddered to a rapidly sinking halt turning over onto her port-side and also going down by the stern. Barely two dozen of her crew were able to scramble into two life-rafts that were hastily thrown into the water.

Approaching the German ship came the two forty-knot missiles. 'Hard a-star-board!' yelled Reitz as he desperately tried to turn *Dresden* to comb the missiles approach as detected by his hydroplane operators.

Too late!

One of the torpedoes scraped past the bows and raced down *Dresden*'s port-side but the other slammed into her starboard side just forward of 'Anton', the foremost of the two big gun turrets in the forepart of the battlecruiser. Turrets that immediately fell silent as the tracking mechanisms were badly damaged in the torpedo's blast. Like her big sister battlecruiser *Scharnhorst* that had been hit by a torpedo fired from the brave sinking destroyer *Acasta* off Norway in June 1940, *Dresden* was able to contain the savage blow. The few survivors of *Hurst* saw their torpedo hit their large opponent but at first it carried on steaming as if not seriously damaged. Then one of them noticed the stern wake of the big ship gradually decrease although the vessel they'd hit continued to disappear over the limited horizon of their life raft.

Had they but known but that one torpedo hit gave the German battlecruiser her worst damage so far of the war. Within moments, *Dresden* was down at the bows and took a six-degree list to starboard. Reitz was forced to reduce speed to only five knots as the damage control teams, guided by Hiltzern and his team strove to check the inrush of water and to shore up any threatened bulkheads in the bows of the warship.

There were no more thoughts of a bombardment or even of a breakthrough voyage back to German waters. *Dresden* was a cripple and all Reitz could think about was getting his near-helpless ship back to Rabaul. Power to the big guns as well as to some of the ammunition hoists to the secondary guns was lost due to the explosion. Hiltzern's damage control team had one priority. To secure their ship from sinking. She was moving at a slow shambling crawl hid only by the cloak of the darkness of those night hours but in five hours it would be dawn and the work to repair the damage was desperately urgent. The hammering and cutting went on and on to restrict the flooding. Auxiliary pumps were positioned to help rid the bows of unwanted water.

Down in the Sick Berth, Doctor Lebers together with Andrea and their attendants worked desperately to patch up the wounded that had been dragged out of the damage area. More than one sailor lost an arm or had a leg amputated due to their irreparable limbs. For the first time whilst he'd been on the German ship, Andrea felt acutely sorry for the men she was treating. Although they were strictly enemy, she'd become every popular with many whose wounds she was now treating. Nearly all of them she knew had been hoping for the chance to return to Germany. Now here they were on a crippled ship with no immediate hope of that return to their loved ones at home. In fact they could well soon be the target of American aircraft hell bent on sending them to the bottom of the ocean within the next few hours. Andrea tried to keep her mind on the medical work that she was doing and not on the thoughts that seemed so horrifying. She thought of Helmut, as she knew he was with the damage control teams trying to save the ship.

Padré Jervaulx's thoughts were with the men who'd been killed by the torpedo blast. At the latest count twenty-seven corpses had already been dragged out and placed into canvas bags. The chaplain said what inadequate prayers he could for his mind was numb with the closeness that he and all still alive on the battlecruiser had been to death itself. Then he made his way to the Sick Berth to help give comfort, if that were possible, to the living trying to cope with their dreadful wounds.

Reitz didn't sleep as he paced the bridge receiving the news of the work of the damage control teams. Astern of his ship on the horizon he could see the glow from the burning *Hiei.* No doubt her damage control teams were facing an even more horrific task than the men on his own ship. Whatever it was the bombardment attempt had been a failure. Of the big ships, only battlecruiser *Kirishima* seemed to have escaped unscathed. Never mind the half-dozen American destroyers that had been sunk. Should either the *Dresden* or *Hiei* succumb to their damage, the sea-fight and its aftermath would go down as an Axis defeat. The first that the Japanese had suffered in these waters.

Just as the first signs of dawn began to glimmer in the eastern sky, Hiltzern was able to report that the damage was now contained and that the pumps were pumping all except the sealed off area dry of water. Speed could be increased from the five knots that *Dresden* had been crawling at since initially slowing down.

Gradually the German warship picked up her speed. To seven, then ten, and eventually twelve knots. As dawn lightened the sky, the distance between *Dresden* and the destroyers with the crippled *Hiei* increased until all that could be seen was the brown smudge of smoke marking the painful progress of the bigger Japanese battlecruiser.

A smudge of smoke that was to attract the attention of avenging American pilots from Henderson Field and offshore carriers. Their briefing instructed them 'To find a crippled Jap battle-wagon and sink it!' Some how in the confusion of the night action, and even with the accounts by the few survivors of *Hurst*, no-one on the American side seemed to have come to the conclusion that there were two crippled enemy battle-wagons that needed to be eliminated. So many conflicting claims from other ships about shelling or torpedoing a 'big Jap' seemed to lead the briefing officers in thinking that only one of the Japanese capital ships would still be within range by the time the attacking planes would be ready to take-off.

It didn't take the Americans very long to find *Hiei* and her escort crawling slowly towards Rabaul. Elated at discovering 'the big Jap battle-wagon' the aircraft swooped to the attack with bombs and torpedoes. Even on board *Dresden* they could see the brown puffs of the anti-aircraft barrage put up by the defending Japanese ships. Evidently *Hiei* still had plenty of fight left in her. The attacks seemed to go on all morning until at last *Dresden* was out of visual and eventually radar range. The set's operators reported the presence of *Hiei*'s blip on their screens until the whole group disappeared off the edge. Anxious lookouts scanned the sky for any American aircraft. The radar lads also watched their screens but no planes came their way. It was if the pent-up fury for revenge against the Japanese was being entirely directed at the luckless *Hiei*. Nevertheless she absorbed an immense amount of punishment whilst at the same time she and her escorts fought back until some of their guns either over-heated or ran out of ammunition. It wasn't until mid-afternoon did the constant attacks finally batter *Hiei* to a burning, sinking halt. Her surviving crew were taken off during a lull in the attacks by her escort destroyers which then drew away off at high speed as scuttling charges blew out enough of *Hiei* to cause her to slip below the waves thus becoming Japan's first capital ship loss of the war.

By dawn the next morning *Dresden*, still slightly down at the bows and with a two-degree list, dropped anchor along-side *Berengia* and *Olaf* in the Rabaul anchorage. Her exhausted, drained and dispirited crew were at last able to take a rest and a chance to contemplate their future. Hiltzern's damage control teams had made their ship as seaworthy as was possible but everyone knew that the battlecruiser would have to return to a Japanese dockyard.

Soon after she'd dropped anchor, a motor-launch came alongside the German ship. From it came Admiral Mikawa and some of his staff. Reitz received them in his main cabin. Mikawa thanked Reitz for all of *Dresden*'s efforts that had been so successful even though regrettably she'd been torpedoed. Japan would immediately see to it that the required repairs would be carried out as soon as she was docked at Kure. He expressed his sympathies for the crew members who'd lost their lives. Reitz in turn asked if *Hiei* had survived. Mikawa's face told him of the answer before the Japanese even replied. However he said that during the forthcoming night, *Kirishima* would be returning to try and get at the airfield. If she failed, then the American hold on Guadalcanal would only get stronger and the future for the whole area would be one of grim defence for the Japanese forces. With his navy's carriers sunk at Midway and in the Coral Sea, Mikawa told Reitz that air power was beginning to show that it could supersede any capital ship without air cover.

It was a sober, thoughtful meeting, which didn't fill Reitz with any firm degree of confidence. He realised that the high days of the surface raider were coming to an end in any area that the enemy could cover with their aircraft. It seemed even more important that the repairs should be completed, the crew worked-up again and a breakthrough back to Germany for the following winter season in the North Atlantic be an earnest contemplation.

Even more sobering was the funeral conducted by Padré Jervaulx as twenty-nine weighted bags were dropped into the bay, two badly wounded amputees having succumbed to their appalling injuries. The crews of *Berengia* and *Olaf* lined their ships in company with the battlecruiser's men. Colonel Tibbetts, still in Kriegsmarine fatigues, with his men watching from the big supply ship, crossed over to *Dresden* to attend and after the service, Reitz received him in his cabin. There the German told him that he was, with his men, going to be returned to Europe on *Berengia.* As they parted, Tibbetts stuck out his right hand and shook hands with Reitz repeating his thanks at not being sent to a Japanese prison camp. He smiled somewhat ironically as the riposte came from the German that maybe Allied cruisers would intercept them!

The next day *Berengia* churned out of the bay and a few hours later, *Dresden* and *Olaf* with an escort of three destroyers, all needing repairs following battle damage, also left Rabaul but bound for Japan.

On the voyage northwards, Reitz and his crew received more bad news. Merchant raider *Thor* had been destroyed in a Japanese harbour along with her supply ship *Uckermark* due to an internal explosion aboard the latter causing such a fire that the raider had been caught up in the oil-fuelled blaze. Germany's sole active representative outside home waters was another merchant-ship raider, *Michel* which at that time was in the South Atlantic with orders to make for Japan, rather than Germany. The noose of war was tightening ever so more seriously against the Axis nations and Reitz would have to bolster his men's morale a great deal once the repairs were completed. He knew that he'd have to go a-raiding first in a quietish area in order to build his crew up before attempting a return to home waters. Not for him this next time an involvement with Japan's Imperial Fleet's struggle with the Americans. His ship was best suited in an independent role, not in a fleet action, where there was every possibility of being exposed to an aerial assault such as the one that had overcome the unfortunate *Hiei.*

He also knew that the chance to see Elle was gone. For the time being. Perhaps for a year at least. He just hoped that Wenneker and his staff could somehow pass on to Grand-Admiral Raeder the accuracy of *Dresden*'s fate and he in turn pass it on to SKL in Northern France and thus it would reach Elle.

He missed her so very much.

Chapter 9

'You are making us dizzy'

The Pacific Ocean, when given its name, must have been in one of its quieter moods for as *Dresden* and her merchant vessel consorts pushed steadily north-westwards into the ocean's grey swells, topped with white breaking waves, the mood of that ocean was anything but peaceful. Reitz had told his crew that this cruise towards the Alaskan coast was to help them find their sea-legs again and to work up to a full war footing in a long preparation for their attempt to break-through the Allied sea-lanes during the winter months. So, he said, that is why they were here, in early September, out at sea rather than swinging at their anchors in Kure Bay. Their Japanese escort, of two minesweepers, perhaps fearful of attacks by American submarines, suddenly and without any warning, turned about and putting on as full a speed as they could, sailed quickly out of sight for now distant Hokkaido Island. Even though that this storm had been with them then, as it was now two days later, Reitz knew that it was difficult to keep a submarine at the correct trim during rough seas and reckoned that this storm, foul as it was, constituted the best weather for *Dresden*, and her fellow ships, to break-out for this shake-down cruise. He watched some of his crew rigging safety-lines which he'd deemed necessary as the pitch of the seas was getting bad enough for the battlecruiser, despite her flared bows, to bury herself into the steepening waves.

Reitz knew that for *Dresden*, her crew as well as for the Axis partnership that the war was going less favourably than during the time the battlecruiser had been in dry-dock undergoing her repairs following that torpedoing from the brave attack mounted by the American destroyer. Even braver had been the actions of one of their Japanese escorts when she'd crossed *Dresden*'s bows and taken a full spread of four torpedoes, fired from an American submarine, along her whole length. Not that the attacker had escaped for the other three escorts mounted such a ferocious counter-attack which resulted in oil and wreckage coming to the surface soon afterwards. Mingling with that of the torpedoed destroyer. For seven long months in Kure, the *Dresden*'s crew and Japanese dockyard workers strove to get the battlecruiser back into a war-worthy condition. Other warships of the Imperial Fleet were also in Kure awaiting or undergoing repairs, testimony of not only the furious battles around Guadalcanal but also in the contests for other islands that the Americans were beginning to invade and wrest from the Japanese. It was obvious, that despite *Dresden*'s brilliant efforts off Guadalcanal, that the tide of war was turning against Japan. Their little Admiral friend, Tanaka of the 'Tokyo Express' with his destroyers had been able to evacuate the remnants of the Japanese army from that island during the first two months of this year. 1943.

A year that saw the noose of potential defeat tightening harder on the Axis. Not only were Japanese forces on the defensive, so also were the Germans. A hopeless defence at Stalingrad together with even Rommel's famed Afrika Korps retreating in North Africa to their final surrender in May meant that the German armies lost over half-a-million personnel. Reitz had done his best, based on scant information, to keep his crew members informed but they all knew that their homeland was also under a vicious aerial bombardment from Allied aircraft that were breaking through the Luftwaffe's defences. They knew this for enough information filtered through the letters to the crew, delivered by a successful blockade-runner from France to Japan, despite the attentions of Nazi censors. More than one crew member had been to see their senior officers to voice their concerns for family and friends back home but none of them ever put in a request to transfer to a ship trying to sail the ever-increasingly difficult journey to France.

Other news, from SKL, was equally despondent. Apparently an attack on an Arctic convoy by *Lutzow* and *Hipper* at the turn of the year ended in such disgrace that the Fuhrer's first order upon receiving the news was to initiate the scrapping of all the Kriegsmarine's main surface vessels. In disgust, Grand Admiral Erich Raeder tendered his resignation and it was only the superb skills of soothing down the enraged leader of Nazi Germany by his successor, Karl Doenitz, that the order was rescinded. A message from the new Grand-Admiral relayed to Reitz told him to keep up the excellent work done by *Dresden* and her crew and to hurt the Allies where appropriate once back on the high seas.

Some hint at the Kriegsmarine's difficulties came in letters from Elle. She was now at the Headquarters for the Northern operations based in Trondheim, Norway. Apparently only two of the Navy's big ships were still based in Norwegian waters – battleship *Tirpitz* and battlecruiser *Scharnhorst*, together with about ten destroyers. She'd even visited *Scharnhorst* with her crew chafing at the endless days just swinging at their anchors in the desolate base at Altenfjord. Some of the crew had even spoke to her wishing that they were on *Dresden*. Anything to be out at sea striking at Allied shipping. She also added that she was billetted with a most hospitable Norwegian family and that she was trying to learn their language.

In every letter she said that she loved him, missed him, wished him well and hoped that he and *Dresden* would be able to make it back to their homeland as soon as conditions were considered to be at their most favourable. She signed every one with a smothering of kisses.

One of her last letters mentioned news about a really old warship called the *Rugen*. Apparently the old battleship had even fired her guns when escorting a small convoy. Fortunately her assailants, two British cruisers, sheered off before inflicting any serious damage and the *Rugen* together with the five ships that were in her charge were able to reach the shelter of a fjord. Briefly, the old war-horse's action seemed to overshadow the combined efforts of the rest of the Kriegsmarine put together – excepting *Dresden*, of course. The latest propaganda from the Nazi press even had *Dresden* at sea, sinking an American battleship off Guadalcanal. She even sent him the cutting – sheer Nazi fantasy!

Arabian Nights brought the final batch of letters. She slipped safely into a berth close to *Dresden*'s dry-dock and her captain, Karl Neumans, had described his remarkable voyage from Bordeaux to Kure with some degree of the riskiness of such of a voyage showing up most clearly. Even the ship's departure had been laced with a high degree of luck. The night before, in of all things, two-man canoes, a British commando unit had completed paddling all the way up the Gironde River before attaching limpet mines to the hulls of many merchantmen tied up in the port. After the explosions died down, the port's naval authorities detailed a check of all unaffected ships to be searched. Such a search of *Arabian Nights* revealed an unexploded device on her hull. It was removed but when the launch was only about one hundred metres away from the freighter, it blew up, shredding its crew and the boat into tiny fragments.

Immediately, without waiting for any orders, Neumans cast off and sailed down the Gironde for the open sea and as darkness fell, powered his course as fast as possible to reach a safe distance from land, without the aid of an escort. Flying a Spanish flag he reached the seas just to the south of the Azores when the freighter came across two boatloads of gaunt survivors from a sunken British tanker, sunk by a U-boat some three weeks earlier. Neumans stopped *Arabian Nights* and picked up the seventeen sailors still alive. Gradually they recovered from their ordeal and in the middle of the South Atlantic, Neumans transferred them to a blockade-runner on the last stage of its attempt to reach Bordeaux.

Rounding the Cape of Good Hope, his faster freighter passed a Norwegian vessel of similar size. As soon as the stranger disappeared over the horizon, Neumans switched his Spanish flag for a Norwegian, borrowed that freighter's name of *Lofoten* and continued to try and get out into the Indian Ocean and its vastness but not before a British cruiser hove into sight six hours after his ship had overtaken the Norwegian vessel.

The cruiser circled *Arabian Nights* and seemingly satisfied with the replies that Neumans sent across by light signals, suddenly put on speed and vanished, fortunately for Neumans and his company, in the opposite direction to which the real *Lofoten* could have been sailing. As darkness closed, Neumans put on full speed and all through the night, at her full speed of seventeen knots, thrashed her way from that close call. Only when dawn came did Neumans relax the high-speed run and reduce back to a more normal cruising speed of eleven knots.

Arabian Nights reached Penang, the Japanese-controlled port in Western Malaya, where some U-boats were stationed. There Neumans off-loaded the various spare parts needed by those submarines and without waiting too long, set course for the Malacca Straits and then to Singapore. Here she was loaded with cargo for Kure which included East Indies fruits that were placed in her refrigerated holds. She joined up with a convoy of six Japanese merchantmen as well as three escorts, one being a damaged light cruiser. At first all went well until about three days sailing off Kure. Late one afternoon, three violent explosions crashed alongside the cruiser, another hammered one of the smaller escorts and two more torpedoes exploded, one each on two of the merchantmen. The convoy's course had taken it across the track of two waiting American submarines, which had each fired torpedoes at the ships in their sights. Neumans ordered 'full ahead' and as *Arabian Nights* thrashed her way from the danger area, two more of the merchantmen were struck. Neumans ruefully remarked to his fellows on the freighter's bridge 'Well, that's what it must have been like on that African convoy when *Dresden*'s shells were dropping around; except for shells substitute torpedoes. It's us who are now the hunted.' A few murmurs of grim assent were the only reply. Behind them, the fleeing escort dropped a few depth charges before hastening away leaving the struggling survivors from the sunken ships to become further flotsam of war. Pieces of human driftwood.

When *Berengia* arrived in August, Theider was able to give Reitz both good and bad news. The former was that he'd been able to deliver Colonel Tibbetts and his men into the safe hands of a Swiss Red Cross delegation who safely escorted the group to the Spanish border where they were exchanged for a group of badly wounded German personnel released from Allied captivity. Reitz had smiled at the news. He'd liked Tibbetts and his men who had certainly worked willingly enough on his ship rather than be handed over to the Japanese. Perhaps in all strictness he should have handed Tibbetts to them but the incident of the tanker *Marona* still rankled, together with what he'd learned from Tibbetts about some of the horrors that the Englishman had seen at first hand in Malaya and then in Sumatra. Reitz, as he gazed across at *Berengia*, also reflected on Theider's good fortune at getting his ship safely back to Japan from France. Unlike the freighter, *Berengia*'s voyage to Singapore had been relatively trouble-free but on the last lap, like *Arabian Nights*, trouble with a surfaced submarine caused the ship to expose her big guns.

The American vessel surfaced quite unexpectedly and then it opened fire with at least one big deck gun on the diminutive Japanese escort vessel shepherding *Berengia* and two other merchantmen. The little escort ship was hit at once and caught fire. The submarine, seeing that the escort was crippled, turned her gun on Thieder's vessel but received a rude surprise when two of *Berengia*'s big 15cm (5.9 inch) guns revealed themselves and fired back to such an effect that the American submarine put on speed and vanished into the protective cloak of the evening shadows. Watching her go, Theider ceased firing and turned *Berengia* back to the sinking escort. Lowering scrambling nets, forty-seven Japanese sailors were plucked to safety before Theider, not wishing to remain in the area too long, put on speed to race after the other two Japanese merchantmen which had both put on full speed to distance themselves from any more possible lurking enemy submarines.

Berengia's arrival brought a fresh crop of much sought-after correspondence from loved ones or otherwise at home. Even the Commander had received one but it gave Hiltzern a taste of really bad news. Written by his sister it told him of the death of both their parents when their house, in the suburbs of Dortmund, was hit by a rogue cluster of dumped bombs dropped by a damaged English bomber during a raid on the city's industrial quarter. Hiltzern had always fretted over his frail father who'd been badly gassed in the trenches near Verdun during 1916. With the loss of his mother, utterly selfless and devoted to her ailing husband, Reitz noticed the spark of life, that had always kept his big Commander going, seemed to go out. Inwardly, Reitz hoped by getting out to sea, that Hiltzern would become himself once again.

Even the tone of Elle's letters seemed to reflect the general mood of the people back home. A mood bracing itself for the worst news possible. Her general '*Joie-de-vivre*' of her previous letters didn't seem to be there any longer. Of course she was missing him. She desperately hoped that *Dresden* would make it back as soon as possible. So that she could see him again. Then she wrote of her own brother being one of the last evacuated wounded to be flown out of Stalingrad. He'd lost his left arm, blown off when a grenade had exploded close to him and three others in a fox-hole. He'd been the only survivor. Younger brother Max had left his college course to go straight into U-boat training. She hadn't heard from him for three months. She was pleased that George and his ship would soon be sailing and she closed her letters with lots of kisses.

'Ah hem! Sir! Time for you to come off watch.' Helmut Brautsch came up to his captain as he stared at the plunging bows, hands deep in his oilskin coat pockets.

'Ah, Helmut! I was just going over recent events. This and that! Tomorrow if this gale blows itself out, we'll think about launching one of our Arados. Be getting close to their suspected convoy routes. It'll be action at last. Get the crew back into trim. Must be off.' Then Reitz saluted his second officer and went to try and get some rest in his sea-cabin.

Helmut saluted in return before checking on the course. Due to the darkness there wasn't anything to be seen apart from the braking wave-tops. All four ships were blacked out as they pushed through the night. Like his captain, his mind wandered back to the time that he'd spent in Japan. For him it was personally a very happy time. For a week, he, with Andrea and Padré Jervaulx had gone to Nagasaki, the padré to go on a religious retreat whilst he and Andrea spent some time sightseeing around the city. One of the shops that they'd visited was a jeweller's where Andrea chose her engagement ring of a single diamond set in a blue sapphire. Jervaulx blessed the ring and mused how the war produced some very unusual situations of which this one was one of the most romantic. A German naval officer becoming engaged to an English nurse who was pretending to be Spanish, being blessed by a Kriegsmarine officer of French descendants whilst they were all in the Christian-dominated city of Nagasaki in Japan. For the time being Jervaulx was asked to keep the engagement a secret and on their return to *Dresden*, she removed the ring and put it back in its presentation box. Yes, Helmut thought, I am the luckiest and probably the happiest man on this ship.

The wind eased considerably during the next morning watch and Reitz took the opportunity to first refuel from *Olaf* and then to top up provisions from *Arabian Nights.* Then these two ships being unarmed were given instructions for a rendezvous in a month's time some five hundred miles west of Vancouver. Farewells were waved as *Dresden* and *Berengia* continued their north-easterly course whilst their two companions set sail south-eastwards.

The weather came progressively colder as *Dresden* closed in with the Alaskan coast. Ice began to form and Reitz ordered the precious radar aerials to be carefully dismantled. The very next day it was deemed calm enough to fly off an Arado and off it roared from its catapult with Rubens and Stolle inside the little machine.

Two hours later the little seaplane touched down in the lee of *Dresden.* Rubens reported that about fifty miles coming along the coast towards them was a small group of ships.

'Show me!' snapped Reitz with a chart in front of him. Rubens stuck a thumb in an approximate position. 'Good! We'll intercept them. Course 043. Interception time – one hour before dusk. Action Stations two hours beforehand.'

Berengia stood further out to sea whilst *Dresden* closed with the ships. Small ones. But still a target.

'Ships in sight' came the cry from keen-eyed Prebke.

Always the first to make a visual sighting.

Reitz took *Dresden* back out of sight. He wanted the enemy ships to be silhouetted against a lighter western sky whilst he came up from a darker eastern horizon. This was it! Back to doing what *Dresden* was best at. A quick attack. Stop. Rescue survivors.

And then, away.

There were just three relatively small coasters in the convoy under the escort of HMCS *Moonshine*, a corvette of eight-hundred tons. Her captain, Lieutenant Ronald Fewston retd., went off watch as dusk approached. He was an old man for active service in 1939 but at sixty had still volunteered his services. The Canadian Naval

Authorities looked at his record and saw that in October 1918, whilst first officer of a Canadian destroyer, he'd been in charge of the depth-charge crew that forced a German U-boat to the surface. But that had been twenty-one years earlier and Fewston was even then in the reserve section of the navy. So he'd been signed off at the cessation of those hostilities but then, there he was, wanting to return. They gave him *Moonshine* to command and for nearly four years he trundled forwards from Vancouver to Anchorage and back. Always with three or four coasters. An absolute doddle of a placement for an old warhorse, now at sixty-four years old. Every journey saw new recruits for the whole ship apart from some of the petty officers and engineers who may be required to do three trips with the trainees. After their sea experience the trainees were then transferred to the much more demanding war area of the North Atlantic. Even the entry of Japan hadn't shaken Fewston too much. For three runs they'd even had a US destroyer with them but the Japanese, even after having occupied the Aleutians, showed no interest in the convoy runs. The destroyer escort, an old four-stacker, then disappeared and Fewston was again left in sole charge. In two more days he'd be in Anchorage Bay again. Every night he always turned in. Without fail. Whenever the sun was due to set. As it was doing so at that moment.

As Fewston left the bridge to retreat to his tiny cabin, a very young nervous trainee midshipman replaced him, being assigned to stand the first four hours of the night watch. Until another trainee midshipman took over. Every night it was the same. Nothing but the empty rolling darkness of the Pacific heaving their little warship up, down, side to side and every variation of these movement directions that those restless waves could conjure. Occasionally as they neared Anchorage they'd sight a solidly built blunt-bowed fishing trawler. Even rarer still an occasional merchantman running on her own. Probably because the skipper felt it was just as quick and convenient, if not more so, to sail solo, rather than in a small convoy. The war had made no difference to the mercantile traffic along the lengthy coastal run. No Jerry or Jap submarines and nary a whisper from any Jap marauding surface sea-raider.

Nothing to excite the nineteen-year old junior midshipman. He didn't really register the approach of *Dresden* from the ship's stern port quarter because he wasn't looking there. But his more experienced petty officer on the corvette's exposed bridge did sweep the seas in that quarter.

'Ship coming up astern' the petty officer grunted.

'What sort, PO?' asked the still nervous nineteen year old.

'Can't make her out but we'll keep an eye on her' came the reply.

As *Dresden* emerged over the dark south-east horizon, both men now watched her rapid approach.

'Nothing to worry about. She's not a Jap. Doesn't look like one of their ships. Could be a new Yank cruiser doing the same as us. On her first cruise to shake her recruits into place' came the PO's next comment.

'Should I tell the skipper?'

'Ah, best send someone.'

Fewston didn't take all that keenly at being disturbed. For the very first time since taking command of the corvette his night routine had been altered.

'What is it then?' he grumbled on reaching the bridge.

'Over there, sir' said the nineteen-year old, quivering at the thought that he'd made a dreadful mistake.

'Well PO?' snapped Fewston ignoring his nervous junior officer. 'What do –' but he was unable to complete his sentence as the dark ship suddenly blossomed red and yellow. All along her length. Noisy too! Bang, bang, boom!

'Hard-a-starboard' yelled Fewston. Too late. With sickening crunches and heavy blows his little corvette shook and began to disintegrate.

'Abandon ship!'

Those crew still surviving as were all but three of their mates, needed no heeding. Hurriedly, rubber rafts were thrown overboard with the crew-members following in haste, jumping to get away from the sinking corvette.

The dark ship ceased firing. 'Thank goodness' thought Fewston, as with his still scared midshipman and the PO, they were the last three of *Moonshine*'s crew to leap overboard as the corvette keeled over on to her port side. Vaguely Fewston registered the fact that all three coasters were also stopped, two showing signs of having been set on fire.

A big searchlight swept the area. Reitz rarely used it but he needed to find the abandoning crew quickly.

'Crikey!' yelled a man 'The Japs are looking for us. Duck down if you can.' There wasn't much cover on his Carley float.

A metallic voice speaking in accented English echoed out from a loud-hailer.

'Allied sailors. Please show yourselves. All of you. We are here to rescue you. We are from a German warship. Fast motor-launches are on their way to rescue you!'

'Blimey! bleedin' Jerries!'

'Can't be. Not up here.'

'Nah, tellin' fibs that's wot!'

'I don't believe them.'

Before the survivors could re-assemble their thoughts, a large powerful launch with a smaller light shining from its bows, drew close to them.

'Come on. We're here to rescue you.'

'Please hurry. You'll freeze in that water.'

'Here, put your hands up so that we can pull you in.'

Fewston's young midshipman was the first to be hauled into Brautsch's launch. He was whimpering with fright. Saying over and over again 'Not bleedin' Japs! Not bleedin' Japs!' until, to his utter shock and amazement his mind registered an English-speaking woman's voice telling him gently but firmly to keep quiet and to calm down.

The rest of the convoy's survivors paddled or swam across to the rescue launches. All except one boatload of survivors, which as quietly as it could in the shadow of the one merchantman still afloat, rowed until out of range of the searchlights and then switched on their boat's motors and at a low speed escaped into the evening darkness.

For two hours *Dresden*'s boats, and *Berengia*'s for she'd come up to assist, picked up the scattered survivors before Reitz decided that enough was enough. He seemed unaware that a boatload of survivors had managed to escape. He did know, that due to his surprise assault, that only a brief call for help had gone out from one of the coasters before a hail of shells swept the wireless into oblivion. Even so there was just a slight risk of some station picking up the desperate call for help. Most of the survivors, one hundred and twenty-three of them, were transferred to *Berengia* but three wounded ones, as well as the shell-shocked midshipman, were placed into *Dresden*'s Sick Berth.

'Not much of a catch' murmured Reitz to Hiltzern 'but at least we're back in business again.'

'Good practice. We must strike the Allies where least expected' came Hiltzern's guarded response.

'Yes, we must. We'll go towards our rendezvous and pick up what else we can.'

Darkened against the horizon, the boatload of survivors opened up the throttles of their boat as they saw the black bulks of the two enemy ships sail away. Having not heard the conversation of Brautsch and his men, the men in the motorboat still assumed that their attacker was a rogue Japanese cruiser although nearly all of them were surprised that their fellows were rescued, rather than be left or used as machine-gun target practice. Keeping to a speed of three knots and sailing close to the shore, they reckoned that the two hundred mile voyage to Anchorage Bay could well take them about two and a half days to complete.

The small naval presence in that settlement did receive, via a coastguard listening station, the smattering of a help message 'Am being shelled by unident –' and nothing else.

'How close?' asked the lieutenant in charge of the station.

'Difficult to say' came the answer.

'Any news from *Moonshine*'s convoy?'

'No. Be due here in the next twenty-four hours though.'

'Any aircraft for a quick search?'

'Nope. Only one we've got is still in bits, undergoing an overhaul.'

So Anchorage Bay waited. Twenty-four hours. Only a couple of fishing trawlers came in. They hadn't seen anything, let alone *Moonshine*'s convoy.

'We'd better inform Vancouver who can then relay our concern to Seattle.'

As a matter of routine, Seattle informed Hawaii. Which in turn reached Admiral Sir Bernard Collins who had been transferred from Simonstown to Hawaii in order to represent British and Empire interests at the big US naval base where the ever-growing number of warships and their huge number of support ships dwarfed the still very small Union Jack flagged presence.

Receiving the message about a missing Canadian corvette was Collins's new aide – Flag-Lieutenant Julian Scott. At first Scott paid little heed to the message 'HMCS *Moonshine* and convoy overdue at Anchorage Bay.' Again, as a matter of routine he passed it on to Collins who at first had resented his posting to Hawaii – 'Be a rest cure for you. Building up our forces will take time but we need an assertive presence if we're to make any impression on the Americans' had come the memo from Admiralty HQ in London.

Puffing on a pipe he only lightly raised his eyebrows when Scott showed him the message. 'We'll need more details. Contact Anchorage if there are any further developments.'

Twenty-four hours later Scott came in with more details. He gave Collins the news about two dozen survivors from one of the sunken merchantmen having been picked up by a trawler and taken into Anchorage. Their reports quoted a large Japanese cruiser but when asked to describe it hadn't produced anything fitting the known Japanese heavy cruiser designs. At least four of the witness reports stated that the ship possessed two big turrets forward, a single funnel and a single aft turret.

Collins looked up, alarm bells ringing in his brain. 'That's not a Jap, that sounds like *Dresden*!'

Scott raised his eyebrows 'The Jerry raider that rattled a convoy off the Horn about two years ago?'

'Aye, that's the one. Been after her since just before the *Bismarck* episode.' Then after a pause he asked 'Have the Yanks got any planes up there?'

'No sir, only an unarmed spotter plane.'

'Has it been searching?'

'No sir, The Yanks aren't all that bothered. Say if it's a Jap it'll have gone back to base.'

'But we think different. Come on, let's look at the chart.' Scott pointed to where the convoy attack had taken place.

'Mmm. If it is *Dresden* then I think we'd still better contact the Americans. Look, she's struck there. My guess is that she'll mooch around for a week or so and then probably not finding much more she'll come south, cross the shipping lanes to Hawaii and come November, she'll be off Cape Horn and slipping back into the Atlantic to take advantage of the North Atlantic winter storms to hide her return to German-held waters. That's what Reitz will do and that's what I'll tell the Americans.'

Scott still wasn't impressed. 'It's only supposition, sir. We have no definite facts.'

'Ah, Scott, but there is something. It says that the enemy warship stopped to pick up survivors. Even used the searchlights. Now, would the Japanese do that?'

'Only for their own sinister practises although I think that even their sailors don't stoop as low as some of their land colleagues, or do they?'

'Well, we can't go into that right now' commented Collins scratching his chin whilst still studying the chart intently. He felt sure that the attack as well as the aftermath bore all the trademarks of Reitz and his elusive battlecruiser. 'Look, we'll go back on all we know about *Dresden* and if the evidence points strongly that the convoy's attacker was the German, then we'll try to convince the Americans to divert some of their resources to try and catch our elusive Mister Reitz. Come on, let's get on with it, Flags!'

Collins knew that he could offer little help even if the Americans felt the need to mount a hunt for *Dresden.*

The slow old battleships in Colombo were useless. Too far away. Too vulnerable to air attack even if they were transferred and in the course of that move came too close to Japanese air operations which they'd have to in order to reach Hawaii in time. Nothing there. The few modern cruisers and destroyers were still heavily involved in escort duty between Australasia and the rest of the Allied trade routes. The Australians hadn't been able to replace the loss of three of their cruisers and as Collins full well knew, *Dresden*'s distant adversary, the *Wellington* was now in Seattle undergoing a thorough overhaul. Especially to her worn-out engines. Any aircraft-carriers were either still with the Home Fleet or on convoy duty. None from the Royal Navy were as yet available for release on Pacific duties.

Collins felt, even before talking to the Americans, that they wouldn't be persuaded to look for *Dresden.* Either she'd slipped away from Japan via the Malacca Straits and into the Indian Ocean or she was still in a Japanese base. But not off the Alaskan coast.

Scott produced the file on *Dresden* of her known career and also with good guess-work. The raid off Guadalcanal. The furious and torpedo gun battle that had crippled *Hiei* and at least another Japanese heavy cruiser. The coast-watcher's report seeing at least one large crippled warship of 'not known' super-structure after the attacks on *Hiei*. It was the *Hiei* that had been sunk as seen by American aircraft before that coast-watcher's report. So was the big warship, the one hit by that American destroyer *Hurst*? Or had *Hurst* torpedoed *Hiei*? It was a pity that none of her bridge officers had survived her sinking. What if *Hurst* had hit the German battle-cruiser? When was it? Eight months ago. Time for Reitz's ship to have been repaired.

Collins pondered. Scott's report was still full of too many suppositions. Even so, he decided to see his American co-ordinators. To guard the Hawaii-Seattle route. Just in case.

How accurate Scott's report was a privilege that neither Collins nor Scott himself were not to know! Not then! They had accurately guessed that the Alaskan raider was the *Dresden* and to a large extent, her movements. But they had no proof. Slowly Reitz cruised *Dresden* and *Berengia* along the Alaskan coast. In the week after the tussle with the convoy, three large fishing trawlers were all stopped, their bemused crews taken prisoner after as much of their fresh catches were transferred to the German ships and then with the prisoners watching, the trawlers were scuttled and sunk. As Reitz remarked to one of the skippers 'Your boat could, if so required, be converted to an escort vessel. The British and the Japanese have done so in some cases, and so has our Navy. No reason why the Canadian or American navies haven't or won't be needing parts of their fishing fleets as naval auxiliaries. However, you will be transferred to one of my auxiliaries which will, if by good fortune, meet up with a neutral ship and a trans-shipment will be arranged if at all possible to enable you, somehow,to return to your homeland. You will not, under any circumstances be transferred for a journey to a Japanese prisoner-of-war camp. It is but the fortunes of war. On this ship we abide by the Geneva Conventions as far as we can.' The German captain then noticed the original sullen looks of his bewildered captives turn to near smiles of relief and they mumbled their thanks.

But it was small pickings for the battlecruiser, the only real benefit being the working-up together of the crew once again into an efficient naval unit. Reitz eventually ordered *Dresden* away from the bleak coast to the pre-arranged rendezvous with *Olaf* and *Arabian Nights* some five hundred miles off Vancouver. A day before the rendezvous *Berengia* some fifteen miles south-east of the battlecruiser sighted a merchantman and closed with *Dresden* to light signal the discovery. Reitz pushed up his warship's speed to investigate. Sure enough a medium-sized freighter flying the Canadian flag came into view. Pretending to be an American cruiser *Dresden* came up close, and when only about five hundred yards off the freighter's port-side, Reitz revealed his true colours and ordered 'Stop ship. Do not use wireless,' as he had done so when confronting single ships beforehand – back in the heady days of the long cruise from Germany to Japan.

The merchantman, *Caribou Saga*, was sailing from Vancouver to Hawaii and then to Brisbane. Amongst the cargo she carried were thirty lorries and other smaller transport vehicles for units of the Canadian army on duty in the Pacific theatre of war. Her captain, Harvey Sanger had watched *Dresden*'s approach but couldn't credit it when the American flag was exchanged for Reitz's own flag at the mainmast and a swastika at her stern counter.

'Bleedin' 'ell, the bugger's a Jerry. Can't be, can it? They ain't got any in this area.'

'Well, it ain't a Jap' growled the ship's bosun standing next to him. 'Before mi' injury, we was shot up by one off Guadalcanal beach, Some berk of an Admiral 'ad us still there unloading wi' all our deck lights on and then this bleedin' cruiser came and whopped us all.'

'Was it this one then?' asked Sanger 'or them in that boat that's comin' our way?'

'Well, don't know skip. It were dark. Could 'ave been because this bugger must be, well is it? *Dresden*? You know, skip, the Jerry raider that shot the Brits. convoy ter bits off East Africa?'

'You're well versed on these matters' growled Sanger.

'I reads mi' papers, skip. Want me to go down and greet 'em?'

'Aye, you might as well.' Sanger sounded a bit unsure. He felt that if it were a Jerry ship, then maybe they'd be alright but what if it transferred them to a Jap camp? Things were rumoured to be rather nasty in those places.

Brautsch saluted the bosun and introduced himself. Soon the merchantman was under their control. When Reitz received the signal lamp report he signalled back 'Send all the prisoners over to *Berengia* except the captain. Brautsch and his men stay on board until our rendezvous. Caribou Saga to follow us to rendezvous with boarding crew. Sending Luth and engineers. Work out how to ditch cargo and convert to prison ship.'

As soon as Luth and his team started up the captured freighter's engines, *Dresden* led them all steadily southwards towards the rendezvous the next day. At dawn, Rubens took his Arado up to search for *Olaf* and *Arabian Nights*. Both ships were just about where they should have been and soon Rubens reported to Reitz of the waiting support ships. It was a joyful meeting when the five ships met.

Hurriedly Reitz ordered *Olaf* and *Arabian Nights* alongside so that provisioning for the long haul ahead could begin. The freighter, apart from the needs for her own crew, was virtually emptied of her supplies. The Caribou Saga was refuelled from *Olaf* and by the middle of the day cast off and was just about to begin her long journey to France when radar reported a small speck rapidly approaching from the west.

'Aircraft, sir' reported a messenger.

The speck came into view. 'It's American, sir.'

'What signal shall we give it?'

Reitz smiled. 'Oh, let's see what it has to say first! No firing!'

The American Corsair fighter, on exercise from an escort carrier hurrying to join up with the big American Task Force No. 38 flew lower to inspect the close gathering of ships below it displaying large American flags.

'What ships?' flashed a signal 'Have you a voice radio?'

'Mmmm, nosey parkers aren't they?' quipped Reitz. 'Morse back – "Radio on blink, special battle group re-supplying"'

The Corsair waggled its wings and flew off into the distance. Just under half-an-hour later, a further aeroplane appeared. A long-range Hudson reconnaissance.

'Probably been diverted to check out on us – maybe the carrier plane was running out of fuel' murmured Reitz to no-one in particular. *Dresden*'s anti-aircraft guns swivelled on their mounts tracking the circling Hudson. After three circuits, Reitz murmured to his seamen signaller on the port-wing. 'Send them this message' and handed him it, written in English – 'Please fly the other way round. You are making us dizzy.'

Obligingly the Hudson turned and reversed. It was in radio contact with Seattle. Eventually the reply from the naval authorities came back – 'Yes, there is a special battle group in your area headed by new battlecruiser *Lincoln* – two big turrets forward, one aft.' The message omitted to say that the new American battlecruiser's turrets were triple-gunned; or that she had three destroyers and a light cruiser in support. The Hudson's message had stated 'one large battle-wagon and four support ships'.

Seattle wrongly interpreted this and thus sent the message back that failed to identify the ships in sight as any other than American. Like the Corsair, the Hudson waggled its wings and flew off. Unbeknown to the Germans, a camera on the Hudson held by its operator took photographs of their group of ships.

As soon as the aircraft disappeared off *Dresden*'s radar screen, Reitz gave orders for the Caribou Saga and *Arabian Nights* to start their long haul to Europe – the former via the Cape of Good Hope, the latter via the Horn. Both ships changed their American flags – Caribou Saga to a Dutch one and the *Arabian Nights* to the Peruvian emblem. Slowly they disappeared while *Dresden* pushed off in a southerly direction flanked by *Olaf* and *Berengia.* By nightfall, *Dresden* and her ships had the sea to themselves but not for long. Soon after midnight whilst Reitz rested after the aircraft alarms of the previous day, radar picked up a group of ships. The buzzer went in Reitz's cabin. Wearily he answered the telephone.

'Bridge here sir' came Brautsch's voice. 'Possible enemy convoy to the south of us. About fifteen miles distant.'

Reitz acknowledged and shaking off his tiredness, he shrugged on his uniform jacket and shorts and hurried to the bridge.

Something of the original adrenalin and excitement began to flow into Reitz's thoughts. This once more was what he'd expected the role of *Dresden* to be. Attacking a convoy having carefully worked out his approach but this time he had to make the enemy think that his ship was an innocent American.

Reitz, on hearing reports from Japanese commanders, knew that the Americans had a very efficient radar system so the odds were that his three ships were already blips on the principal escort vessel whatever it was. Reitz scratched his chin. He decided on a new tactic. He needed to know the disposition of the ships much more accurately.

'Signal Rimmer on *Olaf* to close with the convoy, overtake it, and then veer off. In the meantime we'll work up ahead of them and meet *Olaf*. Here, these are the co-ordinates.'

Olaf's captain, Karl Rimmer, frowned when he learned of what he was required to do. 'Fly big Yankee flags and pretend that our name is the Olivia D' he muttered to his deputy on the tanker's bridge. 'Hmmm! We'd better close up.'

Gradually the convoy hove in sight as Rimmer edged his big tanker to within three miles of the convoy, slowly overtaking it. A small escort edged out from the ships flashing a signal but seemed satisfied with the tanker's reply and message – '*En route* to Hawaii with urgent fuel supplies.'

Rimmer turned *Olaf* away as soon as he'd identified that the main escort was a light cruiser. With three or four small escorts as well as five well-sized merchantmen, the convoy was estimated to be making an approximate collective speed of twelve knots in the general direction of Hawaii itself.

Olaf pushed ahead and gradually disappeared over the horizon from Lieutenant Shelford and the corvette under his command. The sole British warship with all the other ships flying the Stars and Stripes. A little warship by the designation of HMS *Cantor*. A veteran of the North Atlantic. Like her young commander.

Shelford was a midshipman at the start of the war. Based in Scapa Flow. On a lumbering old non-modernised battleship. *Royal Oak*. At anchor when the rest of her squadron put out to sea with only an equally old seaplane tender with an equally unlikely romantic name of *Pegasus* as company at the far end of the anchorage.

A peaceful dark night. Not midshipman Shelford's idea of war-like activity as he stared over the near deserted upper bridge. Fretting that he was missing out on the real war.

Until the explosions. One after another. That tore the guts out of the old warhorse. To send her turning turtle. A tomb for eight hundred matelots. Shelford was lucky. As the bridge toppled towards those dark black waters with flickers of red from the burning ship dappled across them, he was able to jump almost straight into their icy wateriness and swim, thinking oddly of how all his swimming efficiency badges of younger days were now really meaning something.

Swimming for his life as the stricken battleship groaned and writhed in her death plunge.

Until he splashed alongside a little trawler called *Daisy II* where willing gnarled hands of the fisherman crew dragged him spluttering and shivering from the water.

Eventually, after a short spell in a naval hospital they deemed him fit again for active service. On an old destroyer based at Harwich. Escorting coastal convoys.

At first nothing much happened. From Harwich to London, then round to Dover and on to Southampton. Back they went. To Harwich, Great Yarmouth and even as far north as the river Humber.

Then the balloon went up in April and there came the retreat of the British forces, in Norway and the Low Countries. Shelford's destroyer was diverted to Dunkirk. Huge clouds of oily black smoke from ruptured fuel tanks. And what looked like thin black snakes crawling down the open sand-dune beaches to the deceptively gently lapping blue sea. It was only when their ship edged as close as the captain could to those lines that they realised that they comprised of stoic patient columns of khaki-clad soldiers waiting their turn for rescue.

A three-funnelled French destroyer with a large bridge clock just four hundred yards on their port side was hit when set upon by five dive-bombing Stukas. Desperately, her captain beached his ship as she began to capsize. British soldiers, French soldiers and blue-jacketed French sailors jumped into the relatively shallow water and some swam or paddled their way as fast as they could stumble through the water towards Shelford's destroyer. Memories of *Royal Oak* flashed through the senior midshipman's mind as he leaned over the rail urging both the stricken destroyer's men as well as small boatloads of men from the beach columns to get on board as quickly as they could. Soon nearly fifteen hundred men were hauled on board and with a warning series of whoops from her funnel sirens, the little warship gathered way just as more Stukas appeared. The destroyer's guns opened fire, scaring off the marauding dive-bombers so that they sought easier prey amongst the shallow waters or on the dunes. As Shelford looked back not once did he see the long patient lines break rank. All just waiting for rescue – or death.

His destroyer went back. Twice more. Again further bombing raids. Again near misses but not to a venerable paddle-steamer.

She simply vanished under a hail of bombs. There weren't many survivors that time.

Promoted soon after Dunkirk, Shelford, as a Lieutenant, was given command of a fast, well-armed motor-launch. He was sent to St. Nazaire to cover the last of the withdrawals from a France being rapidly overcome by the invading German armies and once again saw a horrifying sight. The once proud liner, but hurriedly pressed into service as a troopship, the Lancastria, loaded with over three thousand troops had just begun to get away, after interminable delays when German bombers once again appeared, taking as their main target the near stationery troopship. Shelford in his small launch just eight hundred yards acting as a protector against possible German E-boat attacks, could only with his crew, watch helplessly as the liner turned over, trapping nearly all of her crew and troopers. A few climbed over the upturned hulk avoiding the slow-turning propellers and dove into the oil-strewn surface of the ever-so calm waters. Shelford urged his launch in as fast as he dare with his machine-gunners spitting fiery defiance at the last of the bombers managing to set one of them on fire as it streaked for its home base. Just fifteen men were hauled on board Shelford's launch, all covered in oil, with more survivors rescued by other small craft converging on the tragic scene but Shelford knew, as he supervised the efforts of his crew that the scene was but a daylight mirror of the horror he'd been through on *Royal Oak.*

Two of the rescued men on his launch died before Shelford could transfer them to a destroyer with better medical facilities. Bitterly he turned his tiny command back to her base at Devonport but once there, he learned that he was to take command of one of the first of the new escort vessels being rushed into service to try and plug the loss of the destroyer escorts that were often the main warship support, if any, on the hard-pressed Atlantic convoys. The new nine hundred and seventeen ton corvette HMS *Cantor.*

A mere cockleshell to be tossed around in the huge Atlantic rollers. Time after time.

He boarded her at Liverpool in late July 1940. As a junior escort ship to an old V destroyer and an almost as equally old sloop. Three inadequate escorts for nearly forty merchantmen.

The first crossing had been reasonable. Only four of their charges were lost. About ten percent. Apparently this was 'acceptable' by their Lordships who were despairing of finding enough escorts to support the convoys on what their Prime Minister already stated was the whole key to the operation of the war. The Atlantic battleground.

So Shelford and his tough little ship crossed and re-crossed those seemingly endless wastes of grey, green, white-topped rollers that stretched from one horizon to another. For day after day. Except when they were illuminated by a vicious series of orange, yellow and red flashes coupled with gouts of black, brown and grey smoking aftermaths as U-boat fired torpedoes crashed into their unsuspecting victims.

Time after time Shelford wheeled his corvette into the pursuit of those hidden grey wolves, dropping depth charges more in hope than in success.

Then the excitement wore off and it was back to those endless horizons, endless hours, endless plunging, endless rolling.

Two weeks leave and back again.

On and on and on. The same pattern. Through 1941 and into 1942. As that year ended the battle with the U-boats didn't seem to have an end in sight. The enemy may have lost the surface battle; it may be faltering in the deserts of North Africa or amidst the snows of the Russian plains but early in 1943 it seemed to redouble its assault on the admittedly better protected Atlantic convoys.

And then it happened.

Seven hundred miles west of the Fastnet Rock. *Cantor* picked up again a strong Asdic contact of a submerged submarine but this time before the enemy had begun its attack. Shelford followed the line and his crew dropped a varying depth-setted attack of charges. A rolling quick-successive blast of ten charges. As he ordered *Cantor* into the counter-turn and attack, the sea abeam of them began to bubble and ooze oil. Then the U-boat surfaced just three hundred yards away.

Shelford could see a white-capped officer urging the dazed submariners to their deck guns but before the U-boat could defend itself, *Cantor*'s own guns lashed out in a fury. This was the enemy that they'd waited so long to see and now the long black-grey-rust streaked metal shark was there. To be hammered into a useless heap of worthless metal. Who cared if it was manned by human beings? Feelings just didn't matter as the first four-inch shell from *Cantor* exploded on to the conning tower sending 'white cap' into red-blooded fragments that splattered across the foaming seas. Nor when the corvette's newly acquired eight-barrelled Bofors pom-poms knocked over the U-boat's gun crew as if scoring a full house of skittles. All down. No-one getting up again. The gap closed and the U-boat soon began to look like an obscene pepper-pot full of irregularly spaced holes when quite suddenly it reared up, the bows briefly lifting clear of the swell and then it vanished, leaving a swirl of assorted debris including one white cap.

Shelford and his crew didn't cheer. Instead, having given vent to their sudden rage, they just fell completely silent. Numb. Exhausted. Suddenly so desperately tired. Perhaps it was the shock of the violent encounter. Or the complete extinguishing of their enemy. A nameless group of men that they'd feared but never personally known. Nor did they want to know them. They were the enemy.

Later, *Cantor* arrived at her berth in Liverpool. No welcoming brass bands or bunting to mark her success. Just a brass naval hat who came aboard as soon as the gang-plank was lowered and the mooring ropes tightened. Said the brass-hat to Shelford 'New job for you lads. Off you go on leave for three weeks and then come back. Sail with a Venezuelan-bound convoy. Then, go through the Panama Canal. Go to Seattle and then, in due time, sail for Hawaii. The Americans need a bit of our submarine-hunting expertise and your boat will join a few more to add to their escort ships, especially in hunting out the Japs on their little island retreats. Go on. Be a doddle after the North Atlantic.' Then brass hat left, having thrown a hint of promotion to Lieutenant-Commander at Shelford when *Cantor* reached Hawaii.

The Americans repeated that word 'doddle' when they told Shelford that his corvette would be attached as one of five escorts to five merchantmen bound with ammunition and oil for bombarding battleships on softening-up exercises against resisting Japanese on one of the numerous coral-fringed islands that they were stubbornly refusing to surrender. One escort to one merchantman. They'd been lucky to have a ratio as low as one to ten in the North Atlantic.

No wonder that Shelford and his re-invigorated crew, on leaving Seattle, following the light-cruiser Barstow and three destroyers out to the waiting merchantman, could barely believe their apparent change of fortune. A week amongst the bright lights of the big American naval base and city almost left them in a dazed stupor after the darkened shattered streets of bombed-blasted Liverpool and other home cities of the crew. The only solace was that they were fighting a common enemy. Together. An enemy that now in the autumn of 1943 was on the defensive. Almost everywhere. Certainly on the Central Pacific sea-route to Hawaii. 'Nary a sniff of the yellow-men since we give 'em a bloody nose at Pearl Harbor' swaggered one navy captain. 'Odd' thought Shelford, 'as they lost most of their then serviceable battleships and aircraft based at the island, you'd have supposed that it was the Japanese giving the bloody nose then, not receiving it.'

'Nothing to worry about' drawled Barstow's captain. 'You can tell your watchmen to even sleep on duty. Just steer the ship in the direction of Hawaii and wake up when you hit the harbour wall' he guffawed.

'Very amusing, I think not' thought Shelford. 'Perhaps he thinks the Japs have surrendered. Maybe I should tell him to guard against the unexpected.' But he kept his own counsel and his corvette duly settled into her position on the northern flank of the diamond pattern of the smaller escorts. Inside it was another diamond comprised of merchantmen. Then the Barstow. In the centre. Just ambling along. At the convoy speed of ten point three knots. No exercises. No emergency drill. No anti-submarine drill. Nothing. Just ambling along. As if in peace time. Secure in the knowledge that the enemy never ever interfered one tiny weeny teeny itsy bit on the Seattle-Hawaii run. Allowing the Americans to build up their offensive strength. To hit the Japanese. Hard!

No-one considered mentioning the *Dresden*. Even Shelford wasn't briefed about the battlecruiser. Because no-one at Seattle knew for certain where she was.

Nor did Collins. Despite his astute guesswork. But Collins did start to worry when the overdue reports of an innocent fast freighter began to filter into his offices in Hawaii. Caribou Saga.

Collins looked at his chart. Alaskan ships. Small trawlers. Now this freighter. Same ship attacking them? Could be.

Then another seemingly routine message about an American aircraft which reported sighting an American cruiser group. The pilot even passed on the message about flying the other way round because the Navy boys were getting dizzy. With two exclamation marks. An addendum to the report from the Americans said that a special battle group on secret passage was in that area. The new US battlecruiser *Lincoln* with support ships.

Flag Lieutenant Scott duly passed this on to Collins. The Admiral suddenly said 'Oh shit!'

'Beg your pardon sir, but it is genuine. The Americans told us that *Lincoln* was approaching the area near the convoy route some three days ago.'

'Buffoons that they are!' snarled Collins.

'I don't follow you sir!' exclaimed Scott, bewildered at his superior's strange attitude. 'It's only a routine report.'

'No it isn't' snapped the Admiral. 'Look, look at the words of that dozy Yankee pilot – look – fly the other way round you're making us dizzy.' '

'So?' queried Scott in a slightly bemused voice.

'North Atlantic. When the big four-engine German FW-Condors used to fly round our convoys. It was often said that the merchantmen or the escorts used to exchange a similar signal to ask the Condors to fly the other way. Now a new Yank battlecruiser wouldn't have known about that signal, would it?'

'Why not sir?' responded Scott still a bit mystified as to what Collins was trying to develop.

'No, because by the end of forty-one we'd just about managed to combat the Condors by air patrols of our own. The point is, if it wasn't a Yank cruiser, which ship was it? Not Japanese. Not a British one. Or a Dutch cruiser. No!' Collins thumped one fist into another. 'It was Reitz and the bloody *Dresden.* Trying to be clever. Probably heard about the stories from a Luftwaffe aircrew whilst having one schnapps too many in the mess. Whatever way he heard it, his brain said "Let's haf ze American pilot vink ve are ze clever ones" and off the bloody cheeky Jerries go with their signal. Only –' and here Collins tapped his nose '– I know better. I was, Lieutenant Scott, once very much involved in the Atlantic convoy war and I also picked up the story. So I'm putting two and two together and the answer I come up with is *Dresden.* We know she's been in Japan. Now Reitz and his merry lads are out there. Pretending to be Yanks and coming their way is this convoy!' Collins jabbed his finger on the pointer.

'Er, yes' flustered Scott 'I have the details here!' He flicked open the pad.

'USS *Barstow.* She's a light cruiser. Then there are four more escorts and five merchantmen. Small fry, if that.' He muttered.

Then Scott suddenly blurted 'Good gracious! What clots we are! There's a Royal Navy corvette amongst the escort. HMS *Cantor.*'

'Aye. Yes, we knew that she was in Seattle but not with this convoy. Who is her captain?'

'Well sir, a Lieutenant Shelford, DSO and bar.'

'Twice, eh.'

'Shall I look up the details?' Scott asked.

'Mmm.'

Scott soon had them. Collins pursed his lips when he read of the U-boat 'kill' that the corvette had made. 'Mmmm. Tough man. Strange isn't it? How tough and hard the young men of this world are becoming. This chap here is a veteran of the escorts but what is he? Twenty-five, if that?'

'Should we contact him?' ventured Scott 'You know in our own naval code?'

'What about – "Suspect German battlecruiser in area. Can you scare it off?"'

Only Collins wasn't really joking. 'No' he thought, 'I'd better do it properly. Via the US naval authorities, then direct to the Barstow. See what response we get.'

The American naval attaché to the British presence was somewhat cool in his response when Collins broached the possibility that the *Dresden* was in the area.

'No, no way. She's nowhere in the area. Our aircraft reported *Lincoln* and her ships. Not some Nazi Kraut ship. They're all hiding shit-scared in your European waters. Yeah, we know that the Jerry battle-crap's been in Jap waters but heh, buddy, she's probably slipped back to Jerry land by now. Can't imagine why she should want to linger in our waters, can you?'

Putting it that way temporarily threw Collins off guard, but he quickly recovered.

'Now look here' he blustered at the American naval captain, 'we know for certain that the *Dresden* hasn't returned to Jerry-land as you put it. None of our air or sea patrols has picked her up and there's been no report of her presence in German waters from any of our agents. So it is our strong belief that she's still here in the Pacific. Look, this is our evidence.' Scott began to unroll a chart but the American held up his hand 'Now hold your horses Admiral! The cruiser group sighted by our aircraft was exactly where we expected *Lincoln* to be and as she's under strict orders not to use her wireless, we can't contact her. You know, hush-hush mission. Jap ears might be listening. So put your charts away, sonny boy.' Scott looked extremely peeved.

'Look, Admiral what's-your-name. I'll pass your views on to my bosses and maybe we'll get back to you.' With that, the naval captain ushered Collins and Scott to the door.

Collins, never at ease with what seemed to him the somewhat casual attitude or discipline ideas of the Americans, just about exploded outside the building.

'Bloody Yanks! Can't they see the danger that they're in! First Hallett ignored all my warnings and look what happened to that troopship convoy! Before you were with me, Scott, but I can see it all happening again. Reitz has a knack of producing his best when we least expect it.' Collins whose face suffused red with rage then snapped 'Right, get our wireless boys to signal *Cantor* in our code and see if she responds.'

'Message sir?' asked a thoroughly perturbed Lieutenant Scott.

'Use your bloody imagination! Something like "*Dresden* suspected in the area. Keep on your guard. Inform Barstow".'

With the report from *Olaf* together with the careful navigational work by Serle, Reitz soon had all the knowledge he needed to plan an evening attack. Half an hour before sunset *Dresden* would approach the convoy from its western flank. With the setting sun behind him. An attack using torpedoes. Not guns. Make the convoy think that a rogue Japanese submarine was making the attack. It was the best he could think of without revealing to the Americans just exactly what was really attacking them. There'd been no follow-up to the American aircraft sighting his ship. It seemed fairly obvious that the enemy just wouldn't credit the Japanese daring to make a surface attack with a raiding cruiser. 'Actions stations' sounded over *Dresden* as soon as the convoy showed up on the radar screen. Heavy boots clattered all over the ship as the men rushed to their stations. Keeping *Dresden* to just fifteen knots, Reitz carefully approached the convoy.

At the same time Shelford received a wireless message, in code. Hurriedly excusing himself from *Cantor*'s tiny open bridge, he went into the box cabin that served as his private quarters and scrabbled around some untidily stacked files before pulling out the code book. Somewhat hastily he translated the seemingly meaningless jargon as 'Expect enemy surface attack, probably jammy fairly soon.'

'Jammy.' He puzzled over that word. Then it was signed 'Brit. Naval-op. HQ Hawaii.' There was a knock on the door. Sub-Lieutenant Richard O'Brien. Half Irish. Half Scotts. Half wild. Never approved of the top brass. When he heard from his skipper of the message, he quickly translated 'jammy' to 'Jappy' and not 'Jerry' as should have been the original and correct meaning of the coded word.

'Japs sir? Nah. Yer see sir, there was once these two Jap raiders, like and they came across a tanker and an Indian minesweeper and do you know what, one of the raiders was kippered and the other shoved his tail a 'tween his legs and scarpered.'

Shelford grinned. O'Brien had been with the corvette since they'd originally left Liverpool all that time ago. What was it? Nearly three years. All that way. Now here they were, over half way to Hawaii from Seattle and this odd message. In a part of the Pacific Ocean where the Japs hadn't made a significant presence since that infamous first day of their war with the Americans.

O'Brien was continuing, his long lanky hair hopelessly out of regulatory appearance. 'Probably dreamt up by some top brass in between either farting or knocking off the various bits of tit masquerading as secretaries. Anyway, sir, I'll be off to my turn on watch. You get your kip, skip, nothing will come of it.'

Cantor continued to plough at her steady ten-point three knots, plunging and lifting through the long gentle swell of the ocean that for once complied with its peaceful name. O'Brien stared towards the setting sun.

'Ship sir, starboard north-west quarter. Cruiser, I think' muttered a seaman on the starboard wing of the bridge.

O'Brien nodded 'Yes, I've been watching it for the last three minutes. It's definitely not Japanese. Must be one of the new American cruisers.'

'How come sir?'

'Well, those dozy sods on our command ship haven't let us know otherwise. You know our instructions. Keep station unless ordered. So that's what we're doing.' Even so, O'Brien ordered a seaman to go down to the forward four-inch gun, the corvette's principal offensive weapon. The gun that had hit that U-boat. O'Brien smiled as he saw the gun's crew begin to track the distant warship.

But no signal came from the Barstow.

Then the superstructure of one of the merchantmen loomed up and the strange warship momentarily disappeared.

But then so did the merchantmen as it suddenly and horribly exploded into a gigantic ball of flame.

O'Brien pressed the 'Actions Stations' buzzer. Then he told Shelford who was pulling on his white uniform jacket as he stumbled on to the bridge.

'What the hell's happening Number One?'

'Fireworks yonder. Merchantman's just blown up. By all the saints, there goes another and with it, by Jeez, the Barstow. Quite an unusual sight, for the Yanks. For us veterans of the North Atlantic it reminds us of recent regular night occurrences.'

Shelford grinned. O'Brien had a very wry manner of simplifying what was developing into a surprisingly serious situation.

'Anything on Asdic?'

'Nah. We ain't switched it on since leaving Seattle' growled a petty officer.

'Well switch the bloody thing on and then up our speed to the maximum possible with the Asdic working.'

Cantor began to shake up her optimum desired speed of fourteen knots. As the corvette began to close with the stricken ships,

O'Brien yelled 'Look sir, it's that stranger again. Bloody odd? She's firing her smaller guns.'

'Aye, and have you read that signal lamp she's flashing at us?'

'It's trouble. It says 'Jap sub. On surface. Am scaring it away."'

Horribly, two more of the merchantmen suddenly flared up. So also did the leading escort destroyer. Torpedoes or heavy shells.

'O'Brien' yelled Shelford 'You're a bit of an artist. Quick! Sketch that cruiser.'

'Why?'

'Go on, it's a hunch I've got. I reckon that she might possibly be a Jap. Masquerading as a Yank.'

Snatching up a chart, O'Brien quickly sketched what he could see of *Dresden* as she rapidly steamed out of visual range. It wasn't much. Two turrets forward, bridge and funnel close amidships, a single turret aft. No stern mounted catapults. A long lean black shape that stopped firing as she drew away. By the time the sun set, it had disappeared. *Cantor* searched for the supposed Japanese submarine but gave up after thirty minutes of fruitless searching and Shelford turned his little ship back towards Barstow. A curt signal from the seriously crippled light cruiser with her midships almost split to the waterline ordered Shelford to catch up with the sole surviving merchantman and escort it to Hawaii. The remaining two escorts, having searched for survivors, would then escort the cruiser to Hawaii.

Shelford steered his little ship across to the lone merchantman that was steaming northwards to try and escape that devastating attack and pushing her speed up to twelve knots, set course for Hawaii.

En clair Shelford sent a message to the 'brass hat' who'd contacted his corvette only an hour or so, if that, prior to the catastrophe that had overwhelmed the convoy.

Scott took the signal flimsy to Collins. It had been decoded. 'From the *Cantor* sir.'

Collins looked up wearily. He'd received a signal from the American naval attaché just moments before. A suitably crestfallen officer. His parting words were 'Maybe we should have taken note of your hunch.' Even so, Collins read the memo from *Cantor*.

'Severe enemy attack from supposed Jap submarine. One small escort and four merchantman sunk, light cruiser Barstow severely crippled. Also suspect possible surface raider of new heavy cruiser type using torpedoes. Have sketch. Three turrets, two forward. Shelford.'

'By heck, it's her. It's got to be. The convoy's attacker. The bloody *Dresden*. Have the Americans any aircraft in the area? If so, they must find her. Say a two hundred mile radius of the action. Fetch me that American naval attaché. Two turrets forward, one aft. There isn't a really big Jap cruiser afloat of that description. Yes, it's glory boy Reitz and his merry men at it again. Just when we least expect them. Come on Scott! Go on, she'll be there. Two hundred miles south-east by dawn. Ten hours and twenty knots.' Collins jabbed his forefinger on to the map. 'There, there, there' he snarled 'That's where you are. High-tailing it on course for your run back to Europe.'

Collins was uncannily accurate but to his chagrin there were no aircraft capable of reaching the suspected area. The only one available was in ashes. Incinerated on a light cruiser called Barstow.

Reitz steamed a two hundred and fifty mile dash to *Olaf* which had sailed, with *Berengia*, to the planned rendezvous. At noon, on the day after the successful attack on the convoy, *Dresden* slowed to fill her tanks after her recent burst of high-speed steaming. It took but three hours in the now well-practised manoeuvring of the big tanker and battlecruiser to fill the fuel tanks of the warship. As soon as the fuel lines were disengaged the three ships intended to set off on slightly different courses but with an aiming point, as had been worked out by Reitz, Theider and Rimmer during the re-fuelling. The next rendezvous was to be off Juan Fernandez Island near Chile. Then round Cape Horn and into the South Atlantic.

Moto Manuska was a lieutenant-commander in charge of his Imperial Japanese Navy's submarine, the I-273. At six feet and two inches tall, he was literally head and shoulders above all the rest of his crew, but only when he peered through his periscope did he lower himself to about their average height. It was what was in those sights that fascinated him. A large warship, possibly with a tanker and freighter as company. In the sunlight that shone brightly he knew for certain what he was sighting. Part of an American battle group. Flying large 'Stars and Stripes' flags. One of the ships, the freighter, even had such an ensign draped over her amidship side-plating. At long last something that could be called a real target. His huge unwieldy submarine, carrying two float planes as well as a sizeable deck gun, had been despatched across the Pacific to surface off the Californian coast.

There the big submarine's aircraft were launched on what proved to be an utterly pointless exercise. Flying over the ample forests inland of the coastal plain, incendiary bombs were dropped to try and set the forest on fire and for the flames to sweep out of control on to the industrial cities and areas surrounding SanFrancisco. The attempt was a notable disaster for the Japanese plan and after only a brief flare-up, the flames soon died down. Even the exaggerated reports of the airmen could not dissuade Manuska that the attempt had been a hopeless enterprise. No vast clouds of smoke spiralled upwards from the coast and so, feeling badly deflated at the ineptitude of the whole escapade, Manuska turned his cumbersome craft away from the area and by mainly surfacing at night and creeping submerged during the daylight hours, he slowly set upon a return course to Japanese-held waters. It had been another let-down for the submarine warrior of the Samurai race. Like all the other cruises and tasks that he'd already been in this war against the Yankees. Hopeless, time-wasting exercises.

But now, in view through his periscope was at last the target that he'd been waiting for since the start of the hostilities.

A Yankee battleship. The merchantmen he'd deal with later.

It never occurred to him to look up a handy reference to check which Yankee battleship was in view. Or else he wouldn't have found one matching *Dresden*'s silhouette.

Nor did he remember at that excitement of time anything at all about the presence of *Dresden* in a Japanese ship-yard. He'd even sailed past the very repair yard in which the German ship had been in before setting off for his unfruitful mission.

But this was it!

The target of every Nippon Navy commander's dream.

He decided on a spread of three torpedoes.

'Stand by!'

'Fire one!' 'Fire two!' 'Fire three!'

'Torpedoes running, sir!'

Manuska remained glued to the periscope. He couldn't take his eyes from the expected joy of hitting the relatively slow moving target.

Dresden gradually increased speed. 8 – 10 – 12 knots – having been the last of the three ships to get under way. Suddenly, a look out on the port wing of the bridge yelled 'Torpedoes coming in on port bow!'

Hiltzern immediately shouted 'Hard-a-port! Comb those tracks!' even as Reitz re-appeared on the bridge having just left it to snatch a quick nap in his sea-cabin.

'What is it?' he asked, tensely.

'There sir' pointed his first officer. A streak of bubbles past ahead of the bows. 'There's another – oh shit!'

The bubble streak ended on the tip of the bows. There was a brief thud and then the torpedo nose-dived towards the ocean bed many fathoms down.

Still the *Dresden* turned but too late. The third torpedo hit the battlecruiser under Bertha's turret. This time there was a massive eruption of smoke, flame and water towering briefly above the decks before it collapsed wetly over the decks, dispersing rapidly through the scuppers.

Dresden immediately began to list to port. Savagely, a suddenly embittered Reitz ordered the starboard bilges to be flooded in order to counter the list. Hiltzern's damage control team again quickly swung into action closing the watertight doors and by the time the portly commander reached the damaged area, teams were already shoring up bulkheads. To Hiltzern and his men's immense chagrin, at least a dozen men trapped behind the sealed bulkheads had either been killed or drowned.

Further aft in the Sick Berth, Andrea was flung from the bedside of one of the stokers who the day before had trapped a thumb whilst on greasing duty. She screamed, shocked severely by the juddering that shook the battlecruiser so unexpectedly.

The stoker uttered somewhat profoundly 'It's a torpedo, miss. We've been 'it, somewhere up for'ard. Ark, them's the alarm bells. Bit late.'

'But who could have fired it?' asked an equally shocked Doctor Lebers.

'Well it won't be an American' remarked Andrea, rapidly composing herself. 'When I went on deck we were flying huge "Stars and Stripes" from all three ships.'

'Then,' the stoker again, wagging his bandaged hand. 'well, it must 'ave been some cross-eyed Nip submarine commander dreamin' of too many samurais and geishas at the same time. Kinda' gotta bit confused if we was still pretending to be Yankee Doodle Dandy, like.'

Lebers nodded. 'Well, even if you're right – oh dear, there goes our telephone. Come on lass, we'd better see what awaits us.'

Lebers, Andrea and an SBA hurriedly packed their bags and as the request asked, made their way forward towards the Bertha turret area.

The cheers rang through I-273 as their captain gave them graphic detail. The enemy battleship had been hit and was listing. The brief flare of flame was exaggerated to 'enormous gouts of fire.' Suddenly

Manuska snapped 'Down periscope. Enemy has torpedo-boat escorts!'

As soon as *Dresden* stopped, Reitz immediately ordered the two biggest of the ship's motor-launches to be launched and sent to the area where an eagle-eyed Prebke had sighted I-273's malingering periscope. The boats took with them scuttling charges and even as they surged forward, these men were busy arming them to explode at various times in the hopes of scaring away the unidentified submarine that had attacked their ship. Helmut Brautsch, in charge of the leading launch and with one of his crew watching for the signal from *Dresden* that they'd reached the area, stared at the dappled water ahead of him.

As I-273 dropped clumsily and slowly down to assumed safety, her hydroplane operators picked up the engine noises of the approaching launches.

'Two escorts sir. Coming our way.'

A small explosion occurred.

'Obviously not near.'

It did not occur to Manuska that the scuttling charge that the operator had heard was, due to its small size, exploding quite close to them and not far away as had been incorrectly deduced.

'How many charges left?' asked Brautsch as yet another one exploded behind them throwing up a small geyser of water in their wake.

'We had twenty-four. Six left, sir' muttered Schenke getting ready to hurl another one over the side.

'Try over there, Otto' commented Brautsch 'And then equally around this launch.' The first four thrown all duly exploded at about the time guessed to be right but the fifth charge didn't, even though the sixth one did. 'Blast' snarled Schenke 'must 'ave been a mis-fire!'

'Almost over-head' commented one of the hydrophone operators.

'What?' Manuska whirled round. 'I thought you said that they were a long way off.'

'It seemed it sir, but I'm –'

Ccrumpp!

That fifth charge thrown by Schenke had silently dropped deeper. For some reason it's timer didn't work at the set depth but by sheer good fortune for Schenke and hopelessly bad luck for the I-273, it hit the submarine's conning tower and then bounced onto the casing of the big submarine where its percussive cap re-acted, creating to the submariners within the iron hull what seemed to be an enormous blast.

I-273 quivered and shook. Lights went out. Water began to pour in through some thin cracks.

Manuska panicked. He'd never been under an attack. Certainly not one of scuttling charges.

'Surface!' he screamed, and then with his pistol, he fired it wildly at the unfortunate hydrophone operator who, startled, collapsed at his bench, clutching a badly bleeding thigh.

The big submarine plummeted rapidly upwards out of control, crashing out of the water in a massive surge of white-water some three hundred yards from Brautsch's launch.

Almost immediately the smaller guns on *Dresden* opened fire, their shells and tracers racing over the rapidly returning boats. I-273 shuddered from numerous direct hits from the tertiary guns as well as the other smaller calibre weapons. Not one member of her crew appeared out of her conning tower or side hatches before the big submarine suddenly dove bow first under the waves, tilting her stern clear of the water.

'Cease fire!' yelled Reitz who'd been alert to the possibility of the off chance that their attacker could be forced to the surface.

And she had. The guns clattered into silence, the barrels smoking from their rapid firing, just as the rudder and propellers of the stricken I-273 vanished in a flurry of foam, bubbles and oil gushing from serious gashes along her barrel-like side tanks.

'Odd shape for a submarine' murmured Serle 'Seems as if she had an extra deck hatch or something.'

'Perhaps a big gun' commented Reitz. 'Order Brautsch to return to the sinking area to see if there's any tangible debris so as to identify our mystery attacker. Meanwhile we'll get back to saving our ship. Hiltzern's last report seemed reasonably promising in re-assuring us that we won't sink.'

There wasn't much immediately on the surface in the oil slick to give Brautsch or his searching men any clear evidence at all as to the identity of the sunken submarine. Occasionally, large bubbles of air came to the surface from the I-273 as she plunged for her last-ever dive. To the ocean bed two thousand feet below the surface. As she did so, she gradually began to break apart as the strain of over a dozen punctures from *Dresden*'s shells began to split her hull apart. Even specially-strengthened submarines designed for diving to six hundred feet below the surface couldn't withstand the ever-increasing water pressure as it dropped rapidly for the ocean bed. I-273 split in half just before she struck and quite a lot of debris began to slowly drift upwards but by the time it swirled its way to the surface, Brautsch and his launch were back on board and the big warship that had been I-273's target had restarted her engines and left the area.

No one witnessed Manuska's submarine officer's cap bob up and down on the surface. Nor a waterproof case, a few papers and magazines with Japanese printing on their pages.

Not for nearly another two days.

Reitz faced his officers. He looked drained. Shocked. Tired. In just two days the battlecruiser crawled about two hundred and fifty miles. A painful agonising crawl. Amazingly no aircraft had flown over them. Only *Olaf* and *Berengia* kept *Dresden* company with spare members of their crews helping Hiltzern's damage control parties shore up the shattered internal mess of the torpedo blast. Anton and Bertha turrets had been jolted off their training tracks and the ammunition hoists that fed their big shells were also badly out of alignment. Fortunately the torpedo's main blast was confined to a large store-area where it originally exploded and its concussive blast had been deflected away from the shell-holding magazine for the main forward guns. Unlike poor *Resolve*, which had disintegrated from *Dresden*'s three torpedoes, two and a quarter years earlier, the German ship was able to escape a similar awesome and cataclysmic destruction.

Nevertheless she was still badly damaged and everyone on board her knew that their only hope was to crawl yet again back to Japan. The damage teams cut away as much of the jagged metal edges that protruded outwards in many places; the cooks in the canteens repaired their damaged shelves and swept up the large amount of crockery that had been shattered in the blast. Eventually they were able to get about half of their canteen back into working order. Even some of the glassware and delicate medical instruments in the Sick Bay had been broken in the blast that had so severely shaken *Dresden*. Doctor Lebers and Andrea, as well as caring for the alarming influx of nearly fifty men hurt in the blast, were also counting the cost of the damage to their precious medical instruments and supplies.

Deep down in the engine room and boiler rooms there was little apparent initial damage but when Herzog carefully tested the engines he and his men soon found that the port propeller shaft was badly out of alignment. There was nothing that he could do. *Dresden* was a dockyard job on that factor alone.

Padré Jervaulx's normal cheerful features became hardened and heavily lined as he once again conducted a burial service of bodies and bits of bodies. Possibly up to twenty-five men killed. Wrapped in weighted bags they sank out of sight, one by one, as Jervaulx, with Reitz and virtually the whole crew except those on vital watch-keeping duties witnessed the brief service and then the departure to the final resting place of their comrades. Jervaulx knew that a further dozen or so men were in flooded compartments held in by the water-tight doors and that only until the ship was in dry dock could they be given their proper burial, when the flooded areas would be drained and access gained into those sections.

There were only grim faces looking at Reitz as he faced his summoned officers. They knew what he was going to say.

'Fellow officers. *Dresden* has been badly hurt. We are going to return to Japan although getting through these American dominated waters will not be easy. We cannot travel at faster than ten knots but for the time being, we'll keep *Berengia* and *Olaf* in company and still try to pass off as an American battle group. Then one night, I will detach our two support ships to steam as rapidly as they can to try and reach Batavia in Java and there to await further instructions. Whether our Japanese Allies will load them up with supplies I don't know. It may be that after our repairs have been completed, that as part of the bargain for these repairs and supplies we may well once again be expected to assist the Imperial Navy in its battle with the ever increasing strength of the Americans.' He paused, and took a sip of water. Continuing, he said 'Somehow, I have the awful feeling that we shall be in dock for at least six months, if not longer. We shall not be returning to our beloved homeland for at least another year and if the war isn't over by then, who knows what difficulties we shall then have to face. We all know that it no longer goes in Germany or Japan's favour, unless new weapons can be found to counter-attack the Allies strengths. Perhaps Admiral Wenneker will fill us in with details when we reappear outside his smug office!'

At this, there were a few grim titters of suppressed amusement by those officers who'd remembered the attitude of Germany's naval attaché when he'd first visited *Dresden* eighteen months previously.

Yet another pause. Reitz looked over his men again. How long had it been? March 1941 to November 1943. Two and a half years away from home. No ship, German or otherwise had been away in this protracted conflict from a home port for so long. That is, if they survived and reached that base. He knew that was the principal desire for his men and but for their recent torpedoing, *Dresden* would have been well on her way. Should he tell the men what he really suspected? Andrea's report to him of the conversation she'd discussed with the stoker in the Sick Berth only underlined his suspicions. That the submarine which had attacked them had been Japanese. It must have seen them flying the American flag. An American submarine wouldn't have torpedoed, in its own controlled waters, a ship flying its own country's flag. He looked up, feeling even more drained. Suddenly the irony of the situation was there. Savagely he blurted out 'The rumour has it that we've been put into this situation by a Japanese submarine. Well, keep that to yourselves. In our ship's log we shall record "unidentified". But we all feel different. We all feel angry and upset at being so long, and now, even longer away from our loved ones.' Then, waving a clenched fist in the air and recovering his composure, he firmly said 'Our ship hasn't been sunk. We will emerge to try again to return to German-controlled waters. We shall see our loved ones again. We are not finished. We are the *Dresden*, our navy's most successful warship. I salute all of you and I will do my damned hardest to get you all back home!' Suddenly the room erupted in cheers. The men felt uplifted. Thanks to the words uttered so dramatically at them by their captain. Yes, of course, they were *Dresden* men. Not as yet defeated by the enemy. Still a potential thorn in the side of their enemies. Whoever they were.

A Catalina PBY flying boat on a routine flight droned over the three ships at just that moment. Its crew saw the Stars and Stripes flag and paid no further heed. Two hours later it flew over the debris of I-273 and seeing the oil slick, the pilot took his aircraft down to the sea's surface. Mere curiosity. Launching an inflatable, two of the crew paddled over to the water-proof case and sodden papers floating in the water. 'Hey, cop a gander at these' said one of the Americans. 'They're in Nip-Nip script.'

'Aye, and look at this' remarked his companion as he leaned over the side – 'a Nippon Navy man's cap' – fishing Manuska's officer's head-gear out of the water. 'Best tell the skip and get him to fly our crate back to Hawaii. These bits could tell us something that the big-wigs don't know about. That a Jap submarine has been sunk and that none of our lads has claimed it. Something odd about that, eh?'

Reitz asked the officers to be careful with what they said to their men. He bade them 'Good-afternoon' and retired towards his main cabin, feeling suddenly tired but noting the grim looks of the men. No longer cheering. It seemed almost as if they were blaming him for their current predicament. Had he not stopped to re-supply and re-fuel, in that area so relatively soon after the tussle with the convoy, then perhaps they'd be steaming for Cape Horn instead of this dismal trudge towards Japan. Again. Twice now they'd hoped to attempt to cross the dangerous Atlantic in their bid for home-waters and twice luck had turned against them. But most of all Reitz felt that he'd let Elle down. What must she be thinking? That the *Dresden* would soon be alongside *Tirpitz* and *Scharnhorst* ready to gather their combined strength against an Arctic convoy? But she wouldn't know. No-one at home did. Except those here on board the three ships.

Then his thoughts wandered again as he briefly stood by the rails near the stern watching the faint wake murmuring along and slowly receding into the distance. He thought of the lives of his crew already lost. This then developed into the destruction his ship had caused against the Allied vessels that *Dresden* had sunk or captured. So many. And for what? Germany was losing the war. He knew it. Yet he had to go on. Perhaps an honourable peace would be negotiated. But somehow he doubted it. The Allies hated Hitler and all his cronies. Maybe they even regarded him as a Nazi stooge. But he'd spared that big passenger liner. Whenever he could, he'd tried to run his ship according to the humanitarian rules, if there could be any, of waging war at sea. Despite the cooling breeze as late afternoon merged into evening, he began to sweat.

'Steady on sir, thoughts you was 'avin' a dizzy turn there!' Reitz looked up. What was it about Otto Schenke? Always there when I need him. He hardly realised that the big man had hold of him. Keeping him steady. Then his eyes glazed over.

'Come on, skip, me thinks you outa' be in your cabin' gasped Otto as he lifted his now barely conscious captain up and over his shoulder.

'Walters, you lazy git!' he bellowed as he kicked at the cabin door. The steward came running from his tiny pantry where he'd been preparing Reitz's supper and went white in the face when he saw Schenke at the door swaying with his inert captain over his left shoulder. 'Skip's fainted. Let's 'ave 'im on t'bed.' Walters lowered Reitz on to the bed with Schenke taking most of the weight and then immediately rang down to the Sick Berth. Andrea, on duty having just about cleared up the mess as well as checking over her numerous patients, took the call. In a somewhat agitated voice, Walters, who was normally so urbane and polite whenever he spoke to her, stammered out 'Cor, come qu, quick, Miss Andrea. It's the cap'n. He, he's taken ill. Main cabin, Miss. Hurry please.' She beckoned to one of the sick-berth attendants and together they rushed away leaving the other SBA to man the ward. Arriving somewhat breathlessly, Andrea quickly sized up the situation. She felt Reitz's sweaty forehead, alarmed at the high temperature of the skin, then his pulse. With her stethoscope she listened to his heartbeat. 'Mmm,' she said, somewhat thoughtfully, 'he has a touch of tropical fever, probably due to anxiety, stress and not enough rest. When he wakes up' – then she paused. Walters looked alarmed, and Andrea knew that he doted on the captain – 'Don't worry, he will and when he does, give him two of these pills and then four hours later, another two.' Walters looked a little apprehensive.

Andrea continued 'I will tell Doctor Lebers when he comes on duty to relieve me. He will no doubt come along and carry out a fuller medical inspection and data check on Herr Reitz. Now I must go and check on the wounded that we're treating.'

Walters grinned slightly 'Thankyou, Miss Andrea. I'll see to him.'

Andrea bade him goodnight, kissing Walters lightly on his left cheek, for she was fond of the little steward and left the cabin and as she turned to make her way back to the Sick Berth, she ran straight into the arms of Helmut Brautsch. He held her tight. He'd just been down to the Sick Berth where the attendant had told him of the captain's illness and Andrea's hurried departure. Now she was in his arms. He had very little spare time whilst *Dresden* was at sea and the last two days had been very hectic, assisting with the efforts at shoring up the damaged bulkheads or keeping an extra watch out for enemy aircraft. So such a moment to hold Andrea was a rare pleasure for him. He knew that he was the luckiest man on the ship. His woman was in his arms. Their women, if they had one, mother, sister, girlfriend, wife or daughter were half-a-world away. Rarely did they have a quiet few moments before one of the crew would interrupt their time. She looked up at him, and smiled that quizzical one that had first charmed him. On the lifeboat. Even then she'd smiled at him whilst *Dresden* loomed up ever closer and fading in the distance, *Arades*, burning and sinking behind them. A nightmare going to her final resting place. 'Your captain. He's ill. Herr Walters knows what to do. You'll have to manage without him.' Brautsch looked perturbed and relieved at the same time. While Reitz was recovering from whatever it was, he'd be temporarily First Officer. At least there'd be no chasing after other ships. More like trying to avoid them.

He didn't want to let her go. But duty called him. To see Hiltzern who'd now be the temporary captain. So different to the man who'd taken over from Von Munke. Like everyone else Hiltzern had willingly gone about his tasks. Wanting to do them. Not hating them like he had whilst the gutless former captain had been in charge.

Gently he lowered his lips to hers.

For them perhaps there'd be more time together once *Dresden* was back in Japan, providing they could avoid the marauding American submarines that were known to prowl ever deeper into what had once been regarded as safe Japanese-controlled waters. But for the rest of the crew it was to be an extremely wearisome, tiresome, longsome and lonesome wait to endure before the next time that *Dresden* could attempt her breakthrough to home waters. Eventually, after what seemed to be an eternity, the couple released their passionate kiss. Andrea murmured 'Well love, we'll just have to wait until the next opportunity. I'm needed in the Sick Berth or here with your captain; you will be busy with the ship. I must go. Try to come and see me, please.'

'I'll try but no promises.' rejoined Helmut, not wanting time to push its forward movement. Inevitably it had to and did. With a little bow and a quick kiss of her right hand, he turned and traced his steps towards the citadel of responsibility. The bridge.

Andrea moved off reluctantly. She loved him more than ever but every so often a little voice said 'He's the enemy' but a stronger voice overpowered it. 'No. He's your new love in your life, no matter what his nationality!' She was on his ship. Serving on it. Caring for the sick and wounded. Whoever they were. From captain to gunner, stoker to seaman.

The arrival of *Cantor* and her lone merchantmen in Hawaii didn't at first generate much excitement. The American naval authorities duly expressed their gratitude for Shelford carrying out his escort duties so well. They weren't too excited when Shelford tried to interest them in the sketch of the 'big cruiser'. They were still awaiting a response from *Lincoln*'s commander but as his battle-group hadn't completed their special mission, radio silence was being upheld for at least another three days.

Then, an hour or so later, the PBY Catalina carrying the Japanese documents in their waterproof case landed at the harbour limits before fixing to its berth. In a casual-briefing about the patrol, the pilot rather laconically added 'Oh, by the way, found these and this Jap submarine officer's cap in a thin spread of diesel oil. Expect one of our lads bagged the silly sod. Maybe the papers are important.'

His senior officer looked a bit puzzled 'Are you sure? There's been no report of any of our ships sinking an enemy sub in these parts. Still I'll pass the whole lot on to our Cipher Boys who'll work out what's in the papers. Perhaps they'll give us a clue.'

Which they did. Startlingly. The log of I-273 was up-to-date to the point of the scuttling charge forcing the big sub. to the surface. What intrigued the Americans was the writer's claim that I-273 had torpedoed an American battleship and brought it to a halt, before being forced to dive due to the presence of small escort craft. The only trouble was that no American battleships were in the area. The main surface presence was *Lincoln* and her 'battle group' on a classified secret operation. No word of any attack on the group had been received. So if it wasn't *Lincoln*, which ship had I-273 attacked?

Then they received Shelford's report of the vicious attack on the convoy. Plus a copy of the sketch of the 'strange cruiser'. Something niggled the American commander. The attack on the convoy had been serious but what ship had Shelford and his men seen?

'Better call in that Limey Admiral. What's his name? Ah yes, Collins. Seeing that the *Cantor* is a Limey warship, he'd better hear the story.'

Collins and Scott listened intently to what the *Cantor*'s captain had to say but when he produced the sketch, Collins blanched

'Are you sure that this is an accurate sketch?' he blurted out. Shelford put up his defences 'Of course. It was the best that could be done. I've a hunch she's a new Jap cruiser that no-one has ever seen before.'

'No, Lieutenant Shelford,' retorted Scott whilst Collins still remained speechless 'that is the German battlecruiser *Dresden*. That was the ship that attacked the convoy.' Turning to the American naval attaché 'You've been conned. *Dresden* torpedoed the ships in that convoy but pretended to be firing on a surfaced Jap. submarine.'

'Holy smoke, she's crippled Barstow and sank two of the escorts as well as four of the five merchantmen,' gasped the American. 'Almost a complete wipe-out.'

'Now will you listen to us?' snarled Collins, anger mounting in his voice. 'Somehow or other, that German warship has been on my agenda now for two and a half years and no-one has ever listened to me. That ship's captain is, as you Americans would put it is "one hell of a guy". We've chased her in the North Atlantic, lost most of a very important troopship convoy off East Africa, we feel sure she accounted for some ships during the Malayan campaign and if you check your records or witnesses we reckon she was the ship that hit your supply ships off Guadalcanal. Now she's turned up again and smashed one of your convoys. When are you going to stop her?'

'She's probably high-tailing it for Cape Horn' butted in Scott.

The American naval attaché's thoughts were racing. 'Maybe she is, but maybe she ain't. We've just had a peculiar incident. A Jap sub's been sunk in this area. A big one. The I-273. Even carried a float plane. Now hear this. We reckon in the captain's log, which we've recovered, that she torpedoed one of our battle-wagons. But no such deal. We ain't got one of our big boys in the area but if you put two and three together, you might make four.'

'What are you getting at?' snapped Collins.

'What if your German raider, flying an American flag – Shelford here says he thought the ship seen by his crew was flying the Stars and Stripes – was clobbered by I-273 in error?'

'So?' queried Scott. Even Shelford was looking puzzled.

'Somehow, I-273 comes to the surface. Maybe the Krauts lobbed some explosives at her and got lucky. *Dresden* opens fire and sinks it, thinking that the Jap is one of ours.'

'Seems a bit far fetched' muttered Scott.

'Maybe' interjected Collins 'but if that was the case, and she's been torpedoed, then the bloody German can't be all that far away. Say a speed of ten knots. In three days she's only managed no more than six hundred or so miles. Come on, let's have a look on the chart.'

The American found one that covered the area to the south and west. Collins placed his fingers and spread them out 'There. Send up a long-ranged reconnaissance sweep and you'll find her high tailing at about ten knots for Japan. All lonesome and unhappy because if she's been torpedoed, she ain't going for South America. That's where she is. Somewhere there. Go on; send up one of your planes. Pronto. Two more days and she'll be out of range.'

'It's only speculation, Admiral Collins but I'll see what I can do. We'll also wireless all our subs. in Jap. waters to keep an eye open for the German – twin turrets forward, single turret aft, non-Japanese outline. Twenty-odd thousand tons. We'll act on your hunch. *Dresden*'s done us a lot of damage, especially if you say she was the one that banged at our supply ships off Guadalcanal.'

Twelve hours later, a long-range Lockheed Hudson flew over *Dresden* and her two supply ships still with her. Wisely Hiltzern refrained from ordering the anti-aircraft guns to open fire on the aicraft. The observer said 'Nawp, that's not what we're looking for. We're looking for a slow Lone-Ranger. That group down there must be doing at least fifteen knots, if not more.' The 'plane flew on with the pilot just making a small note in his log – 'Small battle-group steaming south-west.'

Just ninety minutes later, at almost sunset, Hiltzern ordered *Olaf* and *Berengia* away to try and reach Batavia. The damage repair team had done so well that as the battlecruiser swung to a more north-westerly course her speed was pushed up to seventeen knots. When dawn came some eight hours later, she was almost three hundred miles from her two support ships and with each turn of her propellers, distanced herself further and further away from Hawaii and nearer to the possible relative security of the naval repair base at Kure.

Dresden escaped the cursory search for her for as the Americans explained to Collins that even if the German battlecruiser was sailing with battle damage for Japan, the war for her would be as good as over by the time she'd be repaired. By then, they reckoned life for enemy surface ships would be very precarious – either from attacks by submarines or from aircraft flying from the various Task Force carriers following up the expected island-hopping campaign by the Army and Marine Forces. When *Dresden* would eventually emerge, they'd soon get her. Collins wasn't impressed by the brash American approach but he had to admit that they held virtually all the aggressive cards in the Pacific theatre of this prolonged conflict.

Nine days later off the southern part of the North Japanese island of Hokkaido, *Dresden* came in sight of land after a surprisingly trouble-free passage. Apart from the high-flying Hudson, they'd seen nothing. Radar alerted them on three occasions to possible enemy ships which Hiltzern, despite the battlecruiser's relative low speed, was able to steer away from before the ship or ships came into view. Every day he and Brautsch reported to Reitz about the ship's progress and their captain did his best to concentrate on them despite his illness. A sporadic spate of ill-discipline was also hastily dealt with and the six culprits spent seventy-two hours in solitary confinement having tried to stir up trouble and inciting others, without success, to down tools and refuse to work unless the ship altered course to attempt the passage home. With her forward twin-turrets out of action there was no way the *Dresden* could have fought off any surface action but the homesick men didn't care. They wanted the chance to return home, even in a crippled warship, but did not want another prolonged stay in Japan. Reitz, on being informed of Hiltzern's punishment to the men, grimaced but knew that his commander was right. He knew that if the trouble had spread, the dis-affection could have wrecked the morale, low that it was, of his crew.

But now, on the tenth day of his illness he struggled to reach the bridge. The dim outline of a headland could be seen as, with grey clouds overhead, the German warship turned south-westwards. A small patrol launch came within a mile, but suddenly and abruptly scuttled off to the security of a nearby base, without signalling.

Soon after, a solo converted Betty bomber, on reconnaissance, lumbered overhead, but it too made no attempt to close with the *Dresden.*

It was almost as if the Japanese feared to make contact just in case the ship that they'd seen was an American cruiser on a daring raid. Or probably that they were so suspicious of any unidentified ship that it had to be checked out. Even so far north of Japan's main bases, American submarines ventured to attack coastal shipping and fishing boats. Why not one of their surface warships?

Darkness came as *Dresden* left Hokkaido behind and approached the north-eastern coast of Japan's main island, Honshu. As dawn came up two more small warships approached the German ship. This time they flashed a message across, in English 'What ship?' Reitz, well enough after another good night's rest, was back on the bridge for a dawn stint on watch. The Japanese ships again asked for *Dresden*'s identity even as the battlecruiser's secondary guns tracked their approach. At last, Reitz deigned to flash back the response 'KM *Dresden* bound for Kure.'

Without ever closing to less than a mile the two small Japanese craft, apparently satisfied with their big consort's reply, kept pace with the fourteen knot progress of the German ship for the next eight hours before turning away as sunset, such that it was, approached and putting on speed, vanished back the way they'd come.

Frank Zeke Hewson, commanding officer of an American P-class submarine had just finished a conference with his three senior offices as the boat cruised, hull-down the next dawn. With no torpedoes left and all but fifteen rounds of four-inch ammunition for the main deck gun used up, he concluded that it was time for his boat to return to Hawaii even if two days early. It had been an extremely successful patrol. Two destroyers, five medium-sized merchantmen, two coastal steamers, three landing craft and four fishing boats in a three-week cruise, all within fifty miles of the enemy coastline. 'Excellent work' he said.

'Our best patrol ever' added his first officer.

'Aye,' said the engineering officer 'but we will have to tail it back home soon. Juice 'll just about last out.'

Their thoughts were interrupted when the diving klaxon sounded, the two look-outs and the junior officer on watch from the conning tower quickly dropped down, slamming the water-tight hatches above them.

'What is it?' snapped Hewson.

'Big warship about four miles astern. Coming up quite fast.'

'Periscope depth. We'll have a look' growled the skipper.

Hewson stared hard at *Dresden* as she came closer.

'Don't recognise it. Looks like a new heavy cruiser. Pity we don't have any of our tin fish left. Take a look, Number One.'

'Mmm. You're right skip. Don't look like a typical Jap.'

'Best take a photo of it. Do the boffins at base good to look at her. She seems to be damaged.'

Totally unaware of the American submarine, *Dresden* pushed past the undersea craft churning her way steadily on course. A little later, Reitz received a message from Wenneker that an escort was due to meet them at noon. The Japanese promised their best to give the German battlecruiser an escort. Apparently they'd been highly pleased with the attack on the ammunition ship convoy. Wenneker would explain in due course.

As soon as the supposed large cruiser disappeared, Hewson surfaced and put on full speed on course for home. He also wirelessed Hawaii and received a curt response. 'Describe your cruiser.'

When the reply came, Hawaii knew that the ship that Hewson had seen was the *Dresden* – two-twin turrets forward, one aft. Heavy central superstructure on 'American' rather than 'Japanese' design.

Collins smiled grimly when he heard the news. 'So Reitz is just about safe for the time being. We'll just have to get him and his ship when he ventures out again. That is, unless the Americans can get their carriers close enough to bomb him to bits in harbour. Mark my words, Scott, we'll have him. Sooner if not later.'

Reitz was shocked by the scene as *Dresden* came to anchor off Kure. Battered warships of all sizes were moored, all seemingly waiting their turn for the repair yards. All testimony to the ever-growing strength of their principal protagonists – the American carrier aircraft. Some of the upper-works looked little better than heaps of unrecognisable lumps of scrap-metal. It almost appeared to Reitz that his ship was one of the least badly damaged, from the viewpoint of an outward appearance. A small launch came fussing up to the battlecruiser soon after she'd come to a halt. It flew the German naval ensign. A civilian climbed the boarding steps to be received by Brautsch. No trill of bosun's pipes this time. Not to someone in a faded grey suit. He introduced himself as one of Admiral Wenneker's staff to Reitz and asked that only the captain and Hiltzern should return with him to the German Embassy.

Wenneker's original bluster of almost two years previously had gone. Instead the German naval attaché looked worn-out. Tired. An almost haunted look on his face. He waved the two officers to a seat. 'Saké? Orange juice?' he asked.

'Get on with it, sir' growled Hiltzern. 'We don't need niceties. All we want is to get back to our ship as quickly as we can. We want her repaired and then to be on our way.'

'Gentlemen, how can I begin? You know that the war is not going too well, mmm?' The two officers just stared back, dreading what was going to follow. It wasn't very enlightening. Wenneker told them, that apart from the home waters in the Baltic and North Sea coastlines, the rest of the world's seas were full of danger for German ships. Off the French coast even night-time sailings were fraught with attacks by fast British torpedo boats and by day were subject to RAF and Coastal Command air attacks. Further afield the few blockade-runners from Japan had less than a fifty-fifty chance of reaching a French port. Even the U-boats in the Atlantic convoy battle were taking such severe losses that only a radical design in their mode of operations such as high underwater speed could reverse their fortunes. German scientists had already come up with a potential design and tests should begin early in the new year.

Much more dismal was the news of the crippling of battleship *Tirpitz* although repairs had begun to try and get her back in action by May of the new year. Battlecruiser *Scharnhorst* was the Kriegsmarine's sole main surface ship left in Arctic waters. There were hopes, if sufficient fuel could be found for the two pocket battleships and the two heavy cruisers to try and break out but the odds on success were somewhat less than hopeful.

The Wehrmacht was on the defensive, retreating, not advancing, in Italy and on the Eastern Front. Losses of men and material were within reasonable limits but again, new weapons and tanks were awaited to try and restore the balance. *Dresden*'s superb attack on that East African convoy had long since faded into one of relative insignificance. The excellent record of the ship still kept her in focus of the people at home, who themselves were under aerial attack from the skies, by day and night. Only occasionally did the Luftwaffe muster enough strength to cause the losses in Allied raiding bombers to be anything close to serious.

'Now to immediate problems' Wenneker continued. 'I have asked our Japanese allies to help us to have *Dresden* repaired as quickly as possible. Unfortunately we are not in a strong position to bargain. They have a lot of their own problems and if they do repair your ship, then once again they will ask for it to be assigned to their battle fleet. Maybe,' and here he spread his arms out 'just maybe, you'll be able to slip away in the course of a fleet action. They need every warship they can muster and have even hinted that if we choose not to agree, they'll either sequestrate *Dresden* into their own fleet here in Kure or sink you out on the high seas. They're a jittery lot. Their all-encompassing Far Eastern Japanese-controlled Empire is taking extremely severe knocks. Just like our own situation in Europe.' Reitz and Hiltzern sat grim-faced. Wenneker grimaced as he thought of his next words. 'Even our own raider *Michel* wasn't safe. She was torpedoed just sixty miles from here and less than half of her crew were rescued. It took me three days to get the Japanese authorities to send out search vessels. They just didn't want to know. You must tell your men to stay within the naval compound. European-type faces aren't at all welcome unless with good reason anywhere else. The country is rife with rumours of American agents landing and infiltrating into the Japanese society. Special passes will be required for sight-seeing tours or like Kapitan Leutenant Brautsch and Nurse Cantrell to visit the monks at Nagasaki again. Their secret police are constantly on the alert. We must be most careful if we want *Dresden* to be repaired. Even so, judging from a brief glance at what is needed, I think you'll be in dockyard hands for at least six months.'

The voice sounded so weary, so tired, but not in a defeatist tone. It echoed throughout and over the now still decks and work places of the German battlecruiser. It told the crew how unfortunate it was that the ship was once again at the mercy or otherwise of their Japanese hosts. The crew would be kept as busy as possible and all would have time to write a letter to be sent, at some risk, on one of the last blockade-runners to attempt a run for Bordeaux. In the ensuing weeks all would have time on shore, like the last visit, but only in groups of no more than twenty at a time. The Japanese Secret Police would not be all that inclined to be very patient should any of them wander out of the naval barracks. Reitz, to whom the voice belonged, said that he'd be leaving the ship in order to fully recover from his fever and to prepare a plan for the break-through to home – controlled waters. Unfortunately the war situation wasn't all that good but the ship's news bulletins would attempt to keep them all informed. Then he re-assured them that he was proud of their efforts, proud to be associated with the ship and that after his rest and the ship's repairs, he'd once more lead them in their new campaign at sea. The speakers clicked off and it took only a moment before the sound of cheering could be heard spreading over the whole ship.

'One thing's for certain' remarked Reitz to the officers and men on the bridge 'This ship's crew still knows how to cheer. We are not down-cast nor are we defeated.'

KM *Dresden* was still a fighting ship.

Even the news within the next two weeks that both *Arabian Nights* and the *Caribou Saga* had both been stopped by Allied cruisers, their crews taken prisoner after the ships were hurriedly scuttled, failed to dampen their spirits for on the plus side, both *Olaf* and *Berengia* had reached Batavia and there they were under the protection of the Japanese Imperial Navy, such that it was, in the area.Some how, even Christmas seemed a muted affair, the only bright part of it being that *Dresden* was now dry-docked and the extent of the damage underwater showed how fortunate that they were not to have been sunk. The outer plating of the battlecruiser was found to be split right down to her keel. It could take a long time before she was a fighting force again. But she would. Eventually, when news filtered through that battlecruiser *Scharnhorst* had been sunk off the North Cape with the loss of nearly all her crew, it somehow made the men feel even more isolated and yet perversely even more determined to get home, as and when the opportunity arose. 1944 promised that opportunity but when and how, they'd simply have to wait for events to unfold.

Chapter 10

'So we dashed in and walloped it'

The sound of a bell tinkling echoed over the confines of the Catholic monastery in the Japanese city of Nagasaki, heralded not one of the many services held in the main church but for a much more unusual occasion within the grounds of the celibate monks. A wedding and that in itself was unusual but this one was more noteworthy. The ceremony met with the full approval of the Catholic Bishop of the city. A German naval officer was marrying an English nurse (although to the Japanese authorities, Andrea was still assumed to be of Spanish nationality) in a country where Christians were a small minority and in the course of the protracted struggle with the Americans were often regarded with a great deal of suspicion, especially by the Tempai, the secret police of that island based Empire.

'I, Helmut, take you Andrea, to be my wedded wife. To have and to hold. To love until death do us part.' Looking resplendent in his best Kriegsmarine naval officer's uniform, Brautsch smiled at his radiant bride. He and Andrea spent a week in the city preparing for their special day. She wore a cream suit comprising a jacket and calf length skirt, with a white carnation in the lapel of her jacket. Her head of light brown hair was hidden in a white veil over which Andrea wore a small clôche hat. She murmured back 'And I, Andrea, will love you until death us do part' and held out her left hand on to which Helmut slid the precious thin gold band.

'With the giving of this ring, I, with the authority of the Holy Trinity, do pronounce you both man and wife' announced the Bishop to the assembled company of monks and to Padré Jervaulx who acted as Helmut's best man.

Brautsch parted the veil and lowered his head towards his new bride. 'I love you, Frau Andrea Brautsch and may I have the honour to kiss you.' She smiled up at him and nodded her willing assent.

Shortly after a simple wedding breakfast, the newly married couple, together with Jervaulx, bade farewell to their hosts counted now as friends and boarded the train for Kure, watched under the baleful gaze of an agent of the Tempai who stepped aboard the last carriage as the labouring locomotive dragged the heavy train on the start of its haul to Japan's big naval port. Taking them all back to the war. To Kure and its bay.

The bay was full of some of the major units of Japan's surface fleet that were still in active service. Still afloat despite the ravages of the ferocious and continuous American onslaught.

Monster battleship *Musashi* as well as smaller capital ships, carriers, cruisers and destroyers. Battle and signal flags flying bravely as the fleet gathered to confront the American Task Force known to be approaching the Marianas group of islands that were now on the front-line of the defence line of Japan's newly-acquired co-prosperity Empire. Joining up with other ships stationed off Borneo.

Dresden's work-up in the Bay was temporarily halted to allow for this build-up of the Imperial Navy's forces which was on the point of departure as Brautsch and his new wife waited for a launch from the German ship to pick them up, and with Jervaulx, return them to the vessel that had brought them together.

Even Reitz, now fully recovered from the fever that had temporarily weakened him so much, was waiting to receive the couple as they climbed back onto the clean, well-scrubbed decks of the resplendent and refurbished warship. He knew where they'd been with Jervaulx. And why.

He was so happy for them. But he also yearned for Elle. 'Welcome back Herr and Frau Brautsch. Please accept these little gifts from myself, the officers and crew and the chef' and in so saying, Schenke standing next to him, stepped forward and gave them a superb model of *Dresden*, shining in its polished steel, salvaged from cut-away parts from the ship's own compartments and plating too badly damaged to be refitted. Then Walters handed them a cake, again based on the ship but instead of a bridge and funnel, there were small miniatures, of a naval officer and a nurse, in marzipan and icing, holding hands, looking at each other.

'My, Rudi, you are such a dear little man. And Otto, well, thanks' murmured Andrea, kissing both men lightly on the cheek. Brautsch also said thank-you to both men, shaking them by the hand. As they looked up, suddenly the whole superstructure of the ship came alive with the crew who unrolled a banner. 'Welcome aboard to the happy couple' it read in German and Spanish. Then the ship echoed to the sound of cheering. 'You see,' said their captain 'you've done something to uplift our morale. Come, both of you to the Petty Officers' mess – they have a little bit more for you both.'

And they had. Quite a spread. Every member of the crew received a plate of beef and rice. Also a slice of fruit cake. Simple fare, maybe, but it meant a lot to all on board. With *Dresden* afloat and ready for her sea-going exercises, they knew that it was a cause for celebration. Not just the marriage of the extremely popular Andrea but the hope that this was the start of their return to home waters. For a third time. Maybe it would really be third time lucky!

It was good, thought Reitz, to see how the marriage of the two members of his crew, a unique event as it was for their war, and only possible through the fortune (or mis-fortune) of the conflict that had put the two together. The Kriegsmarine, in common with other world-wide navies didn't employ females at all as sea-going crew members although women did serve on the various shore bases. However Andrea Brautsch, née Cantrell, was an exception. She was, strictly speaking 'enemy', but yet here she was, married to one of his officers. How he wished that Elle could be with him but she was half-a-world away. A brief message indicated that she'd been transferred to Kiel as the Norwegian bases were being reduced of some personnel now that the Kriegsmarine could no longer mount a serious threat to the Allied convoys sailing to Murmansk. True, *Tirpitz* remained but she'd been badly damaged during an air-attack on her in April.

Now it was 6th June. And there was joy on board. By mid-afternoon the lines were cast off and *Dresden* began slowly feeling her way into the bay as the last of the Japanese Fleet set sail to do battle with the Americans. Suddenly the loudspeakers over the deck crackled into life.

'Captain to the wireless room. Urgent!'

Reitz excused himself and hurried up to the wireless office. 'Well, what is it?' One of the men stood, saluted and said 'Message sir. Direct from Kiel by Grand Admiral Doenitz. It says 'To all units, Normandy beaches under attack by Allied invasion forces. Counter-measures to be set up.' Reitz grimaced. It was happening. If the Allies gained a foothold, German forces would be fighting on three fronts – France, Italy and in the vastness of Eastern Europe.

He knew what he had to do. Broadcast the news to the crew.

There were no cheers after his brief announcement. It was if the euphoria of having a wedding to celebrate had been but a dream. The harsh reality hit them. Hard. So far from home and helpless to even take part in any of the possible counter-measures. More than ever the need to try and get back became paramount. To try and get back before the worst happened, and even though no-one said so, it was there in all their minds. Germany was going under, and their loved ones could eventually be in the firing-line from the land invasions.

It took Reitz two weeks of extensive working-up in the Bay to be satisfied that *Dresden* was fully fit for further action. The sharpness at the way he manoeuvred his ship around the bay astonished the two Japanese liaison officers. Their own ships, when on trials, were never thrown about in the vicious turnings that Reitz subjected his battlecruiser to as her bubbling wake frothed in a furious irregular zig-zag pattern behind her. The Arados, all three of them, tried to drop canvas bags on to the decks simulating air attacks. Hiltzern, Halder and a group of gunners had earlier toured some of the shattered wrecks of Japanese ships, with their ally's full permission, and acquired a dozen extra machine-guns, with ammunition, to try to help strengthen the ship's air-defences, and also cut plating away and then refitted it as extra protection for their own air-gunners. It was a known tactic that the American carrier planes often heavily strafed a warship's air-defence gunners before attempting to land bombs or launch torpedoes. Any gunner was an easy target for the machine-gun bullets unless given a measure of protection. The Japanese on seeing *Dresden*'s men given this shielding were dubious at first but on seeing that the plating didn't restrict the operation of the gunners, they then decided to copy the example set by *Dresden*'s crew.

At the end of the month *Dresden* hauled out of the Bay sailing to the south-east with two Japanese escorts vessels, of a small destroyer type, flanking her. News filtered through that the Marianas conflict had gone badly for the Imperial Navy with the loss of many of their highly trained carrier pilots as well as the sinking of the new *Taiho* and the veteran *Shokaku*, two of Japan's main surviving aircraft-carriers. Those still left were little more than an empty threat. Short of aircraft and even more bereft of the pilots who could have flown them. American air domination in the naval conflict seemed all but complete.

Within hours of *Dresden*'s departure, Admiral Collins was given a note indicating as such. Spies on the Japanese mainland radioed the nearest American submarine which in turn passed the news on to Hawaii. So she's on her way. All the American submarines on patrol were asked to look out for her sailing south-eastwards. But Reitz avoided them by abruptly, once out of sight of land, by altering course to the south-west. Within a couple of days the battlecruiser was holed up in a small bay off the Chinese coast. From then on it was slow progress with little more than sixty miles a night being steamed as the German ship moved from one isolated bay to another, avoiding the submarines that were patrolling further out to sea. Never sailing if the moon was too bright. Always at less than twelve knots so that her wake didn't leave a trail of phosphorescent bubbles to attract any surfaced submarine marauder.

Reitz felt even lonelier as the days went on. A communication from Wenneker still based near Kure indicated, in a very guarded sense, that Admiral Wilhelm Canaris, Head of the Abwehr and instigator of his ship had been removed from office and was under house arrest pending further investigations into the abject failure of Abwehr. Also, thought Reitz, for his anti-Nazi views. The little chain-smoking Admiral would have to be very careful. Even more so when news of an anti-Hitler bomb outrage came through when *Dresden* picked up an Allied English-speaking station. One which had failed. Reitz could only shudder at the thought of what the Nazis would do to the perpetrators of the scheme should they be caught. The need to get *Dresden* back home became even stronger but they had at first to reach Singapore in order to refuel and re-supply under the auspices of the main remnants of Japan's Imperial Navy. Poised to defend the southern part of their Empire against the Americans as they approached to attack that key area. The Philippines. Take that area and the Americans would control the sea lanes connecting the former Dutch East Indies and their vital supplies with the rest of the contracting Japanese Empire.

Reitz also knew that his two faithful supply ships, *Berengia* and *Olaf* would be there to meet his own ship. Both vessels waiting patiently with fresh supplies. A signal from both of them at a pre-arranged time and wavelength indicated that the two merchantmen were already berthed in the Lingga Roadstead.

Early in September, *Dresden* dropped anchor close to her own supply ships. Gradually, during the month, the area began to fill up with units of the Japanese Fleet. By the second week of October all the ships were fuelled and provisioned. Even the massive *Musashi* reached the area to join her slightly bigger sister ship *Yamato*. The biggest battleships in the world. Nine enormous guns, in triple turrets capable of hurling two-ton projectiles nearly thirty miles. Impressive but useless when compared to the combined weight of air attack that the Americans could wage against them. Yet with their flags waving bravely as a cooling breeze whipped across the anchorage, the huge ships, together with three other battleships, older and smaller but still powerful ships represented the last major offensive power still available to the Japanese. With seven heavy cruisers and twenty destroyers already at anchor, the Fleet was gathering as a combined force. Perhaps it would be their last chance for glory. Or annihilation.

As Reitz looked across at the ships he felt both sadness and pride. His Japanese liaison officers had already hinted that *Dresden* with her radar, patched up that it was, after no major renovation since its installation, was going to be the key in the forthcoming operation. Off the Philippines. Wherever the Americans were going to assemble their invasion fleet. It seemed that the idea was to allow the Americans to land their troops but then the Imperial Fleet, led by these warships assembling in the Roadstead, would burst upon their supply ships just like *Dresden* had done so dramatically off Guadalcanal, and destroy them, thus depriving those soldiers of the means of sustaining their mission. The details were going to be outlined in a conference on board the *Yamato* as and when the Japanese were ready to set in motion their plan.

Gradually the fleet was added to – by more supply ships, tankers, destroyers, two more heavy cruisers and finally a light cruiser. IJN *Tanyo*. Captain Imoru Hatsu in charge. Hatsu had been very busy with *Tanyo*. When Tanaka's flagship *Jintsu* was sunk in action in the latter part of the Guadalcanal campaign, it was Rikoyu's light cruiser that was the replacement. She skirmished with the enemy, the 'damned Yankees,' off Truk, Rabaul and various other campaigns, escorting convoys and leading destroyers in an attempt to hunt down enemy submarines. Then, in mid-May 1944 an American submarine surfaced and tried to slug it out with the *Tanyo* but Hatsu, in charge of the cruiser's lighter guns, overwhelmed it and the American vessel sank. Five submariners were pulled aboard and taken prisoner. The next day an American carrier aircraft, on a lone attack, swooped down on the *Tanyo* and in the machine-gun attack, bullets sprayed the exposed upper bridge, killing Rikoyu and three other men. Hatsu, thrust into command, in his fury ordered the American submariners out of their quarters and on to the bridge. 'There' he snarled in his accented English 'this is what one of your aircraft has done to my captain and three of my men. This is what I'll do in return' and suddenly he snatched a machine-pistol from one of the guards and before anyone on the blood-spattered bridge could stop him, he pulled the trigger and sprayed the hapless Americans with a hail of bullets and didn't stop firing until the magazine was empty.

'Throw them overboard. They'll feed the sharks' he snapped at the shocked guard. The war between them and the Americans may have been vicious, the Japanese sailors had seen many of their ships go down but none of them standing on that bridge had ever seen cold-blooded murder carried out before their eyes. 'Well, go on, do as I say! I now command this ship' yelled their new captain waving his gun at the startled men.

A few days later *Tanyo*'s guns were in action again in the great air battle of the Marianas and the light cruiser was credited with shooting down three aircraft that were trying to attack the veteran carrier *Shokaku.* Hatsu handled his ship so well that the men, still smouldering after the murder of the American submariners, forgot their hatred of him as they fought to keep their ship afloat during the air onslaught. It was somewhat ironic that an American submarine eventually accounted for *Shokaku* although *Tanyo* contributed to the furious depth-charge barrage that forced the underwater craft to stay below, deep, deep down for nearly sixteen hours before the counter-attack was called off.

For this effort and his skill at manoeuvring the cruiser so well, Hatsu was promoted to a full time Captain and after his ship was repaired in Singapore from the machine-gun damage, she set sail for the Lingga Roadstead, being the last of the Japanese warships to arrive. As the light cruiser sailed past the massive bulk of the giant battleship, *Musashi,* Hatsu's heart swelled with pride. Soon, he thought, he would be on board her as the behemoth's next captain and with what joy would he give the order for her mighty guns to open fire on American ships. He lined up his crew to honour the salutes from the much bigger ship but as *Tanyo* rounded the stern of *Musashi,* to his shock and dismay at first, Hatsu recognised the ship moored aft of the Japanese battleship. *Dresden.* With her two merchant ship supply vessels. Hatsu hissed. To the tannoy he raced and barked into it 'All men. Back to your positions. Now!' Suddenly an idea came to the warped mind of the cruiser's captain. Yes, that was it. In the heat of the forth coming and expected battle against the Yankees he would close with the German and give her a full volley of Long Lance torpedoes. No-one would know. All he had to do was to sink it. He'd never forgotten the humiliation of that earlier soaking nor the punishment meted out to him by the now dead Ryoku. He could but wait for the opportune time.

Gazing across the anchorage Reitz did not at first see or even recognise the *Tanyo* but Serle had his binoculars trained on the cruiser's bridge. He saw the flurry of men disappear from their saluting positions and then coming into focus materialised the features of Hatsu. 'Hey Helmut,' he murmured to Brautsch standing next to him 'It's your non-swimming pal on the bridge of that cruiser. You know, the one that came on board us off Singapore.'

Brautsch looked through his own binoculars 'Yes, that's him. Looks like he's been promoted to captain judging by the gold bands on his uniform jacket. Maybe his skipper let him off after his involuntary dip. We shall have to see if he can fight his ship better than he can swim.' Serle grunted.

Hatsu stared up at the German ship as *Tanyo* slowly cruised past. Yes. Once the usefulness of the German battlecruiser's radar was over, once the great guns of the Japanese battleships were decimating the American ships; yes, once all that was taking place, he would deal with the German braggarts. Once and for all. Hate welled up inside him. Hate as when he shot the American airmen. He was a Samurai. He didn't need European leeches to show that he was a master figure. He could do without them.

Reitz bade the two Japanese liaison officers farewell. Their job was done. They'd delivered *Dresden* to the rendezvous. Soon would come the conference on board *Yamato* when the final orders would be given. They bowed in unison prior to boarding the launch that had come from the big battleship. They'd been polite enough but it was a relief to Reitz to witness their departure. Now he felt as if one obstacle to his eventual move to break-out had gone. Straight away he called his senior officers for a conference.

'Gentlemen, the next week will be the most dangerous in our time together but providing we survive it, we shall be sailing through the American sector over which, two years ago, we were again with the Japanese fleet, but this time we'll be on our own.

Somehow I have this feeling that the ships out there are not all going to survive their eagerly-looked forward conflict with their enemies. Sometimes I think that the Japanese have a haunted death-wish about their naval policies and to them a sailing to a glorious death, that is if death can be regarded as glorious, is part and parcel of their naval philosophy now that they are on the defensive.

I know that we are ready. Our fuel tanks are full. The extra ones we fitted, thanks to Herr Herzog, during our enforced stay in Japan will have increased our range by an extra two thousand or so miles and with this in mind, when we part company with our faithful *Olaf* and *Berengia*, we shan't see them again until we're in the latitude of northern New Zealand. Here, that is where we shall meet them.' With this, Reitz pointed out an area on the large chart of the Southern Pacific between South America and Australia.

'If we get there, I shall then put forward my plan to try and reach our homeland. I have it in sketch form only. It is almost as if we look to each dawn just to see if we ever reach sunset again.'

He then went into some detail about anti-aircraft procedures, the readiness he required from the Arado crews and to the engine-room staff, to be ready for bursts of high speed, especially in the initial break-away from the Japanese and through the American lines.

Only half-an-hour later a launch took both him and Hiltzern across to the *Yamato* where the Japanese were holding their final conference, led by the Commander in charge, Vice-Admiral Takeo Kurita. The two Germans were the last to arrive and were politely ushered towards their seats at the front. Once again Hiltzern's huge bulk seemed to be the equivalent of at least two of the more diminutive Japanese officers as he waddled his way through their ranks. An aide, speaking excellent German, which surprised Reitz and Hiltzern, showed them to their seats indicating that he was there to help translate the content of what Kurita would be outlining.

Adorning the wall behind where the Admiral would be speaking was a huge map of the sea approaches to the Philippines. There was a murmur of chatter between the various ship captains and their first officers but when a junior officer entered carrying a huge photograph of the Emperor, all present stood, and with the exception of the two Germans who instead saluted, bowed deeply as the portrait was carried to the table at the front. Behind the portrait carrier came Vice-Admiral Kurita, looking somewhat pale with sweat on his forehead. His white uniform was buttoned up to his short neck. His left-hand rested on a ceremonial sword attached to a hip-belt whilst his right-hand carried a sheaf of papers. These he placed on to the small lectern attached to the centre of the table.

After what to Reitz and Hiltzern seemed to be an age, their interpreter hissed 'Sit down please, gentlemen. Kurita is about to speak. I'll whisper the translation as he goes on about the great task we have ahead of us.'

Kurita looked down, worn and tired. He was trying to recover from a bout of a malarial-type fever and initially had protested when he'd been told that he was to lead the main attacking force of the proposed surface attack on the American ships off Leyte Gulf. The Japanese guessed that the enemy would strike in that part of the Philippines. The invaders were even allowed to land their forces virtually unopposed by the defenders whilst the Japanese fleet commander, Admiral Toyoda, based in Tokyo, set in motion the plans for the Imperial Navy's four-pronged assault on the American naval and supply ships off the landing beaches. To anyone not used to the Japanese military mind, the plan, in part, seemed almost suicidal.

Reitz and Hiltzern managed to get the main gist of what Kurita was saying, with his aides proliferating the large-scale map with various symbols as the outline of the plan developed.

The main fleet would sail for North Borneo, refuel, and then pass through the Palawan Passage into the Sibuyan Sea possibly drawing American air and maybe submarine attacks. Then, coming from the North would be four aircraft carriers, with barely an aeroplane between them, under Vice-Admiral Ozawa. Two battleships as well as cruisers and destroyers could be escorting this bait as Kurita put it, for fearful of a Japanese air assault on the landing vessels, the Americans would send their main forces north to attack Ozawa's ships, leaving the way open in the Samara Sea via the San Bernardino

Straits for Kurita's ships as well as two other forces coming through the more southern Surigao Straits; combining as they came through with two battleships, two heavy cruisers and other smaller escorts. For the first time in the war, the Imperial Fleet was committing virtually all its available surface forces including all of its remaining nine battleships. Grimly Reitz thought that it was a case of all 'the eggs in one basket,' exposed to the possible overwhelming might of the American air attacks.

Then Kurita stopped and looked over the faces of the men until his eyes came to rest directly looking at the two Germans.

'Gentlemen, this is a once-and-for-all plan. If we fail, Japan will fail. Naval supremacy for certain will pass over to the Americans. Our common enemy. But we do have one ace up our sleeve, one that has served us very well in the past. The presence of our German friends of the *Dresden*. Perhaps we ask too much of them. They helped us in our initial conquests; later at Guadalcanal and in the Pacific. But for misfortunes with torpedoes, they'd be back in their home waters. Three times our Kure shipyard has repaired their ship. Now we have asked for their help again for they have a radar system better, I regret, than any that we possess. *Dresden* will be in our van giving us the advance warning we shall need for air or surface attacks on our force. We know of her fighting ability. However once action with the enemy's surface ships has been joined,' and here Kurita smiled, a little, 'we expect to say farewell to our friends for they will slip away in the confusion. All we can say is that our best wishes go with them. You have served us well but your need back in your home waters will, we suspect, be even more desired. Needless to say, two of my smaller escorts vessels will sail with your supply ships to the Sunda Straits, for I guess that is where they will be heading. I and my colleagues applaud and thank you.' Then Kurita, smiling even more broadly, began to clap and soon the huge wardroom was echoing to the sound of all the Japanese, bar one, standing up and then applauding with a great deal of enthusiasm. Few of them had met *Dresden*'s captain but nearly all of them knew of his ship's capabilities. One man did not stand. Did not clap. Captain Imoru Hatsu. His action wasn't noticed as Kurita waved the men back down into their seats.

'Gentlemen' Kurita continued, 'we leave this anchorage and rendezvous at our refuelling point off North Borneo where, contrary to what the Americans might think, we still have some of our tankers still afloat' – there was a little ripple of grim laughter for all knew how badly mauled the Japanese mercantile fleet had been by American air and submarine attacks in the past eighteen or so months. 'Then we will be off for the real business; full details in your folders. Now, any sensible questions?'

Just one man stood up. Captain Hatsu. 'What air cover will we receive?'

The answer came from one of the aides. 'None from Ozawa's ships but possibly some support from land bases in the Philippines although they're currently fully engaged with the invasion forces.'

Hiltzern nudged Reitz 'It's him alright. The one who fell in the water' and then noticed the interpreter next to him broadly smiling. 'I hear your whisper. It is as you may say – 'a joke that won't go away.' Captain Hatsu didn't care for his soaking then and from what I hear, still doesn't like to be reminded of the incident. Not a friend of yours, I think!'

Hiltzern nodded.

Then the captain of the *Musashi* stood up. 'May we use our special Sanshiki shells should air attack develop?'

'Have them ready to fire, especially when we're in the Palawan Passage. *Yamato* will have them ready as well' came the reply.

'What are Sanshiki shells?' murmured Reitz.

'Like huge shot-gun pellets. Fired from the main armament. Scatter shrapnel into the path of approaching aircraft. Hopefully, one burst could knock down three or four of them at a time' came back the response from the interpreter.

'Hmm' was the only comment in reply.

Hiltzern was back to his pet theme.

'I suppose Hatsu is still on the *Tanyo*?'

'As always. The *Tanyo*. Your erstwhile companion ship and will be on the voyage. Look in your orders' whispered the interpreter.

'Which ship will you be on, Honourable Admiral?' came another voice.

Kurita looked a little vague 'Not on this one but on cruiser *Atago*, immediately behind *Dresden*. Oh by the way, she will signal us in, regrettably, English but now necessary as she won't be having any of our men aboard her. All of you have been assigned one signals officer who understands English. If you haven't, you must let me know before we depart from Borneo. Reserves can be flown out to us from Singapore by seaplane if so needed. Now, gentlemen, to your tasks. Japan has need of all of us!'

Then Kurita waved the men away but he beckoned the two Germans to him. He saluted them both followed by a short bow. Reitz and Hiltzern clicked heels and returned the salute. Holding out his right hand, Kurita extended it to shake both men by hand and then, to Reitz, in slow, halting English, much to the German's surprise, he said 'Admiral Reitz, Japan salutes you and your ship. On behalf of the Emperor, and his Imperial Navy, I present you with this sword' and so saying he unbuckled his sword belt and with both hands, held out the belt, scabbard and sword over to Reitz.

Reitz nodded in return, stepped back, saluted again and somewhat hoarsely said 'Thankyou.' It was all he could say for as he faced the worn-faced Japanese Admiral he could see a tear dribbling out of the man's left eye.

Somehow Reitz knew that he would never see the Admiral again. Or come to that, he'd only see the destruction of many of the fine ships in the anchorage. It was a poignant moment.

Dawn. Three days later. 23rd October. The shadowy shapes of Kurita's warships were behind her as *Dresden* led the fleet. To starboard, Palawan Island. The Palawan Passage. Four hours and into a wider space. Reitz arrived on the bridge as eight bells struck. Four in the morning. He'd only had a short rest. Somehow he felt that this day or the next would see either the survival or much worse still, the destruction of his battlecruiser. His ship. It was a cheering ship that waved farewell as *Olaf* and *Berengia* churned away from them after the refuelling. With their two diminutive escorts both ships gradually put on speed. Their aim was to pass through the Sunda Straits in darkness, elude any Allied air or sea patrols and then lose themselves into the vastness of the Indian Ocean during the night that would follow this dawn that was glowing ever brighter as *Dresden* pushed her away through the relatively calm waters. To port was the South China Sea. Reitz smiled ruefully to himself remembering the encounter with the brave *Anemone* nearly three years back in the waters much further to the north. Then *Dresden* had been the hunter. But now Reitz felt almost as much like the hunted. Although pushing forward to a target he knew that even in sea areas that their Japanese allies liked to think were their own, the Americans were wresting control. Then the sun began to push itself up over the horizon dappling the German ship's sides with a burnished gold.

Something was wrong. It all seemed too perfect. *Dresden* was in the van flanked by a destroyer and the *Tanyo*. Some three hundred yards astern came heavy cruiser *Atago*, Kurita's attack flagship. Looking aft from the port wing Reitz could see the bigger bulks of the two giant battleships. Every ship ploughing a straight, arrow-like wake. At a steady speed of twenty-two knots.

Then it hit Reitz. There were no air patrols. The destroyers weren't making any anti-submarine sweeps. None of the Japanese cruisers or battleships had any of their float-planes taking off. Surely they should. Even if only to keep down any possible enemy submarine. He flicked on his communication link to the Arado hanger ordering them to send off an aircraft at once. But the men had already anticipated his order. One of the Arados was already warming-up on the catapult.

'Radar to bridge.'

'Yes'.

'Small speck twenty-miles ahead of us. Fishing boat or maybe even a surfaced submarine. Not moving.'

In far off Hawaii a report reached the American Naval HQ.

'Large formation of Japanese battlewagons in Palawan Passage.'

It came from a submarine called the *Darter*. Almost as if expected. The Americans suspected that a Japanese naval strike was on the way to attack their ships at Leyte Gulf. This was their first confirmation. Routinely their liaison officer informed the small British presence. When Collins heard of the message he immediately asked if the submarine had sighted a non-Japanese type ship. If so, it would be *Dresden*. Back came the reply that the *Darter* was getting herself into position to attack.

'Get that bloody Arado aloft. Give them these co-ordinates. Full ahead!' yelled Reitz. The Arado shot into the air from its catapult. *Dresden* began to surge ahead taking the Japanese flotilla behind her by surprise. At the same time a light began to flash from her aimed at *Atago*.

Kurita snapped 'Hurry man, read –' but he was unable to complete his sentence for quite violently, huge columns of water began to soar up from the sides of *Atago* accompanied by heavy explosions and flames. Then to the further horror of Kurita, somewhat taken aback by the sudden torpedoing, another cruiser behind her, the *Takao* was also seen to be shaken by two blasts, causing her to slew out of line. Officers urged him to leave his rapidly sinking cruiser for within a few more minutes, the bows of the now furiously blazing and stricken *Atago* were dipping under the waters.

Suddenly there was another vast explosion. 'What on earth?' screamed Kurita, suddenly losing his balance as he was about to scramble on to an inflatable raft that was being held alongside. The Admiral fell into the sea as sailors desperately grabbed at him and hauled him aboard. Badly shaken, he again enquired as to the origin of that massive explosion. A smoke-begrimed officer told him in a shocked voice that heavy cruiser *Maya*, a sister ship of *Atago* had just blown up and disintegrated. Gone. Probably with few survivors. Behind Kurita, as he clambered on board a destroyer that closed with the sinking cruiser, *Atago* was in her final death throes. Then, in the distance, two rolls of gunfire could be heard. Despite his wet clothes Kurita clambered up to the destroyer's bridge. In the distance the brown cordite smoke clouds of heavy guns firing could be seen drifting in the air away from a speeding warship. '*Dresden*?' he asked.

'Yes sir, firing at an as yet unidentified target' came the reply.

Battleship *Yamato* was slowing down and as Kurita's destroyer came alongside, other destroyers began laying down a furious depth-charge barrage more in hope of keeping the American submarines deep down until the fleet, as well as the crippled but not sinking *Takao* could clear the area.

Stolle yelled into his microphone and short-wave radio contact with *Dresden* 'Come on! up two hundred, enemy submarine is trying to submerge. We'll go in and drop our bombs if ordered.'

Below them was a surfaced American submarine, the USS *Billings* some twenty miles from the Japanese ships which *Dresden*'s radar had picked up on the edge of the screen. Reitz ordered 'Full ahead' to try and close the range. With the help of the Arado spotter he was hoping that the big forward guns could either force the submarine down or better still could damage or perhaps even sink it.

Lieutenant Commander Everard Theophilus Darrian Willis was part relaxing on the conning-tower of his big seventeen hundred ton submarine. The wireless room reported that *Darter* was in contact with the oncoming Japanese. Willis decided on one last cigar before submerging. He knew that it would take probably another half-hour before a visual sighting but by that time, thanks to the radar he'd have them in sight at fifteen or so miles. It had been a good war for him. One flat-top, two cruisers, five escort vessels and about a dozen Jap merchantmen. All scratched into scrap-metal, a-rusting on the seabed. There was nothing to disturb his early-morning patrol. Only the slap-slap-slap of small waves pattering at the casing of his slow-moving submarine.

No-one on the watch saw or heard the drone of the high-flying Arado.

Then two things upset that peaceful scenario. As the blue haze from the captain's cigar flittered astern to mingle with the puttering exhaust of the diesel, Willis was lost totally on the thoughts of his war efforts. He heard a voice yelling 'Sir, sir, radar's on the blink. Loose connection. Be o.k. in about two minutes.' Vaguely he nodded. Then, totally out of the blue, two white splashes hit the sea about three hundred yards ahead of the boat's bows. Seconds later, two more soaring columns of water climbed up out of the clear sun-dappled sea. This time much, much closer.

'What the hell?' yelled Willis, his cigar sent hurling over the side. 'Which lazy sod hasn't seen or heard that Jap bomber?' This was to the two lookouts who'd almost fatally failed to see the Arado. Dreaming. Like their captain. Then the lookouts heard it as did their captain. Like a howling express train.

Whoosh! Whoosh! Whoosh! Crump!

'Radar's working sir. Single large speck three miles ahead of main Jap fleet'

'Shit and damnation! Big shells. How the hell do the Japs know we're here? Prepare to dive!'

Then one of the lookouts yelled 'Aircraft sir!'

Overhead came the Arado, spitting flame from her machine-gun.

Billings began to submerge. More heavy shells. Massive splinters rattling the conning tower. One of the lookouts gave a harsh cry as a shard of metal tore at his shoulder as he prepared to drop down the ladder.

'Sir.' A planesman. 'Sir, forward planes are damaged. Boat can't dive.'

Water was already pouring in up forward.

'Shut all water-tight doors.'

'Already have done.'

'Well come on!' yelled Willis 'Get her down somehow!'

More shells crashed outside. One exploded right on the bows. There was a searing flash. Water simply gushed in through the gaping hole. The electrics failed.

Willis realised the inevitable.

'Blow all tanks. Surface. Abandon the boat!' he yelled.

Willis struggled with the conning tower hatch but a burly petty officer banged back the restraining clips and it burst open with a crash. Water briefly cascaded down the access ladder but Willis ignored it. As he put his head over the conning tower the Arado flew across, a black cross on each wing.

'Holy mother of Mary' yelled Willis 'it's a bleedin' Jerry plane!' He shouted down the tower 'Wireless – get this message off to base and hurry. "USS *Billings* under attack by Germans; suspect *Dresden.* Am sinking. Forced to abandon."'

Men began to pour out of a side hatchway as well as from the conning-tower. As the Arado circled, Stein and Stolle could see the submarine's crew jumping overboard and some trying to launch a rubber raft. They flew in low again but mercifully for the abandoning submariners, they did not open fire. Also the shelling ceased as the airmen radioed the successful effort of the shelling back to *Dresden*.

In Hawaii, Collins received the news of the sinking of the *Billings* with a twisted sense of irony. 'So' he commented to Scott 'the *Dresden* is in there, to the fore, sinking one of their subs. Perhaps the Americans will listen to us now. It's obvious that Reitz and his glory boys have a radar set better than anything that the Japs possess. That is why the Japs must be using Reitz's ship to act as their advance-warning ship. We must tell our reluctant friends to listen to us. *Dresden* is the danger ship, not the bigger Jap battleships.'

Reitz ordered two of *Dresden*'s motor launches to be made ready for imminent launching as soon as they reached the site of the sinking of the American submarine. Stein and Stolle were still circling the two rubber rafts on to which the survivors were gathered after the *Billings* had sunk when *Dresden* hove into view. Seeing their ship, the little plane landed and Stein in broken English shouted through a megaphone 'Do not be afraid. Ve vill take you prisoner. Not ze Japs. Ve vill look after you.' Stein was quite pleased with his efforts from lessons in learning the language of the enemy during the quiet periods on *Dresden*, afloat or when in harbour. Part of a widespread effort on educational and cultural activities as set up by Reitz, for both crew and prisoners alike.

As the German warship drew closer to the site of the demise of the *Billings*, Hiltzern, with deeply furrowed brows remarked to his captain 'Sir, do you think that it is safe to be slowing down? There could be other American subs below the surface which we don't know about!'

'I hear you, Hiltzern' came the response from Reitz, staring at the scene of the little Arado slowly taxiing round the stranded American submariners. 'Look over there. Our aeroplane. She'll have seen any of their underwater sharks if they'd been in the area. From the air these waters are quite clear. If Kurita had given orders for a dawn air-patrol as well as a zigzag progress, he may not have suffered the loss of three of his cruisers. I am certain, as can be, in this very difficult situation, that there are no more of their submarines around and besides, not only do we have to recover our own aircraft but can you think what our Japanese so-called friends would do to those Americans? Sometimes I think that we have to hang on to what is basic humanitarianism, even when we are in such a potentially perilous situation.'

Hiltzern grunted and then Reitz continued 'If the roles were reversed, would the Americans bother to save us if we were sinking? We can't besmirch ourselves ever with the crimes of savagery, vileness, awfulness and general foulness that seems to be so common in this overlong struggle. Now that we're almost stopped it's time to get our plane back into place and our prisoners on board as soon as is possible. So, stop engines!'

Three launches soon splashed into the water with their usual well-practised operation with Brautsch and his boat in the lead.

He called out, via a megaphone 'Hurry up you Americans. We are from *Dresden* and we are not going to hand you over to the Japanese. The quicker, the better or they'll want you instead.'

Then one of his men started firing his machine-pistol over the heads of the swimmers and those on the rubber rafts paddling furiously to reach the launches.

'What the bloody 'ell!' yelled Willis 'Bleedin' soddin, lyin' Krauts!'

One of his men jabbed at his skipper's shoulder 'Nah, skip, them Krauts is not shootin' at us. Its at that o'er there, a bleedin' shark!'

Just beyond the swimming men, the water boiled and bubbled as the wounded and bleeding shark, in the act of closing in on a potential meal of a wounded American submariner suddenly found itself being furiously set upon by other sharks drawn to the threshing and twisting of its death throes. It was a grateful Willis who allowed himself to be hauled into Brautsch's launch 'Sorry' he gasped, 'thought you were shooting at us. Seen too much propaganda about how rotten you lot are supposed to be. Didn't really expect to be rescued until your airmen told us. Still wasn't sure until now.'

Brautsch smiled at him 'You shouldn't believe all propaganda. We are not all nasty Nazees! Ask your men to hurry. We're expecting the Japs to catch us up. Very soon. Ah, there's one of their ships in sight now!'

Within ten minutes, both launches and the Arado were safely back on *Dresden*, just as *Tanyo* drew alongside. A light flashed from her bridge 'What have you just been doing? Kurita wants to know!'

Slowly *Dresden* began to get underway with her reply signal flickering back across the gap to Hatsu's cruiser 'Found a nasty shark that might have eaten you for breakfast but we hooked it first.'

There was no reply from Hatsu's warship. Not that he needed for the *Yamato* was coming up fast and the English-speaking officers (there were three of them) were able to pick up the gist of *Dresden*'s light signal. When they translated the message to Kurita, freshly changed after his soaking, he merely smiled. 'I only wish I had ten men like the German Rear-Admiral and ten of his ships. Victory would then be ours but what do I have? Idiots such as Captain Hatsu. Ah yes, I know of his brush with Reitz. Nothing escapes me!' Two of his staff officers grinned. But really for Kurita, there was little to smile at for his force had lost three heavy cruisers and the Americans knew exactly where he was. But he also knew that he had to push forwards. There was no going back.

As *Dresden* began to pick up speed to take her place at the head of the fleet, Kurita on the huge bridge wing of *Yamato* looked down and across at the handsome lines of the German battlecruiser.

'Have this message sent to Rear-Admiral Reitz – "Congratulations on snaring one American shark. Scratch some more tomorrow of the flying fox variety. Good luck."'

From *Dresden* came just one word. 'Thanks'.

The day wore on and nothing else was sighted until late in the afternoon. *Dresden*'s radar picked them up first. Two specks. Reconnaissance aircraft. They came into sight but far out of gun range. A quick assessment and they soon turned round.

Kurita was thinking. During the hours of darkness the fleet reduced speed, not just to save fuel but also to extend the American aircraft so that perhaps the next day they'd only be able to manage one run each at his ships before shortage of fuel would force them to turn back. Even thirty or forty miles further back than what the Americans would estimate may help as well as delay their attacks. Attacks that Kurita knew would come. Until Ozawa's ships were sighted. The latest message from Ozawa indicated that his ships were exactly where the Japanese wanted them but so far as he knew, the Americans didn't yet know about their existence.

'Bull' Halsey, commander of Task Force 38 with his six big fleet carriers and their escort of modern battleships, cruisers and destroyers knew where Kurita was heading for – the Sibuyan Sea where he planned to hit the Japanese ships with as many air attacks as could be mustered.

He also knew of the other Japanese forces aiming for the Surigao Straits. To counter them he'd placed older battleships, destroyers and torpedo boats across and along the narrowest section. As yet he knew nothing about Ozawa's 'bait' of virtually empty aircraft-carriers. Then he received a terse message from Hawaii – 'Deal with German battlecruiser *Dresden* first, then the Jap battlewagons.'

Halsey snorted. He knew that the biggest surface threat from Kurita were his two monster battleships, probably extremely difficult to sink by his own battleships so they'd have to be eliminated, if possible, from the air attacks. Anyway they could deal with the Jerry ship after Kurita's battlewagons had been sunk or disabled. His plan of attack did not alter.

Soon after dawn, more American reconnaissance planes appeared. When Halsey received their news, he estimated that Kurita was about sixty miles further back than what he'd envisaged.

'Have the Japs got shit in their pants?' he snarled. 'Go on, get our planes airborne as soon as the yellow bastards are in range and take this force nearer to them. We'll give 'em quarter if that's what the little yellow sods want!'

Two precious hours dragged out before Halsey's air commanders were satisfied that Kurita's fleet was within attack range.

It was a tense time for all on *Dresden*. Down in the Sick Bay even the fans couldn't really keep the temperature cool enough to prevent Andrea from sweating. Or was it nerves? Just briefly Helmut came down saying that if they were able to get through the day when the air attacks were expected, then the next should see them attempt the break-through of the American lines. Two wounded Americans in the ward whistled as Andrea and Helmut embraced and kissed before he dashed away to his duties in helping to co-ordinate the ship's air defences. Andrea grinned at the Americans. Suddenly Doctor Lebers burst in carrying lifejackets, even for the four sick crewmen as well as the two prisoners. 'Tell the Americans that they must have these jackets ready to put on. Instructions from officer's conference!'

The two submariners, recovering from cuts received during the shaking that *Billings* had endured during the shelling from *Dresden*, smiled nervously when Andrea explained that they might need them as a result of American air attacks. They weren't the first Allied prisoners to marvel at her cool, firm manner. Nor as to why she was serving on what was really an enemy ship.

Lieutenant-Commander Willis threw as smart as a salute that he could muster when Reitz saluted him after he arrived, as per requested order, to meet the German captain early that morning in his cabin. 'Ah Commander, I am here to let you know that should my ship be torpedoed and bombed by your country's aircraft today to such an extent that we will be forced to abandon it, then you, even as our prisoners, will have the same right of rescue as my own men. Lifejackets will be issued to you all in your quarters and your guards, on knowing that the order to abandon ship has been issued, will release you and escort you on deck. From then on it will be a matter of exiting the ship as quickly as possible. As your quarters are near one of the secondary turrets, we will endeavour to get you out as quickly as possible. I thought I ought to personally tell you about this threat to my ship from your people. Somehow I think they'll target the bigger Japanese battleships astern of my ship but we shall have to wait and see. Please now return to your quarters.'

Reitz clicked his heels and saluted the American captain again. Willis could but mumble 'Thankyou', although his return salute was a trite sketchy to say the least as he was marched away. No offer of a drink as on his first contact with the German captain. Maybe he was still being steelily polite but the tenseness of Willis's replies to Reitz's initial questions about any more American submarine attacks only put Willis on to the defensive. This time he saw a hint of sadness in the German's eyes. Almost as if he felt that the American carrier aircraft would attack and sink his ship, half-a-world away from home. But then his mind hardened as he made his way down from the bridge. American soldiers were being killed as they strove half-a-world away from their home to free Europe from the scourge of Hitler's domination. Furthermore this ship, for all the apparent correctness of Reitz and his crew was a ship fighting on Hitler's side. It deserved to be sunk, even if he and the other survivors from *Billings* were still on board when it was going down. It was almost a relief when the guards slammed his prison room door shut behind him.

Kurita stared impassively ahead from *Yamato*'s armoured citadel. Sister battleship *Musashi* was abeam two miles away. The other three battleships were astern. Smaller and older but still powerful ships. The surviving heavy cruisers, seven of them, were ahead, abreast of each other but Kurita focussed his eyes solely on the relatively slim outline of the German battlecruiser some three miles ahead of *Yamato*.

'The Americans are making us wait' he commented to his staff captain. 'It must be at least three hours since dawn and still they haven't put in an appearance.' Then Kurita stopped. A light was flashing from the rear port wing of the German ship.

'What is it, or do I guess? American aircraft?'

'Yes, Admiral, *Dresden* has American planes on her radar about twenty miles away. Visual expected in five minutes.'

'Tell the gunnery officer to open fire as and when in range' came back Kurita's response. 'We will be ready for them.'

Warning rockets were sent soaring up from *Yamato* as Reitz watched the reaction of the Japanese ships to his messages.

'Aircraft in sight. Thirty degrees off starboard bow' yelled a lookout. Prebke, of course, always the first.

Behind *Dresden* the secondary guns of *Yamato* and *Musashi* opened fire. Dirty brown puff-balls of smoke exploding and drifting ahead of the oncoming aircraft which flew through the barrage and over the cruisers. Their target seemed to be the battleships.

Then the aircraft began to peel off in various groups. Some dropped to almost sea-level. Others came in fast, machine-guns chattering from the wings. The rest flew still high. Straight. Until black dots detached from them to fall vertically downwards. At the battleships. Apart from the main armaments, it seemed as if every Japanese gun was firing. But Reitz held *Dresden*'s fire. It was clear that the American planes weren't attacking his ship or the heavy cruisers. Yet.

The battleships began to turn ponderously to try and avoid the rain of bombs and torpedoes. And stricken aircraft. At least three were hit, bursting into flames and sickeningly spiralled out of control into the sea. From *Dresden*, those able to see the results of the contest saw bursts of flame on both the *Yamato* as well as the smaller Nagato but both battleships continued, speed unchecked. Soon the flames and smoke on both ships died down, the fire-damage teams obviously quickly in control at limiting the scale of any potential destruction. Even big battleship *Musashi*, having taken possibly two torpedo hits and three or four bombs, signalled that she could still maintain the squadron speed of twenty-two knots.

But her turn for further punishment was yet to come. Within an hour, a second wave of aircraft was reported. Again Kurita's ships were ready. Reitz watched intently, pushing *Dresden* up to twenty-five knots and releasing a smoke screen to try and hide his ship and those behind him for he sensed that this time the attackers were aiming for the cruisers as well. The barrage of fire was intense as the bombers dropped their loads astern of the German ship. Oddly enough the Americans concentrated on one of the cruisers, the

Myoko, and she was hit by about five bombs and a torpedo. Painfully she pulled out of line, unable to continue with the squadron. Burning and slowing down, she began to turn away, her crew desperately trying to prevent their ship being yet another sunken casualty.

Astern of her, massive *Musashi* took in more bomb hits and at least another torpedo or two. This time she signalled to Kurita that she would have to slow down whilst her damage-control parties struggled with the increasing, but not yet, fatal destruction on board her huge bulk.

For a third time, at around noon, *Dresden*'s radar again picked up yet another American attack. This time the planes dropped low. In front of *Dresden*.

Reitz yelled 'Torpedo bombers. All guns open fire!'

Flame sparkled all along the length of the German battlecruiser. The tracer bullets hacked at the oncoming planes. Three blew up. Two dropped their loads. Five more sheered away to fly, maybe battered, but still continuing over the cruisers towards the crippled *Musashi* now some five miles astern of the last of the Japanese battleships. Reitz was easily able to con *Dresden* into combing the oncoming torpedoes but as he looked back, he saw massive flames shoot out from *Musashi*. She was using her main armament to fire the special 'Sanshiki' shells at the American aircraft, two of which immediately spiralled out of control. But the rest flew on. To strike the Japanese behemoth with three more torpedo hits. And up to half-a-dozen bombs. The flames and smoke spewing upwards from the massive capital ship grew in fierceness and intensity, clearly visible even from six miles by the men on *Dresden*.

'She's had it' murmured Brautsch to his captain.

'Yes, but she's still afloat and taken a lot of punishment.' came back the reply. 'Trouble is, she's too big. Makes an easier target than us. Perhaps two more attacks and she'll be finished. Her sacrifice could well be our salvation.'

A fourth attack concentrated solely on *Musashi* and her destroyer escorts. She fought back but again took further hits. A desperate signal to Kurita indicated that she was turning for the nearest land in an attempt for a possible beaching. Kurita was shaken and ordered the Fleet's ships to slow down and began a reverse turn of course to possibly assist the battered giant but even as his orders began to take effect, a fifth assault came in. Ignoring the barrage again put up by Kurita's ships, the bombs whistled down and around the struggling *Musashi.* Her own defence was much weaker. Only one attacker was seen to be shot down. Four torpedoes, at least, burst on the starboard side of the slowly sinking battleship. Maybe another six bombs hit her directly as well. As the American aircraft retired, the fliers could see that Kurita's ships were still back-tracking. Not aware that this was still the attempt to help *Musashi,* they concluded that the Japanese ships were retreating due to their onslaught. They were now retreating. None of them noticed that *Dresden,* as well as *Tanyo* and two destroyers were still steaming on the original course for the Samar Sea, Kurita's ultimate destination. Still being tracked, as they flew away, by *Dresden*'s radar. Reitz commented 'That must be their last throw. They've come over every two hours or so and in less than two hours it'll be dusk. Signal that to Kurita and tell him to turn back at dusk. We'll reduce speed and still keep a radar watch!'

Kurita was badly shaken by the continuous attacks, even though the fighting capabilities of the *Yamato* remained fully operational despite the early bomb hit on the massive warship. Turning back to assist the shattered *Musashi,* he saw the wounded, crippled behemoth slowly come to a halt, listing badly with fires burning fiercely from various parts of the decks and superstructure. Destroyers closed in but the rear-admiral on the sinking giant lashed himself to a binnacle on the bridge blaming himself for the loss of his once proud warship. Slowly *Musashi* turned sideways and then capsized almost completely over before she slid beneath the surface taking nearly half of her two and a half thousand strong crew with her. Escorts nearby closed in to pick up her exhausted, oil-covered and grimy survivors.

'Sir' an aide saluted the dazed Kurita. 'Sir, two messages.'

Kurita looked at them. The first one was the latest from *Dresden*, the second from a land-based reconnaissance aircraft with the news that the ships of Halsey's huge task force were altering course to the north but the message was incomplete. It was presumed, said the aide, that the report was unfinished due to the aircraft having been shot down.

Kurita made a decision. 'Yes,' he said, 'We will take the example from Admiral Reitz. We will return to our original course. We still have the bulk of our main strength despite our losses. We must go on. Imperial Japan depends on us. We'll catch up with our German frends by midnight, if not earlier. Come the dawn, or soon after, we could well be upon the American supply ships off Leyte Gulf and the American admiral will be out of reach attacking Ozawa's empty carriers. By the time he comes back, his precious ships will be on the bottom and we shall be sailing back for our bases. Let us hope our Southern Forces will be giving us good news about their break-through in the Surigao Straits.'

Reitz received a signal from Kurita about the fleet's turn back and re-formation of the ships by midnight.

The stand-down to the crew on *Dresden* came as a great relief to everyone. Apart from that one short attack by the Americans the day hadn't fully tested them. They hadn't faced the ordeal that was the eventual fate of the crew of *Musashi*. Despite their valiant defence, the battleship's crew in the end had failed to keep their sixty-eight thousand ton warship afloat.

A junior petty officer unlocked the doors behind which Willis and his men somewhat shakily waited. Behind him were *Dresden* crew members with coffee, hot rolls and cheese 'Hello, Americanos' he announced. 'Food and drink at last for you all. Then exercise on deck. With my Kapitan's complimentos.'

Much to the Americans surprise the sailors then removed the gash buckets and two of them with a mop and bucket swilled and cleaned the soiled area. 'Well, we'll be down soon to let you out and savour the night air. Cheerio!'

It was indeed dark when the prisoners with their guards were let out. Dimly behind the *Dresden* could be seen the shapes of the survivors of Kurita's Central Force catching up with the German battlecruiser as the whole group of ships approached the San Bernardino Straits.

Nothing blinked out of the dark bare one dim blue light at the stern of the *Dresden*. Nothing was detected on the radar screen. Except for the whistling of the breeze around the superstructure, the quiet murmur of crew members on watch and the slap of the waves on the hull of the ship, it was very quiet. Maybe not so peaceful for the next furious phase would surely come in the morning. Even Andrea and her husband, out on the deck abaft Anton turret were reduced to quiet murmurings. Amazingly, despite the initial fraughtness of the earlier part of the day, only one injured man had come down to the Sick Berth to join the two Americans as well as his four sick crewmates. He'd cut himself ducking low to avoid the machine-gun fire from the sole attacking American fighter and in doing so, struck his forehead on a projecting piece of sharp metal. Two stitches and a bandage soon put him right, together with Andrea's tender words. By midnight Kurita's ships were back in position and a signal from *Yamato* raised the squadron's speed back up to its twenty-two knots. Reitz and all his senior officers retired to take a rest for they knew that it would be a long day once the dawn broke.

Kurita, before retiring himself and still feeling a bit weak from the fever, left word for himself to be woken as soon as news came through from the Southern Force at their efforts at breaking towards Leyte via the Surigao Straits.

Unbeknown to him, the Southern Force, soon after midnight was fighting a losing battle against a superior American force of old battleships, cruisers, destroyers and small torpedo boats. Before dawn the Japanese lost two battleships, a heavy cruiser and at least three destroyers. The few survivors, some damaged, turned back without signalling their misfortunes to Kurita.

When dawn came, and with it surprisingly grey skies, the seas were empty. Devoid of ships or aircraft. The way through the San Bernardino Straits into the Samar Sea was achieved without opposition. As Reitz came on to the bridge, a short rain squall swept across *Dresden* momentarily hiding her from Kurita's ships. 'If this weather keeps up, it will be ideal for our breakaway from Kurita, from the Americans and from anyone else' he remarked to the burly Hiltzern as his bulk loomed up alongside him.

'Yes sir, we shall just have to wait and see. Now, with your permission I'll contact all our departments to make sure we're all on the ball. Somehow I think that this is our decisive day – we get free of this lot or go down fighting as long-distance German heroes! Personally, I'd prefer the former option!'

Reitz nodded. 'Agreed. Check with the radar and wireless boys first.'

Their replies were negative but eventually the wireless operators picked up some rapid Japanese and even some distorted American signals but with too much interference to pick up anything definite.

The Japanese chatter was Ozawa contacting Kurita saying that he was under attack. Hawaii picked up both that and Halsey saying that he was cracking open another Japanese egg and going to make it into a monster fry-up. Just like his boys had done to Kurita's lap-dogs. Three battleships and two cruisers had been claimed with the Japs in full retreat. No mention of *Dresden* mused Collins as with Scott he assimilated the news and tried to picture the situation.

'You know, Scott, what if the Americans are over-exaggerating? What if Kurita hasn't been so badly damaged and during the hours of darkness has turned back? If so, that would place him here, clear of the San Bernardino Straits. Yes, just here.' Collins pointed to an area on his chart of the area. 'Ah yes, the Samar Sea. Leyte Gulf?

What is it? Say four hours from dawn? What has Halsey left behind to defend the transports?'

Scott told him.

'What? Destroyers and escort carriers! Oh the bloody fools? If Kurita gets near them, it really will be the cat amongst the pigeons!'

Collins voiced his opinions to the Americans. 'No way' came the reply.'Kurita's got his tail between his legs and he is a-running. We smacked up another load of Nips during the night in the Surigao Straits. Only these carriers to smash up and we've got the lot. Deep, deep down. On the sea-bed!'

Collins wasn't so sure. And where was *Dresden*? Surely Reitz wouldn't be running away. He felt that the German would be trying to make his breakthrough for if Halsey was too far north, Reitz would have a clearer run. Unless *Dresden* was already sunk. Was his ship one of the battleships claimed by the fliers? He told Scott to keep a listening ear for all the transmissions and to try and work out what was happening.

Four bells of the morning watch sounded. Still nothing from the radar room. Where were the Americans? The minutes ticked by, the clouds became greyer and the rain squalls grew in frequency, viciousness and intensity. Reitz walked over to the rear of the port wing noting that their little destroyer was still abeam of them. On the other side he knew that Hatsu's light cruiser still trailed them about four hundred yards astern of their starboard stern quarter. Somehow he'd have to shake them off in the breakthrough. Maybe in a prolonged rain squall. Another hour and he was going to go for it, action or not. He had to. He needed space and time. If the American aircraft had gone after the Northern Force, then he needed to get *Dresden* well away before dark and their possible return.

'Radar to bridge!'

'Yes, what is it?'

'Echoes. Ships ahead of us. Twenty miles. About a dozen or so. Slow-moving. Probably twelve knots.'

Reitz pondered the information. Twelve knots? Supply ships or an escort screen? Better inform Kurita. The Japanese Admiral read *Dresden*'s light message. His sleep had been somewhat restless. Sweaty. The fever hadn't fully gone away.

'Ships' he said to *Yamato*'s captain. 'Slow moving. Have your guns ready. A bit earlier than expected but we have them almost in range!'

Six thirty.

'Should have a visual soon' commented the radar room. 'Twenty degrees off the starboard bow'

'Alter course to cross in front of them. Away from the coast. Let's get out towards a more open sea' ordered Reitz.

Hiltzern and Serle worked out a new course. Whatever ships were over the horizon, *Dresden* was crossing them in front at right angles.

Behind them the Japanese fleet ponderously followed, all their main guns at maximum elevation.

Then a lookout yelled 'Smoke sir, Twenty-five degrees. Five or six ships. At least two of them are aircraft carriers.'

Reitz swung up his binoculars. 'Yes, small carriers. Not their big stuff. Probably the new escort type shielding supply ships. Signal Kurita 'Carriers and smaller warships in sight.' Give him their position and range.'

Dresden's big guns began to track the Americans who still seemed not to have seen their opponents.

'Good God sir, what the heck's that?' yelled Hiltzern.

'Sounds like thunder' offered the junior officer at the voicepipes.

'No such thing. That's the *Yamato*. Her big guns have opened fire' shouted Brautsch gazing over the port wing. Two minutes later *Yamato*'s big guns fired again. A truly awesome spectacle. Massive gouts of flame, a huge brown smoke cloud. All followed by the severe boom of the firing guns. The biggest naval guns in the world.

At first the Americans thought that the massive upheavals of water around them were aircraft bombs but then they saw the familiar outline of Japanese heavy warships coming over the horizon. Spitting flame and spuming smoke. Without hesitation the destroyers turned at once with their carriers towards the oncoming enemy.

Reitz at first couldn't understand. The Americans were not turning away. They were altering course directly for the Japanese. He turned his Zeiss binoculars on to them but it was an anguished yell from lookout Prebke that gave him the answer. 'Aircraft on deck!'

Of course. They were turning into the wind. To fly off their dozen or so planes each. Unless the Japanese shells hit their targets fairly soon, the Americans would be launching the first of a possible seventy plane retaliatory attack.

'Full ahead!' he roared. 'Open fire on the starboard carrier. She's nearest. And make smoke. Lots of it.'

Dresden surged ahead as her forward turrets opened up on the carrier nearest to them. The first salvo was short but then

'Cesar' joined in. Her two shells straddled the carrier's lone escort. It turned and made smoke itself just as *Dresden*'s next full salvo caught the carrier.

With unusual and spectacular results.

The front half of the flight deck suddenly reared up and then curved backwards towards the midships section of the carrier as if it were the opening of a giant sardine can. Then the escort's smoke and an enveloping rain shower hid the two battered American ships from sight, before the squall rushed towards the *Dresden* which steamed at full speed into it.

'This is it!' shouted Reitz. 'Hard-a-port. Steer three forty degrees for ten minutes. Make smoke. Use the extra smoke floats. Load practice shells into main armament. Train them on the Japanese fleet. Down our own ensigns. Up 'Stars and Stripes' on main mast and stern jack. Come on. Hurry. When we come out of this, we'll be masquerading as a United States heavy cruiser. Fire a few rounds of blanks at the Japs. Next rain squall. More smoke and a ninety degree turn to starboard. This is the start! Our breakthrough!'

Behind her, the Japanese heavy cruisers wreathed in smoke from the discharges of their main guns began to weave individual patterns as through the smoke, low cloud and rain, American planes took off from the scattering remains of the carrier force that they'd been shelling, as well as re-inforcements from two other small groups of escort carriers out of sight but within aircraft range, began to bite back at their tormentors. Almost immediately two of the cruisers took torpedo hits. The few destroyers guarding these carriers emerged from a rain squall to further harass the battleships of Kurita's force which took avoiding action from their dangerous threat of torpedoes. In vain Kurita tried to keep his force together but its cohesion was breaking up. He was losing control. Worse still, he couldn't see *Dresden.* She'd vanished. Then to his horror, from out of the smoke some twelve miles off the starboard quarter, a large warship emerged, firing its heavy armament. At his ships. Flying the Stars and Stripes.

Ponderously *Yamato* began to turn her huge guns to train on this apparent new menace. Kurita snapped binoculars to his eyes.

'Don't fire!' Kurita yelled hoarsely. 'It's *Dresden*! Reitz is fooling the Americans by pretending to be one of them.'

'But he's firing. At us!' snapped back the battleship's captain.

'What the blazes?' Kurita stared intently through his binoculars 'One of our cruisers is over there as well. Well? Is it? *Tanyo*? What is Hatsu up to? Don't open fire!'

Hatsu was indeed trying to keep up with *Dresden.* He took his light cruiser at full speed into the dense smoke being thrown out by the German. When it cleared he found, to his great delight, that *Dresden* had altered course and in effect hadn't outdistanced *Tanyo* but most pleasing to him, the German was flying American flags, as well as firing her big guns in the general direction of the confused Japanese fleet.

This was his supreme opportunity for his insane revenge.

'Full ahead! Torpedoes and guns range on that Yankee cruiser. This is our chance of real glory for Japan!'

Tanyo seemed to leap forward trying to close the range. Even his fellow officers could sense his excitement and were just as eager. The big ship flying the 'Stars and Stripes' that had appeared from nowhere so it seemed, although looking a bit like the German ship they'd been shadowing for so long, was not just flying those hated flags so prominently but was firing in the direction of their own cruisers and battleships. Hatsu urged his command ever closer, gripping the bridge rail in front of him until his knuckles went white with tension. Here was his chance. He wanted, above everything else, to exact his revenge. His hatred for that ship.

Lieutenant Richard S. Warkson, acting captain of the US destroyer *Ransome* was also consumed with the desire for revenge. Less than forty minutes earlier, huge shell splashes from the Japanese battleships straddled his speeding destroyer as she was being steered in the defence of the escort carriers. Splinters rattled the *Ransome* and his captain was one of seven fatalities. As Executive Officer, as he was then, he ordered the ship into a rain squall determined to close with the enemy as soon as he could. With rain, and the hazard of a heavy smokescreen, *Ransome* was running almost blind, her radar instruments out of action due to that splinter rattling damage. Occasionally the destroyer came out of the rain to loose off a salvo of her five-inch shells before dashing into another squall so that their enemy couldn't reply.

Coming out of another squall, still twisting and weaving *Ransome*, Warkson saw at a range of about five thousand yards a big vessel that opened fire with heavy guns in the direction of the Japanese. Big, dark, handsome. Flying the 'Stars and Stripes.'

'By heck that's a gorgeous sight! One of Halsey's big boys has come back and is laying out smoke to protect our carriers and is firing at the bleedin' Nips!'

Then a young midshipman, his left arm in a sling, yelled out 'Sir, look!' and pointed at a long, lean, low shape with three funnels emerge from another squall. 'It's a Jap cruiser. By 'ell sir, it'll soon be close enough to try and torpedo our new pal.'

'Aye, but the bugger 'asn't seen us' growled Warkson 'and she's coming perfectly in line for us to blow that three-funnelled load of crap to kingdom come. Right, launch torpedoes as soon as we can bear!'

Reitz saw another rain squall coming over from the starboard side.

'Cease firing. Make smoke. When we're in that rain alter ninety degrees to starboard and full ahead.' To Herzog he yelled down the communication line 'If you haven't got everything screwed down, then do so as soon as we've made the turn. I want everything for a three-hour dash. A hundred miles should get us clear of any immediate enemy search pattern.'

Brautsch interrupted him 'Sir, that Jap cruiser's still off to starboard. Seems to be trying to catch us up. Activity by her torpedoes. Goodness, she's opened fire on – us!'

Reitz dashed over to the starboard wing. 'Tell Halder, all secondary guns to open fire on that Jap heap of tin. It's Hatsu. He thinks we're American!'

Hatsu was fretting. *Tanyo* just couldn't get close enough to fire torpedoes. In desperation he'd ordered the cruiser's main five point five inch guns to open fire. Even killing some of those hated Germans would be something.

Brautsch shouted to Reitz 'Look sir, there's a Yankee destroyer sneaking up on that Jap lump of dung.' Just then, *Dresden*'s guns opened up. For real. On *Tanyo*.

'They're firing on us! Come on, close the range!' screamed Hatsu.

An agitated yell came from behind him. 'Sir, sir, an American destroyer! Off starboard quarter! Closing fast!' It came from an anguished lookout.

'What the –' Hatsu whirled, taken completely off guard just as *Dresden*'s shells crashed around his cruiser, followed by three massive explosions.

Tanyo seemed to jerk up and then crash downwards. Torn apart. Her stern section simply breaking off and vanishing. Then more shells from *Dresden* exploded into the disintegrating warship.

The amidships section turned over and was quickly followed by the bridge and forward part of the ship. The flames from the explosions were soon swallowed up by the engulfing water as the light cruiser turned over and slid rapidly into the sea. Hatsu's last sighting of *Dresden* was of the battlecruiser disappearing into another rain squall and making more thick smoke as she vanished out of sight. He didn't even scream as he, with virtually the whole of *Tanyo*'s crew gurgled their last breath as the sinking cruiser slid rapidly below the surface.

Warkson whooped with delight 'Scratched one Jap!' he exulted, watching *Tanyo* disintegrate but then the excitement drained out of him as *Ransome* circled the wreckage. A few desperate hands waved from the oil-covered surface. Survivors. Whoever they were, foe or friend. Must be rescued.

'Lower scrambling nets. Haul those Nips on board' he said somewhat harshly. Part of him was screaming to let the Japanese sailors drown but most of his inner self urged him to rescue them. The danger was over. He'd got his revenge. The harshness of war. Kill or be killed. Die or be rescued. The code of the sea. Willing hands hauled in about ten desperate survivors aboard as *Ransome* at a very low speed slid through the site of the sinking. The destroyer's sailors hustled them down below for a wash-down, dry clothing and a hot mug of coffee. Their army's code may have been never to surrender but all ten sailors nodded their heads and bowed in thanks. None of them could speak English. None of *Ransome*'s men spoke Japanese.

The job of rescue over, Warkson suddenly remembered the big ship that had almost been caught by the Jap. cruiser. No-one knew where it had gone. Vanished in the rain squalls. Someone thought she'd put out a smoke screen. But gone she had. Probably still chasing after the Japanese fleet.

Kurita was indeed a badly shaken man that afternoon. As his surviving ships fled back the way that they'd so confidently sailed through earlier that day. Kurita knew that the big guns of his battleships and cruisers had been defeated by the brave charge of the American destroyers with their torpedo threats and the relentless attacks by numerous escort carrier aircraft. Buzzing like angry hornets and wasps. Three more of his heavy cruisers sinking behind him. Burning. Two of them having to be scuttled being too badly damaged to be towed out of harm's way.

How many ships had he lost? One super battleship, five heavy cruisers sunk, two others severely crippled. Many other ships damaged. *Tanyo* wasn't responding to signals. That must have been her end when he'd seen the sudden violent flash on the near horizon. From messages to and from Ozawa's force it seemed that all the four carriers had been sunk together with some of their escorts and as for the Southern Force, his staff worked out that at least two battleships, one heavy cruiser and four destroyers had been sunk. The bearing of utter humiliation, not glory, was a sour and bitter pill for Kurita to swallow. He and Japan's Imperial Fleet had been beaten into, for the survivors, a running rabble of big, useless warships. Out-fought, and out-manoeuvred and out-classed by the rampant enemy.

But what of *Dresden*? Had she escaped? Unthinkingly he placed his left hand on where the sword in its scabbard would have rested on his hip. He hoped that it was bringing the German battlecruiser the good luck that had so desperately deserted him that day.

Dresden made just over a hundred miles in the next three hours. Arrow-straight ran her wake as she distanced herself from the life-and death struggle between Kurita's badly-battered heavy warships and their tormentors. Even after that initial dash, Reitz knew a search plane could, in less than an hour, range overhead and query as to why an 'American' cruiser was steaming at high speed away from where the actions were being fought. It was a risk Reitz knew that had to be taken. Twice radar reported slow-moving ships ahead but each time they moved out of range without showing any signs that they'd been concerned about his presence. Perhaps fast-moving individual warships were the norm for the Americans. Nothing diverted from its course to investigate the speeding battlecruiser. The seas, visually, remained empty until when it was two hours to sunset, Reitz ordered his ship to slow down to a cruising speed of fifteen knots. He knew that his fuel reserves had been rapidly reduced in the dash. Now he needed to conserve them. Down below, Herzog breathed a sigh of relief. It had been hot work maintaining and greasing the big, high-speeding engines. Now they settled down to the steady throbbing of normal cruising. The big engineer patted a casing 'Well done beauties' he murmured. 'You've done us proud.'

As sunset approached, Rear-Admiral Clifton Sprague, commander of escort carrier group Taffy-3, recalled all the missing vessels of his gallant ships that had driven off Kurita's battle-fleet. USS *Ransome* was the only vessel with any Japanese prisoners and it was due to this fact that the Rear-Admiral wanted to see Acting-Captain Warkson as soon as his ship was secured to her berth.

Sprague, drained as the day's details unfolded, had been cheered with the news of the air attacks on Kurita's force but when he'd heard of *Ransome*'s success against a Japanese cruiser, it put him back on full charge. Here was a true American determined to do his glory bit to avenge the 'Stars and Stripes' country fully after that dreadful day of infamy of 7th December 1941. The young lieutenant, in a fresh naval uniform, threw up a smart salute as he entered into Sprague's office on his command ship. Sprague looked up as Warkson stood there. Still bright-eyed and enthusiastic. 'Dear God,' Sprague thought. 'How does America find such young men, so keen to serve their country?' He smiled and simply said 'Well, son, how did it go?'

'Well you see sir, we'd just seen our carrier fly off her planes and turn back into a rain squall when we sees one of our big ships come out of another rain shower and start firing her guns at the Japs. Then this bloody Jap cruiser comes between our new buddy and us trying to close on our cruiser and to torpedo it. So I says we ain't going to let that happen so we dashed in and walloped it with three bang, bang, bangs up his jacksy. It blew up at once and vanished under in a very quick time. I slowed down and we picked up ten Nips that we've sent off for information. None of them spoke our lingo, nor we theirs so we could get nothing from 'em, sir!'

'What happened to that "buddy ship"? What was it like?' asked Sprague, drumming a pencil up and down, puzzled at what Warkson was saying.

'Can't really say. Possibly a "San Francisco" class heavy cruiser. Big guns, forward and aft. Flying big American flags. And she fired at that Jap cruiser just before we torpedoed it. Then another rain shower came up and we never saw it again.'

'Hmm! Could have been one of Halsey's cruisers. Maybe I'll check. But, boy, your efforts by scratching another of their ships should earn you the Navy Cross as well as promotion to Lieutenant-Commander and skipper, officially, of *Ransome*. Go on, boy, you've done the Navy proud!'

Warkson threw up another smart salute and turned on his heel. The Navy Cross. Captain of *Ransome*. 'Wow!'

Admiral Wenneker received a three 'D' signal at midnight. As per prior arranement with Reitz. The signal that he and his staff had anxiously awaited for the past three days. They'd been nervously following in their naval attaché rooms, the course of Kurita's Force. Nerves remained on edge with the news of the sinking of the two heavy cruisers from the submarine attack; then came the news of the destruction of the *Billings* by *Dresden*. It cheered them up a little but the sustained air attacks the next day on the Force culminating with the sinking of Japan's super battleship *Musashi*, made them anxious again. Another nervous day followed tracing the battle in the Samar Sea with the American destroyers and air groups. At least three Japanese heavy cruisers all caught and sunk. Kurita's message of retreat and defeat. Another three hours. Darkness. Then a further long wait. Nothing from Reitz. Until those three D's. It meant that *Dresden* was not only safe but clear of an imminent American counter-attack. Reitz had begun his breakthrough.

Yet Wenneker knew he had to give out the exact opposite meaning and so it was that 'Tokyo Rose' announced to her listeners on American radios – 'Japanese naval units have engaged American warships off Leyte Gulf and have inflicted severe damage on the enemy vessels. One of the ships in the Japanese fleet was the famous battlecruiser *Dresden* of the German Navy. The scourge of Allied shipping. It is to our regret that she has not yet reached safety after the battle and was seen firing her guns bravely to the very end. We salute her brave and courageous fighting skill whilst in the service of our Imperial Forces.'

'Very clever' thought Collins, who'd also been following the incoming reports of the battle. Everyone assumes that *Dresden* has been sunk. But does that statement say that *Dresden* has been sunk? Only not reaching safety. Firing her guns. At what? To the very end of what? But then Collins was perhaps the only senior Allied officer on hearing that news who did not cheer. Did not believe that at last *Dresden* had been sunk. Somehow a sixth, maybe even a sixtieth sense twinged in him saying that *Dresden* was covering her tracks and that she was in fact breaking through the strong American presence in the Central Pacific.

The Americans ignored Collins. They were euphoric. Even Halsey's apparent blunder of leaving the San Bernardino Straits open to Kurita's big ships whilst battering Ozawa's Northern Force had in the end been seen to be a brilliant extra turn of the screw that had defeated what was seen to be the last desperate throw by the Imperial Japanese Navy.

No-one even took Collins seriously. *Dresden* must have been sunk in the confused Samar Sea action. She was no longer in the picture. Collins felt deflated. He was still not convinced as October dragged into November and on towards December.

Highly convinced and delighted were the crews of *Olaf* and *Berengia* when to the relief of their radio operators, again as pre-arranged by Reitz, they also picked up that brief transmission at its fixed time on its set frequency at the end of the wireless range. Three 'D's'. *Olaf* responded at once with three 'O's' and *Berengia* with three 'B's' exactly an hour later. Reitz was given their replies as *Dresden* cruised to another dawn.

This one filled with hope. Tension maybe. But the main danger was gone. The actions with the Imperial Navy and the Americans were behind them. Their famous luck had held. Had seen them through. Dawn could never be so fraught again.

Chapter 11

'We think that it's one of ours'

The sun-dappled blue waters through which *Dresden* steadily cruised, flying prominent 'Stars and Stripes' flags, belied the fierceness and intensity of the ferocious naval battles that they'd witnessed just two years previously for deep below the warship's revolving propellers resting on the sea bed lay the barnacle-clad wrecks of sunken cruisers and destroyers. Sunk in the fierce clashes for Guadalcanal. One of those wrecks was the USS *Hurst*. As Reitz reached his position on the bridge after a breakfast of coffee and fruit, Hiltzern murmured 'Bit quieter today than yesterday or two years back.' Reitz nodded, remembering that desperate tussle during which *Hurst* had torpedoed his ship. Now *Dresden* was steaming steadily through these waters, keeping well clear of the inter-island traffic of small coasters, sailing craft and even the occasional native dug-out canoe. If the crews of these small ships saw the *Dresden* they took little notice. The 'Rising Sun' warships had long since gone, together with their army and aeroplanes. The 'Stars and Stripes' represented peace and life returning to normal.

Ashore, *Dresden*'s outline on the horizon aroused little or no interest. Life on land was also returning to normal and the sight of an 'American' warship cruising steadily out at sea was nothing to be commented upon for the fighting was over. On the shorelines of the many islands were various rusting wrecks as the main visible reminder and in places inland, the forest vegetation was growing and climbing over the abandoned guns, shell-cases and other rusting hardware.

Above the German battlecruiser the skies remained clear, even though *Dresden*'s radar tweaked steadily, searching for any signs of a horde of avenging American aircraft. But none came. They were all busy much further north seeking the shattered and demoralised remnants of Kurita's ships still in Philippines waters. Round about noon on that quiet day a speck was sighted on the screen causing the alarm bells to ring and the anti-aircraft guns to swivel upwards tracking the aircraft which young Prebke's eyes sighted first, it streaking a white condensing vapour trail. The aircraft carried on, barely registering *Dresden* many feet below for it was a medical supplies aircraft flying high to avoid any faint chance of a fast-moving warplane. The crew saw the German warship but assumed, like the distant coast watchers, that it was an Allied warship out on patrol duties. Nothing about which to get excited or alarmed.

In his base on Hawaii, Bernard Collins was trying to come to terms with the news that *Dresden* had probably been sunk in the furious action in the Samar Sea. Some sixth, or maybe sixtieth, sense deep down inside his thoughts told him that the German ship hadn't gone down with the battered cruisers of Kurita's Central Force.

Not even a report from the Americans about debris purporting to be of German origin failed to convince him – an oil slick, uniforms, packing cases, food packaging. One thing that wasn't on the list was any mention of bodies. The Americans shrugged their shoulders – 'Jee whiz, what else do ya want? That Kraut ship was sunk in the Samar Sea along with all those Nippon wrecks. If she ain't, she's hightailed it back to Jappo land where we'll get her there but we know, "Tokyo Rose" knows and you now know that she's deep, deep down saying sorry to mermaids for disturbing their tranquil life and soon she'll be the property of the denizens of the deep.'

Collins wasn't convinced. He needed evidence. He knew of the U-boat crews who, when under depth-charging, often released assorted debris to try and convince their attackers that they'd been sunk. Now just suppose Reitz had done the same? Sees that there is every likelihood of a furious battle, gets his crew to dump debris overboard and in one of the many reported early rainsqualls of the action, steams off into one, probably using a smokescreen as extra cover and makes his getaway whilst behind him Kurita's ships are milling around and some are getting sunk. Collins was determined to play on the fact that Reitz and *Dresden* had escaped.

Firstly, he decided to contact Admiralty Headquarters in London. The reply that they gave him to his request proved to be very interesting. Apparently the Nazi Press of Herr Goebbels, either on their wireless or in their papers, made little or no mention of the supposed demise of the warship that once featured so prominently in their often exaggerated propaganda. It was if they were saying something whilst not saying anything at all.

It wasn't much to go on but it was a start. Surely the Nazis, even though *Dresden* was a Canaris ship, would have paid gushing tributes about her heroic fight-to-the-finish. They'd done so with the *Scharnhorst* when she'd been sunk – so why not something like 'Heroic end of our gallant *Dresden*'. But nothing like that. Nothing but a brief mention of her being in action in the Samar Sea fighting American warships. Next, Collins went back to the Americans to press them for more information. A transcript of the reports of not only the destruction of Kurita's Force, but also the Southern Force and Ozawa's empty aircraft carriers that Halsey's Task Force had obliterated. As time wore on, bit by bit, he pieced the whole story together. About the two old Japanese battleships hammered in the Surigao Straits. *Fuso* and *Yamashiro*. Positive identification. No

Dresden. She hadn't left Kurita's Force. All four carriers of Ozawa's ships sunk. One or two abandoned hulks finished off as Halsey's cruisers and destroyers closed in but none of them had been able to catch up with the retreating Kurita. He then read again through the reports of the Samar Sea action. Had he missed something? Yes, that was it! The report from that US destroyer sinking a Jap cruiser. What was her name? *Ransome.* Acting Captain Warkson. The confusing bit was the 'big ship' that Warkson mentioned. A cruiser firing her guns at the Japanese Fleet. Flying 'Stars and Stripes'. Also firing on the Jap. cruiser closing in to try and torpedo it. Both this ship and *Ransome.* Firing at the same target.

Was that ship *Dresden*? If it was, why was she firing at Kurita's retreating ships and the Japanese light cruiser? What was its name? Ah yes, *Tanyo.* Very distinctive with its three funnels. Had *Tanyo* on seeing *Dresden* flying the 'Stars and Stripes', closed in thinking that she was an American? Was that why this ship, assuming it to be *Dresden*, fired back so as to prevent herself being torpedoed. Reitz, trying to escape with *Dresden* must have been determined to use any means available, even if it meant possibly firing on the warships of his erstwhile ally. Maybe his big guns fired inaccurately just to add colour to the whole confusing picture.

Then the reports from the aircraft pilots and destroyers disrupting Kurita's big ships. It was difficult to work out just how many of Kurita's ships had been sunk. At least four cruisers and a battleship were claimed. Could one of them be *Dresden*? Was he being too disbelieving of Warkson's report?

What if *Dresden* had escaped? Where was she headed? How could she obtain fuel and other supplies? No reports of any Allied merchantmen ships under attack had come in from either the Indian, Central or South Pacific Oceans. It was felt almost certain that the German blockade-running attempts from Japanese waters were now ended so any required help for *Dresden* couldn't come from them. Or were there one or two of them still at large? So many questions!

He decided, nearly a week after the Samar Sea actions, to put out a message to all Royal Naval and Dominion ships and aircraft. 'Suspect, repeat suspect German battlecruiser *Dresden* was not sunk, repeat not sunk, in Samar Sea battle. Keep careful watch and report any sightings of her to headquarters without delay.'

Collins felt that he'd now covered all possibilities and that there was little more that he could do in Hawaii. If *Dresden* had been sunk, so be it. Something deep down told him not to be too regretful of her demise, if that was the case, but somehow he felt for Reitz and his crew. Fighting half-a-world away from home. But then his mind hardened. *Dresden* had sunk up to half-a-million tons of Allied shipping. But was she there on the seabed of the Samar Sea? What if she was still afloat and trying to get back to German controlled waters. If she was, she'd be tackling the Atlantic. Sooner, if not later. He knew he needed to be back home. Like *Dresden* he'd been far too long away from his home country. He sent in a request to be transferred back to London. He could but wait for their reply.

When it came in the affirmative for Collins to hand over, temporarily to Lieutenant Scott and to catch the next available aircraft for the first stage of his return series of flights back to London, Sir Bernard felt relieved. Somehow he'd never been able to fully appreciate the sheer dominance of the American efforts in their attempts to crush the arrogance of their Japanese opponents. The Royal Navy's efforts were quite feeble in comparison. Only a few battle-hardened escorts and their crews from the Atlantic seemed to have any lessons to pass on to their American counterparts. The build-up of modern battleships and cruisers released from Atlantic and Mediterranean duties was, even at this stage of the World-wide struggle, proceeding only slowly. New staff personnel would come with them. Men and women with no interest at all with his fixation of his ideas on *Dresden*. Another thing that irked him was the apparent casual attitude and approach of the Americans. Never mind their appalling twist and twang to his ideas of standard English.

Yes, he knew that without their considerable effort since the Pearl Harbor debacle, the Allies would not now be in the strong and winning position that they now found themselves. Individual ships, like *Dresden*, even if she was still afloat, couldn't alter the way the war was going. As his aircraft took off from the sun-drenched airstrip, he steeled himself not to look back on Hawaii and the build-up of even more new ships in the once bomb-blasted naval anchorage, but instead, he tried to turn his mind to the task in front of him. Hunting down *Dresden*. He sensed that Reitz and his ship were still afloat. Somewhere in the vast swathes of the Southern Oceans. That's why, so carefully wrapped up in his baggage, was the photo of the German battlecruiser – at speed, so graceful but yet still so much a thorn in his thoughts.

Flying a large Norwegian flag, *Olaf*, off the south-eastern coast of Australia was sighted, ploughing her easterly course in a straight line with her wake as a faint white sliver of diminishing foam from behind her counter, by an Australian Air Force coastal patrol Sunderland. The big flying-boat lumbered over *Olaf* and continued with her crew taking only a cursory glance at the big tanker. The plane's skipper wrote in his aircraft log that he'd seen a Norwegian tanker, together with its course and speed. Nothing else. His orders were to look for a battlewagon, not an ordinary tanker seemingly on her peaceful duties.

At more or less the same time, a Catalina aircraft's crew flying RAF insignia sighted *Berengia* off the north-east coast of Australia, she having just emerged from the Coral Sea. Down in that aircraft's log went the words 'Dutch merchantman. 14 knots Course south-east together with its position. Before that patrol ended, the Catalina sighted three more merchant ships. No battlecruiser. When her crew reported back to base, their base-commander snarled 'What do they expect us to do? There is no Jerry battlecruiser out there. All that these brass-hatted Admirals can do is to fart in a colander, piss into a gale and then, day's work done, squeeze some secretary's tits and backside just to pass the time! What those memo-typing clots need to do is to get off their backsides and get down to the real job. That is killing as many Japs as we can before this bloody war ends!'

When clear of the Solomons and their outlying islands, reefs and other unhabited lumps of rock, Reitz knew that the seas ahead were clear. Well away from the shipping lanes. Well out of range of searching aircraft, if there were any. As *Dresden* pushed along at a steady thirteen knots, conserving her dwindling fuel stocks, all Reitz could think of was the forthcoming rendezvous with his supply ships. Even the food was rationed for all on board – officers, crewmen and prisoners. The mood of everyone was still apprehensive. They knew that they'd completed the first part of their breakthrough. Here, in these endless empty seas, the Allies possibly had no resources available to waste searching for them. How the gash-bin lads had laughed at the 'evidence' that they'd chucked overboard when they'd first sighted the enemy ships in the Samar Sea. The ship's newspaper had printed out 'Tokyo Rose's' wireless message. *Dresden* didn't exist. She wasn't here. She was rusting on some sandy sea-bed. Crafty one, the captain. But she was here. In a few days time she'd meet up with *Olaf* and *Berengia*. The wireless boys said so. Every day, the briefest of contacts.

What were their loved ones at home thinking? That they were sunk and feeding the sharks? Or had anyone in the Kriegsmarine offices in Kiel told them the real truth? Each turn of the propellers took them nearer to seeing them. The skipper hinted that the time for their return would be soon after Christmas. If they reached Kiel. No, the World must think that they weren't there. They could only get back if the Allies thought that they were no longer there but instead deep down below on the bed of the Samar Sea.

Quite a number of the crew expressed their worries to Padré Jervaulx during his confessional sessions. He told them that it was all up to the Almighty and the captain. When he was alone, Jervaulx fervently prayed and hoped for the peace he knew that was coming. He remembered his happy days as an assistant priest in the Munich parish in which he'd served before his call-up in the Kriegsmarine.

Was the church with its tall thin tower still standing amongst those leafy suburbs? Picture after thought picture raced along. Nothing coherent. Nothing making sense. All testing his faith to its utmost. Despite witnessing the sights of death and destruction he'd been able to witness his captain taking a communion wafer next to captains of the ships that *Dresden* had sunk. Humanity triumphing, in a little way, despite the surrounds of evil and horror. Then the long talks he'd held with Colonel Tibbetts. He'd grown to like the English soldier who, to his eternal sense of gratitude, spoke German fluently. Tibbetts spoke of home, about the peaceful rolling Dorset countryside where he'd spent his childhood contrasting so vividly with the violence of Crete, Malaya and lately Sumatra. Tibbetts, like the other prisoners, all respected Reitz. Their treatment as prisoners was almost as equals of the rest of the battlecruiser's crew. They all seemed grateful that they were on *Dresden.* Not rotting away in some foul prisoner-of-war camp. Of course they'd all said that they hoped that the Allies would win. That the Axis nations would be defeated. They also said that they hoped that when peace came, and if they and the crew of *Dresden* survived, it would be then that they could all be true friends. Not fighting but at peace. Humbly, Jervaulx could only say 'Amen' to all of that.

In his cabin, Reitz stared at Elle's photograph. Time after time in his precious moments of rest. He knew that the greatest test for *Dresden* was still to come. If only he could bring his ship safely home he'd be able to see his Elle again. Did she believe the veiled news that *Dresden* was now lost? Sunk? That he'd not been able to say a final goodbye? He'd been away from her for so long. Too long. The war dragged on and on. He was tired. A lot still needed to be done for him to see Elle again. For his crew to see their loved ones again. Still half-a-world away.

The wind blew cooler. The skies greyer. The wave-tops whiter and the troughs greener. Daily the three ships came nearer. In an isolated area of the vast South Pacific Ocean.

After the initial warning by the radar, it was again Prebke who first saw *Olaf*'s thin masts come into sight over the horizon. What was it about the lad? Always alert. Always cheerful and always the first to sight which others thought was still the unseeable.

Three hundred miles east of New Zealand's South Island. That's where the two ships hove into sight of each other, the rust-streaked plates of both vessels heaving up and down in the grey troughs of the rolling waves. The crews of both ships that could be spared waving at each other. Cheering. None more so than some of Herzog's engineers. They knew that the *Dresden*'s bunkers contained only three more days' supply of oil. There were no more willing men than them as they helped to haul the fuel-pipe-lines across from the tanker to connect with the battlecruiser's own hoses. Soon the vital oil, courtesy of the Japanese-held fields in Batavia, was rumbling and gurgling along the piping and into *Dresden*'s tanks. 'Ship in sight' came Prebke's cry some five hours later. The bulk of *Berengia* became clearer as she closed up towards *Dresden*. The relief of her crew was also obvious as they too deliriously waved their welcome. Until darkness fell and well into the next day, the task of re-supplying Reitz's ship went on without ever once being disrupted. No Allied ships or aircraft were in or over these desolate ocean swells. It was unthinkable that the Germans still had a naval presence in those waters. Yet there were the three of them. Still an active presence. Even so, the wireless operators on *Dresden* then gave Reitz grim news. Battleship *Tirpitz* had been blasted by heavy bombs whilst in a Norwegian fjord. Now Reitz, thanks to the picking-up of that New Zealand radio station, knew that his warship was the only major Kriegsmarine unit still on the high seas outside Germany and the Baltic itself. Alone but still very much a going concern.

Fortunately the wildness threatening in the grey skies held off sufficiently long enough for the re-supplying to be completed. With a heavy heart Reitz waved off *Berengia* as she attempted the run around the Cape of Good Hope whilst Reitz took *Dresden* with *Olaf* in company around Cape Horn. The likelihood of a capital ship sailing with the two merchantmen for company, if sighted by an Allied ship or aircraft, would merit too much attention in these southern non-convoy waters. Back in the Atlantic Reitz was hoping to meet up again with his faithful *Berengia* and somehow try to pass his ships off as a special Allied battle-group as he had done in the Central Pacific. Gradually the big freighter dwindled into the distance whilst *Dresden* and *Olaf* picking up speed themselves, swung towards the South American coast.

The two ships turned slightly northwards so as to try and avoid the worst of the Antarctic winds long-range influence and steadily the seas abated.

A long eight days passed as the two ships hauled their gradual way across a deserted ocean. The war was a thousand or more miles away to the north. Day after day of the rolling seas. Only the occasional albatross. One even landed on *Dresden*'s forward main turret and rested there for three hours. The order went out not to disturb it. The bird was reckoned as an omen of good luck. *Dresden*'s luck.

Then at last, when within two hundred miles of Chile's heavily indented coast-line, at forty-nine degrees south, the two ships turned southwards to trace their course for the Drake Passage. A brief refuelling to top up the battlecruiser's tanks and all was ready for the break-through into the Atlantic.

But first Reitz, with Padré Jervaulx, and with the day being Sunday, brought the crew of *Dresden*, apart from those on watch, to the deck abaft 'Cesar's' turret. Luth's team set up microphones in order to link the ceremony about to take place into the ship's broadcast system so that those crew members on watch could at least hear what was about to take place. Even the American prisoners were invited to attend. All to a man said that they would 'even if just for the fresh air', as one of them commented.

Reitz, Jervaulx and nurse Andrea stood on a platform of shell-cases, facing the assembled crew and prisoners. Reitz cleared his throat as eight bells struck to mark noon. A cool wind slanted across the assembled company. 'Members of my crew, and our guests. We have been together for three and a half years facing many dangers and I know that there are possibly more to come. But today we shall remember colleagues of our ship's predecessor and all the others in Admiral Graf Von Spee's fleet of cruisers who were in these waters thirty years ago. Our sponsor, Admiral Canaris, was on light-cruiser SMS *Dresden* as she sailed with her companion ships to round Cape Horn. This was after she'd helped to defeat a British cruiser force off Coronel. As we know, nearly all of Von Spee's cruisers were overwhelmed when they were chased by British battlecruisers based at the Falklands. Only *Dresden* survived but in the months that followed she eventually retreated to this area and finally surrendered due to her lack of fuel and inferiority to the British warships chasing her. It was when *Dresden* was sinking that the then Leutnant Canaris first began to work out the ideas that eventually took shape in this, our own ship. It is my hope, and I am sure, indeed of all you, is that we succeed where SMS *Dresden* did not and that is to get that warship's namesake back to home waters.' A few men cheered.

Jervaulx held up a hand. 'Please, gentlemen!'

The cheers faded away.

Reitz continued 'To explain further why we are here. Padré Jervaulx will be saying a prayer. Then three wreaths will be thrown into the sea. One by myself, the second one by Nurse Frau Andrea Brautsch.' Some more cheers – she was obviously still very much appreciated by those who had been under her ministrations. 'As Andrea is our sole English-born representative she has agreed to assist us in this ceremony. A third wreath will be thrown into the sea by Lieutenant Commander Willis, captain of the US submarine *Billings* who is our – ahem – guest. Please –' here he stretched out his left arm '– please come up onto this makeshift platform and join us.'

Willis looked somewhat surprised at being called forward. There hadn't been a day since his capture by *Dresden* when he hadn't wished for an Allied warship to appear over the horizon to blast this German battlecruiser to bits or for a fleet of bombers to obliterate her. Yet here was its captain extending a hand for him to join him at this ceremony. His knowledge of German was limited but one of his fellow prisoners had been translating the gist of what Reitz was saying. A junior engineer who had a German-speaking mother.

'Go on sir, go and see what they're going to do' whispered his young crewman.

Willis stepped up. Andrea nodded to him and whispered 'I'll translate for you.'

Reitz shook his hand and motioned to Jervaulx to continue. A sudden cross-wave slapped against the starboard side of the stern quarter and the spray whipped up to blow across the assembled company. Jervaulx wiped the dampness off his now somewhat tired, gaunt face. Even his hair had thinned and become quite grey during the course of this long voyage. He'd volunteered for the Kriegsmarine in the desire of saving the souls of errant sailors and never, like everyone else present, thought that he would have to be away from home for such a length of time. The horror of war, when ever it reared its ugly head, tested his faith and *Resolve* to depths that he hadn't realised but now here, on this platform of empty ammunition cases, he felt that there was the chance to put forward, even if only briefly, his desire for peace. When Reitz first mentioned the idea to him some four days earlier, he'd readily agreed. Retiring to his own small box-room of a cabin he wrote out a prayer and then learnt it off by heart.

He breathed in deeply, closed his hands in supplication and bent his head towards the microphone. His white surplice and purple stole flapped in the wind. A brighter splash of colour in the midst of either the dark grey or navy-blue uniforms of all those present.

'Let us pray.' A silence fell over the company. Just the natural sounds of the sea as an accompaniment. No-one shuffled or moved to disturb the atmosphere. Jervaulx hoped his voice would sound strong enough.

'Dear Lord and Father of us all. We who sail these seas commend our lives to you. We remember those comrades of ours who are no longer with us and we pray that whatever is our future, that we will be in your hands if our time comes to join them. We also commend to you, all those who in the course of these bitter struggles, have found their final resting place in the restless waves of this Earth's great waters.

'We also think of our loved ones at home – wherever they are. We think of the love that connects us with them and pray for their safety. Most of all we think of the love of your Son who gave his life so as to show to us the hope of resurrection.

'We pray that this terrible conflict will soon cease and that those of us who survive, may learn to be brothers and sisters again, shaking hands in a fruitful peace.

'Lord, we commend into your hands all those of our comrades of the Great War who died in these waters and may their sacrifice never be forgotten. A wreath for us Germans, another for the British, and a third one for all people – and for the peace to come, as it will one day.'

He paused. Then he said 'Now, in our own language, shall we all say the words of our Saviour who taught us to say "Our Father" –'

The prayer ended. Reitz took one of the wreaths and handed the others to Andrea and Willis. He jumped off the platform and flung his wreath over the stern for it to land in the slowly-moving wake that came out from the movement of the propellers. It bobbed and weaved in the toss of the waves and gradually floated away. Then Andrea threw her's in shortly followed by the one that Willis hurled into the wake. In silence, they watched the wreaths bob up and curtsey as they increased their distance from the ship. Then Andrea extended out both her arms and held hands with Reitz and Willis. Three people. German, English, American. Joined as if one.

As they stood there, Jervaulx uttered his blessing 'May the God of us all bless, preserve and keep us in his arms, today and always. Amen.'

Reitz released Andrea from his grip as the three wreaths drifted away almost out of sight. 'Thankyou' he said in English.

The engines rumbled into fuller life and the ship began to gather speed. The crew dispersed.

Then the loud speakers intoned 'Captain to the bridge.'

It seemed as if the war was coming back.

Reitz arrived on the bridge. Hiltzern, who'd been standing the watch, saluted him and then said 'Radar's had a small ship for some time. It's now in visual sight. Virtually stationary. Could be a trawler. I've ordered for the White Ensign to be run up.'

It was indeed a fishing trawler. Chilean.

Reitz looked at the stationary vessel as *Dresden* drew closer.

'Send Brautsch across. See if they've a radio on board. Better send Jervaulx as well. He speaks very fluent Spanish even better than Brautsch. Maybe they've some fish on board. Buy it with those forged English fivers that we still have. Warn the boarding party not to speak in German. No Kriegsmarine caps to be worn. Probably only simple fishermen. We must keep up our pretence of being Royal Navy.'

The coal-fired Chilean trawler was totally dwarfed by *Dresden* as the battlecruiser edged to within two hundred yards. The Chileans were pleased to see a 'White Ensign' flying from the warship's main mast. Then they saw two launches hit the water and start up towards them.

A tinny voice through the loud-hailer shouted 'Do you speak English?'

The fishermen looked bemused.

'Spaniardo? Si?' came another voice.

One of the Chileans nodded. 'Si! Si!'

The leading launch drew alongside. Jervaulx asked if they had a radio. The reply was negative. Then he asked if they had any fish. Plenty. How much? Say, ten or more boxes? For crisp English five-pound notes that they could exchange at a bank? Say one hundred English pounds?

The fisherman gasped. A week's profit in just five minutes. Of course the 'Ingleesi' could have as much fish as the boats could carry. It was good quality. Plenty more in the sea.

Twenty cases of fish were transferred, ten each to the two boats. Then their visitors returned to the big warship. The Chileans waved them farewell. All they could think of was all that extra money that they'd just earned. Cash for their families. It was going to be a merry Christmas for them.

They watched the warship steer out towards the western horizon.

After an hour, *Dresden* turned south and rejoined *Olaf* further out at sea whose crew were mightily relieved to see their guardian warship re-appear.

Those late November seas around Cape Horn were doing their best to live up to their 'Roaring Forties' reputation. The seas gradually built up to massive waves, each bent on a mission to hurl anything in their path contemptuously out of the way. Or throwing an object in them like a matchstick in a violent whirlpool. A voracious one at that. Only these matchsticks were a twenty-six thousand ton battlecruiser together with a tanker of nearly twelve thousand tons. Frequently *Olaf* looked more like a submarine at times for her well-decks were submerged in a welter of sea-green water with accompanying white streaks of foam and bubbles. Being the excellent sea-boat that she was, *Dresden*'s flared bows were able to throw most of the waves aside but even at a reduced speed of twelve knots there were times when her triple screws came clear of the water as she topped the plunging crests that carried her in sometimes quite an alarming corkscrew manner as she made her way across the send of the sea which was trying its best to engulf her.

Reitz had rarely witnessed such a storm as wild as this one but he was highly pleased. No-one in their right senses would come searching for them in the violent weather and so he set *Dresden*'s course as close as he could to the tip of Cape Horn. Within thirty miles. Everything possible was battened down and no-one was keeping watch in an exposed position. The precious radar masts had been removed soon after leaving the Chilean trawler. Two cases of fish had also been transferred to *Olaf* before the storm had broke. Not that the chefs could make much use of them for cooking a meal in their galleys was nigh impossible. Movement around the ship was limited only to vitally necessary journeys. Only in the Sick Berth was there anything more than the usual activity as Doctor Lebers, Nurse Andrea and their staff were almost constantly bandaging up sprained wrists and ankles and in some cases, some broken ones as well from sailors who'd been unable to keep their balance in the wild motion that the ship was experiencing. Safety ropes were rigged on deck for anyone who needed to go out to deal with any required emergency work of lashing down. None of the weapons were manned. Nearly all the crew simply lay down when not on duty and even for such hardened seamen, there were quite a number who succumbed to sea-sickness as the battlecruiser rolled and heaved in the wild waters.

But Reitz was pleased. The break-through into the South Atlantic couldn't have had better weather.

3rd December. The five-day storm at last abated and the two ships rounded Cape Horn. They emerged into the South Atlantic and speed was increased to *Olaf*'s near maximum of fifteen knots. The salt that had settled on the superstructure of *Dresden* was washed down and the crew were kept busy on repairing damage, where possible, caused by the storm. One of the smaller boats was found to be badly holed and two of the big emergency rubber inflatables had vanished in the storm. But all-in-all the battlecruiser was soon ready for action again. She'd weathered her worst storm and Reitz set her on a tortuitous course as she and *Olaf* made their way northwards to their hoped for rendezvous with *Berengia.*

But she didn't respond to *Dresden*'s coded signals. Perhaps she'd broken down. Or had been delayed by a storm. Reitz was worried for her safety.

He had every right to bè worried. Theider, by taking a careful route eventually steered his ship into the sea-lanes around Madagascar, flying a Dutch flag, but as she began to draw clear of Cape Town, she came under the scrutiny of Lieutenant Roy Milton, RNVR on board HMS *Dumfries*, a modified 'Mauritius' class cruiser. He was standing the forenoon watch that 8th December half-dreaming when a lookout yelled 'Merchantman in sight.' Radar had already tracked the strange ship on its screens for half-an-hour before the *Berengia* eventually hove into sight.

Milton stared intently at the oncoming merchantman. He was aware of something inside his mind that said that the ship was familiar with him but he couldn't think at that moment for if it was what he thought, the idea seemed to be too preposterous to dare tell his captain, who was probably snoring his head off in his cabin. *Dumfries* and her two escorting destroyers were on their way to join the Royal Navy's build-up to resuming a fuller offensive against Japan.

Bloodied from Atlantic and Arctic convoy duty, the journey to Ceylon, via Simonstown, was looked on by many in the cruiser, as well as on the destroyers, as a sort of holiday cruise. Away from the harshness of the European conflict coming towards its final stages where the Kriegsmarine, on and below the waves was no longer a serious threat. Its last big threat, the *Tirpitz*, was now a bomb-blasted wreck in a Norwegian Fjord.

The war seemed an aeon away.

Until Milton recognised the slowing-down merchantman. According to her flag she was Dutch. Even her colour-scheme suggested as much. He'd seen enough of them whilst on convoy duty. He was sure that the ship wasn't what she purported to be. But was he right? Surely he couldn't be. Not here. Not now. Yes, that was it. He'd been first-mate on a timber ship just leaving the now battered North German port of Lubeck when he was sure that he'd seen this big freighter coming into the harbour area. She was English then. They'd exchanged words. What was her name? Yes, he remembered.

Berengia. Next port-of-call for her was Rotterdam. It was then July 1939. Not been seen since May 1940.

Now she was here. Slowing down. He was sure it was her, even if she was signalling that she was the Dutch ship *Meerberke.* His thoughts were interrupted as the captain, Commander Thomas St. Johnston, a dour Northumbrian, came up to him. St. Johnston was sleeping when the alarm bells started up. He wasn't too pleased to having been disturbed.

'Well Milton? Why the sudden alarm? For just another merchantman? Can't you deal with it, eh?'

'Not this time, sir. You see, I think that she's German. She's already wirelessed that she's been stopped by an unidentified warship. Keeps repeating her name. *Meerberke.* Over and over again.'

'Standard procedure for lone merchantmen. Been either too long at sea or seen too many movies about baddie Jerry raiders. Damn it, Milton, there's none of them left. *Tirpitz* upside down in Norway and *Dresden* sunk fighting for the Japs. You know, Milton, that we have a huge 'White Ensign' flying from our mainmast. Even the thickest merchant skipper can see that we are Royal Navy.'

St. Johnston's voice was heavy with sarcasm. Especially when dealing with RNVR officers. The only trouble was that Milton was never wrong in his judgement.

Dumfries was still over five thousand yards away from the now stopped supposed *Meerberke* and Milton still remembered the crestfallen face of his training officer when he'd broken the news to them about the loss of the *Sydney* when she'd gone in too close to a disguised Nazi raider masquerading as an innocent merchantman.

'Alright, Milton, I'll take over now' said St. Johnston.

'Careful sir. If she's a Jerry, she could have hidden guns.'

'Look 'ere. Jerry last had a blockade runner nearly two years ago. Been no disguised raiders for over a year. Must be getting really desperate if this is one.'

'She is, sir. Last time I saw her she was British. I reckon she's been captured since then and been used as a blockade-runner. Her real name is *Berengia.* I'm sure of it.'

'Mmmm' murmured St. Johnston, impressed with Milton's sure certainty as to the identity of the now stopped stranger which was still repeating her signal, slowly, by a stuttering lamp. '*Meerberke.* Cape Town to Liverpool.' After a long pause, the stranger's lamp also flashed out 'Who are you?'

St. Johnston spluttered 'Cheeky sods! Reply – "HMS *Dumfries* and escort. Stay put. Sending boarding party to check papers". Come on! Get that boat launched and you, Milton, go on. Get across. Let's see if she's a bleedin' Jerry!'

The engines of *Dumfries* went into reverse slowing the cruiser down. Three thousand yards. No nearer.

Milton's launch surged into the ripple of the cruiser's fading wash. 'Hurry' he snapped, 'I think that ship's going to scuttle. They're abandoning her. Come on, move it!' The boat's coxswain opened up the launch's throttles but even as he did so, two muffled explosions came from the big merchantman. Milton swore 'Christ! They are bleeding Jerries. Come on, get closer!'

The coxswain kept his cool. Milton might be a good officer but he was after all RNVR. Too bloody keen! Even when we is supposed to be having a quiet cruise.

Milton's launch came up towards the sinking ship. The two lowered boats, full of crewmen, were getting underway as they picked up the last four men, one an officer, as they slid down rope ladders. The officer, with the ubiquitous white cap, stood up in one of the departing boats, his right arm in a meticulous naval salute as he looked across at his former command now well down at the bows. Her stern came clear. Close-up Milton could just make out the blacked-out letters of her name. *BERENGIA.* Just as he'd thought.

More explosions hastened the big freighter's end. With a final spurt of steam from her stern-situated funnel, she slipped under the South Atlantic surface.

Milton challenged the officer standing in the boat. He noted that there were tears in his eyes. 'You weren't *Meerberke*. Your ship used to be the *Berengia*, an English-owned merchantman that you Germans must have commandeered. Weren't you? A supply ship or perhaps now, a blockade-runner!'

'You know?' came an heavily accented answer in English.

Milton spoke in German 'Captain. I speak German fluently. Yes, I saw her in July of thirty-nine in Lubeck. Your paint work didn't fool me.'

'Ach so. You are quite right. I was captain of the last of the blockade-runners. We had to try. Couldn't stay in Singapore for ever. Now we are your prisoners.'

'Yes, please accept our courtesies and follow my launch to the cruiser.'

'Young man. There is one question that I must ask. Why did you stop us? Seriously.'

'You've never ever been able to alter the cruiser-stern, have you?'

Theider nodded and with a wry smile, sat down as his boat pulled her way across to *Dumfries*. He'd firmly instructed his men to admit that they were a German blockade-runner but to say nothing about *Dresden* or *Olaf*. Unable to bluff his way out from the overwhelming presence of the British warships, he'd sent out his false call for help in the hopes that *Dresden* would pick it up. His wireless man told him that just one letter, 'D', had been picked up in response on their special wavelength. Theider hoped that the British had no idea as to the real purpose of his ship. Very soon, his boat came alongside *Dumfries*. He and his men climbed the proffered ladders to her decks where an armed guard waited for them. Milton's launch was hooked onto her falls and hoisted up to her berth. Milton waited for the Germans as they arrived on deck. Theider saluted him and said 'Thankyou, officer. My men are safe now.'

St Johnston didn't bother to go down and see the prisoners. Rather laconically he sent off a message to their Lordships in London's Admiralty Headquarters Offices 'Guess what we stopped today? One Jerry blockade runner.' Unfortunately he failed to mention the ship's name. Not for three hours until another signal came to his ship now well on course for rounding the Cape for Simonstown.

The reply '*Meerberke*,' the pseudonym for *Berengia*, seemed to satisfy their Lordships. No-one bothered to check the file on *Dresden* for the possible names of her supply ships.

With a heavy heart Reitz realised that his faithful supply ship, which had been so much a close part of all their lives, and a highly important element towards *Dresden*'s success, was no longer. Thank goodness she'd been on her own. He hoped that Theider's men wouldn't disclose his whereabouts if they'd been taken prisoner. Instructing his wireless men to keep a keen watch for any extra activity on the airwaves, he decided to stay in a quiet area of the South Atlantic for a few days, avoiding any Allied ships. If he was to pass off as a Royal Navy warship, or an American one, he wanted a ship that didn't look as if it was one that had been battered too much by gales and heavy seas. The cleaning and repair work continued as the seas grew calmer and the sun became hotter. Each day an Arado took off. Looking for a suitable merchantman to replace *Berengia.*

When, early on Christmas Eve, off the eastern coast of Brazil, one such possible victim was sighted.

Where a somewhat untidy Argentinian captain was scratching his scrawny neck and screwing up his tired eyes as he gazed, without conviction, over the bows of his slow-moving, dirty but ironically well-stocked merchantman carrying frozen meat, eggs, vegetables and fruit.

Europe bound she'd ploughed out of Buenos Aries a few days earlier with her crew ill-motivated to be at sea at Christmas-time, war needs or not.

On that Christmas Eve morning none of the scruffy, scrawny-necked captain's crew sighted a stiff-winged bird but it had seen them, loitering along at nine knots, alone on the shimmering sunlit waters far below it. The 'bird' wheeled away and flew back to *Dresden* with the course and speed of the single merchantman.

Carefully Reitz approached it. Not that it wasn't difficult to find for the freighter trailed a lugubrious smoke-cloud a long way behind her stern. Even when *Dresden* was within two miles of the ship, there was no sign of any of her crew, nor her captain, having noticed the warship coming up astern of them. Perhaps only three of her crew were vaguely awake. The helmsman, the second engineer and a lookout up in the crow's nest of the foremast whose view to the stern was limited seeing all that he did was to stare vaguely and dreamily like his captain ahead of him. Over the bows.

'Merry Christmas to our Argentinian friends. Have you any spare eggs or beef on board?. We're sending a boat' came a somewhat tinny English-speaking voice from *Dresden*'s loud hailer.

Captain Sanchos Alberto da Silva looked up as he heard the voice. Vaguely he stared over the side of the bridge.

'Melly Chrissmus, ze Inglesi' he shouted and waved his arms around. He wasn't really sober. Too much bottle already for the festive season.

'Stop your ship, please' came the voice from which da Silva could now focus on as a very big warship flying a 'White Ensign'.

The helmsman leaned over and pulled the engine-room telegraph to 'stop'.

Before de Silva or his nondescript crew could fully realise what was happening, a motor launch from the warship reached their ship and smart uniformed sailors swarmed on board but to da Silva's surprise, they carried sub-machine guns or rifles.

One of the white-capped men spoke to da Silva, in Spanish, asking him for his ship's papers. As well as the papers, da Silva offered Jervaulx a banana 'Ze gift for zis Christmas, senor Inglesi.'

Jervaulx showed the ship's manifest to Brautsch who quickly understood that the ship had more food on it than enough. Da Silva, with more fake English five-pound notes being thrust under his nose, readily agreed to sell part of his cargo to the 'Inglesi' warship. Brautsch signalled Reitz to bring *Dresden* alongside and in return, da Silva's crew opened up the hatches. Soon carcasses of frozen meat and crates of fresh food were being passed over, using *Dresden*'s cranes, across to the battlecruiser.

Unseen by da Silva, Engineer Luth went down into the engine-room, and with the Brazilian's engine-room crew on deck having a breath of air, he and two of his men succeeded in disabling the freighter's engine to such an extent that the merchantman would only be able to sail at four knots. Similarly, other men entered the wireless room, gave the operator some cigarettes and a bottle of rum for him to enjoy outside. Quickly they cut or removed vital wires and valves from the radio set so as to render it inoperable. Two other sailors checked for small radios in the ship's lifeboats but could find nothing to suggest such an apparatus. When they finished their furtive work, they reported to Brautsch that their task was complete.

Within a couple of hours *Dresden* steamed away from the now crippled *Juanita* having restocked her larder with the *Juanita*'s crew thinking that they'd traded with an English warship. Hurriedly Reitz put on speed to rejoin *Olaf* which had continued on her course out of sight of the meeting with the *Juanita*.

Captain da Silva was perplexed when his engineer said that for some unexplained reason, two vital couplings had broken and that the best he could get out of the ship's engines was little more than a crawl. Dockyard work was the only option open to them, he said.

'But where do we go?' wailed da Silva, slowly sobering up and becoming increasingly suspicious that the warship that had been flying thc English Navy's flag was perhaps not what she had purported to have been.

'Buenos Aries where we came from' was his engineer's reply.

Slowly *Juanita* swung her bows to start her laborious crawl back to her start-point. When the radio officer also reported that his instrument was also inoperable, da Silva's brows furrowed even deeper. It could take at least a week before he could get his ship back to harbour. What would the authorities say? After all, it was Christmas Eve. Oh, what a headache of a dilemma!

Well over the horizon from *Juanita*, *Dresden* caught up with *Olaf* and in the gathering gloom, hurriedly transferred some of *Juanita*'s produce so that *Olaf*'s crew could have enough food to see them through to home-waters.

Then it was full speed for *Olaf* at sixteen knots with *Dresden* as her close companion as they pushed north to get out of the 'narrows' as the area between north-east Brazil and the western coastline of Africa was often called.

Reitz planned their breakthrough into the North Atlantic for Christmas Day in the hopes that Allied vigilance would be at its slackest due to the festive season – even in time of war the celebrations, although muted, would probably still be held, on land and at sea. At least, that was his hope as the two ships furrowed their course into the North Atlantic.

The crews stood their watches on Christmas Day knowing that their survival depended on their vigilance and efforts. The radar tweaked on its mountings and every three hours, throughout the daylight hours, an Arado took off to search the seas and to report on any ship sighted in the vicinity.

'Nothing to report.' The seas were empty.

Only when the night sky darkened did Reitz dare to devote time for a Christmas celebration. Padré Jervaulx conducted three masses for *Dresden*'s crew and at one of them, the American prisoners were allowed to attend. *Olaf* came up close, and using a breeches buoy, the priest went across to conduct a carol service for the tanker's crewmen. *Dresden*'s band played Christmas carols and their sentimental melodies sent many a shiver through those listening as they thought of their loved ones. Perhaps only a couple or so weeks away from them.

Via various shifts, those off-duty shared in a meal of beef and vegetables, followed by a fruit salad, all courtesy of the *Juanita.*

Tough guy Schenke dressed up as Santa Claus and distributed presents to everyone aided by two of the beefiest members of the crew in paper fairy costumes. His troupe went into the prisoner's quarters ending up with much laughter and torn fairy suits as the Americans joined in with the jollities.

Five days passed. The 'White Ensign' was exchanged back for the 'Stars and Stripes'. The course taken was only five hundred miles off the coast of the United States of America. Where American warship groups could possibly be found. So hoped Reitz as he stared at *Olaf* pushing her blunt bows through the grey-green waters. Although a number of aircraft were sighted, only two flew near enough to investigate the two ships but on seeing the flags that *Dresden* and *Olaf* were flying, waggled their wings and flew away. The radar, fortunately still working, on three occasions, picked up a convoy of ships and carefully Reitz veered his two ships away from even a visual sighting. How so different, he thought, from the start of his ship's long sojourn with him when *Dresden* went into the attack against those convoys in 1941.

New Year's Eve. *Juanita* slowly crawled to a berth in Buenos Aries. Amazed, and then angry officials, were certainly not amused by Captain da Silva's explanations. 'Christmas Eve, did you say? Were you celebrating a little too early? Mmm? An English warship. Trading on the high seas? Odd place for it to be – they're all going through the Panama Canal or sail closer to Africa. Very odd. Still at least they paid you. Mmmm! Crisp English money. Ah, so you wanted a bit more money, eh? You're making it all up, Captain! English warships don't trade on the high seas. You've been guilty before of maintaining a poor ship. No, you will not have any leave for the New Year. Now, go on, Captain, smarten yourself up and your crew. Don't tell us such silly stories again! One day for repairs and it's off to sea again for all of you!'

No-one questioned them any further about the mystery warship.

No-one, not even in the small Argentinian Navy, bothered to report the strange incident. Not officially.

Not until it was too late.

The weather grew colder, rougher and darker as *Dresden* and *Olaf* pushed their way into the Iceland-Faroes passage. Reitz knew that it was risky but why skulk through the Denmark Strait when surely an American warship sailing to reinforce an Arctic convoy would more likely use these waters in order to rendezvous off that cold sounding land of Iceland. The Allies didn't know that his warship was there. No more Northern Patrols. The only unlikely suspicion that they'd have if *Dresden* was sighted, was to query why an 'American' battleship, such as Reitz was pretending to be, was sailing in these waters when nearly all the American big ships were now in the Pacific.

The Allies minds would be elsewhere. Breaking down the German defences on both the Western and Eastern Fronts. Bombing German cities. Making sure that no die-hard last-gasp Kriegsmarine unit was trying to break-out of the Baltic. No-one surely would think that there was one unit trying soon to break-in!

The cold, grey, rolling waves swished and gurgled past the bows and down the sides of *Dresden* and *Olaf* as they pushed through them, with every turn of their propellers getting them both closer to their first goal, the Norwegian port of Trondheim.

Then the unexpected happened.

Hiltzern was standing watch whilst Reitz was having a short rest. A bridge lookout suddenly yelled '*Olaf*'s signalling, sir – says she's having engine trouble.'

Hiltzern muttered 'Damn!' Then out loud, he asked 'What speed can she do?'

The reply was translated 'Not much more than six knots until repairs can be completed.'

The seas were too rough to contemplate even launching a boat of Luth's helpers. When Reitz heard the dreaded alarm buzz in his cabin, he dashed on his heavy weather coat and boots and stormed on to the bridge.

'What is it?' he demanded as *Dresden* began to slow down. On being appraised of the situation, he quickly made up his mind.

'Signal *Olaf* to effect repairs and then to try and reach Trondheim, the last leg in darkness if at all possible. If challenged, they're to say that they are *en route* to Murmansk and have had to drop out of a convoy due to engine trouble. Oh, and add, farewell friend and good luck.'

The tanker's reply wished them 'Happy sailing. See you soon' and then, *Olaf* was soon lost to sight as *Dresden*'s screws began to revolve much faster, pushing her up to twenty-five knots. Reitz knew that if *Olaf* was to survive, he had to surge on ahead, perhaps cause a diversion and then hopefully, slip safely to Altenfjord where again he hoped that there would be protection from German forces to assist him and his ship to make the final, and most dangerous run, to home waters – even if such a diversion meant revealing *Dresden*'s whereabouts sooner than he would have desired. Guessing the approximate routing of convoys leaving Reykjavik *en route* for Murmansk, Reitz and Serle plotted *Dresden*'s course and average speed, aiming for a night dash when the Arctic winter light was at its darkest for in those latitudes, gloom was the best one could say to describe even the brightest period of daylight. A night dash from the Allied convoy route to Altenfjord. The northernmost point of German naval influence. So he hoped.

One day later, 3rd January, *Dresden* found herself rolling in waters some three hundred miles north-east of Reykjavik. The air temperature was close to freezing and ice was forming on *Dresden*'s superstructure. Reitz knew that the Arados couldn't fly but he was also worried about the radar aerials. He hoped that the over-worked all-seeing eye wouldn't break down in this, potentially, the most dangerous stretch of the homeward run. He didn't want to run into a convoy too soon that would betray his position. Somehow he doubted whether his American flag disguise would hold much water if challenged but better that flag than even his own German flag. So the 'Stars and Stripes' still flew.

At noon, just as eight bells was being struck on the much battered bridge bell, the loudspeakers clicked in to life, whilst Reitz looked through the lower bridge windows at a group of well-clad seamen with steam hoses hacking at ice building up on the fore deck near Anton's turret.

'Captain to radar room. Urgent.'

The radar operators said that a small speck had appeared quite suddenly when about three miles ahead.

Then, Brautsch came running. With young Prebke who saluted Reitz 'Sir, there's a submarine on the surface – and we think that it is one of ours!'

The U-boat was in a bad way. Six hours earlier, she'd endured a long, seemingly unending, barrage of depth-charges. Her entombed crew cringed at each explosion. The submarine's captain, Kapitan-Leutnant Sigmund Horst, at thirty-nine years old, and one of Germany's last surviving aces, a most experienced submariner, was on a lonely patrol looking for an Arctic convoy off Reykjavik in the process of forming up as American ships joined their British counterparts. Two acoustic torpedoes were fired at the mingling ships. One hit a merchantman, which although damaged, was able to struggle back into Reykjavik's harbour. The other hit a frigate but a rescue tug was able to save all but two of her company as the small warship slowly sank. Other escorts vessels homed in on Horst's boat forcing him to dive as deep as the waters would allow. More by luck, than chance, he found a submarine shelf on which he risked waiting. The effort was to confuse the Asdic echoes of his attackers who earlier hadn't been put off by Horst's tricks of releasing oil, air-bubbles and debris. Silently the U-boat men lay down, the engines stopped and after what seemed an interminable wait, the attacks lessened and finally stopped. Just as well for deadly chlorine gas was beginning to seep out of damaged batteries. Slowly but inexorably.

Gently the electric motors were started up. Slowly and gradually the battered submarine rose to the surface with her crew coughing and spluttering as the obnoxious fumes spread over the interior. At last the U-boat surfaced but her troubles weren't over. Her engineers reported to Horst that when the diesels were engaged, nasty thumps from the propellers and their shafts were experienced indicating damage from the depth-charging. Also from the stern came reports that the men couldn't get at the worsening leaks. The U-boat was filling up. Two of her pumps wouldn't work.

She wallowed like an ungainly, badly wounded whale. The relief when the conning tower hatch was opened, letting in fresh air and realising the gas-fumes, was tempered by the biting cold. Fortunately no vengeful Allied aircraft were overheard to blast the stricken U-boat to her watery grave. Not for the time being at least.

How could Horst get the U-boat back home? She couldn't dive and she was proving difficult to steer. Worse still, as Horst, in his oilskins peering ahead at the oscillating bows of his damaged boat, was startled when a lookout, peering astern, shouted that a large warship was closing rapidly on them.

There was no option. With his stomach churning, Horst ordered a white flag to be waved. By surrendering, he could save his crew. He even began to wave his white muffler when suddenly his executive officer, Rudi Stolz yelled 'Good grief sir! She's one of ours!'

Astonished, Horst replied 'It can't be. All our big ships are in the Baltic. You must be wrong, Rudi. Wrong!'

Stolz grabbed his captain's left arm. Urgently. 'No sir! I know her! It's – it's – it's the *Dresden*!'

'Can't be' gasped Horst. 'She was sunk at Leyte Gulf and if not, she's still in Japan. She – she – she can't be here.'

'But it is her!' shouted Stolz. 'I saw her in nineteen forty when I was serving on *Gneisenau* off Norway.'

'Look! She's signalling!' shouted a lookout, scarcely able to believe what Stolz was saying.

'What's she saying?' gasped Horst. Scarcely able to comprehend what he was seeing or hearing.

'KM *Dresden* to U-boat. Hurry up and abandon your boat. We're sending launches to rescue you.'

It was her. *Dresden*. His country's greatest sea-legend.

'Go on Rudi. Get everyone up and on to the casing. Go on, quickly, it is the *Dresden*. You were right!'

Stolz vanished down the conning tower yelling for everyone to get out of the boat as quick as possible. '*Dresden*'s here!' The exhausted begrimed crew members could scarcely comprehend what their exec. was yelling but as they emerged onto the conning-tower they could see to windward the rust-streaked, ice-encrusted heaving sides of their, yes, their sea legend. The battlecruiser had already launched two of her boats which were ploughing across to the U-boat as it wallowed heavily in the ice-cold troughs.

It was a miracle for even as the launches lurched alongside, the submarine's movement in the waves became heavier. She was sinking.

Strong hands grabbed hold of the submariners as they scrambled into the launches. Maybe not too gently but haste was paramount. None of them noticed the icy spray that lashed over the submarine. Hearing their rescuers yelling out in their native German was the spur to them hastening their progress. Already burly Otto Schenke, now on the submarine's casing, was literally lifting the haggard U-boat men into the launch. In less than three minutes, thirty-seven of the men were shoved into the two launches.

'She's going!' yelled Brautsch.

Schenke grabbed Horst as the U-boat's captain despairingly shouted for Stolz who was still below. The submarine shuddered, but failed to recover. She was in her final dive. Schenke maintained a firm grip on Horst as they trod water and then willing hands reached down to haul the U-boat's captain, and then Schenke, into the launch. The cries of the dozen trapped men still in their dying iron coffin were mercifully drowned into oblivion as she vanished under the waves. Horst lay gasping on the bottom boards of the launch as its engines cut in and powered her across to quickly come under the lee of the battlecruiser's port side.

As soon as both boats were hooked onto their falls, *Dresden*'s engines powered into full life and the warship began to gather speed. The 'Swastika', a flag that Reitz only flew in home area waters was rapidly hauled down and the 'Stars and Stripes' once again hoisted in its place.

Not a moment too soon for even as the first of the survivors were being led out of the launches for the administrations of Doctor Lebers, Nurse Andrea and the rest of the medical staff, a shout went up – 'Aircraft in sight!' As per the accepted norm it came from young Prebke.

Dresden's radar operators then, like an afterthought, also reported the presence of the aeroplane just as the U-boat began sliding to her deep, watery grave. Now it was here. An American Lockheed Hudson searching for the U-boat. Late, maybe, but still searching. Too late to find it but the bubbles and oil showing its sinking were too obviously visible. So close to a large warship.

The pilot of the Hudson, Carl B. Summers, flashed a signal – 'Do you read? Please identify source of oil and bubbles.'

The large warship's signal lamp replied – 'Have just rescued U-boat crew from their sunken boat.'

The reply from Summers – 'Well done lads! One more U-boat scratched.'

Reitz sent a response – 'So long pals' – hoping that this was suitably American phrased.

The Lockheed cumbersomely waggled its wings and after a wide circle of the area climbed slowly into the clouds and vanished to the south-west, apparently satisfied.

Half-an-hour later Reitz summoned the U-boat captain to his sea cabin. When he saw the thin, gaunt, stubbled face of Sigmund Horst, he was somewhat perturbed but the submariner gave him a thin smile, extended his right hand and said 'Thankyou. Admiral Reitz, for being in the right time and the right place to rescue most of my crew. We'd all have perished had you not turned up. The shock was meeting your ship. So unexpected. Believe me, we thought that we were dreaming. You're supposed to have been sunk. How come that you are here?'

Reitz smiled. 'A long story, Kapitan. Briefly, before our last attempt at leaving Japan we left instructions with our naval attaché to announce our disappearance upon receiving our coded instruction and then for him to announce it to the media. We needed that story to be broadcast so that it gave us a chance to break-through the Allied controlled waters and the result is, we're here. Flying either the 'White Ensign' or the 'Stars and Stripes' to help fool any inquisitive aircraft or by the use of our radar, avoiding any ships.'

In reply, Horst gave a faint grin and then, croakily said 'Well Admiral Reitz, where to next? It's dangerous all the way to Norway and home.'

'Mmmm. Glad to have confirmed what I've already guessed. You see, Kapitan, I need to create a diversion. Somewhere to the south of us is our fuel supply on an oil-tanker which has engine-problems. She's going to Trondheim. Now you can help me.'

Horst looked puzzled.

Reitz continued 'Were you, or have you been trailing any convoys around here?'

Horst nodded.

'Mmm. I'm a-thinking of making a surprise attack on your convoy which will let the Allies know that we're alive and kicking.

Then, we'll dash for Altenfjord, refuel, and then steam as fast as we can down the Norwegian coast. What do you think?'

Horst grunted. 'Sir, the last I heard was that we've abandoned Altenfjord but there may still be a couple or so fuel barges up in a fjord to the south of there nearer to Tromso.' Horst asked for a chart. He pointed to a long thin inlet. 'Here, Admiral Reitz. Here at Haarje Fjord. We still have some small warships keeping a limited presence. Nothing big. Except for a rusting relic called *Rugen*.'

This time it was Reitz who raised his eyebrows '*Rugen*? Ah, yes, we have met her. On exercise nearly four years back. So, she's still about?'

'Yes sir. But she mainly fires up using her coal-fired boilers.' Horst then stopped. Exhausted. Still unbelieving that he was on board Germany's most famed warship.

'Admiral Reitz. Whenever you refuel, you must be quick. The Allies have agents everywhere in Norway who as soon as they'll see you, they then radio London who order big bombers to come and blast away any worthwhile target. That's how they did for *Tirpitz*. She stayed in one fjord long enough for heavy Allied bombers to find her.'

Just then Walters arrived with a flask full of hot coffee laced with brandy. Pouring a cup out to Horst he murmured 'A pressie from our Argentinian friends.'

Horst nodded, bleakly 'Argentinian?'

Reitz intervened 'Yes, we borrowed some supplies from one of their ships.'

Horst nodded again. 'Wondered how you all look so well fed as well as steaming half-way round the World. You know, Admiral Reitz, you have been very lucky. The Allies, our so-called enemy, dominate the sea and the land, even near and next to our own country, and their aircraft fly over us with near impunity.' Suddenly, he swayed, spilling his coffee and then he collapsed in his chair. Totally exhausted.

With a feeling of pity, Reitz looked down on the U-boat commander. But, with the arrival of Hiltzern and Serle he said 'Leave him be. We'll guess that Herr Horst was after a convoy. Let's say here.' Here he jabbed his right forefinger on the chart to the seas off

Iceland's east coast. 'Now say he was damaged in an attack. Six hours ago? Convoy speed of ten knots. Convoy must be about a hundred kilometres from here. It's headed for Russia. Keeping to the south and east of Bear Island. Herr Serle, work out for me an interception course, time and speed for us to attack the convoy, say, in three days time.'

Horst stirred. Reitz handed him another brandy, courtesy of *Juanita*. The U-boat commander took a small sip and then, quite suddenly blurted out 'The convoy! You could attack the convoy! The one I attacked!'

Reitz patted him on a shoulder. 'It's alright Kapitan, we're working out what to do. Come, I'll show you on the chart.'

'You'll need to speed up a bit more, Herr Admiral. Convoy's speed will be about twelve knots. So, raise your speed a little bit and don't go too far north. You'll hit the Arctic ice. Pretend to be a Yankee reinforcement battlewagon. Sail on their course. Then overtake slowly before barging in to attack them. Just off Bear Island where we'll probably have U-boats waiting for them. Try to time your attack then. They'll be a bit confused.'

'You've done this before?' grunted Hiltzern.

'Yes, Commander, many times. Here and in the Atlantic. One hundred and seventy thousand tons. I was on my last sortie before a transfer to a new wonder submarine.'

'Oh! and what are they?' Hiltzern asked somewhat sceptically.

'Boats that can do twenty knots below the surface. Much better than the old metal coffins from which you rescued me and my crew.'

'Twenty knots! My, my!' remarked Serle 'You'd be able to get well away after making an attack.'

'That's the general idea. Our boats will be able to regain the initiative but it's hardly worth it now. The Navy isn't too keen on stiff-armed salutes and crashing jack-boots or else Herr Hitler and his fart-arsed cronies would have given us the new U-boats over a year ago. We simply won't have enough of the new boats ready before the Allies finish us all off. We're running out of time – and space.'

Then, again without warning, Horst began to shake. Quite violently. Reitz, somewhat alarmed, flipped the switch at the intercom.

'Sick Berth. Now! At once! To my sea cabin.'

Within three minutes one of Doctor Leber's sick-berth attendants arrived. Albert Werthe. A huge man who negotiated the tricky journey along the heaving deck and then the iced-up ladder steps in order to reach the bridge. Reitz nodded at him. How often Werthe had helped with the emergencies in the past when dealing with either Allied prisoners or his fellow crew members. So big. So firm. Yet, so surprisingly gentle. Another real pillar of strength on the ship. Like Otto Schenke.

'Something up, sir?' asked Werthe.

'Yes, our sea-wolf has collapsed. He seems to be so exhausted. Take him down to the Sick Berth and see if our good doctor as well as Frau Andrea can boost him up, eh?'

'Jawohl, Herr Kapitan.' Werthe clicked his heels and then without too much effort, picked up the inert Horst and hoisted the U-boat man onto his back.

If Werthe noticed the sheets of icy spray on his return journey he showed little indication of its lashings as he clambered back down to reach the eventual warmth of the Sick Berth with Horst, legs dangling, still on his back.

'Ere you are, miss' he gasped as he lowered Horst on to a bunk. ''E's just about knackered.'

Andrea smiled at him as the big man straightened up. She liked him. Rough-edged maybe but highly skilful at his job when administering bandages. Didn't like shirkers. Told them so. Only genuine medical cases were allowed in his ward. Bending down herself, she took Horst's pulse.

'Bit weak. He'll need a day or two's rest. Then he'll be alright.'

* * *

'Are you sure, Summers? That you saw one of our ships? The *Canyon*?' asked the USAAF's base commander at their airfield outside Reykjavik. He'd just read the report of Summer's latest patrol. Something just didn't add up. That's why his somewhat laconic, truculent airman was in his office.

'You know Summers that *Canyon*'s now with Convoy JW97B. Over a hundred miles away. She couldn't have been where you say she was. You didn't see *Canyon*.'

'But it was her, sir. She was flying a huge battle flag. Yer know, our flag with lots of stars and stripes on it.'

'Yes, yes, I do know the American flag when I see one but the point is, since your report, I've wirelessed *Canyon* and she's replied. Here, read for yourself. Didn't sink a Jerry U-boat or pick up any Jerries!'

Summers took the signal copy. He scratched his head 'Jee wiz, sir! If it wa' not *Canyon*, wa' ship wor it?'

'Exactly, which ship was it? Even our Limey pals can't tell us. Not the ones up here.'

'Waal, if it weren't a Limey boat, then it can only be, no, it can't. Can it? Shucks sir, that ain't a Jerry battlewagon out there, is there?' Summers sounded peeved. He'd made a huge gaff if it was. But it couldn't be! Surely not?

The lines of a deep frown etched on the forehead of his commander. 'If it is a Jerry, then it's come from the Baltic, slipped past all our patrols and right now is out on a suicide cruise, manned by square-headed Krauts determined to shout "Heil Hitler" once more as it sinks whilst attacking our convoys. I'm passing on your report to the Limeys in London to see if they can enlighten us. Weather's worsening so we can't mount an immediate search. Whatever it is, it's out there. Somewhere!'

When the news of the unusual sighting by the Americans of an unidentified ship flying the 'Stars and Stripes', somewhere near Iceland and roaming the seas in foul weather reached Collins, a shiver went up and down his spine. It wasn't the cold. It was a twinge caused by the message. The only big German warship that could be at large – no, it couldn't be – but it must be – *Dresden* but he needed to be certain. He called in one of his senior assistants, an elderly commander. 'What details have we of the whereabouts of the Nazi big ships?'

The commander fetched a file. Compilation from reports wirelessed in by agents who risked their lives, daily, to try and keep tabs on the naval movements of the Kriegsmarine. They nearly all tallied. Some in North German ports being repaired. Others out at sea, all eastward bound. None had been seen north of Copenhagen and Danish waters for at least a year. Only the smaller vessels such as minesweepers, E-boats and U-boats went north and then usually at night. None of the big modern ships.

'None of them. Are we absolutely sure?'

The commander nodded. '*Prinz Eugen, Lutzow* and *Scheer* are all on fire support for their Army against the Russians in the Eastern Baltic. *Hipper* seems to be on evacuation work, but we're not absolutely sure. Can we check with our agents?'

'No need to sir. We received reports on all of them only two days back' came the reply. 'So they can't be up there in the Arctic, could they?'

'No, but believe this, or not, but –' here Collins checked himself, almost unsure of himself '– but – oh no, if what I say is true, then we are in the shits, if you'll pardon my expression.'

'Well sir, you believe it to be?' – interrupted the commander.

'Yes, to be *Dresden.*' Collins frowned, almost disbelieving what he suspected to be the truth. 'I, for one, never believed her to be sunk at Leyte. But no-one listened to me. There was not enough evidence – bodies, wreckage or even a Nazi-inspired eulogy over her demise.' He knew that now, here was the proof. Reitz and his crafty lads had pretended to be sunk so as to cover their return through the Atlantic.

Other snippets began to click into place. Odd items that he'd jotted down. Two reports of fake English fivers – in Chile and then in

Argentina. Supposedly from an English warship. No-one had bothered to make a proper investigation. The matter about them to the local authorities had been quickly dropped. Collins put two and two together and found that the sum probably added up to a superb piece of trickery, by who else, but Herr bloody Reitz and his elusive ship.

Then there were at least two reports of aircraft sighting a large warship and a tanker steaming north, parallel to the North American coast. Flying the 'Stars and Stripes'. Again no-one bothered to investigate them further, let alone query the movements of American warships. Even at the time, Collins had pencilled in a question mark by the reports. Now it all added up. *Dresden* and an oil-tanker. Food taken from the two stopped ships; fuel from the tanker. Very clever Herr Reitz. You almost fooled me!

Then the report of the airman. Collins felt certain that Summers would give him the final verification. It must have been the obvious thing to have assumed. *Canyon* trying to join up with convoy JW97B. And all the time, it was really Herr clever Reitz.

A messenger came to him. 'Sir, the American flier, Pilot Officer Summers, has just landed at Croydon. Be with us within the hour.'

Now suppose it was Reitz. Where was he headed? The Norwegian coastline? Probably. Plenty of fjords in which to hide his battle-cruiser. Or was he going to go for the convoy? One of his staff, the elderly retired commander knocked and re-entered the room 'Sir, the American. He's outside.'

'Well, show him in.'

Summers threw a casual-type salute.

Collins nodded. 'Well, Summers, can you recognise the ship that you saw from any of these photographs?' and saying this, he removed a large sheet of paper and underneath were various shots of not only *Dresden* but the *Hipper*, *Prinz Eugen*, *Admiral Scheer* and the *Canyon*. None of them labelled.

Summers scrutinised them carefully as possible. 'Say, Admiral boy. Have yah any air shots? I kinda' don't see battlewagons from sea-level.'

Collins smiled. 'Yes, I have' and removed the top-layer of photos to reveal one each of the ships already shown on the sheet below. Not in the same order. From the air.

Without hesitation Summers stuck a grubby finger on to the only one Collins had of *Dresden.*

'It wah this one, sir!'

'Are you absolutely sure?' Collins asked, feeling a new excitement as well as fear developing within him.

'Sure, pal, yeah, that were the ship ah saw' drawled Summers, still bewildered after his hectic flight from Reykjavik to London.

'Do you know what this ship's called?'

'Waal, ah'm not really certain but is she a Jerry?'

'Too right. That is the German battlecruiser *Dresden,* supposedly sunk fighting with the Japs against your lads at Leyte Gulf'.

'*Dresden*? Ain't she the best ship the Jerries have got – an' yah mean it were her that ah saw?'

Collins again shuddered at the American derivation of what he considered to be King's English. It had jarred him at Hawaii – maybe that was why he could never warm to them – perhaps they thought he was too stuffy – but even so, this American flier had just revealed *Dresden* in the identification. Then the reality hit him.

To the elderly commander he barked 'My aide. Now. At once. A matter of urgency.' Then to Summers, he held out his right hand 'Young man. Your information is of vital importance. We've been after that German ship ever since early nineteen forty-one when her then new commander, by the name of Reitz, took over and sailed her into the Atlantic a few weeks before she was followed by *Bismarck.* We sank her big brother but not her and she's been a thorn in the side of the Allies flesh ever since.' His aide, another older reserve navy lieutenant entered the room.

'Ah, Flags, take this message. Have it sent in code to the

commodore of JW97B – "Urgent. German battlecruiser in your vicinity. Do not scatter if she attacks. Deploy *Canyon* and *Sagina* to drive her off." Sign it in the usual way. And hurry man. I think she's very close to them, if my rusty chart work is still any good. Don't look so surprised. Get on with it!'

Which *Dresden* was, close to the convoy. Despite the bitterly cold temperatures, the Arctic Ocean those last three days did at least not rage or blow around as is often its usual vicious temperament. For the three days after seeing the Lockheed Hudson swing into the fading skies, the battlecruiser, at seventeen knots had pushed steadily north-eastwards. For an hour at each noon day, one of the Arados was able to search ahead and on the third day, the airmen reported the convoy some seventy miles ahead of them. Slowly Reitz worked *Dresden* to the north of the convoy and during the long dark winter night closed the gap, steadily, so as not to excite the radar screens of the escorting Allied warships. That next morning he made his decision. A swift raiding attack like the ones they'd tried in the Atlantic nearly four years ago. Do a bit of damage. Stir up the hornet's nest and then go flat out for northern Norway and Haarje Fjord.

Four U-boats were deployed ahead of JW97B whose position was known to German Naval Command at Trondheim. One of the few JU88's still left flying on naval reconnaissance sighted the convoy some one hundred miles south of Bear Island. But the JU-88 was seen. The convoy's naval commander, Harvey Rosedale, on board the modern and very fast S-class destroyer *Sagina* detailed the convoy's six escorting frigates to search for what he suspected could be a possible deployment of U-boats some five miles ahead of a line of five corvettes. Two other corvettes and three armed trawlers, as well as his destroyer and the US cruiser *Canyon* remained as close support for the twenty-eight merchantmen that ponderously pushed their way towards Murmansk.

One of the frigates was the first to strike. Her captain sent a message *en clair* direct to Rosedale on *Sagina*. It indicated that a

U-boat was being depth-charged. At the same time, radar reported a blip to the north. On the surface. Sixteen knots and increasing. Rosedale couldn't work it out. U-boats ahead of the convoy were being depth-charged but one, on the surface was apparently closing in. Why? He'd never known it ever happen before on the Arctic convoys. Sheer suicide. He sent a message to the corvette nearest the apparent hell-bent U-boat to investigate. Then, from his more central position, he ordered 'Full ahead' as *Sagina* heeled over and putting on increased speed, turned and weaving amongst the slower merchantmen, began to close with the stranger.

Then the wireless office rang through to the bridge. 'Yes?' he barked.

'Sir! Message from Admiralty HQ, London.'

As he listened, Rosedale's normal ruddy complexion, even then largely hidden in his wool-lined helmet, seemed to go paler. Shakily he replaced the receiver. 'Have their Lordship's lost their bleedin' marbles? Apparently there's a bloody Jerry battlecruiser out there – oh no, bleedin' hell, that's it. That's no Nazi submarine commander hell bent on suicide. It must be true!' Hurriedly he looked at the radar repeater. 'Blimey, she's only five miles away!'

Then he saw the *Dresden*. A dark, lean shape closing in from the north-west.

'Full ahead! Maximum revs! Someone tell the wireless lads to signal that we're under attack. All guns – enemy surface raider at two nine five degrees.'

The dark shape spat yellow and orange. Firing her guns at the convoy. At his ship. *Sagina*. A year earlier, Rosedale had been a first lieutenant on a destroyer trying to close up on the speeding German battlecruiser, the *Scharnhorst*. That ship had been running away although her gunnery was well controlled. The difference now was that this one was coming straight for the convoy.

The little corvette was nowhere to be seen. Probably sunk.

'Main armament. Open fire!' 'A' and 'B' turrets, with twin four point seven's, flashed out in the direction of the clearly visible enemy warship.

The enemy fired again. And again. Ripples of flame flashing all along her starboard side.

Sagina ploughed straight into a veritable forested wall of water, splinters clanging and gouging out chunks of her thin plating. Rosedale felt his ship shudder at least three rimes. Almost out-of-control, the once lithe proud destroyer reeled away, smoke puthering in huge black gouts emanating from fierce fires abaft her funnel. She slewed into the swell of the pitiless Arctic Ocean, a beaten vessel.

Rosedale croaked 'Is *Canyon* attacking that Jerry bastard 'cos we're done for? All hands to the task of keeping this ship afloat!' He sagged against the lip of the bridge as he watched the sailors around the funnel struggling with their hoses.

'Sir, look!' One of the bridge signallers pointed out across the convoy. Beyond two burning merchantmen the forward guns of the emerging American cruiser could be seen firing.

'Go on, hit the sod!' growled Rosedale as he watched *Canyon*'s guns open fire. He barely noticed two other merchantmen suddenly blaze up, caught as *Dresden*'s shells dropped amongst them.

'Sir, Jerry's had it. *Canyon*'s scared the shits – oh, my bleedin' 'ell do you see that?'

To the horror and shock of the watchers from *Sagina*, a massive flare-up below *Canyon*'s bridge suddenly burst into a series of pyrotechnic flashes. Her 'B' turret was ablaze from a direct hit. The light cruiser began to turn away and briefly fired a salvo from her rear turrets before putting out a heavy smokescreen to cover her withdrawal.

As the news came in about the convoy's tussle with *Dresden*, the faces of the senior naval officers with Collins became grimmer. One corvette and three merchantmen sunk. *Sagina* and *Canyon* badly damaged. Both returning to Scapa, with four of the convoy's frigates acting as escorts. Two other merchantmen also seriously damaged. Also returning with the warships. Only two crumbs of comfort came in when they heard that the crews of the merchantmen had all been rescued. The other was the news that the attacking German warship had vanished, heading rapidly eastwards.

When Collins heard this, he rounded on the officers gathered round the chart of the convoy battle. He snarled 'Well, what did I tell you? Now, perhaps people like you and higher up the chain of naval command will begin to take notice of me. *Dresden* is alive, too bloody alive. In less than half-an-hour, she has caused more destruction to an Arctic convoy than the rest of the Kriegsmarine's big surface ships put together!' He paused, breathing heavily. The other men downcast their eyes. Even they had been sceptical when he'd arrived in London with the obsession that Collins seemed to have with the German battlecruiser. But here it was. In stark reality. Facts staring at them, in the news that they'd just received.

Collins barked out 'Well, haven't any of you a tongue in your head? Just what have we in our larder to stop Reitz and his glory boys making us all look like complete nincompoops? Nothing in Scapa Flow except a few old slow out-of-date has-beens of a surface fleet. All our big modern stuff, so I understand, has sailed off to try and pick off what remains of the Japanese Fleet.' He paused, glaring at those men around him. Continuing, he stated 'Now we've *Dresden.* Probably streaking like a bat out of hell for one of the northern Norwegian fjords, possibly the ones that Jerry hasn't yet seen fit to retreat from, probably near or in Haarje Fjord, that is if clever dick Reitz knows that Jerry no longer controls Altenfjord.' Then Collins pulled out a chart of Norway, straightened it out and placed a finger on the area north of Tromso. 'Yes, Mr. Reitz, that's where I think that you are heading except that this time I'm ahead of you!' Then turning to the nearest member of his staff he asked him 'Have we still an agent there?'

One of the officers nodded 'One, sir. Actually in Haarje fjord.'

Collins smiled and said 'Well, get in contact with him. Ask him for immediate news of any unusual German naval activity. Meanwhile –' Collins paused. Looked around and then continued '– meanwhile, will someone get in contact with Coastal Command's base in Leuchars for a Mosquito as well as a base in either East Yorkshire or Lincolnshire for them to have a dozen Lancasters bombed up and you'd better warn Air Chief Marshall Harris to see if he'll divert that dozen aircraft?'

'Sir, Haarje Fjord is quite a long way.'

'So, get the airmen to take their big play-toys and land them on a Russian base to refuel. After all, it's our fuel that the Russians are using so we'll have some of it back for the aircraft flying back on their return flight.'

Collins seemed very determined to get *Dresden*. His staff seemed to realise his mood. Hurriedly they each went to their own offices to begin to make the arrangements leaving Collins gazing at the chart.

Even German Naval Command in Trondheim couldn't really take in the incredible news coming in about *Dresden*'s dramatic re-appearance with the attack on that convoy. Using a U-boat code, the battlecruiser's latest message gave an estimated time for her arrival in Haarje Fjord. After contacting naval headquarters in Kiel, the response was 'Have fuel available for *Dresden*.' As if they were the only ones in the know-how about *Dresden*'s dramatic re-appearance.

Shivering on the open bridge of his modern minesweeper *M731*, Leutnant Karl Rittman was concluding a night patrol of the area close to Haarje Fjord with an old coal-fired T-boat. Making sure all was clear for the voyage later that day of another ancient Kriegsmarine relic, Kapitan Franke's *Rugen*. She was due to withdraw to Trondheim as the Kriegsmarine's presence in the region was being scaled down to just the odd small patrol vessel. Suddenly Rittman's wireless operator burst onto the bridge, hurriedly saluted and handed Rittman a message. 'It's really urgent, sir.'

Rittman looked at the signal flimsy – 'New orders coming from *Rugen.* Meet in fjord entrance.'

Half-an-hour later, coming out of the fjord, Rittman saw an E-boat motoring at high speed. It slowed and came alongside the minesweeper. Rittman was a little bit surprised to see *Rugen*'s first officer come aboard. He received the officer in his box of a cabin. 'This has come direct, via a land-line, to us. Can't risk any Allies intercepting our radio traffic' he informed the new arrival.

Rittman looked at the message. It was from Trondheim instructing him to sail out and rendezvous with the *Dresden.* Expected arrival time 0800 hours. To escort her up the fjord and bring her to the anchorage of a small coaster and two fuel barges.

'*Dresden.* Last I knew of her was that she was sunk in the Far East' commented Rittman, feeling edgy about the news.

'Then, sir, you must have a dozy wireless operator on board. A few hours ago *Dresden* struck at an Arctic convoy and having inflicted damage on it, radioed in U-boat code, although how they know about our latest code is still a bit of a mystery, asking for an escort into the anchorage'.

'We don't listen in to U-boat frequencies' came Rittman's weak reply. As *M731* carried only one wireless operator, the man needed to sleep sometime!

Then *Rugen*'s officer left him, climbed back on board the waiting E-boat which then drew away at speed, followed by the old T-boat.

'Head out to sea and everyone keep a sharp lookout!' ordered Rittman, still overwhelmed by the astounding news that he'd just received.

As *M731* began to roll in the open seas beyond the fjord's entrance, coming down the fjord, at her near top speed of thirteen knots, came Franke's old battleship with a heavy pall of coal smoke churning out of her funnels. On reaching the mouth of the fjord, Franke turned *Rugen* southwards, only for her to vanish into the security of a smaller nearby fjord where the battleship stopped after turning round. The heavy smoke dwindled down and to all but the sailors on board her and the T-boat, it was if the ships had become merged with the landscape. Only a light haze came from the funnels as both crews waited. Franke's orders were startling but the old sea-dog was furiously working out an alternative.

Out on the pitching minesweeper at about 07.45, a lookout shouted 'Warship ahead! At 350 degrees. Approaching fast!'

Horst was on the battlecruiser's bridge as the little minesweeper came into sight on that dull grey early January morning. Although he felt relieved that Norway was in sight again, the efficiency of Reitz and his crew in dealing with both the corvette and destroyer as well as the cruiser had opened his eyes. His opinion of the Kriegsmarine's bigger surface ships had always been that bit sarcastic. Even when they were at sea they'd made little impression on the Allies since the demise of battleship *Bismarck*. Except for this ship. *Dresden*. If only Germany possessed other captains and crewmen of the quality of those on this battlecruiser, perhaps the Allied navies would have had a much tougher time. But even this famous ship was now approaching her biggest test of her career. Surely once the Allies knew that she was in Haarje Fjord they'd be sending their bombers with their huge bombs to reduce Reitz and his ship to smithereens.

But for the present he was helping this ship. *M731* fired her identifying rockets. Horst knew the U-boat reply. He guessed it would be the same needed for *Dresden*. 'Signal one red, two whites, one red for today. Herr Admiral' he said as Reitz looked at him.

M731 flashed back 'Welcome home, big brother. Follow me' and then she turned towards the land at her top speed of seventeen knots.

Three hours later, with the snow-covered sides of Haarje Fjord enclosing her, *Dresden* dropped anchor under the lee of the south cliff-face of part of the inlet. The anchors splashed into those icy waters hitting the bed of the fjord and held the ship still for the first time since she'd up-anchored when setting out with Kurita's fleet off North Borneo.

In London, just half-an-hour later, a messenger passed a signal flimsy to Admiral Collins. It was a brief signal from Jans Leiffson, sometime shepherd and fisherman as well as being an agent for the Norwegian Resistance in Haarje Fjord. Collins read it – 'Two warships, one large. Haarje Fjord.' Nothing more. The elderly commander coughed 'Sir, perhaps you don't realise but our agents daren't send long messages for fear of Gestapo listening stations. All we received when *Tirpitz* berthed near Tromso was – 'Big Queen. Tromso'. The locals called *Tirpitz* the 'Lone Queen of the North'. So, that's why we haven't received much information on this message but it seems fairly logical that *Dresden*'s just arrived in Haarje Fjord. What we need to know is exactly where. If we send long-range Lancasters they haven't the fuel reserves to go on a search pattern. Best send up a specially adapted Mosquito off first.'

Collins nodded 'Yes, yes. Go on. Get on with it. We need to nail *Dresden.* I should think that the Germans will try to refuel her – this will take about six-hours – can't have that many big tankers up there now that none of their big ships are still there – well, come on, let's nail her!'

The teleprinter in Coastal Command's lonely sleet-lashed base of Leuchars in Northeast Scotland began to clatter. Soon after, a Mosquito was pulled out of its hanger, despite the grim weather, by the ground-crew. Already fully fuelled with extra long-range tanks and cameras for quick reconnaissance work, the ground crew fired up her twin engines. Her pilot and observer pulled on their flying gear and hauled themselves into the cockpit whilst a tractor cleared slush from the runway. Chocks were pulled away from the wheels and Squadron Leader Brian Mulroan coaxed the aircraft into the air leaving the whirling wet snow disturbed by his Merlin-engine driven propeller blades to eventually settle again as he climbed to three thousand feet and vanished from sight on the flight to the north-east.

Reitz needed time only for a quick top up to his fuel tanks. An old coastal tanker half-a-mile further up the fjord, together with two barges approached the ice-coated sides of the battlecruiser and fuel lines were hurriedly attached. Fuel that was going to be needed for *Dresden*'s high-speed dash to Trondheim and hopefully a rendezvous with *Olaf*. Reitz was hoping that his brief attack on the convoy had stirred enough of a hornet's nest in the British Admiralty so as to divert resources to have a go at his elusive raider and thus enabling the tanker to make it to the port.

M731's young commander came on board in order to hand over his message from *Rugen*. A hurried plan, thought Reitz, but given half-a-chance, it might just fool the Admiralty long enough in order to allow *Dresden* to make her breakthrough. Shortly after mid-day, the expected happened. The roar of the Merlin engines of Mulroan's Mosquito were heard before they were seen. Suddenly she rounded the steep bluff behind which *Dresden* was located and there was only time for a brief burst from one of the minesweeper's machine-guns before the aircraft swept over them and rapidly circled and climbed, its task done. Then it vanished. Soon after it had gone, Reitz ordered the fuel-lines to be disconnected. It was time to go. For all he knew, either carrier aircraft or heavy bombers were on their way to attack his ship. Rittman quickly left and the minesweeper began to head down the fjord to escort the battlecruiser out into the open sea.

Jans Leiffson heard Mulroan's aircraft and smiled. So the British were reacting. Soon would come big bombs and blast this German battleship to bits. Putting on a thick coat he went to the door of his hut, preparing to go out and watch the pending action. Opening it, he cursed as there came a cheerful hail from two German soldiers whom he recognised. Oldish men from one of the anti-aircraft batteries that supposedly guarded the anchorage to protect *Rugen* or the few other German warships that still used the fjord's waters.

'Hallo, Jans. Can we come in?'

Jans was about to raise his hands but then relaxed when the two snow-covered men drew near to him. These weren't Gestapo thugs who may have realised that his hut hid a secret radio set. Just two of the older men that like him, were waiting for the end of the war. The sooner, no doubt, the better.

'Jans. We want your skis.' One of the Germans spoke passable Norwegian.

'Come in.' Once inside the shed, the two soldiers rubbed their hands over the wood store and stamped the snow off their boots.

'Jans. We'll stay a bit. Snow's getting a bit heavy' said one of them going over to pull the door shut. 'Look, we've some real coffee and rolls. Draw up a stool and let's eat and have a smoke. Maybe even some schnapps, eh?'

The old soldiers thumped their stools across the floor and Jans, somewhat resigned to his ill-luck at having to entertain them, pulled his stool up after bringing over a blackened pan filled with water. He placed it on top of the hot plate of his stove.

Down in the snow-swept fjord, *Dresden* slid away through the murk, gathering speed for the entrance. *M731* flashed her farewells and soon afterwards, rounding the headland, came Franke's old warhorse. The second stage was beginning. Providing those old soldiers kept Leiffson talking for the next two hours or so. *Rugen*'s men glimpsed *Dresden*'s disappearing bulk vanishing through the blizzard.

Rugen. The seemingly most useless of Germany's bigger surface vessels and probably the oldest. *Dresden.* The most successful of them all. Both still surviving. Both in full commission. The only two major units of the Kriegsmarine still in active service outside Germany's home waters. Fate, so it seemed was bringing their paths together. Four years after that almost desperate mock convoy attack. Together. Again.

Franke hadn't particularly liked his orders that told him to anchor his ship in at *Dresden*'s recently vacated berth, cover his vessel with tarpaulin and then evacuate his ship, leaving her defenceless against a more than likely probable overwhelming bombing attack. But Otto Franke hadn't kept his old warhorse in active service for all these war years without developing some inner sense of about what were ill-conceived orders. Old *Rugen* wasn't going to be sacrificed so meekly. That was why two of his cronies from the gun battery were diverting Leiffson's attention. Plenty of schnapps and bottles of beer to keep the Norwegian happy. At least for two hours.

Long enough for the rest of his crew to carry out his alternative plan. Desperate that it was.

Mulroan's affirmative sighting quickly spurred the authorities in London into immediate action. Knowing that the chance to catch *Dresden* so relatively easily may not come again, Collins, with the grudging permission of both the Prime Minister and Air Chief Marshall Harris, had already set in motion for the other Mosquito at Mulroan's base to load up with Pathfinder flares and at an East Yorkshire base for twelve Lancasters to be bombed up. All with extra fuel tanks. Then, the aircraft rendezvousing over the North Sea were to fly to Haarje Fjord and give the recently arrived German battlecruiser a pasting. All these aircraft were airborne by the time Mulroan's report came through but Collins knew that it would take at least another three hours before the lumbering bombers would reach their target.

At ten minutes to three, a report reached Franke on the *Rugen* that the approaching bombing formation was in sight. From the fjord below Leiffson's hut, the whooping of the old battleship's siren could be heard. The two soldiers looked at each other, nodded and with a last gulp each of the schnapps in their mugs, they shuffled out into the clear cold air. The blizzard had cleared away and rays of a weak wintry sunshine glinted over the tops to the hills on either side of the fjord. Snapping their feet to Leiffson's spare skis they dug their sticks into the snow and swished off not gracefully but rather more like a pair of rather clumsy penguins with their white ski coats flapping in stark contrast against their dark grey uniforms.

When they were only one hundred or so yards away from the hut, the air suddenly filled with the ever louder rumble of heavy aircraft engines. Both men crunched to a halt. This was what that wily old sea salt of a skipper had told them. Maybe a little bit early but expected.

On the bridge of his old battleship, Otto Franke's smile began to broaden. Ever wider as the first aircraft swept into sight. A dark wide stiff-winged eagle with twin whirling propellers swooping over the choppy waters of the long thin stretch of cold dark water glistening a little with the odd whip of a breaking horse in the fading light. Even as the eagle swooped towards its intended victim, Franke continued to smile. Broadly. Looking directly at the bird of doom.

Smiling also was Jans Leiffson. Those old German soldiers had outstayed their welcome. The ship's blasts must have been a warning but if they were trying to get back to their battery they were hopelessly late. He could hear the heavy sound of aircraft engines intent on one purpose only. To blast that warship below his hut in the fjord into immediate oblivion, if not instant scrap iron. All because of him. And his secret wireless set. Faintly, he could hear some gun batteries opening fire. Fools! Far too late!

As Leiffson peered over a rock face, he could discern a dark long shape of a ship under camouflage but then over the water came a fast aircraft with twin engines dropping a series of flares right over the camouflage.

All the Lancasters needed to do was to drop their huge bombs over the flares. Jans cringed as the bombs began to explode. Massive explosions. He almost felt sorry for the Jerry warship that now merited such enormous punishment. Smoke, flames and further explosions flashed and shook the air causing Jans to cling even tighter to his snow-covered rock. Then it was all over. The fast plane swept back over the fjord. Not a gun was fired at it. Then it too faded away.

Jans looked down. All he could see were some flickering flames on the water from an oil-slick that was spread across the waters of the fjord. A surface so recently terribly disturbed. Jans peered harder. No, there was no ship. Some wreckage. Planks of wood. A small boat upside down. But definitely no big Nazi warship. Gone. Vanished. Destroyed.

He hurriedly traced his steps back to his isolated hut. Taking out his hidden transmitter, he warmed it up, cranking the handle furiously. He needed to tell London. He tapped out his call-sign. After his third try, an acknowledgement came through. Carefully he tapped on his key – 'Big visitor sunk. Leiffson.'

Suddenly, the door to his hut crashed open.

'Naughty, naughty Jans. Hands up!' Two different men in naval uniform and holding Schmeisser machine-pistols, stood in the doorway.

Jans went weak at the knees. He'd been caught. The only crumb of comfort that he could think of was that these men weren't wearing the usual Gestapo long black leather coats. Or their black slouch hats. Or SS uniform. Only naval men. He shuddered, scared witless. The two men advanced. One of them went right up to Jans, the machine-pistol stopping at the Norwegian's stomach. Slowly it was raised by the sailor up towards Jans' face. To stop between his eyes. Seconds dragged. Jans knew that death was a mere fraction of time away. He waited. Visions of his loving wife and daughter came to him.

Brrrm! Brrrm! Brrrm! The other sailor was firing his machine pistol. The wireless transmitter quickly shredded into fragments.

Then the deafening noise ended.

The first sailor, in passable Norwegian, quite suddenly, took his pistol away from Jans and snapped it back into a holster.

'You've been a very naughty boy Jans Leiffson. Our skipper has known about you for nearly six months. There won't be much left for you to report. Only the odd small patrol vessel and that for not much longer. No need to call your London masters at all. Ever again.'

Jans could feel a wet patch in his groin. The sailor looked at him 'Don't worry any more. No need to piss in your pants at us ever again. Go on, look after your sheep and catch your fish. Go back to your wife with our blessing.' Then the two German sailors, from the *Rugen,* left the hut, smiling. Not even bothering to shut the door. Jans watched them go, scarcely able to believe that he was still alive.

Down below on the *Rugen*'s bridge Otto Franke was smiling because the big bombers had unloaded their massive bombs on a sheet of canvas underneath which had been a number of small boats. The canvas, as near as he'd been able to organise, had been spread out in the shape of a ship and in the centre holding it all up had been the small coaster and the emptied fuel barges. Only the coaster's funnel and mast had protruded above the rapidly fitted camouflage of canvas. All that was left now was the pall of smoke over the scene and a scattering of debris. Franke, leaning on the open bridge of *Rugen* about two miles further up the fjord, continued to smile when Mulroan's Mosquito, refuelled at the Murmansk base to which trundled the bomber force, re-appeared only half-an-hour later and flew over the scene taking its photographs.

Not a single gun fired at the aeroplane as it made two runs over the fjord. Again on Franke's orders. Even a scattering of fires on the fjord's sides gave the impression that they were part of the scattered burning debris of a destroyed warship. Franke's men, tending the fires, remained hidden as the Mosquito soared above their heads. Eventually Mulroan was satisfied and gunned his engines as the Mosquito soared higher to climb over the surrounding hills and then out to sea.

Darkness soon came over the fjord after the sound of the Merlin engines faded away. Only then did Franke order 'up anchor' of his old ship and using her coal-fired boilers only, the veteran battleship, struggling hard, worked up to almost ten knots as she began her final journey out of the base for Trondheim. Franke knew that he'd never be returning. His efforts in the region were at an end. *Rugen* wouldn't be needed so far north ever again.

In the still night air, the old warship's coal smoke wafted up and across to the shepherd's hut in which Jans Leiffson still sat on a bench, in amazement that he was still alive. Thank goodness those gun-wielding Germans had been sailors from that old relic of a ship whose crew never upset the locals. As the reek of smoke drifted through the still open door and the sound of *Rugen*'s asthmatic engines could be faintly heard, Leiffson stirred himself and staggering through the snow, he managed to reach his former look-out position just in time to see the glow from *Rugen*'s funnels as the stokers down below worked hard to coax as much speed as they could from the battleship's ancient engines. Gradually the light faded and the swishing sound of the *Rugen*'s progress also diminished as she rounded a bend in the fjord and disappeared out of sight.

Messages from both the Squadron Leader in charge of the Lancasters as well as Mulroan in his returning Mosquito gave their listeners at Admiralty HQ the news that the large warship, presumed to be *Dresden*, was no longer afloat. Destroyed. Sunk. When Sir Bernard Collins read it, he shrugged his shoulders. This was now the second time that sources had pointed to the demise of Reitz's ship. This time he tried to harden himself to the news but somehow he still felt a twinge of regret. Reitz was so close to home after such a long time away but Collins soon steeled himself. *Dresden* had sunk at least half-a-million tons, if not more, of Allied shipping.

Nevertheless something else told him not to accept *Dresden*'s demise until he could analyse Mulroan's photographs. It would only be then would he be able to rest his mind over the German warship. When they did arrive, late the next afternoon, he called for them to be enlarged. Something puzzled him but he couldn't put his finger on it straight away. Half-an-hour later the larger versions were ready. He called in two other senior officers. 'Go on, look at these and tell me what you think' he asked.

After a careful scrutiny, one of them said 'Something's not right, is it?'

'Go on. You tell me' replied Collins, hoping that the man's thoughts were his.

'Well – er – sir, there's not enough wreckage. No bodies. No signs of bits and pieces. At least with *Tirpitz* we had an upturned hull.'

'She was twice *Dresden*'s size' ventured the other staff officer.

Collins came back with a harsher tone to his voice 'Well, if it wasn't *Dresden*, or this –' here he pointed to the just discernible ram-like bows of *Rugen* '– bit of relic that the Allies have never deemed worth the trouble to sink, then on what was it the Lancasters wasted their bombs?'

'A very quickly assembled decoy of small boats and a bit of canvas' ventured the older of the two staff officers.

'Mmmm. Just what I thought. We've been had by the short and curlies, gentlemen. Reitz and his merry lads are now probably steaming, as fit as a well-tuned fiddle, past Trondheim. Another twenty-four hours and she'll be in Kiel.'

Collins went on to ask for details of any possible strike-force that would be able to catch the speeding battlecruiser. The news was somewhat gloomy. Only old slow battleships and one fleet carrier, with serious engine problems, were at Scapa. A small escort carrier had sailed at the time of the news of *Dresden*'s startling re-appearance for the Norwegian coast. HMS *Bempton* with an escort of three destroyers. 'Just in case' one of the staff officers said. Collins nodded, adding that it was better than nothing. She was steering for Trondheim but an order went out for her to alter course as fast as she could for the Stavanger region which *Dresden* would have to get round before entering the Skagerrak.

Even so, Collins feared that she'd be too late. Unless Reitz took *Dresden* in for a further re-fuelling stop.

Unknown to Collins, that was precisely what Reitz was doing at that precise moment. In a quiet, secluded and desolate fjord a few miles south of Trondheim. There *Dresden* took in enough fuel from *Olaf* to top up her tanks. The tanker, having succeeded in repairing her engines, and then completing a dash into Trondheim, the last two hundred miles in darkness, hurriedly moved from her berth on receiving a signal from *Dresden* to go to the fjord which Horst knew. Reitz was grateful for the U-boat man's intimate knowledge of the Norwegian coast, especially this quiet fjord with enough water for both *Dresden* and *Olaf* to find a sheltered anchorage. Reitz considered it to be far too risky to refuel out at sea, thinking that already the appearance of his ship must have caused a great consternation in the Allied naval ranks.

Olaf returned to Trondheim's main harbour, rather than to the nearby U-boat base. Her captain's instructions were not to hand over her remaining fuel for Reitz told Rimmer, before the two ships parted, that *Dresden* may be ordered back to Norway for operations against Arctic convoys. Reflecting on this, Reitz smiled to himself. Without that Japanese fuel, he wouldn't have been on the bridge watching *Dresden*'s bows cleave through the seas had he not agreed to sail with Kurita's ships. He'd helped Kurita. The Japanese had helped him and now *Dresden* was almost home. Get round Stavanger and then into the home straight. He knew it wasn't going to be easy. The proximity to the air bases in the British Isles was going to be negotiated without being too sure of whether *Dresden*'s engines, badly strained as they were, would last out despite the assurances of Herzog and Luth.

Another nervous Norwegian agent, in Trondheim, sent Collins the news that Sir Bernard had more or less expected. A large tanker only recently arrived in the port, had briefly left her berth for about twelve hours but that she was back again. Collins guessed that the tanker could possibly be *Dresden*'s source of refuelling. Then came another terse message. The tanker was a Norwegian one, called *Olaf*, and the agent requested the Allies not to bomb her. She was moored close to a residential area. Could cause unnecessary suffering.

Collins nodded yet again, and added that the tanker would probably be nearly empty of fuel if she'd been with *Dresden* since leaving Far Eastern waters.

'Come here, man, let's work out where *Dresden* could be. Let's say she's doing thirty knots.'

'Here sir, off Stavanger, by mid-day, I should guess.'

'Wow! That'll be within *Bempton*'s range. Get her captain to send off a flight of search aircraft and also warn that Norfolk air base for its Mosquitoes to get bombed-up. We might just find Reitz and get in one raid before dark. Come on, man, hurry. Let's go and catch Reitz – and make sure this time!'

As *Dresden* powered through the cold Norwegian waters little more, at any one time, than thirty miles from the nearest fjord hiding place, down in her Sick Berth Helmut Brautsch, on a rare moment of being off-watch, was murmuring sweet assurances to Andrea as the few patients in their cots settled down to rest after a light mid-day meal. She spoke of her nervousness of being so near to Germany but Helmut assured her that the Spanish nationality papers that she carried, as well as the Spanish passport, would satisfy the home-based authorities of her identity as well as Reitz's covering letter that she'd been a willing worker for the Kreigsmarine whilst serving on *Dresden.* The letter carried the stamp of Admiral Wenneker and thus also the approval of the Navy's chief, Grand-Admiral Doenitz. After a while, she dropped off to sleep, nestling in the crook of his left arm, seemingly satisfied with Helmut's words of reassurance and endearment.

Suddenly alarm bells began to ring. Helmut hurriedly awoke his wife, pulled on his sea-boots and oilskins, gave her a quick kiss and then ran out of the Sick Berth, making his way, to his Action Stations positions on the bridge.

'What is it?' he asked, somewhat breathlessly, as he arrived on the bridge, sensing the *Dresden* keeling over in a tight curve towards the indented coastline.

'Aircraft out at sea. Most likely from a carrier. Radar's picked them up. We're hoping to get in amongst those nearby islands and hopefully lose them before they appear' he was informed.

'Aircraft sir. Coming from astern on the rear starboard quarter.'

'Thankyou Prebke.'

It was just three miles to the shelter of the islands. Perhaps another seven minutes for *Dresden*.

The aircraft were clearly visible. Three of them. One of *Bempton*'s search groups.

Suddenly they swung away. They'd found what they'd been sent out to seek. A large warship going at full speed. Course – approximately south-south west. Rounding Bokna Fjord close to Stavanger.

The leading aircraft, piloted by Flight Lieutenant Roger Tilsome, streaked low over the sea. Tilsome snapped into his voice microphone 'It's her alright. I'm informing our chaps on mother.'

'Back on course' snapped Reitz. '185 degrees. Come on Serle, where's our next hiding place before they send their bomb or torpedo aircraft after us?'

'There sir, round that headland. Thirty kilometres from here.'

Half-an-hour passed. Forty minutes. Then another five. The afternoon sky still remained empty. *Dresden* rounded Norway's south-western extremity. She began to turn for the Skagerrak.

'Sir, radar room here. Aircraft. Twenty miles to west on starboard side.'

Prebke's eyes, as everyone else's in a position to be able to do so, were glued to the skies abaft the starboard midships.

Straining to be the first to obtain a visual sighting. All the available anti-aircraft guns pointed in the air as if tracking the expected attackers. As usual it was Prebke who saw them first. 'Enemy aircraft at one hundred and seventy-five degrees.' Almost due astern.

The aircraft, lightly bombed Seafires, were from *Bempton* with orders to try and slow *Dresden* down before a second wave of attackers, a squadron of Mosquitoes flying from their Norfolk base reached the area. Just before dusk.

Horst knew of a deepish fjord about five miles ahead of the speeding battlecruiser. His fellow U-boat crewmen had all transferred to *Olaf* during the recent re-fuelling stop-over but he knew that he was expected to take command of one of the new Walther

U-boats waiting for him at a base near Kiel. Reitz had been pleased to retain him for his knowledge of the Norwegian coast was far better than his. Horst seemed to have the knack of always being able to suggest *Dresden*'s next refuge point. Suddenly Horst, with the Seafires in clear view, yelled 'They've only got small bombs. More used to striking at U-boats and small surface vessels. Probably from one of their escort carriers. Use only your quick-firers.'

The leading Seafire came in, its wing cannons spitting flame, lashing the sea and then in a menacing whiplash across the battlecruiser's decks from which erupted a vicious return of fire. One answering stream of tracer whisked under one of the Seafire's wings but it dived low and jinked its way out of harm's reach.

Three planes curved in from the land side but *Dresden*'s defensive fire forced them to drop their light bombs too early. One of the planes trailed a thin plume of smoke as it streaked away. Horst yelled 'Six more. Here they come!' Somehow the first five that came in bore a charmed life as they streaked in through the hail of fire that greeted them but Flight Sergeant Driscoll in the last aircraft didn't see the hail of fire for he was already dead as a line of machine gun bullets stitched their scarlet ribbon of death right across his chest. But even as he died he was dealing the battlecruiser a desperate blow. As the leading five planes escaped the fire of *Dresden*'s anger, Driscoll's aircraft in flames, crashed horrendously abaft the funnel on the battlecruiser's starboard side. On top of a four point one inch (10.5cm) gun. Aircraft, bombs, aircraft fuel and ammunition went up simultaneously in a flame-searing explosion. Bright red, yellow and orange flames shot up into the air above the crash site. Shards of metal whizzed around. Three exposed anti-aircraft gunners simply collapsed as splinters smashed into them. Those in the gun turret and also in a five-point-nine (15cm) gun below them were immediately burnt into lumps of charred flesh and then disintegrated into unrecognisable bits. Other men staggered away from the blast, horribly burned and injured.

In the flash of a second, Driscoll had unknowingly dealt *Dresden* one of the most death-dealing blows so far as her crew had ever experienced since she'd first taken to the water after her launching.

Reitz was horrified as he stared down at the plume of smoke trailing behind his speeding warship. From the bridge's starboard wing he could plainly see the damage and then the orange jackets of Hiltzern's fire and damage control crews as they arrived on the scene.

Hoses were soon playing harsh jets of cold sea water on to the flames and within five minutes of the crash, the flames of the aircraft fuel and other associated fires were under control and were gradually being extinguished. Dark smoke mingled with extensive plumes of white vaporised steam trailed well behind the stern. Hiltzern's team with sledgehammers and crowbars began to prize open the entry points of both the gun turrets in the hopes of rescuing anyone left alive but in vain. Having gained access, the would-be rescuers were instead faced with the awesome task of extracting the charred bodies of the gun crews and then dragging them out to the deck. Shovels cleared up the bits that had been bodies and these were hastily emptied into large buckets. The shattered remnants of the Seafire were cut free from the superstructure and then shoved over the side with the dead pilot still inside. There was no time for any niceties. Padré Jervaulx, himself with a cut in his left arm, said as many quick prayers as he could think of as the bits of bodies that couldn't be recognised were dropped overboard, having been transferred into weighted sacks. But the strain of knowing that he didn't know who he was saying his farewell eulogies for was too much for him and he was violently sick. Roughneck Otto Schenke held him steady. Jervaulx muttered his thanks and then shook himself free to carry on with his ministrations to the wounded. Nurse Andrea was already at the scene with two attendants as they hastily patched up wounds and supervised the stretcher cases down to the Sick Berth where Doctor Lebers and his assistants began the gruesome task of amputations, if required, as well as other assistance to the shocked men.

Still on the bridge, Reitz continued to receive regular reports about the damage and the progress at discovering its extent. As well as the two larger gun-turrets, two other sites where smaller anti-aircraft guns positioned nearby were totally inoperable. Not only were their crews killed or seriously wounded but the guns were damaged beyond repair. On her stern starboard quarter *Dresden*'s anti-aircraft defences were now drastically weakened. Fortunately Farsund Fjord was only a couple of miles away and Serle, with Horst, had already plotted the course for entry. A small patrol boat began approaching them but Reitz signalled it to keep clear as the damaged battlecruiser turned for her approach. Horst knew the fjord and indicated where the battlecruiser could moor close enough to its steep sides which would mask any radar search in the gathering dark should Allied aircraft be coming in for a further attack.

The Mosquitoes took off from their Lincolnshire base twenty minutes later than what Collins and his staff had hoped for due to a delay caused by the unexpected puncture to a fuel bowser's tyre. They were to fly as direct routes as possible in order to rendezvous with one of *Bempton*'s Seafires which was going to guide them to the suspected course of the German warship. On board the aircraft carrier the returning nine pilots of the strike against *Dresden* were hurriedly debriefed. Although mortified by the loss of Driscoll, all the men agreed that the *Dresden* was probably quite severely damaged by the Seafire crashing on to her upper-works. However, William Wright, *Bempton*'s captain, asked them if the German ship had slowed down but the pilots couldn't give him much reassurance on that aspect as their aircraft had been so low on fuel that they'd been unable to accurately assess the German ship's damage to its fullest extent.

Wright then turned to his station on the carrier's bridge so as to be in touch with the soon due Flight Y39A of the Norfolk Mosquitos. At a range of thirty miles, *Bempton*'s radar picked up the approaching aircraft and as promised, one of her Seafires took off to make her rendezvous with them and guide them to the probable position of *Dresden* as the darkness of the approaching winter's night began to become more evident in its gloomy presence. Wright just hoped that they'd find the *Dresden* before she in turn could find a fjord in order to mask the radar search of the Mosquito. If she'd been slowed down by the Seafire's crash then they'd stand a chance. If not – well, it would be difficult.

As darkness fell, Farsund Fjord's tall sides enveloped the battlecruiser as she sought its protective shelter. Reitz decided to stay for about two hours in order to give his damage control party time to patch up the worst of the wreckage and to give the ship some semblance of normality again. He knew that every member of the crew was feeling the shock of losing so many of their friends and companions when almost within sight of reaching home. Ninety-three dead at the latest count, with at least another thirty seriously wounded. *Dresden*'s bows were anchored facing the distant sea although the entrance to the fjord was out of sight. Reitz ordered two of her own launches out on patrol at the entrance to give a possible advance warning of the approach of aircraft and hurried signals to the few Germans in the area requested assistance for anti-aircraft warnings. A phone trilled on the bridge. Reitz picked it up 'Yes.' It was Brautsch from one of the launches which had short-range talk radio with him which was linked into the battlecruiser's main wireless centre. 'Flight of aircraft have just gone overhead past the entrance to the fjord.'

Roger Tilsome in his Seafire informed Wing-Commander Chris Synswick who was leading the Mosquito that he expected to sight *Dresden* at any time and was talking to him as the flight flew over Brautsch's barely-moving launch although they were unaware of its presence below them. Synswick reported back that he had nothing on his radar receiver but ordered the flight to spread out. Although more used to strikes against U-boats and coastal craft, he felt sure that they'd find the German warship. They searched the coast for the next one hundred miles but no *Dresden*. Two small patrol boats and a badly-damaged U-boat trying to get across to Kiel on the surface were pounced on by individual members of Flight Y39-A and pounded into destruction in a matter of minutes leaving scattered bits of wreckage, oil slicks and drowned crews as the only evidence of their presence.

But no sign of the battlecruiser.

Reluctantly Synswick ordered the planes to return to base as fuel reserves were running too low for an extended search. There was no way that he could order a long night-time search of every inlet and fjord. If the battlecruiser was there, she'd just look like a rock on the radar receivers. Only daylight would reveal her presence.

Collins was extremely disappointed when he heard of the failure to catch *Dresden*. It was obvious that her damage hadn't restricted her speed and that she'd been able to get her furious flames very quickly under control for they would have been easily seen in the darkness. As yet, none of the local Norwegian agents had sent out a message about the battlecruiser. Maybe he'd hear from one of them soon if *Dresden* was still in the area by daybreak. He could also expect no further help from the Royal Airforce or Coastal Command. All their other operational aircraft were already in night action on pre-ordered duties. Captain Wright from *Bempton* was promising a daylight search of the area but that was at least ten hours away. If the battlecruiser wasn't all that badly damaged he guessed that Reitz would risk a night dash into the Skagerrak and by dawn he'd be masked amongst the Danish islands in her approach to Kiel. Damn that man Reitz! He certainly had luck on his side. Even when damaged, he could still give him the slip.

Collins guessed correctly. Reitz recalled his two patrol launches just an hour after Brautsch's sighting report. Only two hours after anchoring in Farsund's shelter, the battlecruiser was on her way again. As she made her cautious way out to sea, Reitz at last left the bridge to quickly inspect the damage and then with a still badly shaken Jervaulx, hurriedly conducted a hasty burial at sea of the rest of the more recognisable bodies of their recent comrades. Jervaulx's stammered eulogies could barely be heard as he desperately sought for the right words as each weighted bag was dropped overboard. Sixty three men were committed to the waters by the time *Dresden* exited the fjord's protective sides. Then the burial party dispersed and the battlecruiser picked up speed for her final dash for the relative safety of home waters. Soon she was flat out at thirty-three knots. An arrow straight course. Reitz threw caution to the wind. He wanted the darkness to cover his run for home but as he looked behind him he could, despite the darkness, see the tremendous wake that *Dresden* was leaving behind her. There was no moon but a few stars twinkled in the night sky above as the warship tore through waters she'd last crossed nearly four years previously.

At Naval Headquarters in a deep bunker at the naval port of Kiel, Vice-Admiral Bernhard Rogge stared intensely at the chart illumined by his desk lamp. On it, a small boat-shaped lump of wood stood out with an etched shadow. It represented *Dresden.* The chart of the Western Baltic and its exit to the North Sea was not one Rogge had been in the habit of making an intense study within the last six months. Normally he used the ones that showed him the Central and Eastern Baltic for, from those charts, he planned and plotted the moves of the surviving big ships left in a sailable condition for the Kriegsmarine as well as the units of destroyer and smaller, down to the patrol boats and converted fishing craft. And all the merchant ships capable of carrying at least fifty persons. The planning, hurried at first, had begun the previous August when the heavy cruiser *Prinz Eugen* fired on Russian army positions as they advanced towards the German-held coastal areas. One by one Rogge, with his co-planner Vice-Admiral Thiele, organised the bigger units of the Kriegsmarine to provide gunfire support to the hard-pressed Wehrmacht units whilst the smaller vessels went into the shallow waters to bring off wounded and non-fighting military personnel. As the Russian Army advanced towards and eventually into East Prussia, the need to evacuate civilians grew as well. Almost every day ships loaded up and sailed westwards to the temporary haven of the ports of Northern Germany. Rogge often mused 'The Allies had their Dunkirk evacuation but we've one at least ten times worse in the Eastern Baltic.'

But then had come a seemingly impossible miracle. That surprising attack by a ship that he'd thought sunk with all hands on the other side of the World. Fighting Americans. Assisting their ally, the Japanese. Rogge had been grateful for their assistance when he'd commanded merchant ship raider *Atlantis* and like *Dresden*, he'd captured a Norwegian tanker, Ole Jacob, then full of aviation fuel. He'd sent the tanker to Japan and had exchanged her fuel for a supply of diesel fuel oil. Thanks to that he'd been able to extend his raiding cruise for a remarkable six hundred and fifty or so days. A record for a raider up to that time. But here was *Dresden*. Dodging the Allied attempts to catch and sink her. Now on her last leg of the race for home. Rogge had never been in on the ruse set up by Reitz and Wenneker but now he knew why.

The less people that knew, the better the chances were for Reitz to get his ship through the Allied-dominated waters for home. Even Grand Admiral Doenitz hadn't told him until *Dresden* made her brief but scintillating attack on the Arctic convoy.

Rogge remembered at first the surprise amongst his own staff on hearing the news. Then the joy. Finally the reality of the dangerous lap down the Norwegian coast.

Now she was racing from her Farsung Fjord refuge with darkness as her only cover. Ordering his chauffeur to have his battered black Opel Saloon car at the ready, he called an aide. 'Let me know immediately if *Dresden* runs into trouble – and don't bother me about the Eastern situation. It can wait. We must make ready for our famous raider. It's nothing short of a miracle that she's so close. I'm going to the quayside.' Rogge's target was one of Germany's few surviving modern destroyers, in the process of tying up after helping to escort the latest convoy to safety. *ZA-28*. New and modern in late 1943 she now bore the rust-streaked scars of constant war service. Sent to Cherbourg to bolster up the flagging fortunes of the defence of occupied waters of Northern France, she'd been on patrol when the Allies launched their D-Day invasion. The three minesweepers accompanying her had been ordered back to Cherbourg whilst *ZA-28* turned to launch a salvo of torpedoes. Registering two hits on a large landing craft, her captain then swung her through two columns of more advancing craft and in a confused action, aided by frequent smokescreens and limited early morning visibility, the destroyer at full speed, escaped the Allied fleet and fled, first to Calais for a brief refuelling halt and then via Rotterdam, Wilhelmshaven and the Kiel canal, to find security at Kiel and was at once assigned to the growing Kriegsmarine presence in the Eastern Baltic.

Her youngish captain, Fritz Wegener, smoking a long thin black cheroot, leaned over the port-wing of the bridge looking down as the latest batch of ill-clad, gaunt civilian refugees shuttled down the gangplank with two of his blue-uniformed sailors guiding them on their way. Then he saw the black Opel draw up alongside the gangway. 'That's Admiral Bernhard come to pay us a visit. Seems to be in a hurry' he said out loud to no-one in particular. He saw the Admiral get out of the car and start to climb the gangplank with two of his aides gently pushing aside the bewildered civilians who were leaving the destroyer, grateful that they'd been saved but uncertain as to the future ahead of them. With their pathetic bundle of possessions – some had nothing at all – and nearly all with hollow-eyed expressions, they didn't really register who this man in a well-worn Kriegsmarine uniform was as he made his way past them. They didn't know that thanks to his effective organisation that they owed their lives to him.

Rogge saluted the deck officer and asked to be taken to see Wegener. He was escorted to the destroyer captain's small sea-cabin, abaft the main upper bridge. There he shook hands with Wegener and bluntly went into his reasons for coming aboard.

'One hour Kapitan Wegener. One hour only to rid your ship of the evacuees and then refuel – a barge will be alongside within ten minutes. Then set course for the Skagerrak.'

'Are we going a-raiding?' mused the wiry captain of *ZA-28*.

'Not quite. Rather you're to be the chief escort for Germany's greatest raider. You know, battlecruiser *Dresden*.'

'*Dresden*? She's here? Already?'

'Almost. My staff officers here have the co-ordinates for a dawn rendezvous. She left Farsund Fjord about an hour ago. Torpedo boats T8 and T9 will be going with you as well. They arrived about three hours ahead of you – one of my junior officers is giving them their orders. All the instructions are with Rupert here –' he indicated a one-eyed officer behind him '– including your code signal to wireless when within short-wave range of *Dresden*. She's been under air attack and has apparently some damage but she's still capable of full speed.'

Rogge paused. The wry smile of Wegener's lined face had gone. The destroyer man was tired but not all that tired to realise the honour that he'd just been given. The honour of escorting a German sea-legend into safety. Germany may well be within just a few months of losing the war but *Dresden*'s arrival would be just the fillip the beleaguered Kreigsmarine needed at this, its most vital hour.

Wegener spoke quietly 'I've just brought back three hundred evacuees, more than half of them civilians. Some had been waiting more than a week on that freezing cold beach. We went in with cruiser *Köln* lobbing shells at the Russkies over our heads as my boats went to the beach. A desperate situation. You know that – God knows how many we've brought back since November. Five thousand? That's my exec's reckoning. Thousands more on other ships. And now this. *Dresden*. My God sir. it's nothing but a bleedin' miracle!'

'It is a miracle. We thought she'd been done for by the Yanks off Leyte but she's almost here. Go to it Wegener, bring her in – and when you have, there'll be some short leave for all of you – that's if you've anywhere to go!'

'Thanks Admiral.'

With that Rogge shook hands and made his way off *ZA-28*. Even as he did, he noticed that the fuel barge had already arrived and was, via her hoses, pumping oil into the destroyer.

A short time later, *ZA-28* churned out of the basin to begin her dash to rendezvous with *Dresden.* Away from the smell of Kiel that seemed to pervade the area – burning houses, dead bodies, oil from sunken wrecks, burst gas mains – all combining in a general air of gloom and despair. As Royal Airforce Chief Marshall Arthur Harris had once laconically commented 'The Nazis sowed the seed. Now they're suffering from my whirlwind. See how they like it.' Or words to that effect, mused Rogge as he made his way back to his headquarters bunker. Then he thought of the girl. Should he tell her yet? Maybe when he knew for certain that *Dresden* would be arriving.

As he entered his thoughts were decided for him. A dark-haired woman faced him as he passed the reception area. In the uniform of a female auxiliary attached to the Kriegsmarine. She saluted him. '*Dresden* sir? What news?'

Rogge looked at the pleading eyes.

'Sir, I know her captain. George Reitz. We're engaged to be married' The woman blurted out.

'Really Miss Chemnitz!' Rogge raised his eyebrows but his eyes smiled back at Elle.

'Well sir, when's he coming home?'

'Soon. In less than twenty-four hours I should think. If not earlier. Like you –' here Rogge sounded somewhat serious '– I had never given up hope that she'd been able to break through the American hold over the Japanese and manage to get into more open waters. Something deep down told me that she hadn't been sunk. And –' he looked straight at Elle '– now, George Reitz is bringing her home – but to what? A very different Germany from the one he left. Look around us. Did we expect this?'

Elle shook her head, tears welling up.

'Don't worry my dear, he's nearly here. Look, make arrangements for some time off. Say a fortnight. That's all I can guarantee for them. Doenitz has already hinted that he wants *Dresden* turned round as soon as we can. Priority order but keep it quiet. Spies all around – Allied and Nazi ones!' With that he gave a quick bow and turned once again into his main office. God, he was tired. He didn't even know what he was going to do when *Dresden* arrived – if she managed this last lap successfully.

Collins didn't like the idea of *Dresden* getting back to Northern Germany. A stormy telephone call with Air Chief Marshall Harris hadn't gone down at all well. In fact he thought that Harris had been quite rude, pointing out to him that it was no good bleating at him to spare more RAF bombers to sink the battlecruiser when the Navy had miserably failed in that respect over the last four years. Collins winced at the words that had come from Harris but his final sentence really cut him to the quick. 'Well, your naughty baby is now scuttling for home. She can't do any more harm to your Atlantic convoy routes even if she is still afloat. Possibly we'll have a go at her when she gets to Kiel. Stuck there in the harbour she'll be a sitting duck, just like *Tirpitz* was – and we won't be going for any dummies, either.' With that, Harris banged down the telephone and there, so far as he was concerned, the matter rested. For the time being.

'Damn, damn, damn. Pompous ass' snorted Collins 'Can't even spare a dozen aircraft. If she gets back to Kiel the Nazis could make a lot of her return. We'll look right silly fools. It'll probably inspire them to even more fanatical efforts and determination to fight on and on.' He swept his hands through his thinning hair and turned to the Skagerrak chart again. In his mind he could see the handsome warship streaking across the dark seas at full speed for a dawn appearance near a Danish island. Masking her from radar searches and also near Luftwaffe bases – or Kriegsmarine naval escorts units. 'Damn. She's home. After all this time.'

Deep down in the Führer-bunker in central Berlin, Adolf Hitler called for an early morning report from his hastily gathered chiefs-of-staff and their aides. He'd just returned from visiting troops on the Oder front giving some of them words of encouragement as they prepared to face the expected Russian onslaught. At the surface entrance, snow flurries whipped at the faces of the specially selected SS guards as they stood sentry duty. Solidly. Men who knew their duty, and only that.

Down below, the assembled men, some of whom were getting weary of the erratic hours that their leader seemed to favour watched somewhat dully as their black leather-coated Führer entered the conference room well below the cold harsh weather above ground. A gloomy, damp hole. And they were in it. In he came, looking as blank as any of them. A look that they feared. By him smirked one of the Führer's principal henchman, Martin Bormann, a sneer over his bloated face. A secret figure, wheeling and dealing dangerously in the background. Thin-faced Goebbels was on Hitler's other side. Those who looked at him couldn't fail to detect the faintness of a smile on his thin face and almost bloodless, lips. The fourth figure to enter was perhaps the sickest looking of the quartet. Admiral Freydeburg. Unfortunate choice Bormann had thought when Doenitz appointed him to be the Kriegsmarine's chief representative on Hitler's staff. Pale. Seemingly without any humour or real National Socialist party spirit at all. An almost pathetic figure. As if he sensed, more than the others, that the fingers of gloom, despair and death were clutching at his and everyone else's throats the longer Hitler delayed ending the war. Yet for once, there could be detected in Freydeburg's pale face, just that hint of a bit of colour. Of a spark of life in the man.

Hitler stared at them and flipped his right arm in response to the chorus of 'Heil Hitler', stiff-armed salutes and the clicking of well-polished boots. He didn't trust any of them. No-one who was of a military bearing. Not since that dreadful Count Von Stauffenberg had tried to blow him up the previous July. Providence had decreed the dictator's survival. Perhaps it was saving him and Germany for worse horrors to come. If so, Hitler seemed unaware of it. To him Providence was on his side. From some resource, he would still guide Germany to victory.

The group gasped inwardly as the demented dictator opened his mouth with the harsh greeting 'You half-baked, faint-hearted cowards. How often have I told you that you should trust me in everything? How can we lose? The example of our marvellous battlecruiser *Dresden* should be a shining light to us all. Admiral Freydeburg tells me that she will be docking in Kiel this very day. Four years ago she left these shores and now she's back. She has outwitted the Allies. She will lead the Kriegsmarine, and thus Germany, to even greater victories!' No-one dared to interrupt him, that is if they realised and some of them did, that the *Dresden* was the brain child of Admiral Canaris whom the thugs obeying the orders of their Fuhrer had seen fit to arrest and throw into a jail, without even the decency of a trial. Perhaps they also over-looked the fact that the same luckless Admiral made sure that no Nazi Party member was ever appointed to her crew. Maybe they placed into the back of their psychopathic minds, the general scorn and hatred that Hitler poured out about the uselessness of the Kriegsmarine's big ships. Just two years previously only the superb diplomatic skills of the Navy's new supremo Grand Admiral Karl Doenitz, had saved the now Baltic-based ships from being consigned to a heap of Nazi-ordered scrap iron.

Collectively, they feared that there was worse to come. If the anticipated success of the arrival of *Dresden* was momentarily giving their Fuhrer a brief glimpse of military satisfaction, then that moment was indeed a short one. Adolf Hitler's face went very still, blanched white as he paused, glaring at the men around him with those peculiar staring eyes of his. Only Bormann seemed to be smiling. Or was it smirking at the uncomfortable glances from the gathered group. Quite suddenly, Hitler's face started to blotch as he launched into a tirade about the ineptness of the failure of all Germany's armed forces at being totally unable to put up a coherent defence. In the West, after the disastrous failure in the Ardennes against the Jew-inspired Western Allies and in the East, the retreat in front of the criminal Bolshevik hordes. Not once in his tirade did he stop to even consider his own failings for the military disaster that was overtaking his country. Nor did he show the remotest sign of any empathy for the appalling suffering of the millions who had given their lives for his plainly misdirected Nazi-controlled war – those who'd fought for Germany; the civilians who'd perished in the now daily bombing of the Fatherland's cities, towns and villages; nor the countless millions who'd suffered as a result of his extreme orders of bestial brutality – in the labour camps, prisons or the vast areas bordered by barbed wire where the main architectural symbol was a burning chimney.

It was if the homecoming of Germany's most successful sea raider was now utterly wiped out of his mind. Here he was, Adolf Hitler, totally demented but also totally ruthless, haranguing with his wild and unsubstantiated statements the very leaders that he himself had appointed to lead his National Socialist Germany into an expected glorious triumph but instead, still with himself well and truly in the lead, was sending them down the now inevitable slippery slope towards the appalling ruin that none of them, apart from perhaps Bormann, could even in their most dreadful nightmares, have ever envisaged.

It was still dark as destroyer *ZA-28* and her two smaller consorts, steaming at nigh on twenty-five knots came within wireless-range of *Dresden*'s short-wave coded signals. 'We've picked her up' reported the destroyer's excited wireless operator as he saluted his captain.

'Warn the lookouts to keep their eyes peeled' murmured Wegener to his First Officer. 'She'll be about twenty degrees off our port bow. Visual sighting possibly in less than half-an-hour. Just as it will be getting lighter.'

Thirty three minutes later a lookout cried 'Ship in sight. Bearing thirteen degrees off the port bow!'

A little later, the dark silhouette of a large warship with a white-moustache at her bows began to materialise.

'Send up today's recognition rockets.'

Green, green and red flares soared up from *ZA-28*'s mid-ships. Moments later, two reds soared up from *Dresden.*

'It's *Dresden.* Thank goodness' announced Wegener. 'Signal her – "Welcome home; follow us."'

The destroyer heeled over, turning to starboard and then in the lead with the two torpedo boats on either flank of *Dresden*, began the return to Kiel with every member of their crews having a real sense of pride in the honour of being the escort vessels chosen to bring home Germany's famous sea-raider.

'We've done it! We're back!' yelled Hiltzern thumping both fists into the air. Men on *Dresden*'s upper deck started cheering and their rejoicing spread throughout the whole ship. Even men not on duty emerged on deck to witness the sight of ZA28 turning to take the lead. It was if the tension of the long journey from Japan, including the nerve-racking times of the Samar Sea action, and the breakthrough of the Allied-controlled sea-lanes, the sharp action against that Arctic convoy and finally the high speed evasive dash down Norway's indented coastline, suddenly it was all lifted. *Dresden* was nearly home. Those who'd survived the four years away from their homeland were now enormously relieved that they were now so close to home. Close to their loved ones again. This was their moment. Then it was back to reality as the ship's loudspeakers intoned 'All men back to their stations. We're not quite home – yet.'

Few of them on *Dresden* could even dare to envisage the battering that their homeland was still taking. In about six hours they'd be tied up to the quayside at Kiel. The disciplined crew settled back to their duties, happy in the knowledge that soon they'd see their girlfriends, wives, parents, mates and other contacts close to their families. Each crew member tried to collect their thoughts on the hope-for reunion ahead of them. That is if those they expected to see had still survived. Or was still part of their own particular friendship circle.

'Aircraft approaching from the west' reported the radar room.

Eyes swung to the skies on *Dresden*'s starboard side. Soon, silvery trails could be seen in the cool of that clear dawn morning.

The anti-aircraft guns began to track the aircraft that flew very high above the four ships. 'American bombers. Won't be interested in us. Probably going on a high-level bombing run of one of our central Baltic ports' commented Horst to Reitz. 'They aren't all that accurate. Spread their bombs over a wide area. Mainly to batter our civilian personnel as much as anything else.' Reitz grimaced. Horst continued 'Sorry, Herr Kapitan, but daylight bombing is as much an occurrence as night time raids. Our famous Herr Goering's aeroplanes are just about helpless against defending our land. A few do manage a burst of heroics in the new ME-262's but we haven't enough of them.'

'What's an ME-262?' asked a curious Hiltzern.

'The World's best jet fighter but like our so-called new superb subs, we just haven't enough of them' came back Horst's reply.

The trails of the American bombers crossed above the four streaming wakes without altering course. Nor did the ships below alter their course. A course for the Kriegsmarine's main port of Kiel.

Chapter 12

'She doesn't know who I am'

Snow filtered between the myriad of recently opened cracks in the rubble-strewn streets of the much bombed, shattered capital city of National Socialist Germany. Maybe it softened the harsh irregular outline of the numerous wrecked buildings that formed the skyline of once-proud Berlin but sooner, if not later, it would melt away to reveal the city's increasing welter of war scars. Tea on the terraces on either side of the Wilhemstrasse was but a distant long-forgotten memory. The early euphoria of the war's beginnings was now replaced by an air of desperate resignation of no longer believing in whatever the vitriolic vibes that the radio might pronounce. The stark fact was that the Anglo-American bomber fleets almost daily dropped their lethal loathsome loads of destruction without much opposition. Worse was the fact that even some hated Russian bombers were adding to the general air of shattered gloom and despair.

One man, temporarily at least, even as he gazed through a broken window, was albeit briefly elated. Never one to show much emotion, Grand Admiral Karl Doenitz, that early morning weary of his subterranean existence in a damp cold concrete-protected set of underground offices decided to climb up to ground-level. As head of the Kriegsmarine he'd not only witnessed the gradual destruction of his 'sea wolves', the U-boats but also, despite saving them from a Führer ordered scrap-heap, the retreat of all the big surviving surface ships to the Baltic and North German waters where, providing there was enough fuel and the ships were mechanically sound enough, they were proving their worth in the seaward defence against the steadily advancing Russian forces, which at that moment were battering against German positions in East Prussia. As he stared out at the gently swirling snow he allowed himself an inward smile. The secret he and the closest members of his staff was out. He'd forced himself to keep it quiet, even from the Fuhrer himself. Not that he cared what the ex-corporal in his equally damp underground rat-hole thought. Even though Doenitz enjoyed a good working relationship with Hitler. Perhaps it was because he was not afraid to stand his ground. The saving of the big ships had been one example. Another was his constant search for the ultimate U-boat. Now with the new Walther boats almost ready for full active service, maybe his dream would reach reality. But then, it may well be too late. Allied bombings, the loss of experienced personnel and the progress of Germany's enemies approaching the shipyards or training areas were hurting the development programme. Badly.

So Doenitz watched the snow. Some flakes dissipating into virtual instant oblivion. Others settling to form an ever-increasing homogenous mess. It had always fascinated him ever since he was a little boy when out in the country he and his father frolicked in the snowdrifts or on a metal sheet to sledge down steep bankings. It was such a change to emerge and see the outside world. The air. How he wished, at times, that he could escape Berlin and get back – yes – that was it, he would leave the city and go to see the arrival of his secret. He could leave all the immediate administration to his pale, sickly-looking deputy, Admiral Freydeburg who spent quite a lot of his time soaking up the tirades of the Führer in his irregularly held military conferences. It had made a change seeing Freydeburg break into a smile when he'd passed on the Führer's delighted attitude on being told that their long-held secret was making its appearance just a week or so ago off the Norwegian coast.

Now their secret was coming home. She was nearly there. She'd been assumed sunk at Leyte. Even the Allies had thought that. Doenitz had read their news reports. As well as hearing the BBC's newsreaders. How triumphant they'd all sounded – 'Nazi raider sunk with all hands. Scattered wreckage was all that remained. The scourge of Allied shipping at long last destroyed.'

So Doenitz smiled as he shouted for an orderly.

'My car. Now! Templehof airport. Warn the Condor crew.'

He could just recall *Dresden*'s captain although he knew enough of him in the file that he'd often referred to, either by himself or with Canaris, when the latter had still been in favour with the Nazi hierarchy. Suddenly it hit him. Canaris. *Dresden* was the brainchild of the little Admiral who even now languished under house arrest. No longer in favour. Suddenly Doenitz went cold. Just suppose that the SS and Gestapo henchmen attempted to besmirch Reitz and his crew. Yes, he knew he had to meet the battlecruiser on her arrival at Kiel. Not just to welcome her back but to warn her crew. As he sat in the armoured car he tried to visualise the *Dresden*. Dashing in and out of those Norwegian fjords. Thankfully the damage from that stricken aircraft hadn't caused her too much of a delay. It was quite amazing that the Allies hadn't been able to sink her. They must be feeling most displeased. For once, in a period of constant decline for Germany's armed forces, one example was still shining brightly. He knew that he had to protect both the ship and her crew. From both the Allies and the elements of the state that still dreamt of a thousand-year Reich of National Socialism whilst forgetting the reality of the dire immediacy of their country's future.

His mind kept wandering. How quickly could *Dresden* be made ready for sea? For Eastern Baltic action. How superbly the

Kriegsmarine's major surviving units were at last showing their worth. The rescuing of all those military and civilian personnel. Doenitz was a realist. He could see a Germany divided after the war. A Western half under an Anglo-American regime which would be far more flexible in its control than an Eastern sector that would be made to pay for the undoubted crimes of Hitler's appalling policies. The very thought of what he knew was called 'The Final Solution' made him shudder. Feel so unclean. Millions perishing because they were undesirable. They were Jews or gypsies or just people in the wrong place at the wrong time. The advancing Russians were said to be re-enacting the visions of raping and pillage reminiscent of those distant hordes from Mongolia under the leadership of Attila the Hun. Crimes repaid by more crimes.

His ships of the Kriegsmarine were now providing the safest of all the evacuation routes. At last, their guns, strength and armour-plating were proving their worth.

The armoured car lurched over some rubble. Briefly Doenitz peered through one of the narrow vision slits. Into his restricted vision he could see a few civilians shuffling over the piles of brick and snow-covered debris. Grey people on the grey streets of a grey city. Anonymous shapes in human form. What future was for them? Perhaps Providence was stoking up a real hell for them because they had deserted The Divine Being for the now mad orator who'd promised them everything but who now shuffled around, like them, a grey dismal apology of a human in a grey dismal bunker deep under a grey dismal apology of a once proud city. Armageddon was fast approaching but he, Doenitz, was escaping. Temporarily at least. Perhaps for good.

The car swept into the Templehof airfield, the shivering sentry on duty by the guard barrier hurriedly raising it and saluting knowing only that one of the country's brass hats was in the interior of the grey steel-sided eight-wheeler Puma as it swept past him, whirling the snow flakes in its wake and the eddies whipped at the flaps of his almost threadbare great coat.

Turning a corner, the Puma eventually pulled up outside one of the hangars. Waiting on the hurriedly swept tarmac stood one of Germany's last four-engined Condors still in regular service. Behind it, as he emerged from the armoured car, Doenitz could see two FW-190 fighters, again with their engines warming up. These two fighters would act as a vital escort to the bigger aircraft which had once flown thousands of miles over the endless restless waves of the North Atlantic, searching for convoys and reporting their course and speed to the U-boats that were gathering to attack the slow-moving merchantmen. Then the Allies introduced their hastily-built escort carriers that spelt the end of the big lumbering bomber-reconnaissance aircraft. Prudently withdrawn, this Condor was diverted for use by senior Kriegsmarine staff officers shuttling between the capital city and their North German naval centres. As a flying office it had proved to be highly invaluable when Doenitz flitted desperately between Berlin, Kiel and Wilhelmshaven in his efforts to save the Kriegsmarine's big ships from those scrap-heap threats of an enraged Fuhrer only two years ago.

Now with its powerful engines pushing it down the snow-flecked runway it carried Doenitz to a meeting with the one big surface vessel that would never have been considered in Hitler's furiously-stoked up non-naval brain simply because *Dresden* was in Japan at the time of that furore. Luckily for Doenitz, the Kriegsmarine and for the country as a whole, those big ships were now assisting in the biggest evacuation ever attempted by sea in history. 'What was it?' he thought, 'Two, three, maybe even four million people?' Doenitz shuddered as he felt the big aircraft lurch into the air leaving a furious whirl of eddying snow behind it as it left the runway for the slow climb away from, what Doenitz knew, to be in all probability, a city doomed to cede to the advances of the Bolshevik hordes. Dimly through one of the small round windows he could see one of the escorting fighters and bleakly hoped that there would be no need for it or its companion to have to go into action against what were proving to be far superior opponents, the American long-range Mustang fighters.

To his intense relief, although not to his stomach's, the Condor landed safely at an air-base close to Kiel and soon, another armoured car carried him through the streets of another city looking like a smaller but equally battered copy of the capital. Even a covering of snow couldn't disguise the fact that Kiel, despite its defensive anti-aircraft batteries, was in parts in a ruined, shattered state. 'How many naval ports were in an equally battered state?' thought the Grand-Admiral. Hamburg, Wilhelmshaven, Lübeck, Stettin, Kiel. It was amazing that the Kriegsmarine had any surface ships left at all but despite the bombings, the surviving ships had, as yet apart from *Gneisenau* and old veteran Schleswig-Holstein, escaped from any serious damage when in home-ports.

Naval Headquarters near the main waterfront had been prior warned of their Supremo's sudden visit. Rogge simply nodded with the words – 'To be expected when our greatest surface raider is about to come back home after four years at sea.' For Rogge it was a temporary relief for him and his staff to divert their minds from the Eastern Baltic evacuation programme. Night after night, sleep never came easy for him as he wrestled with the problems of which ships to use, which ones to undergo a quick overhaul, where to obtain fuel and other vital necessities; how to feed the crews and when if possible, to give them leave. The latter luxury was now a rare commodity. Perhaps a week at the most whilst the ships were in their home port. But now this. *Dresden* was nearly home and the Grand-Admiral was due at any moment.

Rogge snatched a slice of toast, swallowed a weak ersatz coffee and more than once looked at the chart showing *Dresden*'s final approach. Then he heard an officer call out, the stamp of sentry boots crashing together and the door to his control centre was banged open and in swept the Grand-Admiral brushing snow off his long black leather coat before sweeping the garment from his shoulders and having it taken away by an alert junior officer.

'Bernhard, it's good to see you again,' barked Doenitz as Rogge swept up his right arm in the naval salute. Outwardly cheerful, Doenitz continued 'Well, where shall we begin? Eh? *Heinrich Galster*. She safely docked? Eh?' Rogge gave a brief nod. The big thirty thousand ton ex-'Strength-through-Joy' liner only recently arrived and hopelessly overloaded with an estimated ten-thousand civilians on board, was at that time in the process of mooring in Kiel's main waterfront. Doenitz rubbed his hands 'Yes. Yes. We must continue to rescue as many of our people as is possible. I trust that both you and Admiral Thiele have the situation under control. Any problems re victualling or fuelling, let me know.' Rogge again nodded. Maybe he was wary of Doenitz. When he'd been appointed to the raider *Atlantis*, it was Erich Raeder, a definite non-Nazi, who'd been his supreme head. Somehow, deep down, he wasn't quite sure where Doenitz's political views lay. Maybe he'd come to condemn Reitz and his crew for even daring to return home. Even as he looked up at the Grand Admiral, he could see Doenitz's face become totally expressionless and bleak.

'Where is she? *Dresden*. Show me. Now!'

Rogge inwardly sighed. He knew that Doenitz's journey from Berlin was specifically to ask about the battlecruiser. He indicated to the chart table and bending over it, he pointed to a red marker labelled 'D' showing the *Dresden* within visual range of the approaches to Kiel. 'There sir, we reckon that she'll be docking within the half-hour. I was hoping to get down to the quayside to welcome Reitz and his ship although what they'll make of the present predicament that we are currently facing, I do not know.'

Doenitz grunted. 'Yes and I will be joining you. Now, where exactly are you berthing her?'

An aide produced another chart of the actual berthing area. Rogge pointed to a space 'Here sir, forward of the Kristen Wilhelmina.

She's a half-sunk liner that burst her plates when a bomb landed close to her but she's upright and we still use her upper decks for some of my staff's offices, storage space and even temporary accommodation. She's covered up with camouflaged tarpaulins and we'll do the same for *Dresden*. Hopefully from the air, she'll look like an extension of the waterfront. Even so I guess that the Allies in London will soon learn of her presence.'

Doenitz looked even bleaker. 'All the more reason to try and get her quickly back into action.' Rogge raised his eyebrows. 'Yes Bernhard, I do know that under normal conditions she'd need at least three months, if not longer, to be properly overhauled but damn it, we just don't have that time. The war does not go well. We need every possible surface vessel in the Eastern Baltic. It's going to have to be two weeks, Bernhard. Two weeks and then, off back to sea.'

'Sir! The crew –'

Doenitz savagely interrupted 'They'll have to be told and I will tell them. I know, I know, that they should be returning as heroes. Believe me Bernhard the way things are, they'll be better out at sea. Things look dreadful – the military situation, the food situation, the very structure of the country. All on the defensive, on shortages, on the verge of collapse. But –' here Doenitz paused. His inner thoughts screaming to force him to say what three years ago would have been the unthinkable '– but, Bernhard, our worst enemy is amongst those who serve us. The SS. The Gestapo. The desperate Nazi die-hards. You know. Any enemy of them is an enemy of the state. Instant execution. I know. I've seen and heard of it in Berlin and elsewhere. We are facing horror on a grand scale if we dare to speak out. In here we are safe. Out there –' he pointed upwards '– no-one is.'

Rogge's shoulders slumped. Germany's most famous ship. Coming back to a nightmare. He knew what Doenitz was saying. No mention of the new supposed super weapons. Nothing about the new Walther U-boats. Doenitz was perhaps the only one in the Nazi top hierarchy who was realising the true state of the situation facing

Germany, or maybe Albert Speer, the Armaments Minister did as well.

Then he heard Doenitz talking to him again, his face looking even bleaker. 'Bernhard, I need *Dresden.* One of our agents only recently reported that a sizeable Russian cruiser force is getting ready for surface action – you know, ships that Goering's Luftwaffe failed to sink in Leningrad during, now what was it, ah yes, almost two years.' He paused, perhaps to allow his sarcasm of Goering to come over. It was a well-known fact that co-operation between the Kriegsmarine and Goering sometimes resulted in serious set-backs for both the U-boats and the surface ships. The biggest blunder was the failure to adequately defend the admittedly crippled *Tirpitz* in her fjord refuge from a force of slow lumbering Lancaster bombers flying unescorted to deliver their shattering bombs on the battleship. Rogge waited with pursed lips and steepled fingers for Doenitz to continue.

'Ah well, where was I? Ah yes! Russian cruisers. Could break out and go for one of our isolated units off the Courland Peninsula. Perhaps in three or four weeks time. What can we do to stop such a strike? Apart from expose our ships to possible Russian air onslaught. That's why I need *Dresden.* She's our fastest heavy-gun ship. Reitz could obliterate them knowing his record.'

'But sir, what about our other big ships?'

Doenitz shook his head 'You know as well as I do that all of them have been at full stretch since August. The two panzerschiffes are too slow, *Hipper*'s engines are likely to break down at any time and *Prinz Eugen* is due to dock in Gotenhaven to have her guns re-bored together with other major repairs. She's fast enough but doesn't have a big enough gun advantage to work on her own. If she's ready, we might spare her to work with Reitz or keep her on the gun-line. Even so, the work on the *Prinz* will be probably be the last major overhaul for our ships in that town for my guess is that the Russians will have it by the end of the month. The *Prinz* over there and *Dresden* here. The two quickest major overhauls in sea history of front-line ships in a war situation ever! Some record! Hmmm!'

Rogge nodded. He could see the reasoning behind it all what Doenitz was saying. He also realised the tension that his fellow officers knew and felt. But just how would Reitz and his fellow crew members react?

Doenitz, smiling a bit, was speaking again 'Come on Bernhard, let's get on down to the quayside and welcome our hero ship.'

By the afternoon the scudding grey-clouds with their squally snow showers lifted away to the south-west and the crew members on the upper exposed parts of *Dresden* could distinguish the outline of their homeland for the first time in nearly four long years. A light flashed from ZA28. 'Nearly home. You go where indicated. See you again. Cheerio.' The slim shape of the destroyer and the two torpedo boats diminished as they put on speed with white foam thrashing behind them. Coming between them, those on *Dresden*'s forward section could see a powerful launch again with a signal lamp blinking out a message 'To *Dresden*. Follow me' before it suddenly wheeled round, bobbing up and down like a demented cork as it crossed the send of the short choppy waves. As the small launch led the way, the outlines of Kiel's port area became much clearer. *Dresden* was coming closer to her berthing in her home port.

But what a home!

Bombed out buildings, heaps of rubble, twisted dockyard cranes and some small sunken ships, all buoyed for others to keep clear. Reitz and his crew could not yet see or witness the other difficulties. Vital amenities working fitfully, food shortages, bewildered refugees not knowing where to go and the presence of looters, deserters and other desperate people daring to find that extra bit of sustenance despite the danger of patrols of the SS and Gestapo which were still very much in evidence.

But it was home.

A place where they could at last rest and go their various ways to catch up with families, relatives, friends, associates. On leave. That was why they looked forward so much to the next few hours. Not a leave in a foreign port. This was their home port. More and more of the battlecruiser's crew began to come up on to the salt-stained decks to line their ship's rails. *Dresden*'s band began to play some of Germany's national songs. It was as if she was returning from some idyllic peace-time cruise.

Staring down at the devastation on the land, Hiltzern blanched. So did Lebers and Jervaulx. Andrea held on to her husband's hand. Otto Schenke was near the port bows. 'Bloody mess, ain't it?' he snarled to no-one in particular.

'Nearly there, sir' Hiltzern at last grunted to his captain.

'Yes, Ulrich, nearly home' came the reply.

Hiltzern gulped. So far as he could recall this was the first time that Reitz had ever addressed him by his Christian name. Turning, he saw that his captain was attired in his best uniform and attached to it was the Japanese sword which Admiral Kurita presented to Reitz when they'd been to that conference. It had brought *Dresden* good luck but not the Japanese Admiral.

'Yes, Ulrich. You do the same. I'll see to the docking. You can get changed. I suspect that we may get some top brass.'

The little launch was travelling quite slowly. Another light flashed. 'Go in front of that big liner when we indicate.'

'Engines go slow astern.' Reitz gave his quietly spoken orders. This was it. Nearly, nearly there. Slowly the battlecruiser came to the berth being indicated by an officer on the launch. The big liner was the *Heinrich Galster* and a short distance ahead was the half-sunken *Kristina Wilhelmina*. Carefully, Reitz brought the *Dresden* to the quayside berth that was to be her resting place. Without the aid of tugs, even though a harbour tug steamed up quite close to offer her aid. As *Dresden* slowly crept past *Heinrich Galster*, the decks of the liner came alive with hundreds of people, waving and cheering. White-capped officers, blue-jersey seamen and what seemed like hordes of assorted civilians. All enthusing their welcome for the rust-streaked sided battlecruiser, showing her visible battered scars of serious damage to part of her upper-works where the Seafire had come to grief.

On the quayside a guard of Kriegsmarine sailors and older Wehrmacht soldiers were formed up. Behind them, there assembled quite a large crowd. Dockers, war-weary civilians, boys and girls. Word had spread. Their hero ship was returning and now, here she was. Ropes were thrown ashore to be dragged round the moorings bollards.

'Stop engines.' *Dresden* was home. 'Secure all lines. Run out the gangway ramp.'

A great cheer came from the crowd on the quayside. Also from the civilians emerging from the *Heinrich Galster*. This was their ship. Their brave, heroic ship. Nearly everyone had read or heard of her exploits, true or exaggerated. Now she was home. Back home after such a long time away. Some waved grubby handkerchiefs. A few waved flags. Others cried with tearful emotion. Here was illusory hope in the mounting grimness of their war situation.

There were no tears on the face of the still, grim face of the very senior officer with gold braid on his cap and uniform great-coat. Emerging from a black Mercedes with two armed sailors jumping off its running board as it came to a halt and opening both the rear doors.

A bosun's party was waiting, but high on the bridge, Reitz didn't at first recognise the leader of the gold-braided officers that began to approach the boarding ramp. Leaning over the port wing, Sigmund Horst knew who it was. His boss. In somewhat non-naval language he shouted 'It's the big man himself. Grand Admiral Karl bleedin' Doenitz.'

The band stopped playing and as the Grand Admiral placed his right booted leg on to the ramp the shrill wailing of bosun's pipes known the world over from the decks of naval ships trilled into the keen north-easterly breeze as a welcome for the visitors. Somehow their sound seemed to still the watching crowd into silence as they watched the naval 'brass hats' board the battlecruiser and soon, after initial salutes, they saw the whole entourage disappear from sight. One or two in the crowd shouted up 'Good to see yer' before beginning to disperse. Back to their jobs, their homes or to the cold wind-swept streets not knowing what lay ahead.

Hurrying down from the bridge, Reitz saluted Doenitz as he stepped onto the scarred deck planking.

'Welcome aboard, Herr Grand Admiral. Come, please, follow me to meet my fellow officers.' Reitz also saluted the officer behind Doenitz not knowing who Rogge was except that he was obviously someone of high rank.

As Reitz led Doenitz and his entourage into his main cabin, his officers were lined up. Each was introduced. After he'd introduced Brautsch, Reitz then indicated Andrea. 'Now meet Frau Andrea Brautsch, our angel of the Sick Berth.' Doenitz raised an eyebrow but smiled. A woman. 'I'd better have a word with Herr Reitz and Herr Brautsch about this later!' he thought.

At the end of the line, after Padré Jervaulx, stood the huge muscular frame of Schenke and two other leading petty officers. Reitz introduced them 'as my right and left hand of the middle and lower decks. The men who have really run this ship!'

Finally he led the visitors round the line to where Walters and two stewards were waiting. 'Would you like a drink sir? We even have some Japanese saké in our limited stocks. Or maybe even a British brandy still not drunk from one of our captured ships. You know, a present courtesy of Herr Churchill!'

Doenitz smiled but took just a small fruit juice. Rogge. smiling even broader, asked for a brandy with the words 'Got this habit when I was at sea!'

Reitz looked puzzled.

'Ah, my dear Reitz.' Doenitz smiling again. 'My apologies. I haven't introduced you. This is Vice-Admiral Bernhard Rogge. Now my co-controller of our Baltic surface forces. Earlier he commanded Hilfskreuzer *Atlantis* and I dare say, both of you can exchange similarities. His was the most successful of our disguised merchant ship raiders and you have come home as our most successful regular warship raider. My history is a bit sketchy at the best of times but I think that when we tot up all your efforts, *Dresden* will have been, and maybe will still be, the most successful sea-raider of all time.'

Reitz looked up at Rogge, broke out into a smile and instead of a formal salute, extended his right hand to shake Rogge's. 'I've heard of you but never had the pleasure of meeting you. Yes, we must have a long chat sometime!'

Then suddenly Doenitz barked. 'Gentlemen and Frau Brautsch! Your glasses please! To KM *Dresden* and all who have sailed with her!'

Glasses clinked and a burst of conversation began to bubble but then Doenitz again asked for silence. Facing the assembled company he began, but the smile had gone even though his opening words were 'Welcome back to Germany my brave officers, and men, of this ship. You have brought great credit with your courageous exploits over the last four years. A beaming light in the current darkness of our present war situation. Here you are, having evaded all that our enemy could, despite their apparent superiority, throw at you. Home. Heroes of the Kriegsmarine. Even our Fuhrer has acknowledged your excellent service and on his behalf. I salute you all.'

He paused. He knew that Hitler deep in his Berlin bunker actually cared very little about the *Dresden*. Ever since his outrage against Raeder, the German leader only begrudgingly acknowledged the work of the surface ships, even when they were playing the leading role in the Baltic evacuation. Doenitz then went on to outline the grim situation facing Germany and expanded more when detailing the Kriegsmarine's current work.

Then came the bombshell.

'Your arrival home is a tremendous boost for our morale and an unexpected bonus in our collective plans for the future conduct of the Baltic operations. You will all be given just fourteen days leave. Admiral Rogge's staff are working on the required travel passes for you all. *Dresden* will be restocked and given a quick overhaul in your brief absence. You will consequently all return to your full duties by the twenty-eighth of this month.' Apart from a few grimaces and downcast eyes the officers said nothing. As if the shock of what Doenitz had just said hadn't really sunk in. A few hands clenched quite visibly when the Grand Admiral continued warning them of the travelling problems. Particularly on the battered rail network and then, telling them to be careful as to what they said in case the SS or Gestapo heard them. Even being a crew-member of Germany's most successful ship would not save them or even their long-suffering families or friends. They heard Doenitz say 'You will tell all your men of what I have said. Wear your uniform at all times when travelling. It will give you some measure of security.' Then Doenitz stopped. 'Oh dear, oh dear. What gloom and doom I'm giving you! Here you are, safe from fighting your ship all this time. You are here as my heroes and all I am seeming to say is that due to some demented fools who still dream of a Thousand-Year Reich, that you'd better watch your step. You know. I know. We'll be lucky to have another one hundred days.'

He paused again, taking another sip at his fruit juice. 'Ah, but I haven't finished. Not yet. None of your efforts could have been possible without the inspirational leadership of your captain, Vice-Admiral George Reitz.' No-one seemed to have noticed the promotion of their captain. Perhaps it was a slip of the tongue. Especially after the preceding seemingly stern words from their ultimate naval superior. 'Yes, don't look so shocked, I repeat, Vice-Admiral. Please, George, step forward!' Doenitz reached inside one of his pockets and pulled out a small box. Opening it, he drew out the decoration of The Oak Leaves to the Iron Cross. National Socialist Germany's top honour. 'Vice-Admiral George Reitz. I give you this decoration on behalf of the Fuhrer and our grateful country' and so saying this he pinned it on to Reitz's uniform jacket, stepped back and saluted him. Reitz, a little surprised, clicked his heels and gave Doenitz an immaculate naval salute.

Rogge stepped forward 'Congratulations George, you equal rank me' and shook Reitz's right hand. The tension in the room broke and Hiltzern led the three hurrahs followed by the clapping of all those present.

Rogge held up a hand for silence. As the room went quiet through the slightly open door could be heard the sound of more cheering. Somehow *Dresden*'s 'telegraph' had quickly passed outside and the crew were picking up the news.

'Company of the *Dresden.* You are here safely back home with your ship which is more than I could manage with my *Atlantis.* I know how much your recently promoted captain means to you all here and to the men outside, who if my ears don't deceive me, are as equally pleased with the good news as you are. It is a promotion and a decoration given on behalf of you all, but it is not the only good piece of news that I bring. Perhaps it is captain's privilege but will one of my staff officers please step forward?' Reitz looked quizzical as one of the staff did indeed step forward but suddenly his face changed into the broadest of broad smiles as Elle emerged, removing a naval cap and allowing her long black tresses to cascade over and round her shoulders. She ran forward flinging her arms round Reitz who whispered 'Elle, Elle, Elle. Thank God it's you. Elle, my darling, darling Elle' whilst Elle buried her head on to his right shoulder. He could only think of all those days at sea and in Japan of how she had never left his mind and here she was, in the flesh, murmuring 'George, I love you' over and over again.

Then Rogge was speaking again ' Come on lovebirds! I haven't finished.' Elle lifted up her head trying to wipe away her tears of joy. 'Ladies and gentlemen, I have the great pleasure of announcing the engagement of Vice-Admiral George Reitz to Senior Warrant Officer in the Kriegsmarine's Women's Corps, Fraulein Elle Chemnitz.'

Once again the company broke out into frenzied applause and further cheers. Reitz, still holding on to Elle, gave a weak smile, his cheeks reddened a little and then his face was smothered as Elle's lips came into contact with his.

Four hours later with darkening skies gathering over the snow-covered dockside, Reitz, with Elle holding his left hand, and with both of them clutching a suitcase, walked down *Dresden*'s gangplank and on to the cobbled flagstones of the dockyard. As they left the ship, some of the crew shouted –

'Good on yer skip!'

'See yer soon!'

'Have a safe journey' before the couple walked out of earshot at the yard gates. Showing their leave passes to the sentry, they quickly passed through them, the sentry throwing up a smart salute. Elle whispered 'Look George, old Helmster's waiting for us just as Admiral Rogge promised.' The old man in question was nearly seventy years old and he was at the wheel of a battered black Opel car that Rogge and his staff used. 'He knew Rogge long before the war and has been his chauffeur, general handyman and when, but not recently, even his butler. He's going to drive us to the railway station which isn't very far – perhaps as well because he's not all that good a driver but he is loyal to Rogge!'

'Elle, where are we going?' Reitz whispered back, still trying to find himself. The fraught dash for Kiel, the reception from Doenitz, the wonderful announcement of his engagement to Elle who now wore the single diamond ring, briefly flashing when the sentry shone his torch on it as they produced their leave passes and now, in this rattling car, with the memories of the crowd still milling near the gates shouting – 'That's him –'

'That's our skipper of the *Dresden*.'

'He's with his girl.'

'Good luck on yer both!'

Dockyard workers and even civilian refugees. Then a camera

flashed. A ripple of applause, even from a truckload of disembarking soldiers rounding up bewildered civilians prior to taking them to a dispersal centre.

The car with Helmster grinding through the gears, slowly picked up speed, leaving the well-wishers behind. Elle replied, still whispering 'Oh darling, I haven't had time to tell you. We're going to catch a train and go to my aunt's cottage. It's about ninety kilometres away from here in the countryside. You'll love it. Far from anywhere! Rogge's arranged it all. Did so whilst you were speeding down the Norwegian coast. Guess we all knew you'd succeed in that last lap.' Images of the crashing Seafire, the broken bodies, smashed gun turrets and Padré Jervaulx being sick leaped into Reitz's mind. Elle felt him shudder. 'Soon darling, we'll be able to rest together and temporarily forget this dreadful war. My aunt's cottage is right at the end of a small village. It has a few tiles missing when an enemy bomber crashed and blew up a couple of fields away. It was shot down on its way to attack Kiel. Mind, my aunt saw the airmen floating down on parachutes, and told the village policeman and together, she armed with a pitchfork, they managed to reach the airmen before the SS could hear about it. She even offered them each one of her home-made toffees!'

'She sounds quite a character!'

'She's really lovely and soft-hearted. Anyway, we're nearly at the station.' Elle leaned over and kissed her fiancé lightly on his right cheek.

It was a few minutes before midnight that the blackened, overworked locomotive finally hissed and clanked its way over the last few rails before shuddering to a steam-wheezing halt a short distance from the buffers of the near-deserted village station out in the quiet of the North German Plain. Elle and George stepped out on to the platform relieved to be at the end of a tedious journey that had been stop-go-stop-go-stop-go, or so it seemed all the time. At last, they were almost at journey's end, breathing in the keen, cold, frosty air mingled with whiffs of the coal smoke from the engine as it swirled across and back along the track on which it had just creaked. Reitz's mind was still back on *Dresden.* His conversation with Rogge once Doenitz had bade them all farewell and good luck. Rogge's sympathies gushed out. Just two weeks leave for everyone of the *Dresden*'s crew. Then Rogge, like Doenitz, hardened his attitude. Germany was facing a catastrophic defeat. The whims of a pill-ridden corporal were driving the nation over an abyss. It would be worse in the East. Refugees, military personnel and even vital equipment. All to be brought to the temporary safety of North and West Germany. Rogge continued, still stern, even bitter. 'You know George. When the war ends, with the Allies carving up Germany, those of us in this half of our country will be a lot better under the Anglo-American administration. It's all we've got left to struggle for – a possible better way of life for the people we can rescue. *Dresden* will be needed.'

Reitz, barely able to comprehend what Doenitz and now Rogge had said, felt suddenly very cold inside. So this is what it was all for? He'd fought his beloved battlecruiser back to home waters. For all this? A Germany, riddled with an evil, vile system going down to a chaotic, shattering defeat. And just two weeks leave before going back to all the hurt and pain of war.

Two weeks!

Rogge then gave him and his officers just three hours to leave *Dresden* so that his base staff and dockyard workers could start the hurried overhaul the ship so desperately needed. As Reitz said his farewells to the officers and as many of the crew that he could, the cranes overhead were hauling the protective camouflage tarpaulins into place and the sound of acetylene torches could be heard hissing and spitting as they burnt and cut at the ship's damaged upperworks. Extra anti-aircraft guns were promised as well as new crew members to replace the personnel lost were to be drafted to *Dresden* from survivors of ships already lost in the Baltic struggle. He'd hurried through a mountain of paperwork whilst Elle stayed with Walters, Jervaulx and Schenke in his cabin where they told her of some of the many stories of their long sojourn overseas. Now both of them were now at this remote country station.

Outside the entrance archway stood a man with a horse and trap. Elle, whispering again, told George that this was to be their final transport. 'He's called Albert. Fancies my aunt, I think! She's persuaded him to meet us. He's probably been in the station-master's room with Karl and a bottle of schnapps or beer!'

With a rug around their knees, the couple huddled together as Albert, with a little smile on his face, urged the old horse in the shafts to start trotting. A keen frosty wind swept over the crisp snow as the trap lurched off down the rutted village street to soon rattle past all the houses and finally rock to a halt at a cottage a little way from the last of them. It loomed up as a darker shape in the general shapeless mass of the open fields whispering ever so gently in the frosty air. As they stepped down from the trap, all three of them looked skywards, for coming from the West they could just hear it. The increasing drone of many heavy-sounding aircraft. To the north and south of the village, on the far distant horizons, searchlights briefly shone trying to pick up the intruders but to little avail. Guns opened fire, their exploding shells looking like brief temporary stars and as they stared, one of the aeroplanes almost due south of them suddenly sparkled and began to fall down, like a shooting star, plummeting in an ever-glowing flaming spiral until it vanished over a distant low hill. All three of them heard the distant crump as the broken bomber crashed on to the frozen land.

'I hope that the airmen managed to jump clear' muttered Reitz. 'Just like we always willed for crews of the ships we attacked could get clear of their sinking vessel. Into life-rafts or boats. We sometimes even threw rafts in to the water for them if we couldn't stop. It was the worst part of our whole job. Our targets were the ships, not the crews.'

'Hush, darling. Time for all those stories later. Just remember that those bombers are on their way to smash up the ruins of Kiel or Lubeck or Berlin or whatever city where ordinary people scratch an existence in a damp cellar. Whilst you were away, they bombed Hamburg for a whole week, day and night.'

'Yes, I heard about that whilst we were in Japan. I also know that we've bombed London, Coventry and lots of other towns and cities but I feel for those on the receiving end because I've met them. The captain of that battleship we blew up, that liner we set free; Colonel Tibbetts and recently some American submariners. All grateful that we rescued them.'

'Ssh! It's freezing out here to have a serious chat and besides those aircraft just above have now gone away. We're keeping old Albert waiting' and saying this, she thrust a few coins into his gloved hand. The old man smiled and then climbed into the driving seat, cracked his whip just once and the horse and trap lurched off into the icy darkness.

'Come on, darling, let's get inside' Elle whispered, producing a small torch with just a tiny beam of light which she pointed to a stone near the front door and then lifting the stone, picked up a key. Inserting it into the door, she pushed it open, it creaked a little and then they were nearly in, stamping their boots on a thick door mat at the entrance. Elle stooped under a low doorway, found some matches and striking one, she lit a nearby oil-lamp. 'My aunt's electric supply only comes on for three hours in the early evening. Please be quiet now. She's upstairs, probably asleep. Come on, let's go into what she calls her living room.' A small fire just about glowed in the grate but there were quite a few logs close by and she put three of them on to the embers. The fire blazed back into life. 'See, auntie's left us a pot of stew hanging over the fire.' Elle lifted the lid 'Mmm, smells good. Soon be warm enough!' On the mantle-piece her aunt had left a note – '*Elle. Hope you have your hero in tow. Put him in the spare room. Help yourself to some stew. Love. Auntie Bergetta.*'

The soup, of turnip, carrot and potato with a faint taste of beef soon warmed their insides after Elle doled it into two wooden bowls that she fetched from the kitchen. Sitting in two old well-worn armchairs they slurped into their stew, gazing in turn at each other and the flickering logs, but saying very little. The war seemed long, long away. When he'd finished George yawned 'Gosh, that was just the job but I am very tired. Darling, it's so lovely to be here. It's almost as if I'm dreaming but I'm not, am I?' Elle shook her head. He continued 'I must be off to bed. Where's the little man's room?'

'Follow me but only to your room.' With a little giggle, she added 'The little man's facilities will all be in your room. There's only one bed. Auntie Bergit doesn't approve if we sleep in it together and I don't want to upset her. We're so lucky to be even here!' Taking George by one hand and the oil lamp in the other, she led him up the stairs to what turned out to be a little box-room with just enough room for a single bed, a washstand and a chair. 'Here's your palace!' and with that she pulled him close and kissed him ever so gently. George felt a tear drop from her eyes, roll out and down on to his cheek. 'Goodnight my darling. I do so love, love, love you' and saying this she released him, turned and gently closed the door leaving her fiancé in the darkness of the room. Outside, an overhanging tree branch tweaked in the keening wind, matched almost by the creak of the bed on to which George sat, his eyes becoming used to the dark lit only by a single candle.

Dawn's first light filtered through threadbare curtains when he awoke. Maybe because it was so quiet for outside the wind had died away. Maybe because his bed, despite the creaks, didn't roll from side to side or up and down was why he'd awoken early. Looking at his watch he could see that it was just turned six o'clock. Hurriedly completing toiletry necessaries, he dressed, remembering to wear his Kriegsmarine uniform jacket, complete with the new gold stripe that Walters had sown on just the previous day. Then putting on his winter coat, he crept as quietly as he could down the stairs although nearly every board creaked and squeaked on his way to the front door. He pulled on his sea boots and then he could see the freshness of the light, due to a crispy, very white, new fall of snow. Overhead the last of the stars was still shining. Then a thought struck him. Just twenty-four hours previously he'd been guiding his proud battle-cruiser on her last lap to Kiel and now here he was in the middle of the countryside, engaged to the girl he'd thought of so much during those four long years away.

Elle heard him creaking down the stairs as she was also dressed, having heard his earlier movements. Quickly she crossed her room trying not to wake Aunt Bergetta and likewise creaked her way down the stairs and on closing the door, called 'George!' just as he reached the gate. He turned, smiled and hugged her tight as she ran into his arms.

'I couldn't sleep. Not used to a bed that stays still! Even when we were in Japan, apart from one short stay at the Attaché's house, I invariably slept on board, even when the ship was in dry-dock. Even there, it always seemed to be swaying!' Elle smiled up at him and getting up on tip-toe, kissed him. 'Come on darling, let's go for a stroll. The fresh air will do us good!'

Their booted feet crunched on the crisp snow and as they walked, the vapour from their breathing just seemed to hang in the still clear air with the blueing sky above them with a few vague white trails from aeroplanes high above them slowly dispersing.

Elle chirped up 'It's going to be a beautiful clear day. Look, the sun's coming up! You know darling, when all this is over we'll be able to enjoy lots of mornings like this one. Over and over again.' She twirled in the snow like a little playful girl, dancing into the footsteps behind her and then turning to dance the few steps back to where George stood, his eyes watching this vibrant woman. She cried out 'Try it love. Try to relax. To enjoy this serenity. We're here. Together. Away from this rotten war!'

She again twirled, flinging her arms out and then curling them round him. Embracing. Kissing.

George looked into her sparkling eyes. Of course, he thought, she is right. I must relax. But I can't. Here I am in but a temporary haven. Away from it all but not away. Not here in my mind. Not away from the horror and madness that he'd seen. The battleship *Resolve* blowing up. The pointless destruction of the British tanker when the Japanese had torpedoed it. The bravery of the little destroyers that hadn't turned away but instead aimed for his ship before being overwhelmed. The gaunt survivors with Colonel Tibbetts. The look of resignation by those trawler skippers off Alaska or the American submariners being led off his ship by the Wehrmacht guard. But his mind then turned the other way. If *Dresden* hadn't been so well fought then he wouldn't have been here at all. A prisoner at best. Elle sensed him shudder. He muttered 'It's cold, just standing here. Come on, let's walk down this lane. You're right. I'm still out there. On the tossing restless waves of the ocean. But I'm really here. Kissing the girl I love. I can't hang on to the *Dresden* all my life but I can hang onto you.' She smiled. It hadn't been easy either for her, as she'd plotted the battlecruiser's progress in the chartrooms in France, Norway and now in Kiel. One after another Germany's biggest ships had been eliminated.

Before she'd met George, the *Graf Spee* off Montevideo and then, when George had been at sea, she'd chartered the course of the *Bismarck* until, powerful ship that she'd been, it was overwhelmed. Perhaps the bitterest blow was the sinking of *Scharnhorst* off Norway with the news, via the Red Cross, that only three dozen of her crew of nearly two thousand were rescued by the British. She'd thought of all this and then had come that Leyte Gulf battle. *Dresden* probably sunk. How she had cried and cried. She'd even gone into a nearby Norwegian church and the priest had come in. In her limited grasp of the local language she'd told him that she feared that her man had died but she wasn't sure. The priest had looked kindly down at her and told her to pray. When she left the church she experienced an inner strength in the knowledge that George was alive but whether as a prisoner on a ship she wasn't clear. So she never gave up hope and the day before she'd been drafted to Kiel, she went back to that simple, little Norwegian church. The same priest was still there and saw her coming. She'd blurted out 'I know that he's alive.' He replied that prayer did work but not always in the way expected.

Now here he was. How her heart leapt when Rogge burst into the chartroom. '*Dresden*'s off Northern Norway. Now come on, let's hope she makes it for here!' Nervously, she followed the progress of the battlecruiser as she made her way south. Images of that Norwegian church and the kindly priest. Of steep sided fjords. Of the *Dresden*'s wake bubbling and boiling. Most of all, of George. Guiding her home. She confided in Rogge of her love for him. He said that she should get a ring and then he'd do the announcing. Which he had. Now they were together. Walking hand-in-hand. In this quiet area. Away from it all. Suddenly George broke into the silence 'Come on, race you back to the cottage!'

Panting they reached the garden gate, George a couple of steps ahead of her. Brushing some snow off the gate-post, he made a quick snowball and flung it at her. She dodged and flung a handful back at him.

'Now children! This is no time for larking about!' came a sharp voice from the cottage door. Reitz whirled and saw in the doorway, a small grey-haired woman of about sixty years old with her arms folded and a pinafore around her waist.

'You must be Aunt Bergetta.'

'And you must call me Bergit for short, young Herr famous fiancé Admiral. If you hurry in, not only will I get you both some breakfast, but you'll be in time to hear the latest distortion of the truth which is called the news read on behalf of weasel man Goebbels.'

Reitz, bending down, kissed Bergetta on the left cheek and shook her right hand.

'Come on now. No time for niceties out here in the freezing cold.' She chuckled with a twinkle in her eye. Reitz thought of her as a smaller plumper version of Elle. Whilst they sat tackling a bowl of steaming milk and bread, the reader on the crackling wireless broke into the news after the obligatory stirring propaganda marching tune. What he uttered was the usual diet of Nazi-type hate and mis-truths that Bergetta and Elle had heard so often. German forces were slaughtering the Bolshevik hordes; the Jew-ridden Western Allies were being held at the Rhine crossings; four merchant ships and two destroyers had been sunk by the victorious U-boats in the previous week; new weapons being created would soon cut enormous swathes in the ranks of Germany's enemies; new jet aircraft would shoot down all the 'terrorfliegers' bombing their beloved cities and enemy cities would be erased completely by even more powerful rockets. No mention was made of the huge losses being suffered by Germany's military and civilian personnel nor the crippling shortages in supplies or the dangers of rail or road travel.

Right at the end of the broadcast the nasal monotone of the announcer paused for a moment, the sound of a clearing throat could be heard and then the voice continued 'Now in one of our northern ports, safe after a voyage away from home waters of nearly four years, is our triumphant raider of the high seas, our very own battlecruiser, the KM *Dresden* under the command of newly-promoted Vice-Admiral George Reitz. Despite the efforts of the Western Jew-inspired navies to halt her return, she has triumphed by eluding their puny efforts. The *Dresden* has accounted for no less than half-a-million tons of Allied shipping including a battleship, numerous cruisers and other war-mongering vessels; as well as countless merchant ships. She will soon be back on the high seas to strike yet more terror into the cowardly hearts of our enemies. Long live Germany! Heil Hitler!' and the chords of martial music began to issue forth when Aunt Bergetta rather savagely switched the wireless into silence. 'There, Herr Admiral, that's what passes for news these days. Was the bit about you accurate?'

Reitz replied, nodding his head 'Yes, just about. Odd though that they didn't credit us with a million tons, six battleships et cetera. Perhaps then we might have merited being the first news!'

'Perhaps, for once, they hope that the Allies are really listening. Just to get one true jibe in at their inability from being unable to stop *Dresden* returning safely home' said Elle and then lowering her voice to little more than a whisper added – 'You know Auntie, as I've often said to you on previous leaves, our marvellous cretins who run this country aren't all that proud of what George and his ship have achieved. Do you know, that only my darling here has been awarded a medal or received any promotion? Vice-Admiral Rogge told me, after the reception that we held with Grand-Admiral Doenitz, that only recently, cruiser *Prinz Eugen*'s crew were decorated almost to a man for their recent bombardment efforts. Someone very high up doesn't like George and his merry lads because they're the crew of a ship created by my former Abwehr boss, Admiral Canaris, who, as Rogge told me, is now under house arrest. Herr Canaris disagrees too much with Nazi ideology and his Abwehr made too many mistakes for our Fuhrer's peace of mind.'

'Which piece, if he's got a mind?' quipped Bergetta 'Ah I know, the bit that sits on a toilet seat.'

'Careful, Auntie, there might be a bit of Nazi cow-dung listening outside the door!'

'Nah, love, they haven't even got ears that work! Anyway, who is for some toast?'

'Mmm. Your bread is really tasty' remarked George as he tucked into a thick crusty slice.

'I made it myself. Still got some real wheat flour in the basement. Makes up for the muck that is usually sold as bread these days.'

'Well, yes. Our supply on *Dresden* was courtesy of Mr. Churchill himself. We captured one of his well-laden freighters and she provided us with many supplies of the like we couldn't have obtained here!' responded Reitz, with a chuckle.

Another V-2 exploded to the north of Hampstead Heath as Admiral Collins heard the end of the Goebbels-inspired news broadcast. Being reasonably fluent in German, he often listened to their news whilst having breakfast in his flat. Sometimes he used to think that the BBC wasn't always fully truthful either and listening to their news a bit later he heard the clipped, precise tones of Alvar Liddell say 'It is, with some regret that despite heroic efforts by our navy and airforce units, that we have to announce that the German battlecruiser *Dresden* has been able to reach her home port after being at sea for the past four years. We understand that she has been severely damaged and is unlikely to return to sea in the foreseeable future.'

Collins pondered both broadcasts. Strange, that for once, the Nazis were telling the truth, perhaps a shade more accurately than the 'Beeb'. Now supposing *Dresden* had been a British warship. She'd have been first news. Not added on as a tail-piece. A filler-in. Despite the damage that the battlecruiser had caused to Allied shipping, Collins found himself even admiring her exploits. Damn it, she'd been able to get back to Germany. None of their other big ships had dared to come out of the Baltic in the last twelve months and now here was one ship entering that sea. All the way from the other side of the World and now here. Back in Germany. What was it about Reitz and his ship that bit so deeply into his mind? As he made his way on the underground train to the Admiralty Office the image of the sleek warship just wouldn't go away. Just as well I'm a bachelor. If I'd been married t'missus would have thought that I'm hopelessly obsessed with a rival lover. Except that *Dresden* wasn't a lover. She was real. She was bloody enemy. Time after time he'd tried to forget the battlecruiser. Time after time her exploits had brought her back to the forefront of all his thinking.

As he leafed through his papers at his desk he noticed that the memo he'd sent to Air Chief Marshall Arthur Harris hadn't yet been worthy of a reply. It had bluntly said 'When are you going to blast the *Dresden* to bits?' Stuffed shirt! Thinks he's the only bloke fighting this war! By now the Nazis will have covered their hero warship with camouflage tarpaulins. Short of bombing Kiel completely to the ground to be sure of getting *Dresden* sunk in the process – oh hell, what am I saying? We need an agent there to tell us precisely where the bloody ship's been moored. That's if we've still got an agent there!

Collins even asked the Americans pointing out that *Dresden* had accounted for quite a lot of their ships as well. Guadalcanal.

Pacific convoy. A submarine in the Leyte conflict. Damage to one of their cruisers in that Arctic bash-up. 'Nope. That Kraut ship will be in dock for ages an' by the time she's ready for sea, we'll have wrapped up Mr. Hitler and his baddies in a big black sack for good. Right now we're swooping on their square heads down on the Rhine and their naughty battlewagon will just have to wait but we'll wrap her up in the same sack in due time.' Collins winced, as he always did, when listening to the apparent slack wording and attitude of his American counterparts. He'd never felt at ease with it whilst in Hawaii. Now here in London it irritated him even more but he bit his tongue knowing full well that without the Americans, the Allies wouldn't be even close to winning the war.

Even the Prime Minister's staff gave him more or less the same answer. 'Yes, Collins, bad luck that *Dresden*'s made it back to Kiel but the war will be over before Jerry boy can get her back to sea. You know from all your naval experience, that a ship of that size will need at least three months to be overhauled. If in that time we haven't bombed her to bits, then we'll have won the war. One way or the other she's gone and cooked her own goose by running for home.'

Yet as Collins gazed at the photograph of the battlecruiser he could see her guns opening fire again. But at what? With the other big surviving enemy warships opening up on the Russians in the Eastern Baltic? There'd been a number of reports about such activity over the last three months at least. Or would Reitz have a go at an Arctic convoy? Slip back-up through the Norwegian Leads for one last act of bravado. Just to prove the point that the Allies couldn't beat him?

Idly he fed a few pigeons in Trafalgar Square barely noticing another brief flare-up on the southern horizon of the capital. Maybe another V2 or one of their souped-up JU-88's on a lone sneak raid on behalf of a dying, rotten regime. Reitz and his ship surely wouldn't risk themselves for Hitler's vile cause now that the war was ending. Oh I can't even feed these pesky birds without thinking of that damned battlecruiser. *Dresden. Dresden.* Shoo! Go away!

After breakfast, George and Elle took a brisk walk, on the advice of Auntie Bergit, to a village four miles to the north-west. She knew that the inn-keeper still did a few lunchtime meals even though it was relatively simple stuff. The walk along the crisp snow-covered lane certainly worked up their appetite and to their delight, the innkeeper welcomed them 'Ah, a navy man! Don't see many of you lot around here. Not much sea. Only the peace and quiet of the country. Come in, star-struck lovers. Yes, I can see it in your eyes! Now, what will it be? Some weak ale or perhaps cider. Have to water it down these days. I know that I shouldn't but we've run out of regular supplies. The only people who get them proper-like are those who profess still to be winning this war, you know, toadies of Herr Hitler, Himmler and Goebbels. Still, as you're the only ones here, and being navy, I know you don't like that unholy Trinity. My son was on one of their big ships. Got a message that he was killed when an aeroplane crashed on to his ship. You know, the one that's just come back. What's her name? Ah yes! *Dresden.*'

Elle said 'Ssh! Don't distress yourself. My friend here is one of that ship's crew. Sort of trying to have a few day's leave. In your peace and quiet.'

'Gosh' answered the landlord. 'You know about her captain. Gone and been promoted to Vice-Admiral. Some bloke he must be!'

'Yes, he must be. You see, this is him.' Elle almost whispered this to the apron-clad innkeeper. 'He's been away for nearly four years. Now, can we have something to eat, please?'

'You, him? Pleased to have you here. Drinks and meal on the house.' The innkeeper thrust out a hand to George who smiled back, saying 'I'm sorry your son didn't make it. He did get a Christian burial at sea along with about ninety other men. We do have a padré on board.'

'Thanks. Now will pork and vegetables do?'

A slice of pork with carrots and cabbage followed by a jam-based pudding with thick cream proved to be reasonably filling as well as warming. Elle managed to get the innkeeper to keep quiet about George's presence and in return, they'd return and next time, pay the proper price for a meal. 'No more favours, please' she added.

They then made their way back as a series of snow flurries whipped at their faces and coats. Unused to the exercise, George's legs felt somewhat weak and full of aches by the time they reached Auntie Bergit's house and pausing to remove his boots and top coat, he flopped into the old armchair by the fire and was soon fast asleep.

'Ah ha' whispered Bergetta 'this is what our greatest hero looks like' as she entered the room from her tiny kitchen with two bowls of broth.

'Ssh, auntie, he's so tired. I fear that he's not used to walking!' whispered Elle.

'Well, at least, he's quiet out here. If it had been earlier in the war, you'd have been in Berlin where our rat-faced Goebbels would have put on a big publicity stunt and t'owd Adolf would have pinned a medal on his chest and expected a stiff-arm salute, polished boots banging together and a raucous shout of 'Heil Hitler' in return. Instead they're all no doubt deep underground like frightened rats not daring to come out and breathe the wonderful smoke-laden air in what passes for Berlin these days!'

'Auntie, one day someone will hear you and then Herr Hitler will invite you to be a guest on one of his smelly straw-lined cattle trucks going off to a holiday home complete with watch towers and barbed wire!'

'Sod them my dear! I lost your uncle in forty-one when a bomb obliterated his fire-engine; both my sons, your cousins, gave their lives in Italy and my brother, far too old to be really called up went God knows where, probably under a Russian tank just six-months ago.' Tears welled up in her eyes. 'So you see my dear, you're the only one I've left – and now, him too! I will be careful what I say in public for both your sakes. Even when he was on the seas and you were heaven knows where, you couldn't stop mentioning him in your letters. I realise how precious he is – to you and now he is to me. So we must let him rest' and saying this Bergetta closed her eyes as seated in the other armchair, she too also nodded off to sleep.

Deep down in his damp gloomy Berlin bunker, as Aunt Bergit so correctly surmised, Adolf Hitler and his pasty-faced set of hierarchy grey beings, had all but forgotten the safe arrival of their leading surface raider. After all *Dresden* was a unit of the Kriegsmarine, a service so often discredited in the non-naval minds of the Nazi top brass. For most of the war it had been led by Erich Raeder who'd done his best to instil the basic underlying theme of a common humanity to the enemy providing their own ships weren't in any danger. Even his successor Doenitz, whose absence was scarcely noticed, didn't always follow true Nazi ideologies. Only the SS and Gestapo truly carried out Hitler's vile policies to the letter and even then, some in the bunker suspected that henchman Heinrich Himmler's zeal was beginning to waver now that the spectre of total defeat loomed ever nearer. Perhaps they never realised the revulsion that the rest of the civilised World felt for their rotten regime. Down in that damp, dank hole, deep under Berlin's bomb-blasted streets, maybe some of them still dreamt of a Thousand Year Reich and if not, were determined to drag the country into their own particular blackhole. So to them *Dresden*'s exploits were soon forgotten although the bloated Martin Bormann hadn't. On his desk was a memo from the Nazi gauleiter of Kiel. '*Dresden* crew probably not loyal to the Party. Any out of line we will execute on grounds of treason if outside their naval base.' Bormann, not Himmler, replied 'As you so wish. Act accordingly.'

In Kiel's naval base, Rogge's staff, utterly ignorant of Bormann's ugly mind, were working round the clock with the overhaul of *Dresden.* Within six hours of her arrival the tall overhead dockyard cranes began hauling the six big guns up and loading them on to flat-top train trucks for a short journey so that they could be re-bored and calibrated. Engineers swarmed over the big steam turbines, which surprisingly for a major unit of the Kriegsmarine, had worked very well despite the enormous strain put on them during the long voyage. A hurried coffer dam was fitted around the *Dresden,* it being deemed too risky to place her in a dry-dock. Drained as well as possible, men on pontoons floating in the glutinous mud did their best to steam-clean her hull from the considerable marine growth that *Dresden* had collected. More and more dockers swarmed aboard, all proud to be honoured to work on Germany's main war vessel. This was their ship. Back from being lost. Here. Under their feet. Had sinister henchman Bormann or the Kiel Gauleiter seen the willingness that the men, and some women, set to in their work in this hasty overhaul of the stationary battlecruiser then perhaps they might have rescinded their vile directive. But then, probably not. Their twisted warped brains were totally incapable of logical reason.

They could not have known about Rogge's dilemma as he strove to get *Dresden* back into front-line duty. Already he'd earmarked her to act as possible protection for the next big Strength-through-Joy liner to attempt the Baltic passage, the *Wilhelm Gustloff,* getting ready in Gotenhafen. Then *Dresden* would replace the two armoured ships, *Scheer* and *Lutzow,* to allow them to re-stock on fuel and ammunition. Already heavy cruiser *Prinz Eugen*e was in dockyard hands in Gotenhafen undergoing a similar overhaul as to which *Dresden* was receiving. The cruiser's guns had been in almost daily action for the past two months. Currently only the three fit light cruisers were on the gun-line and they desperately needed big-gun support. Rogge was aware that so far, only smaller units of the Navy had been sunk or disabled in the massive evacuation process. What if the Russians were able to gather up this sizeable cruiser force, to either attack isolated Wehrmacht units scattered around the Courland area or worse still, have a go at the often weakly escorted convoys?

Then there was another ugly memo on Rogge's desk. Had he any spare merchant ships that could be used as what was euphemistically termed 'Accommodation vessels'? One ship suggested was the beautiful former Hamburg-Amerika three-funnelled *Cap Arkona.* Rogge shuddered knowing the hidden truth behind the memo. At the moment only his assistant co-ordinator in the Baltic, Vice-Admiral Thiele as well as Doenitz knew of the memo. In his brief stop-over to welcome *Dresden,* Doenitz hinted that the ships were to be used as overspill for the camps being overrun by the Russians. One name seemed to haunt Rogge. Auschwitz. Never mind Treblinka, Ravensbruck, Sobibor, Dachau or Bergen-Belsen. He'd heard of them from covert conversations with other members of his staff but as it was SS material and under their control, what he did not know was best not enquired about. Especially in the current situation. Constantly his mind wandered back to his days in charge of *Atlantis* and then through the log of *Dresden* so meticulously written up by Reitz in the man's neat handwriting. Always a concern for the survivors and the welfare of any prisoners. Rogge hadn't been surprised when reading about Reitz's views on the *Marona* incident and how it helped him to treat Colonel Tibbetts and his men. Some Japanese, he thought, seemed to have the same base, vile value to human life as the SS scum which he guessed were perpetrating some of the worst, if not the very worst crimes to fellow humans. Just to think that such possible thugs still held sway in the disintegrating Third Reich!

No such burden crossed Elle's mind, not that of her fiancé as the days passed. The war seemed a million miles away despite the daily reminder of vapour trails high in the sky above whenever the clouds cleared. A friendly farmer loaned two ponies for them to ride; they found time, despite the cold, to try a bit of fishing although with no luck at all; they visited more of the local hostelries for a mid-day meal and best of all, enjoyed more and more walks. Colour returned to both their faces; anxious lines faded and day by day their love grew ever stronger for each other. From time to time George would relate his experiences – how his little steward always seemed to know exactly what he wanted at the right time; of the first time he encountered Otto Schenke with one of the ship's cats asleep on his lap; of his chats to the British prisoners including Captains Willis-Wilson and MacLeod as well as to Colonel Tibbetts and later the American, Theophilus Willis; of Padré Jervaulx, Doctor Lebers, Engineers Herzog and Luth. All jumbled up. And then of Andrea. He hoped that Elle wasn't jealous. She'd smiled at him and squeezed his hand. No she wasn't. But she would be if he dared to think of anyone else romantically if it wasn't her! It was Aunt Bergetta's views on life that appeared to be the only stumbling-block on them fulfilling their current relationship to its fullest.

She insisted that the pair of them should be back every evening before dark. 'Too dangerous. You never know which SS lump of dog-dirt might just happen to think that you're deserters!' She also maintained a strict Lutheran approach. Separate bedrooms and no midnight assignations! On the other hand, Auntie produced some quite exquisite evening meals made from an ample store of well-preserved vegetables and fruits from her garden all assiduously picked when ripe in the summer from the numerous lanes and hedgerows around her cottage. George himself, filled with the fresh air and Auntie's good food, slept longer and longer each night as he relaxed. More often than not in the old armchair with Elle holding one of his hands or just simply looking at him. He was her man. Her love. Her fiancé. Soon, he'd be her husband.

Married couple, Helmut and Andrea didn't have an Auntie breathing over them even though their basement flat in a Berlin suburb was the property of one of Helmut's uncles. The sound of aircraft taking off or landing at the not too distant Gatow airfield failed to disturb their many hours locked in each other's arms. Neither did the worn out springs of the mattress of the ancient bedstead deter them from their often fervent lovemaking. They were away from the ship. No duty officer to shout out the watches, no emergency rush of wounded to tend. It was time for them to experience love to its fullest and finest peak, time after time. Occasionally they surfaced to foray into the outside cold grey world. Even in those still tree-lined suburbs of the capital, food was difficult to find in ample enough quantities or even quality.

Once hurrying back in sleety rain for the comparative warmth of their basement, they were accosted by an angry bent old woman carrying a pile of sticks. 'You there, sailor man! You should be fighting the Russians. The Fuhrer is. So should you be.'

Suddenly Andrea lost her cool and pulled back the overcoat of her husband. 'Look here, Fraulein. See this' and she pointed to the brighter gold stripe. 'This is all he's been given for sailing his ship for the last four years. Perhaps you've heard of it? The *Dresden*? Right? Now go back to your sticks and pick on someone else to moan at!'

The old woman spat on the ground without replying and shuffled off. A grey bent shape. In a grey broken background of a broken gap in a broken suburban street. Helmut, initially shocked at his wife's outburst, suddenly held her tight as Andrea began to cry. 'Oh I'm sorry darling. I should have kept my cool. But how can I when I know what we've both been through?' She sobbed and sobbed trying to muffle her cries with her face buried into the crook of his jacket sleeve. 'Come on love, let's get back home. We both know the country's in a mess. We're both shocked by it but we mustn't let it upset us. I don't care if you're English and that I'm German. We're both as one now. Together.' Andrea smiled at him, her sobs ceasing. Helmut helped to dry her tears and she suddenly poked her husband in the ribs 'Come on, superman, catch me before we get back to the flat!'

Navigating officer Alfred Serle's home was in a Kiel suburb about half-an hour's walk from the docks. In a deserted warehouse, he hurriedly changed into civilian clothes, putting his uniform in the bag that he carried. His very particular wife hated him in his Kriegsmarine clothes and he feared her wrath more than a possible arrest from the SS or Gestapo patrols. Mind, only once had she written to him whilst he'd been away. Even that creep Robert Koche had often leered at him when he'd received frequent letters from what Serle could deduce were numerous women. It nagged him. Only once. Was the sod still alive? Carefully he approached his house in a row of still quite neat homes. Except his. The front garden, despite the snow, looked untidy. Paint work on the doors and window sills looked worn and bare wood showed in numerous places. He pushed at the front door. It was locked.

He fumbled for a key at the end of his fob chain. 'My goodness, at least she hasn't changed the lock' he grinned to himself as the door creaked open. He sniffed. A perfumed scent wafted across his nose. Not of cooking but what women wore. Ah yes, his wife had tarted herself up. Just for him. She must have heard about *Dresden*'s return. Then he looked up. Yes, there she was. His Greta. On the landing, clad in a long blue silk nightdress draped provocatively open, showing her well proportioned upper cleavage; in her left hand a cigarette smouldered at the end of its long slim holder.

'Hello darling! I'm back. See you're ready for –' Serle faltered for looking over his wife's shoulder he saw a man dressed in the full uniform of a Colonel of the Waffen SS '– Greta – who's him?' he yelled but Greta merely blew out a smoke ring, tossed her long dark brown hair over her shoulder and turned for the bedroom door, grabbing the Colonel by the crotch of his trousers with her right hand and with the other, still holding the cigarette holder, managed a derisive two-fingered gesture. With a rising surge of rage, Serle rushed up the stairs but the bedroom door slammed shut in his face and Serle heard the key turn in its lock. He shouted 'Open up you bitch!' He kicked at the wood and banged on it with his fists but to no avail. Turning, he raced back down the stairs and ran into the kitchen. Frantically he searched the cupboards and found some cooking oil and fat, as well as some matches. Spreading the oil over the units, on to some paper, as well as on the curtains and piling up the fat, he struck a match, hearing as he did so the bed-springs above creaking furiously. Watching the flames flare into life he ran back into the hall, yelled 'Bitch! Whore!' and then fled the house, slamming the front door and locking it. As he looked up from the garden gate he could see that the flames inside the kitchen were really taking hold. Then he looked up. His half-naked Greta was trying to open the bedroom window. Smoke was beginning to seep out. The fire intensified. As her screams carried out of the now opened window, it was his turn to wave two fingers derisively at her as he began to run back down the street in the direction which so recently he'd come the opposite way. Then he'd been full of hope. Now he could only feel a sense of rage, despair and maybe just a touch of fear as well. What if the SS colonel survived? Hurriedly, he ran harder back to the ship.

The battlecruiser's first officer, Ulrich Hiltzern, never left the ship, despite the hammering, drilling and other frantic dockyard noises echoing through the motionless warship. It wasn't because of an over-riding sense of duty. He simply had nowhere to go. Admiral Rogge had given him the sad details. Both his parents as well as his sole surviving grandmother were lost in the great Hamburg firestorm. There'd been no trace of them and their house. Just a big crater at the roadside. Rogge also told him that his slightly younger brother was presumed killed whilst serving on a torpedo-boat destroyer that, like the raider *Komet* which she'd been escorting, was lost in a furious action in the English Channel. Worst of all, his twin sister was never located after a fast-moving Russian armoured column over-ran the Luftwaffe air-base where she'd been matron in a field hospital. That had been in Hungary only so recently as in late December. She'd been due for leave the next day. Her flat in Wilhelmshaven was now requisitioned for refugees fleeing from the Eastern Baltic. So, Hiltzern with nowhere to go, gruffly told Rogge, without a seeming trace of emotion, that the only place left for him was the ship. Rogge even suggested a sideways promotion for him to take command of the Kriegsmarine's newest destroyer which was just recently commissioned. To this Hiltzern snorted 'What! Leave *Dresden*? Not bloody likely an' I dare say no-other member of t'crew will either!' Then he shuffled off to the ward-room to Doctor Lebers. 'Ah, you here Herr Quack? Well, I'd best join you whilst you tell me a story that I can probably work out for me'self.'

Lebers, like Serle, also lived in Kiel but it was only a few minutes walk away outside the dockyard gates. Quite close to the town centre, it was where he'd briefly had a practice combined with his maternity work at the town's hospital. A rather erratic, well-scattered raid over Kiel just three nights prior to *Dresden*'s arrival dropped its bombs over a wide area without causing too much war-material loss. Only a hundred or so homes. Shops. The old church and meeting hall. Frau Lebers was in the process of packing up to go with her daughter and son-in-law to their village home close to the border with Denmark. All three of them, trying to reach an underground shelter when the air-raid alarms began to wail, vanished in a hail of phosphorous bombs dropped as a marker by one of the RAF's pathfinder Mosquitoes. Lebers found all this out from one of the civil policeman whom he'd known before sailing off in *Dresden*. Seeing the portly first officer in the mess, he simply said 'We've enough schnapps here to drown our sorrows' and then the doctor began to cry. Uncontrollably. The strain was too much. Even from a medical man who'd been as close as anyone could have been on *Dresden* to the horrors of human suffering when there'd been casualties. Now, the feeling of loss, helplessness and utter loneliness simply overwhelmed him.

By utter contrast, Rudi Walters felt no inhibitions about how he was spending his leave. Whilst his captain was leaving the ship, he scurried round tidying up as fast as he could and then in his usual mercurial way, ran down the gangplank, exchanged a quick word with the sentry and was gone. As fast as his spindly legs could take him, the little man wove his way down the streets of the dock area and within ten minutes was in the arms of his buxom lady-of-the-town who soon put up a 'closed' sign that remained there outside her room for the next fourteen days. She may have experienced many customers but wearing her favourite red satin bra and pants set, she and Rudi went through the 'Karma Sutra Bible' and added even further variations when the energy permitted. Rudi was her best customer. He made her feel so good. So wanted. So satisfied. Her charms were undeniably lurid but he cared not. Normally her clients paid her but Rudi was the only one she paid. Not in paper money nor in cash but in kind. Alcohol. Chocolates. Sweets. Cigarettes. Jams and pickles. She didn't want them. She always saved them for her Rudi. He was the only client who'd ever written to her. He was the only one to whom she replied. In the last day of his leave, Rudi asked her 'Gretl, I wish to make an honest woman of you. Will you marry me?' She smiled but didn't reply directly. 'Little Rudi Karma. When the war is over and you no longer need to run back to your boat, no longer need my goodies, then I may consent to be your mercurial lady, but whether I'll make a settled down woman will have to be for the time being almost as much as a mystery to how you keep finding me and when here, so much better entertained than any of my other clients' and with that she grabbed hold of him and began kissing him once again to arouse all that she held to be the best part of her 'Little Rudi.'

In quite a different plane of thought and action, Padré Erich Jervaulx gazed around him outside the suburban railway station of the much-battered city of Munich. He was trying to reach the parish where he'd served as a curate before joining the Kriegsmarine. It wasn't easy to recognise where he was for even out in the more open parts of the city, Allied bombs had flattered considerable swathes of the houses and small factories that once lined the streets. Just as they had in Kiel and also where he'd changed trains at Cologne. With a delay of just over four hours before the Munich-bound train was eventually due to leave, he decided to go to see the cathedral. It shook him to see that the area around that lofty medieval church was virtually all flattened and in parts, where the remnants of previous buildings were still existent, huge piles of rubble were in evidence. Amazingly, the cathedral with its soaring spires, still stood. Defiant. Then he wondered if Coventry's cathedral still stood. Defiant. A symbol that church items worth preserving could still survive despite the violence of human beings. Of power-mad men. Picking his way along the streets he, at last, rounding one particularly more ruined corner, saw his curacy church. Like the cathedral at Cologne he perceived that it was still standing, its tall thin western tower stark against the pale evening wintry sky. Atop it, a gilded cross burnished faintly in the last rays of the setting sun. As he approached it in the gathering gloom, he noted that coming from quite a number of windows, many of them glass-less, a gentle flickering glow. Of course, it was Sunday. Must be the evening service. Then the sound of a hymn floated across to him. Carefully, he opened the main door and inside, the church seemed aglow with a myriad of candles, either in the windows or even held in the hands of worshippers, most of whom were standing. As his eyes adjusted to the gloom, he realised that the church was full. Someone whispered in his ear 'Come in, come in, Everyone is welcome although the service is nearly over.' He stood by one of the pillars. One more verse and the singing came to a halt. In the hush that followed he noticed an old priest step forward. Only an occasional cough disturbed what the priest was saying, even if his voice quavered somewhat nervously at first but it gathered in strength as the prayers progressed.

Finally, in full strength and confidence, the white-cloaked cleric said 'Finally we pray for peace and the end of this disastrous war. May God forgive us for the sins committed in the name of our beloved country. May the clean air of the mountains sweep away all that is evil and vile that besets our land. May the God of Love have mercy on the souls of the Western Allies when, surely as night follows day, they will reach this city. Where we have been brutal may they show kindness; pity where we have been pitiless; compassion where we have been angry, patience where impatience has clouded the air. May He, the God of Peace bring that quality to all of us.' Jervaulx glanced around him, nervously, remembering what Doenitz had said in their meeting only three days previously but there was no sign of a violent mob of black-shirted thugs. The priest went into his final Grace and Benediction and the only other sound amidst the slight hiss of the candles was that of some of the assembled congregation softly crying. The service was ended but no-one tried to leave the church. Then to Jervaulx's surprise, he heard what to him had once been the familiar tinkling of the two small bells from the steeple. Now they were ringing out at the end of the service and only then did some of the people begin to stand, and turn to leave. In the gloom, Jervaulx asked one of them why the bells were ringing. 'Don't you know, sir? They are telling all those outside that we've just been praying for the sins of us all. Even to the Gestapo. We've been doing this for the last month or so since Christmas-time. The war is ending, my friend, and the Nazis will be defeated. Yes, you are a stranger because I saw you come in but I'm sure that I've heard your voice beforehand.'

'I'm a Kriegsmarine naval chaplain.'

'Of course, I know that voice. You are Father Erich, aren't you?'

'Yes I am. I was curate here before the war.'

'By the love of God it's good to see you even in this gloomy light. What ship or ships did you serve on?'

'On the *Dresden*. We've just come back after four years away.'

'Yes, I remember hearing it on the news. Not much although we heard quite a lot about her exploits earlier on, especially when the ship attacked that East African convoy. Now it seems that there isn't much room for heroes in these desperate days.'

'Unless you wave a swastika and shout Herr Hitler's name from the piles of rubble that used to be rooftops!'

'Careful now, a lump of rubble may sprout ears! Anyway where are you staying?'

'I was hoping to ask for lodgings with Father Pierre but I didn't see him in the church.'

'Ah no – well – he hasn't returned since the Gestapo asked him to experience their hospitality some six months ago.'

'Why? Father Pierre never had an angry word about them at all.'

'Only love and peace. Like Father André who you saw. Like you he comes from Alsace-Lorraine and as you know, that part of German territory is now in the hands of the advancing Anglo-Americans. Somehow, Father André hasn't yet been asked to jump into a cattle truck or whatever. You see how brave he is. Not only with his prayers but even with the bells. We aren't supposed to ring them until the Allies are seen approaching the area but Father André is defiant. He says the Word of God is more important than the words uttered by the decaying political regime still trying to organise us. Somehow I think it may be a bit dangerous for you to stay with him. He has only an old housekeeper who pops in to clean his single room and cook a daily meal.'

'Oh, then I –'

'Not likely! You must stay with my wife and I. Our house is still standing even though it's minus a few tiles but we get by. Come on, I'll help you with your bags.'

'That is very kind of you.'

'Yes. We must try to help each other. You in return can regale us with your experiences.'

The two men, in the enveloping darkness, left the church as the sound of the bells faded away, Jervaulx warming to the depth of the new friendship that he'd just found.

Once Lubeck had been a beautiful Baltic port with its Hanseatic wooden houses until during a savage reprisal for an utterly pointless Luftwaffe raid on a city like Exeter, the RAF hammered it into another place of rubble and burnt out ruins. Otto Schenke, tough man that he was, couldn't recognise the place. Nor the place where he'd once lived. There was no hole. No pile of rubble. Just an empty space with a light covering of snow over it. A local resident saw the big sailor in an obvious distressed state of mind 'Hey you!' she said. 'Don't I know you? Why, it is isn't it? You are Otto Schenke.'

'Yes, I am and you are?'

'Otto, you great big ugly oaf. It's me! Marta Lodz. I used to feed your cat when you and your missus used to go on a holiday. Sorry, I've gone a bit grey but you 'aven't changed. Well, maybe you're a bit uglier but you are really as soft as, well, you know, a nice fluffy eiderdown.'

'Where's my house? My darling Letitia? Where is she?' Otto grabbed Marta by the hands, shaking them.

'Look, my house is over there. Where it's always been. Mind I ain't gorra' roof. Mi' ceiling does that job now. Top 'alf got blown off by a bomb. The one that flattened your 'ouse.'

'Where is Letitia?' Otto wanted to shake Marta by the shoulders. Fiercely. Somehow he held back when Marta's eyes looked downcast.

'Look, Otto, come in. Have a cup of what passes for coffee these days' and quite firmly, she took Otto by the hand and led him across the rubble and into her rickety dwelling that still resembled at least half a home. Sitting him down with an ersatz coffee, she told him the story. 'The bomb landed but didn't go off straight away. The "all clear" sounded. People came back to the street. Standing about talking. Why Lubeck? What had their beautiful, historical port done to deserve such a savage deluge of bombs and high-explosives?'

'Marta!' Otto pleaded 'Where is my Letitia?'

Marta's eyes again looked downcast. Tears welled out of her eyes 'Oh, Otto, you've been away for so long. You haven't experienced the horror of seeing your home just vanish. Gone. Knocked over. Everything. Letitia did. She saw just that.'

'You mean, she's alive?'

'Yes, sort of. The blast knocked her off her feet. Whilst I was standing here. When the delayed-action bombs went off, we had no warning.'

'Marta! Where is she?'

'Don't distress yourself Otto. They took her to a special sanatorium. It's out in the countryside. About an hour's quick walk from here.' Marta then gave the big sailor details of how to reach the place. Putting down his coffee and muttering his thanks, Otto staggered out and in his lolloping version of what most people regard as plain walking, he heaved himself as fast as his gait could take him. To find his beloved Letitia.

It was almost dark when, after asking three passers-by to re-affirm that he was going in the correct direction, Otto reached the rambling former count's house that now served as the quietly situated sanatorium. Specialising in those civilians who had been unable to cope with the strain and stress of the war. The mentally ill. What some of the more evil of the Nazi-hierarchy described as the unwanted useless bits of human flotsam cluttering up the march to superiority. Had Otto known of this twisted item of warped Nazi logic he'd have probably found the nearest Party Member and tested its neck to see if it could turn as much as the political brain it supported. But there wasn't a convenient Party member around. Only a puzzled-looking nurse in a pale brown blouse and skirt wondering who the gravel-chiselled faced man was and why he'd been pressing on the door-bell for so long. Only the Gestapo did that. Unless they just decided to kick the door in. For fun and physical exercise. Then she discerned his naval greatcoat. She just fled. Not knowing what to do. Leaving Otto to step into the hall.

'Well, who are you?' The new speaker was a tall grey-haired woman with a starched white head cap of the Matron of the sanatorium.

'My name is Otto Schenke. A Chief Petty Officer in the Kriegsmarine. My wife Letitia. Is she here? What have you done with her?'

Schenke made to grab the matron by the hand. She looked at him. The eyes. Pleading. She folded her arms. 'Frau Letitia Schenke is here. Have you any identity card? You could be anyone.' Otto reached inside his coat and produced his naval pass.

'Here. Now take me to her.'

'Herr Schenke. Yes. I'll take you to her but whether she'll know you I cannot say. She is in a world of her own. We do what we can but there's not much hope. Her hearing's been damaged. Her brain doesn't register all that much. But I will take you to see her. Your friend Frau Marta Lodz managed to ring us up to tell us that you were coming. I'm sorry. She said that she'd met you but was unable to tell you of your wife's real condition.'

Matron then turned, told Otto to follow and led him down a long corridor. In the end room, a small thin woman sat in a rocking chair. 'Letitia! Letitia! It's me, Otto!' There was no response, even though Otto knelt down and held her hand. Murmuring sweet nothings at her. Otto tried and tried to get his wife to respond. For a whole hour. But there was no response. Then Matron re-appeared. 'Come now, Herr Schenke. You may visit her for an hour every day that you're on leave.'

Otto left. Disheartened but determined that he could help his Letitia to recover. He trudged back to Frau Lodz and took lodgings with her, sleeping in the former hall-way on a spare mattress. Marta did her best to lift the cloud of despair from Otto's mind but the only time he seemed to light up was when he prepared himself for his daily walk to see Letitia.

Every remaining day, Matron, warming to the gentleness shown by the ugly squashed-nose brutal-looking sailor allowed him to stay longer, but no matter how long he stayed, there seemed to be no change at all in Letitia's condition.

Otto could not contain his tears as he finally said farewell. To Matron he said 'It's no good. She doesn't know who I am. But when this war is over, the good Lord permitting' here he crossed himself 'I will return'.

Matron watched the huge bulk lollop into the darkness. Then she turned and almost by instinct walked as fast as she could to Letitia's room. There she heard Frau Schenke muttering over and over again.

'That man said he was my husband. My Otto. My husband. My Otto.' Matron smiled. For the first time for more than two years she smiled for Letitia Schenke. Then she stopped smiling and her heart hardened. Not against Letitia. But against the lunatic dictator whose whims at waging war were proving to be so disastrous. May his uncompassionate soul be allowed to have one iota of common sense so that he could see enough was enough and stop the madness. Then perhaps the Otto Schenke's of this world could be reunited with their Letitia's. One ray of hope and Otto Schenke had shambled away not knowing of its brief display. Matron rushed out of the room not knowing how to cry. Her tears had long since dried up in the misery of the human wrecks under her care.

Otto Schenke shambled back to Marta's lodgement, picked up his one bag and left for the railway station. Like so many others of the battlecruiser's crew. Unable to comprehend that this was the Germany that they'd all set their hearts on returning to only to find a country descending into chaos. More than one felt relieved to be on their way back to the ship. All of them felt heartily thankful that *Dresden*'s towering superstructure loomed over them by the dockside. Still safe. Still intact. Still a going concern. Still a fighting ship. Something solid that they understood. Less able to understand had been the crumbling of the country and closer at home, their families, their own domestic affairs. Wives and girlfriends who'd given them up for dead. Children who couldn't recognise their father. Parents who couldn't come to terms that it was their son on the doorstep and all of them unable to work out that the man that they'd known all so briefly was suddenly saying 'Goodbye' and climbing on board a lorry or a clapped-out train. All had a different story to tell and yet the same one. Despair. Fear. Not knowing what further traumas were to come.

On the day that George and Elle were due to go down to the station, quite early in the morning came a knock on their aunt's front door. A very firm hand was obviously hitting the door knocker. So loud was it that auntie dropped her cup of nettle and elder-flower tea on to the stone floor. 'Could be the Gestapo! I must have said something!' she cried, beginning to sob. Elle held her in her arms whilst George, hurriedly putting on his vice-admiral's uniform jacket went to the door. It wasn't the Gestapo, but the sober-suited official wasn't the bearer of good news. 'I'm from the area gauleiter. This house will be home to four refugees from the East until further notice. Frau Oberstein will comply. We all have to assist our country in the hour of its greatest need. This is the official order,' and saying this the man handed over a sheet of paper. Behind the official stood an armed policeman. He touched his helmet on seeing Reitz's uniform but shrugged his shoulders at the same time. Reitz snapped at the official 'Look here, little man, I've been at sea for the last four years and what have I come back to? Eh? To have moronic little worms like you knocking on the door of a widow whose husband and sons have given their lives in the service of the Fatherland. Now you turn up and expect her to feed four more people without I assume any extra help from your office. Eh? I thought not. Go away little worm and thank your lucky stars that my ship's guns can't range on your office or they'd blast it and your fellow faceless morons to even tinier worms than yourself!' With that Reitz slammed the door in the man's face and turned to find Elle, mouth open, standing there. 'Oh darling, you didn't have to shout at him! Perhaps it's as well we're leaving. Poor auntie couldn't have possibly looked after us too!'

Auntie Bergit calmed down sufficiently by the time old Albert and his trap arrived to take George, Elle and their bags to the station. At the station, Bergetta fervently kissed Elle and said 'Make sure that he sees the war through with both of you together. I hope I'll see you both when it's all over.' She also kissed George on both cheeks before they climbed aboard the train which soon hissed and clanked its way out of sight, the smoke clouds mingling with the morning mist.

By late afternoon they were back at the Kiel dockside under the shadow of *Dresden*. Above them they could hear the sounds of men working, orders being shouted and a number of tuneless whistles as men painted out the last of the battle scars. They were glad to be on board to help get the battlecruiser back to sea. Back to the element that they all understood. Rogge met Reitz and Elle at the dockside and all three went on board where the former showed them the extra anti-aircraft gun protection as well as the aerials of a new radar that could see accurately astern of the ship. An added extra to their long-standing much-repaired ex-British set that had served the ship so well in her long cruise. The biggest new weapons that had been fitted to the warship were two twin eighty-eight millimetre guns acquired from Kiel's anti-aircraft defences because Rogge argued successfully that on board *Dresden*, Germany's most famous warship, it would help in her overall defence. They were fitted to replace the damaged fifteen centimetre secondary gun that had been destroyed in the Seafire crash. Rogge rattled out some statistics about how fast the gun could fire and that two of Kiel's air-gunners were now drafted on board to guide the ship's own gunners as to how well to fire the guns. Numerous extra Vierling quadruple batteries had also been fitted. 'All over, aren't they?' mused Elle. 'I wouldn't like to be an airman trying to get in close. I'm sure that they'll help to keep you safe.'

It was obvious to Reitz that Rogge had pulled out every stop in the ship's overhaul. She'd not only been through the dockyard hands but Hiltzern had also put to work every man as soon as they returned from their short leave. The decks were clean and polished, new paint was everywhere. Doors, boats davits and anything else in hinges were all well greased.

'You can be proud of her' murmured Elle. 'No wonder you love this ship so much.'

'Ah darling that I do but not as much as I love you. Besides metal can't kiss you' and saying this, George embraced her. It was time to wish her farewell.' I will see you soon. Take care of yourself.' A final tongue-twirling and in the gathering evening gloom, George could detect a tear or two from Elle as Rogge gently took her and led her back to the gang-way. Reitz turned to go towards his main cabin. Mercurially as Elle started to walk down the gangplank, a little man appeared at her side 'You've got a good 'un there, fraulein, and I 'ave too.' She turned to see who it was but Walters, and his special bag with his 'extras' in it had vanished as only he knew how into the dark shadows of *Dresden*'s superstructure.

When dawn of 29th January began to light up the eastern sky, the ropes fastening *Dresden* to the quayside were released and with her crew lining the rails as if at some peace-time review, she slowly slid away with Vice Admiral Rogge and three of his staff officers at the salute. This was their proud ship. Going back to war although Reitz insisted on spending the first day in exercising the crew, particularly the anti-aircraft gunners. The pre-arranged time to escort *Wilhelm Gustloff* would be put back twenty-four hours. Would the liner wait or sail at the first possible moment? It was a risk that Reitz decided to take. His work-up of the crew came first with one hundred and sixty-three new members to replace the ones that had died off

Norway as well as the extra gunners. Of the original crew who'd arrived in Kiel just fifteen days previously, only nine had apparently deserted. Hiltzern said that it was likely to be for family reasons or that their trains were delayed. Three other members were known to have been killed when a long-range Allied fighter plane had machine-gunned their train. Two officers had also not mustered. Reitz was particularly angry when hearing about Alfred Serle. It was soon after when Elle had left that Rogge came back on board with the grim news. Serle was still in his civilian clothes when an SS squad caught up with him just a stone's throw from the naval compound near the docks. The two Kriegsmarine sentries on duty were unable to stop the SS squad roughly throw Serle against a wall, raise their rifles and summarily execute him. Doctor Lebers reported that in Serle's right-hand was his Kriegsmarine naval pass issued by Rogge's office. Lebers was called by a major of that execution squad to formally identify the body. To Lebers, and Rogge, and now Reitz, it was a warning that outside the Kriegsmarine's sphere of operation, not one member of *Dresden*'s crew was completely safe. The major told Doctor Lebers that Serle had murdered his wife and that his orders to round him up came from a colonel of his same regiment who'd witnessed the whole affair. What the major didn't say was that this self-same colonel was the officer who'd jumped out of Serle's burning house, leaving Frau Serle to her horrific fate.

The other officer was Robert Koch. No-one seemed to know what Koch had done. If they had, they would have been even more apprehensive. Koch's home, like Brautsch's, was in Berlin. Reporting a matter of grave national importance about the apparent traitorous attitude of *Dresden*'s captain, officers and crewmen for failing to follow their Fuhrer's noble Aryan principles to a local gauleiter's office, he'd been taken, via various other officials, each higher ranking in turn, until one day, in a partly-bombed warehouse he came face to face with a rather bloated-looking official in a long black leather greatcoat.

'My name is Martin Bormann. The Fuhrer's representative of all state matters. I understand that you have something of great importance to tell me.'

Koch went weak at the knees. Despite the cold, he began to feel sweat on his brow. He knew that he couldn't go back on what he'd already said. Suddenly he poured it all out. How Reitz often seemed to go against all for what the Fuhrer proclaimed. Rescuing survivors who could have easily made it to shore. Refusing to fly the 'Swastika' from the main-mast. Playing music by Edward Elgar on the ship's loudspeaker system. Or by Scott Joplin or George Gershwin. The band even learning to play the English and American national anthems. Proper burials for the enemy. He just went on and on. Rambling. Exaggerating. And all the time Bormann just listened. Intently.

'Well, it's quite a story isn't it? You see Leutnant Koch, the *Dresden* is currently the one ship that is doing this country's greatest service amongst the other apologies that serve on the seas. However –' Bormann looked through the grimy half-broken windows '– I shall keep all your words in mind. Take him away!' he suddenly barked at two guards standing either side of Koch.

Koch was marched away. Down three floors. A door was flung open. 'In there!' He fell to the floor. A key turned. There were no windows. Nothing. The tread of the guards faded away. Bormann said 'Well, you've all heard nothing. Nothing. Nothing. Do not repeat what that cretin has said. It is now a matter of the utmost secrecy. I alone, with the Fuhrer's direction, will deal with this. Now leave this building. Perhaps the American bombers will knock it down in due course!'

Dresden, with two destroyers on either flank accompanying her, cruised at twenty knots as the next evening approached. On the bridge a buzzer sounded. Brautsch, on watch, took it. It was from the wireless room reporting that the *Wilhelm Gustloff* had set sail. Brautsch took the step of telephoning his captain. The response told

Brautsch to raise the speed to twenty-two knots for as Reitz put it 'She's left twelve hours earlier than what we expected.'

At midnight Reitz himself took over. Even though he was an officer of flag-rank he regarded himself as still capable of taking his turn on the bridge watch rota. Horst was with him, he having stayed with the battlecruiser. Rogge's news for him in Kiel had been hard for him to take. The new Walther U-boat ready for Baltic sea trials was now blasted apart and smothered in chunks of concrete when Lancaster bombers of the RAF's 617 squadron dropped their enormous Tall Boy bombs on its re-inforced pen. By utter misfortune, one bomb exploded over and into the same hole as one just created by a previous bomb. The second bomb penetrated and shattered the U-boat and the pen. So Horst shrugged his shoulders and as Serle had been so cruelly murdered, he gallantly said he'd take over as *Dresden*'s new navigator. Reitz was pleased to see the tall U-boat skipper as part of his crew. The man's navigational skills had already proved invaluable. Horst told his captain just exactly where he thought that the refugee liner would be. 'Here sir, about a hundred miles out into the Danzig Bay. Say six hours at about fifteen knots. We should reach her in about six more hours. Soon after dawn if we're lucky.'

Minutes ticked by. Then the wireless room buzzer sounded again.

'Call the captain. Urgent. *Wilhelm Gustloff* has been torpedoed and is sinking.'

Reitz grimaced when given the news. 'Where is she?' he snapped at Horst.

'Not much further on than the last time I showed you sir.'

'How long?'

'At twenty-five knots for at least another four hours.'

Reitz grunted. At that speed the destroyers may well fall behind or run out of fuel but he knew that he must try and reach the sinking liner.

'Signal the destroyers. We're raising speed and expect them to keep company.'

To Hiltzern whose bulk just then heaved itself on to the bridge, he said 'Lifeboats and life-rafts. Get them ready. Warn anti-aircraft gunners to be on the alert at first light.'

An hour passed. Then Kiel wirelessed them a further message – 'Gustloff has sunk. Numerous casualties.' Heavy cruiser *Hipper* passed them half-an-hour later with more than two thousand military evacuees on board. Soon after her had come the light cruiser *Emden* carrying about five hundred military personnel who had been involved in recovering the coffin of the First World War hero, Field Marshall Hindenburg. She couldn't stop either to search for survivors. Then the long night emerged into yet another dawn. Cold. Bleak.

As the skies brightened,the choppy grey seas could be seen to be littered with the flotsam of the sunken refugee ship. And bodies. All lifeless. Reitz stared aghast as *Dresden* slowed. An old coal-fired torpedo boat approached laden with survivors. She signalled that she'd ended searching for anyone alive. Another small escort vessel was also seemingly overloaded. It too signalled 'No-one left alive. Probably five or more thousand believed to have gone down.' The two small warships together reported that they'd rescued nearly nine hundred souls and were leaving the area. Reitz detailed one of his destroyers to act as an escort and when the weather calmed down, to possibly take some of the survivors on board.

Kiel then signalled *Dresden* new instructions. 'Join up with *ZA-28* for bombardment of Gotenhafen coast.'

Soon the destroyer hove into sight. Otto Wegener, ever cheerful, signalled 'Hello friends. Welcome to the crazy Baltic. Follow us and we'll lob some bricks at naughty Joe's boys.'

The coastline flickered into sight. Low, flattish at first. Without shape. A darker grey line set above a grey sea. Lit up by orange flashes. Lots of them. Then streaks of a lighter colour. Briefly. From left to right before exploding into more brief sparks. Yellow. Red. Over everything to the right above these sparks rose clouds of black smoke.

ZA-28 was signalling – 'You will need your spotter plane for accurate shooting. The Russians are to port, our Army boys are to starboard.' The German army guns flickered feebly in response to what looked like to be an overwhelming barrage. As Reitz acknowledged in the affirmative, two dark shapes near the coastline materialised. Small escort warships. Trying to help the Wehrmacht to give some sort of Kriegsmarine reply. Temporarily bereft of big-ship support the Army was facing extreme difficulty. *Dresden* it seemed had arrived in the nick of time.

Reitz ordered two of his seaplanes into the air. One to act as an artillery spotter, the other to look out for any possible Russian retaliatory air strike.

The co-ordinates of the Russian guns were quickly in Halder's hands. As well as the massing of tanks, lorries and infantry that were moving up to the line behind the barraging guns.

'Open fire!' snarled Reitz.

Dresden's main and starboard secondary guns crashed out. The first salvoes landed a trifle short but then subsequent shells began to hack down the Russian guns. As the battlecruiser slowly closed the shore, her two destroyer escorts also opened fire with their main guns. Smaller. Quicker-firing. The news given by the two Arados was encouraging. Huge gaps were being opened up in the line of barraging Russian artillery. Careful shooting by Halder's guns also created havoc and horror amongst the Russian forces behind their batteries. *Wilhelm Gustloff* was being avenged. Savagely. It took nearly half-an-hour before the Russians accepted that their attempted push forward was no longer a practical concern. The Arado pilots were constantly reporting what seemed like suicidal charges by tanks and other vehicles. They were taking their enormous losses as if nothing fired at them would stop them.

Horst murmured 'They're fanatical. They hate us so much. They just won't give up whatever we throw at them.'

But give up they did as the ground around them became littered with the blasted debris of their fallen comrades. Of craters too huge to cross. Of smashed guns and vehicles. In a somewhat disorderly retreat the Russians withdrew to beyond the range of all but *Dresden*'s heaviest shells, hesitated and then withdrew even further as the battlecruiser's big shells followed them to the edge of an extensive broken expanse of forest.

'Cease fire. Retrieve the Arados!'

Slowly *Dresden* cruised the coastline but the Russians made no effort to reply. An hour passed.

'Horst. Come with me. I need to work out our new course for tomorrow we go to the Courland Peninsula. Kiel had just signalled their congratulations on this job. Perhaps as well we weren't escorting the *Gustloff* after all.'

'Ah sir, we have had our hands full ever since *Prinz Eugen* began the work on the gun-line last August.' replied Horst. 'I know that. My cousin is on her. His job is an anti-aircraft defence co-ordinator.'

'Can we expect trouble? I mean, from the Russians?'

'Perhaps an evening strike. But not to worry. They aren't all that good at speeding warships nor do they carry heavy bombs.'

'Hmmm!' grunted Reitz, turning to go towards his sea-cabin. No longer the youngest sailor in the warship, but still with the keenest eyes, lookout Karl Prebke on the starboard bridge wing saw them first. Flying low over the coastline.

'Aircraft, sir. Off starboard beam.'

More eyes searched for them. The anti-aircraft guns began to poke their muzzles higher up into the air as rather surprisingly the approaching Russian aircraft began to try and gain height.

Reitz and Horst hurried back on to the bridge as the alarm bells rang out their alarm.

'There sir! Twelve of them' came a sharp cry from Prebke, pointing upwards.

Chapter 13

'I tried to hold on to him'

The climbing aircraft were confronted with a sudden hail of brown smoke from exploding shells as the warships below them opened fire.

Horst grunted 'Won't do us much harm. They are Sturmoviks. More used to a tank-busting role. Trying to climb to make their little bombs do more damage.'

Each one of the Russian pilots knew what they had to do – 'Sink the Nazi warships that had recently been responsible for the devastating barrage of destruction on their Army comrades.'

Hurriedly re-armed after a sortie destroying a column of fleeing enemy trucks, they'd taken off with the same type of tank-busting bombs and rockets. Just as Horst predicted. Their only weaponry available. But to the airmen it did not matter. All Nazis were only good when they were dead. When two aircraft of the formation suddenly lost their wings and a third blew up, the others just carried on. Consumed with hate. With revenge. The fact that quick-firing eighty-eights or Vierling machine guns were ripping into them didn't seem to matter. Not at first.

A fourth and a fifth aircraft were hit. To crash into the unforgiving icy-cold water below them. At last realisation hit the brains of the survivors – 'Ditch the bombs and get out!'

Still well short of their moving flame-spitting targets the remaining aircraft turned, dropped their bombs and then flew desperately for a wave-level dash back for safety but not before *Dresden*'s heavier guns caught a sixth one for it just simply disintegrated when a direct hit smashed straight into its relatively fragile construction.

'Cease fire!' yelled Reitz. 'They've had enough.'

Horst grunted 'Pity the surviving pilots. For their failure they'll probably be sent to their army's front line as part of their suicide battalions.' Horst then continued, his voice tinged with a mixture of sadness or was it sarcasm? 'A bit like our glory boys in the U-boats. Off they sail in out-dated Type V11-C boats and if they survive, but most don't, off they go again. Lucky if they survive two outings. We've lost the U-boat war despite the bravery of our fellows. Bit like those Russkies. Whatever their losses they won't give up. The difference is that they're now on the winning side! Believe me sir, they'll be back. Won't be satisfied until one of our little fleet has been sunk.'

Reitz nodded, grim-faced.

One of the destroyers began to signal. 'Running short of fuel. Permission required to refuel in Gotenhafen'

Reitz nodded again. 'Reply in the affirmative' and then to the wireless room he asked for a replacement. The reply from Kiel was swift. 'Sending new torpedo boat from Danzig Bay. She'll meet you tomorrow morning. Stay in your area until she arrives.'

Cruising at fifteen knots just out of sight of the coast that they'd so recently shelled, *Dresden* and *ZA-28* spent a long cold night but there were no calls for their gunfire assistance. It seemed as if the Russians had withdrawn to re-gather their strength.

Dawn. How many had Reitz seen whilst on the bridge since joining *Dresden*? The cold made him shiver despite his thick clothing.

'Ship in sight!' came keen-eyed Prebke's call. Always the first.

It identified itself as *T-75* a brand new torpedo boat of nine hundred tons. Just three weeks in service. The three ships set off for Courland but in the early afternoon, the radar room reported a new Russian air-attack. Flying quite high this time.

The group included four pilots who'd survived that recent debacle against *Dresden* and they were in the lead. This time thirty bombers were in the attack group and their instructions were quite clear. 'Don't come back until you've sunk an enemy ship.' They were rather surprised to see three German warships sailing towards them in waters that they reckoned were now under Russian control.

'Attack, attack those Nazi scum!' yelled the leader.

Down the planes dropped, engines howling as they put on speed. Once again the anti-aircraft barrage was impressive. Vicious. Every gun other than the six biggest on *Dresden,* as well as all the guns on the two smaller escorts began pumping shells at the Russians. Plane after plane seemed to just catch fire and spiral downwards. It made no difference. Those Russian pilots had their orders 'Kill the Nazis or be killed yourself.'

One after another they aimed their aircraft into the hail of red, yellow and orange tracer; into the bursting brown smoke balls of the heavier gunfire; hurtling downwards, seeking their prey which was below them. Twisting and spitting fire. At them.

Those attacking *Dresden* and *ZA-28* met their match and the planes that penetrated the flak defence bombed inaccurately but on the less-experienced *T-75,* with also weaker defensive fire, six of the aircraft bombed sufficiently accurately enough to not only hit the nine-hundred ton warship but also to cause her serious damage. She began to lose speed and to steer erratically. The last three attackers, realising that one of the three ships below them was in trouble, all went in for the kill. The first two aircraft released their bombs that crashed down on the severely-crippled warship but as the final attacker dove down, a stream of defiant tracer ripped at the underside of that Russian aircraft causing it to blow up and crash into the water adjacent to the capsizing bows of *T-75*. Slowly she turned on to her port side with members of her crew desperately jumping from her or trying to launch the few inflatable life-rafts that hadn't been damaged. Reitz stared aghast even though he'd seen many ships destroyed so far in this war which perhaps mercifully was in its closing stages. *T-75* was a new warship, no, had been, a new warship flung into the war with a new crew. Into a campaign with the stamp of hopeless defiance now etched firmly on to it. Hurriedly Reitz sent a signal across to *ZA-28* to turn round and pick up any survivors. The afternoon light was fading as the last of the surviving twelve aircraft vanished over the cloud-dominated horizon. Eighteen of the Russian aircraft had been shot down but this was a fact of little comfort for the doomed *T-75*. Whilst *Dresden* continued onwards at twenty knots, Wegener and his destroyer men closed in to *T-75*'s sinking site and were able to eventually rescue thirty-one of the torpedo boat's crew of ninety-eight. As evening closed in *ZA-28* gave up the search and sped off to catch the battlecruiser.

The surviving pilots duly reported to their commander that despite the losses that they'd suffered, one of the Nazi warships was definitely sunk and the other two vessels, seriously damaged, were retreating westwards. Their Commander nodded. Ships were difficult targets but for once, his aircraft were victorious. More Nazi scum eliminated. Somehow the loss of so many of his own pilots didn't seem to have affected him. Not after the many millions of Soviet citizens who'd already given their lives to rid the Motherland of the Hitlerite invaders.

The next dawn seemed to take a very long time to assert itself over those cold, grey Baltic waters as *Dresden* and *ZA-28* approached their target of the isolated Wehrmacht unit on the Courland Peninsula. As they closed the land, they were sighted by soldier Ernst Keldt on watch, sheltering in a frozen ditch adjacent to the coastal track as it came to the end of the peninsula. During the previous two days, Keldt had cowered in the ditch whilst reporting the presence of an approaching Russian surface force and twice he'd listened to the scream of shells as they passed over him. Fortunately both bombardments were of only about twenty minutes in duration and so far as Ernst knew, they'd caused little extra damage or very few casualties, As he peered through his binoculars, the ships that grew larger into his view were somewhat different. There were only two of them, not the usual five. They were approaching from the south-west, not from the north. They also looked like ones he'd seen when he'd sailed in a destroyer for Norway four years earlier. Keldt twirled the handle of his field telephone.

'Two unidentified warships approaching from the south-west. They look like ours.' At the other end of the line the message was relayed to Feldwebel Friedrich Hahn. ''Bout time the Kriegsmarine gave us a hand' he grunted whilst he pulled on his shabby great coat before clambering out of the cellar of the ruined house that was his section's headquarters. Here he was, a veteran sergeant in the Wehrmacht, knowing that the time for the Wehrmacht trapped on this Peninsula would soon come to a grisly end. No matter what losses the Russians took, they never gave up. Probing, probing. Just like those Russkie warships had done for the last two afternoons. Probing for a response but getting not one German gun to fire back. Their last four '88s' were all facing the land waiting for the awesome Russian T-34 tanks. Not pointing for a seaward assault. Now, coming closer were two units of the Kriegsmarine. Hahn's colonel had earlier hinted that they might be rescued by the Navy and now they were here. Like Private Keldt, he too had experienced life on a warship. To Norway, on board *Hipper* when she'd tangled with *Gloworm* off Norway. He'd left the heavy cruiser when she docked after the action. The larger ship approaching possessed similar lines although he couldn't place her but the destroyer looked similar to one of those which had been part of *Hipper*'s escort screen.

Accordingly, Hahn gave instructions for the captured local fishing boat that had been abandoned by its owners, when the German battle-group reached his part of the coastline in its long retreat, to be made ready in order to meet the newcomers.

Reitz ordered *Dresden* and *ZA-28* to come to a near halt when about a mile offshore although all the big guns of the two warships were trained on the coast. 'Boat approaching from the land; looks like from a breakwater of some sort' murmured Horst.

'Is Brautsch ready?' asked Reitz, knowing that his ever-reliable officer was in position, with his men, in the fast motor-launch on its falls. It was quickly released, the motor already running and soon its frothy wash creamed away from its big parent ship as Brautsch closed up towards the approaching boat. It came alongside and a one-armed sergeant begrimed with dirt and years of war-weariness, sketchily saluted from its bows.

'Feldwebel Hahn. Ready to show you in. And you are?'

'Kapitan Leutnant Brautsch of the KM *Dresden*, with destroyer *ZA-28* accompanying us.'

'Signal your ships to keep moving. Russian aircraft do have the habit of visiting us now and then in daylight hours.'

Brautsch ordered one of his men to flash the signal lamp over to *Dresden* and then he followed Hahn's boat to the breakwater. It turned out to be a line of half submerged trucks, armoured cars, empty oil drums and ammunition boxes. Tying up to a truck behind Hahn's boat, and leaving four of his men behind, Brautsch and his group clambered on to the hastily fitted planks that took them over the tops of the various vehicles. Hahn led them to a semi-ruined Russian Orthodox Church where in the crypt below the sanctuary, the German military leader, Colonel Alexis Von Huffmeyer, had set up his headquarters. Brautsch gasped as he saluted the Colonel who was stooping over a map using a magnifying glass. The Colonel, without a cap, was thickly grey haired, sported a patch over his left eye and his left arm was severed at the elbow with an artificial limb for the lower half. Brautsch didn't know that Huffmeyer was sixty-seven years old. Even quite old for his service at Verdun,

Passchendaele and on the Hindenburg Line in the previous Great War. Retiring from the Army at the cessation of those hostilities, he'd volunteered in 1938 to assist in the training of new officers for what he saw as a revitalised Wehrmacht. With his Prussian Army background, Huffmeyer instilled into his eager-faced young officers the ideas of discipline, good military tactics and respect for any captured forces. He'd been swept along, like many Germans, in the general euphoria of the first two years of the war as the German armed forces scored victory after victory but when the Werhmacht was stopped at the outskirts of Moscow, Huffmeyer realised then that Hitler's planning had far outreached itself and that realism was beginning to set in. A realism that held the spectre of ultimate defeat for Germany. The casualties amongst the young officers began to mount, just like it had done in the killing trenches of the Western Front of 1915 and onwards.

In mid-1943 Huffmeyer requested transference with the latest batch of recruits to the Eastern Front. He found himself in charge of quite a number of mixed divisions holding on to the perimeter south-west of Leningrad. Elsewhere, the Eastern Front was being steadily pushed back towards Germany but not yet outside the city that the German Army, to its chagrin, had failed to subdue. Then the Russians massed their forces and began the process of ridding the city of their hated opponents. The city that bore the name of the first leader of the Bolshevik Revolution. Losses to them didn't matter. Nor the enormous number of shells or Katyusha rockets fired at the Nazi army. Or the aircraft shot down. What mattered was that their heroic forces were hammering at the enemy forcing him back and thus ridding their beloved country of that evil presence.

Huffmeyer didn't really understand the Russian way of thinking. He'd never witnessed the atrocities of the SS, the Gestapo and the vileness accorded to many Russian prisoners. He was an honest old officer caught up in what was turning almost to be a rout of the Wehrmacht. Somehow he disciplined his group to lie still in deep fox-holes as the massive lumbering T-34's came churning in their ponderous approach. 'Wait' he'd ordered 'and then fix the anti-tank bombs on their tracks or rear ends as they pass over.' The faint-hearted panicked and were crushed as they tried to flee or were machine-gunned if they'd been able to avoid the first fate. Those who followed their Colonel's example were able to smile with the satisfaction at seeing the big tanks become crippled or even sometimes, blow up. Smiling despite their own losses. But their limited victories were always counter-balanced with Russian advances elsewhere along the retreating Wehrmacht lines until after almost a continual eighteen-month back-pedal, Huffmeyer's group found itself with the sea at their backs and the Red armies pushing further south and cutting off any chance of a retreat along the coastline.

Mercifully the main bulk of the Russian armies left them, an isolated, war-weary but battle-hardened group and apart from occasional probings and the even rarer limited artillery barrages to interrupt them, they'd been able to build up a reasonably strong defence system but their own recent night patrols reported a build-up of a Russian armoured force arriving, together with a number of artillery pieces. Then came the surprising appearance of the Russian warships, the first ones above motor-torpedo boat size to appear to challenge the Kriegsmarine's naval supremacy in the Baltic to bombard, albeit briefly on the last two successive afternoons, their German-held area. It all seemed to point to an effort, by perhaps a reserve battalion or so of the Red Army, to wipe out the nuisance of Huffmeyer's survivors.

Huffmeyer looked up at Brautsch 'Ah, the Kriegsmarine. Last I heard of you lot, was that you'd all gone down with the *Bismarck*!' Maybe it was being sarcastic but he noted Brautsch's immaculate naval salute and then the well-weathered face and finally the thin smile.

'What ship and what is your mission, man?'

'Kapitan-Leutnant Brautsch of the battlecruiser *Dresden* with destroyer *ZA-28* as escort. We have come to evacuate the worst of your wounded but only after we've dealt with the Red cruisers that appear to be causing you a bit of a problem. If we deal with them, other ships will come to take off the rest of your men.'

'Are you on a ship big enough to hit this area?' grunted the old soldier, pointing a grubby black-leather gloved finger at the map spread out over a table of spent ammunition boxes.

'Scale?' said Brautsch.

'Well, the Russians guns and tanks are about ten kilometres from my front observation posts which in turn are about five kilometres from here.'

'Our main guns will be able to reach beyond your front line but why not expose the Russian units over this open ground here' and with this, Brautsch placed his right hand with the fingers spread out. 'Colonel, I'm a navy man but even our secondary guns could reach this area and destroy your attackers well away from what I assume to be woods back there.'

'For a young man you're quite astute but tell me, how will you be able to range your guns, especially if my outposts aren't being manned?'

'We'll launch our own spotter aircraft and when your men see them, tell them to withdraw. Don't worry, Colonel, we're here hopefully to see you all evacuate this area by later tonight.'

'Perhaps as well. We are on strict food and medical rations. About three months ago, four of your fast motor-torpedo boats did land us some limited supplies but they've just about all gone. What food and fuel we have is what my patrols steal from Russian army depots. We even once managed to drive three of their big petrol-tankers across to our lines. That is what keeps the generators going to supply the power for my limited communications. Don't worry, Kapitan-Leutnant, I am grateful to your ship for turning up. You see, I'm an old man, long past my prime and know nothing of your type of war. You said *Dresden*? My God, you're the ship that attacked that East

African convoy? How long ago was that?' Huffmeyer paused. His eyes fading as he tried to recall that incident. And the many since that. Yes, he was tired. Perhaps he shouldn't have been here at all. Trying still to care for men under his command. Where was his cosy fire and fur-lined slippers? A million light-years away. Then he came back to reality. 'You'd better get back to your ship. Here, have this map. I know it off by heart. Go on, the Russian navy, if they're coming, will be here within three or four hours. Get out to sea and surprise them. They won't be looking for you. They'll be looking at us instead!'

Admiral of the Kronstadt Fleet, Mikhail Polensky sent out his cruiser force again. Same time. Same objective. Extended bombardment this time. After thirty minutes, the one hundred and third armoured reserve brigade with accompanying infantry would advance to crush the pestilent Nazi strongpoint and wipe out the viperous scum completely. The Red Armed Forces could no longer tolerate their presence. In his hand he still held a flimsy stating that Air Force units had sunk the German re-inforcing ships steaming towards that isolated army group. The way was clear. Soon complete victory would be accomplished and the Red Navy would be in control of that part of the Baltic – not with submarines or torpedo boats but with its bigger surviving surface ships. Polensky didn't know that *Dresden* was at that moment temporarily withdrawing to allow the cruiser force to approach Huffmeyer's tenuously held territory.

Brautsch told Reitz of the predicament that Huffmeyer and his men faced. 'It seems that Rogge was right and that we're just in time. At least there's no mention of any surviving Russian battleships being in the group. The trouble is, we aren't sure what is their strength.'

Horst intervened 'Nothing very modern or big. Their best destroyers were active off Murmansk but quite what they have after the Leningrad Siege I'm not sure, but nothing that we can't handle.'

Reitz grunted. Horst was valuable to him with his excellent local knowledge and as a navigator, he was as good as, if not better, that the late lamented Alfred Serle. He shuddered to think how low Germany and some Germans were stooping every time he thought of Serle. Four years away from home and then to be lined up against a wall and shot. Without even a trial! The ruddy face of dear Doctor Lebers after he'd identified Serle's body faded to a pale colour of the whitish pallor. Even Padré Jervaulx took it very badly and visibly shook when trying to conduct the burial service.

'Radar to bridge! Suspect five ships to north-east of us. Speed estimated at seventeen knots. Distance about fifteen kilometres.'

Reitz, with the benefit of a new repeater screen on the bridge – one of Rogge's efforts to update their well-used radar during that hasty refit – began to plot his ship's approach. All the gun crews were closed up. The radar was able to identify five enemy ships with two of them showing up to be slightly larger echoes than the other three.

'Cruisers' murmured Hiltzern. 'But I'll bet that the lead ship is a destroyer. Well, I best be off to the Damage Control area although me thinks, Captain' (he'd never once referred to Reitz as Admiral), 'that if Halder shoots properly, we shouldn't incur any damage. Maybe even Goethe's tidy shelves of supplies won't need to be upset too much' and with a little rumble of a chuckle, off he shambled. Never walked. Shambled or waddled, yes, but walking or marching, never. At least that was the appearance that the big officer gave as he moved around the battlecruiser.

Reitz waved an arm in farewell. He knew that for the four years that he'd known Hiltzern was that he couldn't have had a better commander. Even now he was trying to crack a joke, albeit a poor one, at the expense of the meticulous Supplies Officer. Time after time Reitz reflected on how he'd planned his future strategies for *Dresden* based on the accurate supply lists of food, ammunition and fuel that Goethe gave him on a weekly basis, or on a daily basis if so requested. Only a few hours earlier, Reitz had read the lists on the available ammunition still in stock for the heavy and medium guns. He knew, that despite the recent bombardment, he still had plenty of shells for a sharp naval action and a further bombardment if so required.

That a naval action was looming he knew for certain. Out of sight of the Russian warships, Reitz took *Dresden* so as to eventually follow them on a converging course.

'Enemy in visual sight!' came the cry from Prebke. Still ever-keen. How the lad had matured since those far-off early days. Reitz had promoted him to Leading Seaman in charge of his look-out group. Here he was, first again as usual. 'Thirty degrees off the port bow!'

'Speed to twenty-five knots' murmured Reitz. Horst estimated that the Russians were travelling at about sixteen knots as they closed Huffmeyer's coastline from about three kilometres off-shore.

All eyes on those Russian vessels were on that coastline. A part of Mother Russia still occupied by the Nazi scum. Every crew member felt proud to be part of the first major Russian surface force to be in Baltic action against the enemy. This time, instead of just a cursory bombardment, they were to close the shore and really batter their opponents until their own Army's tanks reached the German lines. Gunnery officers and their staff reeled off the ever-decreasing range. Twenty or so guns between the five ships with shells already in their breeches.

'Open fire!' yelled the captain of each ship. In a ragged broadside, the guns of the two cruisers and three destroyers barked out. Their shells crashed on the shore line as well as amidst the sand-dunes and the ruined landscape of that peninsula. Deep down in their slit trenches or cellars, Huffmeyer's men crouched, hearing the crump of the naval shells as they began to add further to the shattered nature of the land they still held.

No-one on the Russian ships kept a decent watch over to starboard. Nothing was expected from there. Not from the re-inforcing ships of the Kriegsmarine reported to be sunk by the Red

Air Force. Or had turned back. If anyone had been alert, they would have seen the long lean Kriegsmarine shape that had been so visualised by many of *Dresden*'s Allied opponents as they'd watched the battlecruiser approach their vessel. They'd have also seen, that slightly astern of the big warship, was a smaller one. In size and outline very similar to the three fairly modern destroyers of their own squadron. An enemy destroyer.

'Mmm. Bit like Guadalcanal and those supply ships' murmured Reitz. 'They don't seem to have seen us.'

With white froth streaming from either side of her bows and a thin plume of diesel exhaust streaming out of her funnel, Reitz knew that this was *Dresden* in her true element. Exactly in the type of action that her creator Wilhelm Canaris envisaged in his mind when he'd helped to draw up her initial design. Little did Reitz then realise that Canaris now languished in a Gestapo-run prison cell.

Again the Russian ships, all in line ahead, opened fire. In the lead was, as Horst had surmised, a modern destroyer commissioned into the Soviet Navy a month after Hitler's armies had commenced their unprovoked invasion. She was called *Verminsk* and was only slightly damaged during the long German siege of Leningrad. All the other four ships were also survivors of that siege. The second ship was originally laid down as an armoured cruiser and eventually, three years after her keel-plate had been constructed with insufferable delays due to the utter ineptness of the Tsar's naval bureaucrats, she slid into the water early in 1914. War shortages and even more incompetence resulted in her being only eighty-five per cent completed by the time the Bolsheviks succeeded in ousting the Provisional Government of Kerensky. Their initial grasp of naval matters was somewhat shaky and it wasn't until 1923 that the *Admiral Poltava* finally joined the new Russian Navy. All her eight seven-point-one inch (18cm) main guns were mounted in single turrets, being two forward and two aft, both superimposed and two each were mounted between the bridge and her second funnel on either beam. If properly handled, with a top speed of twenty-six knots, she could have been a useful asset in coastal defence but with *Dresden* as an opponent, she'd need to have her crew thoroughly alert and well trained. As she'd been damaged by Stuka bombers early in the Leningrad siege, her sea-going efforts came to nothing as she rested on the river bed but her guns still proved useful in the city's defence. To the credit of the Soviet Navy, she'd been quickly repaired after the German withdrawal and this foray against Huffmeyer's troops was looked on as a useful preparation for further strikes against Nazi outposts, providing that the Kriegsmarine's big surface ships were nowhere near to disrupt her efforts.

Which, unknown to her crew, the most battle-hardened of them all, as the *Poltava*'s crew prepared for a third broadside, was but a mere four miles away from them. Next astern was a smaller and even older cruiser laid down and completed in 1905. Even so she had a battery of six-inch guns, four of which would fire in broadsides. Two more destroyers of an early 1930's design brought up the rear.

Reitz watched the Russians fire their third broadside at the Courland Peninsula. *Dresden*'s six main guns were aimed at an almost point-blank range of less than four miles. 'Open fire!' he suddenly barked. *Dresden*'s big guns opened fire and their first six shells neatly bracketed the *Verminsk* as Reitz, taking his time, had decided that she was the most serious threat to *Dresden* as well as *ZA-28*. At first, no-one on the Russian ships seemed to take any notice. 'Ah, the Nazis over there do have some big guns. Redouble our efforts!' yelled *Verminsk*'s captain still looking land-wards. They were his last words for *Dresden*'s next salvo crashed on and around the bridge and amidships section of his modern destroyer, reducing her to a instant sinking cripple.

An alert junior officer in command of one of the starboard main guns on the *Poltava* saw the flashes of *Dresden*'s armament. Entirely on his own initiative, he ordered his gun crew to train their weapon on the unexpected enemy warship firing at them. *Dresden*'s third salvo, directed at the *Poltava* threw huge waterspouts along her starboard side but two of the big shells crashed on board the old cruiser. Her captain saw and then felt the explosions forward of the bridge and could only open his mouth in astonishment as that section of his command burst into flames. The one gun trained in *Dresden*'s direction did manage to fire a shell before the battlecruiser's fourth salvo crashed on the now burning cruiser's bridge and amidships, causing her to burst into flames and to swing out of control, only for her to collide with the fiercely burning *Verminsk*.

Reitz switched his fire towards the three remaining warships, which now fully alert to their danger, began turning away and with increased amounts of froth at their sterns, tried to make their escape back the way that they'd so confidently come. Signalling *ZA-28* to close in and torpedo the thoroughly locked together and helpless leading two enemy warships, Reitz kept up *Dresden*'s fire on the rapidly retreating remaining Russian ships but not before the light cruiser took three direct hits and one of the destroyers looked like a giant pepper-pot full of holes and leaking like a badly-worn sieve from numerous near misses as sharp pieces of shrapnel rattled on and into her sides and superstructure.

Wegener approached the two crippled enemy warships as they both burned furiously, although curiously, the sinking *Verminsk* seemed temporarily to be kept afloat as she was supported by the burning *Poltava.* As *ZA-28* prepared to launch her torpedoes suddenly the old Russian cruiser disintegrated in a massive explosion that flung gun turrets and her bridge structure upwards and outwards. Wegener's lithe destroyer was struck by considerable shards of the exploding cruiser and fragments pierced her thin sides, wrecking part of her engine-room. It began to flood and desperately her damage control team strove to control the sudden in-rush of water and to try and keep her engines moving. Wegener signalled *Dresden* 'Sorry. Taken in Russian bits. Will try ten knots. Going home. Hope to see you again. Good luck.'

Reitz grimaced and then said 'Send them a message of good luck as well and that we will catch up with them as soon as we can.' Then he turned the *Dresden* for the shore-line but as the battlecruiser, without stopping, passed near the area of the now two sunken Russian warships, the pitifully few survivors in the water saw two orange life-rafts bob up and down in her wake. With a strong on-shore wind, they knew that by climbing aboard them, they'd drift towards the nearby coast but who'd be in charge when they'd stumble ashore, not one of those desperate men could really care. What had surprised them was that this Kriegsmarine warship was giving them a chance to live, one they hadn't expected.

Even as they clambered onto the rafts they saw the enemy warship open fire with her big guns. The few of those Russians in the knowledge of the plans behind their proposed bombardment, gruesomely realised that it was their army comrades who were now at the destruction end of the shelling, just as they'd been so recently on their now sunken ships.

Huffmeyer and his men had watched the Russian warships approach. Apart from the men at the makeshift observation periscopes, all of them crouched as low as they probably could in their various holes in the ground. Then the Russian naval shells started to cannonade around their positions.

The telephone from one of the seaward observation posts rang shrilly in Huffmeyer's crypt position.

'What is it? What do you see?' asked a nervous young major.

'Sir, one, no wait, two of the Russian warships have just blown up and the others are turning tail. It's the *Dresden* sir, She's scaring them away.'

Even Huffmeyer smiled when he heard the news. Another telephone. One of the land outposts. 'Tanks approaching. About two kilometres away.'

Huffmeyer nodded grimly. 'I suppose the enemy still think we're being shelled by their ships, eh? Can we contact our Kriegsmarine friends, Leutnant Hahn?'

'No sir, but I think I hear an aeroplane. Could be the *Dresden*'s own float-plane.'

It was. Rubens and Stolle were already in voice-radio contact with the battlecruiser. Horst and Halder with their teams quickly plotted the positions of the approaching tanks.

Dresden's big guns opened fire. Heavy shells began to land on or around the advancing T-34's much to the surprise and horror of their individual crews. These weren't the anti-tank shells with which the Germans usually tried to stop their ponderous machines. One commander gasped in horror as a T-34 just a few yards in front of his own, suddenly reared up and landed upside down, burning furiously. He didn't, nor did his crew, feel anything when another heavy shell landed right on top of their tank. Only total blackness.

Desperately, the leading tanks tried to accelerate but this only put them in range of *Dresden*'s secondary guns as well as Huffmeyer's battery of four '88s' which also joined in. Six out of eight tanks were struck at once and the other two turned to retreat but were caught in the next salvo of shells. The follow-up infantry, their ranks already decimated, turned and fled for the screen of a wood as fast as their horror-struck minds and legs could take them, for every few seconds, a further heavy shell crashed amongst their thinning ranks cutting down even more of them.

The attack was over. A near miracle for Huffmeyer's beleaguered group but even the Colonel knew that come the departure of the battlecruiser, the Russians would try again. If only to exact their fury and revenge. The old soldier came out of his crypt to gaze over to the plain where the wrecks of the Russian tanks still smouldered and flames still flickered. Then his eyes turned seawards and there she was, that long lean proud battlecruiser that had given him and his men enough precious time to ensure their survival and hopes for a successful evacuation.

Bringing *Dresden* to a near halt. Reitz ordered for all the motor boats to be launched whilst the Arado still circled above watching for any sudden Russian attacks but sensibly, the Russian commanders, fearing more vicious devastation, kept their surviving tanks and men well out-of-sight. The wireless operators passed a message to Reitz that told him that four destroyers and two fast ex-ferries were already on their way to evacuate Huffmeyer's men. *Dresden* was instructed to collect the wounded and make all speed back to the Gulf of Danzig. The main evacuation ships were expected to reach the beachhead by 20.00 hours that evening.

Reitz grunted again. 'Rogge must be very confident about our success seeing we haven't signalled Kiel yet with the news.'

Hiltzern nodded 'Aye sir, 'e must now believe what we already know that this ship is the best in the Kriegsmarine, thanks to you, sir. We is the best and proud of it!'

As Brautsch reached the head of the breakwater, Huffmeyer greeted him with a salute and by saying 'Herr Kapitan-Leutnant! I owe you an apology. The Kriegsmarine have obviously sent their best ship. My observers tell me that your escort was damaged.'

Brautsch answered 'Yes. We're going to catch up with her after evacuating your wounded. We must hurry! Other ships will be coming soon to take off the rest of your men and by tomorrow, the Russians can have back this precious bit of land that by all accounts has cost them dearly in lives.'

Huffmeyer nodded 'Aye. They're welcome to the shell-holes and the remnants of our equipment. Anything we can't carry we'll blow up.'

As the wounded were taken out on stretchers to the waiting boats, Huffmeyer went amongst them giving a word of thanks and comfort for each of them.

By the time that they were all safely aboard *Dresden*, darkness covered the beachhead. Doctor Lebers reported that all available space in his Sick Berth was taken up and that some of the wounded were still on stretchers outside the Berth's doors.

He would do his best but no promises.

Dresden edged away from the land and as she did so, the leading destroyer of the main evacuation effort flashed her recognition signals.

As the battlecruiser surged into the dark, radar reported a single stationery blip. Reitz looked worried as he stared at the repeater screen. 'It's *ZA-28*. Crippled. Prepare our boat crews again.' When would their work end? Picking up survivors. Patching up wounded. Burying the dead.

'Illuminate with searchlight!' barked Reitz as the motionless dark shape of *ZA-28* came ever nearer. The stopped destroyer's stern was seen to be just above the water level of the now choppy sea. She also listed to starboard. Reitz suddenly felt very cold. First it had been the new torpedo boat. Now this chummy destroyer. With a signal flickering from the rear of her bridge – 'Need help big brother. Sinking. Abandoning.'

Hurriedly scrambling nets and ropes were lowered all along *Dresden*'s port side. From her starboard side three launches hit the water. Then Reitz took his ship in as close to the sinking destroyer as he dared for yet another rescue mission but this time it was for their fellow Kriegsmarine sailors. Brautsch yelled desperately 'Come on, get this launch under way' as he clambered into it and quickly the boat was released from its falls, the engine gunned and Brautsch steered it for the sinking destroyer.

'She's going!' one of his men cried out as *ZA-28*'s stern dipped under a swell that broke around her rearmost gun-turret. Even as Brautsch's launch neared the doomed warship, the destroyer's list sharply increased to starboard and she began to roll over. Within seconds she lay flat on the surface and the seas flowed into her twin-funnels. Then she suddenly turned over completely and stern first, vanished in an obscene flurry of bubbles, leaving behind as she sank, varied items of wreckage as well as many of her crew desperately struggling in the cold water, trying to reach the ropes and nets representing safety. Quickly Brautsch's launch with two others scoured the wreckage pulling men, gasping and shaking with cold, into the safe haven of their boats. After sixteen minutes of desperate work, *Dresden*'s sirens boomed out a recall. The shaken survivors, some covered in the oil from *ZA-28*'s ruptured tanks, were hurriedly taken below where Doctor Lebers, Andrea and the other sick-berth staff soon took care of them – removing their sodden clothing, cleaning the oil from them and patching up any wounds. One hundred and two survivors. Only seventeen members of *ZA-28*'s crew were not rescued. The outwardly cheerful Kapitan-Leutnant Wegener was not among the survivors.

Reitz felt sick at heart when he was given the news. He'd witnessed so much of the savagery of war, seeing the viciousness of it on ships of the enemy, on his own ship and also, so recently to two fellow ships of his beloved Kriegsmarine. Somehow the loss of *ZA-28* and her effervescent captain who'd greeted *Dresden* so proudly on her last lap to Kiel struck a particular bitter blow to his sense of duty. Now seventeen of her crew's hopes of seeing out the war were now ended in an ice-cold Baltic Sea.

Steeling himself, he left the bridge and went down to the Sick Berth. He spoke to everyone of *ZA-28*'s survivors, as well as the wounded soldiers brought off that beachhead and also to the army doctors who'd come aboard to assist his own ship's medical staff. Finally, he went over to Andrea. So many of the survivors spoke of how much of a pleasant surprise it had been to be cared for by such a gentle but firm lady doctor. Reitz knew that 'nurse' Andrea really was a qualified doctor. Something of his childhood school history lessons passed through his mind. Ah, that was it! That English nurse, Florence Nightingale. How she'd gone to the Crimea to restore the medical work to wounded soldiers. Yes, that was it. Andrea was *Dresden*'s own 'Miss Nightingale'. Nationality meant nothing to her – German, British, Greek, Dutch, Chinese, American – she cared for them all. Crew or prisoner. Yes, Helmut was a lucky man to have her as his wife. Soon, he hoped, he'd be able to share his life with his Elle. He fervently hoped that she was still safe in Kiel.

Then he saw Padré Jervaulx, murmuring the last rites to three of the wounded soldiers who'd succumbed to their injuries. Again Reitz marvelled at the cleric, who like Andrea, had crossed the nationality barriers without a thought, even with men who hadn't professed to be attached to any religious adherence. Jervaulx always listened, gave advice, help and encouragement where necessary and even offered to write the men's letters when they felt that they hadn't been able to find the required words. Now here he was facing up to the horror of war yet again. Entirely opposed to his ethics of Christian love and forgiveness.

Then a voice cut into Reitz's thoughts 'What you needs, sir, is a tot of what I can find and then a bit of shut eye.' It was Walters, who by instinct had followed Reitz into the Sick Berth and who now took him by the arm, adding 'Look sir, rest of t'lads 'll tek this ship back to safer waters. Tha' needs a kip 'afore next bout of action.'

Back in his cabin Reitz swallowed his whisky-flavoured coffee as directed by his faithful steward and was about to drop into his bunk when there came a knock on his door.

'Beg pardon sir, we've three bodies to commit to the deep.' It was Jervaulx.

'Coming padré' answered Reitz, fiercely gulping the last of the coffee and pulling his boots back on.

Just Reitz, Jervaulx and Walters, with the six stretcher bearers assembled at *Dresden*'s stern. The warship didn't slow down as the three weighted bundles were heaved into the bubbling wake and Jervaulx's words were lost in the keening icy wind.

When he woke up six hours later, Walters was hovering by his captain's table. 'Breakfast sir – toast and this time, as you has time ter savour it, some real coffee.' Where his steward was able to procure real coffee, Reitz just simply couldn't even guess. All the little man did was again to tap his nose and say nothing when asked.

On reaching the bridge, Reitz found that *Dresden* was back in the Danzig roadstead with a former Baltic ferry, the *Heidi* lashed alongside. The ferry was now a hospital ship with huge red crosses on her decks and hung down her sides but as Reitz looked across at her, he suspected that the Russians would probably not respect the insignia of the mercy ship. Looking aft, he could see that the army's wounded were being carried in stretchers and that *Dresden*'s cranes were transferring them across so that *Heidi* could take them on to Kiel. She'd already been on four such voyages since the main evacuation of the Baltic lands had begun.

As Reitz gazed across to the shore, for a change, there seemed to be no serious effort by the encircling Russians to disrupt the evacuation. Perhaps it was the long, lean silhouette of the battlecruiser that had so quickly made her mark with her accurate gunfire that scared them. Twice, once in this area and then so recently off the Courland Peninsula, her guns had savaged attempted Russian attacks.

Then the deceptive peace was shattered by the sound of piercing whistles. *Heidi* was casting off from *Dresden* in order to join the latest of the evacuation convoys, this one being under the charge of the light cruiser *Emden*. She flashed a signal across to *Dresden* – 'See you soon in Kiel. Keep an eye on Stalin's bears' – then the small, out-dated cruiser took up speed to lead her posse of ships away from the Bay.

Emden. Another of the Kriegsmarine principal warships that since Norway had hardly been used (except for training purposes) but now, in the Baltic, she was proving her worth. Evacuating. Bombarding. Escorting. Doing her best. Taking military personnel and civilians trapped after the Red Army circumvented the region and took control of the rocky shoreline to the west, where an evacuation even by the Kriegsmarine, would have been very risky. No safe harbours or beaches. Not like the ones around the Danzig and Oxthoft beaches as well as the Hela Peninsula. Beachheads that the Wehrmacht and the Kriegsmarine were defending.

It was all on the maps that Reitz and Horst studied. It did seem odd that the Russians were holding their fire. Or sensible.

For two whole days the threat from *Dresden*'s guns kept the Russians quiet. Another convoy of merchantmen was loading up. Quickly. Reitz watched them knowing that Kiel was yet to respond for his request to be relieved. His stock of shells for the big guns was somewhat low. Only enough for a limited counter-barrage.

The third morning of *Dresden*'s stay in that Bay again passed peacefully. The convoy was nearly ready to go. Suddenly without warning, mid-way during her third day in the Roadstead, *Dresden*'s crew were taken by surprise when the Russians began a renewed bombardment of the evacuation area. The defending Wehrmacht gunfire seemed feeble in response and very soon, newly arrived light cruiser *Nurnberg* and two destroyers, close inshore, began firing over the beachhead at the Russians, but even their efforts seemed to make little difference on their enemies' guns and rockets.

'Well, what is it?' snapped Reitz rubbing his eyes for he'd been taking a rest in his sea-cabin.

The liaison colonel's eyes told the story. 'We need your help.'

'Hmm. We haven't an awful lot of shells left. Maybe an hour's barrage. Panzerschiffe's *Scheer* and *Lutzow* were expected this morning but Kiel has told us that it'll be later this evening when they'll arrive as our relief. So we'll have to be very accurate with our fire.' The Colonel's eyes seemed to be pleading for help. 'Colonel, are you still in radio-telephone contact with your forward posts? We need to be accurate to be effective.'

The colonel nodded. 'Right, let's have it. One hour's careful firing. We'll see if the Russkie Bearmen can take our medicine!'

Once again *Dresden*'s six main guns opened fire. Reitz and his crew could but imagine the carnage that their big shells were wreaking. Again. Torn bodies and limbs. Somebody's brother. Father. Husband. More wrecked flotsam of war. Being smashed by shells fired from Anton, Bruno and Cesar. Blood and spilled guts. Limbless wounded blinded for life. Horses screaming. Trucks burning. Shattered piles of grass, soil and splintered rock or trees as *Dresden*'s shells fell methodically among and along the lines of Russian guns. Eliminating them one by one. Despite commissar threats of instant execution, the artillery men, one after another, took to their heels leaving their guns, their trucks. Some tried to rescue their horses which had drawn some of the guns to their battle-lines. Or shot the wounded ones. With *Dresden*'s supply of heavy shells down to about only ten shells left for each gun, it was to Reitz's and the colonel's relief that the Russian barrage finally stopped. Forward Wehrmacht observers reported that the surviving Russians were all withdrawing out of sight.

'Cease fire!' ordered Reitz.

Darkness was coming over the sea. The convoy of evacuee ships had assembled and begun to leave. Whilst *Dresden*'s guns fired their lethal cargo over their heads, the process of the small boats collecting the frightened civilians from the beach had continued unabated.

'Message, sir.' A messenger from the wireless office saluted Reitz. It was from Kiel.

'Good. At last we can get away.' Reitz sounded relieved. Always aware of the potential vulnerability that *Dresden* was exposed to as she steamed slowly forwards and backwards off the evacuation beaches. Vulnerability to air or submarine attacks. Fortunately none occurred. Then, a small trawler was seen approaching the battle-cruiser.

'Signal from that trawler, sir!' remarked one of the lookouts peering shorewards.

'Damn! What does it want?' snapped Reitz.

'Can we take some wounded? Just picked them up from the beach.'

Reitz groaned. 'Well, I suppose so. Warn Doctor Lebers!'

Carefully *Dresden*'s cranes hoisted the stretchered wounded from the red-cross flagged trawler's deck and up to willing hands on the battlecruiser. Above them the anti-aircraft guns tweaked on their mountings as they scoured the skies for any sudden Russian threat in the fading light.

The wounded soldiers were all safely brought on board. At last the order to catch up with the convoy was given and Reitz was able to relax just a little as *Dresden* picked up speed away from that darkening coastline.

Russians observers saw her long dark shape fade away over the Western horizon.

The commissars snarled at the still badly shaken artillery gunners 'Get those guns back and start firing at any Nazi swine still on that beach-head.'

They whimpered with fright for the alert ones amongst them had seen two large Nazi warships approaching the beach as the last of the light faded. *Dresden*'s replacement at last. With twelve large guns between them. With full ammunition supplies. Panzerschiffe's *Lutzow* and *Admiral Scheer*. When the first of the Russian guns re-opened fire, the two big warships only needed to fire four salvoes before wisely, the Russian gunners fled. For the second time that day.

From the port bridge wing of the *Dresden*, Reitz caught sight of the distant flare-up but breathed a sigh of relief. Meeting the *Lutzow*, they'd slowed and transferred the Army colonel with all the co-ordinates needed in case the Russians re-opened their barrage. The colonel, perhaps reluctant to have to return to the beachhead, was obviously doing his work well for Reitz didn't need to watch the distant flare-up too long. It died away. Only a dark horizon astern – and in the last of the sun's afterglow the dark shapes of the convoy came into sight, after radar had pointed out their presence.

Dark ships taking their human cargo westwards to the preferred hope of a Germany that would more likely come under an Anglo-American force, one that would be more amenable to conquered people than the Russians could or would be. Not surprising, Reitz thought, having heard stories of the vileness of the SS and Gestapo butchers as they'd tried to extend their evil atrocities over the eastern territories. The wheel had rotated full circle and it was now the turn of unfortunate German civilians to suffer the brutalities of the rapacious Russian troops. They were being battered because of those earlier Nazi-instigated excesses. It was those who escaped the Russian assaults that were enduring the pain of the evacuation. Pain from Russians shells. Pain from the winter cold. Pain from hunger. Pain from exhaustion. But Reitz was experiencing a different pain. A pain from the futility of all his efforts with *Dresden* and witnessing the evacuation only emphasised his sheer feeling of ultimate helplessness. No matter how well the battlecruiser's guns fired, they only served to delay what Reitz and everyone else could see as being the final defeat. Wearily he turned for his cabin. Sleep eluded him as he tossed this way and that on his bunk. He sensed that something more dreadful was going to happen. Restless, he went on to the bridge. Eight bells was striking to end the first of the four-hour watches of the new day. 14th February. The dark shapes of the convoy were grouped on *Dresden*'s port side, she being stationed on the northern flank as the ships pushed westwards. One of the junior officers saluted him, 'All vessels on station, sir.' Reitz merely nodded, staring over the port wing of the bridge.

Five minutes passed. Then one of the new radio operators came up to him. 'Sir, for you. It's in code.' It was a message from Rogge – 'To Captain of *Dresden.* Your name-sake city has been bombed with heavy casualties. Attacks continuing. Will keep you informed. Everyone wishes you safe journey home.'

Reitz guessed that was what he'd been dreading. Briefly whilst on that ever-so-short leave with Elle, he'd contacted, by telephone, his grandparents who lived on the outskirts of the beautiful city. Yes, they said, the city had so far escaped a mass-bombing raid. Everyone knew, even the Allies, that the city was not a war-centre. They were perfectly safe.

Quite a lot of his crew came from the city. Soon after the ship was commissioned, some of the crew paraded proudly, through the streets to the City's Town Hall (Rathaus) where Von Munke accepted a *Dresden*-china plaque of the city's coat-of-arms. Reitz was well aware that Walters always took it off the wall in his main cabin and wrapped it up safely as and when action threatened or a storm began to blow. The little steward, who'd been on that parade, always said that the ship would come to no serious harm providing that its *Dresden* emblem was safe.

Now the city whose name the ship bore was probably burning furiously. Rogge's message gave no details. A city of beautiful churches, art galleries, museums and leafy suburbs. A city whose main fame was found in its delicate and intricate china-pottery manufacturing. A city as unwarlike as York or Canterbury or Bath or Exeter, but the Luftwaffe had been stupidly ordered to bomb those English cities. It appeared that at last the Allies were taking their revenge on Germany's famed beautiful city. Determined to destroy it even if its destruction didn't even alter the general war situation.

Slowly dawn came. Cold as always. Grey seas flecked with white spume. Driven by a north-easterly wind. As the ships rolled in the relatively short-pitched waves, Reitz could see that light cruiser *Nurnberg* had also joined the small convoy. Probably, he thought, her shell-stocks were running low, like *Dresden*'s . Wonder if her crew ever think about the destruction in the city of their name? Destroyed because of its big Nazi rallies in the 1930s. But *Dresden*? It worried him how to tell the crew. Maybe, just maybe, the grape vine already knew. No, they couldn't. That message had been in code. No, they'd know about a coded message but not its contents. He decided to tell them but he'd need more information. *En clair* to Kiel he sent – 'Need more about the coded message, Reitz.' Simple enough. The reply came soon after mid-day – 'Severe casualties in *Dresden* city centre. Americans still random bombing. Firestorm worse than Hamburg.' When Reitz decoded the message, he grimaced. Elle had earlier told him about the burning of Hamburg. The city's centre's flames burned for a whole week. About sixty thousand killed but the Allies fortunately did not make any more follow-up raids. There'd been a partial recovery. Of a sorts. So if *Dresden*'s firestorm was worse, then the casualties, even for just one night and part of a day were likely to be even higher. He shuddered and walked over to the microphone of the ship's public address system.

His voice sounded unsteady at first. 'Members of my loyal crew. Our ship bears the name of our once beautiful city with pride. Unhappily I have to tell you that the city centre has been badly bombed. Casualties are said to be high.' The speakers crackled. The words were difficult to hear. Crew members strained to listen. Then their captain's voice seemed to become clearer. Firmer. 'I know that many of you have homes or relatives in or near the city. I have grandparents in the suburbs. No doubt the naval authorities will give us a clearer picture as and when we return to Kiel. Please keep up your spirits. We have seen our own crew mates killed on board this ship but I tell you this, our ship will continue to serve the Navy for as long as we can, if only to give as high an example as we can, that our fighting spirit has not been diminished. We are still proud to bear our damaged city's name and I will authorise a signal saying as much to the Mayor of *Dresden*.' Again the voice seemed to fade away. The speakers hissed and crackled as if echoing the despair in Reitz's voice. 'I only hope that you can keep up your spirits by the time we reach Kiel. My thoughts are with you all. Thankyou.' The speakers clicked into silence. This time there was no cheering. No doubt many of them felt the same way as Reitz. Numb with shock. Was this what supporting Adolf Hitler's regime meant? Helpless refugees. Beautiful cities destroyed. The Allies were grinding Germany into dust whilst her Nazi-ideologised leaders seemingly refused to accept the inevitability of defeat. Total and utter defeat. Down in the Sick Berth, Andrea and Helmut sat side by side on her cot, hand in hand. Andrea pressed her husband's hand as she listened to Reitz. She knew that Helmut's aged uncle and aunt lived over an antiques shop near the city centre. In her mind's eye she could see them, helpless, as the flames swept over and around them. Silently they sat. Tired and weary. Around them the civilian and military casualties. Two of them nurses. Apparently both had flung themselves over small children as they crouched in a sand dune during the shelling that eventually the guns of *Dresden* silenced but not before shrapnel and stones scarred both their backs. Doctor Lebers and Andrea managed to stop the bleeding but not even the most skilful skin-grafting by a surgeon would ever be able to repair the dreadfully scarred tissue. Mercifully both the young nurses were slowly recovering. Physically, if not mentally.

The convoy, by perforce, waited outside Kiel for twenty-four hours before being allowed to enter. Low-flying RAF Mosquitoes had dropped mines during the night before their supposed entry during the dawn hours of 16th February and the port needed the services of six minesweepers to clear a wide enough sea-lane before the ships could enter.

This time there were no cheering crowds to welcome *Dresden*. Only a very worried looking aide of Bernhard Rogge's who very quickly accompanied Reitz and Hiltzern off the battlecruiser towards the Vice-Admiral's concreted headquarters but not until he passed on strict orders that no-one was to leave the ship apart from the wounded personnel.

Past grimfaced sentries and through at least three steel-plated doors. Down into the nerve centre. Rogge pulled up two chairs to his desk and motioned *Dresden*'s two officers to be seated.

'Good to have you back safe and sound' said Rogge as an opener.

Reitz nodded. He could see the lines of worry on the Vice-Admiral's face. Pale and strained. Like his own. 'Yes it was bad. The Russians take their losses on the chin. Then they shrug and come back for more punishment. Halder and his gunnery team have lost count of the vast numbers of tanks that they are supposed to have destroyed. What with that and the rout of their only creditable force of surface craft bigger than a torpedo boat, plus shooting down a sizeable number of their aircraft. I shouldn't think *Dresden* will be too popular with our eastern enemy. Never mind the British or the Americans.'

Rogge smiled. A vague smile.

'Yes, we're covering you again with camouflage netting. We'll keep you here for about a week and then I'm afraid, it'll be back with the largest convoy that we can muster. At least four of our remaining big liners plus half-a-dozen fast merchantmen. Probably three hospital ships. We have still to get out over a million of our people. The Wehrmacht is doing what it can to keep the Russian military forces at bay as also our naval ships are doing. You know that yourself. We must get them out.' Rogge looked bleak. An hour earlier he'd been in conference with his senior, Vice-Admiral Thiele, who'd been to see the situation himself whilst on board heavy cruiser *Hipper*.

Reitz wasn't really listening. He guessed at what Rogge was going to say. A quickish turn-round.

'Shore leave, Bernhard?'

'No, George. Only into our barracks within the naval perimeter. Beyond that, believe me, life is getting worse. The filth of the SS and Gestapo roam the streets. If you're seen with as much as a loaf of bread, having bought it on the black market for your hungry family, they'll shoot you first, uniform or not and then as likely, pinch the bread for themselves. Why, George, are we serving to prop up such vile creatures in this country of ours?'

'I wish I knew. We spent four years away and we've come back to all this' rumbled Herzog. 'We've not besmirched our name but they have.'

'Careful my friend' replied Rogge. 'Careful you don't repeat such words to anyone you don't know. Even in this base there may be the odd sentry still with such grandiose notions to split on their fellow Kriegsmarine members and then go out through the dockyard gates and have a somewhat nasty natter to those cretinous serpents outside. In here, we are relatively safe. Out there –' Rogge waved a hand through the back wall of his office '– none of us can be sure of even returning. You know what happened to Leutnant Serle. We don't want any more such tragedies.'

Rogge turned to a plan of the naval base. On it were meticulously marked the present moorings of all the Kriegsmarine's vessels occupying the port. *Dresden* being by far the largest unit. Black crosses marked sunken vessels. His pointer rested on the largest warehouse. 'We'll assemble the crew in there. Yes. All of them. In two hours time. My dockyard staff will see to your re-supplying. You see, George, the situation has even more horror for your ship. You know, as well, if not better than me, that *Dresden* was a ship conceived, planned and damn well nearly built by Admiral Canaris. Well, for your information, Wilhelm Canaris is now a prisoner of the scum we so despise, accused of anti-Nazi feelings, Abwehr failings and any other disloyalties that they can fling at him. We know, that with Grand-Admiral Raeder's full approval, that there are no Party members, or ever have been, amongst the members of your crew. You know what that means. If Canaris can be arrested on dubious charges, so can any member of your crew, including both of you. Keep the crew on the ship or at the very least in the base. *Dresden*, despite her superb war record, is of no account to any of those –' and here Rogge stopped, his face suffused with rage – then he continued hoarsely '– those unspeakable lumps of appalling horse-shit out there still masquerading as our law and order upholders.'

Reitz and Herzog looked pale, despite their weatherworn sailor's faces.

Rogge continued. 'When we have no more duties for you, and providing that you're still a sailing concern, I shall issue orders to divert you to either Copenhagen or Southern Norway where the SS and Gestapo can't get so easily at you. Also, it'll be safer there for I feel that the Allies will one day chuck every bomb they possess in the arsenal at us. After all, the big surviving ships of the Kriegsmarine are about the only target they haven't yet eliminated since the bombing of *Tirpitz*. Not once have they seriously tried to destroy our ships here in the Baltic but I'm sure that they'll have a go before hostilities finally cease.'

'Here' he added 'these are your orders for the convoy but act in your own individual way if the need arises.'

At last a thin smile crossed the face of George Reitz.

'Where's Elle?' he asked.

'She'll meet you in the barracks hall. Now go to it, get your men in there.'

Both officers saluted and departed, back to where their proud handsome ship rested at the dockside, her upperworks already shrouded in brick tile paint coloured canvas. An extension, at least from the air, of the dockside building.

It was inside one of these buildings that the crew of the battlecruiser filed in to stand in ranks facing a temporary platform of empty ammunition boxes and packing cases. On to the platform climbed Reitz with Elle at his side, Rogge and two of his aides.

Reitz spoke first. 'Members of my crew, Frau Andrea Brautsch and Ad –' but he was interrupted as cheers broke out. It seemed as if the very name of Andrea was held in such high regard that the mention of her name in any mass gathering only caused the men to voice their affection. Reitz waved them into silence although knowing that such a gesture was indicative of the good morale of his crew, despite the apparent grimness of the war situation. 'As I was trying to say, I have with me Vice-Admiral Bernhard Rogge, former captain of Hilfskreuzer *Atlantis* and now in joint charge of our operations in the Baltic situation where as we all know, the Kriegsmarine is still in full control of the sea lanes connecting our isolated East Baltic territory with the ports here in the north-western part of Germany. Now listen carefully to what Admiral Rogge has to say.'

'Friends' Rogge began. He then went on, outlining Germany's current desperate state. No-one cheered him. No-one smiled. It was as if their faces were carved from stone. Reitz gripped Elle's hand as she sat next to him on a plain wooden chair. Rogge himself looked strained. Worn out. Then they listened again. 'You are heroes of the Kriegsmarine but not of Germany. Has anyone, other than your captain, been awarded an extra special decoration? Have you been allowed an extended leave? No. You've been back to war before you had time to really re-acclimatise. And now. What do I tell you? No more leave. No more rest from war duties. No more going home. Until it's all over.' Rogge's voice came across. Staccato-like. Like a badly firing gun. It then dropped a bit in volume. 'Out there you have no friends. Only SS horse-shit and Gestapo scum. Men who would shoot you down like dogs. And they have ears. Even here in this base. You're not safe nor neither am I if they knew that we disapproved of them. If you say that the war is lost. That we will be on the losing side. You may be my heroes. But not one of their's. Murder is their work-a-day practice. Stay here. No leave passes.'

The disciplined crew intently listened. They'd heard about some of the atrocities to their own people in the Eastern Baltic inflicted by the advancing Russians but now this – their own people murdering, shooting, killing their own kith and kin. The air seemed to breathe that uncleanliness. They knew that they'd be glad to be back at sea. But they also felt the parting from their loved ones although none of them begrudged the sight of the captain with his girl. He'd brought them back to Germany. None of them ever envisaged the state of affairs to be so appallingly bad. It wasn't their captain's fault.

'Gentlemen and ladies' Rogge was continuing. 'Your ship was thought up and partly designed by Admiral Canaris who even now languishes in a Gestapo cell. If an Admiral isn't safe, what hope for the rest of you?'

Then Rogge sat down. Drained. The most depressing speech he'd ever given in his whole career. Reitz, sensing the general air of gloom, rose to his feet.

'Ladies and gentlemen, You –' stretching his arms out wide 'you are the best crew of the best ship in the Kriegsmarine. I repeat' but suddenly led by Otto Schenke, the crew as one rose to their feet cheering and clapping like mad. Almost hysterically. Reitz gave them their moment and then waving his arm, he managed to calm them down. 'Well, you can still shout! – [Quite a bit of laughter] – but you have work to do – [mock groans]. Soon we shall be back at sea. We're taking some troopships to fetch more of our people from the Danzig area. So to it, all of you! Dismiss!'

For the next five days, the crew worked as hard as ever – in the engine room, on the radar – it was already well patched up – restocking with supplies, oiling and cleaning all the guns. From somewhere, Rogge's staff found another two sets of the four-barrelled Vierling guns. Andrea, with Doctor Lebers and the rest of the Sick Berth staff, restocked their severely drained medical supplies for Reitz suspected that the ship could well finish up carrying extra wounded that couldn't be taken by the hospital ships. He himself went over to the three big liners, all twenty-odd thousand tons, including the *Heinrich Galster* which had docked shortly before *Dresden*'s first triumphant return to Kiel. He noted that all three liners had fully tested their lifeboats. The story from the survivors of the ill-fated *Wilhelm Gustloff* was that due to over painting, the crew of that ship were unable to free the launching mechanism of many of the boats before the liner sank. This time the authorities were ensuring that the rescue ships were properly equipped. Reitz stopped to admire the third ship. The beautiful three-funnelled former Hamburg-Amerika liner *Cap Arkona*. Memories of that East African convoy came flooding back as he walked the handsome liner's decks. What was that liner's name? Ah yes! *Aspen Castle*. It was strange how the wheel of war's fortune had turned. Soon he was to be in charge of a convoy sailing to rescue troops and civilians. Off East Africa, the old battleship *Resolve* had been placed in that convoy to protect the three-funnelled Castle liner. Somehow Reitz couldn't envisage a Soviet battleship appearing over the horizon to attack the German rescue ships although they might try air, submarine or torpedo-boat attacks. All three liners were now equipped with numerous light anti-aircraft machine-guns in order to ward off the threat of Russian air attacks.

When he felt that the big liners were ready as well as his own ship, the vessels slipped their mooring ropes one winter's evening late that February and assembled in the Kiel roadstead. Nearly all the gathered ships had previously been to the Danzig region. Skippers and crews knew what to expect. The convoy was one of the biggest to make the journey eastwards but the Kriegsmarine knew that should the convoy succeed, over one hundred thousand people would be rescued in just that one convoy. A massive evacuation that in itself would partially relieve the anxieties of the military personnel trying to organise the withdrawal to the Western sector of a Germany gradually sliding down towards total defeat.

Steadily, at twelve knots, the ships churned away into the gathering gloom. Even as the darkness of Kiel's land mass merged into the general winter night, flashes of red and orange sparkled around the port as her defensive anti-aircraft guns opened fire. *Dresden*'s wireless spluttered into life as Rogge sent a message – 'Small raid only. Little damage done. All naval personnel safe.'

Reitz, a little anxious, breathed an inward sigh of relief. Never mind the convoy, his mind was on Elle just as many of his crew thought of their loved ones. The censor readers in Rogge's staff took great care in reading the letters from *Dresden*'s crew members, carefully looking for any sign of dissent against the Nazi hierarchy or their way of controlling the country. Not once in any of the letters could they fault any member of the battlecruiser's crew. The only concern that they'd all written about was being unable to be with loved ones or families.

The horizon flickered orange and red as night turned into dawn. A signal from *Dresden* ordered the convoy to reduce speed whilst Reitz took his ship forward, with two destroyers as escort to fully investigate the situation at the evacuation beaches. A message to

Dresden from heavy cruiser *Prinz Eugen* whilst the latter was escorting a convoy from the beaches which they'd passed during the night indicated a worsening situation. It seemed that the Russians were determined to wipe out the defending Wehrmacht – and then the helpless wounded and civilians awaiting evacuation. The story was the same as before. The only difference was the precise location.

As *Dresden* drew closer to the shore, the flames from the Russian artillery and accompanying Katyusha rockets became ever clearer in its colour, form and intensity.

'A scene from Dante's Inferno' murmured Horst to Reitz as they stared at the spectacle. Reitz grunted. Same nasty story. Again.

'Yes, one which needs to be quenched quickly if we're to carry out this new evacuation. The longer those liners are waiting for us to smash those guns, the more prone that they will be to either enemy air or submarine attacks' observed Reitz. In a louder voice, he ordered for an Arado to be prepared for imminent take-off and Halder's gunners to range on to those guns.

Two destroyers closer to the shore were trying their best to answer the barrage but their 12.7cm (five-inch) guns, at fullest range were barely making any impressions on the ferocious Russian assault. Even closer in shore, small boats moved slowly waiting for the time when it would be safe enough to start picking up the mass of hopeful evacuees huddling amongst the sand dunes.

From *Dresden*'s bridge this mass of people became clearer as the battlecruiser closed the shore, her forward guns already lined up waiting to open fire.

'Launch approaching from the shore' murmured Hiltzern as he rejoined Reitz. 'It appears to be heading our way.'

'Stop engines. It seems again as if the army wants a word with us judging by the uniform of the officer standing up,' came the observation from Reitz.

Within a few minutes the grey-faced, grey-uniformed major with an eye patch over his right eye began pointing out, on a map, where the main concentration of enemy guns were sited.

'Don't use your spotter plane this time, Admiral Reitz. The Russkies have powerful anti-aircraft guns and two of your Navy's aircraft were downed only yesterday. We'll have to rely on this map and our forward observation posts using their voice radio.' He handed over a generator-powered receiver and then hurried off down to his launch. As he clambered into it, Anton and Bruno's big guns belched flame as they began the counter-barrage against the Russian batteries. After almost fifteen minutes a welcome reinforcement came waddling into the bay. Wreathed in her funnel smoke, the veteran pre-dreadnought battleship *Schlesien*, a slightly younger and more modernised version of *Rugen*, opened fire with her four big guns as soon as the army launch with its grey one-eyed major had paid her a visit.

Reitz murmured to Hiltzern 'Here we are – one modern and one ancient. Ten big guns between us. The strength of the Kriegsmarine and so far, we've hardly dented that barrage. For some crazy reason the Russian gunners don't seem to be bothered with us – yet.'

Dresden signalled *Schlesien* and as they closed the shore, their secondary batteries opened up and the extra weight of shells landing in and around the Russian guns at last began to have an effect as the two ships worked their guns along the enemy line. One by one the batteries were knocked out as the heavy naval shells, with their high explosive impacts burst among the guns, rocket launchers and piles of ammunition for every so often, the Russian lines would violently erupt. The crews of the two ships could only visualise the horror of the carnage that they were bringing on to the soldiers manning those guns. Yet again. Blown apart. Into more human debris. Adding to the millions already sacrificed.

After nearly an hour of heavy naval firing the Russian guns abruptly ceased firing. Jubilant Wehrmacht observers shouted into their communication links that the enemy were racing away, some on foot and others pulling the few guns that had survived with whatever transport vehicle that was still functioning.

Meanwhile on the beach, the greater mass of the evacuees began to emerge from the sand-dunes and other places of shelter and then started to shuffle down to the shoreline and as soon as a small boat approached them, waded into the icy cold water, some holding small children in their arms as they scrambled or were hauled up until their rescue boat was full, often dangerously up to the scuppers. The little boats then moved out to the deeper water where the big vulnerable liners waited to receive their desperate, distraught human cargo.

The speakers on *Dresden*'s bridge intoned 'Aircraft approaching.' One of Halder's gunners ignited three rockets to warn the slow moving or the near stationary ships of the impending air attack.

The two dozen low-flying Russian dive-bombers were taken completely aback as they flew over the ships for every vessel that possessed a gun, opened up with a fierce-some barrage. As the aircraft tried to climb up to bombing height they were at their most vulnerable. Their tactic of a low-flying approach failed them as six of the flight just disintegrated and the others jettisoned their bombs at random.

'Cease fire!' yelled Reitz as the surviving bombers flew as fast as they could from the area, pursued by more bursts of flak as they went.

The work of evacuation continued with a grim purpose but as the day wore on, the northerly breeze grew in strength and the seas became choppy with short-pitched waves. Even on the short trip out to sea to the liners, themselves straining on their anchors, caused more of the already tired evacuees to be desperately sea-sick.

Over their heads now droned one of *Dresden*'s Arados launched by Reitz now that the Russian air threat had failed to seriously materialise. Every so often when the aircrew spotted a Russian battery trying to manoeuvre back into position, the fliers reported back to *Dresden* via their short-wave radios and once again, the battlecruiser's big guns opened fire to repeat the cycle of bursting shells, dismembered bodies and wrecked guns all over again. Again and again.

As the day wore on, Reitz fretted at the continual delays as the evacuation slowly reduced the masses of those patient people on the beach. He knew that the first priority, of the wounded, was the slowest part of the whole process but by mid-afternoon, the procession of red-cross flagged boats waiting to unload their wretched cargo of badly-wounded personnel to the relative safety of *Heidi*'s hospital wards, at last, came to a completed finish.

An hour later the beaches were finally cleared as well and the convoy began to form up for its return journey. After their desperate foray to try and eliminate *Dresden* and other ships, the Red Air Force didn't put in another appearance. Nor were there any submarine alarms. Reitz recalled the outer screen of smaller escort ships who'd been patrolling the seaward edge. Perhaps it was the presence of that protective patrol that had kept the submarines away but whatever the reason, Reitz breathed a huge sigh of relief as the convoy began to show froth from under the counters of each ship as each one of them worked up to reach the convoy's collective speed of fifteen knots.

With *Cap Arkona* in the lead followed by light cruiser Köln (newly arrived from bombardent duties from futher along the beleagured coast) and the other liners, Reitz watched the convoy from *Dresden*'s position on the starboard flank with some sense of anxiety. Flashes of the East African convoy emerging out of that hot August morning came into his mind. That big liner *Aspen Castle*. For that, substitute *Cap Arkona*. For *Llandaff*, now Köln. For old *Resolve*, it was his ship providing the big gun support. How ironic. The wheel's full-circle turning to place his ship in *Resolve*'s protective role. The only crumb of comfort was, as Reitz reminded himself, that no known Russian battleship was likely to haul itself over the horizon, nor any of their cruisers, particularly after the battering they'd suffered in the clash off the Courland Peninsula.

'Coffee, sir?' enquired Walters as he approached his captain leaning over the bridge rail.

Reitz nodded and smiled ever broader when he realised that not only was it real coffee but that it was laced with his favourite tipple.

'How the devil, master steward, do you get hold of this stuff, eh?' but all Walters did, as usual in reply, was to tap his nose, wag a finger and slowly close his left eye. As always.

Reitz grinned although he was certain that the little steward could never have left the ship long enough to have obtained the supplies from who was ever his source. Not during that last leave when security was so prevalent at *Dresden*'s base in Kiel. Little did he really know about this mercurial little man. Not that it mattered. The drink not only warmed his insides but also took his mind away from the anxieties he felt about the safety of the convoy's ships. Thoughts of conversations with Captain Wills-Wilson of *Resolve* came uppermost. How the old battleship's captain must have felt as he'd gazed over his troopships. Now it was his turn and the coffee only partly eased his worries. Temporarily.

Back at the beaches, the Russian colonel in charge of his withdrawn and battered survivors of his artillery teams watched *Dresden* and her ships withdraw out of sight. He'd come to hate that long lean grey silhouette of the battlecruiser that so severely savaged his guns. His men. Now the warships were gone. Even that smoke-wreathed old-fashioned one. Now he could re-assemble his survivors to re-open fire.

Opening fire on corpses, wrecked and abandoned equipment. On piles of sand and empty beaches. The Russian gunners increased their barrage, only dismembering the corpses into even more bloodied mutilations. Not one life was lost. None on the Russians because nothing fired back at them. None on the former German-defended beachhead because there wasn't anyone left. All of them were on the ships, their dark shapes disappearing over the horizon.

The flickering glow of the Russian barrage could only be faintly seen astern of the convoy's rearmost ships. Reitz, watching the darkness creep over the choppy seas, felt slightly less anxious. Then, suddenly, all of his worries came screaming back as soaring up the starboard side of the solid-looking liner in the column adjacent to *Dresden* he could see a white plume of spray with a yellow-red base. *Heinrich Galster* staggered as she recoiled as the torpedo exploded.

'Shit!' expleted Hiltzern as the wall of water was accompanied by the boom of the torpedo hit. The liner began to slow down and veered out of position. Fortunately her captain was soon able to bring his damaged ship under control. Three nearby escorts quickly found the Russian submarine and accurate depth-charging soon brought it to the surface for only a brief appearance. Quick-firing guns sprayed the luckless vessel catching it in a vortex of a myriad of shells. It soon sank in an obscene welter of bubbles. None of its crew appeared to attempt an escape. All her crew and the doomed submarine sank to the uncaring ice-cold depths. For ever.

Reitz took *Dresden* alongside the damaged but still moving *Heinrich Galster*. A signal from the liner indicated that she could still manoeuvre but would welcome a tug and escorts to help her on her way to eventual safety.

Reitz called up one of the two tugs in the convoy and three of the minesweepers to act as close escort and then re-grouped the convoy back on course. *Heinrich Galster*'s captain did not request any medical assistance as five of his human cargo of evacuees were doctors who were capably looking after the ship's wounded.

'Not many' he signalled. 'About forty dead and twice that number injured. What's that compared to the ten thousand we have on board?'

'Optimist, isn't he?' muttered Hiltzern.

'Yes, so long as no other Russian submarine is in the area. We can thank our lucky stars that the torpedo hit *Galster* and not us' replied

Reitz, bitterly. How many more times was he expected to guide *Dresden* out of a dangerous situation?

Hours passed. The convoy drew steadily closer to its Kiel destination. The darkness of the night hid the ships. At last, dawn began to grey itself over the dark seas. As the outline of the other ships became clearer, radar reported three small blips approaching the convoy from the north-west.

Reitz studied the repeater screen and asked Hiltzern 'Has Kiel sent us fresh re-inforcements?' The big man shook his head. Reitz grimaced 'Then we must assume that these ships must be Russians. If so, are they bent on a suicide mission? Better warn Halder.'

When Halder came up to the bridge, having been summoned from resting in his cabin, he murmured 'Yes, they're enemy unless we receive contrary information from Kiel. I'll get up aloft.'

As Reitz studied the repeater, the blips seemed to be much nearer. The horizon was still dark. 'They're enemy sir' said Hiltzern rather sharply, suddenly sounding very sure of himself.

Reitz nodded and added 'By heck, they must be. They've increased speed.'

Halder intoned over the speakers from his gunnery observation post 'Range about ten kilometres.'

Reitz sharply ordered 'Illuminate with starshell!'

One of the secondary guns belched flame. The shell burst over the approaching ships with an incandescent brilliance.

'They're definitely not ours. Small destroyer and two smaller boats – probably torpedo carriers.' Reitz sounded calm but inwardly, as always when action threatened, he was like a coiled spring with his nerves. 'Guns. Open fire!' The tension relaxed only slightly as along *Dresden*'s starboard length, orange ripples of firing guns flashed out, angrily, at the now very quickly approaching Russian warships.

'Signal convoy to alter fifteen degrees to port. Escorts to come with us!'

For a minute or so, despite the German ships desperately trying to hit the enemy vessels, the latter seemed to bear a charmed existence, steering a weaving pattern through a veritable forest of shells splashes.

'Good grief! Bloody hit them, Halder!' screamed Reitz as the enemy ships tried to steam ahead of the German warships and thus amongst the refugee liners attempting to turn away from the threat of their torpedoes.

Suddenly the small destroyer in the lead, trying to manoeuvre briefly away from the shells landing around her, momentarily exposed her full length, and three bursts of shells which hit her were seen as eruptions of flame. More shells struck her as she was seen to stagger, the flames acting as an aiming point. With an awesome sound, she simply and quite literally blew apart.

Undeterred, the two small torpedo boats seemed to put on even more speed trying to cross *Dresden*'s bows. Reitz turned *Dresden* away from them and many of the battlecruiser's anti-aircraft guns lashed out, their tracers hosing the latter of the two smaller boats in a vicious vortex, causing it to burst into flames and like its recently sunk bigger companion, to flare up and also disintegrate as it too blew up.

The other boat, a few yards ahead, crossed in front of *Dresden* trailing an oily smoke plume as flames were burning part of her interior. Even so, as she emerged on *Dresden*'s port side, the little boat's box-like bridge was seen to be on fire, flickering flames bursting around it. One of the boat's crew, his uniform on fire, was seen to stagger off balance as his boat jinked sharply, causing him to topple overboard into the icy waters beneath him. *Dresden*'s port side guns opened fire, together with the guns of an escort and the little Russian torpedo boat, unable to escape, suddenly like its companions, also disintegrated under the welter of fire. No-one on the German ships saw it firing two torpedoes moments before its violent end.

'By heck, that was tough' remarked Brautsch, sweating despite the cold air. 'Those Russians were so fast. So elusive. Steered by madmen totally indifferent to everything that was fired by Halder's gunners.'

'Just like Japanese kamikaze pilots that we heard about when we were over there. Death seems not to matter a jolt' answered Reitz 'but we should have blasted them before they managed to get so close.'

'Well, we did get them. Never had such fast boats to deal – what the hell, look yonder, sir!' Brautsch's reply ending with a sudden raising of his voice.

One of the convoy's ships briefly flared. Then a waterspout reared up her starboard amidships. Even on the exposed part of the bridge they heard the boom of an explosion.

'Which ship?' queried Reitz, nerves again jangling. Just when he assumed the immediate danger was over.

Horst grunted 'That's our friend. Hospital ship *Heidi.*'

Even at a two mile distance Reitz could see the *Heidi* slowing down.

'Hard-a-port!' he yelled. 'We'll get in close.'

The battlecruiser surged forwards turning to reach the stricken ex-ferry. She was struggling but fortunately, not on fire. A hole had been blown into her on the waterline, near her engine-room. As *Dresden* closed up, a hand-lamp began signalling from the *Heidi*'s bridge wing – 'Please help. Engine room flooding. Could do with medics – most doctors on board now killed.'

'Shit!' expleted Reitz, not normally given to bad language. 'We should have stopped those bloody Russians earlier. The last boat – oh shit! Thrice shit!' Then he took a deep breath to try and recover his composure. 'Go on Helmut! Your wife and two SBAs. Over there. You as well.' Then to the engine room he snapped 'Luth and team. On deck. Pumps needed!'

It was *Aspen Castle* all over again. Except it was their own people on the stricken ferry. Also, it was colder. With choppy seas.

Andrea was already on deck with SBA Werthe, the huge man with whom no-one ever picked an argument. With him was a gangly nineteen-year old, Karl Ruddenz, who'd only just joined *Dresden*. Compared to Werthe he resembled a rather uncoordinated stick insect. Even so, he was carrying two big medical bags. Werthe's own load of four stretchers didn't seem to worry him in the slightest.

By the waiting launch, Brautsch briefly kissed Andrea on her right cheek before the boat was winched on its falls down to the icy water that slipped noisily against its sides as the motors cut in. Ruddenz, sitting opposite Andrea, couldn't take his eyes off her. Ever since he'd joined the battlecruiser, he'd become virtually besotted with her. She smiled across at him. Poor young lad. He's got a crush on me!

Nothing could get the young lad's mind off Andrea. Her sheer dedication. Willingness to help. Anything about her created an aura. To him she was like a goddess.

The launch thumped up against the steel plating of *Heidi*.

'Wake up, dreamer!' Werthe poked his young companion in the ribs.

Reitz, high on *Dresden*'s bridge watched the medical team climb up rope ladders dangling over *Heidi*'s starboard side. He murmured to Hiltzern 'Let's get in much closer. Drop fenders over the side. We'll use our cranes to swing Luth's equipment across. Me thinks the sea's getting a bit choppy but I also think that the *Heidi* is in no immediate danger of foundering.'

The two ships closed in side by side. Despite the danger still of further Russian attacks, Reitz decided to pass ropes across to *Heidi* to lash the two ships together. *Heidi*'s decks still rode at almost the same level of *Dresden*'s amidships.

Further signals soon brought two minesweepers and a T-boat up to act as close escort whilst the captain of cruiser *Koln* was instructed to get the rest of the convoy well away from the area as fast as possible.

Reitz knew it was a risk with the battlecruiser lashed side-by-side to the crippled hospital ship but when Luth connected up big hoses, using *Dresden*'s power, to pump out the flooded holds on *Heidi*, and then fairly soon after, sending a report that work was quickly progressing, he felt justified in the risk.

Heidi rode much better on the choppy waters and with metal plating and wooden boards being hammered by Luth's team into place, the situation looked more promising as each minute passed.

With the lashed ropes being gradually tightened as the repair progressed, Brautsch signalled that towing could begin. Slowly *Dresden* took the strain and a slow-forward movement of two knots was attempted. Deep inside *Heidi*'s engine room, Luth and his men worked feverishly to try and restart the ex-ferry's engines.

In the ravaged main saloon, Andrea began to organise order out of the mess. Using some of *Heidi*'s crew, as well of some of *Dresden*'s men, the wreckage was quickly cleared. The saloon's main table became her operating table and Andrea, with Werthe and Ruddenz stitching and bandaging where required, began to deal with the wounded personnel following the torpedo blast. Even *Heidi*'s sole surviving doctor was giving assistance. Young Ruddenz had yanked the whimpering man to his feet with the words 'Call yourself a sawbones? Well, get thi'sen to thi' feet and help our lady doctor 'cos she's got more guts than tha's got garters. War dun't wait fer no-one so tha' best gets a move-on, sharpish like!' Delivered in his quite broad Bavarian accent, the harshness behind the meaning of his words shook the dazed doctor out of his stupor, and soon both he and Andrea's medical coats became ever more splattered with blood as they worked on their patients, most of them already wounded. Now they had further pain and injuries to bear.

Padré Jervaulx was also in the make-shift surgery room trying to mutter words, seemingly so meaningless and jumbled as the working parties shovelled the bits that a few minutes previously had been live bodies into weighted bags. People, despite their wounds, full of renewed hope to be escaping from the hell that they were leaving behind, now consigned to a icy cold watery grave with the minimum of fuss as the bags were dropped over *Heidi*'s sides. Desperately,

Jervaulx attempted to say his Benedictions for the dead but his words, so thin in the frost-laden air, could barely be heard as the bags vanished. More debris of war. When would it end? Never in his calling as a cleric had his faith and calling been so severely tested as it had been in the last two months. First the debris from the crashed Seafire. Then the desolation of Munich despite his host's attempts at general *bonhomie*. Now this. The savagery of war. So close at hand. So meaningless in its horror.

An hour passed by. On *Heidi*'s bridge, Brautsch conferred with her blunt-speaking captain trying to reassure him that with *Dresden*'s help, his ship would soon be operational again. Every so often he went below to see how Luth's team were getting on, and then to the saloon. He didn't want to interrupt his wife's work but to see her there, constantly at work, filled him with even more admiration. Then she looked up. Perhaps sensing his presence and blew him a kiss. He likewise responded with a blown kiss of his own before going back up *Heidi*'s bridge where he met one of Luth's men.

'We're ready to start up the engines, sir!'

'Good. Get on with it.'

Heidi's decks began to shudder as her engines turned over in neutral.

'All personnel to return back on board' came an order shouted, via a loud-hailer, from the battlecruiser's bridge. 'Including Kapitan-Leutnant Brautsch. Medics to assist on *Heidi* if still needed.' Reluctantly, Brautsch left *Heidi*. Another quick kiss to Andrea and then he, with Jervaulx, were soon back on board *Dresden*. Werthe and Ruddenz opted to stay with Andrea. She wouldn't go. There were still too many patients needing her attention. The blast from the torpedo had done more damage, so it seemed, to the personnel on *Heidi* rather than to her engine rooms.

The securing lines were released, one by one. *Heidi*'s engine-room staff shoved their throbbing engines into gear. Slowly, at first, the hospital ship began to move forward. One, two, three knots.

As she gathered way, Andrea looked up from her work. Ruddenz shyly grinned at her. 'Are we under way?' she asked.

Ruddenz nodded 'Aye, miss. But we is staying with you.'

'My husband. Where is he?'

'Back on board t'ship, miss.'

Andrea hurriedly told *Heidi*'s doctor to carry on. 'Be back soon' she called, urgently feeling the need to get on deck to see her beloved Helmut. If he was watching. With Werthe and Ruddenz hot on her heels she emerged on *Heidi*'s decks, waving and looking up at *Dresden*'s bridge as the gap widened between the two ships.

To her pleasant surprise she could just make out her husband waving back at her.

Then she turned on her heels and hurried back to the blood-splattered saloon. Back to her work. Of patching up already badly hurt patients. She knew that some of them wouldn't make it back to Kiel. She also knew that she had to try.

The five slow-moving ships all came into view of Captain Androv Alexovitch as he stared at them through the periscope of his submarine *B-12*. 'Damn!' he cursed 'I shouldn't have tried that long shot at the convoy with our last brace of torpedoes if I'd have known that this easy target was going to come and pass us by.' He could but watch with a furious chagrin as *Dresden, Heidi* and the three escorts slowly began to move away.

Alexovitch had never seen *Dresden* before. Of the hospital ship, he dismissed it as a Nazi cover-up transport for fleeing top officials. He cared not a rouble for any of them. Murderous swine that they were. During the enemy's retreat from Leningrad his village, like so many others, was the scene of a desperate battle between the attacking Red Army and the defending Wehrmacht. Alexovitch, on leave, went to his village hoping to be re-united with his wife and two young daughters.

'Not here, comrade. Not alive. Have a look in the church.'

The ruined shell of the Orthodox church was a mortuary. Of the village's inhabitants. Forced in at the point of Waffen SS bayonets and then burnt as the church was torched. Their crime? One young boy seen stealing a loaf of bread from a Wehrmacht supply truck. Alexovitch's wife and two young daughters were at the end of a row. It was no wonder that he was so full of hate. Of bitterness. Of revenge.

Four times he'd fired torpedoes at his enemy's ships. Four times those salvoes failed to find a target.

And now this one. The easiest to hit of the lot. And *B-12*'s torpedo racks were empty.

Slowly the enemy sailed away. By keeping half-submerged, Alexovitch kept *B-12* at a discreet distance watching the ships. He knew that if his boat couldn't attack, then aircraft could. From the nearest held Russian air-base.

The air colonel-in-charge of Gregor Valutin's air-base received *B-12*'s message whilst a fierce snow-storm raged over the field and huts. A base only thirty miles behind the front line. A front-line savaged in part so fiercely by *Dresden*'s shells. The warship described so carefully by *B-12*. General orders already existed at the base that this particular German warship was enemy surface vessel number one priority to be sunk 'whatever the cost'.

'Out, out, out to your aircraft' screamed the colonel to his clearly unhappy pilots.

'Flying in this white shit?' queried Valutin.

'Yes, yes. Now! This is the position of that very nasty piece of Nazi shit!' yelled the colonel, all reasoning temporarily gone completely out of his brain.

It only returned when the first three planes all crashed trying to take-off.

'Damn, damn, and thrice damn! Abort! Abort the mission!' the colonel yelled into his microphone linked to the pilots headsets.

The surviving pilots heaved a sigh of relief and taxied their planes back to their canvas-covered temporary hangers.

Revenge against *Dresden* was one thing. Futile suicide of his pilots was another. Not to be wasted skidding in deep snow. Aloft and over the target. Well, that was different altogether. Even if they were then shot down.

B-12 received a terse message – 'Continue shadowing. Report if there's a major change in speed or course.'

Dresden's wireless operators picked up *B-12*'s wireless traffic but as none of them understood Russian, they couldn't make any sense of it all. All that they could report was that an enemy ship, of some sort, was about twenty miles astern of them. When Reitz heard about it he surmised that it probably involved a submarine on their track. He alerted his radar team as well as the crews of the escort ships to keep a careful watch for a submarine or even enemy planes. But nothing could be detected. Not yet.

Heidi continued to push slowly forwards carefully watched by Reitz and an ever increasingly worried Helmut Brautsch, fearful of a sudden Russian attack on the defenceless slow moving hospital ship. His wife was on that ship. Working as quickly as she could. Patching up human war debris.

'Helmut, I know what you're thinking. About Andrea.' murmured Reitz.

'Yes, sir. I wish I was still on board the *Heidi*.'

'Your place, Helmut, is here. On this ship. Where you can best co-ordinate our anti-aircraft defences. However if *Heidi* is attacked, I shall ensure that you will be sent over to bring her back. Andrea's high up in my regard too you know!'

'Thank you, sir.'

'Ever since she came aboard our ship and at once rolled up her sleeves to assist Surgeon-Leutnant Lebers she has been in my mind. Your welfare for her I too share, but I also know that you are a member of the Kriegsmarine and your duty, like that of everyone else of this crew, is that when danger threatens, is to assist in whatever way possible, the defence of this ship. The rest of us have our female partners on land. You are the exception. She's only a few hundred metres away. On a ship within view.'

Slowly *Heidi*'s engineers notched up speed – three, four, five and eventually six knots.

Gradually dusk approached. As well as clearing skies. Another half-an-hour and it would be dark. The Russians wouldn't be able to find them and come the morning, they'd be out-of-range of their threats. The minutes ticked slowly – one by one – or so it seemed as Brautsch, the nerves worsening, willed darkness to come over the seas.

On the airbase in East Prussia it also stopped snowing and immediately the air-colonel ordered the snow to be swept off at least one runway. The base's ground-attack aircraft, twelve Sturmoviks, were hauled by tractors out of their shelters. *B-12*'s latest signal still showed that the slow-moving group of German ships were still moving in the same westerly heading but their speed was slowly increasing.

'We'll only get this one chance. Nine of our aircraft are going for the ships and the other three will search nearer waters or land for suitable targets. We should just about reach those infidel craft before darkness. Right, you eight –' here Squadron Commander, Gregor Valutin pointed to the pilots nearest to him '– you will follow me. Three flights of three aircraft. We can only carry smallish bombs so make every one count!' Not one of the pilots questioned the validity of flying over darkening waters when none of them had ever done such a task before. No-one argued with Gregor Valutin, holder of 'Hero of the Soviet Union' medal three times over. No-one argued with the revolver he always carried. Anyone who did never lived to tell the tale. Became disgraced. Family at home as well.

Eight of the nine aircraft took off, snow whirling around them as the propeller of each machine whisked at the powdery particles as the Sturmoviks roared down the hastily prepared runway. The ninth aircraft skidded on the hard-pressed ice, turned over in its take-off dash and exploded as it plunged into a pile of snow at the side of the cleared track. But Valutin knew where he was going. Showing a red tail-light he snarled over his air intercom 'Follow me!'

B-12, now fully on the surface, kept signalling to Valutin's air-group knowing that it was on the way. Alexovitch ordered an orange flare to be lit to guide Valutin's oncoming flight. The faint glow was seen by the ever alert Prebke. Alerted when Reitz broadcast to the ship's look-outs and gunners that due to increased wireless activity astern of *Dresden*, that he believed an air attack was still possible as darkness fell.

'Glow on surface astern!' he shouted.

At the same time, the new stern-searching radar picked up Valutin's flight. Starting to gain height after their near wave-top track towards first *B-12* and now, *Dresden* and her ships.

Valutin was searching for the darker blobs indicating the enemy ships.

With star shells aimed at him and his seven companions.

'Stupid square-headed Nazis! You have shown me where you are!' Valutin smiled grimly to himself even as the bursting shells rattled shrapnel on to the Sturmovik's fuselage as the aircraft flew pell-mell into the fierce-some barrage.

Behind the flight, Alexovitch slammed the conning tower hatch shut as *B-12* began to dive. His job was done. He'd guided his comrades to their target.

'Attack!' yelled Valutin as he angled his Sturmovik into a power dive. 'Attack the Nazi swine below us!' The other aircraft lined up, one after the other to follow their leader to glory – or death.

Somewhat impassively, the pilots of the two aircraft behind Valutin watched their leader's plane lose its starboard wing and begin to spiral hopelessly and helplessly out of control whilst in their headphones they could hear Valutin screaming, as his inter-plane communication was still switched on. It only cut out when his aircraft crashed into the cold unremitting dark waters of the Baltic Sea.

Not that those two men had much longer to live. Both died within seconds of each other as the murderous defensive flak tore their machines apart and their aircraft to follow Valutin's into the icy seas.

Of the other five aircraft, the first four hastily shed their bomb load and attempted to escape but in turning away, two of them were also caught by the barrage and dropped, like heavy stones, to crash to their watery doom.

The last aircraft's pilot, with a bit more sense rather than bravado, dropped quickly to sea-level and unseen by the gunners on their smoke-wreathed ships, flew hurriedly out to sea in a northerly direction.

'Cease fire!' ordered Reitz.

Brautsch said 'Thank goodness that they've gone. Even those that dropped their bombs weren't anywhere near.'

A seaman on the port-wing of the bridge shouted 'Sir, Hiedi's signalling. Our medics have done and could we get them –'

'Aircraft, sir! One, Coming from the north at ninety degrees.' Prebke's ears, as well as his eyes, were the first to hear the eighth, and last, of the Sturmoviks make its approach in the near darkness.

'Shit! Open fire!' snarled Reitz, taken off guard.

Only one of the Vierling batteries was able to open fire as the dark shape of the attacking fighter-bomber flew behind and over *Dresden*'s funnel, screaming its engines, trying to gain bombing height. An alert gunner on torpedo boat T-9, immediately astern, fired a single line of tracer that caught the Sturmovik's' propeller before the pilot could avoid its death-dealing blow. In his desperation, he released his bomb-load. It was his last act for the aircraft spiralled and with increasing speed, crashed and blew up as it hit the sea, adjacent to *Heidi.* Blowing a hole in her sides but not one as big as the one created by the falling bombs that splattered across her upper decks penetrating the thin deck plating and exploding in the saloon below.

Above the rows and rows of wounded soldiers and civilians whom Andrea and the other medics had just treated. With death dealing results. As well as causing the dry ornate wooden panelling and soft furnishings to catch fire.

Within seconds, flames shot high above *Heidi*'s superstructure as the hospital ship took on an orange-yellow appearance. A vicious one.

'Hard-a-port! Get alongside! Fire teams at the ready. Douse those flames' shouted Reitz, his nerves at full stretch. 'Go on, Helmut, get aboard *Heidi*!'

But Brautsch had already gone. Running, leaping, jumping down the access ladders and rushing to deck level where his boat crew were waiting.

'No time for the boat. We'll jump across on ropes when we're alongside' he yelled, scared witless as to what might have happened to Andrea.

The fire-hoses began to gush out jets of water on to *Heidi*'s upper deck as Reitz conned *Dresden* alongside. Clouds of vapourised steam as well as gouts of smoke began to rise from the stricken ex-ferry.

Although the flames burning top-sides on *Heidi* were being extinguished by the hoses jetting out from *Dresden*, below her main deck they were burning fiercely. Brautsch and his team of nine men all succeeded in dropping on to *Heidi*'s aft deck where they were met by some of the hospital ship's crew. 'This way! Your men and lady doctor are near the saloon' one of the men shouted. 'Hurry! We must try to get the wounded out!'

Led by the seaman, Brautsch flicked on a torch as he followed him down a smoke-filled part-burning passage-way that led into the saloon. There he met Werthe, bleeding from a head wound where part of the burning ceiling had hit him.

'Where's my wife?' asked Brautsch as he grabbed the big semi-dazed medic by his tunic. 'Doctor Frau Brautsch? Nurse Andrea to you!'

Werthe jerked his head. 'Over there. Wouldn't leave the wounded. It's hell sir, the ceiling collapsed.'

Brautsch stared across at the flames and then without a thought, began to run over the burning cots and mattresses, Werthe close behind.

'There sir!' he gasped.

In the smoke could be seen young Ruddenz holding up a burning beam with one hand and trying to pull an unconscious Andrea out from under it. Brautsch bent down and with Werthe, heaved the beam out of the way. He never noticed the heat nor the burns on his hands as he picked up his senseless wife. Retching for air, and following the two medics, he ran through the searing flames as they puckered at his singed uniform coat.

It seemed to be an age, although in reality only a few seconds as Brautsch, hardly aware of the flames around him, carried Andrea, his beloved wife, to safety. Then he was through the flames as he emerged into the smouldering end of the saloon. Still he didn't put her down. Werthe and Ruddenz led him down the smoke-filled passageway back the way he'd come. At the end they reached the deck. There, hardly able to fathom out what had happened, Brautsch finally stopped, his lungs heaving for air, his uniform badly singed, and the pain from his burnt hands beginning to register.

To his horror, *Dresden* was now more than fifty metres away. Reitz had taken his warship away from the clearly doomed *Heidi.*

Clear of the threat of the flames or explosions

'Sir! Sir! We'll take Andrea now. We've a stretcher for her.' In a daze, Brautsch let Werthe take Andrea and lower her on to the stretcher before strapping her in. She was lowered on ropes into a boat, already loaded with nearly twenty other cases. One of *Dresden*'s boats. Its motor deepened as with Andrea on board it puttered away, back across to the battlecruiser.

Brautsch, Werthe and Ruddenz plunged back into the smoke and began dragging as many of the wounded out of the burning saloon. Three of *Heidi*'s crew helped as they paired with the three *Dresden* men to carry the men out on to the hospital ship's decks.

On their sixth journey a wild-looking sailor came up to them. 'I'm from the captain. We're to abandon ship. We've no more power to our pumps and we're sinking.'

Brautsch pushed him out of the way 'We've more wounded in there and one of our boats is alongside and we're going to load it up. So, miserable worm, you stay here and help lower these desperately wounded people down into that boat.' Then he smacked the seaman across the face and shook him, until the man nodded in agreement.

For five minutes, Brautsch and his men carried more of the wounded out but then *Heidi* suddenly lurched taking on a serious list to port. It was time to abandon. Really time.

The last of *Dresden*'s over-laden boats moved away leaving Brautsch and his fellow rescuers to slide down ropes and plunge into the icy water. It took their breath away and soon Brautsch was struggling. Ruddenz grabbed hold of him and desperately made his way through the choppy, icy waters.

It was a struggle but eventually they both came under the lee of *Dresden*. Behind them, *Heidi* lay on her beam-ends, with huge clouds of grey steam gushing and billowing above her as the cold Baltic waters smothered her burning interior as she now rapidly sank.

Spluttering and shivering, Ruddenz guided Brautsch to a scrambling net but the officer was barely conscious, with the pain of his burnt hands as well as the shock of the severe cold together with the constant taste and retching of the salty water. Above them they could hear shouts of encouragement. Werthe, already on the net, leant down to grab his nineteen old companion and succeeded in hauling him on to the net. Otto Schenke and a new midshipman, Andres Feld, came down the nets to try and heave Brautsch out of the water but just as Feld grabbed at his tattered uniform jacket, *Dresden* gave an unexpected lurch throwing both midshipmen and Brautsch off the net and into the ice-cold waters. Feld struggled with trying to hold on to Brautsch but felt the man's uniform jacket rip and all he found himself holding was a small piece of ragged cloth. Desperately he searched, even diving under the surface but as he came up spluttering and gasping for breath, the strong hands of Otto Schenke grabbed his left arm and hauled him, shaking with cold and the desperation of losing Brautsch, on to the net and moments later, pulled him completely out of the water.

'T'officer's gone, young sir. Come on, back on deck!' bawled Schenke.

Feld turned, trying to jump back into the dark grey waters even though he could hardly see anything for the darkness of the night.

'No sir, come on up!' Schenke sounded angry and young Feld knew that he couldn't argue. He may have been good swimmer but out of water, he was no match for a bruising confrontation with the ugly-scarred appearance of the brawny chief petty officer.

Gasping for breath as he lay on the deck-planking he heard Schenke say, in his rough accent 'You did yer best lad. Now go and get the'sen changed afore ye gets a cold.'

Feld smiled, weakly, still trying to cough sea-water out of his lungs. 'I tried to hold onto him but he slipped away. It was the cold.'

'Go on, lad, probably t'skipper'll want ter know as well.'

Andrea lay in a cot, breathing shallowly. Doctor Lebers was holding her pulse but looked up when he saw a visibly-shocked Reitz looking down at him.

'She'll live, sir. It's just the shock of what's been happening to her, I expect.'

Reitz nodded and then saw Andrea's eyes slowly open.

She said 'I know that I'm back on *Dresden* but please, tell me, how I got here. The last I knew was seeing Helmut bending over me. Did he bring me here?'

Reitz nodded again. How could he tell her that her husband, having rescued her had gone back into the burning saloon and with help, had pulled about two dozen badly wounded, all of whom were in the Sick Berth occupying every bed? How could he tell her that he, Werthe and Ruddenz, together with the three hospital ship crewmen had jumped into the water to try and swim back to *Dresden.* How all but her badly-burned husband had made it back. How midshipman Feld had done his best to haul Helmut out of the water and had even jumped back to try and reach Helmut but had been unable to find him. How one of the escorts on patrol had picked up a submarine on its underwater detection gear and that he'd, for safety, ordered *Dresden*'s engines to 'Full ahead'. How the escort had then reported 'False Alarm' and how another escort, torpedo boat T-9 had picked up a body and the identity tag on it identified it as her dead husband.

But he did tell her and all the while, Andrea tried to take in the unfolding horror of it all.

'He's dead, isn't he, Herr Reitz?'

Reitz nodded grimly and impulsively held her hand. Why had the war been so cruel to this wonderful woman? Damn, damn, damn! Why her?

This was his moment of deep despair. He'd lost the one officer that he could regard as almost a close friend. *Heidi* had sunk with the loss of eighty per cent of those on board. Some of her crew were on board his ship as well as the wounded that Brautsch and his men had rescued. He thought of *Heidi*'s struggle only for the ex-ferry to sink so quickly. Just sixteen minutes after the bombs had struck. Only enough time for her topsides crew to launch four of her boats before the fire below made life on deck unbearable. A fire that had burnt out *Heidi* so rapidly. Now she was gone. Brautsch was a lifeless corpse on T-9. And he, supposed hero of *Dresden* and of the Kriegsmarine, had been unable to prevent it.

He let go of Andrea's hand and almost savagely left the Sick Berth to return to the bridge, leaving Andrea sobbing gently, she knowing that the child growing inside her would never ever meet its father. Doctor Lebers knew that she was pregnant and also knew that despite the trauma of the last few hours that the unborn child was safe. He hadn't been in a maternity ward before the war for nothing.

Dresden surged ahead at seventeen knots, the fastest that the minesweepers could manage. A curt signal to *Koln* informed the cruiser's captain of the tragic loss of the *Heidi*. When *Koln* replied, Horst was able to more accurately work out an interception course.

The only pleasing note was that the convoy was out of range of Russian air and submarine attacks. So also was *Heinrich Galster*. The big liner, closer into the coast was making good progress – at ten knots and she'd been able to limit the damage from her torpedoing.

Utterly weary, Reitz decided to turn in for a couple of hours before dawn. Drained of energy as well as emotion. Try as he could, sleep just wouldn't come. He saw the *Arades* in flames, then the *Resolve* and *Marona* blowing up, the helpless troopships off Guadalcanal; the Pacific convoy's ships being torpedoed; the surprise of the Arctic merchant-ships as his shells crashed on and around them; the Seafire plummeting on to *Dresden*; the guns firing salvo after salvo of indescribable destruction into the Russian ranks but all of this paled into insignificance as he saw those flames shoot out of *Heidi*'s decks and he knew that he had to rescue Andrea. Now she was, like so many others, a lonely pregnant widow. Eventually he turned his mind to Elle. He saw her clearly smiling and laughing. Blotting out the vicious memories of this sickening war. He even tried to say a 'thank you' to her but even that, in his mind, sounded so inadequate.

Half-way through the next day, *Dresden* and her escort caught up with her convoy. Soon after, another of the Kriegsmarine's big ships joined them for the last twenty hours sailing to Kiel. Heavy cruiser *Prinz Eugen*. Returning from bombardment duties after her refit in Gotenhafen.

As they neared Kiel, a signal from the port's authorities diverted *Koln* to the Kiel Canal and then to dock in Wilhelmshaven for a hasty refit and to prepare her for defensive mine-laying duties in that port's North Sea approaches.

Still out of sight of Kiel, the rest of the convoy approached the port whilst *Koln* put on speed, her captain no doubt thankful that his ship wasn't going back to Eastern Baltic duties any more.

Off the entrance to the Kiel Canal, a Swedish timber ship was told to wait until a warship of the Kriegsmarine had entered the Canal. Leaning over the rails, one of her crew shouted down to a hovering tug. 'Hey you!' – to one of the tugboat men – 'Which ship are you waiting for?'

'Aye, and what do you want ter know for?' came back the reply.

'Oh, just nosey like what we neutrals are!' came back the jocular reply 'Heard that some of your big ships have been sunk like in the East!'

'Don't be daft. Now that we've got *Dresden* back how can we possibly fail?'

'Is *Dresden* that ship over there?' asked the persistent timber-ship crewman.

'Could be. We're escorting her to the locks so be seein' you, like!' and with that, the tugboat churned off round the headland to catch up with the approaching warship.

Deep down in the Admiralty-bunker under London's busy thorough-fares, Admiral Collins looked up as the elderly commander on his staff entered his office.

'Sir! We've just received this message from an agent on a Swedish timber-ship.'

It read – 'Suspect *Dresden* in Kiel. ETA 17.00 hours Wilhelmshaven on 30th.'

Collins reached for his telephone. 'Get me Air Chief Marshall Harris. At once!'

Harris listened to what Collins told him. 'The thirtieth, you say? Hmmm! Well, if what the agent says is true and seeing we've a few bombers spare, what say you that we give Wilhelmshaven a merry pasting at about midnight. You agree? Right! I'll sort it out!'

Collins gazed at the photograph of *Dresden*. The handsome lines of the speeding battlecruiser. Yes, in just over twenty-four hours she'd be blasted in the 'pasting of Wilhelmshaven' – as Harris put it. This time, Herr Reitz, this time you won't escape.

Chapter 14

'No roses bloom'

Time after time the bombs cascaded on to the near hapless town of Wilhelmshaven creating fresh swathes of destruction. Euphemistically termed 'carpet-bombing', the bombers of the RAF and their Canadian assistants dropped their explosive loads all over the port area without aiming specifically at any set target. 'Bound to have hit something' Harris told Collins when the latter rang up to enquire if the *Dresden* had been destroyed. Whatever the final analysis of the raid would prove there was little doubt that the days of Wilhelmshaven serving as an active port for the Kriegsmarine in the war were just about extinguished. Despite the deluge of bombs, none actually scored a direct hit on the only large surface unit of the German Navy berthed in the port. Near misses caused her below-water plates to crack and water poured in to the hull of light cruiser *Koln* but the crew still on board her kept their nerve and by careful counter-flooding were able to allow the cruiser to settle on the dockside bed whilst still remaining upright. No doubt, given time, the cruiser could be repaired but neither the Kriegsmarine nor the political masters of Nazi Germany could spare the time or resources to consider such an effort. Her days as an active sea-going unit were over.

As the smoke of the fires cleared away, a high-flying Mosquito reconnaissance aircraft took photographs of the battered city and in particular, the port area.

When the photographs of the port area landed on his desk, Collins studied them with a keen intensity, scrutinising them with the aid of a magnifying glass. 'Damn! Oh the stupid sods! That's not the bloody *Dresden*. It's one of their tin-pot shit-scared light cruisers – *Koln* or *Nurnberg*. It appears that mister bloody Reitz and his glory boys weren't in Wilhelmshaven after all!'

An aide, new to the staff, nervously suggested 'Perhaps sir, the *Dresden* doubled back to Kiel. She's very elusive, isn't she?'

'Too bloody right.'

'Sir, what is it about that ship?'

Collins looked at the scared face of the young lieutenant. 'Well sonny boy, I've been after her for the best part of four years.' He then went on outlining to the young officer just how *Dresden* had always figured in his thoughts. How the Allies never seemed to be able to catch her. How they'd eliminated all the other big ships above heavy cruiser size – *Bismarck*, *Tirpitz*, *Scharnhorst* and *Gneisenau* but this one, she was still a going concern.

The lieutenant ventured 'But sir, she can't do all that much more damage can she? The war will be over soon I should think?'

Collins gave him a glare 'Whilst ever she's afloat she can do us harm. What's to stop her coming out of the Baltic for a last glory gung-ho dash at our convoys? You know, go down in a blaze of Nazi hero-worship?' With that Collins snatched up the photographs, and swept out the room, slamming the door behind him.

Martin Bormann heard about the Wilhelmshaven raid as well. He also knew that *Dresden* was somewhere near Kiel. He also knew that her creator Admiral Canaris was being subjected to intense interrogation. 'Soon, soon, Herr Admiral Reitz. You will be in the place of Canaris. Next time you dock in Kiel, my boys will be waiting for you.'

The thinning grey hair of Padré Jervaulx blew in untidy twirls as the funeral service of Helmut Brautsch proceeded. Somehow the padré felt that this time the war had gone on long enough. How many men had he committed to the deep? Grimly he tried to focus on his task as four sailors prepared to drop the weighted canvas-shrouded body over the stern rails of the slowly-moving battle-cruiser. 'May the God of love give eternal rest to this our departed brother' and then the body was gone with a splash into the grey waters. Andrea, supported on either side by Reitz and Walters, threw a wreath of a few hastily gathered flowers collected in the brief stop-over in Kiel. Boatswain's pipes trilled a shrill lament and then the big drum of the ship's band beat a slow thumping as the crew dispersed back to their duties. Walters led Andrea back to the captain's main cabin but she really didn't know what was happening. The man who'd rescued her from a burning freighter, who had befriended her and with whom she'd fallen in love and married, had gone. Dying, attempting to save others. Saving her and her unborn child. Their child.

Walters handed her a port-and-lemon and then gave his captain a tot of his favourite whisky. Even at this melancholic moment Reitz couldn't work out how his loyal steward managed to procure the liquid. 'Must have slipped ashore during our two-hour stay' he thought keeping the notion to himself. 'Probably whilst I went to see Bernhard Rogge.'

Rogge hadn't been all that pleased that Reitz had hazarded his ship in the attempted rescue of the doomed *Heidi*. Then his attitude changed when Reitz told him that Brautsch had been lost. Rogge knew what must be going through his fellow Admiral's mind. To lose men in humanitarian work was so tragic. So unnecessary. 'George' he continued 'you've one more trip to make and then we're pulling you out of the main evacuation programme. All our fit ships will be sent to Copenhagen. Only ships that are needing a major overhaul will be berthed in German ports – *Scheer* here in Kiel, *Lutzow* and *Schlesien* to Swinemunde. In due course, *Hipper* will come here as well. You will receive your instructions in due time. It depends on how much fuel I can scrape up. I know about *Olaf* in Trondheim. Perhaps you'll be able to take *Dresden* there although it'll be risky. Allied air patrols are quite intense off the Norwegian coast.'

Then Reitz was able to see Elle. They met in the base's gloomy canteen having a cup of ersatz coffee, a slice of rye bread and some plain biscuits. She'd been shocked to see her fiancé looking so strained.

'Not the most romantic meal, is it?' George muttered. Elle, her eyes filling up with tears whispered back 'Every meal with you is romantic. Just having you here is marvellous.'

George held her hand 'Darling, what a lovely thing to say. You will still marry me, won't you when all this is over? Maybe Padré Jervaulx will do the honours.'

Elle couldn't stop her tears. 'Yes, yes. Of course. As soon as we can after the war has ended.'

George leaned over the strained table and gently dabbed at her tears. 'Thankyou darling. Thankyou.' Getting up, he helped Elle to her feet and kissed her. Gently. Breaking off, he looked straight into her eyes. 'Darling. I have one more cruise to do and when I come back I'm going to try and get you on board. It won't be safe here and Admiral Rogge will just have to do without you! However whilst I'm away you can do one thing for me. Contact our Naval HQ in Trondheim and pass this message on to *Olaf*'s captain "Your master will soon require your services." Do this as soon as you can and give him this short-wave radio frequency to listen to from April tenth onwards.' So saying this, George gave Elle a piece of paper with the frequency.

Elle nodded. 'Yes my darling. Secrecy is the word, I presume, as well?'

George grinned 'That's more like it my girl.'

In his cabin Reitz looked across at Andrea as she held her drink. He raised his glass and said 'To the memory of Helmut. May your child to be always be a reminder of your love for him.'

'You know?' gasped Andrea.

'There's not much that our good doctor Herr Lebers doesn't know even if he's not been in a maternity ward for the last four or so years!'

'Captain' Andrea looked up at Reitz. 'You have been very kind to me and I have tried to work my passage on this ship, as it were. I fell in love with Helmut and as you appear to know, I now carry our child. I have been informed that it will be born, God willing, early in October. Perhaps the war will have finished by then. Where we'll all be, I just don't know. How the Allies will treat me, I don't know. Perhaps they'll think that I've been a traitor, even if only in an humanitarian form.' The words simply tumbled out of her. 'Whatever happens, every time I feel myself, every time I will look at our child, I shall think of Helmut, of the four years that I've been on this ship. Of you. Of the dangers we've all faced. Of being rescued by your ship when our lives were in danger on *Arades*. We were counting our lives in minutes just before *Dresden* arrived. So without you, I wouldn't be here with our baby alive inside me. I only wish that Helmut could have been with us. What will become of us?' Then she paused, tears beginning to stream down her cheeks. Sobbing, she went on 'Captain, what a long speech for me. Oh dear, I don't know what to say or do anymore. Helmut's gone. What do I do? What do we all do?'

Reitz gripped her hand and before he could reply, Padré Jervaulx, also in the cabin, intervened 'Frau Brautsch, we are all God's people. Out of this dreadful war I am sure we shall all become friends again. The horror of it all has, in a strange way, drawn us all closer together. Once the evil of Nazism has been eradicated by the Allies as it surely will in the next few weeks, there will be a time of pain and recrimination, and then a new combined Europe will arise. We will all join hands in friendship. Out of evil comes good. Those of us, on either side, who have fought an honourable war, as I believe our ship has done, will find it easier to shake hands with our former enemies. Indeed, although it may be difficult at first, I shall look forward to the New Era that is going to come. Perhaps, even as a prisoner of the Allies, I shall try to go to Coventry to pray for the new friendship in the ruins of the Cathedral we bombed in November nineteen forty. Perhaps people from Coventry will pray with me in the ruins of the church where I was a minister. When we were sent on leave, I went back and there, despite only a rough tarpaulin over what had been the roof, the church was full that day with people praying that the war would end soon and that we could all be friends all over again. You see, Frau Brautsch, we have on this ship been enlightened by your example to make friends with us. In your way you have shown it possible for enemies to become friends. You are in our debt for the selfless love for the wounded on this warship that you have shown. May God be with you and your child.'

'Mmm, seems as if everything has been said' murmured Reitz, releasing Andrea's hand. 'Now I must get back to the bridge. We have orders to proceed to Swinemunde.' He left for his position aloft, thoughts racing through his mind. So far, like he'd done when he'd first taken over the battlecruiser, he kept his final plans to himself. He was in no doubt that by the time *Dresden* returned from what could well be her final war patrol, the war would have reached virtually its last dying stages. Even as he climbed up to the bridge, he could see the anti-aircraft guns pointed upwards at a steep angle tracking some high silvery specks. American daylight bombers. Able to roam almost at will over Germany's air space as the Luftwaffe was virtually a spent force. The high-flying aircraft flew on to a distant, unknown eastern target ignoring the battlecruiser. Even if they had seen her.

The target hadn't been Swinemunde for the town looked to be relatively intact. No major fires. A few wrecks near the harbour entrance but as *Dresden* approached, an E-boat was seen to detach itself from the harbour wall and begin to close-in on *Dresden*, signalling the battlecruiser to come to a halt. The little warship, dwarfed by the bulk of *Dresden*, came about. A neat trim boat, her captain obviously still taking pride in his vessel for its brass binnacles burnished in the pale noonday sun that shone on the glistening waters of the fairway where the battlecruiser had come to a gentle stop.

From the *Dresden*'s bridge the officers could just make out the fore-tops of two of the Kriegsmarine's larger warships anchored near the main channel of the port. Old battleship *Schlesien* and the pocket-battleship *Lutzow*. Both with worn-out engines and guns. For the past nine months they'd been constantly in fire-support of the retreating German forces in the Eastern Baltic. At long last, after a somewhat inglorious war career, the *Lutzow* had at last been able to prove herself. But now no longer. She was, to all intents and purposes, little more than a floating gun battery with her guns already pointing eastwards ready for a final dual with the advancing Russian armies. Unless the Allied bombers got to her first. All but her gunners and some engineers had been sent ashore. As was the crew of the ancient *Schlesien*.

As the E-boat came alongside, a naval captain and an army officer clambered aboard *Dresden* where they were piped aboard in the traditional naval manner. Discipline was still a keyword on board *Dresden*, whatever the war situation. The news the men brought Reitz only confirmed the desperateness of the situation. Reitz was to take *Dresden* forwards to the Eastern Baltic again, give fire support where required and be principal escort for a convoy back to the Western ports. As before, except that this time it would be the last appearance by a major Kriegsmarine unit in those waters. There wasn't enough fuel for another sortie by any of the ships of cruiser size or above. Ammunition was also in short supply.

Nothing else needed to have been said. It was written on the faces of the two officers as they saluted Reitz before returning to the

E-boat. The war was lost. The Kriegsmarine had done its best to rescue nearly three million personnel with relatively few losses from the Eastern Baltic. The job of evacuation was nearly over.

Off the beleaguered Hela peninsula, *Dresden* seemed to dwarf all the other vessels in the area. Two destroyers and four minesweepers were scuttling back and forth trying to assemble the convoy of small, fairly fast merchantmen. Very rarely did Russian aircraft put in an appearance and as soon as the battlecruiser appeared, the Russian guns remained almost universally silent. Perhaps some observant officer recognised the big warship and was a survivor of a previous bombardment. Whatever it was, the two Arados that Reitz ordered to be launched could only find a few tanks and half-a-dozen salvoes from *Dresden*'s big guns soon saw them trying to race for cover providing that they were able to escape the fearsome shells as they exploded in and around the area.

Within a few hours of her arrival, the convoy was ready to proceed and under *Dresden*'s protection, heaved its way westwards gearing itself up to twelve knots. Leaving the junior officers in charge, Reitz called up all his senior staff as well as some of the leading petty officers to the officers' wardroom. 'Gentlemen' he began, 'this has been our last war operation supporting the army here in the Baltic. We shall be in Kiel fairly soon and after that, it's up to us. We can stay there and probably be bombed to bits or we can try and reach Copenhagen. Heavy cruiser *Prinz Eugen* together with light cruisers *Nurnberg* and *Leipzig* are already there awaiting either further orders or plainly to remain intact when the war ends for end it surely will very soon.' He looked round at the familiar faces. 'Four years we've been together. And now, this. The final instructions.' No-one spoke or even offered a comment. 'That could be our position but if you agree, with the fuel we've still on board plus any we can scrounge in Kiel, I intend to try for a breakout back to Trondheim where *Olaf* is waiting with more fuel. Maybe a last Arctic convoy attack or a surge into the North Atlantic as a final gesture. Or whatever. Perhaps straight into a Royal Naval fleet. At least we can surrender on the high seas rather than tamely in a port. In your envelopes I have added some ideas to my plans. Keep them to yourselves until we leave Kiel although I'm sure my ideas will soon be over the whole ship!' With that he turned on his heel and left the wardroom. Distantly he could her cheering. Morale was still high. *Dresden* wasn't defeated – yet.

Gradually the convoy turned away from the main danger area. The Russians made no serious effort to hinder its progress. Perhaps their aircraft were earmarked for the final push to smash Hitler's armies in the battle for Berlin. They'd seen enough of *Dresden* and signalled the Western Allies to get her when she reached Kiel. Certainly Harris intimated as such to Collins when the latter told him that the Russians had sent a message about this latest convoy. The big battlecruiser, as the Russians called *Dresden*, was guarding the ships. Estimated date of arrival in Kiel – 9th April.

'Alright' Harris snarled 'we'll get her then. Two for the price of one as *Scheer*'s already there undergoing repairs. We'll do for them both, but I have still to keep up the pressure on the retreating Nazis on our Western Front.' With that, Harris slammed the 'phone down. Every time Collins contacted him about *Dresden*, it hit a raw nerve with him. What was it about that bloody battlecruiser, anyway? War'll end soon. She can't do that much more damage, can she?

Even from a mile offshore where the battlecruiser dropped anchor, Kiel looked a shattered wreck of a town after the night raid by Harris's heavy four-engined bombers. Smoke poured into the dawn sky of that morning from the shattered docks,

Prudently Reitz halted the convoy, which had reached Kiel a day later than anticipated, just before midnight off the port when messages from the naval headquarters warned him of the approach of enemy aircraft. The convoy split into various sections and dispersed to other ports on the northern German coast between Swinemunde and Kiel although nearly half of the ships were still with

Dresden awaiting to enter Kiel. Now that the dawn revealed the burning city, Reitz realised that his move to stay off-shore had been a wise one. What ships there were in Kiel all looked to have been sunk or utterly wrecked at their moorings.

Even Germany's most successful panzerschiffe *Admiral Scheer* succumbed to the bombs for she'd turned turtle and her upper works were now in the silt of the dock basin where she'd been moored.

Whilst the pall of smoke partly covered *Dresden*'s convoy, new Allied aircraft were seen, high above Kiel. Reconnaissance planes. No doubt taking photographs of the previous night's raid. As soon as they circled away back to the West, Reitz gave orders for the battlecruiser's main launch to be lowered on its falls so that he could go in to assess the viability of the berthing of the convoy as well as his own ship.

Even he was shocked at the destruction as the launch threaded its way into the main part of the port. Utter devastation in both the naval and merchant ship dockyards. Two shattered destroyers lay on their sides wedged against a dock wall. Dockside cranes crazily toppled over into the basins. Buildings all around reduced to a few shattered walls and heaps of rubble. Smoke. Dust. The smell of death. It was a wonder if anyone ashore was still alive. They found some stone steps and hastily made fast to a broken iron strut. Reitz leaped onto the steps followed by four well-armed members of his crew. Then with midshipman Feld in charge of the launch, he ordered him to keep the launch in mid-harbour and to 'get the hell out of it for *Dresden* should a daylight raid occur – or that the Nazis get too inquisitive.' Then, at a run, and with a drawn pistol, Reitz led his four sailors to the Naval Headquarters. No-one was on surface guard and the door to the bunker opened as Reitz pushed at it. He motioned for his men to keep guard at the entrance corridor. At the next set of doors stood two armed sailors who demanded for his pass. He showed it to them and they saluted. 'Of course, Admiral Reitz, I think that you're expected' one of them stuttered rather nervously. Then through two heavy doors and into the main control area. Straight into Elle's arms.

'Darling, thank God, you've come back ' she murmured as he hugged her.

'You too. Now look, hurry. Where's Rogge?'

'In there. I think he was hoping that you'd get back. Just like myself. Last night was sheer bloody murder.' After the briefest of knocks, Reitz entered to see the former commerce raider captain look up, eyes dull with fatigue. He looked up at Reitz as if he'd seen a ghost.

'By heck, George, you've made it! How? We thought that you'd been sunk. Your wireless made no reply to our messages!'

'Bernhard. Good to see you. We kept wireless silence once we heard that Kiel was under attack. The convoy's safe – still in the roads. Signal *Dresden* if you think that it's alright for the ships to come in and disembark.'

'Was it a bad passage?'

'No, the Russians held off. A minor submarine threat the first day out but two of the escorts scared it off. The worst bit seems to be here. As if the Allies thought that the convoy was already in Kiel and not at sea.'

'Aye, you did well to keep them out of the way' grunted Rogge, beginning to regain his correctness and composure. 'I'm afraid last night was sheer hell. Even had to withdraw the surface guards. It was bang, crash, wallop for the best part of six hours. *Admiral Scheer* copped it. Fortunately very few of her crew were on board. Seems indicative of the end of Germany. Even our best ships are succumbing in the final act.'

'Ah, Bernhard but they haven't got us yet!' remarked Reitz.

'George, get away as quickly as you can. Go north. Lubeck and Swinemunde will be the next targets. No safe harbours for our ships. Only the cripples can't escape. Like *Hipper* and *Lutzow*.'

'Can I take Elle?'

'Yes. Get her out. We're not organising any more big ship movements. There's one fuel barge still intact near the north pier. Here –' he thrust a piece of paper into Reitz's hands '– I've sent my authorisation for it to meet your ship and give you all of its fuel – should be enough to get you to Southern Norway if you want to – you'll then be able to contact your tanker *Olaf*. She's not off loaded her fuel to the U-boats. Go on. Get out to her. Run for the Atlantic. The Azores. America. Where ever – but get *Dresden* away.'

'As you say, Bernhard.'

'You must. The SS and Nazis aren't too keen about you and your crew. Even in these last few weeks they'll still be capable of even worse atrocious acts. What with that madman lunatic still ranting and raving in Berlin, even with the Russians only twenty miles from the outskirts, who knows what crazy orders he'll issue at the last moment!'

'Careful, Bernhard.'

'No Nazi shit in this bunker' snapped Rogge. 'If they were I'd shoot the buggers myself. You know, George, ordinary Germans have fought fairly and squarely without ever knowing the real truth behind the filth and muck that we are now hearing about. Good God, George, it's incredibly awful! Almost beyond belief. To think that I sailed *Atlantis* for six hundred and fifty days and that you kept *Dresden* afloat these last four years for that shit to finally reveal itself – I've heard about Auschwitz, Treblinka, Belsen, Dachau and many more. Millions murdered and tortured in the name of Germany. Even those of us who have fought as fair a war, if war can be called fair, in the Kriegsmarine will be tainted with the murdering scum that has now ruined our beloved country.'

Reitz was shocked at Rogge's outburst.

'Don't dally George. Right now, SS lorries are lined up outside our own shattered area. Keep *Dresden* out at sea. Go on. Get off for Norway. If we can, we'll send you out fresh instructions. Nothing left for any of us here.'

Down in his deep underground office with a single electric bulb swinging on its flex as it shook to the distant explosions many feet above, Martin Bormann rubbed his hands. The Kiel units were waiting to pick up *Dresden*. The battlecruiser was said to be waiting to enter the port. It was reported that she was due for another hasty overhaul. Perhaps for two or three days before sailing to Copenhagen where other units of the Kriegsmarine had already fled.

'Yes, yes. We've got you, you traitorous cowards' smirked Bormann.

When Reitz left Rogge's office he'd been shocked at the man's outburst. Although he'd known Rogge for only a few weeks, he knew that the punctilious ever-correct naval officer never raised his voice in real anger yet now; the despair of the situation had broken through. He knew that he had to get Elle out. Where was she?

'Not so good, my love.' Elle's voice penetrated into the fog of Reitz's despair. He turned to see her at his shoulder. He looked at her, grim-faced. 'Darling. Come with me. Nothing left here. I'll get you on board *Dresden* and we'll sail to a safer area. Perhaps to Southern Norway. Hurry. Just go and get your necessaries and change into some trousers and seaman's boots. Two minutes. Somehow I think that even the Nazi thugs will be marching down this corridor before too long. Even the Kriegsmarine may not be safe from their madness!'

She was away just three minutes. Her long black hair was tucked up into a sailor's cap. An extra pair of socks helped to keep her boots tighter to her feet. Navy-blue trousers and a Kriegsmarine overcoat completed the outer ensemble.

It was as if she'd been prepared for the move. She had. She'd been hoping that George would appear to take her away. He had. There he was. Waiting for her.

'Come on! We must be quick. Four of my men are outside. Follow me!' They emerged out into the gloomy exterior of that smoke filled dawn with clouds of the grey smelly stuff still swirling over the shattered dock side buildings. The four sailors fell in behind as Reitz explained that a new SBA had joined them, with the permission of Vice-Admiral Rogge. None of them guessed that the matelot behind their skipper was a woman. Not that they cared. They'd heard firing whilst waiting for Reitz to re-appear. SS death squads after anyone found or suspected of looting. Desperate people risking their lives for an extra scrap of food. A quick line-up against a wall. Bloodied bodies collapsing on to the pavement. The sailors wanted to get away from the horrors of land. Back to the environment they knew best of all.

The cold grey sea somewhere out there.

Feld saw them at the steps and quickly conned his launch so that the group were soon speeding away into the murk that lay at the entrance to the dock.

As they cleared the obstacles of the sunken ships they could see the battlecruiser still at anchor although she looked clearer as the smoke from the shattered port was thinning out. Hurriedly the boat was hooked up and hoisted back to the battlecruiser's deck. Even as Reitz clambered back onto the deck he felt the engines rumble into life as the anchors came clear of the silt that had held the battlecruiser in position.

Dresden was on the move again. Away from the disaster that was Kiel. Away from Bormann's thugs.

Luck was on the side of the reconnaissance aircraft later that morning as it flew over Kiel. The smoke-clouds had cleared sufficiently to allow good photographs to be taken.

'By God we've got her, at last!' exclaimed Collins as he saw the outline of a big ship with her upturned hull lying in the main naval basin of the port.

'Ah hmm!' An aide coughed nervously. 'That's not the – er – *Dresden*.'

'What the heck do you mean?' snapped Collins.

'Sir. That's the *Scheer*. She was reported to be there undergoing repairs. Look. She's only two propeller shafts. *Dresden* has three.'

Collins scrutinised the upturned hull. 'Damn! You're right.'

Another aide spoke up. 'Rumour has it that *Dresden*'s been seen off Swinemunde or at least has been diverted to that port. Harris has told us that he's designated 617 Squadron to blast that port. *Lutzow*'s there. So is the old battleship *Schlesien*. If *Dresden*'s there, we'll be able to bag all three.'

'Huh! We shall see. Twice we've missed her. Will it be third time lucky?'

The ship in question lay in the lee of a small island off the Danish coast. Awnings were spread over her bow and stern and four of *Dresden*'s launches towed camouflage netting fore and aft of the ship in a further attempt to disguise her outline as she swung at anchor waiting for darkness.

As darkness fell, the loudspeakers clicked into life. The ship's crew heard the familiar voice of their captain. Reitz broadcast to his crew. 'Members of the best ship of the Kriegsmarine – and I mean, the best.' Faint cheers could be heard from some parts of the ship reaching up to the bridge. Those men around their captain smiled. It was clearly evident that morale on the ship was still very high. 'Those of you who have been with me these past four long years and who have survived, God be praised, will know what I mean. Some of you have only been with the ship since our return from our overseas venture but I think, no, I'm sure, that you will already realise what a splendid ship that you have joined. I make no apologies but we have done our duty to the best of our collective ability. No member of this crew is more important to the success of this ship than his neighbour. We've all learnt to work together and that's one reason why we're still afloat despite the dangers that now beset us. You are all aware that the war is coming to an end and that the Nazi regime that has resulted in the devastation of our country will soon be brought to account by the advancing forces from the east and west.' He paused. The only sound, if any, was the rustle of the wind through the rigging and on the canvas shrouding as well as the slap of the short pitched waves as they surged against the worn plates of the battlecruiser as she strained at her anchors.

The crew was listening. Very carefully.

Reitz continued. 'Maybe from the ruins of our country, a new stronger Germany will arise, but this time to live in peace with our neighbours. Until this does happen, life will be difficult for all of us. Especially these next few weeks.' Another pause. Then the voice came over again, a bit quieter. 'I am going to take this ship northwards away from the hell that is encroaching Germany. Away from those we know and love so that we can survive and in due course of time, return to help them.' Again he paused slightly and then continued 'We sail but not to surrender. The fuel we collected from that barge in Kiel will enable us to make a high speed dash across the Skagerrak to Trondheim where the air is cleaner. Further away from the rottenness that is across our land. At Trondheim I shall make a further decision to our collective purpose. Maybe as a final threat to the Allies. As a bargaining counter. Even a run into the Atlantic. Whatever course, it will not be easy. First we shall up anchor as soon as it is dark and make that high speed dash across the Skagerrak. Away from the threat of the Allied night bombers seeking to destroy the last vestiges of the Kreigsmarine still in Germany's own harbours. We are still a fighting ship. Do your duty, all of you. God bless you all. Thank you.'

Even down in the empty sick bay Elle could hear the renewed cheering that erupted over the whole ship. Doctor Lebers and the other men broke out into spontaneous applause. She was in a curtained-off section holding Andrea's hand. George had told her of Andrea's existence and of her sense of deep shock after the tragic death of Helmut Brautsch as their launch sped away from Kiel. He'd briefly introduced Elle to Lebers before leaving to resume command of the battlecruiser. Elle shook her long dark hair out of the sailor's cap.

Andrea looked up at her and weakly smiled 'You're the captain's girl, aren't you?'

Elle nodded. 'Yes. He came back especially for me. Out of the hell that had been that air-raid. I'd stayed in the naval headquarters deep underground in a concrete bunker rather than risk going back to my flat. I knew that *Dresden* was approaching Kiel and just hoped that I'd be there when George would have come. He did, so now I'm here.'

'Was it really bad?'

'Yes. They did for the *Scheer*. If this ship had been in the dock, we wouldn't be here now, that's for sure. Bombs all over the place for the best part of six hours. Non-stop explosions. Even deep down we could hear and feel the battering that Kiel was getting. Not all the Navy's girls who left for their bed-sits came back to work. Presumably dead. It was horrible!' The words simply just swelled out of her.

Andrea smiled and patted Elle's right arm. 'You're lucky. You still have your man. All I have is a reminder –' she placed both her hands near her navel '– here it is. Our baby. Growing inside me. Helmut never knew. Doctor Lebers did. Just before I went on to the hospital ship he examined me. I just didn't have time to tell Helmut. I just didn't' but Andrea couldn't finish. She began to cry again.

It was Elle's turn to comfort her. 'We heard that *Dresden* tried to rescue the people from *Heidi*. I knew that an officer had been lost saving lives. So you see, we've both seen suffering but I'm sure that George will see us safe. Come now. Let's get to work. Give this place a real clean. For something to do!'

By the time the anchors came up, the Sick Berth was gleaming clean again.

Dresden upped her speed as she left the Danish island astern. Down in the engine room, Herzog and Luth with their well-practised team watched their charges whirring ever faster into motion, dreading the time should the engines ever fail. Now, perhaps more than ever, they needed them to function at full capacity.

Crew members on the upper deck watched the bubbling white phosphorescence of the *Dresden*'s wake stretch out in a straight line in the dark sea as the battlecruiser pushed forward into the night at a fraction over thirty knots.

Escaping from the grim fate overtaking Germany.

Overtaking the two big warships anchored off Swinemunde. 617 Squadron's Lancaster dropped their big bombs on and around the port area but without their usual accuracy. Not one of their explosive devices directly hit *Lutzow*. Near misses though damaged her underwater plates but her crew, like that of cruiser *Koln* three weeks earlier in Wilhelmshaven, were able, with careful counter-flooding, to settle the pocket-battleship in an upright position to the river bed with most of her upper works still above water and some of her guns still in a working order. Pointing in the direction of the expected Russians. Still capable of firing a last defiant barrage. Even old *Schlesien* was also aground and still capable of firing her guns as well, despite the raid.

'Shit!' Collins snarled 'can't the RAF get anything right? That's not the blasted *Dresden*. It's their bleedin' flop-wagon *Lutzow*. They can't even sink that old pre-dreadnought wreck. Look, they've still got their guns pointing eastwards. Now –' here he thumped at the table '– now, I want *Dresden*. Where the hell is she? Get me Harris. I want the whole Baltic searched from top to bloody bottom.' His aides winced. Collins really did have a bee in his bonnet about the elusive battlecruiser.

'Harris,' he snapped down the telephone 'your lot's missed again. Search for the bloody ship. Everywhere. We must know where she is. Christ, what if she comes out on to the Arctic or Atlantic lanes – how many more Allied sailors are going to die at that ship's hands if she's escaped? Search the whole bloody area from the Skaggerak southwards. Every harbour. Every inlet. Now!' and then he slammed the telephone back on to its Bakelite stand, almost breaking it in the process.

Harris grunted as he replaced his receiver. He knew he'd virtually assured Collins that his bombers would get *Dresden* but it appeared that she was an awkward target. Her captain obviously kept her well-repaired and fuelled when the rest of the Kriegsmarine's big ships were in dock awaiting non-existent fuel or desperately in need of an overhaul. Either way, like the two pocket battleships, they were sitting ducks. Wearily he contacted the reconnaissance section of both the Royal Air Force and Coastal Command bluntly telling them that it was of paramount importance that every bit of the Western Baltic and the Skagerrak as far as Southern Norway be searched. Unless *Dresden* re-appeared in the Eastern Baltic, then she was to be found. Without fail. First light they promised.

Dawn. *Dresden* was covered in camouflage in a narrow inlet in the southern coast of Norway. A deserted one. Arrow-straight she'd fled that night until just as the first hint of the new day began to creep into the eastern sky, the Norwegian coast came into sight. Horst found a three mile long inlet deep enough and isolated, into which the battlecruiser could anchor, close to a convenient overhanging cliff.

The RAF searched. Even Canadian and United States airforce aircraft searched. Sixty aircraft. Two were lost. Shot down by the one Luftwaffe Me-262 that was scrambled to investigate. But no *Dresden*. The Russian reply was equally negative. She wasn't in the Eastern Baltic. Already the Danes in Copenhagen had told Collins that three cruisers were sheltering there – a crippled one, a light cruiser and the *Prinz Eugen*. But no battlecruiser. No *Dresden*.

'Damn, damn, damn! Where the hell is she? Where?' snarled Collins. He scrutinised the whole of the Baltic and its western entrances. Where could Reitz have taken his mercurial ship? Not even anything from his Kiel contact. Not since that raid. Probably killed in that air-raid. Silly sod! 'Could be bloody anywhere' he chuntered to no-one in particular. Indeed, it was to no-one. Even his aides recognised the need to put distance between themselves and Collins when the latter was in one of his rages over *Dresden*. On the wall at the side of the map there was now a large photograph of the battlecruiser in pre-war days.

At full speed. For a warship she was graceful. Collins found himself again looking at her lines etched out in that black and white photograph. Speeding. Lithe and fast.

Then he knew the answer. Whilst 617 Squadron was blasting Swinemunde, Reitz must have taken his ship at full speed, probably bursting her guts for southern Norway. But exactly where? Hundreds of fjords. Useless for a radar search. Too many confusing echoes. But that's where she was. There. He jabbed at the area with his right forefinger.

'You there! Yes. You! And you!' he shouted. 'I've got her. She's there! I know it.'

Nervously the other naval officers drew closer.

'How sir?' ventured an elderly white-haired commander.

'Her speed – and her commander's cunning' grunted his boss. 'She's capable of over thirty knots. Full ahead. Twelve or so hours from her hiding place in Danish waters and she's there. Snug in some bloody fjord. Laughing his Nazi socks off at us!'

The elderly commander winced at the vehemence from Collins but ventured, quietly 'Sir, *Dresden* is a Canaris ship. No Nazis, so our intelligence told us, are part of her crew. In fact, that can be applied to most of their Navy's ships. Again our intelligence tells us that Canaris is under house arrest or maybe by now languishing in one of their prison cells.'

'Oh, don't be so bloody officious!' rattled Collins, irritated by the accuracy of what he knew to be true in what the commander had just said. '*Dresden*'s there. In a bloody fjord.' Then trying to get back on track he continued 'Trouble is, which one? There's hundreds of 'em. Now look here, signal Coastal Command as well as the *Bempton* to get off their bums and to go off and search. The carrier, with at least two escorts vessels, will have to detach from her Arctic convoy and when in range of Trondheim, start searching the coast. It's a pity that she's the only one currently available. Signal her to search to the north of Trondheim and to Coastal Command to search from there to as far south as Stavanger. Oh, try and contact any of our agents as well – and add to any of the pilots that if they see any Nazi bit of shit fleeing for a bit of Norwegian crumpet then they can send some bullets up their arses.' The commander blanched at the crudeness of what Collins passed off as humour.

Collins, trying to gather his thoughts, lit up a cigarette. Not his usual pipe. The navy's favourite. Player's Navy cut.

For four long years this one warship had dominated his thoughts. The war in Europe was coming to an end. Somehow he had to get the damned battlecruiser before peace came. Soon the Yanks and Russkies would be meeting in the middle of Nazi Germany. Berlin was under siege and presumably that rat, Herr mister bloody Hitler would soon be getting his come-uppence. The Allies had virtual air supremacy and on the seas, the U-boats had just about been reduced to a small nuisance threat. It was nearly over but not quite. Not whilst *Dresden* still floated. Wherever that might be. She still represented a potential threat. Collins drew his last puff of smoke and then stabbed out the butt round and round his ashtray. Savagely. Damn! The very thought that *Dresden* was still out there really narked him.

Carefully relying on Horst's superb navigational skills, Reitz took *Dresden* for three or so hours every night from one fjord to another, creeping in the darkness at low speed so as not to excite the radar screens of any possible searching aircraft, to eventually a slightly bigger than normal fjord some seven miles south of Trondheim. There, near yet another steep overhang, *Dresden* came to a halt. Above the overhang, fir trees whispered in the chilly wind whilst below them the battlecruiser's anchors splashed into the relatively calm waters of her new shelter. Two islets at the mouth of the fjord would help to deflect any radar searches. As *Dresden* passed these islets, Reitz sent out a coded message on a pre-arranged wavelength to tanker *Olaf* still moored in Trondheim's main harbour. A messenger went up to *Olaf*'s captain, Karl Rimmer. Ever since the ex-merchant skipper assigned to the tanker as her captain, Rimmer, day by day, controlled and ran his ship with the co-operation of quite a few of her original crew on the promise that not only would they be paid but if *Olaf* ever returned to Norway, then when hostilities would cease, that the ship would be handed intact back to its original owners. Intact.

Now here she was, in a Norwegian harbour. One of the crew was allowed shore-leave to contact the local Resistance group to beg them not to tell the Allies to bomb the ship as there were Norwegian nationals on board and that the tanker would return, after the hostilities ceased, to Norwegian ownership. The Resistance leader nodded his head in agreement. He'd already heard the story of Jans Leiffson and how the Germans had let him go, even though they'd caught him at his illegal radio transmitter. Not only that but Trondheim had so far never been bombed by the Allies and for them to bomb the tanker would almost inevitably lead to further civilian casualties as well.

When Rimmer received the message of *Dresden*'s arrival, preparations were made to get the big tanker under way. Shortly before midnight she slipped her lines and steamed out into the fairway. Earlier that very day, German port officials had come into his cabin with requests for his supply of fuel-oil to be allocated to the U-boats in their nearby concreted base but Rimmer refused all their requests despite their pleas that the oil could supply up to fifty or so U-boat sorties aimed at the coastal lanes around the British Isles where some successes were being scored. 'Ah, but at what cost?' Rimmer asked 'A tiddler of a coaster for two U-boats lost. It's just not worth it. You should also know that I've had a wireless message from Kiel as to my orders. Signed by Doenitz himself, as well as Vice-Admirals Thiele and Rogge. My oil is for *Dresden* should she return from her activities in the Baltic.'

An official was still in his cabin when *Dresden*'s signal came through. Rimmer, never one for pompous brass hats, smiled at the official, thrusting the signal under his face.

'Well, go and tell your boss that *Dresden*'s not very far away and if you've got any sense, you'll get what's left of our Wehrmacht round here and send them off to set up blocks on all roads leading to that fjord and also set up any spare anti-aircraft batteries to give our ship some form of protection.' With that Rimmer opened his cabin door and ushered out the seething official.

Now *Olaf* was making her way to the ship that she had succoured for now nearly four years since her capture in the Antarctic Ocean in July 1941.

A minesweeper flashed a signal – 'Follow me to *Dresden*' – and accordingly, Rimmer, keeping his eye on the little warship's faint red light shining dimly at her stern, took up position as indicated. Just under an hour later, the bulk of the battlecruiser loomed up as a slightly lighter shade of dark grey as she lay moored up in her sheltered position. *Olaf* was quickly lashed alongside the battle-cruiser and soon her welcome supply of oil helped to fill the *Dresden*'s tanks to almost a third full in the next two hours before Reitz gave the order for the refuelling to stop.

'Just as well' murmured Rimmer when he received the message 'We haven't all that much left in our own tanks.' Certainly the tanker rode higher in the water than he'd ever known.

Without ever meeting Reitz, Rimmer ordered *Olaf* to back out, turn round and again following the minesweeper, to make her way back to Trondheim.

Dawn was just breaking as the big tanker nudged alongside her recently vacated berth.

'Finish with engines.' Rimmer called up Karl Larsen, *Olaf*'s former captain. 'Here,' he said in passable Norwegian – he'd taken the trouble to learn the basics of their language – 'as I promised. We've finished with your ship. I've kept my word. I trust that you'll keep your word not to tell your pals ashore where I've been with this tanker. If they're curious tell them we've been offloading our oil into the U-boats tanks. There's going to be no more fighting from

Dresden. A message to that effect came from Reitz. What he's going to do with her I don't know. Probably stay hidden until the war ends and it will soon be ending. Maybe by the end of this month or in early May. Anyway we'll soon be leaving this ship. She's yours now and I shall be saying the same to your local town mayor.'

Rimmer then saluted Larsen and in return, the Norwegian who'd stayed on the tanker all the time since her capture, extended his hand saying 'Captain Rimmer. My thanks. We have got on well together and you've kept your promise. In return I give you my word.' The two hands met. An act of friendship of enemies whilst at war. An act of common sense and the bond of united humans. Tired of the war. Both yearning for peace.

With the departure of the tanker, crew members of *Dresden* made busy with her camouflage. Other men crossed over to the fjord's shore with saws and axes, and using only hooded lights from torches, cut down greenery from a widish area so as for it not to be discernible from any searching aircraft. With their loads they returned to their boats and when back on board *Dresden,* draped the foliage over the camouflage so that from the air the battlecruiser would like a continuation of the forest on the slopes of that overhanging rock.

When dawn came all activity ceased, although in shifts, the anti-aircraft guns were still manned whilst the rest of the crew took a meal-break or rested.

During the day, three high-flying Allied aircraft were heard and watched through the few gaps in the camouflage but the planes flew on, unaware, so it seemed, of the extra bulge in the fjord's sides. A bulge comprising the battlecruiser KM *Dresden.*

Down in the Sick Berth Andrea and Elle rested in the now clean unused area. Not one casualty was in their care. No more wounded. No-one. Just the medical staff. Reitz decided to go down to visit Elle and to continue to comfort Andrea. When he reached them, he saw them whispering gently to each other. It appeared that Elle and Andrea had found a comforting friendship with each other. Elle looked up as he came into the Berth and hushed him up 'Ssh! Herr Lebers and his staff are asleep. Come, sit by me on this bunk.'

Reitz sat down and soon tiredness came over him. Gently kissing Elle he murmured 'I'm tired, darling. We must all try to relax and get some sleep' and then he laid his head on the bunk's pillow and was soon asleep. Elle and Andrea quickly followed his example and soon all three of them were asleep. Quiet came over the Berth. Just the gentle sound of breathing. Rest, at last, for all of them. For a short time.

For nearly a fortnight the *Dresden* lay hidden. Each day crew members adjusted her camouflage and helped to man road blocks on the fjord sides with the few Wehrmacht soldiers still in the area. If there were any Norwegian agents in the vicinity, they made no attempt to contact London. To them the war was coming to an end. No point in having more destruction.

Deep down in his beleaguered bunker, Adolf Hitler shot himself. His body, and that of his wife of but a few hours, were taken up the dank steps to the outside into a badly blasted courtyard and there, with the aid of a few cans of filched petrol, were set alight. In the gathering darkness, lit by the frequent flashes of Russian shells, the rest of his henchmen made their preparations either to drown their sorrows and await the arrival of the Russians or to attempt to escape into the labyrinth of Berlin's ruined streets. Martin Bormann, determined not to give up, was making his final preparations. He'd hid his fury when the Führer announced that Grand-Admiral Karl Doenitz, now near Kiel, was to be his successor. A Navy man and one that Bormann was certain did not follow the Führer's National Socialist ideals to the full. Especially one of his ships. *Dresden.* The blasted ship had escaped his clutches. Now if he could get to Northern Germany before the war ended he might just get his hands on her. The chance was there. Very fleetingly, as dust swept down on to his desk as more Russian shells exploded above on to the already shattered Chancellory buildings, Bormann rose and left his room, the memo about *Dresden* falling unnoticed to the dust-covered floor. Climbing the steps he collected three of his faithful SS bodyguard and together all four reached the surface doorway. Dust and smoke swirled in the gloom, lit by frequent fires burning all over Berlin's broken centre. The four of them flitted across the courtyard. No-one ever saw any of them again. Alive. Dead. No-one even cared. Not then.

That same evening Reitz was sitting in his main cabin sharing a frugal meal with Walters. The telephone rang. 'Wireless office here, sir. Please come.' The message read 'Adolf Hitler has died. Fighting to the last.'

'Good riddance' was the unspoken thought from Collins as he prepared to leave his office when an aide told him the news of Hitler's end. 'Soon the sods will all surrender.' Then, deep down, he knew that the prize that he'd been chasing for so long was perhaps going to elude him after all. Perhaps one last major effort could be made to find the *Dresden* but news of her whereabouts seemed to have dried up. Perhaps the Norwegians, realising that the war was ending were not risking any last-gasp retaliation by die hard Nazi fanatics who had nothing better to do than shoot and murder their way to the bitter end rather then retreat into the fact that the 'game was up'. For them. Once and for all.

The sketchy information that he'd received about the tanker in Trondheim was that she was Norwegian. Riding high. Virtually empty of fuel. She'd probably been supplying the U-boats. Or the ancient wreck of a vulnerable old battleship. What was her name? Ah, yes! *Rugen.* A battered old survivor probably acting as the tanker's guard warship.

The elderly commander came up to him 'Sir, At last! A message from an agent with access to the whereabouts of Kreigsmarine warships – "Large warship recently brought into the Kiel naval docks. Twin-gun turrets. Nazis trying to disguise her. Suspect *Dresden.* Thought to be damaged."'

Damaged? That was real news. Hurriedly Collins contacted Harris with the news. The Air Chief Marshall, almost in desperation, said that he would send bombers over to Kiel and 'sink whatever the Nazi's have still afloat.' Raids on 3rd and 5th May. Before the Nazis drag themselves to properly surrender.

Collins knew of the warships moored in Copenhagen. But what if this 'damaged ship' wasn't Reitz's elusive ship?

What if *Dresden* was hiding in a Norwegian fjord that *Bempton*'s aircraft or Coastal Command hadn't yet found? Waiting for a last dash of glory against an Arctic convoy. One was assembling off Reykjavik right at this moment. Thinly protected. Should he give it a covering force? Not much hope of a modern one. All the 'KG5's' were scheduled for Far Eastern waters.

Then he saw the name of his old command. Still in Scapa Flow. Yes, that was it! He'd get up to Scapa and order her out to sea. Join up with *Bempton* and her escort screen of two light cruisers and four destroyers. They'd be able to cruise off the Trondheim waters. Just in case Reitz's ship wherever she was aiming for that Arctic convoy. A U-boat had already wirelessed the convoy's position before being eliminated. Must be something that the Nazis were still planning.

Well, thought Collins, with my old command and *Bempton*, I'll be able to form the Royal Navy's last major hunting group of the war. 'Yes' thought Collins inspired by his impulsive thinking 'This could be my last chance to finally try and nail the *Dresden*.' Hurriedly he gave out his orders. Aeroplane from Croydon airport to fly him to Kirkwall in the Shetlands and then either by MTB or a flying-boat to the Scapa Flow anchorage.

As he watched London recede below him, Collins allowed his mind to go over the history of his old flagship, the *Monck*. It would be good to tread her decks again. A sister ship to *Rodney* and *Nelson* she'd experienced a relative quiet war since the start of the *Bismarck* episode. Somehow she'd always just missed the real action. A serious fault with her main guns had caused her to abort her efforts at sailing in the hunt for the big German battleship. Later in the war she'd covered the Arctic convoy prior to the one searched for by *Scharnhorst*, which as Collins well knew was sunk by the *Duke of York* and other ships.

Now he could get *Monck* out at sea, join up with the *Bempton* off Norway and hope that Reitz would come out with guns blazing. A final dash for even more pyrrhic glory. A fighting end. Surely, given his record, he wouldn't allow his ship to tamely surrender.

Would he?

But he had to find *Dresden* before anything else could materialise.

Cheering broke out all over *Dresden* when the news of Hitler's death was broadcast over the loud speakers. Down in the Sick Berth Elle hugged Andrea 'Soon we'll be able to be free of this war.'

Andrea, coming back into reality, felt a sudden relief come over her. 'Yes' she whispered back 'My baby will be safe.'

The loudspeakers clicked into life again. It was Hiltzern's voice. 'Attention all crew! The captain will now speak to you all.' A hush went over the whole vessel, still nestling under her makeshift camouflage.

'Ladies and my loyal crew.' An acknowledgement from Reitz of the esteem that he held obviously for Elle as well as Andrea.

'The war will soon be over. This ship will undertake one more cruise. We are going to sail this evening. We will be joined by our compatriots of the old battleship *Rugen*. Our destination will be Scapa Flow where we shall surrender our ships. Intact.' Then Reitz paused. In a lower tone he continued. 'Should any member of the crew wish to be transferred to Trondheim rather than risk this last admittedly still dangerous voyage, then he may do so without any feeling of blame or guilt, by transferring to the minesweeper currently alongside us on our port side.' Another pause. 'Thankyou to you all for being my loyal crew. That is all for now.'

Columns of dirty brown smoke floated upwards out of the tall ungainly funnels of *Rugen* as she lay alongside Trondheim's quayside. In an odd sort of way the old battleship had come to be almost adopted by the Norwegians. Over the last few years her antiquated outlines were usually seen sailing up and down their coast protecting the various convoys of slow merchantmen of which she'd been the big-gun escort. From Narvik down to Trondheim and Stavanger. Then back up again. Time after time. She'd been the replacement for the patrol cruiser *Bremse* which the Germans had lost four years earlier when *Brems*e tackled two British cruisers as they'd swept in to attack her small convoy of three merchantmen. *Bremse* was sunk with guns firing. The merchantmen all escaped to the shelter of a nearby fjord.

Whilst in harbour, Otto Franke's crew always behaved impeccably with their Norwegian hosts. The story about the incident with Jans the shepherd from Altenfjord filtered down the coast and as to how Franke's sailors released the shepherd instead of shooting him.

So the Trondheim locals watched his old ship with interest. Something was afoot. The old warship was preparing to leave. Even coal had been loaded into the ship's bunkers. Maybe she was returning to Germany.

'Cast off' shouted Franke. 'Engines. Slow astern!' Slowly *Rugen* backed away. As she churned past *Olaf*, Franke could see members of the tanker's crew waving their farewells knowing that they would soon be fully handing their ship back to her Norwegian owners. Franke gazed ahead of him as *Rugen* went about in the main fairway. He knew that if Allied aircraft or warships were sighted and that they'd fail to see his white flag of surrender, then his beloved old veteran would stand no chance under any determined assault. Yet he felt an inner sense of pride when a week earlier a launch with Horst on board came alongside and the ex-submarine captain delivered Reitz's request for *Rugen* to accompany *Dresden* on a possible voyage to Scapa. Just six hours earlier the message had come, via *Olaf*'s wireless officer, that *Dresden* would rendezvous with his old ship outside Trondheim.

So she waddled off, smoke pouring out of her funnels as with both her coal and oil-fired boilers linking up, Franke endeavoured to attain fifteen knots, the fastest he felt that *Rugen*'s ancient engines could safely reach. The smoke lay heavily over the still waters of Trondheim's sheltered fjord waters before eventually dispersing. As she neared the open sea, her old-fashioned ram bows began to dip into the increasing swell and as they did so, the seas broke over onto her forecastle to wash up to her two big guns, the spray then whipping into the faces of the men on her open bridge. Kapitan Franke smiled. His old warhorse was tasting the open sea again. Probably at the start of her final voyage. He'd have to wait to see what Vice-Admiral Reitz fully intended. It was a proud moment to be associated with Reitz's ship.

'*Dresden* in sight, sir!' came a lookout's shout. 'Port-side. Two eighty degrees.'

Franke watched as the powerful shape of Reitz's warship came into view, the white moustache at her bows diminishing as she slowed to match old *Rugen*'s efforts. A light flashed from *Dresden*'s bridge – 'Welcome old friend. Follow us. Further instructions to be sent later.'

Someone else also saw the light signal but being unable to read Morse, or understand German, as well as the signals being too far away to be discernible, Gef Hornsen could only surmise that for a reason best known to themselves, two big German warships were meeting up for an unknown destination. Even he had felt some admiration for the *Rugen* and her old man of a captain. For nearly three and a half years he'd watched the old battleship sailing in and out of Trondheim, up and down the coast, as escort to a variety of merchant ships, not just supplying the enemy garrisons but also carrying trade for Norwegian concerns.

Somehow he sensed that this time it was different. *Rugen* wasn't hugging the coastline. What ship she met out there, Hornsen could but guess. Jerry didn't have any really big battleships left since the

RAF had blasted out the *Tirpitz*. The one he'd seen on the horizon looked powerful enough but why did it meet up with the *Rugen*? Perhaps some Nazi Admiral had ordered them out on a last suicide mission. So what? Let them go. He might tell London but then he might not. Why risk a Gestapo search team, even at this stage of the war, getting a fix on his wireless and coming along to blast him and the wireless to bits. Not the same as when Jans Leiffson had been told to look after his sheep by two of the sailors from that old bit of scrap-iron. He'd also heard the story. No, it wasn't worth the risk. The Allies would soon find those two ships – and send those glory-boys to the seabed. Maybe he'd send a vague message. Say in twelve hours time.

Not one crew member on *Dresden* took up the offer to transfer to the minesweeper. Instead, tough guy Otto Schenke and two of his rough pals clambered up to the bridge and requested to have a word with Reitz. Schenke saluted his captain as smartly as he could and in his gravelly voice he growled out 'Herr Kapitan! We is *Dresden* men and we is proud of 'er. If yer thinks that any of us is leavin' this ship then you 'as anuvver think comin'. We an't bin wiv yer fer us to 'ave a last fart with U-boat men.' As always, Reitz winced at hearing the tough man's way of speaking. Always in a rough accent. Always hopelessly with incorrect grammar. But he also knew that the man represented all that was good and loyal with the lower deck for whom he was chief spokesman. Tough and reliable. Competent to a very high degree. Extremely loyal. Just as Schenke was now uttering. Smiling broadly, Reitz extended his right hand and pressed it into Schenke's 'Otto Schenke. Ever since I first met you I knew that you were a rough, loyal diamond. You still are. You probably always will be. But not to your wife who I hear is making a good recovery. I know that you are gentle to her. Even to this ship's cats. But rough to everyone who crosses your path. I am proud of you, your friends here and to all the crew you represent.' Stepping back he saluted all three men and dismissed them. He knew that the big ugly petty officer figured frequently to the forefront of much of the dangerous action concerning the ship. Time after time.

Reitz pondered over Schenke's efforts as he recalled that last message from the shore authorities – 'Inform Otto Schenke that his wife, Letitia, is well on the way to a full recovery.' It had come from the Matron of that nursing home via Kiel's naval authorities.

Reitz could see Schenke in Brautsch's boat boarding the blazing *Arades*, helping to rescue Andrea from those flames. He knew that the big man was always the first in the rescue parties to drag out fellow shipmates when *Dresden* had been torpedoed. Dazed, shocked shipmates feeling his huge paws pulling them to safety. He'd watched him on the scrambling nets heaving Horst's U-boat men on to *Dresden*'s decks. Charging into the flames to drag out burning crew members after the Seafire had smashed on to the ship. His last dangerous mission had been to pull up the shaken survivors from the sinking *Heidi* up the ice-grimed nets as they'd struggled out of the cold Baltic waters. The despair on his face as he'd learned of the failure to rescue Helmut Brautsch was clear to everyone near him.

Reitz also knew that Schenke was protective to the weaker members of his ship. No-one bullied when Schenke was around or else they were soon clutching at a bloodied nose or swelling black eye. Far too often the big man's version of law-making clashed with the general rule of discipline which Reitz had been forced to dispense to the broken-nosed sailor. Demoted. Promoted. Demoted. Promoted. Always the same. Bash up someone who couldn't defend themselves and they'd feel Otto's big fist. Yet no-one was gentler to the ship's cats who knew that his bunk was the best to sleep on when Otto was there. Yes, he'd seen the big man with the two cats curled up. One on his shoulder. The other by his chest. Purring softly as their guardian snored.

Schenke in return saluted his captain, turned and clattered his way down the steps. Back to his torpedo tubes. And cats.

All that had taken place six hours previously. Now *Dresden* was back in her natural element. The wave-tossed open sea. Just before reaching it, three Seafires flew over the entrance of her hiding-place but passed on down the coast showing no signs of having seen the emerging battlecruiser. Now as dusk crept over the heaving restless sea, Reitz could make out the rolling dark shape of the old pre-dreadnought as the *Rugen* gamely took station at, what was to her an almost engine-bursting top speed of fifteen knots. Even in the growing dark, Reitz could see the faint glow at the top of *Rugen*'s spindly trio of funnels and then the dark smudge of coal smoke whipping flat and wide over the port flanks as the brisk northerly wind swirled the smoke into dispersed shreds of soot.

The tannoy above Reitz's head crackled into life. 'Captain. Wireless room. We have an urgent message.' Dashing as quickly as he could from his sea-cabin to the wireless room, he there read the flimsy giving the news. 'From Doenitz. C-in-C Kriegsmarine.

To all U-boats and surface units. All U-boats to surface and surrender. If near Allied waters sail to nearest port.'

The war was obviously very close to an end. All their sacrifices. And for what? This. Surrender. No more killing. The chance for peace. After nearly six long weary years.

'This time boys let me tell the crew. Not your bush telegraph!' warned Reitz and there was no twinkle in his eyes. Only a deep sadness. He knew that it wasn't at all unexpected, which was why both *Dresden* and *Rugen* were surging steadily on their course. Southwest. Towards Scapa Flow. Not Reykjavik.

An hour before Doenitz's broadcast, Collins in his admiral's quarters on the *Monck* received a message from Naval Headquarters that had originated from Trondheim – 'Two German warships leaving Trondheim. H.' That was all. Nothing else. He'd pondered it. Two? What size? Must be big enough for the agent to risk sending it. Even at this nervy time. Collins shuddered. He guessed at the risk the brave Norwegians were always at when wirelessing. End of the war or not, Gestapo scum were just that. Scum. Always scum. Trigger and torture-happy.

Again, two? What if one of them was *Dresden*? Last suicide dash for an Arctic convoy? Big ships? Only small patrol craft and U-boats. Wait. He had it. Jerry's old pre-dreadnought heap of scrap-iron. What was her name? *Rugen.* That was it. Could it be that she was linking up with *Dresden*? Surely not. A racehorse with a three-funnelled cripple? No, they weren't going for an Arctic convoy. Be scuttling back to Germany. Or Copenhagen. Now, wait a minute. Can't be either or why would Reitz have risked *Dresden* to escape, so he presumed, to Norway. Oh hell, damnation upon damnation! What the heck was Reitz up to? If it was Reitz and his bloody ship! Collins' temper was coming up to boil. Careful now. T'old doctor's going to be having a fit if my heart gives a funny turn. But the thought of *Dresden* just wouldn't go away. It had been part of him for the last four years. Day after day. Week after week. Year in. Year out.

A knock came to his cabin door. Captain Reynolds entered and saluted Collins. Inwardly the captain had cursed when the Sunderland flying-boat landed near his venerable battleship and out of it had come this fire-and-brimstone Admiral, wanting to sweep the seas for that blasted bleedin' Jerry raider, the battlecruiser *Dresden.* How the hell could his slow unwieldy tub catch the speedier German raider? Yet this bloody Admiral snorted when he ordered him to up-anchor and hare off on a wild-goose chase. Thank goodness his chief in the engine-room contacted him with the news that a new coupling-rod needed to be fitted to replace one that had just fractured. Had brains that one!

Why risk dear old *Monck* when the war was all but over. No-one relished the thought of her big sixteen-inch guns firing broadsides. Probably shake the old tub to pieces. Reynolds gazed up at the oil-painting of the seventeenth century admiral whose name the ship bore. In charge of Charles II's fleet he'd fought a raiding Dutch fleet under Van Tromp to a standstill, probably saving England from some sort of invasion. Well, this old *Monck* wasn't going to perform any heroics, never mind what her namesake had done! The war was ending. The German fleet wasn't the enemy. It was the clock. It just wasn't ticking fast enough.

Reynolds handed Collins the message from the wireless room giving the contents of the announcement from Doenitz. The Admiral snorted on reading the signal. Gone were his hopes, however faint, for a final gun-for-gun confrontation with Reitz's battlecruiser. Perhaps they'd soon hear of her return to Trondheim. Even *Bempton*'s aircraft, quite close to that port, had failed to find the elusive German raider. Then suddenly Collins slumped in his chair. The end was near. He'd not been able to catch her. Somehow Reitz had eluded him. Four long years. Now this. The bleedin' Jerry ships had been told, no, ordered by their Nazi boss to surrender. Reynolds watched the Admiral. The glaze seemed to only slowly lift. Perhaps he was going to explain. Reynolds waited. It was obvious that the gold-braided man in his chair desperately wanted to catch the *Dresden*. But why him? Then Collins looked up. How many times had he tried to explain *Dresden*'s place in his thinking and work to people who'd asked? He sighed and began, starting with the time he'd first had to deal with the elusive German warship when he'd last been on board this battleship.

Finally he said 'The last we heard of her, but a few days ago, was that she was probably in southern Norway, in range of a tanker called *Olaf* which we now know to have been captured by *Dresden*. Oddly enough next to the *Olaf* in Trondheim was another old survivor of this whole saga. Their oldest commissioned ship, an old pre-dreadnought called the *Rugen*. Have you heard of her?

Reynolds nodded. 'Aye. She once even fired her guns at a friend of mine when his ship tried to get at the convoy the old ship was escorting. It's quite an achievement for Jerry to still have her afloat and in working order.'

Collins nodded. 'Yes. Both of them. Out at sea. Are they going for Copenhagen and risking the last of our air strikes over the Skagerrak? If not, where are they? Surely not for an Arctic convoy. *Rugen*'s too slow.'

Reynolds interrupted 'I know where they are.' He sounded very calm, puffing on his pipe. Pointing with his right index finger to the chart on a nearby table he continued 'Here, sir.'

'What! Approaching Scapa Flow?'

'Aye. To surrender if I'm not mistaken. Trying to imitate the surrender of the Kaiser's fleet at the end of the Great War. Their oldest capital ship with their best modern ship. Linked together. Surrendering this time of their own choosing. With a sense of history and possibly even honour.'

'Hmm!' grunted Collins too taken aback at what he guessed to be the truth.

'Sir. May I suggest we ask Coastal Command to mount a search for them, say on a one hundred mile sweep east of here? We make preparations to sail even at reduced speed and when we get the news that Jerry's been sighted, then off we go to receive

'My God mister' growled Collins. 'Fancy being an Admiral, eh?' Then he chuckled at one of his gruff jokes. Maybe his last of the war.

Grey. A colour so often associated with the North Sea. Not sparkling blue with the sun shining brilliantly over it causing the white wavelets to glisten in its welcoming rays. There was no glisten about the heaving stomach-lurching dawn waters where the armed trawler *Northern Sapphire* plunged sickeningly into each short-pitched roller some forty miles to the east of Scapa Flow. Every time her bow smashed into the next oncoming wave, sea spray hissed over her bows drenching her somewhat wet and cold forward gun-crew manning a three-inch (7.5cm) gun. Still standing a war-watch on the specific orders of the trawler's young skipper, Lieutenant Edward Beach, DSO, RNVR. A chemistry graduate before the war, Beach now sipped at a mug of semi-hot over-sweet tea in the trawler's tiny wheelhouse whilst doing his best to keep his balance and also to search the waters around him for any possible surrendering Nazi U-boat. Some of these submarines may still be manned by die-hard fanatics determined to still fight for their now deceased Führer. Hence the gun-crew being in position. So as to deter them from any such crazy notions of a last bitter confrontation.

Beach's war had been unpleasant. After joining up soon after hostilities broke out, he quickly went through the Navy's officer training and was then assigned as First Mate to a motor gun boat with the rank of midshipman.

One foggy day when out on patrol in the English Channel, an E-boat loomed out of a swirling fog bank and machine-gunned his craft before vanishing out of sight. The gun-boat, catching fire, began to sink. With his skipper dead, Beach yelled at the crew to jump clear and then dashed down below to help pull the wounded out on to the deck. Then, with his jacket on fire and being the last to leave the stricken vessel, he also jumped overboard as the gun-boat sank beneath him. Luckily another boat in their patrol group heard the E-boat's firing and in the grey shrouds of the fog saw the glow of the burning gun-boat. It closed up on the few survivors and managed to rescue thirteen of Beach's men before, finally, Beach himself. Due to the testimony of his crew, Beach was eventually awarded the Distinguished Service Order. The badly-scarred midshipman then spent a long time in hospital and in after-care recuperating from his horrific ordeal. When fit he took on a shore placement, but soon after D-Day he was promoted to Sub-Lieutenant and posted to one of the Navy's newest motor-torpedo boats in the Harwich Force.

Further promotion to Lieutenant, he found himself in command of *Northern Sapphire*, escorting East Coast convoys before moving up to Scapa as part of the anchorage's anti-submarine patrol. The Admiralty, in their wisdom, thought that some suicidally-minded U-boat skipper might try, as a last valiant gesture to end the war as it had started by emulating U-47's efforts at torpedoing the old *Royal*

Oak. Almost, but not quite as old, another battleship was there providing a tempting target. *Monck.* She'd been at Scapa since January. So Beach and his little trawler beat their way into the pitching seas of that early dawn of May 8th.

Standing next to his skipper, a young nineteen year old peered through his binoculars through the open side window on the starboard side of the pitching trawler's bridge. 'Ah be gorra sir but yon thur is two bluidy big sheeps bearin' a dooan an 'oos!'

Beach winced, doing his best to understand the barely comprehensible Scottish accent of Robert McTaggart, the boy whose voice had just penetrated into his private thoughts.

He followed the boy's arm. 'Thur, sir, outa' thur!'

There was no mistake. Two large grey warships were indeed coming ever closer to the little trawler. Instinctively Beach yelled.

'Actions Stations. Warships off our starboard quarter. Man all guns!'

McTaggart murmured 'Begorrah sirr. Them's are Jerries.' Beach felt weak at the knees. 'Jerries? Oh, shit! Do you think that they know that they are supposed to have surrendered?' He knew, as the rest of his crew knew, that just one big shell from those enemy warships could blast *Northern Sapphire* to smithereens. As he watched them, he noticed that the big guns of the leading warship were pointing fore and aft in the rest position. As the two big ships drew closer, a light signal flashed out from the nearest one that Beach guessed to be at least a heavy cruiser. He racked his brains to work out which one. Probably the *Prinz Eugen* or the *Hipper.* The other vessel was really old. Three smoke-shrouded funnels. An ungainly heavy mast. One big turret only in her bows. Vaguely in the recesses of his mind from reading a dusty old book about ships in the last war he had a vision of an old pre-dreadnought battleship. Surely this second warship wasn't one, was it?

The flickering message, carefully and slowly in English, spelt out – 'We are Kriegsmarine ships. *Dresden* and *Rugen.* Please come alongside me and accept our surrender. We request an officer to guide us to Scapa Flow. What ship is yours?'

Both the German ships were slowing down as they bore down on the armed trawler. Beach had heard of *Dresden.* Principle enemy surface raider, Scourge of the Allied war effort at sea. Yet here she was, surrendering to his little trawler.

He said to Chief Petty Officer Irons who'd just entered the wheelhouse. 'Reply to them – "We are HMS *Northern Sapphire.* Prepare your port-side to receive our captain."' Then to Irons he continued 'Take charge Chief. I'll be boarding that ship and I'll take Leading Seaman Burtoft with me. Look after Mister McTaggart for me whilst I'm away.'

'Aye, aye, sir. I'll look after t'lad.'

Burtoft was relieved to get away from his position with the three-incher. Always wet there. Even in a quiet period he and his gun crew always seemed to be cleaning and polishing it. No-one could ever remember having been asked to actually fire the thing! Now for him it would be quite a change to get on board a real ship. One with lots of guns. Even if it was an enemy one!

Beach conned *Northern Sapphire* into the lee of the now barely moving *Dresden.* A scrambling net was already in position.

'Take over now, Irons. I'm going aboard. Come on, Beach, and bring your trusty rifle with you!'

The two men grabbed at the net as Irons neatly placed the trawler's sides adjacent to it. Huge hands from Schenke and one of his pals hoisted them on to the net and before they realised it, helped them quickly up on to the deck of the gently heaving German ship. So much smoother than the tossing corkscrew motion of *Northern Sapphire.* As they looked down, the little trawler was already putting on speed to draw ahead of the almost motionless *Dresden.*

Schenke sketchily saluted Beach and Burtoft and then motioned them to follow him to the bridge. To the two Englishmen it seemed to take an age to clamber up the numerous steps but then, quite suddenly, they saw the big German sailor in front of them smash his boots together and salute an officer. Beach looked across to Reitz and to his astonishment the German officer, in a very smart uniform with lots and lots of gold on it, saluted him with a proper decent naval one. None of your 'up your right arm as stiff as a poker' Nazi load of bollocks. Still in a daze, Beach did his best to fashion a salute back to him, although he winced with pain as he did so. His wounds were hurting. Must be all that climbing.

Then he heard the German speaking in excellent English 'My name is Vice-Admiral George Reitz.' Beach gasped. No wonder the Jerry wore so much gold. A bleedin' Admiral. Must be the same in both navies, all gold, spit an' bleedin' polish. Wonder if he'd ever dirtied his hands. Then he heard Reitz continuing 'I am captain of this warship, the *Dresden* and have been so for the last four years. I now surrender this ship to you but as I do, I would like to know your name.'

Beach gasped again. He was a captain as well as being a bleedin' Admiral. Blimey, this was the bloke who'd been skipper of this tub whilst she was shooting up all our ships. Somehow he straightened himself and as authoritatively as he could, he answered 'Lieutenant Edward Beach. RNVR Captain of the armed trawler *Northern Sapphire*.' It sounded so weak. Then pointing to Burtoft, he added 'And this is Leading Seaman Nathan Burtoft in charge of our main gun.' It sounded ever so ridiculous having to explain himself to this high trumped-up load of Nazi tripe. Probably still wishing that he was hoping to end his war firing all his big guns in some last mad Nazi-inspired act of sea-going lunacy! Reitz spoke again, guessing at the young officer's obvious look of amazement on his face. 'I know of the Royal Naval Volunteer Reserve. To you goes the honour of receiving my surrender and as a token of it, I give you my pistol.' Then Reitz removed a Luger from a side holster and handed it to Beach, smiling as he did so 'Go on, take it. Keep it as a souvenir.'

Beach looked into the German's eyes. They seemed sad. It must be painful for him with all that gold braid on him to have to hand over his beloved pistol. He heard Reitz again 'Lieutenant Beach. I am glad that we didn't meet earlier on. I fear that even Seaman Burtoft's gun couldn't have done us much damage! You see, you may be surprised to learn that I have never agreed with unnecessary killing. We have fought this ship to the best of our Navy's traditions but not for the evils of Nazi crimes. It would have been like a crime to have sunk your little trawler had you tried to fight, which I am sure that you would have done. As it is, my ship has now finished her role as a fighting unit of the Kriegsmarine. She is now under your command.'

Beach couldn't take it all in. From a small, almost insignificant, Royal Navy warship. Now to this. In temporary command, at least, of Jerry's most feared surface raider. All that he'd read about her whilst in hospital. True or exaggerated. What was it? She'd virtually destroyed an Allied convoy somewhere off Africa. Only recently she'd re-appeared to rattle away at a surprised convoy going to Russia. Now here he was. In command of it. Even if only temporarily.

Weakly he said 'Thankyou sir. Your English is very good. My superiors will enjoy talking to you.'

'Your superiors?' queried Reitz.

'Yes, the admiral on board the old *Monck*. Flew up from his London headquarters about two days ago. Word is that he's been after your ship for the last four years. One of the old battleship's junior officers told me about it just before we left to go out on patrol. Told me to steam away as fast as we could if we saw your ship. Now I'm here. Ugh!' Reitz thought that Beach's grimace was a sort of expression of surprise that the young lieutenant was actually on board *Dresden* when it really ought to have been the admiral from London. He didn't realise that Beach was reacting from a nasty twinge as a result of his still badly scarred back.

'Mmm' murmured Reitz. 'When we sail into Scapa I shall be delighted to make your Admiral's acquaintance. As for my English, I did spend some time in your country in the years before this war started.' Looking at the two Royal Navy representatives, he tut-tutted 'Oh dear, how remiss of me! Here I am acting as a gracious host but yet not inviting you, as victors, to share some refreshments with me in my sea-cabin just aft of where we are standing. Come. My steward will look after our needs. He understands English and can even speak it fairly well – I've helped him and others on this ship to learn English. We had quite long periods when we weren't fighting and to help pass the time, we set up educational classes. We had to do something positive during those long years when we were away from our country. Ah ha! I rattle on too much – sometimes a fault of mine – so – let's go and see what Herr Walters has on offer.' Reitz smiled. There was even a twinkle back in his eyes.

Just as they were about to leave the bridge, a shout came up from one of the lookouts. 'Aircraft astern off the port quarter!' A lumbering Sunderland came into view. Reitz did his best to translate what his men were saying.

'It's signalling' Horst commented. 'Telling us to heave to and surrender.'

Reitz replied 'Tell them that we have already surrendered to HM Armed Trawler *Northern Sapphire* with Lieutenant Beach on board who is directing us towards Scapa Flow. Compliments from KM ships *Dresden* and *Rugen*.'

The slow flying-boat came even nearer, circling the three ships. Reitz commented to Beach as they followed the aircraft with their eyes 'No doubt taking good propaganda film of us – something like 'Mighty German battle-fleet surrenders to puny armed trawler' – should make good newsreel footage for British, French and American cinemas!'

Slowly the Sunderland lumbered off into the distance and when it had disappeared, Reitz turned to Beach 'Come on, our beer and beef awaits us.'

Walters, in a very clean white steward's uniform, bowed courteously to Beach and Burtoft. 'Vot is your pleasure, mein gentlemen? Beer? Whisky? Sherry? Gin?' Beach chose a gin, Burtoft a beer. The beef sandwiches were delicious. Courtesy of *Olaf*, from a Norwegian butcher who'd supplied Rimmer whilst the tanker had been in Trondheim. A butcher grateful to be re-united with his sea-faring brother. An engineer's assistant on *Olaf*.

Somewhat speechless, Beach smiled back at Reitz who held up his whisky 'Gentlemen. I toast you both – to the Allied victory and to peace between our two countries. Come, how often have you been able to have a drink with an enemy Admiral?'

Burtoft raised his beer. 'Cor, this would be summat' to tell his mates. Scoffin' wi' officers!!'

Beach cut into his thoughts of such superior associations. 'Admiral Reitz. Your war may be over but we aren't at peace yet. We've the Japs to deal with and then, you watch it, the bleedin' Russians will be next. Smacking down Adolf was only part of their dream. Trouble is they'll borrow 'is ideas. You know. Total domination for the Commies. Nothing else.' Suddenly the young officer gasped again, dropping his glass to the floor as quite involuntarily, with both hands, he clasped at his back 'Damn, oh damn shit' he winced out as he looked at the blood that was seeping through his shirt and on to his hands. He tried to take his jacket off but Reitz stepped forward 'Walters. Call the Sick Bay. Quick! This officer is hurt.'

Savagely Beach turned round, lifting his shirt clear of his trousers. Reitz gasped as he saw the bleeding scarred skin. 'Good grief man! How come?'

'One of your bloody E-boats. Shot up my boat when we were on patrol in the Channel. Three or so years ago. It's never mended proper like. Must have caught it climbing up your scrambling net. My own bloody fault I suppose!'

A knock came on the cabin door. Sick Berth attendant Werthe entered, with Ruddenz carrying a stretcher.

'I can walk captain' snapped Beach, wincing with pain.

'Ah, but these two gentlemen are well versed with stretcher work. They'll have you in the ship's hospital in no time at all. Two ticks, I think, is your English expression. Please, let them take you!'

Beach soon found himself strapped on to the stretcher and as quickly, but also as carefully as they could, was carried off down the various steps and what to him, was a virtual labyrinth of narrow steel-lined passage ways until he reached the Sick Berth where Andrea and Elle, both in starched white nursing apparel waited for him.

'Women? Two of you? On this tub?' he weakly croaked as he was lifted on to a bed.

'Yes, Lieutenant. My name is Doctor Andrea Brautsch and this is Fraulein Elle Chemnitz.'

'But, but on this warship?'

'Hush. It's a very long story. By the way, I am English. My husband was an officer on this ship but lost his life when he rescued me and others on a burning hospital ship in the Baltic. Now, please, so I have been told, your back is the problem. Please turn over and I'll take a look.'

Beach obediently turned over. He heard Elle gasp as she looked down at him 'Not very pretty is it?' he snapped.

'Ssh!' hushed Andrea. 'Fraulein Chemnitz doesn't understand English. She's the captain's fiancée and we rescued her from the clutches of the Nazis only a few weeks ago. She has been a great help in comforting me over my widowhood. Now, let's see. Badly burnt? Some attempts at plastic surgery? Hmmm! They didn't do too good a job did they? I'm surprised that you went back to active service. You need careful attention before you go back to see the Captain. Yes, though he's a Vice-Admiral everyone here still call him as captain. Ah, here he is now!' she said turning her head to the door as Reitz entered. He went up to Elle, squeezed her left hand and looked down at Andrea working on Beach's back 'Look after him well, doctor. He's our temporary captain. When you've finished with him, please have him escorted to the bridge. Lieutenant Beach, you are being handled by what my men think is an angel in disguise. I'll see you soon.' With that Reitz clicked his heels, turned, kissed Elle lightly on her cheek and left the Sick Berth.

Back on the bridge Hiltzern handed him a signal flimsy 'From the wireless room, sir.'

Reitz looked at it – 'From Admiral Collins to Vice-Admiral Reitz, captain of KM*Dresden.* Expect rendezvous outside Scapa Flow. 0930 hours. Battleship *Monck* will accept your surrender. Will board your ship on anchoring.'

Again Reitz murmured 'Mmm. So this must be the London admiral that Lieutenant Beach mentioned. It'll be quite a pleasure to see his face when he treads on our decks. Ulrich?

'Yes, Herr Kapitan'

'Tell the principal officers to meet me in my main cabin dressed in their best uniform, for a reception with this Royal Naval admiral when we anchor in Scapa Flow. Kapitan Leutnant Horst will stand the watch on the bridge. He knows what to do!'

Hiltzern saluted and shambled off.

Reitz leaned forward watching *Northern Sapphire* gamely pushing ahead, dipping her bows into the short steep waves as she tried to make her top speed of ten knots. Burtoft, with his rifle at his side, stood stolidly a yard behind him. His thoughts were that here he was not getting cold and wet even if it was on an enemy ship. And a big one at that!

There was a crash of boots behind him. This time he recognised the ugly face of the Petty Officer who'd pulled him aboard. His voice sounded as if it was full of gravel. Reitz also turned 'Ah, Schenke, what brings you here?' he asked as the chief petty officer tried to make a passable version of a salute.

'The English officer, sir!' Another crash of his enormous boots. Damned if he knew what size his boots were!

'Thankyou, Schenke.' Then facing Beach he asked 'Are you better now?'

'Yes sir. Your doctor Andrea. She was very gentle and careful. Just like the angel that you said she was. It is no wonder that she is so well regarded. One of the men in the Sick Berth indicated as much when I left. So did that ugly giant who half-carried me up the steps. Plucked me off my feet as if I weighed nothing at all!'

'Aha. Herr Schenke. He may be ugly but he really is quite gentle. Unless you pick a fight with him. Most inadvisable!' chuckled Reitz.

Beach stood next to the German thinking back to the way Andrea had first gently cleaned the scarred bloodied skin on his back with a warm, mild, antiseptic wash; then she'd softly dabbed at his skin making sure it was quite dry before applying some gentle soothing cream. Gentle. That was what he remembered. So different from some of the nurses who'd treated him at the various hospitals. They'd always seemed to be in a rush. But this one. Gentle but quick. In seemingly no time at all she'd firmly bandaged him up but yet, her touch had been so gentle. Yes. Gentle. He knew that something inside told him that he had to try and see her again before he returned to *Northern Sapphire*.

Now he had to concentrate on the task. He ventured a question to Reitz whilst watching the trawler swaying from side to side and the spray swirling over and around her tiny bridge. Pertinently he asked 'Captain Reitz – yes, your doctor Andrea says that everyone still calls you captain – well, why have you risked your ship to come here to surrender? If the RAF had found you they'd have done their best to send you to the bottom, war ending or not!'

'Better out at sea, Herr Lieutenant, than in one of our harbours. Your airforces have blasted some of our best remaining ships in the last month of this war whilst they sought shelter in one of our ports.

Another reason – and you may be surprised at this. We did not want to be arrested by the Nazis.'

Beach pursed his lips and raised his eyebrows at what Reitz had just said.

'By the Nazis?' he queried.

'Yes, Lieutenant. By the scum masquerading as the representatives of our political leaders. You see, this ship was the brainchild of a Wilhelm Canaris, an admiral like me but even being of such a high rank did not stop him from being arrested by the Nazis. I received a signal just before setting out on this voyage that Admiral Canaris was actually executed by the Nazis. Who knows what they would have done with us had we stayed in Kiel, or even in Copenhagen. We were advised, that despite the risks, to make for a remote fjord in southern Norway where the Nazis would have found it very difficult to get at the ship. We are patriotic Germans as much as you have your pride in representing your country. Admiral Canaris made quite sure so far as he could, that no Nazis were ever appointed to the crew of this ship although after our one short recent spell of leave, one of my junior officers in charge of our aft main turret failed to return. The report, from a Nazi official, was that his body had been found in a basement cellar after one of the bombing raids on Berlin. That officer was the only one on this ship who I suspected had secret leanings to the Nazi ideologies but as he's dead, I'll never be absolutely certain. So, you see, we are loyal Kriegsmarine sailors who've done our duty to the best of our ability. We are the losers. You're on the winning side. The war is over. I know that you're finding it hard to accept what I've been saying to you as I see you frowning so much. If doctor Andrea can make you feel better, I hope that I can as well.' Reitz looked directly at Beach. Then he smiled. 'Lieutenant. I am no longer your enemy. Come, please, let us shake hands.' Reitz held out his right hand. Hesitantly Beach extended his. The grip was firm but also gentle. Genuine. Not false. Not limp. Here he was. An English man with a German. Shaking hands.

'Sir!' Reitz looked up. 'Sir, large blip on the radar screen. Two smaller ones as well.'

Horst murmured 'It'll be the English battleship and her escorts.'

Reitz translated this to Beach and showed him the radar repeater screen. Beach, with more puzzlement on his face, stuttered and said 'You have radar? Thought your lot was a bit down in that department.'

Reitz grinned 'Well, let me tell you one of our secrets. This radar was originally a captured British one. We've updated it from time to time but it has been one of the factors in our overall level of action successes.'

'Captured?'

'Aha! Off one of your cruisers now under the Mediterranean Sea. Before she sank, one of our special units boarded it and removed its radar. Set and aerials. Even the instruction book as well.'

Beach nodded. 'So you lot's got commandos as well?'

'Sort of, although not on this ship.' replied Reitz.

Then, in a gruff badly accented English, Ulrich Hiltzern, puffing as he returned from his round of the ship said 'Herr Beach. Ve haf ze guns, ze torps, ze speed and ze crew. Best haf all ve has ze gut Kapitan. Very gut Herr Kapitan.'

'Danke, mein Herr officer' replied Beach in his best long-forgotten schoolboy German.

Reitz continued to smile. It was so near the end. No more battles or worries. Soon *Dresden* would be at rest. After formally surrendering. The last triumphant act. Getting both her and old *Rugen* to where he'd planned. Getting them there in safety.

'Smoke! Fine on the port bow' sang out a lookout as the *Monck* laboured through the choppy waves just two hours and twenty-seven miles out from Scapa Flow. On her squat box-like solid bridge structure Collins raised binoculars to his eyes. This was the moment that he'd waited for over these last four years. Sighting the *Dresden*.

The ship making the smoke was not the sleek German battle-cruiser as Collins, focussing his eye-pieces, made out the ungainly trio of funnels and stubby mast. Third in line of three ships approaching *Monck*, Collins realised that this was the old pre-dreadnought that the Allies had never bothered to waste any destructive weapons on and thus sink her. Memories of that late May evening of 1916 came into his mind's vision. This could have been one of Mauve's pre-dreadnoughts that had trailed after Scheer's battleships but which, on the German turn-away found themselves in the thick of the conflict. He could remember seeing one of them blow up and vanish. This must be the last one of them, old smoke-pouring veteran that she was. Collins swung his binoculars but this time too far to the left. The little armed trawler, even at that distance, kept almost disappearing out of sight as she bobbed up and down. Carefully Collins swung his sights. There. That was her. Even at that distance she still looked powerful. Sleek. The legendary German battlecruiser. His *bête-noir*. The focus of his mind. There. In view. Flying a 'White Ensign' atop her main mast behind the single squat capped funnel. Then he saw a white flag being raised to eventually flutter below the 'White Ensign'. The sign of surrender.

Monck began to turn when about two miles away from *Northern Sapphire*. At that distance Collins was able to watch the two German ships, keeping station behind the little trawler, without the aid of his binoculars. Yes. Come on. Two hours time and I'll be on your deck, mister bloody cock-a-hoop Admiral Reitz. As the battleship completed her turn, Collins went to the starboard wing of her bridge. To gaze. Hardly ever taking his eyes from the *Dresden* as she followed the four British warships ahead of her. Behind her, smoke still poured out from old *Rugen*'s spindly funnels, dissipating into shards of black soot over the choppy seas on her port-quarter.

The heavy splash of *Monck*'s anchors echoed across the relative grey stillness of Scapa. Nearer to the shore her two escorting destroyers also dropped anchor. On *Dresden*'s bridge Beach murmured to Reitz 'You'd better drop your anchors too' as the battlecruiser's engines, rumbling in reverse, brought her to a gentle drifting motion. Over the deepest part of the Flow.

'Drop all anchors. Finished with engines.' ordered Reitz. Behind her, the former plumes of black smoke from *Rugen* were being replaced by a steady greyish-white cloud as well as steam as her stokers began to rake out her hot coals and release excess steam from out of her boilers. *Rugen*'s war was at an end as well. Her tired ancient engines had spun their last revolution.

Gently, with a modicum of splash, the battleship's principal launch hit the water with Admiral Sir Bernard Collins seated in the stern-sheets. This was it. He was going over to the *Dresden.* A few moments earlier Reynolds gave him a message from one of his petty officers. It had flashed across from the German ship. 'To Admiral Collins. Please come aboard. Reitz.'

Collins looked up as he approached the flared bows of the *Dresden* towering over his launch. Faintly he could hear the sounds of a military band playing, oh what the heck was that damned tune? Blimey! Not dear old 'Hearts of Oak'. Blimey again! The cheeky Nazi bastards can play one of our tunes! Hmm! Then as his launch hooked onto the side-steps placed on the starboard midships section of their warship, Collins heard the tune change to – no – well, the bloody cheek! 'God save the King'! As he clambered to the top of the steps the tune ended, only to be altered to the shrill wail of bosun's pipes. The traditional Navy salute for senior officers. 'By heck. Jerry does the same as us!' thought a now quite bewildered Collins as he stepped on to the deck of the battlecruiser. The wailing came to its shrill ending and as Collins looked up, he saw a British naval officer saluting him. 'Welcome aboard sir! I am Lieutenant Beach, captain of the trawler *Northern Sapphire* and acting captain of this ship, the Kreigsmarine's battlecruiser, the *Dresden.*'

Collins gave a perfunctory salute looking over Beach's shoulder. The man standing behind him giving an ever-so punctilious salute carried a lot of gold braid on his cap and uniform sleeves. 'Must be him. Bleedin' Vice-Admiralty bloody Reitz' thought Collins 'Looks quite ordinary. The sod's even smiling.'

Beach cut in. 'May I introduce Vice-Admiral Reitz, the former captain of this warship.' This time Collins made an effort and gave Reitz the best salute that he could muster although inwardly what he really wanted to do was to chuck the seemingly smirking Kraut overboard.

He heard Reitz say, in perfect English 'Welcome, Admiral Collins. Please come with me to my main cabin where my officers await to offer their surrender. I have already given my pistol to this very brave English officer here, Lieutenant Beach, as a sign of my surrender.' Then, in German, Reitz ordered 'Guard party, attention!'

The feet crashed out as the sailors, with Reitz, Beach and then Collins between them, marched along the deck planking until they reached the door leading down towards Reitz's main cabin. Collins couldn't really believe that he was on the deck of *Dresden*. Behind the honour guard came *Monck*'s gunnery officer and two of the battleship's junior lieutenants. As support to Collins.

As they entered the cabin Reitz began to introduce his officers. Their names meant nothing to Collins until he heard the German say 'This is our padré, Erich Jervaulx.' Collins' ears pricked up. A bleedin' padré. On one of that bleedin' Nazi bastard Hitler's ships? That swine didn't believe in God and all that stuff. But Reitz hadn't quite finished. 'Finally this is Doctor Lebers and his principal assistant, Frau Doctor Andrea Brautsch, née Cantrell.'

'What now? A bleedin' Kraut woman!' Collins even winced to himself. Not the fact that he was being introduced to a woman but that he'd thought of a German being a Kraut. An American term! He shuddered.

Reitz looked at Collins noticing, but not correctly interpreting, the look on the man's face 'Ah! We rescued Miss Cantrell, as she then was, from a burning freighter in the South Atlantic that had been set on fire by one of our U-boats. Ironic I suppose that her rescuers were us Germans. She's been with us ever since, entirely of her own volition. Married one of my officers but he died only recently whilst in the process of a rescue attempt from a burning hospital ship in the Eastern Baltic.' The words didn't register all that much to Collins for he was staring at another woman. Two of them? Surely not another turncoat? Reitz saved him from any further incorrect thoughts about Andrea as he took Elle's hand and introduced her to Collins. 'Finally, but certainly not last. This is my fiancée Leutnant Elle Chemnitz of the former Abwehr and Kriegsmarine Intelligence Services. She joined us a few weeks ago at Kiel being under threat of possible arrest by the Gestapo.' Collins' jaw dropped. Former Abwehr? Arrest by the Gestapo? How many more surprises could he take?

Then Lieutenant Beach came up to salute Collins.

'Beg pardon sir, my vessel has come alongside and I must return, with Burtoft, to resume our patrolling.' Then to Reitz, he also saluted. 'I didn't like you or your ship at first or what she had done in this war but perhaps now, in just these few hours that I've been on board, my perceptions have changed. May we meet again in the future.' He stepped back and turned to go but then caught sight of Andrea, so he went up to her and gave her a salute as well. 'Thankyou, Doctor Brautsch. I am feeling much better.' To his surprise, she leaned forward and kissed him on his left cheek, murmuring 'Thankyou, Lieutenant. You have restored my faith in humanity. Write to me when you can. I would like to get to know you better.' Astonished, Beach reddened a little and stammered 'I'll try. See you too again, I hope.' Then he turned, rejoined Burtoft and with Schenke, Werthe and Ruddenz waving their farewells, clambered down the boarding steps to where *Northern Sapphire*, heaving gently in the slight swell, waited for him.

'Cast off' he ordered and with a gentle putting from her exhaust the little trawler turned, heading for Oxna Sound and the North Sea.

For a long time, until the two German ships could no longer be seen, Beach stared at them, knowing that he'd probably never see their like again. Knowing also that on board the *Dresden* was a woman that he yearned to see again. To get to see her again. To get to really know her. Even if she was pregnant with her dead husband's child.

'Gentlemen – and – ahem, ladies.' Reitz clapped his hands. 'Please join myself, Admiral Collins and the officers from HMS *Monck* for refreshments whilst we have the time. I'm sure that the British don't require our presence on shore with them just yet!'

Walters had managed to concoct quite a display of small snacks out of the almost depleted supplies from *Dresden*'s larder. Together with some limited amounts of drinks – schnapps, whisky, gin and beer – as well as some real coffee. The gathering of British and German officers soon gave the atmosphere of quite a jolly party. The war in Europe was over. The tension of former enemies soon dissipated as they did their best to converse with each other. Collins was quite amazed yet again. Jerry's naval boys behave just like ours. Even to having a decent tot. Even the gin in his glass never seemed to empty. That steward was always totting it up – he didn't even need to ask. This was VE Day. Prime Minister Churchill surely wouldn't mind. After all he was probably knocking it back with HM King George in London. So if he could do it down there, why shouldn't he up here? Even if it was on an enemy warship. He deserved to relax. We've won the war. The Nazis had been defeated – but this lot, well, they seemed to be a really decent bunch of chaps, even if they can't speak our lingo, very well. Apart from Herr bloody know-it-all Reitz.

Collins wanted to really ask Reitz how he'd been able to keep his ship in such order and still afloat. After all, none of the other big Jerry warships had escaped retribution. Only a handful of cruisers and destroyers still left.

Then in his ear he heard *Monck*'s gunnery officer whisper 'Sir, I think we've got them off guard. Can't even see many of their blokes out on the decks. Probably all having a good piss-up in their own messes. Reynolds and *Monck's* marines will soon be here. I saw their boats being launched about five minutes ago when I went out on deck.'

Through his gin befuddled brain, Collins could vaguely recall the plan put to him by Reynolds. 'Give Jerry half-an-hour or so and we'll board her. Once *Northern Sapphire* is out of the way we'll come across. Arrest bloody Reitz and his glory boys. Our Navy interrogation teams will soon try to work out that all this non-Nazi stuff from them is really phoney. When we've got them off their ship, we'll go through it with a fine tooth comb. Any Nazi lump of evidence we'll keep.'

Vaguely Collins nodded 'See to it, man.'

Just then Captain Reynolds with heavy-booted marines burst through the doors. 'Silence all of you! I am sorry to interrupt you but all of you must –' He got no further.

Muffled explosions from deep down inside the *Dresden* could be heard, shaking the ship. Moments later, she seemed to lurch. Then settle. Ever so slightly towards her bows.

'Damn you Collins! What's bleedin' Jerry up to?' shouted Reynolds. More muffled explosions followed.

Reitz held up his hand. 'I'm sorry, Captain. We are scuttling our ship. We don't need her any more. Neither do I suspect that your navy will. This is where the High Seas Fleet ended their career in nineteen-nineteen. This is where we end this ship's career. Please. Everything is ready. The boats, gentlemen – and ladies. I'm sure that the Royal Navy will see to our needs once we're on shore.'

Then came the strident call of klaxons over the whole ship and as if by some pre-arranged order, suddenly the whole vessel came alive as her still-disciplined crew appeared in ranks, some by each of the launches where junior officers and the petty officers were getting the men on board. Others were going down the embarkation steps or scrambling down nets where rubber inflatable boats waited for them. Everything as if it had all been previously practised. Which it had. In a quiet Norwegian fjord.

Usually at least once a day. For nearly two weeks.

Up on *Dresden*'s bridge, Kapitan-Leutnant Horst pulled the last of the switches to set off the final scuttling charge. All the watertight bulkheads and doors were jammed wide open. *Dresden* was settling very carefully down by the bows. On an even keel. Just as had been prepared and planned. In that quiet Norwegian fjord.

Astern of the battlecruiser, old *Rugen* was also sinking. A bit quicker than the *Dresden*. But she was sinking. That was for definite.

It took both Reitz and Hiltzern to get a rather unsteady Admiral Collins to his feet. Walters held up six fingers. Six neat pink gins.

All especially for the Admiral. 'Come on, Sir Bernhard, I am sure that your captain will see you to his barge.'

Reynolds came over to Reitz 'I'll take him now.'

He didn't bother to salute Reitz. The German admiral had foiled his plans to take over the ship. It was all patently obvious that it was all part of a plan. Well, let the Intelligence boys sort it out. It was back to *Monck* for him. The destroyers would soon be around to pick up these cocky sods and if any of them drowned, so what!

In next to no time, or so it seemed, *Dresden*'s crew left their ship, each clutching just a small bag of their most personal possessions. Schenke held both the cats in a basket. Emerging on the now clearly sloping deck of his beloved, but sinking warship, Reitz holding Elle's hand, could feel the tears of emotion welling up. Elle squeezed his hand. 'Come on, darling, we seem to be about the last.' Silently they went over to where Reitz's own boat waited in its falls. Reitz helped Elle and Andrea to take their seat. Joining his principal officers. Then he boarded it and the seamen carefully released the launch down to sea-level. The motors cut in and she purred away towards the bows which were just above the surface. The last of the crew aboard her scrambled down nets into their rafts which were carefully paddled away from the clearly sinking battlecruiser, now listing slightly to starboard. Elle hugged her fiancé still standing in the centre of the launch, tears in her eyes as well. Then *Dresden*'s bows dipped under the surface, the sea soon surging to Anton turret, round it and up to Bruno's twin guns. Reitz raised his arm to salute his sinking ship, tears rolling down his cheeks. Around him on the boats he could make out others of his men all either at the salute or silently watching. Watching their ship as she quite sedately settled towards her final resting place. To deep water where the remnants of the scuttled Kaiser's Fleet were also at rest. Too deep for raising back to the surface.

'George!' Elle tugged at Reitz's sleeve. 'Someone's waving from the bridge!' and then she was pointing. A white-shirted figure was waving even as the sea sought to engulf the bridge structure.

Reitz whipped up the binoculars that he'd earlier strapped around him and focussed them on the small white-shirted figure. 'It's Horst. He hasn't bothered to save himself.'

'Darling, we must get closer. Can't we save him?'

Reitz shook his head. Horst vanished from view. The bridge dropped further into the sea. Then Reitz knew why. Horst had earlier told him that all his family had perished in the bombing of Hamburg. Every-one of them. Grandparents. His wife. His son and baby daughter. Then, twice, he'd lost crew members on two occasions when his U-boat was sunk beneath him. The first time in early 1944 when his boat hit a drifting mine whilst on a training exercise in the Baltic. The second when *Dresden* so surprisingly appeared to the rescue. There was nothing left for Horst. Guilt. Sorrow. The need to be re-united with his lost wife.

He'd never really given up grieving for her. Or for his young children.

'She's going!' shouted a sailor from a nearby raft. *Dresden*'s stern came out of the water, her propellers and rudder dripping as they came above the surface. Astern of her, old *Rugen* lay on her side, the sea entering all three of her funnels. Quite suddenly the old remnant of Pre-dreadnought days turned completely over, She rocked violently from side to side and then rapidly slid out of sight with creaks, groans and bubbles.

Soon after, *Dresden* began her final plunge with her stern well clear of the surface. Slowly, but then gathering speed, she slid down to her final resting place. At her sternpost fluttering in the breeze Reitz could see his naval flag, the one that he'd designed. He didn't know that in the confusion of the evacuation, Otto Schenke, his ever so loyal crew-member to the very end, had hurriedly fitted that special flag. It was the last artefact of *Dresden* that the watchers saw as with a final flurry of foam, bubbles and escaping oil, the battlecruiser slid down under the surface to her final watery resting-place.

'*Auf dem Grab eines Seemanns bluhen Keine Rosen*' (No roses bloom upon a sailor's grave) murmured Reitz as he finally lowered his saluting arm, the tears still streaming down his face. He'd seen, like the rest of his crew, their home, for most of them for the last four years, sink below the waves. They'd never see her again.

'*Ah, aber nur de Tranen des Meeres, Die ihre Gesichter waschen*' (Ah, but with only the tears of the sea to wash their faces) came a voice from another launch that had just come alongside. Reitz turned to see a grey-haired officer with a neat trim goatee beard saluting him from that launch. The man lowered his arm and continued in a gruff voice 'Aye, Admiral Reitz, My old bird was almost as tough as yours.' Then Reitz knew who the older man was. Franke. *Rugen*'s captain. He heard Franke say 'Aye, we've met quite a few times though we've not done so in person, until now, if you gets my meaning.'

'Yes, Herr Kapitan Franke, I do. Remember that crazy exercise with the dummy torpedoes on your old warhorse? Then your ship had to pretend to be my ship on at least two occasions in Norwegian fjords. And now here. At the end. Both ships together.

At rest on the sea bed of Scapa. It's a pleasure to make your acquaintance, my friend.'

On another boat, one of *Dresden*'s bands-men struck up a sailor's lament on his cornet. When he'd finished, another man played a sea-shanty on his accordion. No-one stopped them. It seemed to take an age before the men slumped back into or onto their seats for the journey to the shore. The two destroyers and other vessels including what looked like a steam yacht, in naval grey paint, which could not disguise its handsome if old-fashioned lines, steamed up to them and the men in the rubber boats and rafts paddled towards them. With armed sailors flanking them, they clambered up to the decks of the nearest vessel and disciplined as ever, lined up in silent rows before these ships, followed by *Dresden*'s and *Rugen*'s powered boats, took them to flimsy-looking wooden jetties for disembarkation.

Somewhere on *Monck* a bugle sounded. The call for the mid-day meal in the various messes. Slumped in the officers' wardroom in an over-comfortable armchair, Collins groaned. It had all been too much of an unreal dream that morning. Sighting *Dresden* and that other relic. Boarding her in the relatively stiller waters of the Scapa anchorage. Meeting Reitz. Not the epitome of some cocky-farted Nazi crew-cutted thug. No, quite a sane, normal Naval Officer. Quite human. Almost as if he was a Royal Navy man. Almost equal ranked him. Spoke damn good English. All his officers. Perfectly correct and polite. Then the padré. Odd how all parsons seem to have that same benign smile. Except that Jerry's padré seemed to have lines of great sadness on his face as well. Then those two women. One looking as if she was a bit preggars. Have to be careful with her. The Intelligence boys, that is. Collins shuddered as to how he'd been seemingly duped with all those drinks just so that they could go and scuttle their bloody ships and he'd been able to do nothing about it at all. Damn it! He hadn't been able to properly appreciate the battlecruiser before he'd found himself back on *Monck*'s launch. The Jerries even saluted as their ship was sinking. It was if they had won, not lost, this blasted war. Reitz had ended it all on his terms. He'd given the orders. Shouldn't have scuttled his ship.

But he had done.

The bugle called again.

Oh damn in hell! Dinner-time! More gin and tonics would no doubt be downed to celebrate the end of the European war. Collins groaned as he felt himself being hoisted to his feet. 'Come on, Admiral, It's time for food. Our job's over.' Captain Reynolds was even allowing himself to smile as he ushered Collins into the officer's dining area. Vaguely Collins registered that the men, standing at their places, were applauding. 'For you, sir' murmured Reynolds 'and I suspect, for *Dresden*'s final act. It's over. She's gone.'

Epilogue

'Ah, Colonel, you have our guests'

When the members of the British War Cabinet met as soon as they could after the euphoria of the VE Celebrations, their collective minds were focussed on the effort to defeat the last remaining Axis partner – Japan. The sinking of the two German warships in Scapa Flow barely caused a comment, at least, an official one.

Even on the BBC, generally so meticulous in its news bulletins, the scuttling of the notorious (to them) raider *Dresden* or the ancient pre-dreadnought *Rugen* was put towards the end of the news bulletins which instead, with Richard Dimbleby in particular, concentrated on the unfolding discoveries of the horrors of the vast scale of human tragedies emerging what the Allied forces found to be the undeniable foulness of the now defeated National Socialist regime – names such as Bergen – Belsen, Dachau, Treblinka, Auschwitz, Ravensbruck.

The hunt for the top Nazi leaders went on – Goering was captured in the mountains of Bavaria, Himmler committed suicide when trying to pass off as a disguised soldier and Doenitz, clearly shaken by the calamity that had overtaken Germany, did his job of surrendering as carefully and diplomatically as possible. He'd done what he could to delay the final surrender whilst ever his smaller ships were still bringing out refugees from the Eastern Baltic. No-one as yet had found the elusive Martin Bormann. He'd seemingly had just disappeared.

Western Europe certainly did its best to celebrate the end of the principal fighting. In England, crowds gathered outside Buckingham Palace to cheer the King and Queen, who with Prime Minister Churchill, cheerfully waved back at them. The bells of St. Paul's Cathedral as well as Westminster Abbey rang out their joyful peals of freedom before and after Thanksgiving Services, a sound echoed throughout the rest of the land. Pubs were full, celebrations were held in the streets, bonfires were set alight and best of all, the street lamps once again lit up the once dark streets of the war's blacked-out towns and villages.

The furore of the celebrations didn't last too long. Rationing was still in place. Loved ones were still fighting in Burma. The Americans suffered large casualties over the struggle for a volcanic island called Okinawa. It seemed as if everyone sensed that the recovery from six long years of war wasn't going to be achieved overnight.

Somehow the fate of those two German warships was lost in the detritus of other more pressing events. Even Churchill only grunted when told of the event. Somehow he blamed his Air Chief Marshall for not having sunk the ships before they'd set off on their final voyage. Very wisely 'Bomber' Harris kept his counsel. He knew that, at a key stage in the war, only Bomber Command was able to keep up an offensive pressure on the Nazis, and had done so with a great deal of bravery by literally thousands of RAF personnel and their aircraft. The war was over. He knew that he'd done his best. Sinking another two German ships was small fry when compared to his staff's total war effort.

Sir Bernard Collins wisely handed in his resignation from the Navy as soon as he could. It had been a long tiring war and his health wasn't all that good. He went off to a small bungalow in the tiny Suffolk village of Walberswick which overlooked the peace and quiet of Southwold harbour. Contentedly on the days when the sun shone, he would get out his deckchair, sit on the lawn and when the tide allowed, watch the movement of small boats as they shuttled up and down the creek near the bottom of his garden. In his home, on the wall above the fireplace in the lounge, he fitted to it the photograph that he'd carried around with him whilst on his various war assignments. The one of a handsome speeding battlecruiser. Every time he looked at it he would say to himself 'Ah, I did at least tread on your decks.' Sometimes he carried on thinking of that vessel shrouded in the depths of Scapa Flow. He couldn't remember too much of seeing *Dresden* sinking but he knew that as long as he lived, that the image of first sighting her, and of the old *Rugen*, steaming in to surrender, would never ever go away.

Naval Intelligence did its best to piece together the story of the raiding battlecruiser. Each and everyone of her crew was carefully interrogated in the hopes of finding a tiny scrap of Nazi-inspired savagery in the workings of the warship. It was soon obvious that the crew members were hiding nothing. Time after time they praised Reitz. Time after time they spoke of their moments of hope when talking to their Allied prisoners. Not one of them vented any anger or arrogance. Another common theme was their collective distaste, not of the bombing or food shortages that they'd endured when they'd returned after their four years away, but of their own Gestapo. All of them suggested that someone very high up in the Nazi hierarchy had them all marked as potential traitors. The Intelligence at the same time received reports of captured memos from Kiel, Wilhelmshaven and other North German ports that the local gauleiters were to arrest any *Dresden* crew-member. Orders all dated April 1945, particularly after the 20th., Hitler's fifty-sixth birthday. This was when the Führer let it be known that he viewed with displeasure of the apparent lack of National Socialistic zeal emanating from the crew of the battlecruiser. Martin Bormann's signature or a mention of him was on all the relevant captured documents. So far the Nazi henchman had not been traced in the ruins of Berlin or anywhere else. It seemed that Reitz and his crew were prepared to risk the possibility of being at the receiving end of an Allied air-strike on their ship rather than be extra victims to twisted Nazi minds.

The Intelligence read with great interest *Dresden*'s log-book so carefully written up by Reitz and other officers. The day-by-day account of her whole war-career. Six volumes of it. All had been carefully stowed in a waterproof bag by Ulrich Hiltzern and then without fear or prejudice it was all presented to them. There were even occasional entries by captured Allied prisoners from various ships that had become *Dresden*'s victims. From the bosun of the *Rampleton*, to the Honourable Wills-Wilson of *Resolve* – right up to the words written by the American submarine captain of the *Billings*. It was all there. Complete honesty. Nothing hidden at all. Every so often praise for the way George Reitz was handling his ship. From fellow crew members and his former Allied prisoners. Highest in the plaudits were the notes from Colonel Tibbetts.

When the news of all these items of evidence was handed on to Winston Churchill, he issued his own memo to the effect that the crews of *Dresden* and *Rugen* should be treated as well as the post-war conditions could allow and that he would, if he succeeded, in his bid to win the forth-coming General Election, see to it that those crew members would be at the forefront for an early release. If he didn't succeed then he would ensure that the Labour leader, Clement Attlee, would be fully acquainted with his line of thinking.

At first, unusual as it was, Churchill also received various notes on the well-behaved efforts of *Dresden*'s crew towards their prisoners from those ex-prisoners themselves, most notably from Colonel Tibbetts. Churchill had met Tibbetts soon after his release from German hands which took place following Tibbett's transfer to

Spain. He'd also received a long letter from Captain Morris of the *Aspen Castle* actually praising the efforts of *Dresden*'s crew. Then surprisingly via the Norwegian Ambassador, he was given high words of praise as well for the crew of the *Rugen*. It really was most perplexing. How often had he said during the war that the only good German was a dead one? Now here were people actually praising them! Hadn't Captain Morris seen the destruction on his own ship? Then all he could do was praise the *Dresden*'s crew! Or those Norwegians? How many of them had suffered during the Nazi occupation? Yet, for *Rugen*'s crew, nothing but praise for their civil behaviour!

When the crews of both sunken German ships assembled on shore, they were soon, with an armed guard, ferried to the Scottish mainland. Once there, they were split up into small groups, interviewed and dispersed to various prisoner-of-war camps. Reitz, though, was separated from everyone else as soon as he set foot on Orkney soil and by aeroplane, was flown south to Edinburgh. For three weeks he related his account of *Dresden*'s voyages, taking his Royal Naval interviewee considerably by surprise with his frank and full account. His early war efforts on the various destroyers, his efforts at trying to help save *Gloworm*'s survivors, to his meeting with Canaris and then through the whole story of his time on *Dresden* until the final moments of her scuttling in Scapa. The naval officers carrying out the interrogations were not surprised to hear Reitz repeat the last entry that he'd written in *Dresden*'s log for they knew about it as well as having relieved Hiltzern of the saved volumes – '*Dresden* sinking with *Rugen*. Crew evacuating ship for eventual internment by Royal Navy. Log ends. Reitz, Commanding Officer. 11.49. May 1945.' There was no sense of bitterness at being on the losing side. Only a strong feeling of pride in the collective achievements of his crew and their ship.

From Edinburgh, Reitz was sent even further south into England to finish up, well away from any other naval prisoners, at the P-O-W camp of Lodge Moor on the western outskirts of the steel city of

Sheffield. To his pleasant surprise Rudi Walters was already there, his red hair still as untidy as ever but the sparse cabin was neat and tidy, just as if the man had never left *Dresden.* Every day Reitz was allowed to write to Elle who'd been parted from him, almost as soon as they'd stepped ashore, by the marine guard from *Monck.* She and Andrea were in a camp for civilian internees somewhere near Leicester even though both women had worked for the German military. Somehow their English interrogators couldn't quite work out why Andrea had stayed on the *Dresden* whilst the rest of the nurses, including Elfrida Ramsdale – who was now engaged to newly promoted Lieutenant-Commander Briggs – had chosen to return to Occupied Europe and through the auspices of the German Red Cross, as requested by Reitz, were released at the French-Spanish border, and soon after had arrived on English soil. When Andrea replied by crying, it had taken very gentle talking to her for them to realise the depth of her love for Helmut Brautsch. The baby developing inside her added further credence of that love. Then the interrogators read the further testimonies from Reitz, Doctor Lebers, Padré Jervaulx, Albert Morris, Angus MacLeod and again most importantly from Colonel Tibbetts and some of his men and they then knew that Andrea Brautsch was a very special heroine of the sea. To their pleasant surprise, both women were kept in a relaxed attitude in their camp, and both of them received letters from the men in their lives. Elle from Reitz, Andrea from her new love, again recently promoted, Lieutenant-Commander Beach, now in charge of a whole group of the Navy's newest minesweepers as well as with five captured German minesweepers, still with most of their crews on board, who were involved in the task of clearing the North Sea of their deadly mines, Allied or German. When Andrea wrote back she wished him well, a safe return and hoped that she'd soon see him. Signed. With a kiss.

As the summer developed, Reitz was allowed out of his camp, with only one armed guard as well as a naval officer, to visit the countryside to the west of the steel city whose smoking chimneys could be discerned on clear days in the valleys towards the east. Driven out to the Pennine foothills in a naval car, he was allowed to view the Loxley Valley reservoirs and then to a village perched high on a hillside at the eastern edge of the Pennines. Allowed to stretch his legs when the car parked in the village pub's yard, he and his escort by chance met the local vicar on a walk after visiting one of his parishioners who stopped, not realising whom he'd just greeted and enthused so much about his beautiful church that Reitz felt almost duty bound to go and visit it. The stunning view from the churchyard over the valley and reservoirs was well-matched by the sense of history inside the centuries-old building. The vicar, by now realising that Reitz was probably a naval prisoner-of-war (he was in his spare uniform), showed him the church's Saxon cross. 'Are you from Saxony?' he asked, ' for that's where some of us English came from. You see, there's not all that much difference really between us!' Reitz smiled but shook his head. Then the vicar took him to the east end of the church and showed him a sunken vestry complete with a fireplace. He told Reitz that this was where monks from another village used to stay the night before taking services on a Sunday. 'A bit before my time!' he quipped. Again Reitz smiled, warming to the earnestness of the clerical gentleman. As they stood outside the porch, the clock in the church tower chimed three o'clock and the vicar said 'Ah, time for a cuppa'. Care to come with me? It is alright –' this to the escorting naval officer '– my wife's quite used to strangers popping in even though we've three small children. During the war men from the military guns guarding the reservoirs that you can see in the distance –' here he pointed out over the valley '– used to come for a cuppa' on hot Sunday afternoons. Then I used to get them to help swell our evening congregation.' Here he chuckled.

'Come on, it's just up this bit of a hill.' He carried on chattering – about the village, the trees, the smells from a nearby farm, about his hopes for a lasting peace.

After tea – on the lawn in the warm early June sunshine, Reitz shook the vicar's hand whilst watching one of the vicar's young sons trying to catch a butterfly. 'Thankyou Padré. This has been a most welcome change, If I'm allowed to come again, I'll bring my steward. Two extra bodies at one of your services. Mmm?'

'Yes, yes, of course you must come.' To the naval officer 'I'm sure something can be arranged, can't it?'

It did develop. Reitz and Walters went over to the vicar's for the next four weekends having given their honour word to the guard. They stayed overnight on the Saturday and the next morning, after Walters assisted the vicar's wife with breakfast, they walked down to the church with the bells ringing out. 'Reminds me of my youth, Rudi, when I pulled a rope. I seem to remember mentioning that to Jervaulx when I first met him although by the sounds of it, the English way of bell ringing is quite a bit different.' The vicar, himself a bell ringer, invited them to watch the local team. During each of the services, Reitz read a lesson with hardly a trace of his German accent. The congregation seemed to take it all in their stride. There were always strangers at the vicarage. None of them guessed that their apparently civilian guests were German prisoners-of-war. Not until a villager saw the Royal Navy van picking up Reitz and Walters during Sunday evening. When someone approached the vicar about as to the identity of the two strangers, they were taken aback when the vicar replied. 'Oh, yes, two more of our brothers in faith. Does it really matter now that the fighting has stopped that we welcome them as friends? What now were Christ's words in his Sermon on the Mount? Ah yes, "Blessed are the peace-makers." Do I need to say more?'

It was the start of a new friendship as word spread. Soon, on a weekly or fortnightly basis, other church members hosted more English-speaking prisoners from the camp.

In early July, Reitz read in a paper that the British electorate had voted in what they called a Labour Party and that Winston Churchill was no longer the Prime Minister. A few days later, soon after an early breakfast of tea and toast, Reitz sat down to write his daily letter to Elle. She'd been quite envious about his visits to the vicar, his family and to the village church. Even more so when George told her of Walters taking up the household chores – preparing an evening meal and then keeping the vicar's three sons awake in bed with his playful antics and his version of bed-time fairy stories.

Suddenly, as he started to phrase out his first sentence, the door to his three-roomed hut flew open. A Royal Navy captain, whom Reitz had never seen before, stood in the doorway. 'My compliments, Admiral Reitz. Please change into your best uniform and then come with me.' Walters quickly laid out his uniform complete with Kurita's sword and belt and his Oak Leaves decoration. 'Should I take them?' asked Reitz. Walters nodded. He'd already been told that Reitz could wear his war honours and decorations. The night before when he'd been quietly informed. Outside, four armed guards as well as the captain, waited by two cars. One guard and the captain followed Reitz into the first car. Walters, unseen by Reitz, was ushered into the other car with the other three guards.

It didn't take them long to reach Sheffield's Midland Railway Station where the captain and the guard with Reitz between them, led him through the entrance with the minimum of fuss and then onto the platform where the 'Master Cutler' train was waiting for its usual early morning start on its run to London. The faint hiss of steamy vapour filtered out between the couplings of the long line of carriages as Reitz was marched down the whole length of the train to the first carriage, and once inside to the compartment immediately behind the hiss and steam of the big black Stanier locomotive. There was a table in his compartment and a white-jacketed train steward brought in a jug of coffee, with cream, and a tray of biscuits. Outside in the corridor, two naval military guards made sure that no-one else was allowed to visit Reitz and it was made plain to him that he could only leave the compartment for toiletry needs, and for nothing else.

Whistles blew. A guard waved his green flag and with puffing clouds of black and grey smoke, the locomotive hissed and chugged its way out of the gloom of the station and into the brighter, sunlit air. Sipping at his coffee and mystified as to why he was in solitary confinement on this train, Reitz gazed out of the window watching the city streets of Sheffield soon give way to the open countryside. As the engine gathered speed, the plume of now grey and white smoke drifted amongst the trees, hedges and bushes as well as over fields of corn, potatoes and other crops. Children going to school stopped to wave and in the fields, cattle lumbered clumsily away as the shadows of smoke chased after them. The train slowed to pass through a station. Chesterfield. The name meant nothing to Reitz although by then he'd worked out that the train was moving in a generally southerly direction. Time dragged allowing for yet another coffee. More names. Derby. And then, Leicester. Leicester? That's where Elle was. The train hissed to a stop. Elle. It would be marvellous if by some miracle he could catch a glimpse of her. She'd once written that her camp was near a railway line for she often heard trains whistling and chugging and rattling as they passed nearby.

Then the compartment door slid open. She was standing there. Elle. His Elle. The woman that he wanted so much. George rose to his feet and fervently hugged and kissed her, almost overbalancing as the train jerked back into motion.

Ever southwards the whirring pistons of the chugging Stanier drove her big driving wheels along the burnished rails. One more stop. Peterborough. Then again, on the journey, a visual sight of blurred motion at speed.

During the journey Elle blurted out, amidst her tears of happiness that both she and Andrea had been taken out of their camp, without explanation, and driven in a closed van, to arrive at the railway station of Leicester. Just before she'd been separated from Andrea, Lieutenant-Commander Beach turned up and so far as she knew, escorted her to a carriage further back on this same train. She repeated what she'd written in her letters about their fair treatment in the detention centre. Medical staff had seen Andrea on many occasions. Her pregnancy was going well. The baby would be due in October. It seemed that the Intelligence people accepted all her accounts of her war work and even more importantly, the role of Andrea on the *Dresden*.

Both George and Elle, as they either held hands or sipped at more fresh coffee and ate some sandwiches brought in by the white-coated steward, wondered as to the reason why they, as well as Andrea and her new love were on the train. Reitz, trying to remember the geography of England, guessed that the eventual destination would be London. Elle gripped his hand. Were they going to be tried as Nazi criminals? She shuddered at the thought and gripped George's hand even harder as the train began to slow down as it began its final haul through the suburbs of London. Every so often, the engine-driver carefully applied the brakes so as to bring the long heavy train to rattle slowly over the points outside the immediate entrance to London's St. Pancras Station. Finally, just a couple of yards from the buffers, the black locomotive hissed as it came to a steam and smoke shrouded halt.

After a long wait, the door to their compartment was finally pushed open by the same naval captain that Reitz had last seen in Sheffield. As they alighted from the train the platform was relatively empty, apart from a few station staff. Only the panting of the Stanier made a louder noise than the crashing boots of the sailor guard as they began to escort George and Elle towards their eventual exit from the station.

Outside, two more Royal Navy marked cars waited. Reitz and Elle were ushered into the front one with the captain who muttered to the driver 'Go on man, to our destination.' The captain proved to be quite a chatterbox and Reitz translated to Elle as quickly as he could as to what the captain was pointing to – the Bank of England, St. Paul's Cathedral, Tower

Bridge, The Houses of Parliament, Westminster Abbey, St. James' Park. It seemed like a tour of London's most famous landmarks.

Then the car slowed down and passed through a pair of open iron-worked gates with a glimpse of a red-jacketed sentry on either side. Slowly it rolled along a curved gravel pathway until it halted beneath a stone pillared canopy with bullet holes flecked into its columns.

'Your Luftwaffe did those' remarked the naval captain. Reitz raised his eyebrows. The captain continued 'You do know where you are Admiral Reitz and Fraulein Chemnitz, don't you?'

Inwardly Reitz had a believable guess but what he couldn't work out was why he and Elle had been brought here. Of all places. Buckingham Palace. He was sure it was this famous place. But why?

As he emerged from the car, two sentries either side of him in smart red jackets, white creased trousers and tall shiny black boots both gave him an immaculate salute. 'Must be my uniform' thought the bewildered Reitz but training and discipline made him return their salutes with his own perfect naval salute. Behind him, Elle felt equally bewildered.

Then Reitz heard a voice that he instantly recognised. 'Ah ha! Vice-Admiral Reitz. It is so good to see you again. I presume that the lady is your fiancée, Fraulein Chemnitz. I am very pleased to make your acquaintance.' Coming from the main entrance, Reitz looked straight into the eyes of the smart uniformed man with outstretched hand, and smiled. Colonel Arthur Tibbetts shook him by the hand smiling broadly. Images of a dishevelled, desperate group of soldiers in a disabled launch came into Reitz's mind. Then the colonel in his Kreigsmarine overalls leaving *Dresden* in order to board *Berengia* at Rabaul prior to his journey to France. Reitz murmured to Elle 'This is Colonel Tibbetts whom I rescued in the Sunda Straits.' Elle nodded. George had mentioned him in conversations and letters. The Colonel stepped up to her, saluted and kissed her right hand and in German said 'I am very pleased to meet you. Your fiancé saved my life.'

Then to them both he said 'Well, let's not dally here. Our hosts are waiting for us and if I'm not mistaken, here is the first of them.'

A deep booming voice came out from the entrance doorway. 'Ah, Colonel Tibbetts, you have our guests.' More amazing flash-backs went through Reitz's mind. Out on patrol in the North Sea and English Channel whilst sortieing with his destroyer, he'd often tuned into the BBC. That speech about defending our island on the beaches and in the hills – their finest hour – only one person had that famous voice. Yes. It was him. A stout bald man in a dinner jacket and black bow-tie.

'Yes, sir, they are here' answered Tibbetts, beckoning Reitz and Elle to follow him and Mr. Winston Churchill. Through the door and along passageways. Past more men standing to attention in rather colourful uniforms and white breeches. Meeting up with a slim smallish man with thinning hair and dressed in a grey suit. Introduced to them as Clement Attlee, the new Prime Minister. Following them, they entered a room full of people, all standing. All facing the front. Some in civilian clothes. Others in Naval or army uniform. Reitz glanced upwards at the beautifully ornate ceiling and the sparkling crystal-glass chandeliers that hung down from it, their soft light glimmering over the heads of the assembled company.

Tibbetts turned and gestured to Reitz and Elle to follow him down the central gangway to the front passing the rows of people all firmly facing forwards. Past their red-cushioned chairs. Reitz was in a complete daze. He was sure that even from the backs of the standing people he could recognise some of them. But why here?

Then he and Elle were at the front. Churchill and the other civilian stepped to the right. Colonel Tibbetts moved over to the left, ushering Reitz and equally surprised Elle to stand level with him.

In front of them, standing by an ornate fireplace, stood a pale thin man dressed in a much gold-braided naval uniform nervously smoking a cigarette. Seeing the arrival of Colonel Tibbetts, he crushed it into an ashtray, turned slightly and stammered 'Ah, ah.

W.W.W. Winston and col. Col Tibb, Tibb. Tibbetts. You, you have our gu, guests here?'

Tibbetts saluted 'Yes, your Majesty.'

King George VI of the United Kingdom and the British Empire smiled and faced a now even more thoroughly amazed and startled George Reitz.

'So, Colonel' the stammer gone. 'You've managed it after all. As you said you would.' Tibbetts nodded. Then to Reitz and Elle he said 'You know who I am?'

Desperately still trying to understand and throwing up as smart as a salute that he could muster, Reitz answered 'Yes, sir, sorry, I mean, your Majesty.' Elle gripped George's left hand, helplessly nervous but somehow she managed to bow her head.

The King said, smiling 'Well, Vice-Admiral Reitz and Fraulein Chemnitz, as they say in naval parlance, at ease. Please remain standing.' Then in a louder voice 'Ladies and gentlemen! Please be seated.' When the shuffling of the company into their seats ended only the King, his equerry, Colonel Tibbetts, Reitz and Elle were still standing.

The King spoke again. 'Three months ago the most horrific war in European history ended. Even now, whilst we finally deal with Japan, I am sure that we have still yet to uncover the true nature of the vile crimes perpetrated by the now defeated Nazi rulers of Germany. However, today, I have summoned you all here to meet one of only two members of our former German enemies that myself or members of my wartime government felt any respect as to their manner of conducting their part in the war. The first of them was Field-Marshall Erwin Rommel who gave strict orders that any prisoners taken by his men were to be treated according to the rules of the Geneva Convention. We also admired his skills of leadership and tactics, both when on the offensive as well as when retreating. I have met many Allied personnel who can vouch for all of this.'

The King then stopped so as to take a sip of water from a glass on a small table on his left-hand side. Turning, he again directly faced Reitz and Elle, and then continued. 'Erwin Rommel was, whilst defending German-held territory, unfortunately and from what we can gather, unfairly implicated in a plot to dispose of Herr Hitler and as a result, his Nazi masters made him commit suicide rather than have his family executed as well.' He paused again and in a slightly lower but firmer voice, he said 'The other German we admired is with us here. Vice-Admiral George Reitz, captain of the Kriegsmarine's battlecruiser *Dresden*. It may surprise some of you to learn that despite the successes of the *Dresden*, that in the last few weeks of the war, there was a plot by the Nazi hierarchy to have the whole crew of that warship arrested and like Erwin Rommel, probably executed as well. Apparently, Admiral Reitz and his company did not carry out Nazi ideals properly. Fortunately, Admiral Reitz's superior, a Vice-Admiral Bernhard Rogge learnt of their evil planning and advised Reitz to take his ship to southern Norway so as to hide in the fjords and then to use his discretion as to where to go next. Admiral Reitz chose to sail to Scapa Flow to surrender in company with another German warship, the old battleship *Rugen* whose captain in the course of his duties also did his best to respect the people of Norway with whom he came in contact.'

Another pause. Inwardly the King craved for another cigarette but he knew that he had to finish his speech which he and Colonel Tibbetts had prepared over the previous two weeks. He coughed and continued 'Er – ah – well – Admiral Reitz – er – you met Colonel Tibbetts in er – rather unusual circumstances, so I gather. We, the Allies, were highly relieved when he re-appeared in the exchange of prisoners that was acted upon by your instructions. You see, Admiral Reitz, Colonel Tibbets is in reality a general but never likes to be known for this rank, whether on active service or even today. To his men he was "the colonel", to me he is a colonel and to you he was always a colonel. One of our Navy's vessels pulled him out of Dunkirk on the last day of the evacuation there. The information he gave to our chiefs-of-staff as to the further movement of your Panzer forces was most invaluable. He was on HMS *Kelly* commanded by Lord Louis Mountbatten when that ship was bombed off Crete. His third narrow escape from death came when you rescued him in the Sunda Straits and then kept him on your ship, rather than hand him over to the Japanese who, due to who he was, would no doubt have tortured him prior to execution. He would have been far more important to them than the luckless General Percival. When Colonel Tibbetts came back to us in England, not only did he help in the planning of our invasion of Occupied Europe but he also landed, via the same civilian boat that much earlier in the war had rescued him from Dunkirk, a day or two early so as to hinder any probable advance by Rommel's units. So you see Admiral Reitz, the man you saved, helped us in no small measure to win the struggle against your evil political masters.'

Reitz, still totally fazed by what the King was saying, could not yet understand all of what the King was saying nor of the reason for it all. Why him? Why here? Why all this about Colonel Tibbetts?

The King took another sip of water. Then, slightly louder he continued 'Not only did Colonel Tibbetts play his important part in the war but he rarely stopped talking or telling us accounts of your conduct Admiral Reitz. Of your humanity. Of the way you handled your prisoners, attending and seeing to their welfare. He has gone out of his way to gather even more evidence, corroborated when your ship's log fell into the hands of our Intelligence Service. You have your Chief Officer Hiltzern to thank for that – he brought the whole record of *Dresden*'s log ashore. Perhaps you know that. We know how you rescued the medical ladies on the *Arades*, of you dropping life-rafts for HMS *Resolve*'s few survivors, of you sparing the civilian liner *Aspen Castle* and of many more acts of humanity even to the sacrifice of Kapitan-Leutnant Brautsch when trying to aid one of your own hospital ships in the Baltic. We know that you fought your war as honestly as possible without resorting to acts of crime or revenge on the ships or crews which had no means of reply.'

Then King George VI waved his left arm at the people seated behind Reitz and Elle. 'Admiral Reitz, I now ask you to turn round. See whom Colonel Tibbetts, Mr. Churchill, and our present Prime Minister Mr. Attlee and I have invited to be here to witness this occasion. Go on, please, turn round.'

Still bemused, Reitz and Elle turned. On the front row were Andrea with Lieutenant-Commander Beach, as well as Elfrida and her 'Briggsie'. Then on the same row was Kapitan Franke sitting next to Hiltzern and the other main officers from *Dresden*. On the other side were more associates from the ships that *Dresden* had encountered. Wills-Wilson from *Resolve*, MacLeod from *Llandaff*, Morris from *Aspen Castle*, the American submarine captain Commander Willis. Behind them and his own officers were many men from his own crew, some with women next to them. Prominent on the second row with his ugly, scarred face was Otto Schenke with a tiny, thin woman clutching his left arm, Letitia. Specially brought from the nursing home from where Otto had last seen her. Almost fully recovered. As Reitz looked at Otto, Letitia even managed to smile.

In a third block of seats at the front were Winston Churchill, Clement Attlee, Anthony Eden and a host of other politicians with their wives who had all served in the British War Cabinet. Reitz didn't recognise them but inwardly guessed that they must be important.

The King coughed slightly. Reitz and Elle turned back to face him.

'Admiral Reitz. I cannot give you any medal or the chance to have honours or letters after your name like I have done with countless men and women who have served my country's cause these last six long years. You after all were one of my country's enemies and your ship under your captaincy caused the Allies much concern with your depredations. However, here you are with people who, I hope, you can count as friends, myself included. With the express wish of Colonel Tibbetts, my wartime Prime-Minister Mr. Churchill as well as Mr. Attlee and members of this country's new government I can give you this.' The equerry standing behind the King stepped forward with a scroll bound in a red ribbon and sealed with the Royal Seal, and handed it to King George who then turned and held it out towards Reitz in his left hand and announced 'Admiral George Reitz. I give you this in recognition, that often at risk to yourself, your crew and your ship, that you showed the highest standards of humanity and seamanship in endeavouring to save lives wherever possible during the conduct of your sea voyages. To me and to many of us here, you will be a legend of the sea, even if you were on our opposing side.'

Then King George VI stepped forward and shook Reitz's right-hand whilst handing him the scroll with the left. Stepping back, hardly able to comprehend as to what had just taken place, Reitz again threw up yet another immaculate salute. 'Thank-you your Majesty' he croaked as Elle gripped him. Turning, he saw a dribble of tears coming down her cheeks. She knew. He knew. Everyone of his crew who were present knew. They were now free people. Best of all they were amongst friends. Old and new. Known and unknown. The war was over. For both sides.

Suddenly Elle clasped her arms around her George murmuring 'I love you, I love you' and then, fervently began kissing him whilst around them, the beautifully decorated drawing room of Buckingham Palace resounded with a spontaneous burst of applause.